PENGUIN MODERN CLASSICS

The Art of Joy

GOLIARDA SAPIENZA

The Art of Joy

Translated by Anne Milano Appel
WITH A PREFACE BY ANGELO PELLEGRINO

PENGUIN BOOKS

PENGUIN CLASSICS

Published by the Penguin Group
Penguin Books Ltd, 80 Strand, London WC2R 0RL, England
Penguin Group (USA) Inc., 375 Hudson Street, New York, New York 10014, USA
Penguin Group (Canada), 90 Eglinton Avenue East, Suite 700, Toronto, Ontario, Canada M4P 2Y3
(a division of Pearson Canada Inc.)
Penguin Ireland, 25 St Stephen's Green, Dublin 2, Ireland (a division of Penguin Books Ltd)
Penguin Group (Australia), 707 Collins Street, Melbourne, Victoria 3008,
Australia (a division of Pearson Australia Group Pty Ltd)
Penguin Books India Pvt Ltd, 11 Community Centre,
Panchsheel Park, New Delhi – 110 017, India
Penguin Group (NZ), 67 Apollo Drive, Rosedale, Auckland 0632, New Zealand
(a division of Pearson New Zealand Ltd)
Penguin Books (South Africa) (Pty) Ltd, Block D, Rosebank Office Park,
181 Jan Smuts Avenue, Parktown North, Gauteng 2193, South Africa

Penguin Books Ltd, Registered Offices: 80 Strand, London WC2R 0RL, England

www.penguin.com

First published in Italian under the title *L'Arte della gioia* 1998
This translation first published 2013
001

Typeset in 12/15 pt Dante by Palimpsest Book Production Limited, Falkirk, Stirlingshire
Printed and bound in Great Britain by Clays Ltd, St Ives plc

ISBN: 978-0-241-95699-1

www.greenpenguin.co.uk

ALWAYS LEARNING   **PEARSON**

Contents

Preface

The Long Journey of *The Art of Joy*

If it's true that every book has a destiny, then I myself certainly played a part in that of *The Art of Joy*, from the time I met Goliarda in 1975 through the editing of the novel that Goliarda delegated entirely to me. Her sudden death in 1996 subsequently bound me inextricably to that destiny since at that point, the responsibility of letting Modesta's story – completed years earlier in 1976 – live or die was mine alone. Repeatedly rejected by major publishers in its day, the manuscript lay for decades in a chest in my office, awaiting more fortunate times. Those times never came. Until Goliarda died.

Then I had a thousand copies of *The Art of Joy* published at my own expense under the imprint of Stampa Alternativa. The year was 1998. Copies were sent to a number of critics and writers. The book was passed over in silence. I remember going each day to a Feltrinelli bookstore which kept two copies of the novel behind some other volumes high on a shelf hidden behind a column. Each time I asked myself: who on earth is going to buy it? One day I noticed that one of the copies was missing. I don't know what I would have given to know the identity of that one lone buyer. After a time the other copy disappeared as well. It was astounding.

Three years went by and nothing more happened. Then, thanks to the enthusiastic interest of Loredana Rotondo, director of Rai Tre, a programme about Goliarda was created as part of the series *Vuoti di memoria* (*Memory Lapses*). Entitled 'Goliarda Sapienza, the Art of

Living', it was a melancholy but evocative production full of numerous testimonials, including mine. It was aired more than once, a rare occurrence, though scheduled at times that as usual were impractical.

The show was not in vain. It served to arouse the interest of the all-powerful distributors, ever sensitive to media support, who pushed the publisher Stampa Alternativa for a more sizeable reprint, which came out in 2003. This time a certain interest began to develop, more to do with morality issues than those of a strictly literary nature; this has always been the case with the critical fortunes of Goliarda's work.

Outside of Italy, *The Art of Joy* enjoyed a decidedly better fate. When the 1998 edition came out, I gave the novel to a young literary agent who dealt with German-speaking countries. She aroused the interest of Waltraud Schwarze in Frankfurt, who had a resourceful way of discovering little-known texts. The book thus came to be published in Berlin by Aufbau-Verlag. Or at least the first part came out: in Germany the volume was divided into two parts. But Waltraud Schwarze had meanwhile telephoned Viviane Hamy in Paris, an apprentice at Robert Laffont, a publisher known to be daring, recommending that she read a novel *paru en Italie en 1998 dans une petite maison d'édition que personne ne connaît. Le texte est un peu bizarre, il fait 600 pages. Il va coûter une fortune en traduction, il y a peu de chance pour qu'il y ait plus de personnes qui le lise à l'étranger qu'en Italie, mais c'est vraiment merveilleux. That is, the text is a bit unusual, and it's 600 pages. It will cost a fortune to translate, but it is really marvellous.*

Hamy immediately sent the novel to her translator, Nathalie Castagné, she too a novelist, who called her five days later, both excited and anxious. The excitement was the result of reading the book; the anxiety came from a fear that, on the one hand, Viviane Hamy might decide not to have the novel translated, while on the other hand, if she agreed to do so, she, Hamy, might become responsible for the publisher's ruin.

That was how the successful coup of *The Art of Joy* in France came about, through the group effort of three extraordinary women, unconcerned about competition and ready to roll up their sleeves. The critics did the rest, and did it well. All I can do, as an Italian writer, is point out an interesting phenomenon I observed from my reading of the immense body of press clippings: in France, critics actually read the books they review. Maybe only when they seem like good books, but then they read them all the way through.

Today *The Art of Joy* has appeared in translation in many countries of the world. When the prospect of publishing her book in its entirety arose in the spring of 1996, Goliarda, preparing to revise *The Art of Joy* twenty years after she had completed it, set in front of her a reminder of sorts with the following words: 'Thirty years have passed since the first notes about Modesta. Careful, Goliarda, don't fall into the trap of self-censorship!' She was afraid that two decades of rejection by the publishing world, and three decades of living with her novel's protagonist, might have blunted the force of the original idea; she worried about slipping into the sin of censoring herself, the most serious lapse for a writer like her. She feared being shamed and embarrassed by the most idiotic form of betrayal, her own story.

Anyone in her place would have had good reason to doubt herself. The two greatest Italian critics of the time had expressed judgements along those lines. The first: 'It's a pile of iniquity. As long as I live I will not allow the publication of such a book.' The second, a more elegant free spirit, and a rather close friend of Goliarda, had once answered the phone with some irritation: 'What does that kind of work have to do with me?!'

The Art of Joy must be cursed: because of it Goliarda was reduced to absolute poverty, and even ended up going to jail. She had begun writing it the year after those first notes, that is, in 1967. She had already completed *Lettera aperta* (*Open Letter*), scheduled to be released that year, and *Il filo di mezzogiorno* (*The Meridian Hour*), which would come out two years later. They are the first two novels of a series of five autobiographical works which Goliarda interrupted for nine years, literally possessed by the urge to give life to her character, Modesta. (Such irony in that name: 'Modesty'!)

She usually wrote in the morning, starting around nine-thirty and continuing on until one-thirty or two o'clock. She wrote every day, trying to avoid – though it wasn't easy – the numerous invitations to lunch outdoors in Rome's sunshine during those blissful, excited years. She always said that writing meant stealing time away even from happiness. On Sundays she religiously rested. She smoked a lot, like just about everyone did back then. Her workday often ended with a hot bath. In the late afternoon a much younger friend, Pilù – reddish-brown hair with delicate freckles on her face and big eyeglasses – would ring the doorbell. They smoked and drank together, but most of all Goliarda read her what she had written that morning. I think the regularity of Pilù's listening ear was critical to the progress of a work that is certainly not a short story, like so many [books] that have qualified as novels for some years now. Pilù listened with interest – not the attention of a professional, but that of a well-read, avid reader. On the other hand, Goliarda sometimes also let Peppino read what she wrote: he was the refined and sensitive, much-loved doorkeeper of the building on Via Denza.

Goliarda and Pilù would carry on like that until evening. Afterwards Goliarda cooked a quick supper. She was an extraordinarily talented cook. She could cook anything, with anything, and above all with the utmost insouciance. She wanted so much for this talent of hers to be recognized. Let them say she was a mediocre writer, fine, but not a bad cook. She seems to have inherited the art from her mother, Maria Giudice, who between peasant uprisings, strikes, rallies and a bevy of children was not above preparing sumptuous little dinners that were even appreciated by Mussolini, who, during a common exile in Switzerland, was still a destitute revolutionary.

But often Goliarda and Pilù would join a group of friends who lived on nearby Via Paolo Frisi and would end the evening there, drinking wine after having gone out to dinner together. The following morning, after the inevitable black coffee on an empty stomach favoured by Sicilians, Goliarda would go back upstairs, high up amid the sky and clouds – a curious attic room converted from a space for drying clothes, with a huge window overlooking Villa Glori's expanse of wistful pines. There she would sit in a low baroque armchair, place an empty cardboard box on her knees as a desk – the box had contained old 33 rpm records, Bach's *Fantasias* performed by Gieseking, I think – and resume her writing, surrounded by a sea of notes scattered all over the floor.

She always wrote on ordinary sheets of typing paper – folded in two because, she said, the reduced format gave her a sense of moderation, though I think it had to do with nostalgia, a need to reproduce the dimensions of her old childhood notebook – on which the words were inscribed in a rather minute handwriting, each line gradually more indented until it was reduced to one or two words, then she would start all over again with a complete line. The result was a curious design, a kind of electrocardiogram of words, indeed, a writing of the heart.

Goliarda always wrote by hand, using a simple fine-tip black Bic; she said she needed to feel the emotion throbbing in her pulse. She consumed dozens of pens, mainly because she left them scattered everywhere, then couldn't find them again.

And so the days, months and years passed, with nothing out of the ordinary happening, aside from a trip to the eastern borders of Turkey (but Goliarda was never a stalwart traveller in a geographic sense) and the publication of the first two novels. Meanwhile paintings, drawings and sculptures by many fine artists went away, while bailiffs, property seizures and eviction notices arrived. Until I came along. I remember that on one of the first days that I lived on Via Denza, as I was climbing the stairs I ran into an eighteenth-century Austrian chest that was being hauled off to auction, confiscated following a labour dispute with a maid who had gone unpaid for too long: the nonetheless adored Argia, to whom Goliarda remained forever grateful for the help her much-appreciated domestic services afforded her during the years she was taken up with writing *The Art of Joy*.

Subsequent to the time of our meeting, Goliarda wrote the entire fourth and final part of the novel, which was completed in my own house at Gaeta on 21 October 1976. I myself affixed the date to the manuscript, and together we began its revision, which after a few months I continued on my own. The editing was completed by mid-1978, the year we left for China after sending the novel out, through a well-known critic, to be read by one of the major publishers. When we returned, at the end of that year, we found the first of what would be a long series of negative responses. Then life became more and more pressing. *The Art of Joy* was put aside; other works were urgently calling Goliarda. And so we come to 1994, the year in which I oversaw the publication of the first part of the novel by Stampa Alternativa, a publishing house that was not new to courageous ventures. It was then that they decided to proceed with publishing the entire work. Goliarda's sudden death meant that it was once again I who would prepare the novel for publication in its complete edition.

Goliarda will not see her Modesta in bookstores. But I know that the sorrow is no longer hers; it's all mine for her. Goliarda is no longer with us. But Modesta exists. The joy of a writer, we know, is her work itself, seeing her characters and their stories grow page after page in the tenuous strokes of the written words, seeing them come alive and take shape, ready to go out into the world. The rest, the volume on the bookseller's shelf, is satisfying – and also cause for anxiety – but has nothing to do with that joy.

I can still see Goliarda climbing the stairs to the attic in the morning with a pot of tea and her inevitable cigarettes. I recall perfectly how she would come down a few hours later, in a breathless state of joyful apprehension, sometimes weeping without sobbing. She seemed to slowly re-emerge into the light from an abysmal pit, whose depths housed the dense colony of her creations, the numerous characters of the novel. Figures who were in large part herself, with stories that belonged to others. Goliarda did not identify with Modesta to any great extent – after all, *The Art of Joy* is not an autobiographical novel. She always replied a little uneasily that Modesta was better than her, an indication that – at least insofar as an author may be her own character – Modesta may be said to be Goliarda, but summed up in a blend of Beatrice, Carlo, Bambù, Nina, Mattia, and even Nonna Gaia. Whereas there is almost nothing of Joyce, Carmine, Pietro, Prando and Stella in Goliarda, nor anything of Jacopo or Carluzzu. Those who knew her well can in part confirm it.

I am sure that readers will see the abundance of life contained in this novel, as if Goliarda were getting even with fate that had not let her have children – she who'd wanted as many as her mother, who had borne eight young ones. I will never forget the dedication that the poet Ignazio Buttitta penned in a volume of poems that he gave her:

'A G. *ca è matri di tutti e un havi figghi*': To G. who is a mother to all yet has no children.

So yes, the countless characters in *The Art of Joy* are Goliarda herself, manifested in numerous offspring, Modesta first of all.

Over time, the more judicious critics will draw attention to the stylistic and structural aspects of the novel. Maybe they will end up confirming that Mody is the most vivid female protagonist in our twentieth century, despite being born between avant-gardism and minimalism – which rejected the traditional form of the novel and its strong character development – and that Goliarda's fusion of cinema and psychoanalysis restored the novel's natural tempo, ending the era of the antinovel, though without turning the narrative into pure cinema or television. But all of that, though she was far from being unaware of it, was of little interest to Goliarda. She wrote the way she read, as a reader. She wrote for pure, unbiased readers who were far away, with lucid yet passionate abandon, tender and sensuous, attentive to the work's heartbeats, rather than to types and forms.

But ideas were a different matter. She was very attentive to ideas. In fact, she described herself as an ideological writer, clearly doing herself an injustice. Yes, the heart and ideas were her sole source of literary nourishment. For the rest she truly wrote for sincere, distant readers, the only ones to whom she felt fraternally close.

Angelo Pellegrino
May 1997 – January 2006

A Note to the Reader
Asterisks within the text indicate terms explained in the end notes.

The Art of Joy

PART ONE

I

I'm four or five years old, in a muddy place, dragging a huge piece of wood. There are no trees or houses around. Only me, sweating, as I struggle to drag that rough log, my palms burning, scraped raw by the wood. I sink into the mud up to my ankles but I have to keep tugging. I don't know why, but I have to. Let's leave this early memory of mine just as it is: I don't want to correct or invent things. I want to tell you how it was without changing anything.

So, I was dragging that piece of wood. And after hiding it or leaving it behind, I entered a large opening in the wall, closed off only by a black curtain swarming with flies. Now I'm in the dark room where we slept and where we ate bread and olives, bread and onions. We cooked only on Sundays. My mother is sewing in a corner, her eyes wide in silence. She never speaks, my mother. She either shouts or keeps quiet. Her heavy fall of black hair is matted with flies. My sister, sitting on the ground, stares at her from two dark slits buried in folds of fat. All her life, at least as long as their lives lasted, my sister tracked her constantly, staring at her that way. And if my mother went out – which happened rarely – she had to lock her in the toilet, because my sister wouldn't hear of being separated from her. Locked in that little room my sister would scream, tear her hair and bang her head against the wall until my mother came back, took her in her arms and silently stroked her.

For years I'd heard her scream like that without paying any attention to it, until one day, tired of dragging that wood, lying on the ground and hearing her scream, I felt a kind of sweetness spreading through my body. A sweetness that then became shivers of pleasure, so that little by little, I began to hope each day that my mother would go out so that I could listen, ear pressed to the toilet door, and take pleasure from those screams.

When it happened, I would close my eyes and imagine that my sister was tearing her flesh, harming herself. And so, touching myself in the spot where pee-pee comes out, my hands urged on by the screams, I discovered a pleasure greater than that of eating freshly baked bread, or fruit.

My mother said that my sister Tina – 'the cross that God justly sent us because of your father's evil ways' – was twenty years old. But she was only as tall as me, and so fat that, if you could remove her head, she would look like the trunk that Nonno always kept locked. Nonno, who had been a seaman, was 'even more wicked than his son'. I had no idea what a seaman did. Tuzzu said they were men who lived on ships and went to sea . . . but what was the sea?

Tina looked just like Nonno's trunk, and when I was bored I would close my eyes and lop off her head. Since she was twenty years old and female, all females at twenty must surely become like her, or like my mother. For males it was different: Tuzzu was tall and had no missing teeth like Tina; his were strong and white, like the summer sky when you get up early to bake bread. His father was like him too: vigorous, with teeth that shone like Tuzzu's when he laughed. He was always laughing, Tuzzu's father. Our mother never laughed, and this too must have been because she was a female. But even though she never laughed and had no teeth, I hoped to turn out like her; at least she was tall and her eyes were large and gentle, and she had black hair. Tina didn't even have hair: just a few thin strands that Mama combed out trying to cover the top of that egg.

The screams have stopped. Mama must be back, hushing Tina by stroking her head. Who knows if Mama too has discovered how much pleasure you can feel by touching yourself in that spot? And Tuzzu, I wonder if Tuzzu knows? He must be harvesting reeds.

The sun is high. I have to go look for him and ask him about this touching, and about the sea too. Will he still be there?

2

The light makes my eyes burn. Whenever I leave the room, the light always burns my eyes; when I go inside though, the darkness blinds me. The heat has let up and the mountains have turned black as Mama's hair again. The mountains always turn black as her hair when the heat lets up, but when the heat intensifies they turn blue, like the Sunday dress that Mama is sewing for Tina. Dresses for her all the time, and ribbons too! Even white shoes, she bought her. For me, nothing. 'You have your health, *figlia mia*, my dresses are good enough for you if I shorten them. What do you need dresses for, when you have your health? Give thanks to God, instead of complaining, give thanks to God!' She's always talking about this God, but if you ask her to explain, not a word: 'Pray to Him to protect you and that's that! What else do you want to know? Pray to Him, that's all.'

The heat has really lessened and the air is fresh. In a short time the mud has dried up and the wind has died down; the reed bed is still, and isn't screeching like it was yesterday. I have to look closely: wherever the reeds are stirring, that's where Tuzzu is.

'What are you doing there like a silly ninny? Catching flies?'

'I was looking for you, and I'm not a silly ninny! I came looking for you. Are you finished?'

'No, I'm not done. I'm taking a rest. And smoking a cigarette. Are you blind, besides being a halfwit like your sister? Can't you see I'm lying in the shade with a cigarette in my mouth?'

'So now you smoke? I never saw you smoke before.'

'Of course I smoke. I started two days ago. It was about time, right?'

He shut up and took the cigarette out of his mouth. He wouldn't talk anymore now. Whenever Tuzzu shut his mouth he wouldn't open it again for hours, so his father said. And if he used to do that before, imagine, now that he smoked! How grown up he looked lying there like that! Had he gotten bigger, or was it the cigarette that made him look older? How can I talk to him now that he's so grown up? He'll laugh in my face and say I'm a silly little baby, like he always does. All I could do was sit near him and keep quiet. At least I could look at him. I looked at him a long time and I'm looking at him now: his sun-darkened face was scored by two huge, limpid wounds – certainly not eyes – which wept a deep, cool blue water. I watched the assured way he brought the cigarette to his mouth and then took it out, the way his father did.

That self-assurance made me shiver.

No, he wouldn't talk to me anymore, and maybe he wouldn't even let me watch him anymore. The thought made me feel so cold that I had to close my eyes and lie down, because my head was spinning like the time I had a fever. I closed my eyes and waited for him to pass sentence. He wouldn't even let me watch him anymore.

'What are you doing, *scimuzza*, falling asleep, you little silly?'

'No, I'm not sleeping. I was thinking.'

'Oh, you mean you think too? A silly *scimuzza* who thinks, huh! What were you thinking about? May I have the honour of knowing?'

'I was thinking of asking you . . .'

'What? Come on, tell me! A chicken about to have its neck wrung – that's what you look like! What is it? Talk!'

'Oh, nothing . . . nothing. I wanted to ask you what the sea is.'

'Not again! Enough about this sea! Thick-headed, you are! I've explained it to you a hundred times. A hundred times! The sea is a vast stretch of water as deep as the water in the well between our farm and that hovel you live in. Only it's blue, and no matter where you look you can't see where it ends. What more do you want to know! *Locca*, a crazy fool, that's what you are! And even if you weren't *locca*, females, as my father says, have never understood a thing, not since the world began.

'But I do understand: water deep as the one in the well, only blue.'

'*Brava!* Congratulations! So, stand up and look around! Do you see the *chiana*, the plain around us?* What's the name of this plain, huh? Let's see if you're capable of learning.'

'This plain is the Chiana del Bove.'

'Well then, the sea is a plain of blue water, but without the mountains of lava that we see out there. When we look at the sea's expanse, we don't see anything out there, nothing that limits our view, or rather, we see a thin line that is nothing more than the sea merging with the sky. And that line is called the horizon.'

'What's a horizon?'

'I just told you: it's where the vast stretch of blue water ends there at the sky. Way out there, where the eye can't reach.'

'A stretch of water blue as your eyes that meet the sky of your forehead.'

'Just look at that, what a thought! A troubadour, that's you. I swear to God, you're like a troubadour! What happened? Did you tumble out of bed this morning? Is that why you're having such poetic thoughts?'

'And you, did you tumble out of bed this morning, is that why you're smoking like a grown-up? You smoke and I'll . . . can I look at your eyes? If I look at them, I'll have a better idea of what the sea is like.'

'Go ahead! Who said you couldn't? If it gives you so much pleasure to know what the sea is like, go right ahead. It must give you a lot of pleasure, seeing how you're blushing. You're cute, even if you're *locca*. Really cute! Who knows who knocked up your mother?'

'A man of course, and a seaman too, from what she says.'

'So, now we're being funny. What happened? The last time you were like a mummy! What happened? Did you wake up all of a sudden last night?'

'Yes, I woke up, and not last night. I wanted to ask you about that too . . .'

'What? How should I know about your waking up! Go ask your

mother. The sea is one thing but . . . Hey, you're red as a beet. Have you been drinking? What else did you want to ask? Tell me, and stop staring at me! Enough! I'm tired of this. So help me God, all this staring is making my head spin. You have beautiful eyes up close like this. I hadn't noticed before. Honey, that's what they look like . . . who knows who knocked up your mother? I'm going back to work now. Enough of this! Hey! Why are you holding me like that? Are you out of your head?'

The heat was rising again, the earth was steaming and the mountains receded, blue again. I couldn't let him get away, I had to ask him why – when I was watching him before, and now that I was holding his arm – why I felt that urge to touch myself in the spot where . . .

'What kind of question is that to ask! At your age! You're a scourge! My father is right: a scourge! Aren't you ashamed of yourself?'

'Why should I be ashamed? I discovered it myself. Nobody told me, so it must mean that everyone knows about it.'

'Good for you! What logic! Watch out, *picciridda*! Let go of my arm, little girl, or you'll be sorry. You're making me lose my temper, watch it!'

'Why should I watch out? I'm not scared of you, and you have to answer me. So answer me, did you know about it?'

'Of course I knew about it! What do you take me for, a dunce? I'm a man and if you don't let me go, I'll touch you myself and we'll make a *frittata*.'

'So let's make this *frittata*. I'm not scared! You're the one who's scared. Some man you are! You're all shaky.'

He had pulled away and was getting up. Strangely, I had no strength left in my arms, but when I saw him standing there picking up his *coppola*** without looking at me, I rolled on the ground, unable to get up, and grabbed his ankles with both my arms. I was afraid he might kick me but instead, cap in hand, he first leaned down with his hands out as if to push me aside, then dropped to his knees and fell on top of me. His eyes were closed. Had he hurt himself falling? Had he fainted? An eternity went by. I didn't dare say anything. I was afraid he would get off of me. Besides, even if I had wanted to, I didn't have the energy even to move my lips now. That strange languor was unfamiliar to me, a sweet lassitude, awash with shivers that kept me afloat. Behind my back a precipice had surely opened up, making me dizzy, but those shivers kept me suspended in space. I opened my eyes and heard my voice saying, 'Now I know what the sea is like.'

He didn't answer. Staring at me without moving, he pulled down my skirt, lifted my petticoat and tore off my panties. He didn't move, but with his fingers, continuing to stare at me, he began to stroke me just like I did when Tina screamed. Abruptly he turned his face away with a shudder. Was he leaving?

'No, I'm here. Where do you think I'm going? This is where I should be now.'

Reassured, I closed my eyes. Tina was screaming, and my whole body was shaken by those tremors I knew so well. Then the stroking went so deep that . . . what was he doing? I looked at him. He had spread my legs, and he sank his face between my thighs, caressing me with his tongue. Of course I wouldn't have known if I hadn't looked at him. That was something I couldn't do by myself. This thought made me shudder so deeply that Tina's screams were silenced, and I was the one screaming loudly, louder than she cried out when Mama locked her in the toilet . . . Had I fainted or had I fallen asleep? When I opened my eyes there was a profound silence in the *chiana*.

'We have to stop here now, *bambinella*. Even though you're a naughty little girl, I don't want to ruin you. Put on your panties and scram. Just be thankful I managed to get my head straight after you made me lose control. Oh, you really made me lose my head, so help me God. Who would have thought it? You're tempting, really tempting, but I don't want to ruin you. On your feet, beat it!'

3

I got up and put on my panties, but I didn't run off, even though his voice was gruff and he wouldn't look at me. It wasn't like before. I wasn't scared of him anymore, and I didn't even say goodbye. I walked home slowly, teetering from fatigue and the recollection of those tremors that made me stumble at every step. It had been beautiful.

The earlier stroking seemed like day-old bread compared to Tuzzu's caresses. I had been right to ask Tuzzu. He knew everything, and although he got a little angry, he answered. Even now, staring at that lopsided wall that Mama called a house, I knew that beyond the distant mountains that appeared and disappeared like the spirits of the dead there were other, real houses, and roads, and the sea.

The old woman who came once a month always talked about the spirits . . . She must be coming today or tomorrow, that old woman. She must be because this morning Mama fired the oven and made bread. Mama always makes bread when the old woman comes, and along with the bread she bakes cookies that she then serves with *rosolio*.

I can hear talking behind the curtain. It must be the old woman with her bag full of rags that Mama will later sew together side by side.

Pushing aside the black curtain, I stood in the doorway, frozen. Right there in front of me, sitting at the table as if waiting for me, was a tall, vigorous man, taller and more vigorous than Tuzzu's father. A giant with a mass of tangled hair falling over his forehead and a blue jacket in a shiny, furry fabric I had never seen. He was staring at me, smiling, with eyes as blue as his jacket. His teeth were white like Tuzzu's and his father's.

'Well, well, just look at what a fine piece of skirt my daughter turns out to be! I'm happy, truly pleased! I was sure your mother would produce nothing but Tinas. I'm delighted to see that it's not so, my darling daughter. It's a great satisfaction to see the flesh of your flesh turn into such a striking bit of skirt like you.'

'Stop it! Don't talk that way. Leave Modesta alone! She's not a piece of skirt. She's still a child, a little girl! Get out of here! I've been telling you that all evening. Get out, go away or I'll call the police!'

'Listen to her! The police! And where do you think you'll find them? Around the corner? Go ahead, go! Run down to the *chiana*, it'll do you good! You've turned into a fat cow. Look at me, what a fine figure I am. I've run all my life!'

Saying this, he stood up to his full height, tapping his robust chest and hips that revealed not a trace of fat. After twirling around to display himself, he came toward me, laughing. His voice was soft like the fabric of his jacket. I had never touched a fabric like that. He took my chin in his hands and stared at me, still laughing.

'You're tall, too, and round and red like a pomegranate.'

So this was the man who had knocked up my mother! I liked talking and laughing with him. Neither my mother nor Tina ever spoke. Now with him I could talk, instead of venting my feelings to the wind as I usually did . . . His hand tilted my chin and I raised my eyes to get a better look at that smile. But then my mother started shouting. I had never heard her yell like that. She rushed between me and that man and began dragging me off to the corner to get me away from him. Those screams made me desire Tuzzu's kisses and I closed my eyes. My mother, her voice like Tina's, tugged and screamed while he went on laughing. I pushed her away with all the strength I had. I didn't want to budge. I wanted to stay there and listen to him.

'It's no use shrieking, you idiot! Can't you see she wants to stay here with her dear old papa? Ah, the call of blood never lies, never! Isn't it true that you want to stay with your daddy? Tell your mother you want to be with your papa.'

'Yes, I want to stay with him!'

I had barely gotten the words out when my mother, still screaming, threw herself at me, grabbing me by the hair. But with his big hand, he slapped her away from me, saying mildly, 'Careful, make sure you don't lay a hand on the flesh of my flesh! Take your hands off her, or I'll wring that shrivelled chicken's neck of yours.'

In his grip my mother sagged like an empty dress: she looked like a heap of rags. And like a heap of rags, the big hands picked her up and threw her into the toilet. When the door opened, I saw Tina huddled in the corner. Surely it must have been he who put her there earlier. Now Mama went to join Tina, one rag pile on another. Then he calmly locked the toilet with a key and turning to me, made the comical gesture of washing his hands. My blood rejoiced, proud of his strength.

When he lifted me into his arms, my own stroking and Tuzzu's caresses faded in comparison to the pleasure I felt between my legs, held by those hands, so heavy yet so gentle, covered with soft, blond hair. I waited. I knew what he wanted by the way he stared at me.

'I didn't scare you, did I? I didn't hurt her. I just got her out of the way for a while. She's too annoying, and I want to enjoy this fine daughter I didn't know I had in peace and quiet. A true gift of destiny . . . are you afraid?'

'I'm not scared. You did the right thing. That will teach her for always yelling at me and punishing me for everything.'

'Good. I see we have the same blood and it gives me pleasure, great pleasure . . .'

He kept repeating the word pleasure, more and more softly and with growing urgency, as he placed me effortlessly on the bed. He was so strong that I felt as light as the skein of wool I always had to bring Mama when she was working. Now she wasn't working. After being silent for a while, she started screaming behind the door with Tina. Or was it Tina? Or maybe it was both of them, but I didn't care a fig. I myself had cried like that many times. Now it was her turn. I didn't care. What mattered to me was following the big hairy hands as they undressed me. When I was completely naked he touched my chest and stopped whispering, laughing softly instead. 'Look here, two little buds sprouting. Does it hurt if I touch them?'

'No.'

'Do you know what these little bumps are?'

'No. Pimples, maybe?'

'Silly! They're your breasts beginning to develop. I bet you'll have big, firm breasts like my sister Adelina. When she was your age, your aunt Adelina had the same colour nipples as yours, rosy pink.'

'So where is this Adelina? I've never seen her.'

'Aunt Adelina, you should say, Aunt Adelina. If you do what I tell you, I'll take you to her. She's in a big city with shops, theatres, markets . . . there's even a big port.'

'If there's a port, then there's also the sea?'

'Of course there's the sea. Ships too, and buildings. Adelina has become a fine lady! If you do what I tell you, I'll take you with me to see her. I'll not only let you meet this aunt of yours, the great lady, I'll show you things you can't even imagine, spectacular things. What do you say? Do you want to make your dear papa happy? If you make him happy, afterwards he'll make you happy.'

4

And he seemed happy lying there next to me, naked. I had never seen a naked man. Without the blue jacket his shoulders looked like the white rocks in the stream in mulberry season when the *ceusa** ripened and the sun, high overhead, hung in the centre of the sky for days and days and months. I opened my eyes and there it was, pinned there. I closed them, but it was still there, motionless behind the window pane. Spying? I had to sleep. Even with my eyes closed, the sun's gleaming blades pierced my eyelids and I had to sleep all curled up to hide from that light that peered in at me.

'What are you doing? Trying to hide, all curled up like that? Are you afraid of your papa?'

How did he know? All naked and white like that, he was scary, but I mustn't show it. I had to be strong, like him. If he sees that I'm scared, he'll think I'm like Mama and he won't take me away with him.

'I'm not afraid. It's those *scimunite*, those silly ninnies crying in there . . . they make me sick. If it's true that you're my father and you're like me, use your fist to make them shut up.'

The rocks beside me were now slowly moving. He was burning and the wispy hair, blond as a field of rye, rose from his wrists to his shoulders. The rye was on fire. When had it been? We were gathering mulberries, Mama and I, and Tina was laughing under the fig tree, when a chunk of that stationary sun high above fell, and like a fiery serpent began slithering and burning everything around it. The blond

16

hair was burning, the poppies, the clothes that Mama had hung out to dry, Tina's skirts . . . the smoke from that scorched hair was choking me too.

'How can I, *figlietta*, how can I shut those squawking chickens up when you're caressing me like that? What a flower you are! A real rosebud.'

The blond rye was burning and the smoky serpent was strangling her throat, she had to get away . . . She had to run and climb the fig tree and scream like that time . . . Tuzzu would come and take her in his arms when he heard her screams.

'*How did you save me from the fire, Tuzzu?*'

'*You under one arm and poor Tina under the other: so singed she looked like a piece of wood when you make charcoal.*'

'*Why didn't you leave her there to burn? You should have saved only me.*'

'*Just listen to this wicked* picciridda, *what a heart this little girl has! If you say it again, I'll let you burn, so help me God, even if you are white and plump as a dove.*'

She had to get away, but the rock had slowly rolled over on her, crushing her against the wooden planks of the big bed, and the flames were rising. Tina was screaming, but those screams gave her no pleasure. That man wasn't holding her under his arm, wasn't caressing her like Tuzzu did. Instead, he roughly spread her legs and stuck something hard and cutting in the hole where pee-pee comes out. He must have taken the kitchen knife and wanted to cut her up like Mama quartered the lamb with Tuzzu's help at Easter. The blade was entering the lamb's quivering thighs – the big hand sank into the blood to divide, split apart – and she would be left there on the planks of the bed, torn to pieces.

★

You couldn't see anything. Had the sun gone down? Or was she already dead, quartered like the lamb? The knife's pain was still there, rising up past her belly button into her stomach, then further up, shattering her chest. Yet she was able to move her arms. She searched for the knife with her fingers; there it was, shoved in from behind. Her chest was intact and her belly too, intact. Only the torn flesh below her belly burned and something thick and slimy, a strange fluid, oozed: not pee, blood. She didn't need to look: she had known it for ever.

Better to lie still with my eyes closed and sleep, but the sun is splitting my head and I have to open my eyes: that glow isn't the sun but the oil lamp that Mama used to light before so she could work . . . such a long time ago, before that naked man who was now asleep beside me had come – and with him the painful blood. Mama too, when the blood came, would press her stomach and cry; then piles of red-stained cloths would accumulate in the basin.

The pain was gone now and her father seemed happy in his sleep. Soon he would wake up and would certainly want to do again the thing that had made him so happy. Mama always said: 'It's a misfortune to be born a woman; once the blood comes, goodbye peace and contentment! All they want is their own pleasure, they quarter you from top to bottom, never satisfied.'

Before, I was a child, but now I'm a woman, and I have to be careful: he's already moving. I have to get away. But where? It's dark outside.

The toilet? All I had to do was turn the key and take refuge in Mama's arms. But no sound came from that door, plus Mama had never hugged me; she only hugged Tina. Even now, pressing an ear to the wood, I could hear them sleeping in each other's arms. I could hear Tina's heavy breathing and Mama's lighter breath, just like every night in the big bed: me at the foot of the bed and those two clasped together up there. No, she wouldn't open the door; she just wanted to know if even there on the floor they were hugging. Maybe she could see through the cracks with the lamp. Nothing, you couldn't see anything . . . I have to wake them up, I have to wake them with the lamplight . . . All I do is set the lamp down near the door and remove the glass that protects the flame: like the sun, the flame blazes up and scorches my forehead, making me step back. Almost immediately it creeps swiftly along the parched wood. It hasn't rained for months.

Tuzzu had been wrong to save Tina from the fire that time. He had been wrong. He should have saved only me. But this time he wasn't there, and even if it meant dying for fear of those flames, that smoke that was nearly choking me, I would not call for help, or scream.

5

'Poor creature! Poor child! If I hadn't seen it with my own eyes and heard it with my own ears, I wouldn't believe it! Leave her be, *maresciallo*, leave her alone. Don't harass her anymore. Can't you see how she's trembling? What more do you want to know? You've been questioning her for three days and regrettably, it's all so clear! So terrible it feels like we're living in the Middle Ages instead of the year 1909. That's because God-fearing people no longer run the country, and the godless ones . . .'

'Forgive me, Mother, but politics has nothing to do with this. With your permission, during the past three days I have only been doing my duty. Unfortunately these things happen a hell of a lot . . . Oh! Forgive me, *Voscenza*,* Reverend Mother, I only meant that . . . I, well, yes, I've seen so very many cases that I can't keep count anymore. It's my duty to get to the bottom of the incident, to protect this creature as well.'

'Oh, Holy Virgin! Be quiet, be quiet! Can't you see that the moment she hears you speak she has another attack?'

This sweet, gentle voice – can't you hear how sweet it is? – is the voice of Mother Leonora suggesting that I faint. It was easy: all I had to do was squeeze my eyelids shut and make tight fists, until my eyes began to tear and my nails, digging into the flesh of my palms, made me tremble like Tina did when Mama went out. I had learned it from her, and like her – I could see her stamped on my tightly shut eyelids – I was really trembling.

20

'Have you no heart at all, *maresciallo*? Leave her be! Didn't you hear what Dr Milazzo said? She mustn't be reminded of anything that happened that infernal night, nothing! The child must forget . . . You see? As soon as she saw you she grew pale as a little corpse, and as soon as you mentioned that nasty business . . . there, you see, she's having another attack. What more do you need to know? Everything was confirmed by Tuzzu and his father when they brought her here, and afterwards, on several other occasions . . .'

'With your permission, Mother, not quite everything.'

'What do you mean? Those are just details.'

'But we haven't found the man who claimed to be her father, neither among her mother and sister's remains, nor . . . And, well, you see, Mother, we have to find him!'

'It's up to you to find him. You found the jacket, didn't you? It was even blue velvet, like this poor tormented child said. In the name of Saint Agatha who suffered torment like this little girl, don't torture her any further! Can't you see how she's thrashing about? Go away, in the name of God who is our witness! You have no Christian soul, you *carabinieri*. And you, Sister Costanza, instead of standing there frozen like a mummy, help me lay Modesta on the bed. That's it. Poor child! Do you feel what a dead weight she is? This is surely an epileptic seizure. She didn't suffer from them before, from what Tuzzu told us, but this tragedy has ruined her for ever.'

Once again Mother Leonora's voice let me know what I had to do: clench my fists even tighter so that the nails would drive more deeply into the flesh. Enduring this pain was better than answering that man with the black moustache, his eyes hard as stones: if he kept questioning me, he might make me say something I didn't want to say. My eyelids hurt so much by now that I began to scream loudly, my cries genuine. So genuine that those two officers, confused by my tears and by Mother Leonora's sweet supplications, vanished amid the frantic swishing of the long skirts those strange, tall women wore. Only when all was silent, except for Mother Leonora's faint breathing, did I relax my fingers, but slowly, so she wouldn't notice. I had to calm down slowly, so she wouldn't become aware of my strategy. I had to follow the suggestions of that sweet voice. What was she saying now? What was it I had to do?

'There now, there my child. Those dreadful men are gone and I am here with you. They won't harass you anymore, my poor little martyr, body and soul tormented like our patron Saint Agatha! That's it, take your time, don't worry. Don't be afraid, the wicked men are gone.'

I knew it, but I also knew that it was not time to open my eyes. This she had not yet told me.

'They're gone. Don't you believe me? You're right not to believe anyone anymore, after what you've been through. Yes, you're right. But I will restore your faith. You must believe me. Open your eyes. Give me the consolation of seeing in your beautiful eyes that you believe me.'

There, she said it. I could open my eyes at last. One moment more and I would open them. She had guided me not only with her voice, but also with her smooth white hands, even smoother than that downy soft blanket, whiter and more fragrant than those sheets that had magically replaced the coarse grimy ones in the big bed where I had always slept before . . . before the blood had come. Fortunately, I had withstood my fear of the fire without running to Tuzzu. If I hadn't had the strength to hold out, Tuzzu – with those legs of his that could run like a hare – would certainly have saved those two again.

'There, that's it. Look at me with those beautiful eyes. Beautiful and limpid. Think no more about that fire that clouds your gaze. Don't think about it anymore; pray instead. Pray to Saint Agatha to perform a miracle, to make you forget everything and heal your tormented body and soul.'

'Who is Saint Agatha?'

6

'Oh Jesus and Mary, don't you know? The things one sees in this piti-able country of ours! They haven't taught you a thing, not a thing. Nothing but misery and suffering. If you promise me you'll do what Dr Milazzo said . . .'

'What did he say?'

'He told you to forget, forget everything. If you do that, I will teach you . . .'

The voice promised a warm, gentle lullaby of fragrant sheets and daring adventures of queens and regents, sieges, wars and exploits. In Mother Leonora's sweet lilting voice, armies advanced with gold and silver breastplates. Enemy troops and savage hordes fled, driven off by her hand, rising toward the sun like the wing of a dove. Dreadful, wicked men, multitudes of godless individuals to be subjugated by the righteous law dictated by the Cross. The small room smelling of sugared almonds was populated with knights and paladins, saints and virgins consecrated to God, who could not be turned against their faith by anyone, despite snares and persecutions. Saint Agatha was very beautiful. I was right to ask who she was. Her severed breasts on a tray made me shudder even more than Mother Leonora's delicate, gentle hands, which caressed me whenever I had an epileptic seizure.

And I had these seizures often. At least every two or three days. Not more often, or she might become suspicious. Something in her gestures, her voice, told me that she did not touch herself, and that if she found out about me she would surely send me to hell. The story about hell and heaven was really boring, but every so often I had to put up with it; it didn't last long, after all. And soon enough Saint Agatha would be evoked by Mother Leonora's raised finger. Tall and fair, she would appear with her wavy, long blond hair falling softly down her garment of blue and silver brocade. Through the gossamer hair, fine as gold dust, her small rosy breasts could be glimpsed.

There was Saint Agatha, coming through the door; and nearby, in a dark corner of the room, before our eyes, two men, black as sin, ripped out those small breasts with red-hot forceps and arranged them, still warm and tremulous, on a silver tray . . . At that point in the story, Mother Leonora always looked into my eyes and asked: 'It scared you, didn't it? Were you scared?'

I understood what her eyes were trying to suggest – eyes blue as the sky illuminated by numerous tiny gold stars – and I began to tremble, but only a little, just enough to make her take me in her arms. In those arms I rested my head on her bosom, feeling its fullness and warmth beneath the white fabric. Mine was still no bigger than two small bumps. 'How thin and undernourished you are, poor creature! Such a skimpy chest!' she'd told me. 'Let's hope this chest develops, that it grows and develops, since tuberculosis is quick to strike!'

I didn't like that word, 'tuberculosis', or those little bumps: I shuddered at the thought that those bumps might not develop like hers. I trembled, my cheeks buried in that warm, fragrant swelling.

And as the red-hot forceps tore the white fabric and ripped out the tender flesh of her breasts, a thrill of pleasure started up inside me. And when she, seeing me continue to tremble and fearing that I might fall, held me even closer, the thrill became so intense and protracted that I had to clamp my teeth so I wouldn't scream. Unfortunately this never happened to me again, that is, without even touching myself, as I'd had to do until then.

7

The cool air, smelling of sugared almonds, made me fly through dim corridors, the darkness barely relieved by numerous small whitewashed doors that were always kept closed. Behind them, no doubt, were many small cubicles like mine which the swarm of tall, white-robed women sometimes entered, and sometimes left, their swift, cautious tread so light that it was easier to hear the rustle of their skirts than the sound of their footsteps. Those women were always sighing. Maybe because they never spoke? Or because they didn't stroke themselves and never saw any men? How long had it been since I myself had seen a man? There was the gardener, but talking to him was forbidden. Sometimes another man came, but he wore a long skirt like the women did, though his was black. I later learned that in addition to a host of women who laboured – as Mother Leonora said – to spread the word of God on earth, there was also a host of men who, again in Mother Leonora's words, were mankind's blessing. Afterwards I realized that these men who wore skirts were the priests of whom my mother always spoke so lovingly, the ones Tuzzu's father hated, often calling them 'filthy priests, fucking priests, asshole priests'. Such wicked words! Mother Leonora had been right to scold me that time, but I had just arrived then and didn't know any better. What was it I had said? Oh, yes: 'damn it'. From that day on, I abandoned all those bad words without any regret. It wasn't easy – even though I tried to forget them, I couldn't get them out of my head – but I devised a system, a discipline, to use Mother Leonora's word (such a beautiful word, though, 'discipline'). Every time I felt them rising in my throat, I bit my tongue. The pain made me forget them. I had no regrets. From Mother Leonora's tender, rosy lips – sometimes she let me touch them – I learned so many beautiful new words that at first, listening closely so I could catch them all, my head would spin and I felt breathless. Tomorrow morning, too, who knows how many I will learn? . . . I must sleep, that way it will soon be light. And with the light, in that room lined with cupboards as high as the ceiling, with windows so clean that it seemed there was no glass, Mother Leonora would begin to speak, standing upright, pointer in hand in front of those immense cupboards. Except that instead of cups and plates and glasses, like in Mama's cupboard, Mother Leonora's shelves were full of books. And those books were full of all those words and stories that Mother Leonora taught me. I wonder if she's read them all?

'So many books, Mother! Have you read them all?'

'What are you saying, you silly little thing! I've studied, yes, I know some things, but I'm not a learned scholar. Only the doctors of the Church hold all the world's knowledge in their hands.'

'I'm going to become a scholar too!'

'What a silly creature you are! What good would it do you, being a female? A woman can never attain the wisdom of a man.'

'What about Saint Teresa then?'

'But Saint Teresa, as the word "saint" tells you, was one of God's chosen, you silly little thing! Be careful not to fall into the sin of conceit. It pleases me to see how much you like to study and I certainly have to admit that your memory and determination are uncommon. But be careful, because intelligence can lead you to fall into the dark web of sin. Pray and embroider, besides studying! Embroider and pray. Embroidery accustoms you to humility and obedience, which are the only sure defences against sin. And while we're on the subject: Sister Angelica has complained. She says you're not as attentive at the embroidery hoop as you are with me and at the piano. She was very resentful about this apathy of yours. Try to make her happy in the future. Sister Angelica knows much more about humility than we do, and only from her patient hands can you learn it. I worry about your intelligence . . . you're a female . . . a woman . . . Sister Angelica . . .'

When she spoke like that her voice rose shrilly, almost like Mama's voice. But it was pointless to contradict her; she didn't understand. How could I apply myself with Sister Angelica? She was so homely that she almost reminded me of Tina. At the piano it was different. Sister Teresa, though she was neither beautiful nor homely, spoke through her hands. She made such sweet sounds come from the keyboard that it was like listening to Mother Leonora's voice . . .

'Modesta! You weren't listening to me! You mustn't let your mind wander like that when you are being scolded. It's a sign that the devil is flirting with you, making it hopeless for us to try to straighten your young branches, which are inclined toward darkness rather than the light. A child is a fragile plant that tends to be weak-willed and playful. Only by securing it tightly with the cords of discipline can you make it grow straight, its body and soul free of deformities. This distraction of yours is indeed a sin. Go to the chapel after class and recite ten Hail Marys and ten Our Fathers! That way you'll learn to listen when you are scolded.'

Sinfulness! The devil! She was truly tiresome when she acted like that and even her face changed: it got withered and twisted. That was why Modesta looked away, not to see her that way. She only wanted to see her beautiful.

'Modesta! What are you looking at? Did you hear me?'
'I heard.'

She had to be patient, and besides, those awful words like 'evil', 'hell', 'obedience', 'sin', didn't go on for long. She knew how to put a stop to those protests: all she had to do was lower her eyes and start crying. It was a bit taxing. But afterwards, Mother Leonora's voice, composed again and sweet as always, would once more start murmuring beautiful words, like 'infinity', 'blue', 'gentle', 'celestial', 'magnolias' . . . How beautiful the names of flowers were: 'geraniums', 'hydrangeas', 'jasmine' . . . what marvellous sounds! Now once she wrote the words down on the blank page, in black and white, she would never lose them, never again forget them. They were hers, hers alone. She had stolen them, stolen them from all those books, through Mother Leonora's mouth.

8

And she had to steal more of them, accumulate as many as possible even there in that enormous room they called the parlour; it was the only room in the convent with tall windows, full of gilded furniture. Amid the glitter of gold, the black piano held precious notes and chords free for the taking. All she had to do was follow Sister Teresa's voice, not sweet like Mother Leonora's, but really rather coarse.

'Today after the vocal drills and the piano exercises we will also learn to write the notes . . . Oh, what is it this morning, my child? Your eyes are so radiant that you look like the Virgin Mary being lifted up to everlasting glory by the angels. Ah, youth, how beautiful and resplendent it is!'

'It's not youth, Sister Teresa: it's that after months and months of promising and putting it off, Mother Leonora is going to show me the stars.'

'I'm glad. You see, being good and obedient has quickly brought you a reward!'

Actually, not so quickly. For months she had toiled over that damn embroidery frame under the harpy-like eyes of that shrewish Sister Angelica.

'"Only good bringeth forth good!"* And tonight you will go . . . it's tonight you're going, isn't it? You will go with her where none of us has ever set foot. Actually, I should say "has never laid eyes", because it's about seeing with your eyes!'

'Not even you, Sister Teresa?'

'Good heavens, no! Aside from the fact that going round and round up that iron staircase would make me drop from vertigo before reaching the top of that slender tower. How slender it is! It may be my impression, but when it's windy, it appears to sway like a banner. Then too, I don't suffer from insomnia. I sleep at night, by God's grace, and I wouldn't trade my sleep for all the stars in the firmament.'

'What does insomnia have to do with it, if I may ask?'

'It has everything to do with it! And don't act so simpering with me. "May I" this, "may I" that. Save all that decorum for Mother Leonora.'

'So what does insomnia have to do with it?'

'It has a lot to do with it.'

'How?'

'If I say it does, it does! You're so pig-headed! Come on, vocal exercises. Let's go. Forget insomnia and do your scales.'

'But isn't insomnia the malady that afflicts you at night and doesn't let you sleep?'

'Of course! It's the malady that props your eyelids open with its iron claws and won't let you close your eyes, or, as they say, will not grant you the blessing of sleep.'

'But isn't it the malady that by the hand of God strikes those who are in mortal sin?'

'What are you saying! Who tells you such nonsense? Oh, you haven't been speaking to the gardener, have you?'

I had spoken with Mimmo, but I replied promptly: 'No! God forbid! I never speak to men!'

'A proper answer! So was it that prattler Sister Angelica? Don't listen to her. That woman has ruined her eyesight with her embroidery and all she sees are tangles of colour . . . Well! Never mind. We're not here to embroider. Come on, sing your scales now, in groups of four: one, two, three, four, one . . .'

'Who is it, then, who suffers from insomnia?'

'Stubborn as a mule, she is, oh! A real horse fly, this *picciridda* is, when she wants to know something. It's partly true that insomnia is a

punishment that God inflicts on those who have sinned. But sometimes – though rarely – it's like a warning, an alarm bell for those who
possess great intelligence and, without insomnia cautioning them to
beware, might fall into sins of presumption, of . . . What do I care
about sins! Let Mother Leonora tell you about them. All I know about
are notes! The convent's physician says that all great minds suffer
from insomnia and that it's also hereditary. But that fellow is a heretic,
and except for castor oil or some pill, it's best not to listen to him.'

'Ah! Then it's Mother Leonora who suffers from insomnia?'

'Exactly, and when this malady struck her – I think it was two or
three years after she came here to fill the position vacated by Mother
Giovanna, who died . . . never mind how she died, may God forgive
her! – a medical specialist, sent from Palermo only in exceptional
cases, after examining and re-examining her obtained the bishop's dispensation for her to bring her father's telescope here. He was a great
astronomer. And she installed it on the tower. The dispensation also
stated that she could spend as many hours as she wished studying the
stars, like her father. That, too, is a family affliction. It's inherited
along with intelligence, wealth and power. You should know that
Mother Leonora is from one of the oldest noble families on our
island, one of the most affluent. I can't tell you the name because, as
you know, when we take the vows we no longer have family members
nor . . . Are you surprised? Your surprise tells me how many acts of
humility Mother Leonora must have performed in her heart to cleanse
away the arrogance she must have had. I saw her mother, once. Such
arrogance! Beautiful, like her, the same eyes, same forehead, same
nose. And then, you too: why do you think you were able to stay here
after that night when Tuzzu and his father brought you here? They
say it was because the convent was close by, but I think it was because
they were afraid of the police . . . So why do you think you were
allowed to stay here?'

'I don't know.'

'Oh, that's a good one! She doesn't know! It was because of Mother
Leonora's influence! If you only knew how she fought, afterwards, to
keep you here and not send you to some orphanage with its bedbugs
and hunger. Of course, I shouldn't say that, because the orphanages

too are run by nuns, but you know how I am: I can't help speaking plainly. The fact is that these orphanages are run by nuns from poor families, of low extraction. Lower-class individuals who come from rural areas or from the same wretched orphanages. It's not like it is here. This, too, is something I shouldn't say – may God forgive me – but here there isn't one of us who isn't the daughter of a baron at least. Even the immensely wealthy have never interfered in here and never will.'

'And you, Sister Teresa, are the daughter of . . .'

'A baron, that's right. But you should have said *were* the daughter of, not *are* the daughter. Repeat the question.'

'And you, Sister Teresa, whose daughter were you?'

'As I said, of a baron, but a poor one, not from a very old family. That's another reason why I will never be a Mother Superior! But what does it matter? Less worries and more time for music and for teaching it to the novices and to you . . . But enough now. Forget the scales and let me hear Clementi's *Sonatina*. It's a joy to teach, especially someone like you. Listen to that touch! The touch of an angel. But that's enough now, that will do. We have to start learning to write music. Here, come over here: see this sheet of paper with the lines? The lines were made by the novice from the continent.* Now you will fill them in for me . . . No, no, you must do it as if drawing a mouth. There, first the outlines: firmly now . . .'

The pressure of my fingers marked the shapes of notes between the lines, trapping them there: no one would ever be able to take them from me anymore. They were mine, stolen like the adjectives, nouns, verbs and adverbs . . .

9

And she had to steal more of them, collect as many as possible on the lined notebook pages. And numbers too, copious numbers added to the words, the musical notes, the stars. The stars! That night she had seen the stars so close up that it seemed she could touch them with her fingers. Through the telescope, on the high, scary tower – a defiant finger pointed at the heavens? – Mother Leonora had shown her Ursa Major and Ursa Minor, the Little and Big Dipper, and shining Sirius: the brightest star in the firmament.

'Firmament! What a beautiful word, perhaps the most beautiful word . . . the brightest in the firmament of words.'

'What did you say, Modesta? How wonderful! What did you say, dear heart? Tell me again.'

I said it again.

'How wonderful! It sounds like a poem. You're extraordinary! Not only intelligent, conscientious and good, but with an imagination that is almost frightening! You will be a poetess: a nun and a poetess. That way you will be able to sing the high praises of the Lord!'

A poetess, maybe, but I wasn't too sure about the nun. Of course, we had it good there. Every day we ate as if it were Sunday, and the rooms, the sheets smelled of sugared almonds. But an entire life there?

'How many years have you been here, Mother?'

'That's not the way to say it, Modesta! Repeat the question properly.'

'How many years has it been, Mother, since you took your vows?'

'Good! That's the way. You have to be vigilant, Modesta. Sometimes you have a worldly tone – who knows where you picked it up – that does not befit a future novice . . . It's been many years, my child, since I entered this peaceful oasis. Oh, if only I had entered it sooner, at your age! At the pure, chaste age that you were when you came to us. Unfortunately, I lived in a fatuous world which was almost never touched by the word of God. I should not talk about worldly matters, but in this case it is permissible because it will help you understand how the Virgin protected you by making you come here among us, even though it was through misfortune. She chose you right away, partly because you are of humble origins and she protects the unprivileged, whereas for me, perhaps because of the sin of heresy that had possessed several members of my family, the path was long and painful. For years I lived a life of light-hearted luxury, until a terrible dejection overcame me and made me suspect I was in error, as my confessor, to whom I owe my salvation, repeated to me every Sunday. He opposed everyone in my family to bring me closer to faith. My parents said that my depression was a bodily illness – anaemia, they said. But it was my young, pure soul that was suffering from all that luxury, from all that immoral, hopeless talk which my uncle in particular – God rest his soul – was fond of. The source of my suffering was unclear, torn as I was between the lofty, moral words of my confessor and the learned superficiality of the others.

'It was at the debutantes' ball that Our Lady, to whom I had prayed so much, enlightened me as to my malady, which no medicine had been able to relieve. A malady that manifested itself in endless ennui and depression. Until the day before the dance, what am I saying? until that very morning, I didn't know. On the contrary, the joyous preparations, the ribbons, the gowns, the flowers, seemed to have revived me, a momentary diversion from my ennui and dejection. But that evening, as I put on the immaculate, white organdy gown customary for debutantes, I began to feel supremely anxious and started trembling all over. I was already promised to a young cavalry officer whom I had not yet met. I had caught a glimpse of him from the balcony, marching with his platoon. He was tall, with a moustache and eyes so black they seemed like pitch. I have always found dark men repulsive. They said he was handsome, but to me he was frightening like all swarthy men. He was tall and muscular, and his cheeks bore the numerous scars of various duels, as I was able to observe when I saw him up close. He had already killed three men back in his own country. He was a German aristocrat. May God forgive him! At the age of twenty-three or twenty-four, three deaths already weighed on his conscience. Just think, three men dead, killed for trivial reasons of worldly honour. That man had already frightened me from a distance, but up close, as we danced the quadrille, with those scars reminding me of his crimes, the horror that lay concealed behind that dazzling uniform, resplendent with medals and chevrons, was passed on to the splendour of the silks, the candelabra, the women's tiaras, revealing an orgy of sin and crime concealed by all that luxury.'

Silks, candelabra, dazzling tiaras, his scarred cheeks . . . A pang in my stomach, like when I was hungry, made me shiver from Mother Leonora's trembling and I had to run into her arms and hide my face. In part because she looked so beautiful when she got excited that way, and also to hide the desire that had overcome me to be embraced by that officer. A desire that surely could be read on my face, even in the dark . . . Tuzzu, where was Tuzzu? His cheeks weren't scarred, but a blue sea welled out of the wounds of his eyes, and his hands were strong when they caressed me. Tuzzu's hands caress me in the dark; he always caresses me like that when the reeds grow dark and silent. No, these are not Tuzzu's hands. These are the soft, trembling palms of Mother Leonora, which rise from my waist to my shoulders barely brushing my breast with a rustling of wings.

'What's wrong? Did you get scared? Were you frightened at the thought of my going to perdition had I remained in the world? But the Madonna enlightened me in time, as she will with you. Come now, don't be afraid. The danger is past. You're a big, strong girl now. You mustn't get scared like you did when you were a child. See how well your chest has developed? Remember how we worried that it would remain flat and shrivelled like Sister Teresa's?'

Yes, my breasts had thankfully grown, but those hands no longer gave me the shivers. They were spineless and they never dared to do anything. Many times I had hoped, but she never went further than a few timid caresses. At first I had thought that Mother Leonora didn't stroke herself because she was pure and holy, like everyone in the convent kept saying, but now I knew that at night she too stroked herself the same as I did. I realized it the night she brought me to sleep in her bed, using the storm as an excuse. Then, believing that I was asleep, she began touching herself and moaning. Some saint! A coward is what she was! A coward, and that's why all she talked about was hell and punishment . . .

What had I said? A long scream, followed by a fluttering of white wings, pushes me away. What had I said? Crazy! I must have said something terrible, because Mother Leonora is now running around the tower like a bat blinded by the light; something terrible, since she falls to her knees and begins making the sign of the cross, crying desperately:

'*Mea culpa, mea culpa, mea maxima culpa.*'

How to make amends?

10

A high fever took care of making amends, gripping me the instant I saw Mother Leonora shut me out as she went on praying, frozen as a corpse. A fever caused by fear, I think. How could I have been so foolish as to tell Mother Leonora what I was thinking? Shivering, my teeth chattering, I tried to make sense of what had happened to me. The terrible fever lasted three days and three nights, gouging my brain with the question: why did you do it? I had done it because like a fool, I who thought I was so clever had put too much faith in Mother Leonora. And so the disillusionment of seeing her cowardice day after day, and consequently, no longer loving her, had made me commit one of the most predictable errors. Once I realized my mistake, the fever went away. But not the terror of being exiled from all those women who, though fatuous and contemptible, were essential to me. For years they had seemed so sweet and beautiful and tall! They weren't even tall. At fifteen I was already taller than Sister Costanza, who was the homeliest, true, but also the tallest. Too bad. I almost wished I could go back to the time when I admired them and tried to walk and talk like them. Careful, Modesta, even this desire to return to a past that can no longer be is a sentimental trap that can cost you dearly. No! Look at the reality: what happened happened and could not have been otherwise. Now I have to get out of this exile in which Mother Leonora has plunged me. In three days I haven't seen anyone except the nursing sister and the old, bald doctor. If he were at least young! I wonder where Tuzzu is? Maybe he went to sea.

The sea . . . now I knew what it was. I had glimpsed it in so many reproductions of famous paintings, they almost made me forget the desire I once had to see it.

'What is the sea like, Tuzzu?'

'A vast stretch of water as far as the eye can see. See, it's like this stony ground you see before you from morning till night. Only instead of these rocks and mud and – let's not even mention the eyesores! – there's water, blue water. Sometimes calm like the water in the well, sometimes tossing like the reeds when the fagoniu* blows.'

'So it's just like in the paintings in the nuns' house?'

'What are you saying, you silly ninny! Those pieces of canvas hung on the walls are fake, false and deceitful. Nature can't be painted or bought. Besides, what can you expect from those shrivelled-up mummies? They've betrayed their own nature and all of nature, as my father and my uncle, God rest his soul, used to say. He could even read and write too. Barren, is what they are! They chose to be barren like the treacherous, deceitful sand. Never mind paintings! Come on, let's walk a little, come . . .'

Tuzzu led me by the hand along an endless expanse of springy blue grass that swayed so much it made you feel like you do after drinking rosolio at Easter.

'Such a silly monkey this picciridda is! First she pesters you like a fly because she wants to see the sea, then when you take her there she doesn't even recognize it.'

The grass gave way beneath my feet and pulled me down; I clung to Tuzzu's arm, terrorized . . . How did you save us from the fire, Tuzzu?

'Don't be afraid! Can't you see I'm holding you? As long as I'm holding you, you don't have to fear either water or fire.'

And it was so. I didn't sink. And we walked along, hand in hand, in the blue sea of Tuzzu's eyes. His hand was hot and gripped me tight . . .

No, it wasn't Tuzzu. It was that bald little man with the lizard eyes, gripping my wrist and shouting. He was always shouting, that little man. Maybe because he didn't wear either a white or a black skirt?

'Look, a seizure! And to make matters worse, her fever has risen again! This girl is going to die on us! Run, Sister Costanza, go immediately to Mother Leonora, and tell her that whatever sin this child has committed, she'd better come quickly or this one will die!'

So that was how to get out of there. That little man wasn't as bad as he seemed. He must also be intelligent. I had to do as he said, and not be quiet and good like I had been those three days.

I closed my eyes to rejoin Tuzzu and the sea that left me fearful and breathless. And with all the strength inspired by desire and terror, I cried out loudly, but with one small variation. Instead of Tuzzu's name, I said: 'Mother! Forgive me, Mother!' And I thought of Tuzzu, whom I had forgotten for so long: 'Forgive me, Mother, forgive me!'

II

Everyone was moved, but Mother Leonora did not appear. She sent word via Sister Costanza's sour, toothless mouth that she had forgiven me, but that she was waiting for God to give me a sign of His forgiveness before she could consider seeing me again.

How will I know when God has forgiven me?

As if she had read my thoughts, Sister Costanza added: 'Don't worry. If this sign manifests itself, Mother Leonora will know about it. We were not deaf to your intention to repent. But intention cannot yet be called repentance. There was too much passion in your tears. Nevertheless, given the state of your health and your good resolve, we accepted Dr Milazzo's suggestion that starting tomorrow, you may go out for a few hours during the day. But take care not to disturb our quiet in the corridors and in the garden with your tears and sighs. This is a great favour that you have been granted; remember that. And pray for the doctor as well, since he interceded for you with such great affection.'

While waiting for God to give me a sign of His forgiveness, I began roaming through the corridors, the colonnade, the garden. That garden had seemed enormous to me when I raced across it so as not to miss a single new word, an adjective, a musical note. Now, like in dreams, it had grown smaller, a shrunken, crowded space. All those women knew but, as if by tacit agreement, they pretended not to see me even when I brushed by them. Exiled from their severe, impassive faces, I felt transparent: only my hands and shoulders felt heavy, forcing me to bend my head toward the ground. I had no appetite anymore. All I longed for was Mother Leonora's smile in the morning, there in the room with the bookshelves that I thought were cupboards when I was little. How Mother Leonora had laughed once when I told her that.

Can such longing weigh you down even if you no longer love her as you did before? Having nothing better to do, I began trying to understand what that longing was. Never mind repenting. What I had to do was study myself and others like you study grammar and music, and stop indulging in my emotions. Such a beautiful word, 'emotions'! But I had no time for words now. I had to think about what that longing was.

After days and days of meditation, I understood. It wasn't Mother Leonora I missed, but all the privileges and attention those women had heaped on me solely for fear of Mother Leonora. Indeed, she gave the orders. Those tears and sighs were nothing but anger over no longer being the darling of the mistress of those handmaidens. Once I realized this, I stopped crying. Because affection, once it's gone, doesn't return.

It had been that way with the lay sister Annina as well. She had seemed so sweet, Annina! We had become such close friends and then she, too, had proved to be a coward. No, affection no longer returns, but favour, yes. You could win back favour.

To do this she had to continue studying her actions and those of others and not forget anything. Forgetting had also been a mistake. Mother Leonora had urged her to forget the past as if it could never return. Instead, a few misguided words were all it took to cast her back into an isolation marked by dry bread and a few bland soups identical to those when, as a child, she would wander about the *chiana* looking for Tuzzu.

Tuzzu was the only thing she remembered . . . why him? Maybe it was natural to try to remember only pleasant times. But if that was so, maybe it wasn't a good thing. Because you learn more from your enemies – she had read that somewhere – and from the bad things of the past that . . . Yes, that must be so. And I decided that from that day on I would always remember everything about the past – both the good things and the bad – in order to bear it in mind and at least avoid repeating the mistakes that had already been made.

'Don't worry about it, princess! There's a cure for everything, except for *La Certa*, Death!'*

Mimmo's voice! It had been more than a month since anyone had spoken to me and I looked at him, startled. As usual, he was leaning against a tree, smoking and smiling. From afar his body, clad in dark brown velvet, looked like another trunk, which by some quirk of nature had sprung up from the oak.

'For those like me who work among the trees, it's an ancient custom to wear nature's colours, to satisfy her whims and be protected by that lady. Nature is a woman and capricious. Take these nuns . . . Oh, not to speak ill of anyone, but with such a small plot of land, who would think they'd have me planting geraniums and hydrangeas . . .'

We had chatted together many times there where the woods were so dense that you couldn't see anything from half a yard away. But given my situation, I couldn't take the chance. Too bad. Not answering, I lowered my head and turned away from him. Truly a pity. Mimmo always had nice things to say to me and hundreds of names for me when I used to run about without a care and would hardly listen to him. He called me sunflower, little missy, princess . . .

'Why princess, Mimmo? I'm not a princess.'

'But you are, you are! A princess by a caprice of Nature, who sometimes enjoys making a royal princess bowlegged while giving a willowy, regal bearing to a nobody. Ah, little princess, my heart aches at the thought that this lily-white skin of yours is destined to wither away among these four walls. Last night at sunset, may God strike me if I'm lying, you looked like a pale rose gilded by the sun. And if I were a bee I would have no other desire than to alight upon the rosebud of your sweet lips.'

Rising on tiptoe, facing him, I responded by closing my eyes:

'Go on Mimmo, make believe you're that bee and alight on me.' But he didn't move. Only when I opened my eyes did he say:

'With your eyes closed, no, princess. The flower and the bee kiss with their eyes open.'

And moving close he placed his large hand between my shoulder and my neck with a touch lighter than I ever thought an oak could possess.

'Besides, my attentions aren't self-serving, princess. Or rather, their only interest is feeling this silky, swanlike neck beneath my fingers. Once I was in Catania, a large city that is far, far away from here, down by the sea. In this city there was an immense park called Villa Bellini – who knows if it's still there? I'm talking about many years ago. They told me that this Bellini had been a great local figure, one of the men whose statues are all around amid the trees. So many statues! And there are not only statues. There's also a kind of platform, where the band plays, not like in theatres where you have to pay, but free for everybody. And then there are a lot of old men sitting under the trees near the statues, ready to tell ancient stories of adventure to those who stop. These old men make you pay, but not much, just a few cents. The best thing in the park is a big lake, full of swans that you can pet if you're polite. And I can assure you, princess, that your skin is as delicate and smooth as . . .'

Incredible. It was true that he had good manners and showed no self-interest. In fact, without finishing the sentence he removed his hand from my neck and touched his cap, departing with a 'Good day, princess'. So not all men were interested in only one thing, as my mother and the nuns insisted. Especially now that I had fallen into disgrace, what interest could he have in talking to me?

'Don't you feel well, princess? Collapsing on the ground like a frightened little chick?'

A voice, after more than a month! I'd like to run away, but he goes on: 'It's damp here, my little chick, extremely damp.'

'That's true, Mimmo, thank you. Now I have to go.'

'Go where? From riches to rags, eh, princess? But don't take it to heart. It happens to everyone at least once. If only it were just once in a lifetime! But you certainly caused a stir! Who would have thought so, a little thing like you! You caused such an uproar that the whole convent is still reeling from it!'

'So you think when someone falls, Mimmo, she can choose whether to fall down hard or gently?'

'*Brava*, princess! I see you haven't lost your sense of humour! A good sign. To tell you the truth, I was a little worried seeing you wandering around like a sleepwalker, all bent over. I said to myself: don't tell me she's becoming hunchbacked from all that praying and penance! You wouldn't be the first young girl I've seen enter these walls nice and straight as a ramrod, who little by little becomes stooped like a beast of burden until she withers away and goes out feet first, pardon the expression, without ever experiencing the rewards of a long, happy old age. My wife and my sister-in-law have white hair, yet they're content, having escaped hunger and illness. But these nuns . . . who can understand them? They say they live chastely, yet they're bowed down as though bearing the most grievous sins.'

Before, when Mimmo started talking that way about the sisters and the convent, I would run away, but now his remarks entered my blood like a soothing balm. I felt the need to straighten up and raise my head.

'There, that's better, *brava*, princess, *brava*: stand straight like you did before.'

'It's just that my hands and arms feel so heavy.'

'Of course. When the body loses its vital spirit, whether due to grief or disgrace or lack of food, the hands and arms sag lifelessly. But that's a bad sign. It means the soul is tired of the body and wants to die. It happened to me when I got the notice that my oldest son, Nunziato, had died in the war in Libya. My arms felt heavy; they were pulling me toward him. And to keep going – six children, flesh of my flesh, were depending on me for bread – to keep going, I had to cut off those arms. Now they work, they move, but I don't feel them anymore. They're gone along with him, princess.'

'I have to go now, Mimmo; they might come.'

'No, for now no one is coming: the oak is silent. But if you feel uneasy, go. But nice and straight, eh! Grab yourself by the hair and pull your spirit up. Because all they're waiting for, even if they don't know it, is to see you stoop so far over that you'll find yourself six feet under.'

'No, don't say that, Mimmo. You're such a good man, why do you talk like that?'

'Because it's the truth. What do you think? That a good person can't see the truth? You know who you have to thank for at least being able to go outside?'

'Of course I know: the doctor.'

'That's right, the doctor. But the doctor alone wouldn't have been able to do it if a novice hadn't died eight or ten years ago. She was your age more or less and, like you, she too was a protégée of Mother Leonora.'

'How did she die?'

'She killed herself, dear child. And who could blame her? Locked up in that room for more than a month, she became despondent and jumped from the window. See, that one over there. I found her splattered on the ground at daybreak. No one had heard a thing. These convents have thick walls, bomb-proof walls, so as not to hear either the tears or the joys of this world. Look, that's the window.'

'That's the room I'm in.'

'Of course! Because it's the cell adjacent to Mother Leonora's. That's where her protégées end up.'

'But how did she do it? There are iron grilles . . .'

'No, they put those in afterwards. As they say in Catania, Saint Agatha's sanctuary was robbed first, then later they put in a gate . . . Anyway, as I was telling you, the doctor – who just so you know is a man of pure mind and heart, who knows the law besides medicine – the doctor was able to obtain approval for you to have a breath of fresh air and some recreation by reminding them of that suicide which everybody here, apart from me, had forgotten. Of course, now they've sent him away. But he is a man of true conviction, and he went away untroubled. I'll say goodbye now, princess. The oak tree is telling me that the troops are on the move and that you and I had better go our separate ways.'

The oak is telling me . . . It was actually true. All he had to do was lean his head against the gnarled trunk to know if there was any movement in the woods. I tried it too, but the tree said nothing to me. Yet after a few minutes the white skirts of the novices began to appear amidst the low-growing shrubbery. They came toward me and then pretended to be startled, scampering away in exaggerated terror punctuated by shrieks and laughter. The oak did not speak to me, but it had been right to warn Mimmo. That's it, come and laugh as much as you please. Now I know how to put a stop to all this fun you're having. Enjoy yourselves while the farce lasts since, as Mimmo says, 'he who laughs last laughs best'.

12

To get out of that situation, I had to die. And die just the way Mimmo had suggested to me: that is, by jumping out of the window. But which one? Fortunately there were bars on mine, because it would have been too high and, on top of that, there were no geranium beds, no trees or shrubs that would keep me from breaking all my bones. I cared about this body of mine, which had given me so much joy.

I searched for three days without finding a single window that did not have those loathsome iron grilles. Finally, discouraged, I sat on the grass and leaned my head against the rusty rim of the well. The flock of sheep, as Mimmo called them, never ventured there. Why not? Indeed, why was it they never came near the old well, and when one of them glimpsed it from afar, she swiftly crossed herself three times and looked away? That's their business. For me it was better this way. I had at least found a place where I could concentrate undisturbed in the sun, since by this time I was no longer able to either think or read in my cell. How could I manage to die if all the windows had bars? '*E caddi come corpo morto cade*'. . .* How could I appear perfectly dead, 'even as a dead body falls', to quote the Poet, without really ending up in the odious arms of *La Certa*?

'Did the princess by chance call for me? If you'll excuse my saying so, you should not let yourself be lulled into sleep like that, under the April sun. April entices us with her false warmth. She caresses you with caring hands, but she's ready to abandon you to the venomous dampness as soon as shadows fall.'

'Who told you I was looking for you, the oak tree?'

'As usual, and it was right. Even now, your eyes are calling to me, princess, but they don't know whether to trust a stranger or not. Because, even though I've seen you grow with the tenacity of a healthy plant, we're still strangers, aren't we?'

'Do you know why the sisters never come near this well and why, when they see it, they cross themselves as if they've seen the devil?'

'I see that since they've kept you in quarantine you've sharpened your tongue, eh, princess?'

'Not just my tongue, Mimmo, I've sharpened my wits as well. It's just that . . .'

'What? The well? It worries you, this well? Stay away from it, child!'

'Why?'

'Because it lures tormented souls. I myself have counted two of them who listened to its voice.'

'Whose voice?'

'The well's water of oblivion, princess. And they jumped in. I fished two of them out myself, with these arms. My father, in his day, pulled another one out. My grandfather, God rest his soul, who knows how many! But he was of the old school, and kept quiet about it. At that time people kept quiet about everything. Even at home, with one's own blood, you didn't talk. People were mute in those days! But things have been changing these past twenty years. In the villages down in the valley people are beginning to talk, guardedly, of course, but they talk. And on the continent, from what my son tells me – he's a merchant, so he comes and goes – there's a flurry of talk and new ideas. They even speak out against this war that has broken out. When did people ever speak out against a war, before! This son of mine, Giovanni, says that the wind of rebellion is coming here too, stirring people's minds, especially in the sulphur mines and saltworks . . . You should hear him! He's really passionate about these new rebellious ideas.'

'Rebellion against whom?'

'Who else do the poor rebel against? Against the rich, the barons, the Church.'

'So the doctor was one of these?'

'Of course. Not at first, but in the last few years he changed, like my son Giovanni.'

'But he's not poor. He's a doctor.'

'He must be an exception. Although my Giovanni tells me that over there, on the continent, there are many doctors and teachers and lawyers who are on the side of the people.'

'But can what your son tells you be true?'

'Of course! And I'm worried. He's always talking about these things. He's a hothead, my Giovanni! I'm afraid that one fine day . . .'

'And what do you think about it?'

'Me, princess? I'm wary by nature. Then too, even though I criticize the rules of this convent and many, many other things about the Church that aren't clear, I still believe in God. Oh yes, I believe in God.'

'Ah, why, don't they believe in God?'

'Well, if it were simply that they didn't believe in Him, child, that I could understand. But they hate and oppose Him. That's what makes me wary, you see. Without the Gospel's teachings, our young people have only a dark future ahead of them . . . You're all flushed. What is it? Is it the thought of all these godless people? Eh, it's Mimmo's fault! You're right, my child. Mimmo talks too much!'

What could I say? That discovering that I was not alone in doubting God had brought on a heat flash, forcing me to clamp my mouth shut to keep from screaming with joy? Lowering my head and clenching my fists to drive my nails into my palms (this would make me grow pale, I knew), I said, 'Don't worry, I'm all right, Mimmo.'

'It worries me seeing you hanging around this well. I told you, I pulled two of them out myself, with my own arms.'

His anxiety showed me I was right on the mark. He wouldn't let me out of his sight again, not for a moment. My eyes rolling, the pallor increasing as my nails dug into my palms, I stood up, lurching so that he had to hold me up.

'Don't worry, Mimmo, it was the sun and the dampness. You were right. Good thing you woke me. Although now . . . Maybe it would have been a blessing for me to get acute double pneumonia and go to be with God . . . Thank you, Mimmo. Goodbye.'

Without looking back, I set off toward the convent with an unsteady step, as they say in novels. Behind me I sensed him standing stock-still, frozen by his concern, and I almost felt pity for him. The urge to turn around and run to reassure him was so strong that I staggered for real. Yet this was no time for pity. It was time to act.

13

But acting did not turn out to be as easy as I'd thought. For days and days, masses of clouds raced over the convent like the immense wings of crazed birds, and I was afraid. I went to the well, I stared into its depths, but there too, the cloud masses flapped their dark wings against the slippery walls, only to end up being sucked under by the stagnant water at the bottom. I was shivering with cold. Mimmo was certainly always around now, like a sentinel, and this assured me that his concern was ever vigilant. But he did not approach me again. Surely his apprehension had overcome his relish for chatting with someone, which always did him good. He himself had once told me:

'Forgive me, *Voscenza*, if I don't talk today, princess. It's just that I'm gripped by thoughts that kill my appetite and my desire to talk.'

And coward that I am, I couldn't make up my mind to take the leap that would have liberated both him and me. How could I? I didn't even dare think of those lava walls that slid round and round all the way down to the invisible depths. By day I pounded my head and chest, accusing myself of being cowardly. At night the well's eye never left me, staring at me from the dark corners of the cell, keeping me awake and clinging to the sheets for fear of falling in. I could never do it. It was hopeless. If only I'd known how to swim! If only Tuzzu had taken me to see the sea and taught me to swim! He said it was easy even for a silly ninny, a *scemuzza*, like me.

'First you have to learn to do the dead-man's float: you just lie on the water like you lie on the grass, on your back, confident, and spread your arms and legs. If you're not afraid, then the water holds you up just like the earth does now.'

The dark grass parted under the weight of my dead body, dragging me off to slap against the convent's outer wall, while the sun's fiery globe succumbed and went smiling into the lava arms of *La Certa*. The sun was lying: he knew he would never die . . .

No, I would never have done it if the sign of God's forgiveness had not come from Sister Costanza's toothless mouth.

'God has forgiven you. Here is a suitcase. Gather your things: sweaters, skirts, stockings, a change of sheets and pillowcases, a blanket and all your personal items, including the gold rosary with mother-of-pearl beads that Mother Leonora gave you. Prayer books too, of course, but not the others. You will not have the opportunity to study where you are going, but in return you will have the privilege of learning a skill. You will choose it yourself: seamstress, embroiderer, cook. You will choose among these humble skills that are the only suitable ones for a woman. Studying is a luxury that corrupts, as our Superior from Turin used to say. I have never opened a book that was not a prayer book. And when, God willing, I become the leader of this community, there will be an end to this waste of time and money. In two or three days, when the next coach comes by, you will go to the orphanage in Pietraperzia, which is well known for its strictness and discipline.* Mother Leonora herself will assume the responsibility of paying the monthly fee. And so that you may be aware of her magnanimity and adopt it as a model, you should know that – provided your conduct improves over the years – you will not have to worry about your future when you come of age and find yourself back in the world. Because she has remembered you in her will. She is very ill.

'I see that you are not rejoicing at the good news that I have brought you. And that tells me, contrary to what Mother Leonora insisted – she is always too good, much too good to keep a firm hold on the reins of this convent – that the isolation of these past months was not enough to take you down a peg or two and make you realize how many sins of pride you have committed during these years. Not to mention other sins I don't know about and don't want to know about. It was of no use at all. We, the older ones, have never been wrong: our decision was the right one. Where you are going you will learn humility and abnegation, the only disciplines that can lead to the soul's salvation. We elders thought only of this: saving your soul.

'Goodbye for now, Modesta. We will say our farewells properly before you leave this house. You have been granted permission to bid us all adieu in a formal ceremony. First, so that your departure may be impressed more deeply in your mind, and then to provide an example to the other young women, so that they may know what is lost by being sinfully arrogant. Have you nothing to say?'

'Will Mother Leonora be there? Will I . . .'

'No.'

And with that she vanished, the door closing behind her, burying the one faint hope that had appeared in that avalanche of words. If I could only see her! She couldn't be so uncaring toward me if she had remembered me in her will. I had to see her! I had to die to see her again: there was no other way. Or had I been dreaming? No, the suitcase lying on the bed was real, and it was filling up with small dark creatures: bedbugs. I knew all about bedbugs. Soon they would infest the white walls and drive me out. Without realizing it, I found myself clinging to the bars of the window. Fortunately, the sun was still high.

If the sun was out, Mimmo had to be out there too. Rigid with apprehension, Mimmo would be in his place keeping watch . . . There he was, among the trees. He must have spotted me, because with a little leap he went and hid behind a bigger trunk. I ran, so I wouldn't get cold feet, and tried not to think about the well's gaping mouth. Sister Costanza's voice spurred me on: '*No books where you're going . . . they won't be of any use where you're going . . . you'll learn a skill . . . humility . . .*'

My sweaty hands slipped on the polished stone. Twice I fell to the ground and got back up, but eventually I was standing on the brink. So Mimmo could see me clearly . . . And maybe because I had run so hard, or because Sister Costanza's voice echoing in my head made me lose my balance, or because the edge of the well was smooth and slippery, I slid down without even having to summon the courage I had so anxiously sought for so long.

14

I'd like to tell you how it felt to plunge into that dark bottomless pit but I can't, because for the first and last time in my life I fainted – for real, not on purpose as I had always done. So neither you nor I will ever know anything about it. What I learned was that Mimmo saved me. And that while I wasn't hurt, except for some scrapes and a few small cuts on my face and legs, Mimmo broke his arm. I was a bit remorseful, but since he went around telling anyone who pitied him, 'It's nothing! Nothing serious. A broken arm can be reset, but there's no way to recall a soul once it leaves a body!', if he's happy, I'm happy.

As for me, lying between the lily-white sheets of my reclaimed bed, with my eyes closed so no one could see my joy, I was happier than God Himself in His paradise, as they say.* I listened to Mother Leonora's voice as she spoke, though it was not her earlier voice. Her voice had faded a little, as though worn out. Nevertheless, it was still her voice, at last. She said that everyone in the convent was moved – about time! – and that even though I had fallen into mortal sin by attempting to take my own life, there was no denying that it was also a sign: that I should remain there, with them, within those walls. Together we would pray to cleanse ourselves (what an ugly word, I thought) of this sin as well. If she kept me there and let me study like before, I would gladly pray. Night and day I would pray, and I would truly repent my naivety and imprudence.

I had grown up now. And though earlier I had been careful enough to measure every word, every gesture, now I was nothing but prudent: a cluster of nerves and veins firmly linked by fear of acting rashly. Even now, although she kept asking me to open my eyes, I didn't dare look at her. That face had stirred too much emotion in me. The fear of seeing it again after so long, that something in its features might set off some odd notion in my brain, told me that it would be better to wait at least until the next visit.

'Till tomorrow, Modesta. Our time is up. Rest quietly and pray. Pray like you're doing now. I can tell, you know, by the way your lips are moving.'

Only when the swish of her skirt told me that she was about to go out the door, only then did I open my eyes a slit and get a glimpse of her: she had become very small, like a scrap of cloth that has shrunk after too many washings. It was a good thing I hadn't opened my eyes before, because my heart leapt and I was shaken. Unable to help it, I started crying and sobbing. But for real, with real tears, as the Poet says.*

My tears curdled, froze in astonishment, when I saw her the next day. She was no longer herself. Two harsh lines at the corners of her mouth drew her lips into a pinched grimace. Was this the reason her voice was now shrill and metallic and spoke of nothing but sin, hell, repentance and death? As soon as she left, I wished never to see her again, something I would have thought impossible at one time. I decided to get better quickly so I wouldn't have to be subjected to that hour of fire-and-brimstone. Each day I had her find me dressed, my cheeks rosy and fresh thanks to pinching and a splash of cold water.

'Excellent, Modesta. I see you have responded well, and haven't let yourself be sinfully lulled by the languor of convalescence. I am quite pleased to see how you have grown these past months. In bed you looked very small, like you once were. But you've grown tall and strong. Don't let it be a source of pride, however. Temptation may lurk even in bodily well-being. Pray! This healthiness of yours is all due to prayer, and to Saint Agatha who has watched over you. I've dreamt of her constantly in recent months and, at times, I saw her living and breathing as I see you now. She came to me, and with her eyes told me not to worry because she was watching over you. Now I must go. My visits would only be an indulgence now that I see you are back on your feet. I must go at once; other afflicted souls are awaiting me. Starting tomorrow, we will see each other only at prayer in the chapel, and during classes. Sister Angelica will be happy to see you back at the embroidery frame again. She says that since you've been absent, the tapestry has not progressed as before.'

At last that stranger's voice fell silent, and she left. By now I hated her. Unexpectedly, that feeling of hate – which they said was a sin – gave me a burst of joy so intense that I had to clench my fists and clamp my mouth shut to keep from singing and jumping up and down. As soon as I felt calm again, I timidly whispered *I hate her* to see whether the effect would repeat itself or whether a lightning bolt would strike my head. It was raining outside. My voice hit me like a fresh breeze that set me free from dread and dejection. How could those forbidden words give me so much energy? I would think about it later. Now I just had to repeat them out loud, so they would never again elude me: *I hate her, I hate her, I hate her*, I shouted, after making sure that the door was firmly shut. The carapace of depression broke off my body in pieces as my chest expanded, jolted by the energy of that feeling. Wrapped in my smock, I can't breathe anymore. What is it that's still squeezing my chest?

Tearing off my smock and shirt, my hands found those tight strips 'so your breasts won't show,' which until that moment had felt like a second skin to me. A seemingly compliant skin that bound me with its reassuring whiteness. I took the scissors and cut them to shreds. I had to breathe. And finally naked – how long had it been since I'd felt my naked body? we even had to bathe with our shirts on – I rediscover my flesh. My released breasts explode beneath my palms and I stroke myself there on the floor, taking pleasure in the caresses which those magic words had triggered.

15

No lightning struck my head while outside the rain continued beating against the window panes. My naked body, flushed with pleasure, felt it falling faintly. A gentle April rain between my breasts, hips wide open to welcome spring's freshness. I had rediscovered my body. During those months of exile, locked up in that armour of despair, I had stopped stroking myself. Blinded by terror, I had forgotten that I had breasts, a belly, legs. So sorrow, humiliation and fear were not, as they said, a source of purification and beatitude. They were slimy thieves that took advantage of sleep to creep to your bedside in the night and rob you of the joy of being alive. Those women didn't make a sound when they passed you or went in and out of their cells: they had no body. I didn't want to become insubstantial like them. And now that I had rediscovered the intensity of my pleasure, I would never again surrender to the renunciation and humiliation that they preached so much. I had those words to fight back with. And my physical exercise – that's how I thought of it now. In the chapel, a rosary between my fingers, I kept repeating: *I hate*. Bent over the embroidery frame under Sister Angelica's dull gaze, I said over and over again: *I hate*. At night before going to sleep: *I hate*. From that day on, this was my new prayer.

Along with praying, I studied. I searched for the meaning of those words in books. But other than God's wrath and Lucifer's envy, I didn't find anything. Maybe all those people who hated the Church

58

had different books. Mimmo had talked about them with respect and fear: 'I don't agree with them, but I have to admit that since Giovanni made contact with those people, he seems like a different man: confident, forceful . . .'

So they, too, were happy by virtue of hatred. How could I get to know them? The doctor had been one of them, but I was just a child then. What could I know? Now he was gone. Too bad! I resigned myself to not knowing anything about it. But if I continued studying with that hatred in my body which was more nutritious than bread and which gave me the strength to apply myself day and night – everyone in the convent marvelled at it – I could become a teacher. From what they said, women were beginning to teach on the continent. And as a teacher I would certainly meet those people. Plus, Mother Leonora had remembered me in her will . . . I just had to be patient. Mother Leonora was suffering from an incurable disease. Another year or two, and I would be free. But even Mother Leonora's affliction must have had enormous magical powers, because, despite her illness, each day she appeared straighter and less gaunt . . . and she'd gotten her wind back! Far from having breathing difficulties, all she did was talk. And they weren't tremulous, humble words like before, but insidious, confident words, not open to discussion. Listen to this:

'I've been sentenced, Modesta. The doctor gave me five or six years at the most. But I thank God for these years that He has still granted me because I know that they will be enough to mould you and make your vocation blossom from your soul. I can tell you keep it hidden in your breast like a precious jewel. I will close my eyes only when I see you wearing this habit that I, too, wear. Because you should know that my entire trousseau as Christ's bride will go to you when I die. A costly trousseau, which fits you perfectly, as though it were a sign from God. When I was your age, I was the same size as you.'

Did you hear that? There's more:

'Don't be frightened, Modesta. You're frightened because you don't yet know the blissful sweetness of renunciation and humility. Your youthful fibre is still too full of animal vitality, of physical well-being. In fact, I spoke to Sister Costanza about it. We would like you, please, to decrease your food intake, at least in the evening. By now you are all grown up and healthy. Any denial at the table can only help you pray. Starting tomorrow, your supper will be bread and milk like the lay sisters. But, as I said, don't be frightened. I won't force you, and to prove it to you, I would like you to read a copy of my will. The original has been entrusted to a notary in Modica, for safekeeping . . . You see? It says that you will receive this annuity even if God does not grant you the grace to become part of His ranks. And so sincere is my desire to do nothing but honour your wishes that, here, attached to the will, is a document signed by the doctor confirming that you lost your virginity due to causes . . . but never mind. I don't want to remind you of all those terrible things, that infernal suffering. The important thing is that if after my death you would prefer to re-enter the world, this document will be of help to you, since you must know that no man will wed a girl unless he is assured of her physical and moral integrity.'

And on and on for days, for months. Here's more, even if you no longer care to listen:

'Don't be afraid, these documents are proof that I do not wish to force you to do anything, and that, whether I am dead or alive, you will only take your vows when and if you are ready. But I also know that God will not call me to Him before I have carried out this charge. Perhaps all my suffering had only this as its purpose: to lead you to Him.'

Whether because of this steady stream day after day, or the supper of bread and milk that made me wake up hungry and tired, the effect of that hatred deserted me. The doctor had given her five or six years, at least. And what if the illness that was buoying her up was so powerful that it might actually sustain her until she completed her mission? Oh, no! That was too many years, even if I had achieved the power of hate and the cunning of prudence. Indeed, it was precisely because of these achievements that I now recognized the fragility of my nature and all natures. I was afraid I would not be able to keep up the lie for such a long time. No! Even just five or six years were too many. I either had to run away from here or be fortunate enough to have her God call her back to His eternal side as soon as possible.

16

Running away was unthinkable. Where could she go? Even if she were able to get across the lava wall that surrounded the convent, which wouldn't be easy, Mimmo said it took five or six hours to reach the town on foot . . . what was its name? To her dismay, she realized that in all those years she had studied French, even Latin, but she had not spoken to anyone who wasn't a nun or a priest. She sensed that their language was different from the one she would have to speak outside, in the world. With Mimmo it was different. Like it or not, he was part of the convent.

Thinking about these things, the hatred left her, giving way to a lassitude that spread through her chest and arms, forcing her to lie down on the sun-warmed bench. Was hate deserting her? Or was all that milk they made her drink in the evening diluting the strong feeling that had earlier sustained her? Even if she wanted to dream, like in a novel, once she reached the town, would she be able to elude the *carabinieri*? Could she find a position as a maid – how charming she would look with her apron and starched white cap – in a house where she would meet an officer, a friend of the family – or better yet, why not? the son himself – who, beguiled by her charm, would ask her to marry him? Where had she read all this? Ah yes! It was that pathetic Annina, the lay sister, who was punished endlessly for reading that drivel. But even if that officer asked her to be his wife, she wouldn't be able to marry him. Men don't marry women who have lost their virginity. Mother

Leonora had me in her grip. There was no way out. If only I had that certificate! Then too, if I ran away I would lose the inheritance I had worked so hard to come by. Maybe it was better to stay. On the whole, Mother Leonora was kind to me; she had forgiven me, after all. And perhaps in time she would become gentle again, like before . . .

Mimmo's face, blurred by the sun, appears against the sky, up there among the vine leaves . . .

'You shouldn't give in to the lure of the sun like that, princess. Being poor is a venom that weakens us; the lack of food muddles the brain. I have to agree with Giovanni on this. He says that the poor fancy the rich as being kind and generous so that they won't feel even more humiliated at having to kowtow and revere them.'

Mimmo was right, that sun was harmful. It had muddled my thinking. It was only my awareness of being poor that made Mother Leonora seem kind and beautiful to me . . . I shouldn't fall asleep in the sun; it had happened once before and I fell into the well. My eyes snapped open. How long had I slept? Mimmo wasn't there, yet I had heard his voice. Had I been dreaming? I was about to get up – the bench beneath me had lost its warmth and shivers were running down my arms – when Mimmo's voice once more pinned me to the chilly surface. Mimmo had spoken, but not to me, and now his lilting voice was trying to persuade someone there behind the hedge. Something told me I should listen. You could tell from the way they spoke that they hadn't seen me. Plus, the hedge that separated us was tall and dense. I closed my eyes again, pretending to be asleep.

'*Voscenza* will forgive me, Mother Leonora, for being so bold as to contradict you. For once, listen to an old man who, though ignorant, knows about these things. That balustrade you lean on at night is rotted. It should be replaced.'

'But it's made of iron, and besides it's very old. As long as I'm alive I won't allow that masterpiece to be replaced by that horrible railing the village blacksmith made.'

'But the blacksmith is a fine craftsman, Mother, if I may say so, and he made it to look like the other one in every detail.'

'How can you say that! You can tell it's an imitation, and a poor one at that.'

'True, Mother. But what harm is there? We're only going to remove it; it's not like we're discarding it. We'll remove it carefully and put it someplace else, where you can see it whenever you like. But do me this favour, Mother. I don't like to think of you going around that tower, leaning here and there.'

'But it's made of iron, Mimmo!'

'Iron, yes, but corroded, eaten away by age and bad weather. In some places – just yesterday I went to check – there are spots that look like they've been sawn. Sawn, I swear to God! With all due respect, *Voscenza,* I wouldn't want to see you go tumbling down some night . . .'

The voice went on imploring, but I'd stopped listening. That *sawn* reinspired the lost hate that had been drowned in all that milk they made me drink in the evening. Besides, I never liked milk.

17

Starting that night, I got busy. I had to work quickly, because Mimmo was very good at convincing people, rich and poor, men and women, animals and devils, as Sister Teresa said.

A saw was easy to find in the equipment shed behind the kitchen. There were saws of all shapes and sizes. And after gulping down the milk and soft, bland bread among all those flaccid white faces – I swear! what other colouring could all those future brides of Christ have? – instead of going to bed I waited until all the doors were closed before slipping out. Hugging the walls closely – I knew every stone of those corridors, every corner and every door – I climbed up toward the cool darkness, even darker than the pitch-black of the stairs. Luckily there was neither moon nor stars. Though the mornings were sunny, for days and days a dense cloud covering descended from sunset to dawn, obscuring Mother Leonora's firmament. She moaned about it – it wasn't the cloudy season – but for me it was a sign that I had to act, or saw, if you prefer. For several nights I sawed until dawn, protected by that mass of clouds until the first light of day. I sawed at four places, the four points that supported the weight of the telescope. When my work was done, I threw myself on my bed, exhausted – I hadn't slept for days and days – and contented. At last I could sleep. Now all I had to do was wait for a clear night.

Strangely enough, however, I couldn't sleep a wink, maybe because

I had become used to sleeping little or not at all, or because I was worried that the balustrade might be replaced. I would fall asleep but then quickly wake up, obsessed with keeping an eye on it. A clear night did not come. It rained now, even in the daytime.

'What a shame, princess, just this year when nature promised such a great harvest! There hasn't been such a spell of foul weather around here as long as anyone can remember. All that good wheat and hay will be ruined if this continues.' I prayed along with Mimmo that the skies would clear, because otherwise my wheat and hay would rot as well if things went on like this.

There was nothing I could do. At night, clinging to the window bars, I almost wept with rage. Not a star could be seen, not a breath of wind stirred that dark, dense mass. Exhausted, I sank onto the bed. Let it all rot, wheat and rye and hay. That night I would sleep. I'd had enough. And I slept so deeply that, according to what they told me afterwards, only Sister Costanza's slaps – she never missed an opportunity – were able to wake me up. Howling, weeping, doors slamming in the wake of the frantic clanging of the bell, dragged me out of bed terrified. I thought: an earthquake!

'Worse than that, child! Worse! Hurry, come to the chapel, you're the only one missing. We're all in the chapel, praying. Mother Leonora fell from the tower! Who would have expected it?'

I had never heard such joy in Sister Costanza's sorrowful voice.

'Who would have thought she'd go up to her observatory! There's been nothing but thunder and lightning all night. Who would have imagined it! Come, hurry! Mimmo has laid her out as best he could; he's the one who heard the scream. Come to the chapel to see her one last time and keep vigil for her!'

Keep vigil? Me? All night and maybe the next morning too, when I was dying for some sleep? I wouldn't dream of it.

'Come, child, get a move on! Don't stand there in a daze. Naturally, I understand how you feel; you are the one most affected by this tragedy. You were so devoted to her and she loved you so much! But take heart. Accept this great trial that God has sent you.'

So then, if I were the most affected, I could very well faint out of grief and thus avoid the ordeal they wanted to inflict on me. *E caddi come corpo morto cade*, I fell like a dead body falls, as the Poet and master of life says. And there was no way to wake me, either that night or the following day.

18

I woke up only when my bowels, which had become a hard knot in the prior twenty-four hours, began turning into countless burning tentacles. My tongue – at first I didn't know I had a tongue – was so swollen and parched that the nursing sister had difficulty getting me to swallow a teaspoonful of a warm, fragrant liquid.

'Poor child! How she's suffering! Look at the state she's in! Three days without eating or drinking! And still she's spitting out this little bit of broth!'

I wasn't the one spitting it out; on the contrary, I liked it. It was my tongue, which no longer obeyed me. Had I perhaps taken too many of those pills? I'll explain: in order to be able to sleep for so long, every night and every morning during those three days I had swallowed some of those capsules that make you sleep. The doctor had introduced me to them a long time ago. Veronal, they were called, and every night he would give me one to quiet me. At that time, despite my fear, I had never swallowed them; instead I had hidden them away for a time when I might perhaps need them. And it was a good thing, because they spared me a final meeting with Mother Leonora, and, from what I now learned, her funeral as well. The pills had proved useful, but I was so afraid of having taken too many – the doctor had told me that they could be toxic – that I couldn't help asking, 'Am I dying?'

'No, daughter, no, don't say that word again. You've done nothing but repeat that word these past three days. No, the doctor examined you. There's nothing wrong with you. Just grief and malnutrition, that's what he said, and that all we could do was hope you might regain the will to live. I see that this will has returned, since you are afraid of dying. Eat, child, and pray. Wanting to die is a terrible sin. Mother Leonora would be saddened. Think of her, and take heart. What a pity you didn't see her! Her body was all shattered, but her face was untouched, beautiful and serene. The face of a saint.'

If a doctor – I wonder who this new doctor was? – had said there was nothing wrong with me, I had nothing to worry about, so I gulped down that good broth that flowed into my stomach like liquid sunshine.

'Good girl, Modesta, *brava*! That's the way to make Mother Leonora happy, not by wanting to die, as you've done these past days! That's how Mother Leonora wanted to see you. Eat, eat. Don't disappoint her now that she's dead, just as you would not have disappointed her when she was alive.'

So as not to disappoint Mother Leonora, I ate so much that in a few days I was back on my feet and able to listen to Sister Costanza's cackling voice without much fear of the suitcase – it was an obsession with her – that she laid on my bed when she came in.

'Gather your things, Modesta. You may take with you your precious rosary, the picture of Saint Agatha and the books that Mother Leonora in her immense generosity gave you, your personal undergarments and the bands. Don't forget the bands: continue binding your chest even after you are exposed to all the worldly dangers where you are going.'

I didn't dare ask for an explanation, or take my eyes off the suitcase where already some small bedbugs evoked by Sister Costanza's words began to dot the tan-coloured leather with black.

'I am not permitted to utter worldly names and places; we no longer belong to that world. But you must not worry, because Mother Leonora has thought of you. In her magnanimity she wanted you to be the one to choose whether to join the ranks of the Lord or remain out in the world. And so that you might make this choice freely, in full awareness, she also decided that you should first come to learn about the world. That is all. They will come for you in the afternoon . . . I see your bewilderment, my daughter. Like you, I disagree with this, because the Lord sent you here when you were nothing but a defiled, terrified little creature and your place is here with us. But that is what her will states and that is what must be done. Go in peace. My heart is untroubled: I know that we shall meet again.'

I was bewildered by the unfamiliar quality that shone through every word Sister Costanza spoke and by the gentleness her voice now held. I decided to look at her, and I nearly fainted for real. She was almost beautiful. It was as if something had straightened her up, and her lips were smiling as her eyes wandered vaguely around the room. She was dreaming about Mother Leonora's chapel stall; it was the rigid back of that oak seat that had straightened her. I almost regretted being the one who had brought about that happiness of hers. But there was no time for regret. I had to pack quickly.

Troubled by that unfamiliar presence, I began gathering my things . . . '*Don't forget the bands, continue binding your chest . . . dangers . . . where you are going . . .*' That *where you are going* made my hands shaky and I kept dropping things. I couldn't find anything. The binding strips slipped out of my fingers and rolled into the corners, between the feet of the bed, and I had to start all over again. The suitcase was too small; it wouldn't close. Sweating, I finally managed to close it by kneeling heavily on the lid. And whether it was the exertion or Sister Costanza's radiant face that made me really angry, I sat on the suitcase and started to cry, appealing to Mother Leonora to at least tell me where she was sending me. Did she mean to take revenge?

19

She had undoubtedly chosen some horrible place where I would necessarily find my vocation. Sister Costanza had been very certain when she said: 'I know that we shall meet again.' With my fists clenched to my temples, which were bursting from that *I know that we shall meet again*, I didn't hear the door open.

'What's the matter? Are you crying, princess? You loved her so much, did you? Well, I did too. I don't cry, because it's not something men do, but inside, well . . .! She was a great lady! But come now, come along. It's best for you to go. Dark times are ahead for this convent. Just now, a sealed letter from Palermo arrived. Sister Costanza is replacing Mother Leonora! Dark times! Come, get up, let me take your suitcase. I'll carry it for you. Sister Costanza sent me to you because they mustn't watch you leave . . . What's wrong? Are you trembling? Don't be upset! Weep for her, of course, because it's fitting that the dead be remembered with tears; she loved you like a daughter. But now come, come with me. You'll see that even though she's dead, she hasn't abandoned you.'

I clung to Mimmo's arm – before I would never have been able to do that. I no longer felt like one of them. What could they do to me now, even if they were watching me from the half-closed shutters of all those windows in the courtyard? – I gripped his arm tightly, when my eyes fell upon something so grand it made my legs shakier than my earlier fear had: a carriage without horses. Or were the horses under that long tube that gleamed in the sun? Surely the horses must be in there, looking out from those big glass eyes framed in gold.

'It's not a carriage, princess, it's a modern-day deviltry that runs as if there were ten horses pulling it . . . I'm old-fashioned and I don't care for all these new contraptions. I'm wary of them. I saw one down in the village, and it seemed like a freak of nature to me, a giant cockroach. What do I know! But I swear to God, this one takes your breath away, it's so beautiful. It looks like a cathedral!'

Assisted by Mimmo and a tall gentleman – surely an officer – wearing a dark uniform and a shirt so white that the sisters' wimples seemed grey by comparison, I climbed into that cathedral, though I did not let go of Mimmo's hand.

'There you are, sit right here, *signorina*. If you feel sick or something makes you uncomfortable during the trip, see this? It's a receiver: pick it up and talk into it. That way I can hear you through the glass if need be.'

'Did you hear that, princess? If you hurt yourself – because this thing runs; it's not like a carriage, it runs like the devil – just lift up that tube and tell him.'

'But who is he, Mimmo? An officer?'

'No, a driver is . . . is like a coachman . . . I'll say goodbye now, princess. I know we won't see each other again. This carriage-automobile is grand and Mother Leonora is watching over you. But whatever you may need – by God's grace you are able to write – know that I am here. Remember: Mimmo Insanguine, gardener at the convent of the Sisters of the Sorrowful Mother, Sciarascura. Remember that. Farewell, princess.'

The coachman drew my hand from Mimmo's, saying gently, 'Forgive me, *signorina*, but it's getting late.'

And he closed the door. Mimmo's hand lost, I clung to the window glass and looked at him: his arm was raised in farewell. I watched him until his large body, sheathed in brown velvet, blended among the tree trunks, merging with the oaks that surrounded the convent's immense lava wall.

20

When Mimmo was taken from me, swallowed up by that sea of oaks, a great weariness made me slump on that soft seat, softer than my bed and all the sofas and chairs in the music room. The carriage – what did Mimmo say it was called? – was like a small room in dark velvet. There were even windows with pleated shades, which filtered in a gentle green light like the leaves in the woods do when the sun is high and scorching. Now that I had said goodbye to Mimmo, I closed the shades on that window as well. What good did it do to look at all those mountains, as bare as Sister Teresa's bald head? I had seen it for myself, that head! How had it happened? It was very hot, I had gone to the lesson way too early and she had hastened to put her coif back on.

'Oh Modesta, no, you shouldn't enter like that without knocking. No, no, you mustn't do that!'

'But I knocked . . .'

'Well then, that tells me I'm getting deaf, as well as blind! It's high time, for that matter. I'm really beginning to feel I can't take any more of these exercises and scales, all those stupid girls banging the keys as if they were monkeys and not God's creatures . . . Bah! All in all, growing old isn't as bad as they say, Modesta. There's the advantage of no longer seeing Sister Costanza's ugly puss, may God forgive me, of no longer hearing . . . but don't get me started! Plus, as you see, only old age has allowed me the consolation of wearing this light coif when the sun is so hot. But come, let's get started. You keep me talking here and nothing gets accomplished. Let's go, in groups of four: one, two, three, four . . . one, two, three, four . . .'

She had been right to close those green shades and not see Sister Teresa's bald head multiplying up, up, amid the dust and heat, to where the last cranium joined the sky . . . Terrified, she raised her hands to her head. No, they hadn't shaved her. The thick, sturdy braids were still there, having escaped Sister Costanza's scissor-sharp fingers just in time.

'You must call me Mother Costanza now, Modesta, say it: Mother Costanza . . .'

Or maybe now that she held the convent's reins, the woman had had second thoughts and was chasing after her. Maybe she would stop the carriage with those strong hands of hers?

'Does the *signorina* feel ill? If I may say so, I saw your head swaying left and right in the rear-view mirror and I took it upon myself to stop.'

'No, I'm not ill, sir, thank you. It's just that I have a hollow feeling here, in my stomach, and I feel drowsy.'

'Don't be alarmed, *signorina*. It's nothing. The automobile has this effect on all the women and young ladies. Here, sniff this little bottle. Now I must get back to driving because it's very late. They're expecting you at the villa. I see you're feeling better. Good! You wouldn't think so, but these salts work. Now you know that they're here in the armrest in case you feel ill again. See, there's ammonia in this little round bottle.'

He was kind, that coachman, and once she sat up straight, the automobile ran so swiftly that Mother Costanza would never be able to catch up with a carriage that, as Mimmo said, ran faster than the wind.

Repeating to myself *I have to sit up straight; otherwise the man inside the glass enclosure will stop again*, I fell asleep.

When I opened my eyes the glass enclosure was still full of light. But there was no sign of the gentleman . . . the driver, that's what he was called. The automobile was still moving, however. Placing her hand on the wall to feel the velvet again, she felt something silky smooth instead. That unexpected touch made her open her eyes. She was no longer in the small, dark velvet room speeding along. This one was stationary and was much larger, and the walls, though covered with fabric like those of the automobile, did not have those little windows all around, only a single, very large one, barely shielded by a length of white transparent cloth. Just like the wedding veil the novices wore when they went to the altar for the divine marriage ceremony.

She wanted to jump out of bed and run to look outside, but she restrained herself. Who knew if it was permitted by the rules of the house? She had learned to be prudent, and although her stomach began complaining of hunger, she stayed where she was and settled for just moving her eyes. Her suitcase wasn't there, but her books were arranged neatly on a small desk, so glossy it looked like glass. The picture of Saint Agatha hung above her, a little below the large crucifix in the middle of the wall. Her smock was arranged so carefully on a small chair at the foot of the bed that if it had had a head it would have seemed that she was sitting there watching herself. Slipping her hands under the blanket, she felt her coarse nightgown and the bands binding her chest. Her hair had been spared, but those bands, it seemed, she had to keep. Never mind! But who could have arranged everything so neatly while she slept? As if in answer to her question, the door opened and a young girl wearing a smock and a white cap – had she ended up in another convent? – entered the room, smiling. The smile reassured her: she had never heard of being allowed to smile like that in convents, brazenly showing one's teeth.

'Please excuse me, *signorina*, the Princess wishes you a good morning and wants to know if you slept well and if you're satisfied with the way I arranged your things.'

I didn't know what to say. Could I speak, or was it better to remain silent? But seeing that her smile was wilting into a pout, I got up my courage and said: 'Very satisfied.'

The smile reappeared.

'Thank you, *signorina*, I will let the Princess know. The Princess asks me to tell you that you may do whatever you wish: go out, walk in the garden, explore the library, the music room. And if you're hungry, you may go down to the kitchen where you will find the cook at your disposal . . . Here is a sheet of paper. It's for you, so that you will know how to act. May I go now? If you need me, pull that cord to your left and I will come right away. I'm very swift, *signorina*, so swift that the Princess has honoured me by calling me Argento-vivo, Quicksilver. She never calls me by my real name, only that one. Oh, by the way, my name is Luigia. The fact is, I'm not from here. And as the Princess says – I myself would never presume to pass judgement on the town I live in – the women here are slow, if not somewhat lazy . . . As I was saying, I was born in Tuscany, in Poggi-bonsi, to be exact. There, *signorina*, if you don't hustle, you don't eat, my dear *signorina* . . .

And was she ever quick! Within seconds she had rattled off all those words with a smile, while rearranging anything she didn't feel was quite in order. She drew the curtains, tying them back with a perfect bow, then disappeared from sight, leaving me blinded by the sun, holding that sheet of paper, light and delicate as silk – was the whole house made of silk? – on which a tiny, flawless script told me the times when I was permitted to leave that room. I was allowed to go anywhere, but only during the hours which the pen had written elegantly but firmly on that precious piece of paper.

21

The entire house wasn't made of silk, but almost. There were wooden doors and tables, velvet drapes. Outside, however, everything was made of marble: staircases, fountains and statues that, when you least expected them, peeped out from a green niche, not marble of course, but leaves and flowers so lovely that if Mimmo could see them he would be wild with joy. No, better that he wasn't there to see them; he would have felt bad. He was so proud of his geraniums, even though he grumbled: 'Eh, princess, there are flowers that are more beautiful. I wish with all my heart that one day you may see them as I did in Catania . . . If you could see that villa! I was in Catania when I was a soldier. But here, amid the lava, on this meagre scrap of land that we manage to reclaim from it, we have to grow beans, tomatoes, things to eat . . .'

As Mimmo had wished for her, she now saw those flowers. Sometimes she even touched them, but she didn't know their names. And after days and days of that silky silence which made her slip from her room into the corridor, and out to the garden, she found the courage to enter the library to find the names of those flowers. She had been right: there were huge volumes full of illustrations where you could find all of them if you looked.

All the names were in Latin. She had to learn them by heart. Now she had something to keep her busy: going from the library to the garden, from the garden to the library to engrave all those strange, difficult names firmly on her mind.

Mimmo always told the truth. Those plants truly were beautiful. If only he were there to break the silence with his sturdy, unhurried voice! Instead, there were only the rushed words of that frivolous creature from the continent, who raced around the room always saying the same things. She didn't even listen to her anymore. Or rather she stopped listening to her, until she said:

'The Princess is very pleased to know that you are less sad, and that you go to the library.'

So then, the house wasn't deserted. They knew what she was doing. Heartened by it, she even dared to enter the music room that day, and with trembling hands, opened the lid of the piano that was at least three times longer than the one in the convent; it wasn't brown, but black and shiny like the marble columns of the entry staircase. The brilliant gloss was intimidating, but she couldn't stand that silky silence anymore, so she resumed her practice. Could she be disturbing anyone? At the convent they only allowed her one hour. Her eyes and her fingers were entranced by the whiteness and pliancy of those keys. She barely had to touch them and the sound rang out powerful and pure like an organ. It wasn't a piano – or maybe, as with the automobile, there were three of them hidden under that long hood . . .

'The Princess bids you good morning and asks me to tell you that you have a marvellous touch. She also said that she admires how you have resumed studying and practising the piano, despite your grief over what happened . . . The Princess would like to know if the food in our house is to your liking and why you don't take tea at five o'clock. Oh! I see, at the convent they didn't take tea . . . Forgive me, *signorina*, but the Princess has instructed me to measure your shoulders and waist and the circumference of your chest. What's this you're wearing under your shirt, *signorina*? Why is it so tight? Oh, of course, the convent's rules. I will report it to the Princess if I may . . . The Princess asks if you would please – provided you don't mind too much – she asks that you please take off those bands for a moment so that I can take the exact measurement of your chest . . . The Princess asked me if you have a photograph of yourself. No photographs? Of course: the convent. Too bad. The Princess asks me to tell you that, knowing how devout you are, she has ordered the driver to take you to Mass tomorrow morning in the village. Only since it's a two-hour drive she would like to know if you prefer to go to the eight o'clock Mass or the one at noon . . . at eight? Very well, I'll tell her.'

How many days had I been there? If the next day was Sunday it must have only been a week or eight days. It seemed like months! Would they leave her by herself for ever? Of course she could read and study, the food was good, but . . . here she comes again with her "Princess":

'The Princess requested that I bring you these three dresses. She asks that you please wear one of these for tea this afternoon, though she is well aware of how important those smocks of yours are to you since they remind you of your vocation. I will come to pick you up since you are not familiar with that wing of the house. She also told me to be sure to tell you not to worry: you only have to wear the dress at five o'clock. After tea, you can go back to wearing your smocks.'

There were three dresses: one pink, one white with gorgeous lace, and a blue one, shiny and flashy, but at least it had the highest neck-line. A pity! The pink dress and the white one with the lace appealed to her, but she had to be prudent. So she contented herself by not taking her eyes off them as she dressed and combed her hair – she didn't have much time. She had never seen anything so beautiful; she felt like crying.

'What is it? Are you crying, *signorina*? Come now, it's not the end of the world if you wear a dress for one hour. The Princess had expected this. If you knew how intelligent she is, the Princess! She had actually predicted that you would cry if you had to take off that smock. Come, dry those tears. You don't want to make the Princess sad, do you? She has already suffered so much these past few years: misfortunes one after the other, and then Mother Leonora's . . . There, that's it, go right in. And smile for once, *signorina*, smile, if only not to remind the Princess of her grief.'

Maybe she was right; I should smile. But prudence stopped me; my lips froze. Confused by Argentovivo's chatter and surprised that, even if I had wanted to smile, my lips would barely move, I found myself in the middle of a room so spacious, so crammed with tables and sofas and armchairs and settees, that my confusion turned to dismay.

There was no one, only a desert of furniture: here, too, no one was waiting for me. Resigned, I decided to wait for Argentovivo to return, since I would never on my own have found my way back to my room down those corridors and rooms that all looked alike.

'I assure you, Maman, she's pretty. A bit solemn but pretty, I assure you!'

Appearing in front of me – where had she come from? – a small, pale face nearly hidden by a mass of fine, blond silky hair (silk here, too) was studying me from head to toe, circling around me just as I did the statues in the garden. Finally, taking me by the hand, she led me safely – how she managed not to overturn the maze of little tables loaded with figurines, boxes, lamps, God only knows! – toward the rear of a narrow, high-backed chair with padded armrests. Seated in the chair was the Princess who had sent me all those messages through Argentovivo's voice. She was as I had imagined her. Except that when she spoke, had it not been for the little hand that held me, I would have run away.

'Thank God she's not actually one of those monsters who infest our convents! Thank God she looks human! And you, Cavallina, you could have told me, couldn't you? that she was normal. If not beautiful, normal. You could have told me, couldn't you?'

'But I did tell you, Maman, and Argentovivo also told you. It's just that you never trust anyone.'

'Of course I don't trust anyone! I'm surrounded by *cafoni*, boors! No one who inherited my good taste or that of your father, *buon-anima*! God rest his soul! Come here, child . . . What is your name? What's that? Modesta? Dear God, what a hideous name! Don't be offended, my girl. It's just that to me, names . . . well, there isn't one that seems fitting to me. Or rather, there's not a name that resembles the person who bears it. The two always clash. Does it seem to you that I should be called Gaia? What's cheerful about me? Bah! As for Modesta, how dreadful! Forgive me, I . . . Oh, Cavallina, she's not only normal! Now that she's worked up . . . are you offended because of your name? Well, now that this offence, or whatever it is, made you blush a little, I can really see that you are lovely. That's enough now! Go away, the two of you! I've tired myself out. The sight of youth is tiring. Go ahead, off with you.'

The little hand tugged at me and I clung to it. We were already out of the room when the voice boomed behind us:

'Just look at that! Now that she's running I can see that she is also graceful! Listen, Cavallina, since she isn't homely, let's let her come with us, shall we! What do you think?'

'Of course, Maman, it would make me very happy.'

'Good! All right then! Agreed. But now, off you go. And you, girl, do you understand? Tomorrow, instead of making that drive to the village, you can come to Mass with us, at noon. Be sure to be on time! And put on a decent dress, for the love of God! A dress in a more cheerful colour, for Heaven's sake. Because that blue is depressing, so dismal that the sadness of a winter evening has washed over me since you've been here. Go on, be off!'

22

We raced off, or rather the small hand pulled me, because, to tell the truth, I didn't have the strength either to stand there or move. The little hand dragged me through corridors and stairways until I began to recognize the draperies of the corridor leading to my room. The thought of having to go back in there alone made me slow up and squeeze her fingers hard. I apologized, because she almost fell.

'Oh, I'm sorry!'

'It's nothing! I didn't hurt myself, see? I didn't even fall.'

I looked at her: standing still like that, there was something lopsided about her slim little figure, as if one shoulder were lower than the other.

'Did my mother scare you? Is that why you're looking at me like that and gripping my hand so tight? She has this effect on everyone the first time, but then you get used to her.'

Something in that silky little face – even her eyelashes shone golden there in the dim sunlight – warmed me and made me forget prudence for a moment.

'No, it's my room that frightens me.'

'Your room? What's wrong with your room? If you want, I'll come in with you and take a look. Maybe it's gloomy . . . there are a lot of bleak rooms in this house . . . rooms with depressing stories. I hope they haven't given you one of those. May I come in, or would you rather be alone to pray like you always do?'

I was about to say: pray? not on your life! In fact, I was afraid I had said it, but luckily the practice of prudence acted on its own and I heard my voice reply, 'No, come in, it would please me. I'll pray later. I've prayed so much and shed so many tears over Mother Leonora that I consider your kind concern for me a sign from God, *Principessina*. I was so cold before.'

'Yes, I can see that. I also see that you speak like my aunt. You must have loved her very much to have her voice and her way of expressing herself. There's a photograph of her when she was young in the rose-coloured parlour. I'll show it to you; you look like her.'

'You look like her too, *Principessina*.'

'Naturally! But don't call me *Principessina*. Call me Beatrice.'

'Beatrice? But your mother . . .'

'Cavallina, yes, she nicknamed me Filly . . . for various reasons. She says that Beatrice doesn't suit me, that Papa was wrong to name me after Dante's Beatrice. She was too perfect, she says. But the fact is that Dante was Papa's favourite poet. But let's go in, let's see this room. Come on . . .'

Still tugging me by the hand that now burned in hers, she opened the door with assurance, and I happily followed her. Just like the poet, I too had my Beatrice, halo and all, to confront the inferno that room had been for me.

When I stepped in, Beatrice so illuminated it with her mass of golden hair that I felt almost ashamed of having found fault with it. But after standing in the centre of the room for a moment, staring at the floor, she said, 'Of course, it's not exactly a beautiful room, but I can assure you that no one died in here. None of these objects is associated with any misfortune. No, no one died here. On the contrary, a while ago there was an English girl who left us to get married. Unfortunately for us, because not only was she quite charming, but she was also a very good teacher. For a year now my mother has been looking for another one, but the only photographs that have come from London are those of ugly old hags. This month alone I rejected ten of them. Just imagine if Mama had seen them!'

My little filly laughed as she wandered around the room touching the walls, examining the drapes. Until she suddenly stopped, as if she had lost her balance; she was out of breath, yet she hadn't been running. She looked at me and became serious, staring at the hem of her dress. So that was it. My Beatrice wasn't perfect like the poet's inspiration: she limped. Seeing her pallor, I tried to smile at her, but my damned lips wouldn't move. I would have to come up with some exercises to learn how to smile.

'Such a sad, sad smile . . .'

Yes, I must think up some exercises.

'What is it . . . do you feel sorry for me?'

That *do you feel sorry for me* loosened the knots of prudence that bound me and I found myself so close to her that I was almost embracing her.

'Feel sorry for you? Of course not, Beatrice. You're so beautiful, and even though . . .'

'Then you noticed? Thank goodness! That way with you at least I won't have to force myself anymore.'

'Force yourself to do what?'

'You see, Modesta, when I'm with my mother I have to force myself to limp as little as possible; otherwise she starts yelling. You've heard what she's like, haven't you? I have to make sure I hide this flaw of mine from strangers. But since you've noticed it and won't say anything to her, I don't have to strain myself anymore. I can see that you're sincere. What a relief! My leg hurts so much when I force it like that.'

And it must have been so, because Cavallina continued her inspection of the room hopping and skipping with joy.

The small dissonant note of her left foot somehow lent her slim waist a certain tenderness, making you want to hold it in your hands like a precious thing that might break at any moment. Summoning back the prudence that was abandoning me, I did not grasp her waist. But to justify my hands, which were too close to it, I said: 'What a lovely belt! What a wonderful shade of red!'

'But it's not red, Modesta, it's claret. Oh, forgive me, these things are all new to you and are of no interest to you . . . This is exactly the reason I couldn't decide whether or not to tell you why this room isn't as cheerful as mine. You're always praying, and you're so serious!'

'Don't be silly, Beatrice. Tell me. I'd like to know.'

'It's because it's missing a mirror. Here, you see? See that mark on the wallpaper? There was a mirror here. They're beautiful, you know, their frames carved with gilded flowers. I have one in my room . . . I wonder why they took it down? That's what's making the room dismal. Oh, I know why! In the convent there were no mirrors in the rooms, right? And you certainly wouldn't want one: it's frivolous. Argentovivo told me that even when you comb your hair, you never even look at yourself in the mirror that's in the toilette.'

'No, we aren't allowed to look at ourselves in a mirror.'

'Of course. And that's why the room is gloomy. If there were a mirror in here, even with the faint sunlight we have today, the room would absorb and reflect it . . . See how it was hung here purposely to catch even the smallest ray of light from the window? Naturally, without it all this wallpaper seems drab. If you'd like . . . maybe it wouldn't do any harm. And maybe you could pray just the same, if you want . . .'

'I'll think about it.'

23

And I did. Instead of praying, I thought. Had I bungled things with them as I had with the dress? Should I perhaps abandon all that prudence? Or did they too, like Mother Leonora and Sister Costanza, perhaps say one thing and think another?

When I was with Beatrice in the garden, in the music room or in the peacock-blue drawing room for tea, everything seemed clear to me. Everything, including her faltering step, told me that I could trust her, that I could smile. But when I was alone, doubt crept up on me and set me back on the old path of prudence. A sad path that led only to the convent. But at least it was familiar, that path. *'Chi lassa la strata vecchia. . .'*,* as my mother used to say, 'Better the devil you know than the devil you don't know'. And if that were to be my destiny . . . 'Destiny', another of my mother's words. Was there such a thing as destiny?

'Destiny, what destiny! This land was destined to remain a desert of lava, yet in three generations we've made it as fertile as the valley below. Destiny! The idle prattle of silly women!'

Mimmo was right. I would not be a silly woman. Like the Princess, that's how I wanted to be. Now there was a woman who was as strong and wilful as a man. If only she had continued to yell! After the first outburst, she had fallen silent. Each day she had tea with us, followed us with her eyes, but remained silent. And that silence was more terrifying than her earlier shouting. I, too, should keep my mouth shut and listen. Listen to Beatrice. Maybe, by following her voice – just like the poet – I could discover a way out of that jungle of silks, marble, allure and riches. She looked just like Doré's Beatrice* when she pointed out a closed window on the top floor, raising her arms as if poised over an abyss because of the strain of standing up straight.

'You must have noticed that it's always closed, haven't you? That's where the "thing" is, as my mother calls him.'

Or, when she suddenly flew nimbly up the stairs and would disappear around the corner of a corridor for a moment, then reappear and, with her small, swift hand – the wing of a bird? – urge me to follow her.

'Look: all these portraits are our ancestors. Mama stashed them away up here. She hates them. Down in the drawing room, as you saw, there are only landscapes, madonnas and crucifixions. Here it's all family . . . I like them though! They're all here, except Nonna. They didn't want her here because she was a bourgeoise commoner, but I made such a fuss that I had her brought to my room. I'll show her to you later. She's portrayed on horseback . . . And now that I've introduced you to more or less all of them, come, and I'll take you to Ildebrando.'

I entered a small, tidy room without much furniture, but full of toys, trains, boats. On a table was a large house built almost entirely with blocks. I looked around, but saw only a wheelchair. I wanted to hold my tongue, but I couldn't help asking, 'Is he out?'

'No, he's dead. It's just that according to the Prince's will – my father, that is – all the rooms must remain untouched so that, if they want to, those who are gone may come back. His room too, up there, is untouched. Sometimes I have the feeling I can smell the aroma of his tobacco. He smoked a pipe. Here, though, I can't smell anything, maybe because I never met him. Who knows? He was Maman's oldest brother, and he died before I was born, when he was ten or twelve. From what they've told me, he was stricken with rheumatoid arthritis and . . . then consumption, I'm not sure, his heart – I think – and he passed away . . . If you want to know him better, his photograph is over there. See, his face is beautiful. He looks like a woman, doesn't he? But his body . . . Come on, let's go and see Aunt Adelaide.'

By now I knew I wouldn't find anyone behind the door that Beatrice was opening and privately I hoped I wouldn't be surprised again. Surprise is the enemy of prudence. But the chirping of a hundred birds that struck me as I went in turned me to salt, as Tuzzu used to say.

'Look, isn't it marvellous! She had the cages brought here from Paris. They look like little cathedrals, don't they? She wanted her birds to feel like they were free.'

'But did she sleep in here? With all this racket?'

'Yes, in that bed over there. Besides, birds sleep at night too. See these drapes around the cages? In the evening, Argentovivo closes them and they go to sleep. When Aunt Adelaide was alive, she did it herself. Her little creatures were all she lived for. There used to be a lot more of them, but since she died they too have been gradually passing away. And it wasn't only birds she kept; she also had goslings, cats, and pigeons up in the dovecote. Now the gardener's son takes care of them. I'll take you there someday. When she was alive, I used to like to come and visit her, only she didn't want anyone, not even me. Maybe because I reminded her of Aunt Leonora. It seems she didn't want to see anyone anymore from the day Leonora entered the convent. She hated my father; she said it was his fault. She saw everyone as her enemy, and was only interested in looking after God's little creatures, as she called them. I don't know if it's true, but they told me that whenever the mother of some little creature died, leaving the eggs, she herself would incubate them. They told me that she managed to hatch a chick more than once. Maybe it's just someone's fabrication . . . I don't know; I'm just telling you what they told me. Now come on, enough about the family. I would so much like to play the piano with you. I know you're more talented, but I like plodding along with you. Besides, as Maman said, since I've been playing with you, my touch has improved a lot.'

Soon her tiny hands would plod along behind mine, as she put it. Instead of annoying me, those tremulous, shaky notes filled my chest with a tenderness I had never felt. Besides, playing four-handed, I would have her close beside me for an hour or two at least.

24

'This morning I'll take you to the other side of the villa. Come on, let's go. But what's wrong? Have you been crying? You have dark shadows under your eyes. I'll bet you were crying over Aunt Leonora. I don't want you to cry! I won't let you. Come on . . .'

The memory of that sonata and its sweetness had kept me from sleeping a wink: scales and scales played together, Clementi's *Sonatinas* – my fingers as shaky and uncertain as hers! – her rolling step through the empty corridors, the golden mass of her hair that shimmered with light at every window . . . Cavallina was dangerous. That silent old woman, shut up in some room, was following us. Argentovivo was right: the Princess knew everything. Plus, she was Mother Leonora's sister. I must never forget that.

'Here we are. This is Uncle Jacopo's room. Close your eyes for a few seconds so you'll get used to the dimness. "Only at sunset is that malevolent lamp acceptable," he used to tell me. At other times he joked: "Would you mind turning off this shitty sun!" He always said *merde*, maybe because he had studied in Paris and was a republican. Uncle Jacopo was Maman's favourite brother, only they argued all the time. That's because he was also a heretic. In this room there are only scandalous books. Reading them is forbidden. I've always been very curious, but I never dared take one, even though the key is right there in the vase where he left it . . .

'What is it, why are you so pale? Is it because he was a heretic? Yes,

I know, they're against God and they read all those books against God, but he was a good man, believe me. Or is it the skeleton and all these strange contraptions that scare you? They scared me too when I was little. But then, hearing them talk about him, I got over my fear. If you only knew what a gentle voice he had! I always came here to help him with his collections of butterflies, shells and minerals. He kept live things in these little jars. I don't know why . . . he did experiments. He wrote and published many books, in Rome and in France. Maman says you can't understand a word of what he wrote. He was a physician and also a chemist, did you know? Complicated things . . . I loved him very much, even though he swore against God and the priests. Besides, he did me a great favour. By yelling and shouting he convinced Maman not to make me embroider anymore. It was torture for me. He said that embroidering made women stupid. Only once did I manage to get him to tell me why he didn't believe in God. He said that the invention of God is too simple an explanation – or maybe he said convenient, I don't recall – to account for the beauty and mystery of butterflies. He also said that ugliness and beauty are one and the same thing, and cannot be separated, that . . . wait, how did he put it? Oh yes, that beauty is born from ugliness, ugliness from beauty, and so on. It's very tricky. When he spoke like that it was difficult to understand him and . . . All this was the reason he wanted to be cremated. Don't ever let it slip out of your mouth. See that vase on the mantelpiece? That's where his ashes are. Come on, let's go. Why are you standing there like a statue? He wasn't a bad man, Modesta, really, even though . . .'

At last I had found another heretic. Those books flirting with me in the dim light attracted me more than Beatrice's brisk, caressing voice. If she hadn't been there I would promptly have taken one of those books, at least one . . . but she was tugging at me now, and I had to be prudent. I let myself be led away by her warm little hand, down the stairs to the last room on the right overlooking the small lake. The room was so different that I didn't dare go in. Windows took up all the walls, from floor to ceiling, allowing the light and the trees to spill onto long, pale wood tables, their strange lamps like slender snakes with large bent heads. In addition to the tables, there were bookcases along a single wall. In front of them was a cot with a grey-green blanket, sheets and a pillow neatly straightened, waiting . . .

'Yes, that's where he slept. It's lovely here, isn't it? But it was lovelier when Ignazio was alive. Too bad you didn't get to know him. He died the very day you arrived. How come I'm not wearing mourning? Maman doesn't want me to. She says her brother Jacopo was right, at least on this issue. Uncle Jacopo said that wearing mourning is barbaric . . . that if someone is truly grieving he bears his sorrow in his heart, without the need for pointless exhibitionism. And I am truly grieving.

'Come, look how handsome Ignazio was. This is where he kept the things that were most dear to him. Look: a receipt from the London Underground . . . here's a ticket from the Paris Opera; a postcard from Weimar. He studied in London and in Germany . . . And here, his photograph in civilian clothes: that's me he's holding, when I was little. But come, look at this one above the cot, in uniform. He was even more handsome, wasn't he? It's from when he entered the air force. He also designed airplanes, did you know? He always said that the world's future would be decided in the sky, on these wings. See, these are his drawings. He was always working, even at night, under these big lamps. The large windows too, he had them put in. He needed a lot of light, before. Later, he no longer wanted to look out and he had those dark drapes hung. When he died I opened them, because I only want to remember when he was handsome and fit. These bookcases too are full of his designs and calculations.

'You're amazed at all those photos of airplanes, aren't you? The photo above the cot, the one with him in it, I put it there myself, afterwards . . . All he wanted on the walls were airplanes. That's why Maman used to say that he didn't love anyone, only his infernal machines. But it's not true; he loved me. I was the only one he wanted around after the tragedy. A year he lay paralysed on this cot. He was wounded just three months after the war began. He had enlisted voluntarily. He said the war would end quickly because of the airplanes, and instead . . . this war is never ending. Why won't it ever end? . . . Every afternoon I would come and find him increasingly thinner and paler on this cot, and he would talk to me about the war, about the

Socialists, about a certain Mussolini whom he greatly admired: he said he was a man who believed in youth, not in those old men in parliament who pretend they're taking care of Italy, while instead they're digging her grave. He loved Italy very much. He smoked constantly, and when he fell silent he would make smoke rings . . . like men do. But of course, you have no experience with these things. I can tell, you know, that when I talk about men you become distracted, and maybe I shouldn't speak about them. Still, it's too bad you didn't get to know him.'

Dazzled by Ignazio's good looks as he stared at me from the photograph, I heard my voice say: 'Too bad . . .'

Terrified, I glanced at Beatrice, but, captivated by her Ignazio, she hadn't understood.

'Yes, unfortunately, because now the family will die out. He was the only male left, the youngest of the Brandiforti. And if he hadn't let himself get caught up in politics, as Maman says . . . she's right about that. What do we Sicilians care about a war that the King of Italy is waging for his own gain? On this point Maman and Uncle Jacopo were in agreement. But Ignazio, up in Rome at the university, got carried away and so he enlisted. He was shot down after only three months. But I already told you that. Sorry. It's just that I loved him so much. I would read to him. I was the only one he wanted to see. Sometimes he got tired. He turned his head to the wall and I kept silent. Once I was getting up to leave, but he said: "No, stay here, little one. It's just that I'm tired, but I like knowing you're there, as long as you aren't bored." Bored! I lived for those hours in the afternoon when I came here. After a while, maybe half an hour, twenty minutes, he would turn his head back and I continued reading. I was happy with him . . .'

At the word 'happy', perhaps because she was smiling, her unexpected, desperate tears blinded me. Or had the sun gone down? There was darkness all around. How long had I been listening to her voice? In the dark, in response to her sobbing, I embrace her. She's trembling all over. I feel her silky hair against my neck and cheek and, what surprises me even more, I begin cradling her, singing something I didn't know I knew:*

'*Si Beatrice nun voli durmiri coppa nno' culu sa quantu n'ha aviri . . .*'. *If Beatrice won't go to sleep, whack goes the ladle on her little behind . . .*

And, seeing that a few giggles began to be heard amid the tremors and tears, I continued cradling her, my hands encircling the slimmest, dearest little body that I could ever imagine existed on earth.

25

'Ooh, ooh, ooh, dormi figghia, fa la "O". E si Beatrice nun voli durmiri coppa nno' culu sa quantu n'ha aviri . . . ooh, ooh, ooh . . . dormi bedda, fa la "O" . . . Sleep, little one, go to beddy-bye . . .'

Beatrice's ability to go from tears to laughter was something that took my breath away. She was laughing now, curled up in my lap.

'Do you know why I'm laughing?'

'How would I know that?'

'Because you're singing the same lullaby that my *tata* used to sing to me.'

'Your *tata*?'

'Yes, my nanny, the wet nurse. They say *tata* on the continent, and that's what they taught me to call her. It seems more elegant to them, except that my *tata* was Sicilian, and I know there's a bad word in that lullaby.'

'So you understand Sicilian then?'

'Of course I understand it. With my *tata*, when we were alone, '*u parravamu sempri*, we always spoke it. I like it a lot, but in our home it's forbidden: French, English, Italian, anything but Sicilian. So many things my *tata* told me! She always spoke to me in Sicilian, or rather in Palermitano. She was from Palermo, and she was very proud of it. She hated Catania: "*Catanisi soldu fausu*," she always said, "The Catanesi are false."* And I enjoyed needling her. She would get angry, but then we laughed and made up. What good times those were,

Modesta, there in Catania! The house was always full. They were all alive, then, and we didn't have this damn war. We came to the villa only in the summer, but here too, the house was always full of people. Ignazio's friends . . . if you knew how many he had! And all young. When they came to see him they would shut themselves up in his room and talk loudly, you know, like men do. I always stood behind the door, not to eavesdrop, but I liked to hear the voices and smell the aroma of tobacco that filtered through the cracks. Later they came for dinner or tea with their sisters . . . Then, in 1915, they began leaving. Everyone said that the war would last only six months, thanks to some extraordinary weapons or other that . . . Well! Almost two years have gone by and it's still not over. And the losses aren't over either . . . cousin Manfredi died right after Ignazio . . . as if he had called him. And two months ago Alberto, too, disappeared at the front in . . . I don't remember where. And so all the houses are closed up. Those doors draped in black are so sad. Then there was Alessandra's tragedy, poor child: she was Ignazio's fiancée.'

She stopped talking, and her head felt heavy on my shoulder.

'Are you asleep?'

'No. Why haven't you asked me about Alessandra?'

'I don't know.'

'It's really true what Maman says. You were born for the convent. You're not at all curious. But me, I'm curious about everything! Is it a sin?'

'Why should it be a sin? Come on, cheer up, don't be so sad. And to show you it's not a sin, I'll admit . . .'

'Address me familiarly, as "tu".'

'I'll admit that I'm curious about Alessandra too. So?'

'But you're asking without being really interested! Ask me properly! Otherwise I'll think it's a sin.'

'Would you please tell me . . . What is the tragedy that concerns Alessandra?'

'Address me as "tu".'

'All right, so tell me about it.'

'She killed herself when she found out that Ignazio was paralysed.'

'Dear God! How did she kill herself? May God forgive her! This is definitely a sin.'

'We never knew. It's a mystery. Some say she starved herself to death, some say she poisoned herself, some say . . .'

'What?'

'It's terrible, but some say – and it seems that this is really the truth – that she hanged herself in the bathroom with a rope. Yes, a rope.'

As she spoke, she clung to me and hid her face in my neck. Was it an embrace? Was it possible that she also felt those shivers? I, too, had done that with Mother Leonora. So then she hadn't been a coward after all; it was just because I was a child that she behaved that way. Now I was Mother Leonora, and like her I had to be prudent. But how to stop the little hand that innocently grasped my breast, or rather the bands that bound my bosom?

'What on earth are you wearing under your smock, Modesta? It feels like a cuirass! Let me see . . .'

'No, no, *Principessina*, it's not permitted. Those are the bands that all the novices wear.'

'Oh! Why? Won't you answer? . . . I see. I can feel that your breasts are bigger than mine. It's so that they don't show, for the sake of modesty.'

'Exactly. No, don't do that. Don't loosen them, Beatrice. Besides, you're tickling me.'

'Strange; I'm not ticklish there. You don't believe me? Put your hand here. You see? I'm not ticklish. It makes me feel warm. When I was little I would always put my hand on my *tata*'s breast to fall asleep . . . I'm sleepy! Will you let me put my hand there?'

It was hopeless to try and stop her. Her quick little hand had found an opening between one binding strip and the other, in part because I didn't fasten them as tightly as in the convent, and now she was holding a breast in her palm. Supported by her hand that way, it looked like Saint Agatha's severed breast. I closed my eyes so I wouldn't see those fingers now playing with my nipple, plunging me into a prolonged shiver . . . Poor Mother Leonora, what she must have gone through! Motionless as she had been, I let myself come agonizingly. Don't let the child notice, for God's sake, don't let her see! . . . She fell asleep like that, clutching my breast. From the tall windows the moon peered in, suspicious: under her spiteful gaze Beatrice's hair shone like silver. I didn't know what to do. The effort to resist caressing her was so strong that I felt as tired as I did when I used to run through the reeds all day looking for Tuzzu. Beneath the moon's gaze Tuzzu stared at me, the wounds of his eyes bleeding a blue sea . . .

'*D'accordo ca nenti pisi, picciridda, ma non poi stari cca' tuttu 'u santu jornu, e poi t'haiu a purtari in vrazza menzu addurmintata . . . It's true you don't weigh a thing, little girl, but you can't stay here the whole blessed day and then make me have to carry you in my arms, half asleep . . .*'

Sleep tugged at my hair, my forehead . . . *nenti pisa 'sta picciridda*, weightless, this little girl is: a small kitten on my lap. Either I had grown taller or she was smaller than normal. How old could she be? I don't know what's happening anymore, Tuzzu, I'm sleepy and muddled, confused by Ignazio's eyes winking sweetly and malevolently in the darkness, more malevolent than the moon. They weren't the eyes of a boy, but those of a grown man. Her brother? How could it be? Should I wake her? I didn't dare. Sleep there? She would catch cold.

'*Are you taking care of the Principessina? Be careful, you know! The Principessina must absolutely not catch cold. Her health is delicate, very delicate!*'

'Signorina, Signorina Modesta! Oh, thank goodness I found you! I was looking for you. It's supper time. You know the *Principessina* is delicate, delicate and distracted, as the Princess says, and must be looked after. She even forgets to eat when she's reading or roaming around the house . . . Oh, she's sleeping! Oh dear God, Signorina Modesta, you have no idea, you can't imagine the worry she causes us. Always having to look for her! Yes, yes, I'll help you carry her. This always happens when she comes to this room! I even took the liberty of suggesting to the Princess that this room be kept locked. And you know what she told me? In this house, we don't lock anything up. If Cavallina wants to break her neck running through the garden or wants to sleep with Ignazio, she's welcome to! Here, everyone is his own master, free to live and die as he pleases. One of a kind, the Princess! But I firmly believe that this room should be locked. Listen, I'm not a superstitious ignoramus, as the Princess calls the village women, but this room is maleficent for the *Principessina*. Evil! When she comes in here, after hours and hours I find her crying or else asleep, all

dishevelled like she is now. It's not natural. Good thing we have you
here now! Now the responsibility isn't all mine, like it was before . . .'

I decided to answer her just to stop the flood of words.

'Don't worry, Argentovivo. I'll see to Beatrice. There, that's right,
let's carry her to her room.'

'What about supper?'

'Maybe it's best if she sleeps.'

We carried her up to her room, but as soon as she was in bed Beatrice opened her eyes and said, 'I'm hungry!'

'You see how she acts, Signorina Modesta, you see?'

'I'm hungry!'

'Supper is served in the green drawing room.'

'No, I want to eat here, with Modesta. Here, I said! Go on, go! And
don't say a word! One of these days I'm going to sew that mouth of
yours shut. Shut up and go away. I want to eat here, with Modesta!'

I felt my blood run cold. I had never heard Cavallina utter harsh
words, and her shouts thundered like those of the Princess.

'Come here, Modesta. I purposely pretended to be asleep to make
you come to my room. I was afraid you wouldn't want to come. Do
you like it?'

Saying that I did, very much, I moved closer and tried to guess how
old she was. Up close like that, tiny wrinkles were beginning to line
her pale forehead. Or was it those shouts that had aged her? I had
never seen such transparent skin.

'See, this is the mirror I told you about. See how bright and
cheerful it is? Haven't you made up your mind yet? And this is our
grandmother. Look how beautiful she was! The Englishwoman,
not an aristocrat but very wealthy, remember? None of us inherited her beauty, as Maman says. We only managed to inherit her
money, or rather, steal it, she says. Grandfather was in sad straits,
as is often the case with aristocrats. And so, again in Maman's
words, that ingenuous bourgeoise was providential in keeping the
family afloat. She makes me laugh so when she says that all aristocrats are thieves! Beginning with the Savoia, who are aristocrats up
to a certain point. How funny! She's beautiful, isn't she? She looks
like Ignazio, doesn't she?'

'Yes, and Mother Leonora as well.'

'You want to become a nun like her, right?'

'Yes.'

'When did your vocation come to you?'

'In the convent.'

'What exactly is a vocation? How does it feel? What do you hear?'

Not having any idea, I responded in the words of Mother Leonora: 'It's like the singing of birds.'

'She too used to say that, Maman told me. I barely knew her. Maman also says that for Aunt Leonora it was a tragedy because she was rich and could have made a good match. But that for you it's different. It's good that you have this vocation because in the convent, with Mother Leonora's modest stipend and trousseau, you'll be better off than married to some servant or perhaps a lowly clerk. With your intelligence, she says, and with our support, you can even become Mother Superior.'

Argentovivo was right: her Princess had a keen eye.

'That's why she told me not to deter you from your vocation. Though I'm sorry about it, because it means that in three months you'll go away, and I like being with you. I told her that, you know. But she said I should leave you in peace and that I'm impetuous. It's true, somewhat . . . it's a pity, though, because if you didn't have a vocation you could stay here with me for ever, since I too will never be able to marry.'

'Why not? You're wealthy.'

'Yes, yes, I know, but Maman says that no one must find out that a Brandiforti is a cripple. Many have asked to marry me. You see, all the Brandiforti up until Grandfather's generation were fine-looking and healthy. Then something in the blood deteriorated. The first sign was the fact that the Englishwoman had only one child, my father . . . Then the birth of the "thing" who, as I told you, is in the room where the window is always closed. No one has ever seen him, not even me. Of course, there was Ignazio, handsome and strong, but Maman says that he too was rotten – his brain, that is. Maybe that's why he died. So Maman says that our lineage must dry up like a river that is no longer fed by the Mountain. We're from Catania. There, the

Mountain bestows life with its snow and death with its lava. Maman says that she can recall seeing many other fertile estates and families wither and die out as willed by God and the Mountain.'

26

'Good morning, *signorina*. Did you sleep well? The *Principessina* woke up fresh as a daisy this morning, fresh as a daisy! She wants you to know that the music teacher will be here after breakfast. You should see how excited she is about taking a lesson with you! Oh, since you've been here, the *Principessina* has flourished! Flourished, there's no other word for it! . . . Did you make up your mind about the mirror? She told me about the mirror, too.'

'No, no mirrors.'

'So be it. The Princess will be happy, but the *Principessina* will be sorry about it. She's truly so disconsolate that she can't take dance lessons with you too! Well! No mirrors. No dance lessons. Dancing isn't appropriate for a nun. The Princess says it's better that way!'

I had been right to be prudent. Imagine marrying a servant! Better a nun. Imagine becoming like *that one*! Now that I knew, that cheerful exuberance of hers could be seen as raging envy obliged to masquer-ade behind humble words and jolly remarks. Those stubby fingers, the forced smile stuck onto the corners of her mouth, that body stuffed into that shapeless smock . . . Oh, no! She would keep her vocation. At least she could continue to study history, maths, the piano . . . The piano! Beatrice had said that her teacher had been a great Rus-sian concert performer. And if she said he was good, it was definitely so. The tutor, too, had such a wealth of learning that Mother Leonora seemed ignorant by comparison. Philosophy . . . that she might not be able to study in the convent . . . She should find out. Such a rich, mysterious world 'the world of ideas' was; that's what the tutor had said. He had also said:

'Excellent, *signorina*, you associate concepts just like a man!'

Of course she had heard something about Plato from Mother Leonora, but the Sophists, the Epicureans . . . And that Greek philosopher who said that everything happened by chance . . . what was his name? She had to ask. The tutor would tell her.

To be able to ask without fear. This would not be possible in the convent. But at least she could read. In those few months she had to ask, ask that gentle, smiling old man. Too bad the tutor wasn't young. She had been so hopeful, but by now she knew that the music teacher too would be an old man. In that house there were only women and old men. Who knows why Mother Leonora had fled this rich convent to retreat within those lava walls on the Mountain? In the end, it was the same thing . . .

'What are you doing there in a daze? Thinking? Maybe you were praying. Sorry! I'm so eager to introduce you to maestro Beliajev. You'll see, he'll be thrilled about you!'

Beatrice swayed in the partly open doorway, one hand resting on the doorjamb, her fragile torso hidden by soft white folds. She almost always wore white.

'Do you know, you look just like Doré's Beatrice?'

'You think so? I don't remember her; what is it, a painting?'

'No! The illustrations in the book down in the library.'

'Oh, yes. That huge tome belonged to Papa. You notice everything. You think I look like her? You'll have to show it to me later. Come on, give me your hand. You don't want to? How come?'

How could I, after having held her in my arms? Just the thought of feeling her palms put me in peril of losing both prudence and my vocation. But it didn't stop her. There she goes, grabbing my wrist with her quick hand. Good thing I tied the bands on properly this morning.

'What is it, Beatrice? What's wrong?'

'Oh God! He's here, he's coming. Don't you hear him stomping up the stairs?'

Indeed, a heavy stride – the tread of someone wearing hobnailed boots or wooden shoes – was making the stairs rumble.

'Close the door. I'm scared.'

'Yes, but what's wrong?'

Now safely inside the room, clinging to me, she slowly opened the door again, and mutely pointed to a huge man, a giant who was tramping down the corridor, coming toward us. He had to be over six feet tall, solid as a door, with broad shoulders and a small, round, bald head on a neck that looked like a column. That round knob seemed more like a continuation of his thick, muscular neck than a head. The neck had two bulging eyes, so pale they seemed colourless.

'Who is he?'

'Come, I'll go speak to him. With you, I'm not afraid of anything . . . Good day, Pietro.'

'My respects, *Principessina*.'

'How is Ippolito?'

'Fine, *Principessina*, everything is fine.'

From his great height, he stared down at us blankly. Although you couldn't tell from his face, his surprise at being spoken to completely froze him. Rigid like that, he looked like a metal statue.

'Does *Voscenza* require some service, *Principessina*?'

The slow voice was equally expressionless.

'No, thank you, Pietro. I merely wanted to ask about Ippolito.'

'He is well, thank God, he is well. May I go now? *Bacio le mani a Vossignoria*, my respects to your ladyship.'

Rigid, he turned to the right and continued climbing the stairs with his iron tread. So that was the noise I heard every morning.

'He's scary, isn't he, Modesta?'

'Of course he's scary. But who is he?'

'He's the one who takes care of Ippolito. See, he's going to the top floor. He's the only one who can deal with "the thing", as Maman says. How scary! Make sure you close the door. I had never spoken to him before, brrr . . . what a dreadful voice! This wing of the house is awful: "the thing", Papa's room . . . brrr! . . .'

'You've shown me all the rooms, but not the Prince's room, your father's.'

'That room frightens me. It's not nice, perhaps, to talk about a dead person like that, but I can't hide anything from you. The fact is that I . . . I don't remember when . . . oh, yes, when he began to make me go to him each afternoon to read aloud and study astronomy. I must have been ten years old. Of course, I'm not as intelligent as Maman, or you. Even the tutor – have you noticed how he always addresses you when he's explaining something? Well, so . . . I didn't understand astronomy and he would get angry. So when I went to his room I would start shaking . . . You see, just talking about it makes my hands shake. I didn't know what was happening. Ignazio said I read well, whereas with Grandfather, I got flustered.'

'Did you say Grandfather? Wasn't the Prince your father?'

'Yes, yes, I made a mistake. I got flustered, like with him . . . I, I . . .'

As if cowering in trepidation, she huddled in my arms. How could she seem so tall from a distance, yet so small in my arms? How did she manage to go from tears to laughter so quickly it made you dizzy?

'May I ask how old you are, Beatrice?'

'You noticed, didn't you, Modesta? You see and notice everything.'

'No, I don't see. As a matter of fact, I'm beginning to feel really confused with all these names, these aunts and uncles, grandparents . . . Really, I'm sorry to ask you so many questions, it's just to . . .'

'But I like it when you ask questions! You seem less like a nun . . . Oh, sorry! I meant less serious, more like me. Your hair, is it thick? You wear it so tightly pulled back, I can't tell. Let me undo this bun, this *tuppo* is just like the one my *tata* had . . . Let me, just this once!'

'Of course, go ahead if it makes you happy. I see you're smiling again.'

'Come over here, beside the window. Dear God, all those hairpins! You'll damage your hair this way. It's harmful to pull it so tight.'

'I won't need it where I'm going. After the novitiate they'll cut it.'

'Don't say that! You mustn't say that! I can't bear to think about it . . . Two more months and . . . do you realize we've known each other for a month? Don't go away! Don't leave!'

She was crying now, in the farthest corner of the room. It was her way of distancing me. But by now I knew how to get her to come back and how to make her smile. All I had to do was distract her with something new. I finished removing all my hairpins, and with my heavy braids thumping behind me at each step . . . how long had it been since I felt that vital weight? like when I would go and look for Tuzzu . . .

'*If you don't keep quiet I'll cut off your braids and go and sell them in the village. Nice and thick they are, sturdy. So help me God, if I can make even a lira I'll do it!*'

'*Are they worth that much?*'

'*Of course!*'

'*What do they do with them?*'

'*Make wigs for old people.*'

'*What are wigs?*'

'*Uffa! What a nuisance! Always questions and more questions! I don't have time and I don't feel like answering you. Be quiet, I have work to do!*'

'Be quiet, Beatrice! Hush! Look, look what a surprise. Hold the hairpins, come on, look!'

'How thick they are! One of yours would make braids for me and two others . . . What's wrong? You have tears in your eyes. Oh God, I've never seen you cry! Oh God! No one will tell Maman. Have you lost your vocation?'

'No, I haven't lost it. Mother Leonora gave it to me and . . .'

'So then you're crying because, even though you haven't lost your vocation, you're sorry to leave me, right? Tell me, are you sorry?'

'Yes, I'm sorry.'

'That makes me feel better. I was afraid, because they say that people in the convent love no one but God. That's what Aunt Leonora used to say . . . How strange; with your braids you look even younger. And you, how old are you?'

'I was born on 1 January 1900. That's what the archivist at the convent told me. She said that with me it was easy to keep count.'

'So that makes you seventeen, like . . .'

'Like who?'

'Like me.'

27

'Go on, you realized it! I can tell you're not surprised. Maman is right: you see and notice everything. She also says she hasn't met many young women as intelligent and determined as you. And she's very annoyed because she can't seem to come up with a nickname for you. She says you're the opposite of your given name and . . . why are you turning pale? She's not angry with you! You know how she is; she's just irritated that she can't manage to find you a nickname.'

Terrified, I was about to draw my hair back up in a bun. Beatrice was naive, but the Princess was not; it would mean trouble for me if she were to see my braids!

'What are you doing? No, no, leave them down! Besides I have the hairpins now and I'm not giving them to you! I'm so glad you realized it! That way I don't have to pretend not to be lame, or older . . . But please, don't let Nonna know you know.'

'So then the Princess is your grandmother, and not your mother?'

'How could she have had me? I don't know how old she is. She seemed very young to me too, before Ignazio left for the war, but then when they brought him back on a stretcher, in just a few months she became all ashen and shrivelled. I hate seeing her that way. Up until two years ago, you should have seen her ride a horse . . . Not even Carmine could keep up with her.'

'Who is Carmine?'

'Indeed. That's the point. Will you let me undo your braids?'

'No, Beatrice, no. It's not permitted. But then, whose daughter are you?'

'That I can't tell you. I really can't. I might cause you to lose your vocation and like Nonna says, your vocation is the only asset you have.'

'It's not as easy as you may think. When it's deeply rooted, as it is in me, nothing can change it. But wait: you said you might cause me to lose . . .'

'There, you figured it out! Yes, because Mother Leonora was my mother. Dear God, how pale you are! But I didn't tell you! You realized it yourself, didn't you? You figured it out yourself! I don't want to take away your vocation.'

'It's all right, Beatrice. No, you didn't tell me. I realized it myself.'

'Still it's one thing to assume something and another thing to know for sure, isn't it? How pale you are!'

'Just a minute. I'm going to wash my face.'

In the small bathroom I leaned over the sink and nearly vomited. I was trembling all over but not because I was upset, as Beatrice thought . . . That abominable woman . . . The appalling fiancé, the debutantes' ball, her panic in the face of worldly corruption . . . Not to mention the Madonna who had enlightened her about the man's dreadfulness. God's grace, her vocation! Yet all the while she had had a man!

To cool that hatred, I began slapping myself with cold water, until I saw the face of a serene, unsmiling nun in the mirror. As I went back to Beatrice, who was waiting anxiously, her hands full of hairpins, I kept thinking *damn you, you liar, I hate you.*

'I didn't tell you, Modesta! It was you who realized it, you!'

'Of course, Beatrice, of course.'

'How calm you are now! Did Mother Leonora's sin make you lose your vocation?'

'"Let he who is without sin cast the first stone", Beatrice. Besides, Mother Leonora completely atoned for her sin in solitude and prayer. Though I haven't sinned, none the less I feel unworthy compared to her!'

Horrified, I could hear Mother Leonora's voice speaking through my lips. Could the hatred have reawakened her inside me? The prayer of hatred can do anything; it can bestow both life and death, anything.

'Now tell me, there's a good girl, tell me. Who was your father? The officer to whom she had been promised?'

'If you let me undo your braids here, in the sunlight, I'll tell you.'

'Go ahead, little one.'

'How sweet your voice is now. You're a saint, Modesta! You let people do anything to you and you accept it all without rebelling. How do you do it? I wish I were like you! Such beautiful hair! Can I comb it for you?'

'Tell me who your father was. Or don't you know?'

'Someday I'll show him to you.'

'You have a photograph?'

'There's no need for one.'

'Then it's someone who lives in this house.'

'You're getting colder . . . Not really, he comes sometimes . . . Haven't you noticed him?'

I did a quick review: the priest, too old . . . the tutor? the Russian concert artist? No, both too old . . . That skinny man who came to examine 'the thing'?

'The doctor, Beatrice? Is it him?'

'Cold, colder . . .'

'The notary who came the other night?'

'Colder, colder . . .'

'That man who comes every once in a while?'

'Warm, warmer . . . warmer . . .'

'No! Then it's . . .'

'Hot! Come here, look, he's coming up the terrace . . . I always run away when he comes.'

Behind the window, standing close together, we followed the slow steps of a tall, strapping man . . . As if he felt our gaze, he raised his head, with its curly white hair, and looked in our direction. For a moment, a pair of blue eyes fixed on us. Glints of gold flashed in those dark blue depths. He was dressed in velvet like Mimmo, except that instead of being brown, the velvet he wore was a blue so dark it seemed black.

'Who is he? The gardener?'

'No, the *gabellotto*, the estate manager.* Don't you see the shotgun he's carrying?'

Of course! That man dressed and moved like Mimmo, but he carried a shotgun slung over his shoulder. A doubt struck me. Beatrice was impetuous, so the Princess had said, capricious and unreliable. Could she be teasing me, as she often did with Argentovivo and the other women? I mustn't lose sight of the fact that she was the mistress, and that only a 'consecrated veil' kept me from being a servant in that house.

'That can't be, Beatrice. And even if it were true, you wouldn't know about it. These things are difficult to find out.'

Pulling away from me and hurling herself onto the bed, she's screaming now and crying, thumping the cover and thrashing the air.

'You're calling me a liar! To protect your Mother Leonora, you're calling me a liar! She was such a coward! A coward, like you! She abandoned me here, leaving me with these madmen! If it hadn't been for my *tata* and then Ignazio, I would have died. Died of loneliness, concealed from everyone. They kept me hidden away, don't you see? Earlier I told you about all the people who came, in Catania too . . . but I only saw them from a distance, or from behind a door. Go away! Go like that coward who abandoned me!'

She seemed sincere. What should I do? I had to make her quiet down. Not so much for her sake – something inside me told me that those tears were good for her, a healthy outburst that would leave her calm and serene – but because Argentovivo might hear her. And the only way to silence her was to embrace her.

'You're right, Beatrice. It was cowardly of me not to believe you, but you have to understand . . .'

She smiled, the tears running down her chin and neck. Those tears were begging to be dried – by now I knew it – and taking her in my arms I caressed her cheeks, her chin, her neck.

'Ignazio used to dry my tears like that too when I cried. He called me his personal fountain. Once he said to me: "I'm thirsty, will you let me drink these tears?" And you, aren't you thirsty?'

I was very thirsty, and my lips sucked up those tears. I didn't know they were so salty.

'How salty they are!'

'Didn't you know that?'

'No.'

'Why? Haven't you ever cried?'

'Yes, but . . .'

'You've cried and you never tasted them? How strange! I did it right away . . . ever since I can remember. And then I discovered that they tasted like sea water – less salty, but the same taste.'

'Have you seen the sea?'

'Of course! Haven't you? That's incredible! It's not possible!'

'Now it's you calling me a liar. Watch out or I'll start crying like you.'

'Go ahead! That way I can drink too. But how come you've never seen it?'

'I was born in the mountains, but there was someone who always talked to me about it.'

'Your brother?'

'Almost.'

'You never talk about yourself.'

'It's not permitted.'

'Liar!'

'Watch out, or I'll start crying and screaming.'

'That's what I want.'

'Why?'

'I told you, because I'm thirsty, and sleepy too. Will you let me put my hand on your breast?'

She didn't wait for me to answer. She quickly untied my smock and, shifting aside the bands, wasn't satisfied to place her hand on my breast like before, but pulled it out altogether. I closed my eyes to resist the tantalizing arousal until, hearing her so quiet, I thought she had fallen asleep. Then I looked at her. She wasn't sleeping. She was staring at my breasts, wide-eyed.

'How big and firm they are! They're more beautiful than my *tata*'s, even the nipples . . . they're pale. My *tata*'s were dark. Will you give me some milk?'

Without giving me time to say anything, her lips began sucking me as though she were really drinking.

'I'm not thirsty anymore now. It's your turn.'

With a sure gesture she pulled out her breast and forced me, her hand unexpectedly strong, to drink from her nipple as she had done from mine.

'That's it, like that, drink. You have to close your eyes; you'll satisfy your thirst better.'

28

I squeezed my eyes shut. I froze in astonishment.

'Go on, suck me. Be a good little *picciridda*. If you don't eat you won't grow. You'll wither away, and gaunt *La Certa* will come and gather your bones. There, eat and you'll grow . . . Hush, hush, *picciridda*, relax.'

I couldn't relax. I was frozen, embarrassed, seeing her play with my breasts, my hair, my ears. How was it possible?

'You're all chilled and sweaty, Modesta. Here, I'll dry you. You don't think it's a sin, do you? What harm is there? After all, we're both women. We won't get pregnant.'

That made me laugh out loud . . . Tuzzu used to laugh when I . . . '*Listen to this picciridda – a retort worthy of the impudent scamp she is!*'

I thought I was laughing and instead, to my surprise, I found myself crying on her chest. She was tall now, and her arms sheltered me.

'Oh, are you crying? Don't cry. It's not a sin, I promise you. Here, come, let me drink all those nice salty tears.'

I submitted. I felt cold.

But little by little her caresses slowly melted the chill of my surprise, and a warmth I had never felt before made me say, 'No, Beatrice, it's not a sin.'

And so, for the first time in my life, *fui amata amando*, I loved and was loved in return, as the aria goes.* Something so rare that even now, I can recall the feeling of lightness that made me open my eyes in the morning, secure in the new adventure that was born from our embrace. Together we ran through the rooms, the garden, the avenue lined with palm trees . . . Our lessons and afternoon tea were the only interruptions in our solitude as a twosome. But they were brief interruptions, since a look, or a caress under the table, or her brushing my shoulder as we played the piano always reassured us that we would soon be together again.

'Shall we play baby and *tata*?'

'Yes.'

'This time you be the *tata* and I'll be the baby.'

'Which do you prefer, being the *tata* or the baby?'

'Oh, it makes no difference to me, as long as I can be near you and hold you.'

'Me too.'

Surrendering to her, I left behind that inferno of qualms and bands and lava walls. The convent receded when I stared into her eyes. It collapsed behind me and I could see the stars again. Was that what paradise was: love? I didn't know what that word meant: 'the Love that moves the sun and the other stars'.*

Naturally, when she embraced me everything revolved around me. It wasn't like with Tuzzu or with Mother Leonora. A tenderness I had never known before made me feel serene among the trees that revolved around the sun, confident that I would not fall.

When she undressed me, I learned from her what colour my skin was, how many moles I had on my back . . .

'You have a slim waist too. It's just that you don't wear a corset. See, it's almost as slender as mine. Don't you believe me? Here, I'll get the measuring tape. Plus you're taller and have wider hips, and you're not lame.'

That word was always followed by tears. To make them stop I just had to kiss the leg that was slightly thinner and shorter than the other.

'Don't you find it repulsive?'

'Repulsive? Of course not! I only find it moving, Beatrice. Don't be silly.'

'My *tata* said the same thing. Will you give me some milk like she did?'

114

'First I'll cover you with my hair.'

'Oh yes, I'm so cold!'

And she pretended to be so cold – there in the sun – that it made her tremble.

'And what's this, between your legs?'

'A meadow.'

'Can I rest my lips there and feel how soft the grass is?'

29

But the grass down in the meadow was damp that morning.

'Did you hear that storm we had last night? The first thunderstorm this summer. Soon it will be autumn, Modesta.'

Huge clouds looming on the horizon shut off our view, like a lofty wall of lava. I had forgotten that wall.

'Soon you'll have to leave . . . Stay here with me, Modesta!' By now she said it in a whisper, like you say a prayer that will never be granted, or like a faint refrain: 'Stay, stay.' I hugged her so she wouldn't see how much I wanted to stay. Only by burying my face in her shoulder could I say: 'God is calling me.'

I no longer wanted to go away, now that Beatrice was kissing every inch of my naked body, and now that I too could kiss her endlessly whenever I wanted. What did it matter if that house was essentially a convent, and that there were no men? What did I care about men now that I had her? All I would have in the place I had to go back to was that solitary love I now knew was called masturbation. Such a sad thing, I thought, what nuns do, and I had to laugh.

'What are you doing, laughing?'

'Yes.'

'Why?'

'I don't know.'

'Do you know, you look like a different person now that you're laughing? If you would only take off those bands and wear a corset!

Or at least let Argentovivo comb your hair to look softer, with a curl or two hanging down, like mine. She's very skilful.'

'I would never let Argentovivo touch me!'

'If that's the case, I can comb your hair myself, and make a chignon.'

'I can't, Beatrice. Besides, what good is it for such a short time? Twenty more days and . . .'

How could I not go back? How could I lose my vocation so suddenly in the eyes of the Princess and Beatrice herself? And what if Beatrice tired of me? I had no choice.

'I told her, you know. I told Nonna not to make you leave. Two days ago. But she didn't answer. Then yesterday she sent me this note. Look: "Leave that girl alone. You're just headstrong and thoughtless like your mother was. And you know it!"'

'Does she mean your mother, Mother Leonora? So you've spoken about her?'

'Once, many years ago. You can understand, can't you? It wasn't just capriciousness; I wanted to know. Here, and even in Catania, I had heard rumours. So I kept insisting until she sent for me and said: "All right, since you must know, so much the worse for you." That much I remember, but I don't remember anything else about that conversation. It's odd, but maybe because I was nervous I only remember the beginning and the end . . . The end was: "And now that you know, call me Nonna in private, face to face, because you are not my real daughter." But I don't want you to think she said it hatefully. You know how she is; she yells and shouts but then . . .'

'And did she also tell you about Carmine?'

'Of course. She always says that either you lie completely, or you tell everything.'

Look at that! I was learning so many things from that mute old woman. She was right.

'What upset me the most wasn't learning the truth, which I had more or less guessed, but . . .'

'What?'

'Well, Nonna said that when Leonora found herself pregnant, she could easily have ended my life before I was born – for me it would have been a blessing – and then married just the same, or she could have kept me and passed me off as her sister. Not exactly a tragedy! Even the Milazzos, neither rich nor noble as we are, have a daughter whom they pass off as their youngest but who is actually the child of their eldest daughter.'

'So why didn't she?'

'Who knows! She said either ending my life or letting me live was a sin, and she chose the convent. What do I know? Maybe you can understand; she had a vocation.'

'And Carmine? Why does he still come here?'

'He was left a widower and never remarried.'

'What has that got to do with it?'

'I wonder why he never remarried. Nonna pressed him to marry Agata three years ago . . .'

'I didn't mean that, I meant why . . .'

'Why what?'

'Well, if Carmine got a Brandiforti woman in trouble, why didn't your grandfather, your uncles. . .'

'What do you mean! We're noble and he's just a peasant. Do you expect someone in our family to dirty his hands over a commoner? Of course, if he had been someone of our class, or an officer maybe, a bourgeois, but a commoner . . . Imagine challenging a commoner to a duel!'

'But he wasn't thrown out or anything . . .'

'Thrown out? What are you saying! Nonno adored him and always said: "It's one thing to lose a daughter, who besides being a woman is foolish to boot, and another thing to lose a *gabellotto* like Carmine. Without a daughter you have fewer worries and you're spared a dowry, but without a *gabellotto* like Carmine, who's going to look after your lands?" Naturally! He manages everything and has trained so many men with his shotgun that they protect the estates and are as submissive as dogs. He frightens me!'

'But he's your father!'

'Some father! As my *tata* used to say, he's a *pedi 'ncritati*, a coarse peasant.* I've never looked at him directly. I don't like him and he scares me . . . I'm cold. Everything here scares me. Look how overcast the sky is! It's going to rain, Modesta. It's a sign that you're going away.'

'Let's go back inside, Beatrice. You're shivering. I wouldn't want you to come down with something.'

'I wish I would get sick. That way you'd have to . . .'

'Come now, Beatrice, come! I'm responsible for your health.'

I tried to pull her but she wouldn't budge. I didn't think she was that strong; I couldn't make her take a step. And I wouldn't have managed to if a gust of wind hadn't made her wobble. I grabbed her around the waist just in time to withstand the second squall that hit us from behind. Drops as big as flintstones battered our faces and made the villa's white facade appear to waver. Beatrice murmured, 'Dear God! The rain, it's a sign. You see? They closed all the shutters. They closed everything up . . . Oh God! Modesta, look, look! . . . The wind blew open the window on the second floor! God, I'm scared. I've never seen it open!'

It wasn't the wind: two arms now reached out, almost as if someone wanted to climb onto the windowsill and jump.

'It's Pietro, Modesta! It's Pietro shouting. What's happened?'

'Don't look, don't look!'

I pressed her head against my shoulder, so she wouldn't see all that blood covering Pietro's face. Only the hands and arms could be distinguished.

'Why wouldn't you let me look? What is it, Modesta? What's wrong? You look like a ghost.'

'Never mind, Beatrice. Go dry yourself off and find Argentovivo. Have her send for the doctor right away.'

'The doctor? Where are you going, Modesta? No!'

Peeling off her hands, which were clinging to my skirt, I raced up the stairs. I just had to get to my door and from there climb the last flight of stairs. I knew the route Pietro took. Every morning I had followed that iron tread. This was the corridor . . . It must be one of those doors. I was running down a long hall similar to mine, when a door at the end opened and Pietro slowly stepped out, blood trickling down his face.

'Watch out, *signorina*! Go back downstairs. I have him under control. Go back down and have them send for the doctor. This is no place for you, *signorina*!'

He was calm, but he must have been in a lot of pain because he slumped on a bench. His voice was loud and threatening. Maybe he was right, but I wanted to know. So, holding my breath to overcome my fear, I entered the room and saw the 'thing', his hands tied. Hunched in a chair, he was writhing and biting, his mouth oozing saliva. The 'thing' was nothing but a stumpy, fat man with a round head who was staring at me with Tina's eyes. I stepped back, and for the first time I had my doubts about whether the dead could return. Seeing me, that male Tina stopped thrashing and whining, and gaped at me open-mouthed, just as if he recognized me.

Drawn by the resemblance, I couldn't stop my legs from rigidly approaching him. He waited, his eyes spellbound. Only when I was nearly close enough to touch him was I sure it wasn't Tina, and to overcome the fear that had seized me, I smiled and kept telling myself: take a closer look, it's a man. He probably just has the same malady Tina had. Tina wasn't a monster or a 'thing', she was just sick. The doctor at the convent had told me about it: mongolism. I smile to make sure it's not Tina, and I start calling his name softly: Ippolito, Ippolito! He screws up his face in what he must mean to be a smile, and with his big, bound hands begins pushing at my skirt, but slowly, almost gently. It's not Tina.

'It's a miracle! A miracle!'

Pietro stares at me, ecstatic, wiping off the blood.

'You shouldn't have done it, *signorina*, but it's a miracle! Prince Ippolito has never done that with anyone . . . only with me, twice in ten years. You are a saint, *signorina*. Just look at that, he's quieted down. It's a miracle! And without pills or injections. He saw you and he calmed down.'

There! That's what would free me from my vocation: that miracle. But to substantiate it I had to stay there, so everyone could see me and know.

'You see, Pietro, nothing is going to happen. Go and treat your cuts or you'll bleed to death. Go ahead, and if you really want to put your mind at ease, send someone to stay outside. Nothing is going to happen to me. The Madonna led me here. I myself will watch over this poor soul!'

And unafraid, touched by Jesus, as they later said, I reached out and put my hand on that head. What fear could I possibly have, having grown up with a 'thing' like this? In fact, he had more hair than Tina. I began stroking it, and he lowered his head delightedly just as Tina used to do with Mama. He had no other way to show that he liked me.

In less than a quarter of an hour the news had spread throughout the villa. They came running. I could hear them behind the door, in the corridor, praying. Beatrice was there too. I could not retreat; the victory had to be complete. I loosened his ties as he watched me docilely, his eyes black and moist like a dog's. After I untied him I knelt in front of him, staring into his eyes. Then he lowered his eyes to my skirt and began to stroke it shyly. I was beginning to understand. The 'thing' had never seen anyone but Pietro, the doctor and maybe the priest. Probably my size or my gentle voice – I continued calling his name and telling him 'good boy, good boy' – or maybe the colour of my skirt amazed and captivated him. I let him go on until, confident by now, I began saying: 'Me Mama, me Mama . . .' He must have been breastfed by someone, the poor soul. Then I took his hand and placed it on my breast, repeating: 'Mama, Mama . . .' Then, something that astounded even me – I was beginning to sweat from the effort of repeating and looking into his eyes – he said awkwardly between his teeth: 'Mama, Mama, Mama.'

I heard something like a shudder pass through the corridor in response to the announcement someone had made: 'He called her Mama!' And after a silence, the word 'miracle', loudly shouted by everyone.

It was done. I held in my hand – a true miracle indeed – something that would enable me not to lose my vocation, but to change it as I pleased.

*

'So, my dear girl, from what I heard, your Mother Leonora appeared to you and you wish to sacrifice your vocation to devote yourself to our family?'

The voice that had been silent for so long was now booming again, more terrifying than the thunder and rain that had continued unabated outside. If only Beatrice were there! This time I was alone with the Princess. Her mocking grey eyes held my gaze, as mine tried vainly to look away.

'Well, answer me! It's true you're quite pretty when you get worked up! Too bad it only happens once in a blue moon! Answer! Do you think I care about your vocation? If you must know: in this house we believe in God, but very, very little in priests and nuns. Then too, if this can reassure you, I'm glad to know that when I die – I'm old now and although the idea of death doesn't thrill me, every so often I have to think about it. What a shame to have to die! What was I saying? Ah, yes, I'm glad to know that Cavallina and that 'thing' up there will not end up in the care of servants, but someone who, though taken in, is still part of the family, for better or for worse. Can't you speak? All right then! Answer me this at least: have you meditated seriously about the decision you've made? This isn't just a passing storm, is it? You're happy here? You won't regret leaving the convent, afterwards? You're young! Think before you answer, because you see, my girl, I won't tolerate whining women. Afterwards, you won't be able to complain. Do you understand? It's true you haven't complained these past months and you haven't gone around snivelling, but you never know with you women! It's better to be clear up front. *Patti chiari e inimicizia eterna*, clear understandings breed eternal animosity.* Well, answer me!'

'I've meditated, madam Princess. My place is here.'

'Fine. Tomorrow I shall write to those withered old ladies who've lost you, and have them send back the dowry and trousseau. I want to write a nice, polite letter and laugh, thinking of the disappointment and rage each line will cause Mother Costanza. I'll make them send back every last thing. Then, with the trousseau we'll have some ball gowns made for you. Because, see here, my girl, let's be clear: if you must sacrifice yourself, don't let it show. To begin with, tomorrow when the dance teacher comes for Cavallina, you too will take lessons. The waltz, the mazurka, the quadrille and all the rest! If you've made up your mind, you must learn to dance and to smile, because sourpusses and graceless bumblers really get on my nerves. Understood? Now off with you. I have to write a little line or two to Mother Costanza.'

Not expecting anything further, I started to run off to Beatrice. But when I was at the door, she added: 'Oh! You'll also have to learn to ride a horse . . . and we must see to that damned name of yours, my girl!'

*

My slim waist clinched by a corset, my breasts free, clasped only by a flimsy lace brassiere, I advanced toward Beatrice who was acting as my cavalier in that complicated quadrille of curtsies and glancing embraces, twists and turns. Whether it was the magic of the corset that helped me stand erect, or the patent-leather boots, glossier than the marble floor, I was really much taller than Beatrice. And when she held me around the waist as the teacher changed the rhythm at the piano – one-two-three, one-two-three for the waltz – I went flying around the great hall, surrounded only by empty and waiting chairs and sofas. 'Now, counterpoint! Turn!' Nimbly, Beatrice twirled around. She was incredible: when she danced, her limp nearly disappeared, and her strong hands held me firmly as I spun around the walls, the drapes, the chandeliers.

'Oh, *signorine*, what a delight it is to the eyes to look at you: two angels, I swear to God! Two angels embracing as they soar up, up into the clouds! It was time the *Principessina* had a partner! No, no, it's your turn now, Signorina Modesta, you're already proficient at being led. Come, it's your turn now to be the cavalier! Don't be afraid. Beatrice will guide you by letting herself be led. Don't worry, that's always the way. I swear to God, the pattern never changes: the lady pretends she's being led while instead she leads, leads, leads . . . There, that's it! Excellent! Turn, twirl, twirl. Bravo! Bravo! Bravo! What more can I say . . .'

That small instructor, smaller than Beatrice, though not old, was slight and smiling and curiously honed. Maybe because he had neither whiskers nor a moustache? On the other hand, he wore numerous rings and his pink fingernails seemed polished. When he arrived, all the women whispered and laughed together. If he approached to correct the placement of a hand, Beatrice stroked the black curls, slick with sweat and perfume, that tumbled over his temples when he ran over to us from the piano.

'Oh, come on, Modesta, don't you get it? It's not because he's a dancer or has to be able to dance the part of a man or a woman . . . Or that may be partly it. How astute you are! But be that as it may, it's that he's a woman like us. Can't you see that tiny waist? Just think! He doesn't even wear a corset! What fun it would be if we could put a corset on him . . .'

By now we were laughing together, and he, impassioned by our joy, instructed:

'No, no, Signorina Modesta, not so heavy! She's the cavalier who's leading now . . . Lightly, lightly, lightness, femininity! There, that's it, don't cling to the *Principessina*'s shoulders as if you were afraid of falling into a ravine. A lady, believe me, is not afraid of her cavalier; she knows that with a light touch . . . there, like that . . . such a lovely hand! it will be she who leads her partner. How I envy him! Then up, up into paradise . . . in three beats: one-two-three, one-two-three, one-two . . .'

We laughed in three beats: one-two-three . . .

'Now, both of you, without missing a beat, kindly take me round the waist . . . That's the way. And now, the grand finale, the galop. Ready? Go!'

30

We were so good – according to Argentovivo – that often one of the legion of maids would come to watch us from behind the glass doors. One day even the Princess deigned to attend a lesson to observe my progress. After ten minutes she stood up, and going through the door shouted, 'Fine, fine. Excellent, girls! Just look at that: three Graces without a cavalier! I'm going. The accounts await me. You three, make the best of it.'

She spoke so loudly that all three of us stopped, not daring even to look at each other. The thud of the door made us jump. The Princess was always slamming the door. The instructor, white as a sheet, was moving toward the piano where the young lady had stopped playing, when the door opened again.

'You made me lose my train of thought. I had come for a specific reason and you three with those leaps and twirls . . . Oh, yes! Mody, when you're done with this little party, I'll expect you in my study. I have a thing or two to tell you. And you, why are you standing there? Do you or do you not intend to make this lesson productive? Note that I pay you handsomely and I don't like to have my girls' time wasted. Go on, hop to it!'

The instructor hastily gave orders to restart the waltz, and Beatrice had already taken hold of my waist, but my legs wouldn't support me and I let myself be pulled along by her . . . She had a thing or two to tell me. What could be wrong? Had I been laughing too much? Had I shown too much interest in the dressmaker? Had I spent too much time with Ippolito? Or was it the accounts? Had I bungled the accounts? Dragging my legs, which did not want to move, I knocked on the door.

'Come in, come in, Mody. Please, close the door softly. I can't stand the slamming of doors. Why are you standing there frozen? Come, sit down. Carmine and I have a couple of little things to make clear to you . . . Have you met her, Carmine?'

I sat down just in time because my legs were no longer working. The man was staring at me with a blue gaze as opaque as majolica.

'I haven't yet had the honour of meeting Signorina Modesta.'

'Mody, Carmine, Mody!'

'*Voscenza* will pardon me, Princess, but I don't like these foreign names.'

'And yet, in my presence at least, you'll have to get used to it.'

'With all due respect, what nationality would this "Mody" be?'

'English. First I thought of Modesty, but it's almost as ugly as the Italian, so I shortened it to suit me. I have no idea if it's correct. But the British, a grand people, are very permissive when it comes to names. Do you know what the mother of my consort, the Prince, God rest his soul, used to say, Mody? Yes, that bourgeoise commoner whom we robbed. And don't blush, of course that chatterbox Beatrice must have told you all about it! The Englishwoman used to say that to keep a horse happy all you have to do is tie him with a longer rope. So the British are firmly tied but with a rope so long they're not even aware of it and think they're free. Oh, yes, I learned quite a few things from that bourgeoise lady. She was clever! She read, instead of wearing herself out by having babies. But why are you letting me go on! This isn't why we're here. Listen, Carmine, to finish our discussion I'm telling you that this girl is skilful and gifted. For two months now she's been keeping all the household accounts, and never one mistake. Everything balances better than when I kept them, and she's even saved me some money.'

'I don't doubt it. But the house is one thing, it's another thing to . . .'

'And what about me? It seems to me I've been taking care of everything for ten years, haven't I?'

'Forgive me for what may seem like an impropriety, but *Voscenza*, Princess, are an exception: you were born to be a man!'

'And I'm telling you that Mody is like me! I've been watching her for months! Besides I can use a hand; my eyesight is worsening. I have to train someone who will be able to look after things when I am gone. Leonora of course was impetuous like Beatrice, but she had good taste and intelligence. It's as if she found the girl and raised her just to relieve me during these final years. Yes, I admit it: I'm tired, and someone must take my place.'

'But . . .'

'We've talked too much about it today. Mody is here. Leonora sent her to us and starting tomorrow, 3 November 1917, she will meet with us every Monday to learn to manage everything. You see her speechless because she's afraid of me, but the tutor told me that she has quite a glib tongue! I will teach her to deal with those thieving attorneys and notaries and you will instruct her about the lands and the tenants. Understood?'

'But, if I may say so, the *signorina* is young.'

'Young or not, that's my decision . . . You don't agree?'

'I'd rather not answer that.'

'You – when you were a boy, who taught you?'

'The Prince, God rest his soul, and *Voscenza*, Princess.'

'So then, why won't you respond about the girl?'

'Because, with your permission, I prefer not to.'

'Don't respond then, given how obstinate you are. But starting today, here, in my presence, you must call her *Padrona*. Understood, Carmine? Mistress. Say it.'

'I have to call the *signorina* Mistress?'

'Mistress.'

'Since *Voscenza* insists, but given that she's just a little slip of a girl, *'na scazzidda di carusa*, can I at least call her *Padroncina*?'

'Oh, all right. Now go. I'm tired. And you, girl, why are you still standing there? I said you may go, didn't I? I'm sure you understood everything. And try to command the respect of that man of honour.'*

31

And to command his respect I began poring over maps of the property to study the boundaries, lands and dividing walls of those immense estates. There was always some legal action underway. The princess had given me the civil code, saying: 'Study it. It's the only way to avoid being seriously robbed by lawyers, brokers and notaries.'

Every Monday I listened to Carmine report on the new crops, the harvest . . . Labour was in short supply because of the general mobilization . . . The *sovrastanti*, his trusted men, and the *braccianti*, the farm hands, were demanding more and more . . . In Licata, a lamb had been found in the fields with its legs broken. It was a warning: we must negotiate with them or all the livestock would end up in the woods of Ficuzza – who could set foot in those woodlands? – and there become tinned food for the front. South of the Valle del Bove, a lava flow had destroyed acres and acres of olive groves. Nothing got through from the north anymore. Strikes at Fiat had blocked everything and prices were rising sky-high: bread which in 1915 cost 53 cents a pound had risen to 56 cents a pound, pasta from 71 cents to 95. And to make matters worse, in August, on the continent – specifically in Turin – there had been a bread riot.

'Here too, believe me, *Voscenza*, discontent is growing. At the front the soldiers are full of these rebellious ideas. And sooner or later they'll come back . . . the *senzadio*, those godless atheists, can rear their heads here too. Let's not forget 1893. Today there isn't a man like

Crispi on the island. Keep in mind that in Turin they also looted and burned the church of San Bernardino . . .'

Now I knew who those wretched *senzadio* were. And I also knew that Crispi had stopped the revolution with bloodshed. I had learned it from Jacopo. In a book by Voltaire, in the margin, there was a box with a black border where he had written:

'I should rejoice over Crispi's bloody victory, but the general jubilation finds no echo in my heart. I know all too well that we are a class that's done for, but I would rather we died at the hands of the peasants than be bled dry by the *gabellotti*. Because that will be our end.'

I had known I could find information in his room, but I would never have imagined the treasures contained in that small library. I had to study, to prepare myself for when I met them, those socialists. They also said that women were equal to men. In the margin of a book by Augusto Bebel, Jacopo's clear handwriting read:

'October 21, 1913. How I have tried to instil at least some of these ideas in Beatrice! But it's difficult to uproot her from this barbaric setting that surrounds her. It will take a century before women can hear your voice, old Augusto!'

I soaked up those faint lines, erased by time in some places, as though I were Beatrice . . . I stole her place. I could hear Jacopo's voice from those pages, instructing me not to read chaotically, as he put it, but systematically, his method. At the end of *Candide* a note said: 'reread Diderot's *Interpretation of Nature*'.* When I opened the book, the words 'Young man, open this book and read on' grabbed me by the throat, but the postscript especially moved me: 'One more word before I take my leave. Always bear in mind that *nature* is not *God*, that a *man* is not a *machine* and that a *hypothesis* is not a *fact*; you may be sure that if you think you have found something here which conflicts with these principles, you will have failed to understand me.'

Diderot warned against certain philosophers: 'Great abstractions' – he wrote – 'glow with only a pale light. There is a type of obfuscation which could be defined as *the affectation of the great masters*. It serves as a veil which they enjoy drawing between nature and the public.'

Jacopo had underlined that last sentence, and next to it was the name of a certain Marx: which meant that he must be someone who said more or less the same thing. Maybe he was in the section where Voltaire was. Could he have been one of them? . . . Jacopo, Jacopo, his books, his fine handwriting, his serene brow in the photo, which did not belie his notes; his ashes in a vase to make it clear that he did not believe in any god and that he had died without fear.

'*Uffa*, how tiresome, Modesta! All you do is ask about Jacopo. I've told you everything! Besides, he travelled a lot, it's not like he was always here. No, he never married. He didn't want children; that much I know. *Uffa!* You have so little time for me now, why? I'm bored all morning without you!'

It was true; though recently, as I had foreseen, Beatrice had become less attentive toward me now that she was no longer worried about my leaving. As for me, having been advised by the Princess, I threw myself wholeheartedly into caring for Prince Ippolito, not only in the mornings, as I had before, but also in the afternoons. And since I spent almost the entire day with him and had grown used to sweet-scented surroundings – how quickly one learns to appreciate pleasurable things! – I couldn't stand seeing him dirty. With Pietro's help I managed to keep him clean. Pietro was very happy with the progress of his dear Prince. He was devoted to me by now and fawned over me like a puppy dog, hovering with his immense bulk.

'By God, a woman is what was needed here! I did whatever I could, but the hand of a woman has a different touch, as my father used to say. Who would have thought that my *signor* Prince, in such a short time, would be eating with a fork. A miracle! A miracle that only a woman can perform! Even in my house, when my mother died, everything grew dim with dust and tears. And only when that sainted soul, my aunt, came to live with us did cleanliness and brightness return . . .'

'You even go to the "thing" at breakfast time, Modesta! And I have to eat alone! *Uffa*, what a pain! Why?'

I responded to this refrain with one of my own. 'Don't get upset, Beatrice. It's my obligation. Keep in mind that I was destined for the convent, and although I've learned to dance and dress properly, and spend my evenings with you, I have a duty to perform and nothing can come before this duty that Mother Leonora assigned me in place of my vocation.'

She sulked and grumbled, but meanwhile her interest in me came back even stronger. She didn't know why, but I did. Hadn't Mimmo always said: '*What do you expect, principessina? Even if the soup is tasty and served graciously, if that's what you always have in front of you, you get tired of it . . .*'

'You don't even come to tea anymore!'

In fact I didn't like tea, and that way I avoided the Princess's silence; her Monday morning shouting was enough for me. Besides, in addition to Ippolito, the accounts and the lessons, I had my own studying to do. I'm poor, right, Mimmo? Poor, and I have to become strong by reading and studying, finding in myself and others the key to not succumbing. There had been many who, born poor, had been saved by their intelligence and the strength that knowledge affords . . . There, spread out before me in rows in the immense library, their names shone on the brown and gold spines of those volumes.

32

Thanks to the doctor, a gentle old man who now gaped at me with constant reverence, I had obtained the Princess's permission to open the window in that room. As a result, the air had swept away the terrible odour that no amount of scrubbing had ever been able to eliminate.

With Pietro watching over me and his dear Prince, that room was my home. No one could come in, and Pietro couldn't read, so I could blithely take Jacopo's books in there and study them undisturbed. Over time, I discovered that Ippolito was happy not only when I sang or told him stories, but also when I read aloud (maybe because I pronounced the words slowly, syllable by syllable). He listened, captivated, and I learned more and more, as Jacopo's instructions guided me . . . So that even the tutor, whom I had thought was a genius only seven or eight months before, now seemed like an insignificant philistine who couldn't be relied upon. And if Mother Leonora was merely a *religeuse*, he seemed like a poor Candide, happy and content with his servitude, full of enthusiasm and naivety. Voltaire said that to be naive at twenty was a sin. I was still naive, but I wasn't twenty years old yet. I attended lessons, yes, but only to later dismantle them, strip them, and extract solely the concepts that could be of use to me. Ippolito listened happily, unaware of my efforts. Because it was an effort! My skirts hung loose at the waist and a strange sweat broke out when I helped Pietro bathe and dress Ippolito in the morning.

'You're a saint, Modesta, a saint! But you should take care of yourself; it's alarming how thin you've become! Yes, I know, it's your duty, but now you're all mine, right? You're not thinking about that ugly "thing" up there even now, are you? At least in the evening you're all mine, right? Come on, let's play . . .'

I too eagerly awaited evening. I wanted nothing more than to caress her and hold her in my arms. And even though I was tired, as soon as she touched my hair, my sleepiness vanished.

'. . . Is it true that Ippolito eats with a fork? How did you do it?'

'. . . Is it true that he lets himself be bathed? Yes, of course, Pietro bathes him, but you help him dress him, comb his hair. Argentovivo told me that Pietro has spruced himself up too.'

'. . . What on earth do you do all those hours with him? Argentovivo says that Pietro told her that you read and the "thing" listens. Can it be?'

'. . . Is it true you've managed to get him to pray? Father Antonio is happy to come and give him Holy Communion every Sunday.'

'. . . Is he terribly ugly, Modesta? Is he really as monstrous as Nonna says?'

'Of course not, Beatrice. Besides, no soul of God is monstrous. He's just fat and stumpy, but his eyes are not exactly like Ti— I mean, they're ugly but expressive.'

'What are you thinking about, Modesta? You're not thinking about him, are you? You don't love him more than me, do you? Sometimes it makes me angry to think that you spend so many hours with him, that you comb his hair. You don't caress him, do you? You don't sing him a lullaby like you do for me, do you?'

'What are you saying, Beatrice! Ippolito, even though he's ill, is still a man! And I, although I didn't go into the convent, will always be God's bride, vowed to chastity.'

'Good thing. That way at least I'll always have you all to myself. I hate men.'

Of course. Even though he was ill, he was a man, and a prince. Beatrice was right. How come I hadn't thought of it before? Had I been working, studying too hard? Or had the serenity I felt in Beatrice's arms softened me, as Mimmo used to say? *'Eh, princess!*

When love is too great it makes you soft. It happened to me once. From the sturdy labourer I had been, I melted away like a candle. No living creature should surrender to it.'

I used to run away when Mimmo talked like that. But was what I felt for Beatrice love? All those daunting books that spoke of love! They were delightful to read, but the passions they described were as fanatical, Voltaire would have said, as religious passion. Not to mention that for some reason, it was always the women who had to submit . . . Jacopo said the reason for it was that women are brought up only to love . . . She had to be wary of Beatrice and think about her own life. What had she done since she'd been in that villa? Of course she had studied, and she had won the Princess's complete confidence, something she hadn't hoped for. And although Carmine wouldn't deign to glance at her, he had no choice but to accept her now.

The 'thing' was still a man. I had seen him touch himself several times as he looked at me. And each time, Pietro had promptly sent me away with some excuse. Had I wasted all that time? Yet it had taken time for Ippolito to get used to me. One day when I was late, I found him tied up, drooling, and Pietro desperate. That's what I had to do: get sick and let them stew in their own broth, as Mimmo would say.

The next morning I awoke with a severe headache, unable to swallow any food. And tossing out all the pills, drops and purgatives the doctor brought me, I held out against Beatrice's desperate tears, the Princess's demands – by now she was saying, 'Without her, I feel like I've lost my right arm' – and Pietro's entreaties. He was no longer able to manage his dear Prince, who had been up to all sorts of mischief since he'd stopped seeing me in his room.

I couldn't imagine what would happen when I saw him again. However: 'One action leads to another action, and eliminates inaction which, though restful, in the long run turns into a quagmire.' In that year I was able to ascertain that Ippolito's degree of idiocy was not as extensive as Tina's. His brutishness had been caused simply by his having been abandoned. At least now he spoke a few words: 'hungry', 'sleepy', 'peepee', 'Mama', and, oddly, he called Pietro 'Uncle'.

Ten days later, when I showed up, nothing important seemed to happen. Ippolito, after crying and drooling with excitement, was quiet all day. But in the evening, when it was time for me to leave, he began screaming and holding on to my skirt. Overcome by my long absence, he was now afraid that I would not return. Pietro struggled to pry his hands loose, but the entire night was hell, and we had to resort to the straitjacket and the pills like before. Something had happened.

In the days that followed, they assembled in the rose-coloured parlour in fighting trim, arguing in front of me without seeing me.

The doctor: 'And I insist that, since he has not calmed down either the first or second or third night, another solution must be found. With all those baths, bromides and the straitjacket, we'll end up killing him. I cannot assume the responsibility for a murder. My duty as a doctor—'

The doctor again: 'It is my duty to advise those responsible – and you are responsible as well, my dear *signorina* – that as of this morning Ippolito has been refusing to eat. Pietro is unable to make him swallow anything, not even by opening his jaws with forceps. My duty as a doctor—'

The Princess: 'From the very beginning, my dear *signor* doctor, with all your duty, I said it was folly to leave a girl with that "thing". Who, though he may be a "thing", is still a man. I'm well aware of how much those little "visits" of his cost me.'

The doctor: 'Those little "visits" are one thing; it's clear that Signorina Modesta is another matter. I insist—'

Don Antonio: 'And I forbid it! And I will be forced, if you insist, to appeal to the Curia. We clergy cannot allow one of our sheep, pledged to God, to be compromised by sleeping in the room of a man, even as a nurse. I remind everyone that the spiritual journey of this soul is very dear to His Eminence. There is not one time that he does not ask after her.'

Beatrice wept silently, staring at everyone so wide-eyed that it was frightening to see.

The Princess: 'Well then, bring him a more attractive girl, since he's become so picky.'

The doctor: 'We did, Princess! And we went even further. We called Carmela back.'

The Princess: 'Who is this Carmela?'

The doctor: 'The one he was once so fond of . . . That's right, Princess, the daughter of that petty thief who was killed in the citrus grove in Licosa, the one who didn't want to come anymore after she got married, remember? Just as well. Anyway, yesterday she agreed, even though she has three children. The result? While he wouldn't even look at the others, he would have strangled Carmela if Pietro hadn't been there. There's no doubt about it. My Ippolito has fallen in love. Basically, even though he doesn't have all the right feelings, it's clear that after being with a decent girl he doesn't want anything to do with those earlier trollops. Even Pietro realized it. When he brings him a new one, the Prince turns his head and repeats stupidly: 'Mama, Mama, Mama.'

The Princess: 'What does Mama have to do with it?'

The doctor: 'That's the point. Since the first day, he's called Signorina Modesta Mama.'

The Princess: 'Imagine that!'

*

I had hoped for something to happen, but the uproar of slammed doors, shouts and screams, commands and countermands forced me back to bed. There was nothing else I could do, because the Princess now looked at me with eyes whose gaze I dared not meet. In my safe haven, I received news from Argentovivo and the doctor. The Princess's latest decision was that I should not see him and that they should continue bringing the 'thing' those girls. She was certain he would forget me. But the doctor, when he was with me, sniggered and kept repeating, 'Say what you will. I may be crazy, but I'm not sorry my Ippolito has fallen in love.'

The days passed and, forced to stay in that bed, I began to feel sick for real, when one fine evening the door swung open so unexpectedly and so loudly that I huddled against the wall holding my head in my hands. Who could it be? Sister Costanza, surely. She was the Mother Superior now. And if she used to do it before 'to discover the hidden little vices of all those little sinners', imagine now that the convent was in her hands.

'Girl! Pardon me for entering your room, but they told me that you

are not well. And I'm sick and tired of both your illness and all the talk
and nonsense that your presence in that room has caused. So we have
to make a decision. I spoke with Carmine, and he agrees. He admitted that there is no other solution, partly because, like it or not, the
blame for all this havoc is yours, and you must be the one to take
responsibility for it. All in all, given that in a hundred years I'll be food
for worms, as that joker Hamlet says, it wouldn't hurt for you to be
part of the family legally as well. You will be better able to look after
affairs, at least as long as Beatrice and the "thing" are alive. But take
heed! I don't want any grandchildren. This family of cripples and
imbeciles must end with my husband. There's no use in your protest-
ing. It's your fault and the fault of that impetuous Leonora, who, for
each thing she did right, always did a hundred things wrong. I'll give
you three days to recover. Because Don Antonio is going to marry
you in the private chapel, at night. Don't count on my presence. I
haven't seen the "thing" since he was born, and I certainly have no
intention of seeing him now. The doctor and Pietro will be your wit-
nesses, because no one – understood? – no one must see him. Oh,
another thing: tell your friend Cavallina to stop it. For ten days now
she's been plaguing me with her tears and sighs. Try to get her to
calm down unless you want me to send her off to some boarding
school in Switzerland. Do we understand each other? Good night.'

The door slammed more forcefully than before, but, strangely, her
shouting had brought a warmth to my cheeks and a peace I had never
known before. Like after a job well done, eh, Mimmo? Basking snugly
in that peace, I sought out Mimmo on the silk-covered walls, along
the plush velvet drapes that protected me from the night. A job truly
well done, right, Mimmo?

'That's right, Principessina, and afterwards one can enjoy the most satisfying exhaustion there is.'

Mimmo was always right. Even though married to a monster, I was
still a *principessina*. And the languor that very slowly crept over me
was indeed the well-deserved sleep that follows a hard day's labour in
the fields.

33

I slept so deeply, under Mimmo's watchful eye, that when I opened my eyes I was afraid the Princess's visit had been only a dream. Especially since someone was crying in the room.

'It's horrible, horrible! I can't even think about it, Modesta. You shouldn't have agreed. You can't sacrifice yourself like that! It's all the fault of that crazy doctor and Don Antonio. It's dreadful! Why must your goodness be repaid this way?'

Beatrice never understood a thing. If she were more intelligent, as Jacopo had wanted her to be, I would have made her my accomplice. It's hard to do battle by yourself. But there was no other way. I had to continue embroidering that canvas alone, to protect myself and to protect her.

'It's my destiny, Beatrice.'

'But you'll sleep with him!'

'It's my destiny. Don't be upset. Think about the fact that this pious sacrifice will allow us to be together for ever. Have you thought about that?'

I was sure she hadn't thought about it, and in fact:

'It's true! I hadn't thought about it.'

'Darling Beatrice, why don't you try and think of the bright side of whatever happens? Nothing is completely negative in life.'

'God, Modesta, you talk like Uncle Jacopo! I've noticed it for months now. I didn't say anything because I was afraid you might get mad.'

Beatrice was scatterbrained, yet at times discerning. The similarity that her little head had grasped was dangerous; best to change the subject.

'Will you come to the wedding?'

'Modesta, no! Don't ask that of me. I could never. I've never seen the "thing", and besides Nonna said that no one must see him, even if he's getting married.'

So much the better. If they had seen Ippolito they would have realized that he wasn't as monstrous as their imagination had drawn him. Never refuse to see the unpleasant aspects of life; by remaining unseen, they are actually magnified in the imagination, transformed into irrepressible demons.

'There, you see, you withdraw from me, just like Uncle Jacopo, following who knows what thoughts. You've changed a lot, Modesta.'

Luckily she always warned me. This inability to keep her mouth shut, as the Princess said, was convenient.

'It's not that I've changed, Beatrice, it's that soon I will have yet another cross to bear and I'm preparing for it. And please, don't go on crying like that. How would I manage to bear all this if you were far away?'

'Far away? What do you mean?'

'The Princess told me that if you continue crying, she'll send you off to some boarding school in Switzerland. You know that when she says she'll do something, she does it.'

Thanks to the Princess, the crying stopped. It was unbearable for me, too, to see her that way. Now she dried her tears and tried to smile.

'Oh God, Modesta, for God's sake, I won't cry anymore. I promise you! Tell her I won't cry anymore!'

She appealed to me. I was the one who maintained contact with the Princess, now, and in just one year! Careful, Modesta, one must be cautious with power. Above all, never lose old friends, as Shakespeare says.* Beatrice's humble way of imploring me could signal disaffection on her part.

'My darling Beatrice, let's not think about unpleasant things. Come

now, smile. When you smile, everything becomes beautiful for me.'
Where had I read that nonsense that young girls are so fond of? Still,
it came in handy.

'When you smile, the sun shines for me even if the sky is cloudy.
Come, hold me close. In your arms I will find the courage to face the
painful task that awaits me.'

'Oh, Modesta, how gentle you are with me again, and what sweet
things you say! You've been so serious these three weeks that I was
beginning to be afraid of you.'

There, she'd said it. I had to rid her of that fear to have her as an
ally, even an unsuspecting one. Fear and humiliation are the seeds of
hatred and antagonism. And even envy, so they said. It would be difficult, but now that I was beginning to have some power, I had to find
a way, like a wise old monarch, not to attract too much envy, even
from the servants.

After allowing myself to be comforted by Beatrice's embrace, I got
up.

'Now leave me, Beatrice. I have to pray and find strength.'

Those of you who are reading are surely already thinking that my
triumph would necessarily require something very distasteful: sleeping with an individual who was disabled, if not monstrously ugly. The
fact is that you are reading this story, and you are ahead of me,
whereas I'm living it. I am still living it.

All at once I realize what's in store for me. What did that monster
do with all the girls who had been brought to his room? And whom
could I ask? Certainly not Pietro. The doctor? How could I? He too
was a little goody-goody. My saintly reputation did not allow me even
to graze certain subjects. A cold sweat began sliding down my back
and for a moment I began to have doubts about what had earlier
seemed to be a victory. Instinctively, old habit made me fall to my
knees with my head in my hands. I wasn't praying – don't worry – I
was just trying to overcome the wave of disgust that clouded my
brain. I must not give in to that disgust. Besides, if so many girls had
been in that room and had survived, I too could do it. I tried to remember one of those names. Carmela, that's it, the one who was Ippolito's
favourite, according to the doctor . . .

'Forgive me for disturbing you, *signorina*. The Princess has asked me to tell you that for the ceremony you must wear the dress that Mother Leonora wore when she became the bride of Christ. If you please, I have come to take it, to freshen it.'

Argentovivo had never been so respectful. She spoke more slowly now, keeping her eyes lowered, and didn't bustle about the room like a madwoman anymore.

'May I take the dress, *signorina*?'

Of course. She was waiting for my order. That waiting restored the self-confidence I had lost. I was part of the family now. And to bolster that self-confidence I let her wait a few minutes. Her respectful still-ness and bowed head completely calmed my tremors. And with com-posure, my ideas began to flow clearly again. At least I no longer had to fear the walls, the drapes, the servants of that house, as I had in the past.

'One moment, Argentovivo – I have a question to ask you. Do you know a certain Carmela Licari?'

'No, I don't know her. She's just a peasant who lives down in the shanties. As you know, we in this house have no contact with those kinds of people.'

'You may take the dress.'

Curtsying – before making a move she even curtsied now – she ventured to say, 'But the *signorina* mustn't think about that one. Those women were paid to come and . . .'

'I didn't ask for your opinion.'

The Princess would have replied that way, and the effect was imme-diate.

'Oh, I'm sorry! I didn't mean . . . Forgive me if I disturbed you. *Riverisco*, my respects, *signorina*.'

★

It was risky, but I had to know. Luckily I hadn't spent a single penny of the money the Princess had given me each month since I'd taken over the management of the house.

When the sun was high, thereby ensuring that all the men were in the fields and that everyone in the villa was shut in to escape the intense heat, I put on an old smock, covered my head, like the farm women, with the least conspicuous kerchief I could find, and ran down to the white walls behind the trees. There was an opening guarded only by the dog Menelik, who knew me, and in a moment I was out. I had never been outside, and a sloping expanse of wheat, swaying in the wind as far as the eye could see, lashed my legs and brow. The wind was strong, and I couldn't move. I wasn't used to walking without a wall to mark the boundaries of the outside world. And to think that as a child all I did was wander through the lava plain, the *chiana* . . . Those years in the convent and in the villa had weakened me. I couldn't even look at that dancing expanse of gold. For a moment I thought of turning back. No! I had to get over it. And lowering my head, eyes fixed only on the white shanties that could be seen down at the bottom, I started running as though pursued, pausing only when my hands found a wall where I could regain the equilibrium I had lost. It was a drinking trough, teeming with donkeys and children.

'Ma chi dici chista 'cca! Iu nun la capisciu, e tu? What is she saying? I don't understand her, do you?'

As I knew from the time I was with the nuns, outside the wall they spoke another language.

'Ma chi dici? 'Na straniera havi a essiri, e chi voli? What is she saying? She must be a foreigner. What does she want?'

It was a good thing I hadn't run away from the convent back then. But now I had money, and without another word, repeating only the name Carmela Licari, I handed out coins.

'Ah, Carmela, she's looking for Carmela, *chidda ca parra comu 'na signura*, the one who talks like a grand lady.'

One of them gestured with his head and, without saying a word, took me to a doorway closed off by a black curtain. But instead of letting me go in, he stood in front of the doorway, straightened his *coppola* like an adult and, spreading his legs, held out his open hand. I gave him more coins and he went back to the others shouting something that must surely have been an insult. I called out and when the curtain parted I was plunged back in time. A darkness smelling of mildew and sweat assailed me, making me feel like a little girl again. Flies buzzed around, knocking against the walls. Three beds had been added to the big bed where Mama slept with Tina. In back, the fire in the stove was out as usual.

'What do you want?'

The voice wasn't shrill like Mama's.

'Oh, holy God, it's Signorina Modesta! What are you doing here, *signorina*? Is something wrong? Have you run away? Oh God, *signorina*, this is no place for you! You haven't come to make trouble in this house, already so wretched, have you?'

Terrified in turn by her fear, I cried out without meaning to, 'No, Carmela, no, I haven't run away! I just want some information . . .'

'Yes, yes, I understand. I too was very frightened the first time they took me to him. And to think – we're both women after all – to think that I, due to poverty and bad luck, was experienced when I set foot in there. And that experience saved me. I'm not telling you these things for money, *figghia*.* It's just that I wouldn't want anyone to go through what I did as I waited to enter that room . . . I'll take the money, but only half of it. And only because, as you see, we are in great need. But I see that you are in a hurry. If they find out that you ran off, woe to you and to me. Look, *figghia*, for me it wasn't hard, but you have to bear up. I'll tell you. You should know that I was the first female the poor soul had seen. Now, even though you're a woman, I don't know where to begin . . . To make it brief and less embarrassing for you and for me, I – and don't look at me like that or I'll feel ashamed! – when I went there I thought he had been instructed. There was a doctor there too, but that's another story. What do I know! I thought that the Prince had somehow been taught what a man does. And so, closing my eyes and not taking off my clothes – there are some who like to undress you . . . so then, closing my eyes – and to think I was ten years old when they put a man between my legs – I waited. A century passed, and from him, not a move. I opened my eyes, and that poor soul, fully clothed and with his . . . how can I say it? Well, all right, with his thing out, was touching himself, in a frenzy. In short, I learned that he didn't know what to do with his thing, which, hard as a rock, must surely have been painful. And so, may the Madonna forgive me! With blessed patience . . .'

'What?'

'Since he knew nothing, and since it was convenient for me, I taught him to stroke himself up and down like men do. It couldn't hurt him, that much I knew. A seaman told me that men do this when they are on ships, at sea for months and months. Even the ship's doctor told him that it was not harmful to one's health. In fact, he even confided to me that it gave him more satisfaction almost than doing it the regular way. Oh, *figghia*, how shameful to have to tell you these things. But you gave me a lot of money. Now you know. There is only the uncertainty of all the young women who came after me. That I can't tell you. But now, tell me, what is it that's really bothering you? That he's ugly? He's ugly, true, but he's good, I can guarantee you that. Docile. Or since they are making him marry you, maybe you're worried about not having children? Of course, with children your position would be stronger, but I wouldn't have any with the Prince. I'm not telling you anything, you're young! Look around you . . . I know these are vile things to say as far as religion goes, but don't do as I did, being too trusting . . . look around you!

'Now go, I hear them coming back from the fields. Go, *figghia*, my Michele is violently jealous. He is overcome with raging jealousy toward everyone in the villa . . . No, I don't want all the money, it's too much. No, no! All right, if you insist, I'll take it. I see that you have a good heart, and I'll accept the money, but only if you promise to think of me as being in your debt. Now run, run home, and don't come out again . . .'

★

As I went out, the light blinded me as it had many years before, but men were approaching and I mustn't think about the past. I had to run, as Carmela had told me. Going uphill, the endless gold of the wheat was less intimidating. And without looking, head lowered, I raced toward the dark patch of woods beyond which a high wall protected against the poverty which I had managed to escape, at least up till now, but which awaited me, unchanged, with a child's open mouth and outstretched hand. I would never again go outside that wall.

'My *Padroncina*, my young mistress, has good legs! I swear to God, I would never have imagined it! From a distance, if it weren't for the colour of your hair, I would have taken you for a field hand or a hare.'

Riveted, I brought my hands to my head. In my eagerness to run from poverty I had lost my kerchief. I cursed my past and my cowardice. Now it was hopeless to try and get away. I clenched my fists and confronted him, staring right at him. For months I hadn't looked at him. Maybe because from up there on his horse he seemed bigger, or because outdoors the majolica blue of his eyes held red flames, or because he was laughing, but the earlier terror gripped me even more sharply.

'You must have run a long way, *Padroncina*; you're all flushed. If you will permit me, I can take you back on Orlando. Going downhill, all the saints are there to assist, but uphill is uphill. Whoa there, Orlando, easy now you rascal. Allow me to introduce my *Padroncina*. Orlando is the one who spotted you moving through the wheat, and made me turn off. So, if you like, I'll take you. Don't worry, not inside the wall. Carmine is a man of discretion. And if you don't cross him, he sees nothing and hears nothing. I'll leave you at the spot where you came out . . . I'll follow along on foot.'

'But I—'

'You mean you don't know how to ride bareback?'

'I don't know how to ride a horse.'

'Well then, it's unavoidable: even if you don't like it, you'll have to climb up in front of me . . . Here, put one foot there. Now leap up. *Brava!* You're nimble . . . I apologize for having to sit behind you.'

That voice filled me with profound terror. When I felt him bent over behind me holding the reins, it was as if I were completely surrounded by chains. He had trapped me; that's why he was smiling.

'Why are you trembling like that, *Padroncina?* Maybe you're afraid of the horse? It happens to everyone the first time. But you must get used to it, because in the future, once you're a princess, you will have to oversee your lands not only on paper, but also in person.'

'Yes, of course, but . . . he scares me a little. What's his name?'

'Orlando, *Padroncina*. I hope it's only the animal who scares you and not its master.'

His voice and the wind made me sway left and right. From up there, the dancing immensity of gold began to make my head spin, so that without meaning to I grabbed hold of his arms.

'Oh, no, *Padroncina*, you have to leave my arms free. Orlando is very jealous. And if he becomes too aware of you, he's apt to change his mood and make us break our necks. Lean back on me. Naturally, with skirts it's difficult. There, that's it . . . can you feel how I do it? Thighs and knees lightly gripping the flanks. *Brava!* That's the way. I bet in a month you'll be as upright as *Principessina* Beatrice and even better. When you want, I'll teach you.'

The horse's flanks were steaming. By contrast, the arms and chest of that man gave off a dry heat, like when you're in front of a fireplace. I didn't open my eyes for fear the strange dizziness would return. I should have said something, but my mouth was pasty. If only he had gone on talking . . . But now not a word from him. In the silence, my dizziness increased with each slight tug he gave the reins, and I was mortified to feel the sweat seep from my back onto his shirt. Soon I could no longer distinguish my fabric from his. He did not speak again until the horse came to a stop and he climbed down, offering me his arm.

'Here we are, *Padroncina*. If I may say so, you shouldn't be so afraid of the animal. You gave me a bath, sweating like that. He's a good animal if you treat him right. Come now, down you go.'

His hands around my waist, before I could open my eyes he swept me off; I was taken aback and to my shame heard myself say, 'Oh, forgive me for sweating like that!'

'No need to apologize for sweating: it's fragrant! I swear to God, I would never have believed that sweat could smell like orange blossoms, not even if my mother had told me so! *Baciamo le mani*, my respects, *Padroncina*.'

Laughing, he mounted his horse without giving me another look.

My legs were shaking so much that I was barely able to watch him ride away before sagging to the ground. Even seated, I was still shaking. And as the sweaty heat from the horse gradually dissipated, a bitter chill began to creep over my body. Yet the sun was still high . . . Look at him there, that white head of his racing along . . . Goddamned old man! Outside the villa he could laugh. He was master, there. Beatrice was right to hate her father.

The chill wouldn't leave me. And neither would my loathing for those powerful arms, that confident laugh.

*

Angrily I tore off my clothes and washed myself, as if the water could erase the memory of that old man's magnetism. I mustn't think about him anymore.

What was it that had disturbed me so? His strength? The ease with which he had lifted me up as if I were a feather? If so, then what I was feeling was not a healthy hatred, as I had imagined. No, that hatred masked my fear of him. It was hard to acknowledge feeling weak and cowardly, but I had to face that reality. My foray from the villa had been a real test. Within its walls I felt strong and confident, but all it took was that hovel, that child at the water trough to make the past return. That's how the past came back . . . not with the same characters, like in novels, but with new ones that trigger the memory of fears that haven't been expunged. And that was very dangerous. I mustn't try to forget the past, as I had thought while running from Carmela's house; instead I should remember it all, so I could keep it under control and use it to strengthen myself against the new experiences that surely lay in wait. Carmela had reminded me of my mother. It was the old fear that had made me lose my kerchief. Carmine too scared me, but not like Mother Leonora had. And the Princess, what kind of fear did she arouse? There, I was on the right track: it was necessary to study the emotions that others awaken in us, just as we study grammar or music.

The feeling of warmth and release that filled me as a result of these thoughts confirmed to me that I had discovered something meaningful. I closed my eyes and saw myself running through the wheat, trembling like a seven- or eight-year-old child. That foray had helped me grow, provided I always keep in mind that that child, with her foolish fears, could be reawakened in me by a look, a wall, a certain light, a face. And that her fear could lead to the undoing of all my present plans and prosperity. In a few months I would turn eighteen. In three days, or rather two, I would be a princess, even if this meant . . . If only things might still be as Carmela had described!

*

Things were still as Carmela had said. And it wasn't so terrible, because Pietro, instead of preparing the big bed, had brought in another smaller one, separated by a night stand. A bell on the head-board provided reassurance. It rang directly over Pietro's head, as he kept watch in the room next door. The first couple of weeks were hard, but only because Ippolito, as soon as I took a step toward the door, would grab me gently by the skirt. Carmela was right; he was docile. And so I always had to be there with him, shut up in that room. But later on he began to settle down, and I was able to resume my life. Life was wonderful with a little security underfoot. Now I could run up and down through the bedrooms, the parlours, the gardens, without fearing – as I had before – that someone would pull the rug out from under me. I was part of the family. I could see it in the way the servants, the maids, the dance teacher, the tutor stepped aside for me when I ran into them. Even Don Antonio – something I would never have imagined – no longer addressed me directly as he used to, but circumspectly, bowing his head slightly. As I had planned beforehand, I became a kindly old monarch. I was very considerate with everyone, I bestowed gifts prudently and at times I let them show sympathy for my misfortune.

'Such a beautiful, saintly girl, sacrificed to a monster for her entire life!'

On this point I held firmly, both with Father Antonio in the confessional, and with the others. They must not forget my trial. That was the only way I could gain their full consent and appease their potential jealousy. With Argentovivo, it was a real success. Whenever she saw me I made sure a slight sadness crept into my eyes. Once she actually threw herself at my feet, weeping.

'My poor *signorina*, how good you are to be so cheerful and serene, given your great sacrifice!'

Sacrifice! I had slept for years with Tina.

And so, slowly but surely, my long familiarity with monsters, and Pietro's care – he kept his dear Prince neat and clean – helped me overlook Ippolito's ugliness. In fact, I felt a sort of tenderness when he sat there very quietly, watching me like a dog. Seeing his happiness when I let his big misshapen hands hold mine conveyed something sweet and indistinct that aroused forgotten shivers in me. But I did not add anything new to what Carmela had told me. I never undressed or appeared naked, and for bed I chose the most high-necked night-shirts I could find. But of course, at that time they were all quite high-necked. I nearly forgot . . .

34

That Monday the Princess surprised me with her acuity, as Argento-vivo would have said. I always learned something new from her. Listen to this:

'You tire yourself out too much, Mody! You've become skin and bones. Watch out! If you become ugly, I'll have the "thing" disown you. Before, it was a joy to the eye to see you. You work too hard. You have the house on your back, that "thing" to look after, and you still study! Granted, this proves that you have intelligence. At first I used to think that your interest in books was due to your having to acquire a position, but now I see that it is truly a scholarly interest. But I don't like to see you like this. Therefore, either find a way to gain some weight and get back a bit of colour, or I shall forbid you to take any more lessons. Is that clear? Then too, maybe the doctor is right: you should get out in the air more. Starting tomorrow you will take riding lessons. That way, when you catch up to Beatrice, who isn't bad on a horse, you two can go riding a little. You must do it for Beatrice's sake as well: with the excuse that you can't ride a horse, she's becoming fat and flabby on me. These blondes! As soon as they pass adolescence they blow up like balloons. I want her thinner, and you fatter. You too, Carmine, do you understand? We must give Mody lessons. Now, enough talking, get to work.'

I didn't know myself why I persisted in studying that way. But now that the threat had been issued, the thought of not being allowed to study anymore made me finish off two bowls of pasta that evening and lots of mashed potato; potatoes were said to be fattening. And in the morning milk, butter and heaps of jam. However, the idea of seeing Orlando again made me tremble with fear. Was it really Orlando I was afraid of, or Carmine?

Since our encounter I hadn't thought of him again, nor had I looked at him, not even when he stood in front of me in the old woman's study . . . There he was, coming down the broad lane, laughing. That smug laugh was insufferable. Outside the wall he was master. You could tell by the way the other man listened to him, one step behind, leading Orlando and another horse by the reins.

'Good day, *Padroncina*. I am very pleased that you have decided to confront the horse. I leave you to Rosario; he's the best riding master we have, and he will teach you properly. Remember, Rosario, the *Principessina* is a little frightened. With you, I feel confident. *Riverisco*, *Padroncina*, my respects.'

Rosario quickly linked his fingers together and positioned his hands to give me a boost up. But you could tell he was holding back. I felt so angry toward that deferential snotnose that I fell over the animal's flank.

'Forgive me, *Voscenza*, forgive me. I didn't think you already knew how to leap up. Luckily you weren't hurt! You weren't hurt, were you?'

'I'm fine. Don't cower so! Where did Don Carmine go?'

'Actually he must have gone back home . . .'

'And where is that?'

'Well, on foot it's far. By horse, a good ten minutes.'

'Take me there on the horse, then.'

'But I have orders to . . .'

'I'm the one who gives the orders here! Help me climb on and try not to let me fall again!'

He went on apologizing profusely. Feeling him behind me on the saddle, thin and spindly, was so disgusting to me that, using my thighs and knees, I managed not to lean on him.

'Why, *Voscenza* is in perfect balance! That was my mistake, believe me, Don Carmine didn't tell me. He said you were still afraid . . . That was my mistake.'

'That wasn't the mistake. Let's go, I'm in a hurry!'

*

'What's this, *Padroncina*? You're telling me that Rosario made you tumble? Bravo, Rosario! I didn't know you also had the knack of making beautiful girls tumble! Good for you . . . What? You don't want him to teach you? Did you hear that, Rosario? It's clear you didn't make her fall hard. Now what do we do, *Padroncina*? We'll have to talk about it. I don't have the time. What do you say, Rosario, should we try Beppe? . . . No, she says? It has to be me? All right then. You go back to work, Rosario, or we'll waste all day here. I'll try to settle things with the *Principessina*.'

He opened the door to let Rosario out, and when he had shut it again he leaned his back against it, staring at me. He was no longer smiling.

'So then, it really has to be me?'

I couldn't open my mouth, I was so angry over those words.

'Well, answer me! And why are you trembling like that? We're not on the horse. Say something.'

The familiar *tu* thrown in my face, him standing right there in front of me, made me raise my arms and pound his chest with clenched fists. I wanted to scratch his face, but he was too tall.

'You're beautiful. Strong too, and you want me. Do you know you want me?'

I was about to hit him again, but the truth of those words struck me like a lightning bolt. It was true. How could I have known it if he hadn't told me? And here I thought that the trembling that gripped me in his presence was simple hatred. Should I run away? But why? I had never felt the frenzy that was coursing through my blood in the guise of hatred. It was a terrifying pleasure I had never experienced, and in order to feel it once more, I started striking him again. He let me do it. My arms and fists hurt from pounding that marble chest, making me sink into his motionless arms. That was his signal. As if that were all he had been waiting for, his hands close around my waist and lift me up, making me soar, light as a feather. It was like looking into a ravine. The greater the terror, the greater my desire to plunge in. I found myself on the floor with him on top of me. He had not undressed me, nor had he undressed. I felt him inside me. He wasn't hurting me; he was moving gently. When he slid out, I knew he must have come just by the way his head slumped against my shoulder. But he said nothing, and I was burning all over since no shivers had come to relieve me.

'I'm sorry about being in such a hurry, *picciridda*; it's just that I've wanted you for so long, and you really don't know anything. Slowly, in time, I'll teach you to come too. Your mothers don't teach you anything, so it's up to the man . . .'

★

And teach me he did. Every morning, just after sunrise. First to understand the horse, and later, there at his house, in that small bare room that smelled of tobacco.

'It's like with the horse. You have to tighten your thighs around me, and you have to move with me. It's like being horse and rider. Let yourself go, *figghia*, don't stiffen up as though I wanted to kill you. By now you know the animal, and I want to give you pleasure like you give me. You see, *figghia*, love isn't what so many men who aren't men say it is – and women too who aren't women – the ones who go running from one lover to the next, barely feeling anything. With love, when you find it . . . to me it only happened once . . . no, not with Beatrice's mother; that one was sick in the head like all of them in the villa, full of impulsive whims; one day she wanted it and the next day she cried . . . No, with a real woman whom I had for years; then she died on me. But that's not what I wanted to say. The truth is that when you find the right woman or the right man, then it's your duty to get to know one another. The body is a delicate instrument, more so than a guitar, and the more you study it and attune it to the other person, the more perfect the sound and the more intense the pleasure. But you have to help yourself and help me. You mustn't feel ashamed. Here now, I'll move very, very slowly and you follow me. And when you feel the heat building you have to tell me, so I'll wait for you, and we'll climax together. Why don't you want to tell me, eh, *picciridda*, when you feel ready? If you don't want to say it out loud, give me a sign, squeeze me tight, bite my ear, whatever you like. You're warm and trembling all over, but I know you feel only a faint pleasure. That's it, take your time, don't be ashamed.'

How could I have known it if he hadn't told me? Ever so slowly, I learned to follow him on that deep wave that held such thrills. And the first time I really came the pleasure was so intense I thought I had been struck by lightning.

'*Brava*, now you're really a woman, and I cried out with you. I bet you didn't even hear me, you were screaming so loudly when you came.'

For days and days I thought I had not learned the lesson well. And if I slid on the saddle, I was afraid of falling off . . . And when he, not speaking, grabbed me by the waist and tossed me onto the bed so that I felt my legs tense, I was always afraid that I might not reach that thrilling, satisfying shudder. But Carmine was skilful and patient. With his palms he guided me, easing the anxiety that made me rigid, and always after riding with him I plunged into that alluring, bottomless ravine.

'That's it, *figghia*, gallop! Yesterday you were a little scared, but today if you don't let fear erase the memory of pleasure, you won't be afraid anymore. Fear, like destructive thoughts, is a hardy weed and you must uproot it from your body immediately.'

He laughed, swiftly overtaking me with his Orlando and urging me to gallop toward the valley. And that loud laugh, along with the steely curls on his head, filled me with a sweet terror that drove me to catch up with him, grab those wiry ringlets and pull and pull. I hated him, I wanted to hurt him, but when I was away from him that mysterious chill gripped me again and I had to go back.

'Of course you're hurting me! What am I, made of iron?'

'You're made of iron, and I can't stand the sight of you!'

'Fine, *figghia*, so don't look at me. Anyway, for some reason people make love with their eyes closed. You're a real woman, real and forceful. And to think, I swear to God, that I thought you only liked the caresses of other women! Just look at that. Even an old man like me can be wrong!'

How did he know? My surprise made me tug too hard on the reins and Morella almost threw me off.

'What is it? Are you upset over a silly thing like that? What do you think, that you're the first to be initiated by a woman's hand? There's nothing wrong with it, *figghia*. And don't worry, you're a woman, a real woman, even if you wake up with whiskers one of these days.

35

What I learned from Carmine I tried to relay to Beatrice. My caresses became more watchful and more penetrating. Of course, I wasn't a man, but I entered her more deeply with my hand and she came more intensely. Besides, as Carmine said, I was preparing her for when she would meet the right man. Naturally it was difficult there, but the war would end, and in Catania . . .

'Can you see the sea from our palazzo in Catania?'

'Not only the sea, Modesta: shops, the market. Look how big our beautiful Catania is . . .'

Her small hand feverishly pointed out streets and piazzas on the map. She showed me photographs of the palazzo with many shops nearby, full of marvellous things.

'And this is the villa at Ognina, amid the orange groves. That's what orange groves are like! Here there are only these woods; woods are gloomy! An orange grove is something else, because you know the sea is nearby even if you don't see it. These woods are dismal because they're so far from the sea. It seems like a century since I've been back there! Damn this war! Why are men always at war, Modesta?'

'Gains, Beatrice. Simply for profits and gains disguised as ideals. And maybe for something else that's more difficult to understand.'

'Oh God, there you go, answering me like Uncle Jacopo! What a pity you didn't know him.'

'I've come to know him through you.'

'Sometimes I almost believe this game you play. Sometimes I actually think you knew him somehow.'

'It's thanks to you. Through you I've come to know him so well that sometimes, in sleep, he visits me and tells me what we should think, do . . .'

'Oh, yes, Modesta, tell me about it. I like it when you tell me stories. What did he say we will do? When did you see him? Did he tell you what we will be doing in two or three years? . . . Will I marry? Did he tell you whether I'll get married? Nonna doesn't want me to, and besides, I'm afraid of men. You're the only one I want.'

No matter how I put the subject of men, she wept and clung to me. Something had to be done. She was crying so hard that I didn't hear Argentovivo yelling behind the door.

'What is it, Modesta? Who's shrieking like that? And in the courtyard too, do you hear how they're shouting?'

I barely had time to open the door when we were swept down to the courtyard where a crowd of peasants and servants nearly crushed us. I had never seen so many of them all together. Some carried flags, some were tossing their caps in the air like a discus, others were weeping and hugging. Everyone was shouting something different. You couldn't understand a thing. Until my ears began to grasp the underlying cry that linked all those exclamations: 'The war is over! The war is over!' A few are shoving me now, saying over and over: 'The war is over!' Overwhelmed by hugs and handshakes, I can't find Beatrice anymore, until a familiar, high-pitched voice from above yells more loudly than all the others: 'Not for us!'

With a final whisper, all those voices fell silent and the upturned faces quickly bowed their heads, speechless. The Princess, pale, very tall, gripping the balcony, hurled her words into the silence a second time: 'Not for us!'

Then after a pause:

'And you, Mody, Beatrice, up here with me, immediately!'

★

'Have you lost your minds mingling with those foolish beggars? They even dragged out the Italian flag! The same ones who were screaming for war earlier. Sit down! And lest this vulgarity be infectious, let me make our position clear to you. For us, the war is not over. With Ignazio's death, for me the war will never be over. And I shall never allow anyone to imply the contrary. We will not budge from here. I can see it in your eyes; I can see it's what you had hoped! I will never agree to go back to Catania or Palermo, where I saw him going about strong and healthy. And when I, too, am gone, you two will remain here to care for my room, as if I might always return. Just as my husband, God rest his soul, insisted on for himself and for the others. And to make it absolutely clear, I've drawn up a will attesting to this. Anyone who crosses the threshold to leave this house will become a stranger to the family, and the money will go to whoever remains. And if no one remains, the money will go to a pious institution whose name I will not tell you. Now, go and tell those imbeciles not to let me see them laughing and smiling. Advise the tutor and dance instructor as well. Not a word about this peace that doesn't pertain to me. For me and for you, the mourning continues.'

I didn't dare look at Beatrice who, white as a sheet, let me drag her to her room where I settled her on the bed as best I could before rushing off to warn everyone about that madwoman's orders not to celebrate. So why all those dance lessons, all those dresses, as if to prepare us for life, only to then decide that the villa would become our tomb? She had gone mad. As I spoke to the servants, I read on their pallid faces the uncertain looks that the prospect of insanity arouses in us all. She had gone mad, and for the moment it was best not to oppose her.

'But, *Voscenza*, but . . .'

'No buts. The Princess wants it that way and that's how it must be. Send all those people away. Yes, of course, offer them a little wine, but quietly please. Then off they go, back to work. Today is a day like any other.'

36

Gaia was not crazy, nor had she ever been. By now I was beginning to understand the human animal, and I knew that any intent others have seems like madness to us if it is contrary to our wishes, while that which serves our purposes and leaves us content with our way of thinking appears reasonable. It wasn't madness. She was determined to die, taking us all with her. And she was firmly determined! I trembled before another individual's resolve, which I was facing once again, but I was no longer panic-stricken. And since I had my own objective, or plan, or intent, call it what you will, which might seem crazy to others, I would deal with this madness with the same firm hand as that grand old woman whom I so admired. I admired her, but she had to die. How? There was time. Both Beatrice and I were only eighteen years old. We had to be patient and go along with her without making her suspicious. The opportunity would come. The first thing I had to do was reassure Beatrice, then see to the will. Find out where she kept it, at least. Not lose sight of it.

'I see, Mody, that I did well to place my trust in you. You're the only one in recent months who hasn't regarded me as insane, and whose disposition hasn't changed. Yesterday I tossed out Don Antonio. He started acting crafty – like an elephant in a china shop, though! – asking me about my will: whether my wishes are in a safe place, whether I deposited the will with a notary, if it was here, if it was there, and on and on. As if I needed anyone besides myself. The will is here . . . As if I needed a notary or a doctor, or whatever. What that old fool was really trying to say is that I'm crazy, right, Mody?'

'You aren't crazy, Princess.'

'Is that really what you think?'

'Really. You've decided what's best for you, and it's only right to do it.'

'*Brava*, Mody! But I'm selfish, is that what you think?'

'Of course I think so.'

'Indeed. I never said I was altruistic . . . Now get to work! And you, Carmine, tell me what's new, given this insidious peace that has fallen upon us.'

'What's new, Princess, is that everything is going up. Naturally, increases were expected, but costs are rising sky-high, and unless we take steps . . .'

As he spoke, Carmine looked at me with admiration. It was the first time. I had managed to gain the respect of that man of honour. Two victories in one morning. Now I knew for certain that the will was in the house. I bided my time, and in just three months Gaia told me so in her own words. Until that moment I had searched the study and her bedroom, but only very perfunctorily. Because it's one thing to hope and another thing to be certain. And now I was certain: the will was not far off. I went back to rummaging through the study and the bedroom more meticulously than before. I discovered the secret drawers in the study. I leafed through her personal books, page by page, and carefully examined the bindings. In so doing, I learned the type of reading she preferred; there weren't many volumes and they were all poetry. It took me about a month to complete this operation, until I was certain that it could not be in those two rooms. It would take me an entire year to search the whole house as thoroughly as I had the study and the bedroom. The only solution was to study her, hoping to find some small hint that would lead me to uncover the hiding place. Using the pretext of not understanding poetry, I asked her permission to borrow some of her books.

As I read all those French and English poets, I realized that I had never understood poetry, not really. Of course, I had read Dante, Petrarch, Leopardi, but without grasping the secret of their verse. Truthfully, I had preferred reading philosophical essays, historical and political texts, and biographies. I was so struck by that discovery that I almost forgot about the will. I must have shown such persistence in my reading that even the Princess noticed it.

'Look, Mody, reading all that poetry isn't making you unfocused, is it? I won't lend you anything anymore if you keep staring into space with those big wide eyes. It's like you're searching for something . . .'

It was curious, however, that in the midst of all those books of exceptional poetry there were two prose works: Manzoni's *I promessi sposi* and the *Tales* of Edgar Allan Poe. This made me very suspicious. Leaving aside *I promessi sposi*, with which I was familiar, I began reading Poe's *Tales*. That night I came across the finest stories I had ever read. I couldn't stop reading, not even at dawn, when lack of sleep made my eyes burn a little. Those mysterious lines, in which the even more mysterious faces of young women appeared in magical settings and underground gardens, had so captured my emotions that I failed to understand a sentence in 'The Purloined Letter' which was the key to my feverish search: 'Perhaps it is the very simplicity of the thing which puts you at fault . . .' I was about to go on to 'The Gold-Bug' when I jumped up in bed, turned off the light – by now it was broad daylight – and began leafing through the pages of that story, until I realized that the will, like the famous purloined letter, might be somewhere in plain view where I had never thought to look. I quickly checked the desk in the study – I confess I had been hoping – as well as the tables and bookcases in the library, the musical scores . . .

I found it on Ignazio's nightstand, in a folder of sketches. Our destiny lay there, among those drawings signed by Ignazio, who stared at me, troubled, from the photograph above. Not a speck of dust on that night table which, like everything else, was dusted each day. Who would ever think of rummaging through those drawings made by the hand of a dead man? In fact, my fingers were shaking when I picked up the document. Ignazio's eyes froze me. That gaze wanted to live on, to pin us all in place by his death. But I too wanted to live, and though shaking, I put the will back in place. Slowly, Modesta: make sure no one suspects that anything has been touched. The venom of fear can make us slip up.

★

The next morning, buoyed by my discovery and by sleep, the last thing I would imagine was that Ignazio's wrath would show itself so soon. A thunderbolt had struck in the night, shattering the large window in her room, and all of Aunt Adelaide's birds were found dead. Terrified, I went with Beatrice to verify that what Argentovivo said was true. In the large cage, all of her remaining little birds lay stone-dead, or dying. To make matters worse, at the sight of them Beatrice doubled over, pressing her mouth with clenched fists. I held her in my arms as she vomited a dark liquid mixed with blood. Argentovivo began screaming so loudly that I had to slap her as best I could, still holding Beatrice in my arms, in order to bring her to her senses.

'Run, instead of screaming! Go and find the doctor while I lay her on the bed.'

Even there on the bed, the vomiting continued. I got a basin and with a damp towel, one of Aunt Adelaide's, I tried to wipe her brow which, once the vomiting stopped, had suddenly turned yellow and cold as marble. Then the vomiting resumed and with it her face started burning up, covered with red spots. An eternity passed in that spasmodic seesawing before the doctor arrived. I too felt like vomiting, due to fear and the sour odour of decay that had filled the room.

'It's started! Just yesterday I got word that Catania has been infected by it. All the hospitals are full, corridors, stairwells, every available space . . . If you feel like vomiting, don't hold back. Better to throw up and release the poison.'

'But what is it?'

'The *spagnola*, Modesta, the Spanish flu.'*

'The Spanish flu?'

'It appears that the soldiers returning from the front are carriers. Forgive my bluntness, but I must be frank with someone: it's quite serious. It hasn't been a week since the outbreak began in Catania and already there are countless dead. I was hoping it wouldn't reach here, so far from the populated areas and with all this clean, fresh air. I didn't say anything, so as not to scare you unnecessarily . . . No, no, don't worry. Beatrice can't understand me; she has other things to worry about. Her fever is high. Help me lift her so I can listen to her lungs. Now go and give orders that no one should approach. Everyone's in quarantine. Don't let the Princess come here. We need to get Lysoform. Boil everything in the kitchens. All the bed linens must be boiled. Good, Modesta, I see you've recovered. May I feel your pulse? Your tongue? Normal . . . Has the nausea passed?'

'Yes, it's gone. It was just the power of suggestion. Tell me what else I must do.'

★

In a week's time the villa became a hospital. The stink of disinfectant and vomit was everywhere. And everyone, dragged down by the sickly sweet, sour stench of death, sprawled in beds that had to be changed three or four times a day. Except for me, Pietro and Carmine, who was assigned to maintain contact with the outside world, they were all burning up with fever. Two nurses arrived from Catania, but within days they, too, took to their beds. In the servants' wing only Argentovivo and two others were still standing. The doctor, also ill, sent orders from his home. Don Antonio, from his bed, sent word telling us to pray. The small dance instructor no longer came, but he hadn't died like so many others in the area.

Carmine brought us news every evening when he returned from his rounds, and if it hadn't been for him we wouldn't even have had any salt, sugar or medicines. He said that all the shops were closed, many draped in mourning. The hospitals were overflowing with the sick and dying. In the province of Messina, all the prisoners had managed to escape. In the larger towns, these criminals and other impromptu thieves looted houses while sick people watched, powerless to stop them. Every doctor had been pressed into service, along with students with only one or two years of medical school. The battle against the rats had begun. Even there, in the villa, they began to appear, big as cats and ravenous. For weeks we struggled with exhaustion, filth and fear. My only consolation throughout this nightmare was a small hope: in addition to children, the virulent disease they called the *spagnola* – to make it seem less frightening – killed older people in particular. Yet when the Princess sent for me, and I saw the strength of spirit as well as the physical power of that grand old woman, who sat up in bed as firm and proud as if she were on a throne, I was almost happy to hear her shouting in her usual voice.

'Well then, how is Cavallina?'

'Better. The danger is past.'

Beatrice, who was the first to fall ill, had been out of danger for just a few days. And so thin and shaky that my throat tightened at the thought that, instead of the Princess, it was she I had almost lost.

'And Argentovivo?'

'Fine, just fine.'

'She was a big help to you, wasn't she?'

'An enormous help.'

'I will repay her. That's not why I called you, but rather to tell you that I cannot move my legs, and this arm as well. To make a long story short, I am unable to move my entire left side. Not a word! Don't betray my trust. Not a tear, not a word to anyone. I don't want anyone to know! No one must see me like this, except for the doctor, of course. Therefore, given that, as I said, I do not wish to be seen by anyone, from now on you will be in the room next door at all times and you will look after me. But not a word to anyone. Not even after I am dead. I don't want to be pitied, either alive or dead. Now off with you. Go get your things, your books, and come back here immediately. Here, because in case of an attack you must immediately run to the doctor after giving me these pills, even if you have to pry open my mouth with pliers.'

In the three weeks we spent together, my admiration for her only grew. Not one complaint, not when the attacks came, nor when she laboured to rest or talk to me. She talked about everything, but especially poetry. She asked me who my favourite poet was, now that I understood poetry, and had me read her something. The more I admired her, the more I waited for the moment of her death. One reason was that now, no matter how much I tightened my corset, my waist was swelling, and she, though ill, stared at my hips with increasing suspicion.

'How come you've put on so much weight, Mody? You're not playing tricks on me, are you? I told you that I don't want any children from that "thing"! Tell me if that's the case, since in the early months, with a good doctor, it's child's play to get rid of it.'

'Don't worry, Princess, there's nothing to tell. It's just that I've been eating too much lately.'

'So then, eat less. I don't like you this way. You lose your gracefulness, and your peasant origins show in those puffy cheeks.'

She had to die. My insane will to live against her insane will to die.

'Oh, Mody, this letter here on the nightstand is for Don Carmine. If anything final happens to me, you are to give it to him immediately. Understood?'

She had to die. I had waited too long. And when another attack came, instead of giving her the pills and running to the doctor, as I had always done, I stood behind the closed door and waited until the last moan fell silent in that room. Then I went back in. Were the bulging eyes looking at me? No, they were staring at the door. I looked away; that wasn't what I had come back for. After closing her eyes I took the letter and read it. It was not a new will. The letter told Carmine that the will was where he knew it was, and so on and so forth.

With the letter in hand, I ran to get the will, which I slipped into a large Chinese vase at the foot of the staircase, along with the letter. I would burn them afterwards. Now I had to run to the doctor. Ten or fifteen minutes could go unnoticed, but any longer would strain even the credulity of that myopic old man with his fine, flyaway hair like a child's.

37

The will could not be found. Everyone bustled around looking for it, and I too of course, right behind them, but only to keep an eye on Carmine.

As I knew he would, he went to Ignazio's room followed by Don Antonio and the doctor, and after glancing at the papers on the nightstand, he turned to the three of us who had trailed after him in single file.

'If there's nothing here, I can assure you, Don Antonio, that there is no will.'

'No will? How can that be? She told me many times . . .'

'Of course, me too. But you know what the Princess was like, God rest her soul . . . You, like me, were with her for twenty years.'

'And what was she like? Tell us.'

'Don't you think she liked to play tricks at times?'

'That's true, but . . .'

'The facts speak for themselves. We searched the whole villa with a fine-tooth comb. If it's not even in here, her favourite room, it means she changed her mind, or that she never made a will. But what are you upset about, Don Antonio? About the construction of the church? There's no need. We have the Princess Modesta here who knows what should be done. She's the last person to have heard the spoken wishes of the Princess, her mother-in-law, and surely she knows what is to go to the church and everyone else. Am I right, Princess?'

Carmine did not look at me, but he was showing me what I must do. What could I have known about inheritances if he hadn't told me? As best I could, I reassured Don Antonio, who followed me everywhere, even into the Princess's study where, after hours of discussions, we came to an agreement. I would never have imagined such tenacity and determination in that churchly old man. As soon as the black skirt disappeared behind the door, Carmine burst out laughing so loudly that I almost fell off my chair. I hadn't heard him laugh in months.

'How does it feel to be in that chair, *figghia*? It doesn't look too comfortable to me. You'll have to do a lot of practising to keep the wind from blowing you out of the saddle.'

I hated it when he talked to me like that.

'What are you trying to say?'

'I'm not saying anything. Did you see, I didn't say a word? I just observe.'

'Did you know that I'm expecting your child?'

'I hadn't been told yet, but I've noticed. I observe, as I said.'

'Why didn't you tell me it could happen? You're an old man.'

'There's young sap in this old tree. Why are you sorry? You shouldn't be sorry since, if you ask me, *'stu figghiu*, this baby, comes just at the right time. Once it's born, especially if it's a boy, it will stop all those tongues down in Catania from wagging. If I were you, *figghia*, I wouldn't be sorry and I would give up this mania for the city that has come over you. I can read it in your eyes; it's unwholesome. And I'll even tell you why: first, because Catania is still infected with influenza, and second, because it's better if you show up bolstered by a fine male Brandiforti.'

I couldn't understand what he was really thinking, but I had to restrain myself. What would I do without him? Even now that he stood up, and without a word held my head in his hands, I would have liked to throw him out. But the dry heat of his palms calmed me.

'You're not sorry, are you? No answer? All right. It stands to reason. You hate me and you don't want to give me the satisfaction. But I observe. And I can see that you're not sorry. From the way you carry your belly it's clear that you're not sorry.'

Not only wasn't I sorry, but now that my nausea was gone and the stench of vomit had faded in the villa, day by day everything was coming back to new life. The draperies, the drawing rooms, the light, people's gestures. A hunger I'd never experienced before made all food seem like a marvellous gift of fortune. I craved it all: fruit, water, milk, and especially bread. I had forgotten the taste of warm bread, fresh from the oven, sprinkled with olive oil and salt. I could have eaten nothing but that. And with the hunger, the light became warmer and more intense, the grass fresher and greener, the peaches and figs sweeter and riper. Picking them and holding them in my hand each morning, it was as if a stream of forgotten sensations returned to get reacquainted, flowing from a distant past that I kept hidden in some remote corner of my memory. Even sleep had become a carnal pleasure. As soon as I got into bed, shadows and thoughts bent over me, lulling me. To prolong that sensation of peace I tried to elude sleep, but it was hopeless: dreams glided over me in streams of light and colour. When I was no longer able to wear a corset and saw my huge, misshapen waist and swollen belly in the mirror, instead of despairing, as I had at first thought I would, I laughed as if it were a funny trick of no great concern that life had played on me. I couldn't manage to be serious. The only nuisance was the sorrow I had to simulate for everyone over the Princess's death.

With Ippolito it was easy. As soon as the Princess died I allowed him to come out of that prison of a room and, as I had thought, once outside, accompanied by Pietro, his attention was distracted from my person. He had bonded to me because, aside from those who were paid, I was the only woman he had ever seen. To gain more freedom, I had a skilled nurse come from Turin. I chose the prettiest one. And when Signorina Inès began bustling around him with her brown ringlets and her sprightly, competent ways, he forgot all about me. So much so that I was nearly upset by his 'fickleness'. But I didn't feel the need for anybody; I recalled Beatrice's caresses and Carmine's embraces as though in a fog . . .

Carmine never came around anymore. All the work had fallen on my shoulders. I didn't need books either, or the piano. I was a bit frightened by that discovery. Will I always be that way? But I soon understood. Just as I was now swelling, afterwards I would deflate, and would surely go back to being as I was before, if I didn't die. Yes, that's what that languor was which my body imposed in the form of contented dreaminess, along with hours of sleep. Nature was preparing me for the labour I would have to face. At the same time, I sensed that gradually this languor, when repeated numerous times in women who did nothing but give birth, generated a state of dull-witted deficiency that isolated them from life. Of course, how could that preparation on the part of both body and mind – for the most mysterious, most risky undertaking a human being can confront – how could it not make everything else seem, in the long run, pointless and dull?

When the moment announced itself with a fierce spasm that slashed down from the stomach, tearing hips, kidneys and intestines, she knew she had to awaken from that torpor and fight. It wasn't just labour, as she had thought. It was a battle to the death that raged inside her as if her body, whole at first, had split in two, and one part was struggling to eat the other.

'Scream! Scream, it will help you!'

'The position is right. Good it's coming. Scream and push! You can do it!'

Who can do it? That overwhelming wave of pain? Was she supposed to follow that wave? Her body was fighting the other body that, like an iron ram, kept battering the wall of her belly to get out. The enemy was there, in that ram that kept pounding to get out of its prison and live at the cost of tearing, destroying her body which, though prepared, couldn't manage to expel the enemy and not succumb.

'There, *brava*, that's the way. Not writhing all around, but pushing down; that way you help it and you help yourself.'

Yes, she had to push him out, that stranger who already had a strong will to live his own life. She felt that he was determined to live even if it meant killing her. And with one last push, which from her shoulders ripped through her, sending a sharp spasm to her lower abdomen and thighs, she felt him slip out of her with a silent thud and fall into space.

No. They had caught him. Hands held him up, slapping him against the milky light from the window. It must be dawn; the birds were screeching. Birds always screech at dawn. In there, too, slapped by those hands, wails came from the mutilated part of her exhausted body.

Why was he screaming like that? Was he crying for the life he had won, or because, in the mystery of that carnal act, the creature knew he had nearly killed for his life? Only my body and his knew the secret meaning of that mortal, non-hostile struggle: each battling for his own life.

38

I came back from that long journey just in time to see that I was about to lose Beatrice, for the second time. How had I managed not to notice those lifeless, staring eyes, the drawn-back hair that made her look like an old woman?

'We must stay here and honour Nonna's wishes. Even though she didn't leave a will, this is what she wanted. And nothing must change. I look after her room too now, which must remain as if she might return at any time.'

I had stayed away too long, and Gaia and all the family dead had seized the opportunity to worm their way into her. Suddenly I knew what that thing called destiny was: the unconscious desire to continue what for years has been insinuated, imposed and repeated to us as being the only right path to follow. My throat tightened. I didn't want to lose her, and that sad, haggard face masquerading as Gaia drove me out of bed and into action. To act, I must not contradict her. I resumed caring for those rooms with her and I did not force her to see the 'thing's son', as she called the tender dumpling that clung to my breast just as she had once done.

'You're breast-feeding him yourself? It's a disgrace. A real princess would have immediately brought in a wet-nurse!'

She slammed doors now, like her grandmother. The noise woke Eriprando, who started crying and screaming. He was always wailing and squirming in those swaddling strips that bound his torso and limbs. Tight, sturdy strips to make him grow straight and strong. Rigid strips to educate and correct – or to cause body and mind to become unbending? I couldn't stand hearing those screams. I leaped up, enraged by all those constraints which, coming back from that long journey inside my body, on the sidelines of life, appeared to me with a clarity I had never seen. And I too began shouting, something I'd never done:

'Enough! Enough! Enough!'

I didn't want to hate Beatrice, but she had put on a harsh face that I had to destroy. I threw open the door and went running down the corridor, screaming my hatred. I could hear my voice but I couldn't understand what I was saying. Until I came upon a trembling Argentovivo. I started slapping her. And between my shouting and her tears I heard her voice saying, 'Of course, Princess! I won't swaddle him anymore! Don't fret so! Oh God! Yes, yes, you're right! . . . The *Principessina* is in her room . . . Yes, yes, I'll bring her here!'

When Beatrice too stood before me, trembling – with that obscure will that she was unable to oppose making her look old – I grabbed her by the head and pulled out the hairpins, yanking her hair. Feeling her tremble even more as I did this, an insane fury made me raise my hand to her, and slapping and kicking her, I dragged her to my room, slamming the door in Argentovivo's face as she wept. I didn't want to hate her, but I couldn't stop my hand. Only when I saw her collapse at my feet did I leave her there in the middle of the room and, locking myself in the bathroom, put my head in a basin of cold water. I didn't care about anything anymore. If she wanted war, war it would be, but open warfare. I couldn't act toward her as I did with others. We two were equals, bound together. The cold water calmed me and I went back into the room.

Eriprando, still tightly wrapped like a sausage in his swaddling strips, was screaming. Beatrice, all huddled up on the floor, wasn't moving. I leaned against the door and stared at her. Thin trickles of blood ran down the part of her forehead that could be glimpsed through her hair. They were knocking at the door and I had to open up. I started to move, but suddenly two arms grabbed me around the knees.

'Forgive me, Modesta! I've been awful! You're right, awful! It's just that Nonna was so good to me.'

Stunned, I lifted her up. Her clear eyes shone and her swollen lips were smiling. Her hair fell onto her soft, inviting shoulders. And paying no attention to the calls coming from behind the door, we kissed each other the way we used to do in times past.

39

Eriprando, freed from the swaddling strips, no longer cried; he played with my nipple and with Beatrice's hair which, loosened there in the sun, attracted him. When he pulled harder Beatrice yelled, and to get back at him took over my other breast and sucked. They fought over my body, and in that joyful tussle they became friends. I took advantage of it to rest, surrendering to those two creatures to whom, for the first time in my life, I felt wholly connected.

I needed rest. I was tired. Was that weariness perhaps a sign that I was no longer young? I had never felt tired before. Or was it knowing that I was now alone in having to nourish and protect them? That was it. I wasn't old. I had just emerged from my early youth and I already had a past. That fatigue was merely a longing for something that one has had and thinks will never return.

It was that same yearning that prompted me to record my youth on these pages, because I don't want silence to obliterate Beatrice's long hair, illuminated by the sun, which held us with its inimitable narcotic warmth. I would like to stay in this moment. But even now, as I write, the sun is going down, someone is knocking at the door, a car is waiting at the gate . . .

The impressive Lancia Trikappa* was waiting, gleaming in the sun, and even now that I knew it wasn't a coach, the idea of a second trip into the unknown blurred my vision. Like an echo of fear, a feeling from the past crept into the joy of the moment, poisoning it. It was the child-me who edged her way between me and the present time. Closing my eyes, I saw myself as I was then, clutching Mimmo's arm. I had to banish that little girl who would not be reassured no matter what. I turned my gaze to Beatrice, who was silent beside me, wholly absorbed in stroking Eriprando's hair. She was always holding him. It was she, now, who didn't want a wet-nurse to care for him, not even to wash or feed him, and she was a help to me as well. With the Princess's death my work had doubled, and despite Carmine's help I had very little time to myself . . .

The car was moving. Beatrice was laughing softly. She didn't even turn to look at the villa, completely taken with her little nephew. They looked alike, two peas in a pod. For months and months everyone in the villa had been saying so. It was natural, but there, in that odd setting, the similarity was truly striking, even for children of the same father. I too did not look back. I wasn't leaving anything in that house. Mimmo wasn't there, and all of Jacopo's books had already been sent off in a trunk with Signorina Inès, Ippolito and Pietro, who was pained by the devoted gaze his dear Prince, now reserved only for his new passion.

'I'm aggrieved, Princess. Truly disappointed! I was hoping that in a month or so this infatuation for the Torinese woman would subside, but . . . ah well, men! You mustn't take it to heart. You must have patience! Men, they're all alike! Even my father, God rest his soul, was captivated by every new skirt! But you must believe me, it's you my Prince loves, *Voscenza* . . . It embarrasses me to speak to you about such things. But, well, given the way things are, I think that in Catania – *Voscenza* will forgive me – I think we will need to distract him with some *picciotta*,* ahem, yes, like we did in the days when the Princess, God rest her soul, was alive because – the point is – the Torinese is a virgin . . . what is it, are you crying?'

Poor Pietro! Certainly not crying! I had covered my face with my hands because I was about to burst out laughing. In Catania, the longed for Catania, I would have a large room all to myself with Jacopo's books. So longed for and, to me, seemingly so far away that I nearly panicked when I heard Beatrice cry out:

'Catania! Catania! Look how beautiful it is, Modesta, look! You too, Eriprando, look at your city!'

Stunned by its proximity, I opened my eyes and shut them again, dazzled by the expanse of dark rooftops shining in the sun, plunging into a blue sky that stretched to infinity, as far as the eye could see: the sea! Tuzzu's blue sea!

'Yes, yes, it's the sea! And who is Tuzzu? . . . Yes, where it gets lighter, that's the horizon.'

My eyes filled with that uncontainable expanse of light, which wouldn't fade even with my eyelids tightly shut. I heard myself say:

'Let's go see it up close, now!'

At Beatrice's command, the swift car began racing as though pursued by those high, dark walls, with their many windows and iron balconies, which hurtled behind us.

As soon as the car stopped I jumped out, breathless, followed by Beatrice. And maybe because I expected to see it from above like before, I had to look up to find that inverted liquid sky which flowed serenely toward boundless freedom. Great white birds glided in the dizzying wind. My lungs, released, opened up and I breathed for the first time. For the first time, tears of gratefulness rolled down my face. Or was it the strong, pungent taste of that wind that bent over my mouth to kiss me?

PART TWO

40

But the promise of freedom, repeated by the waves and the wind, shattered against the walls of palazzos springing with roses and vines sculpted from sharp lava.* There was no freedom in those back streets and narrow alleyways, those confusing piazzas swarming only with arrogant men sporting straw hats and canes, watched by shadowy female figures hidden behind curtains or from the darkness of ground-floor doors, always partly open. The palazzo on Via Etnea opened its doors to a string of unwelcome receptions at which, two days after our arrival, a procession of impeccably dressed women, with white or black gloves and flowery hats, began parading in front of us, opening and closing their fans and offering protection and advice.

'Oh, Jesus and Mary! No! Go alone to the Opera? *Gesummaria*, no! There's our box, my dear niece . . .'

'Absolutely! Indeed there was much talk about your absence on Sunday! Of course, you were both tired from the journey, naturally. But please, my little doves, Mass at noon on Sundays. It's tradition. Absolutely.'

'Go to the café by yourselves? Oh no, it's unacceptable, dear cousin, unacceptable! . . .'

'Of course, it's quite unfortunate not to have a brother, a husband!'

'Go to the cinema? That modern devilry? Oh no! We never go except on rare occasions, and always provided that one of our men makes certain beforehand that the film isn't too licentious . . .'

'An historical film, you say, cousin? Nonsense! History as a front for indecorous scenes, women in low-cut dresses, orgies. . . Not on your life! Everyone is still talking about that *Cabiria*!* A true disgrace! And those in parliament who go around spouting high-sounding words about freedom. But what can you expect with all those socialists in the government? And our Holy Father a prisoner!* Meanwhile, immorality is rampant in our own homes as well! Yesterday I nearly had a stroke hearing my nephew, only fourteen years old . . . what a barren generation of misfits and selfish egotists we're raising! . . . but what was I saying? Oh yes, I nearly had a stroke hearing my nephew urging his sister to cut her hair like all those lunatics on the continent, the suffragettes. My husband, who saw them in Milan, says they look like men, with short hair and no corsets. All we need is for them to start wearing trousers and amen! Everything is being turned upside down, everything! . . .'

'If I may say so, my dear girls, you read too much. It's not good for the eyes. My uncle, a doctor, claims that reading causes wrinkles . . . Gaia permitted you to? Well of course, always one of a kind! A woman of great merit, no question, but too, too . . .'

'Last Sunday at Mass, the Baronello Ortesi showed a real interest in our darling Beatrice. Of course they're not from an old family, but these barons are wealthy! We must have him meet Beatrice . . . Oh no! Not here! You two are women alone and cannot receive men. You could accept cousin Esmeralda's thoughtfulness, since she so kindly offered to arrange a tea. Oh, it would be nice if there were a man in this house . . . !'

Beatrice grew pale, and I no longer slept, increasingly oppressed by figures and accounts. Tossing and turning in bed, I banged my head against the walls of that prison of payments, property taxes, tenancy agreements . . . The *campieri*, the estate's armed guards, and the *sovrastanti*, the *gabellotto*'s trusted men, were struggling to collect the rents, the peasants were rising up, the land wasn't yielding, wages tripled. To read a book I sacrificed hours and hours of sleep. The piano was silent. Jacopo's trunk, still closed, stood forgotten in a corner of the room next door. What kind of trap had I fallen into?

I pressed on, managing that seemingly immense realm which was leaking on all sides. And that odd house kept like a royal palace? *'I would suggest that* Voscenza *refresh the drapes in the spring,'* the major-domo had respectfully directed. Which meant having them remade. The country villa, Carmelo, was still open, serving as a hotel, await-ing the return of all the deceased; twenty mouths to feed, twenty wages to pay each month. I couldn't sleep anymore. Gaia had also suffered from insomnia. Now I understood her obsessed look, the way she remained shut up in her study intent on fighting that impos-sible battle. What had she sacrificed herself for? Out of duty, for a name to be held high in other people's eyes or her own? In fact, all those lawyers, bankers and notaries had the same impervious gaze she had, fixed in one direction. Not Carmine. In my memory, Car-mine, his white curls unruffled in the breeze, rode toward me on his horse, laughing . . . For months I had only seen him surrounded by notaries and attorneys imprisoned in their close-fitting black vests and jackets. As soon as he could, he fled. I too had to get away from those walls and those men whom I had so admired when I managed Carmelo, but who now seemed like inmates in a prison that they themselves had built day by day. *'If I may say so, Princess,* Voscenza *should have been born a man.'* At one time I had thought those words were the highest recognition one could receive from other people, but now the terror of becoming like Gaia tightened my chest so that I couldn't breathe.

The city taught me. The power of those majestic domes, of the rapacious palazzos and towers barely refined by haughty, ornamental gates, kept out the wretched swarm that was bled dry serving and smiling, and reminded everyone, rich and poor alike, that amassing wealth was a way to contend with the fear of death, a word that in reality is no more frightful than the words 'illness', 'slavery', 'torture'. I would no longer worry about death, that final destination which, once it's no longer feared, makes each hour enjoyed to the fullest seem eternal. But you had to be free, you had to take advantage of every moment, experience every step of the walk we call life. Free to observe, to study, to gaze out the window, to look beyond that jungle of palazzos and glimpse whatever light from the sea might filter in through the shutters . . . Someone had turned off all the streetlamps, the port's siren saluted an unseen ship, the clatter of shutters arose as they were opened, one by one. A fishmonger's cry went up from the narrow back streets surrounding Via Etnea, interrupting the call of the snow vendor, who reminded people of the heat in order to sell the 'Mountain's saliva'. . .

But all this was out there, not here on this elegant boulevard of heavy bank doors, sumptuous as coffins. They had opened the doors of the Bank of Sicily, and here came the first employee crossing the street. You could tell from the perfect cut of his dark suit and his jaunty, polished cane that he wasn't a mere clerk. The man surely had the same insistent, focused gaze as Attorney Santangelo and was preparing for his day as a manager, pleased to give orders and humiliate people. No, I would not become an employee to my inheritance. To begin with, I would not receive anyone that day.

Jacopo, with his ironic smile, is calling to me from inside the trunk. I must open that trunk. At one time he spoke to me about wealth and poverty, but I was too young then. Somehow he told me that both one and the other can bestow life and death: *'From Carmelo, 27 March 1912. I leave tomorrow. I'm resuming my travels. There is no life in these minds obliterated by pride. I feel contemptible leaving the entire burden on Gaia's shoulders. But what good is it to oppose history? My duty would be to shut myself up in this prison with her and go along with her absurd hope of keeping up a mentality and wealth obtained on the backs of the poor, and soon to be swallowed up by a middle class fortified by a new greed. And if not that . . . a spectre is haunting Europe. I declare myself a coward, but I am resuming my life. The only regret and guilt I'll take with me – a heavy burden – is Beatrice. We should prepare her for life, make her study; the new world will belong to doctors, engineers, chemists. I'm leaving, and the rest is silence.'*

Beatrice said that Jacopo would have been as handsome as Ignazio if he hadn't had a curved back . . . Stooped under his burden, Jacopo walks along paths unknown to me, long dark paths with no trees or houses. Where was he going?

'You see, Beatrice, he's always doing that. He speaks to me and then he goes away.'

'Don't say that; it frightens me! God, it's so scary, Modesta! What did he tell you?'

'Many good and proper things that he wants for your happiness and mine.'

'Oh God! That's enough now. Let's go to sleep. Hold me! I'm afraid I'll see him too.'

Beatrice clings to me. I like to feel her trembling: the way it starts up, how slowly but surely she calms down in my arms until her hand drops or the pressure of her head on my chest plunges me with her into a deep sleep that holds no memories. According to what I was told, I slept for two days and two nights.

41

'I'm selling everything. I said I'm selling everything. I'll rent the palazzo to the bank. Attorney Santangelo agrees: turn everything into gold and some shares. Then we'll see. Before long it will take a suitcase full of paper to buy a crust of bread. The seaside villa will do, and it will also be good for Ippolito: here he can't go out in the street and his health is suffering. At Carmelo he had grown used to working with the gardener, to being outdoors, to—'

'And it was a mistake! Word about his deformity spread throughout the fields. It's one thing to imagine it and another thing to see it, *figghia*, and you've lost standing! If, in addition to this first error, you now want to add, as you're telling me, that of retreating to a small house without a household staff, it will be difficult to keep up your prestige.'

'But I don't want to keep up any prestige, Carmine. Maybe I wasn't clear. I want to dispose of the lands as well.'

'The lands too? No, that I didn't understand! The Princess, God rest her soul, and I placed our trust in you, but I can see you're just an indolent woman. Are you tired of working so soon?'

'That's my business. You can't understand. I don't like this work. I want to study!'

'Study? Listen to her! And what does that mean, study?'

'You see? You can't understand. All right, so I'm lazy and a woman, call it whatever you want.'

'I won't say another word. But when they know you're selling, word will get around and you won't find anyone who will offer you the real value of the land: they'll give you next to nothing, like what happened last month with the Suormarchesa estate in the Serradifalco territory: it had to be sold at public auction and Don Calò bought it for a song.'

'So don't wait for a public auction and for Don Calò to arrive. Buy it yourself. Carry out the plan you've had for twenty years.'

'I see you're perceptive. But I didn't steal anything; I took what was coming to me by my labour, while the Prince and his offspring, not to speak ill of the dead, fooled around studying books and gazing at the stars. Besides, I did it for my sons.'

'Your sons? What sons?'

'I have two sons . . . didn't you know?'

'How could I know when you didn't tell me?'

'I had to tell you? You observe, *figghia*, you listen. You've become like these *signori*. Always taken up with useless things . . . I've been very worried during these four years of war. But as God willed, Mattia returned when you gave birth, and now Vincenzo is coming home after he was said to be missing. You too have a son; did you forget that? If you sell everything, what will you leave him? You may have enough to live on for ten or twenty years, but lands give children status. And you have a son!'

'He's your son too.'

'He doesn't have my name!'

'You talk like the old man you are: "name", "status"! My son will make his way on his own. We younger people are different.'

'That may be! But as you say, I'm an old-fashioned man, and for me my duty as a father comes first. And while we're on the subject: my sons mustn't know about my weaknesses. You're a child, just a few years between you and Mattia.'

'So?'

'We can't see each other like we used to. My sons mustn't know.'

I lunged forward to strike him, but this time he didn't let me hit him. He blocked me with his hand and, holding me at a distance, said in a frigid tone that I didn't recognize:

'Stop right there, *carusa*, the time for fun and games is over, little girl! You have to keep quiet. Understood? And forget. Carmine has forgotten. Always at your command, Princess.'

★

'This one we absolutely must take; it's a unique painting, and this landscape too, look! Even if you don't like them very much, we must keep them. We'll put them all in one room. Uncle Jacopo used to say that over time they would become priceless. Fortunately he made a note of the ones he thought were valuable. He knew everything about painting, about sculpture, even architecture. Such freedom, Modesta! Have you noticed how my colour has returned, like you wanted, and that I've even gained weight? Come on, give me a hug and smile. I just can't stand to see you so sad. Let's hope that this ill-ness will soon pass. What did the doctor call it . . . anaemia? Is that what he said? I want so much to take driving lessons with you. What a good idea you had to sell that hearse and buy a small car. Without a driver we'll be free to go wherever we want. We'll drive ourselves, just think what fun! How do you feel? Better? Come with me, there's a really nice Empire-style table that I'd like to take with us, but I want your opinion.'

Did you hear how Beatrice talks? Carmine is gone and she senses the emptiness I'm left with, and that I need her.

Until a few minutes ago I had meant to skip over the episode of Carmine's desertion, recalling that being abandoned or abandoning is one of the obligatory phases that life imposes on us. But as always happens in 'affairs of the heart', his words assumed the right to live without my intellect's permission. Don't worry. I won't give you a blow-by-blow description of the struggle that everyone comes to know and tries to forget. I suffered just like everyone else. But love is neither absolute nor eternal, and love doesn't only exist between a man and woman, possibly consecrated. You could love a man, a woman, a tree and maybe even a jackass, as Shakespeare tells us.

The harm lies in the words which tradition presents as absolute, in the distorted meanings those words continue to hold. The word 'love' is a lie, just like the word 'death'. Many words lied, almost all of them lied. That was what I had to do: study words exactly as one studies plants, animals . . . And then, wipe away the mould, free them from the deposits of centuries of tradition, invent new ones, and above all discard and no longer use those that common practice most often adopts, the most corrupt ones, such as 'sublime', 'duty', 'tradition', 'self-denial', 'humility', 'soul', 'modesty', 'heart', 'heroism', 'feeling', 'compassion', 'sacrifice', 'resignation'.

I learned to read books in a different way. As I came across a certain word, a certain adjective, I extracted them from their context and analysed them to see if they could be used in 'my' context. In that first attempt to identify the lie hidden in words that were evocative even to me, I realized how many of them there were, and accordingly how many false concepts I had fallen victim to. And my hatred grew, day by day: the hatred of discovering that I had been deceived.

I found the words to kill Carmine. I found what all the poets know: that you can kill with words, just as well as with a knife or with poison:

> You kill me, but my face
> remains glazed
> in your eyes.
> At night
> your eyelids weep,
> nailed shut.

And thinking back to Beatrice in the early days of our love, to the Beatrice of that time, before I forget her:

> What drives you on
> through obscure, unsettled
> seasons,
> you who pale at the slightest
> heat
> and collapse, shattered,
> at the slightest stir
> of shadows on the lawn?

Don't be afraid. I won't recite all the poems that flooded my mind like a swollen torrent.

*

'What are you doing, Modesta? You shouldn't work so hard. Forgive me for coming to look for you. It's so nice down at the shore with this heat. We've prepared a fire; tonight we'll dine on the beach. Pietro caught a lot of fish this morning. He's so funny, he wants us to think that Ippolito caught some too! Come on, we're all so cheerful, the only thing we're missing is you.'

And they all seemed really happy to scurry around under Beatrice's orders. In a short time, she had transformed the small cove into a dining-room glittering with silver cutlery and porcelain plates, lit by bright acetylene lamps on the boats. The happiest of all was Ippolito who, hand in hand with his Signorina Inès, sat staring at the sea. Did the sea whisper freedom to him as well? It must have been so, because those big eyes with no eyelashes, always teary, widened as they stared at the water. A distant echo of recollection seemed to appear in his eyes when he turned his gaze on me. Terrified, I had the precise feeling that those eyes were looking at me with recognition, as he repeated: 'Boo-tiful, Mama, boo-tiful.' Fortunately, Signorina Inès burst into one of those sudden laughs that shook her dark ringlets, her neck and her breasts. Fortunately, because I was about to run away when I heard him address me as 'Mama'.

'Did you hear that, Princess? He said "beautiful". With me he's already said it, and many other words as well. But, just as I thought, in front of you he's embarrassed. Do you see how much weight he's lost? And do you know, he's just about finished painting the vegetable garden fence with the gardener's help, and his hands have almost stopped shaking.'

With growing dread I watched that poor thing's eyes as he followed Inès's lips and then looked at me with a kind of satisfaction at hearing his aunt, as he now called her, tell of his accomplishments. He had a strong sense of family, the poor creature. I tried to laugh silently. But the thought that he had been lost to life only as long as they had kept him locked up, and the recognition of the progress that he had made even at his age just because someone took pains with him, brought sobs to my throat; I had to return quickly to my room, where I wept for hours and hours. Was I crying for Ippolito?

42

The sea was waiting. I looked at it with the childlike gaze of Eriprando, wide-eyed, roving. It was summer, and I had to steal a bit of freedom from that grudging sea. To do so I had to understand it, touch it with my body as Beatrice was able to do. It was curious, but as she ran along the beach Beatrice barely limped anymore, like when she danced. Making up my mind to enter the water was the hardest thing I'd had to do so far. The sea was harsh, and rejected me, resentfully. I struggled to grasp that fluid body that eluded me, surprising me on all sides. I kept losing my balance, hurriedly retreating on all fours to find myself coughed up on the beach, breathless.

'Forgive me for intruding, *signorina*, but you will never learn if you continue fighting the waves like that. You have to surrender to the sea. I've been watching you for ten minutes and . . . actually I meant to ask you how to get to Villa Suvarita. I'm looking for Princess Brandiforti.'

A voice whose soft r's rolled down on the sand without disturbing the silence made me raise my eyes, still stinging from the salt, but all I could see was a white shirt gleaming in the sun.

'Pardon my impertinence, *signorina*, but you need a swimming instructor and I need a villa that I can't seem to find. The villa of a certain—'

'I heard you. I am the Princess. Go ahead, speak.'

'Oh, I'm sorry! I didn't think . . . But what am I saying? Sorry again.

I didn't mean to disturb you. If you will be so kind as to tell me where the villa is, I will go and wait for you there.'

'Why, were you looking for me or the villa?'

'You, but . . . just a moment, I'll put on my jacket. It was very hot in the woods.'

'Well then?'

'Oh! Carlo Civardi, physician. The attorney, Santangelo, sent me. I see that you are looking at me doubtfully. I'm used to it and to reassure you I will tell you that I am not as young as I look. In a month I'll be twenty-eight. But if my appearance doesn't inspire your confidence, don't worry. I'm used to that too. I understand. All in all, I came with very little hope. I like Sicily very much, but unfortunately I see that here, too, the preconceived notion of *in senectute sapientia* prevails, even more so than in my region.'

'And where are you from?'

'From Milan, Princess, a very beautiful city, but somewhat damp. To be frank, I've had some mild discomfort in my joints that politely suggests that I be wary of the poetic mists of the north, and that has, let's say, driven me south in search of the sun. How beautiful this island of yours is! I travelled it far and wide before stopping here in Catania.'

'And why did you stop here in Catania?'

'The usual story, common and simple: my uncle is Dr Lenzi, a friend of Attorney Santangelo. I work with him. I see that you're puzzled. I'll go back to my uncle: his hair is completely white and this obviously inspires confidence. I see that fortunately you're smiling, even though it's at me. I was beginning to think that what Santangelo says about you was true.'

'What does Santangelo say?'

'Well, that you have an iron will. That . . .'

'. . . That I don't trust anyone, that I'm cold, aloof and tightfisted.'

'Well, not exactly.'

'Yes, exactly. Santangelo is right.'

'Well then, if you will allow me, I won't disturb you any further.'

'Where are you going? Not only do you look like a young boy, but you give up quickly like a little boy.'

'You think so?'

'Why don't you disguise yourself as an old man?'

'Pardon?'

'Like actors do: eye glasses, whitened hair, a fake beard. In fact, why don't you grow a beard?'

'But I have a moustache! Besides, up north hardly anyone wears a beard anymore. It's more sanitary.'

'Really? The problem is that men still wear them here. Why don't you grow one? It would help you look at least twenty-four or twenty-five, instead of eighteen.'

'Oh, dear God, only eighteen? I see. Forgive me for bothering you.'

'Just a minute, please. Do you know how to swim?'

'What?'

'If you know how to swim and will teach me, I'll overlook your age and entrust the Prince to your care.'

'Blackmail?'

'Take it any way you like. I must learn how to swim.'

'It's not very dignified for a doctor, but I can't afford to refuse. I have only two patients, and on top of it all they don't pay . . . So then, may I see the Prince? Is it something serious?'

'No, no! It's just that his old doctor died. You may see him tomorrow, but come with a bathing suit. Now please leave me. Talking in the sun is tiring. Good day!'

As you probably realized, not knowing how to behave with that young man, I had adopted the abrupt manner of the Princess, God rest her soul. It always worked. After a moment's uncertainty, I heard him stumbling hastily into the woods.

I had learned so many things from that grand old woman! I felt her rise up inside me in her proud solitude, while Modesta, intimidated by that stranger, clung to her. Could it be that Gaia also shouted so much because she was sometimes afraid of people, just as I had been afraid of that well-spoken doctor? What was the reason for that fear? I close my eyes to question the past and a procession of nuns, old men, and lay sisters with their ageless faces comes marching toward me. The doctor was the first young man I had ever met. I had done the right thing asking him to return. I had to interrupt that procession that now seemed restful to me in comparison with that boy's intense gaze. To my astonishment, I realized that I was afraid of his young age. But I was only twenty-one and, fearful or not, I had to meet his youth head-on with mine.

'Who was that, Modesta?'

'The new doctor.'

'I don't believe it. He looks like a boy. And besides, even if he were a doctor, is that the way to receive him, Modesta? You shouldn't have!'

I find myself on my feet slapping her, but not hard enough to hurt her, like the first time. I now know how to deal with those prejudices which, from the depths of twenty years of custom and convention, resurfaced darkly in the blue lake of her eyes. Crying calms her, and whether it's because she's afraid of me or because my slaps enable her to feel justified in her own eyes, she accepts life and is happy again.

*

Beatrice now laughs with the doctor, whom she didn't want to have anything to do with earlier; they're amused by my clumsy attempts to stay afloat. I must look really comical as I founder in the water just a few yards from shore. They swim away blithely, confidently cutting through the sea and laughing, but meanwhile I manage to float and do a few strokes, provided I can see the bottom. Who knows when I'll be able to go out where all you can see is an expanse of dark water probed by the sun? For hours, from the boat I had watched those slow tentacles patiently plumbing those mysterious depths. Another month or two – autumn was still far off, fortunately! – and with the help of that young man I would do it . . . They're laughing again . . . they've reached the rock of the Prophet. That rock had become my aspiration. I studied, read, took care of Eriprando, but deep inside me that rock rose up like a promise.

The days passed, revolving around that promise, that lava silhouette that emerged – at times pensive, at other times glowering – in a pool of water which from the beach always appeared green, until I was able to see up close that it was not an optical illusion, that in fact the sea was always green around the Prophet's colossal head. With

Carlo's help, I had done it. Just in time; large clouds were already appearing on the horizon. I was trembling with elation over the swim and because the air had turned cool overnight. Carlo, too, was elated. He stood aside, silent, after helping me climb onto the Prophet's tresses. He never spoke when we were alone; I had to wait for Beatrice to hear his voice. Gaia had worked all too well . . . But by this time I couldn't undo it. Maybe it was better that way. I couldn't get used to that youthfulness and intelligence that assailed me with a fervour and language that were new to me. I had to steal that mastery of his: his ability to play the keyboard of words the way I could make a hundred nuances echo from the notes on the piano. For months now, I had been grasping each new word on the spot and repeating it to myself so I wouldn't forget it. In time, I would talk like him, just as in time I was able to feel the remote, unreachable lava of that small island beneath my feet.

★

'Lying in the sun without an umbrella, Modesta? You'll ruin your skin! How many times must I tell you? You're already so dark! It's unattractive, that dark skin, like a peasant woman's.'

'On the contrary, if I may say so, the Princess is ahead of her time. And perhaps she knows it. In Riccione there are many women who have accepted heliotherapy upon the advice of us doctors. The healing properties of the sun have been known for some time, only this medical truth clashed, as always, with modesty, or rather with an aesthetic ideal it hides behind. Last summer we saw swimsuits that were actually scandalous – for the husbands, of course! But times change. You can't stop progress, and the Princess, dear Beatrice, perhaps consciously, or following her instinct or love for the sun, as she likes to call it, is doing something to promote women's liberation. Paleness and fragility, after all, are nothing but subtle bridles to curb and tame female nature, just like the Chinese bind their little girls' feet in the name of beauty. Now, now, Beatrice, don't get upset. I can see I'm boring you. It's the fault of my job: a professional deviation.'

'I'm not bored, Carlo. It's just that I feel like playing croquet. Shall we go?'

The two run off to look for mallets. Beatrice has given him permission to call her by name. It's normal; they're just kids. 'Consciously', 'heliotherapy', 'professional deviation'. What marvellous expressions!

★

'No, Beatrice, no! You're very kind, but it's hopeless for you to go to so much trouble to see that the Princess takes an interest in me. Don't you see that even when I speak, she not only doesn't listen to me but she closes her eyes as if . . .'

'On the contrary, I do listen to you, and to prove it to you I can tell you that you're sympathetic toward those socialists you talk so much about.'

'May I ask how you realized that?'

'From the way you spoke, some days ago, about women.'

'And you weren't scandalized? You didn't send me away?'

'Why should I have?'

'Well . . . Attorney Santangelo had advised me . . .'

'Santangelo doesn't interest me. What interests me, instead, are these sympathies of yours. Well? No answer?'

'Forgive me, Princess, I'm very confused. You have the ability to surprise me continually. I never imagined that you were interested in politics.'

'No, we're not at all interested in politics! Modesta! How can you think of joking about these things? Can't you see you're embarrassing him? Carlo has no sympathy for those godless atheists! I don't like it when you act like that! I'm going to take a swim.'

'No, Doctor, I would advise you not to follow her; you'd lose her. Let her swim. Later we'll explain to her that there's nothing wrong with those socialists. It takes patience with Beatrice, and time. I can see you're puzzled. Believe me, it's better this way. Sooner or later it would have come out. Or were you hoping that Beatrice would never find out? Why are you staring at me in a daze?'

'It's not that. It's just . . . the fact is that I've never heard you speak so gently and at such length. It's your voice that enchants me. You should speak more often.'

'You haven't answered my question. How did you become a socialist?'

'It was at university. Two or three critical meetings, and everything became clear to me.'

'Are there many socialists in Milan?'

'Many, yes. And even more in Turin. Even here in Sicily there are many.'

'Are you serious?'

'Yes.'

'And you know them?'

'To be honest, I'm here in Catania to make contact with comrades.'

'Ah! Now I understand why you haven't bothered to look for other patients besides us these past months. I found it very surprising. But I attributed it to family affluence and – forgive me – indolence.'

'I must admit, you don't miss a thing. Your diagnosis was nearly accurate. No, definitely not indolence! But a certain economic stability that allowed me to see my actions clearly. I'll explain. For some years my calling as a doctor has come up against many situations that stripped it of the aura of sanctity I had seen in it as a youth. I realized that being a doctor in this society is nothing more than trying to repair the damage caused by working conditions in mines and factories, by prejudices or by circumstances of poverty and filth – damage created at a rapid rate, much too fast for good intentions and the paltry efforts of individual doctors. What good does it do – in a lifetime – to save a hundred people, ninety-nine of them wealthy or well off, when you've realized that medicine must first and foremost prevent illness for everyone, indiscriminately? A doctor's profession in such conditions is equivalent to that of a missionary who goes to Africa to heal the lepers and save some souls . . . above all his own! Come to think of it, they're no fools: if they truly eradicated suffering, how could they continue to enjoy those playthings they call the soul, evil and redemption? I was joking. Partly because I'm becoming pompous. And so to conclude this very pedantic little speech: a doctor's profession is only valid if accompanied by political action that aims to provide everyone with healthful, liveable homes and genuinely efficient hospitals. To do this it is necessary to act, act deep down at the root causes. There is no other way.'

'Is that what socialism is?'

'Yes, but I can see you're preoccupied. I'm afraid I've bored you.'

'You know very well that not only did you not bore me but . . . don't be coy!'

'You're right.'

'You resort to acting demure because I'm a woman, and this allows you to presume that your talk is too profound for . . .'

'Touché! I apologize. But it's so rare to find women—!There are some extraordinary women, truly extraordinary, among the socialists, but still very few, unfortunately very few!'

'You taught me to swim, didn't you?'

'Yes.'

'Would you teach me . . . would you introduce me to some of these socialists?'

'I'd like to kiss your hand. Such a lovely hand! Thank you for not withdrawing it. I love you, Princess!'

'Weren't you in love with Beatrice?'

'I am very fond of Beatrice, but since I've heard you speak, I realize that I was clinging to Beatrice to get to you. Forgive me. No, don't pull your hand away! *I am not fond of love.* I've already suffered too much in the name of love. If you intend to quash all hope, with your permission I will stop coming here. There are many doctors in the city. Now I must go, Princess. No! Don't be angry with me if I don't come tomorrow. I have no hope, I can see that! Think me vile if you like, but don't hold it against me, because I loved you for an hour.'

43

The first week of Carlo's absence

'Will he really no longer come? But why, Modesta, why?'

It was best not to answer . . . *'Think me vile if you like, but don't hold it against me, because I loved you for an hour.'* He had spirit, that lanky young man with his awkward gait.

The second week of Carlo's absence

'So what you found out about him was true? It wasn't a joke?'

'What did I find out, Beatrice?'

'Have you already forgotten? Go on, of course you remember! That he was a socialist! Is that why you sent him away?'

'You yourself pointed out that we have the good fortune of not knowing any of those atheists.'

'So it was true? It seems impossible. What a pity, he was so cheerful!'

It was best not to respond.

'Why don't you answer when I talk about him? You're insufferable when you do that! You remind me of Nonna Gaia. You're just like her, distant and self-centred. You never think about me.'

'And why do you say I never think about you?'

'Oh, of course! What do you care if Carlo doesn't come anymore? You're always shut up in that damn room, working! *Uffa*, what a bore! In the morning with Attorney Santangelo, in the afternoon by yourself, and later you're always with Eriprando and . . .'

'And with you, it seems to me, no?'

'Oh, sure, scraps . . . And I get bored, *uffa*! Especially now with these clouds. *Uffa*, how tedious!'

'It's autumn, Beatrice.'

'At least before, we could go to the beach. Then too, it's not as if I don't love Eriprando. But he's little. How can you expect me to talk to him? With Carlo we could have such interesting talks!'

'But he was a socialist, Beatrice; don't forget that.'

'I haven't forgotten. It's a very serious thing, I know. It's serious, isn't it, Modesta?'

The third week of Carlo's absence

'All those amusing things he taught me! Remember when he came with tambourines? You have no idea how much fun it was to play the tambourines. You can't imagine; you never wanted to learn. He'd promised to bring me several new games, once summer ended . . . When summer is over and we're forced to stay shut up indoors, it's important, he said, to think up diversions to amuse ourselves, to distract us from nature's lethargy. He also said that autumn and winter are the most difficult seasons but also the most . . . the most . . .'

'Productive, Beatrice.'

'Ah, yes, productive! That's right, for the imagination! And that summer, though beguiling, can be more fruitless in the long run. How well those from the continent express themselves! Maybe it's because, as he said, they have long winters and are forced to think a lot?'

'You could also say: to play with their intellects.'

'Oh, yes, that's what he said, delightful, isn't it? It's strange, but I thought people on the continent were all blond and sombre, but he has dark hair, dark eyes too, and he's always joking. Of course, his hands are pale; remember how white his hands are? What am I saying? You never looked at him; how could you remember! But why does everyone have it in for those socialists, Modesta? He doesn't seem like a monster. Maybe he's an exception, like Uncle Jacopo, who was so gentle even though he didn't believe in God.'

'He must be an exception, Beatrice.'

'Well then, in that case, why don't you write to him and let him come back? Maybe then, in time and with your influence, he'll stop being a socialist.'

'If you miss him so much why don't you write to him yourself and ask him to return?'

'Me? Have you lost your mind? I'm a Brandiforti and an unmarried young lady!'

'I haven't lost my mind. You're the one who misses him, so it should be you . . .'

'You're jealous, that's what! You're jealous and that's why you don't want to write to him. I figured it out, you know! You used the fact that he's a socialist as an excuse to shut me up. You're jealous . . .'

It was better not to respond and to let her cry, though those tears led me to take her in my arms and made me aware of that sad, unbearable tremor which for some days had been causing her to limp more.

'You're jealous of Carlo. Tell the truth! You're jealous!'

Two days after the third week of Carlo's absence

'I decided to write to Carlo because I realize you didn't send him away because he's a socialist, but because you're jealous. Besides, as Uncle Jacopo used to say, maybe being a socialist is not as horrible as they say.'

'You're free to do what you like, Beatrice.'

'What does that mean? Nonna used to say that too and then . . . What does that mean? That you'll give him a cold reception, or that you won't receive him at all? Tell me now, at least. So I'll know what to do!'

Now that she was finally rebelling – and because I did not want her to confuse me with Gaia – I could speak. Taking her in my arms, I tried to still for a moment those curls shaken by years of fears and insecurities. I had to still that little face that started at the slightest sound or shadow.

I take her cheeks in my hands, and like before, her hair falls softly over my fingers. And though not one shiver now blurs my gaze, the touch of her hair fills me with a peace which, while holding no surprises, is perhaps deeper than the pleasure of the past.

'Listen to me, Beatrice. For once, listen to me! I am not like your grandmother, even though I learned many things from her. I love you in a different way than she did. All I want is your contentment. I'm not opposed to Carlo. I have a lot of confidence in you, and the fact that you care so much for him convinces me that perhaps there is nothing wrong with being a socialist. What do we know, right?'

'Nothing, actually. Nothing.'

'Who was it who spoke ill of the socialists, hmm? Try and remember.'

'Well, Attorney Santangelo, my aunts and . . . all those others.'

'But those people are all *antipatiche*, disagreeable, aren't they, Beatrice? Tedious.'

'Oh, for heaven's sake, Modesta, don't even speak of them! So then you don't find Carlo *antipatico*?'

'Beatrice, hold your little head still for a moment; try to look me in the eye. I don't find Carlo either likeable or unlikeable. For me he was just a doctor who came to check on the health of Ippolito and Eriprando. But if his company is important to you, I will try to get to know him and love him as you love him.'

'But I don't love him, Modesta! What are you saying? It's just that I enjoy myself with him!'

'All right! Then I'll try to enjoy his conversation as well.'

'Oh, yes! That's just what I wanted, Modesta! Thank goodness you understand. I was feeling resentful toward you. It's just that when you won't talk, it scares me. I'm not intelligent like you, like Nonna, who understand even when something is unspoken. Uncle Jacopo was like you too, but I, I . . . I need you to explain things to me, and now that you've spoken, I believe you. I believe you and I love you so, so much. It's you I love, not him. You mustn't be jealous. It's just that I have fun with him.'

'When is he coming?'

A deep blush rising from her neck to her cheeks, which I had never seen in her before, disturbed me so that for a moment I felt as though the old passion for her was coming over me again. I closed my eyes to try to understand. No, it was only recollection of a time when I trembled at her sudden, unpredictable changes – recollection or nostalgia? – as we walked hand in hand through the corridors and gardens.

'Why did you close your eyes, Modesta? Don't you feel well? How

201

lovely you are with your eyes closed! When you close your eyes you're more beautiful and I always want to kiss you, but we can't.'

'And why can't we?'

'Because I have things to do.'

'But did Carlo reply? When is he coming?'

'He's down in the parlour, waiting. That's why I can't kiss you. I was afraid you wouldn't want to see him, so I told Argentovivo to have him wait downstairs. He's been waiting quite a while. Come on. Now that everything is cleared up, come down with me.'

'Why don't you go by yourself?'

'But it isn't appropriate, Modesta! I'm an unmarried young lady. Come on, come with me!'

'Yes, of course, I'll come, but just for today. In the future, I permit you to see him alone. I'm the head of this household, aren't I? Times have changed, Beatrice.'

'But what will people say?'

'Didn't we decide not to be concerned about what people say, as Jacopo advised us?'

'You're right. Later on I'll see, but not today! I'm afraid!'

Her small, trembling hand pulled me along as it had in the past (how many years ago had it been?). But back then her pallid face did not blush with that deep red that now makes her seem like a stranger. A stranger, but dear to me. The way it should be.

In the parlour, in Carlo's presence, the blush vanished as swiftly as it had arisen. So swiftly that I became concerned (how could that small body stand so much excitement?) and put my arm around her slender waist for fear that she might shatter. Grateful, Beatrice leaned on me and together we went to greet the young man, who seemed taller and more serious now that he wore a double-breasted winter jacket, as though he had aged.

'You see, Princess, I followed your advice and I've grown a beard. And just as you predicted, I gained years and patients as a result. You are invaluable, Princess!'

'I am happy to have been of help to you, Doctor, and besides, the beard suits you. Isn't that right, Beatrice? Doesn't it suit him?'

'Well, it can't yet be called a bona fide beard like the ones you see in Catania . . . It will take another month or two before the scraggly thing can be called such. So I hope, at least.'

'Nevertheless, it becomes you. Doesn't it, Beatrice?'

Beatrice was rigid. Her back weighed so heavily on my chest that I was almost unable to speak. Carlo could not sit down in front of ladies who insisted on standing; that was the rule. So the three of us, standing stock-still in the middle of the room, looked like tin soldiers awaiting an order to attack.

'I'm afraid Beatrice doesn't approve of my beard. She's looking at me as though she doesn't recognize me.'

Beatrice didn't answer. And while I, beginning to sweat, tried to nudge her toward a chair, Carlo's smile turned into a disappointed pout.

'Clearly my beard has not been as successful here, among friends, as it has been out there among foes. What would the Princess say if I were to go home and shave and come back in about an hour? That way we can begin all over again, as if this beard had never existed.'

Unexpectedly turning to me and hugging me, Beatrice burst out laughing so hard that Carlo jumped back and I had to dig in my heels not to totter.

'Oh God, how funny he is, Modesta! Did you see how he was plucking at those few hairs when he said "clearly"? Oh God, Carlo, how funny you look with that beard! I've never laughed so much in my life! I'm laughing so hard I can't breathe!'

Little by little her contagious laughter spread to us, too, and somehow we frozen tin soldiers found ourselves huddling on the sofa, all three of us in hysterics. 'Just like kids,' Carlo said, and added, 'kids who claim to have a beard, of course!'

The laughter we had managed to stifle seized us feverishly again until Beatrice stood up and yelled, 'Enough! Enough, Carlo! Have mercy, I'm dying!'

'Have mercy? I should have mercy for you who showed no mercy at my attempt to enter the austere world of our masculine, bearded heroes with these few hairs of mine?'

'No! Don't say that word again. I can't take anymore!'

'All right, I won't utter the scandalous word "bearded" anymore,

Signorina Beatrice! But it's my duty to plead the cause of the beard, which has always been and always will be a symbol of genius and virility! At least in our country, where hair is abundantly profuse. Would you laugh, little girl, at the beard of Garibaldi, Galileo Galilei or Turati?'

'And who is this Turati? Do you know him, Modesta?'

'Ah, foolish girl, ignorant and unaware! Yours is an act of true irreverence, not only toward our ancient forefathers, but also toward the luminous greatness of our contemporaries who, with their elaborate beards, have erected the pillars of our bearded culture.'

'Oh God, Modesta, bearded culture! Bearded culture!'

And we doubled up laughing, until Argentovivo came in carrying tea. Exhausted from the hysterics, we fell upon the cakes and biscuits in silence; I didn't know fun could be so tiring.

'It's true, Princess, I haven't felt so tired since I was six or seven years old. But it's a good, pleasant fatigue . . . I had forgotten! It reminds me of a time many, many years ago when I still lived with my parents in the country . . .'

44

'No, we're not from Milan, but from the countryside. Oh, yes, Princess, there's a big difference, just like here in Sicily, for that matter. My ancestors came from northern Europe: wealthy farmers, but not rich enough to live a prosperous life in town, they went in search of fertile, affordable lands. In our "clan", as we called that band of seven families of thirty or forty individuals – I never did a proper count – those pioneer-forefathers were vaguely described as a tribe of heroes. But as my father used to say, they were merely the usual predators who have always roamed around our country, robbing here and there. Come to think of it, they could actually be called colonialists. *"A strong, sturdy stock bred by the cold, by austere customs, and by no contamination from indigenous elements"*. . . . And by constant stealing, I would mentally add to the end of this sermon, which some uncle fed us before dinner at least three times a week. You're laughing, aren't you, Beatrice? It's no laughing matter. I would have liked to see you deal with it! I was so afraid of that strong breed! Not to mention the women! I still remember how frightened I was by my grandmother's voice. So frightened that, after her death, I could no longer recall her face, just her voice. Yet throughout my childhood she sat before me at breakfast, lunch and dinner. That's right, laugh all you want! But I can still hear Nonna Valentina's terrifying voice thunder as she stared at me: "Why, he's a midget! This child isn't growing!" So it was steak at every meal. I exuded the smell of meat from every pore. I, who always despised meat! Or maybe I began to despise it afterwards? It doesn't matter; psychology doesn't interest me. God how boring all those subtle psychological novels are! Let's leave them to our dear comrade Montessori. Dear God, how tedious she is!'

'And who is this Montessori?'

'A comrade of ours who deals with child psychology. I haven't read anything of hers, but they say she's worthy of note. I think she invented a new methodology for educating children. I see this interests you, Princess. I will procure her writings for you.'

'They don't interest you because they are written by a woman?'

'No, no, Princess, what I said was that psychology doesn't interest me.'

'*Uffa!* There you go, quarrelling. Never mind, Carlo. Tell me about Nonna Valentina and the clan. What were they, British?'

'British? Not on your life! They came from some barbaric north, loaded down with household chattels and poultry, playing the long horn as they made their way through the Alps. You should have seen my grandmother's firm hand when she gripped the musket to chase off some unfortunate chicken thief, or in the big kitchen, when she wielded the knife to carve a piece of meat for the midget . . .'

'Why, were you small?'

'Small? Of course not, Beatrice! This went on until I was fourteen years old! She would grab me by the ear and pull me towards her yelling: "Are you going to grow or not, midget?"'

'You, a midget?'

'Yes, and I believed it! Afterwards, in Pavia, in Milan – in the civilized world I mean – I realized that while I wasn't exceptionally tall, neither was I a midget. But there, surrounded by those tall, blond uncles and cousins . . .'

'But you're dark-haired.'

'My mother's fault.'

'Oh God, you're so funny, Carlo! Did you hear what he said, Modesta?'

'At least that's what Nonna Valentina kept saying: blame my mother, and above all my father. A fine, decent member of the family, but absent-minded and without the slightest sense of reality, interested only in his microscope. And so, in his distraction, in Milan, a city possessed by Satan, he went and fell in love with a tiny young girl, dwarfish and very, very dark, a Neapolitan to boot, though aristocratic and wealthy. *Bambolina*, little doll, Grandmother called her with insincere sweetness: *"Oh no! Bambolina is delicate, it's better if you go. Bambolina already climbed the stairs twice today! She's so thin, I wouldn't want her to get sick like last year!"* Still, I was fond of that name because she really did look like a porcelain doll, with her black wavy hair, her small rosy lips and eyelashes so long that when she lowered her gaze they cast a shadow on her cheeks. I remember that at fourteen, I could already pick her up when she was tired and carry her up the stairs to her room. I remember that even the last time, I was the one who lifted her up from the armchair where it seemed she had fallen asleep. At that moment I didn't realize. She was only slightly heavier than other times.'

'Was she dead?'

'Oh, yes! Of tuberculosis. I owe my weak lungs to her, besides my being a midget. Or so they said. Yet all those horrors that Bambolina bequeathed me are dear to me and I consider them precious gifts.'

'Why do you refer to her as Bambolina? Didn't you call her Mama?'

'Of course! But since she died, I don't know why, I can't think of her without calling her that. Maybe because my father and I always called her that. He loved her very much. He never got over her death. And while before he used to disappear from the house for weeks at a time, afterwards we hardly ever saw him. By then, all he cared about was politics.'

'Oh! Your father too was involved in politics?'

'Yes, of course, Princess. That was another thing my grandmother Valentina fumed about: why at the most unlikely moments she was given to frequent fits of impervious mumbling to which she gave vent as she walked, or rather, marched, up and down the parlour with those long, gnarled legs of hers. I, when I heard the thud of those heavy feet on the parquet floor . . . in my house we didn't have rugs, they were considered a luxury! Only Bambolina's room had carpets. I used to like to run around that warm, colourful room, when she was in bed. She let me take off my shoes and . . .'

'And Nonna Valentina didn't get angry?'

'She never went into Bambolina's room. In fact, once when Mama was in bed with a fever, I heard her say to the doctor: "I won't step foot in that room again. It's suffocating! Not only does she never open the window, but as if that weren't enough, she drenches herself in perfume like a . . . Never mind. These women from the south! They could transform even a church into . . ." – may I, Princess? – "into a brothel!"'

'Did she actually say that word?'

'Oh, yes! She swore, too, sometimes. But please believe me, always in order to express her chaste indignation over the world's permissive ways.'

'You were telling us about when you heard those thuds on the floor.'

'Oh, yes! When I heard those thuds, I would go and hide under the bed in my room.'

'And what did you do under the bed?'

'Well, I would doze off so I wouldn't hear that martial stride thumping up and down, or else I'd read all my father's forbidden books.'

'What books were they, Carlo?'

'Political books.'

'Political? So you were already grown up then?'

'It's awful to admit, Beatrice, but I've never had the makings of a hero. Yes, I was fourteen when I hid under the bed and began to get interested in politics, falling victim, like my father and grandfather, to this curse some witch must have cast on our family's sound, lucid thinking. My relatives would walk past my grandfather's library quickly, throwing blistering glances at the books and journals: instruments of corruption that the devil forged at night in some cauldron. Only the hefty tome of the Bible was permitted in the other clan houses.'

'And they didn't say anything? How come?'

'For an old, compelling reason, Beatrice, at least since the time Ecclesiastes took pleasure in cogitating and writing about what he cogitated.'

'What do you mean, Ecclesiastes in the Bible?'

'Of course, dear Beatrice: "... *money is the answer for everything ...* *Do not revile the king even in your thoughts, or curse the rich in your bedroom, because a bird in the sky may carry your words ...*"* We were the richest of the clan. And then there was Aunt Clara, a sharp spinster, serene and hard-working, who soothed everyone with her absolute optimism about the vigour of our sturdy, enduring stock. She would always say: *"Now, now! Let's not exaggerate, this politics is merely a childhood disease that my Federico came down with."* Federico was her brother and my grandfather, just to be clear. Except that this childhood disease persisted until his death: *"A mild childhood disease,"* Aunt Clara kept repeating, throughout her long life. I wouldn't say it was so "mild", however, considering the massive purchases of expensive books, the frequent night-time visits by certain Carbonari,* the pranks in Rome peppered here and there by the occasional drowning of a papal informer in the Blond Tiber.* All silly trifles that never impressed Aunt Clara. But when Federico officially followed that outlaw Garibaldi to Sicily, the outrage was horrific! And he would no longer have been able to return to the clan if Garibaldi had not met with the gentleman king in Teano.* Afterwards, despite the bitterness that gripped him, whenever he spoke to me of his lost dream of an Italian republic, deep down I was grateful for the "General's betrayal" which had allowed me to get to know him. He was a big, bearded, childlike man, with a vulnerable look ... How can I describe him to you, Beatrice? He appeared to be straight out of a storybook. When he recounted his wartime experiences – atrocious, really – he could clothe them in such an aura of adventure and mystery that he made them as exciting and soothing as a good fairy tale.'

'Why do you say "good", Carlo? Aren't all fairy tales good?'

'Oh no, Beatrice, not all fairy tales are good. Indeed, as our comrade Montessori says, and I agree with her in this respect, almost all fairy tales are evil: they are a tool to terrorize children and teach them to fear law and authority. We spoke about this at length, or rather, she talked to me about it, urging me to write a new kind of fairy tale. I remember that in Rome, as soon as she broached the subject of fairy tales, everyone fled. Certainly her stance against the tales of Andersen, Grimm and many others is a valid one. But to expect all comrades –

doctors, engineers or firemen – to force themselves to come up with different plots and adventures for the revolution every evening instead of sleeping . . .'

'A revolution through fairy tales! It's a nice idea, though.'

'Of course, Princess. But first there are slightly more serious problems to solve: unemployment, hunger . . .'

'It seems to me that Montessori counts fairy tales among these serious problems. Fairy tales, along with bread, are children's food, and it's important that this food be different from what they are usually offered.'

'You never fail to amaze me, Princess! If only Montessori expressed her ideas so clearly . . .'

'*Uffa!* There you two go again! Carlo is right, Modesta, this Montessori is boring. Why do you keep interrupting him? Let him talk.'

Without realizing it, Beatrice was calling me a bore. Everything changes. Eriprando wriggles out of my arms; playing horsey on my legs bores him now that he can balance on an almost real horse and rock himself up and down. For me too: Beatrice's coy flirtatiousness, which enthrals Carlo, now leaves me indifferent and at times irritates me.

'And you, Carlo, stop bringing Modesta more and more books. All she does is read! It's not good for her. Plus, they make her become even more serious than she's always been.'

'Just listen to our Beatrice, talking like Nonna Valentina.'

'What do you mean! I'm not against books, but this is overdoing it a bit, it seems to me. Come on, finish your story, it's almost time for dinner. I hear Argentovivo setting the table. But afterwards you'll stay with us, won't you? That way we can play Shanghai Rummy.'

'What story, Beatrice? I lost my train of thought at the idea of the delicious dishes Argentovivo must have prepared. A real Paganini, your Argentovivo, she never repeats herself.'

'The one about the childhood disease! God, how funny to call something as serious as politics by that name. Because I understand it's something serious. What do you think Modesta? I know it; you needn't look at me with such a stern face.'

'Oh, yes, Aunt Clara. Poor thing! It was terrible for her to have to acknowledge that Grandfather's childhood disease had become hereditary. The same evening, back in 1889, that my father came to dinner with Turati to celebrate the birth of the Socialist League and Turati himself drank a toast to my father calling him comrade, she was unable to bear the blow, and died.'

'Your aunt?'

'Yes, Aunt Clara. She died of grief, poor woman! At least that's what my grandmother used to remind us of at the table, staring at my father with rancour. But he would respond mildly: "What grief, Mama? Old age is making you muddled. You know very well she died of indigestion."'

'So you too inherited the disease?'

'It must be so, although medical history has no record of the fact that the germ of an idea may penetrate a mother's chaste womb. However, even assuming that this can happen, the symptoms of this hereditary disease were slow to emerge, hampered by the recollection of my grandfather's heartache over Garibaldi's betrayal and by the disappointment Turati had caused my father as he walked along Via Volta in May of 1898.'*

'Your father was also betrayed? Betrayed how, if he was out walking?'

'Walking, yes – in a manner of speaking! If you think about it, ours must be a family destiny. In each generation, a betrayal. Not so bad though; not everyone can say that. What do you think?'

'But Doctor, do you mean Turati . . .'

'Yes, the very one, the same Filippo Turati who's still active in the Chamber today.'

'But he must be ancient!'

'You should know, you ignorant, sweet girl, that God or his representative grants petty politicos, not politicians, a very long life. Assuming some anarchist doesn't think of . . .'

'Oh God, Carlo, what would this anarchist do? Who are these anarchists?'

'Individuals who are gentle, moral and impetuous like you. The Princess can tell you. By now she knows as much about them as I do, if not more. Our Princess has a real talent for politics.'

'Oh, I see, Carlo. Turati betrayed your father by becoming a monarchist as well?'

'Oh God, Beatrice! Now it's you who's making *me* die laughing! Did you hear that, Princess? It's an ingenious idea, and not all that far from reality. Beatrice has squarely grasped the essence of Turati's socialism. Let me explain: the socialists fell into the psychological trap of liberal thinking. They too believe in the fundamental goodness of democratic institutions. Whereas we know, after the success of the Russian Revolution, that it's perfectly useless to tinker with the laws here and there, correct them timidly, if you don't change everything from the very foundations. We must abolish private property, abolish the class structure, and involve everyone in the control of power.'

'Oh God, Carlo, stop, I don't understand a thing. Why do you say "they believe"? Don't you believe that?'

'I belong to the communist faction, which is waiting to be established as the Italian Communist Party. It will happen soon, within a few months. But I see by the glazed expression on our Beatrice's little face that I'm becoming boring. Forgive me; I let myself get carried away. Well then, my father found himself caught up in the events of 1898. A spontaneous uprising to protest the inhumane working conditions of an eleven- – yes, eleven- – hour workday. The incident was occasioned by the Pirelli clothing factory, Pirelli being a great friend of my father for that matter, except in politics, I mean . . . Do you know what they called him? May I, Princess?'

'Of course, Doctor, as you please.'

'They called him "women's secret procurer".'

'How funny! Why?'

'Because he was the one who "perfected" women and young ladies whose breasts, shoulders, hips and thighs were deficient. Calves too, I think, though I wouldn't swear to it.'

'Of course, since at that time all those curves were stylish. I've seen them in the weekly *Domenica del Corriere*. How comical they were!'

'Well, the revolt broke out suddenly and was terrible. The troops under General Bava Beccaris's command came armed with all the deadly weapons of the modern era. My father was on the barricades with his trusty sling shirt full of stones. Many fell, but others held out, while our Turati, during pauses in the fighting, was carried around on the shoulders of two comrades, yelling and urging everyone to cease fighting. I can just hear him; even now all he does is preach peace and nonviolence . . . So, then he said: "As deputy of your constituency I invoke your calmness and patience! Not the patience of a jackass, mind you, but the patience of reason. Listen to my advice: I tell you in good conscience, the time has not yet come, it has not come!" It was then that a worker, a comrade, next to him shouted: *"E quand l'è ch'el vegnerà donc el dì?* When will the day come then?" Did you understand? I see you're laughing; good thing, I don't like translating foreign languages . . . To end the story: those "God-fearing" socialists, as my father called them, allowed themselves to be swayed and let the workers pay for a revolt that for better or worse might also have . . . who knows!'

'And so your father never spoke again, the poor thing? It's a sad story, Carlo. I don't know why, but it's sad! It's not like the others.'

'In fact, it's so sad that to me, as a boy, these stories served as an antidote to the poison of politics. And I would never, ever, have taken an interest in it if I hadn't met a midget like me in Turin . . . indeed, thinking back, I listened to him not only because of the intelligence and goodness his face inspired, but because I could finally look someone in the eye.'

'And who was this midget?'

'Who *is*, you should say, Beatrice. He's alive and well, fortunately. His name is Antonio Gramsci.'

45

From Beatrice's diary, found many years later by Modesta

7 January 1921

Why can't one be happy for ever? Why does something always get in the way of our happiness?

It's been a year since I turned to you, dear diary, and that's because I was so happy and had so many things to do: get ready for the evening, rummage through the wardrobes or chest for a blouse or shawl to smarten up the dresses and skirts that Modesta had made for me when we were wealthy.

What beautiful things Grandmother had! Who would have imagined! I found so many ribbons and belts! And then, with Argentovivo, I would try new ways to wear my hair. How important it is to change one's hairstyle! Modesta should do it too, I've told her so many times. All it takes is a new comb, a ribbon, some flowers; but of course, she's like Nonna; she doesn't care much about her personal appearance. Maybe because like Nonna she's too intelligent. But it's a shame because whenever I've managed to persuade her to let me do her hair, she looked fabulous, as even Carlo noted. Then too, it was so wonderful to find new flowers for the parlour and dining room, in the garden or at the market, and with Argentovivo, discover Carlo's tastes – they have very different tastes on the continent – so that he wouldn't tire of our food. It wasn't easy because, as Argentovivo rightly says, men don't like to talk about cooking and you have to be deft at discovering their preferences without asking. What's more, they like to eat well even if they are intelligent and preoccupied like Carlo. Dear diary, I think I will stop here because seeing his name in writing hurts so much. It's been a month since he left for Livorno to organize the birth of this new party. Who knows why it's taking such a long time! Besides, everything should already be done according to what he said. What if that midget and the communist party that frightens me so still need him, and won't ever let him come back?

5 March 1921

The more time passes, the more I hate this new party and all those comrades of his. What a disaster, that Sunday he took us to them. Before, we always spent evenings down in the parlour, and on Sunday afternoons he took us to the movies or the theatre. But that Sunday Modesta insisted so much . . . I have to stop because it makes me cry to think of those Sundays in that big sad, cold house, but at least he was still with us. It's really true what Dante says:

There is no greater sorrow
than thinking back upon a happy time
in misery.*

I must stop because I can already see tears spotting the paper. I don't want to stain you, dear diary.

12 March 1921, five o'clock in the afternoon

I've wept so much, dear diary, but now I'm here with you again. Talking with you gives me great consolation. Another week has passed and no word from Carlo. Modesta doesn't know when he'll be back either. Or does she know he won't ever return and doesn't want to upset me? She must know, since she spends all her time with those socialists now, afternoons and even evenings. She comes to dinner and then runs off to them. I hate them, plus I just don't see how she can enjoy being in that big room full of dusty books with only a table and some uncomfortable chairs – there isn't even a sofa – with all those badly dressed men who talk loudly and smoke, with no respect for us women. I was so uncomfortable that Sunday! Not only were we practically the only women in there, but no one stood up when we entered. Not that I think they're rude; they're Carlo's friends. It's just that when they start debating, they're not aware of anything anymore, as that woman told me. The only woman who was there besides us.

12 March 1921, 10:30 p.m.

I'm ashamed to tell even you, dear diary, but I'm jealous of that woman. She stole Modesta from me with her glib tongue and that high forehead, her hair cut short just like a man. Modesta doesn't say so, but I know she admires her greatly. All she does is read. As if the books and magazines Carlo gave her weren't enough! Now she always comes back with bundles of newspapers. She told me they're back issues of the newspaper that this woman edits. Besides going to her house, I'm afraid she also goes to the print shop because she sometimes comes back with ink stains on her blouse. Of course I shouldn't speak about it and I would never do so with strangers, but you are my one true friend. We've known each other since I was eleven years old and you have never betrayed me. I know I shouldn't judge that woman and be jealous of her, and I ask forgiveness here before you and God, but I can't help it. I hate her and, what's even more shameful, it's because she's so beautiful . . . There, I said it. I'll leave you now so I can go and pray and try to rid myself of this vile feeling that haunts me night and day.

13 March

I prayed and I hope I can manage to think of her neutrally, even if not as a friend. Mainly because she is a good friend of Carlo and, as Carlo told us, a champion of their 'ideal'. She's worked with the unions since she was a young girl; she's been imprisoned and tortured many times.* She must not be as young as she seems, because Carlo said she was a comrade who took part in the strikes up on the continent – she isn't Sicilian either – to promote a nine-hour day instead of the eleven hours which is the workday for all workers today. I remember now that on the few occasions that I went to her place, she insisted that a man can't work for more than six hours a day. I did the wrong thing with Modesta, and now I'm paying the price for it. I should have let her talk when she wanted to speak with Carlo, rather than always interrupting her and acting silly. Nonna was right: I'm spoiled and lazy, but that will change, I swear to you and to God. And if Carlo comes back – I pray to the Madonna every night to grant me this favour – if he comes back, I'll let them talk about anything they want and I too will try to study those books. I'll do it for Modesta and to correct this self-centred nature of mine.

15 March

I tried to read the Communist Party Manifesto, but I couldn't get through more than one page, at least for today. I understand it, but it makes me feel sad. I don't know why, but it makes me sad and a little fearful. Can it be because of that spectre* that is haunting Europe? Why did Marx choose that dreadful word, 'spectre'? Couldn't he have found another word, 'angel', maybe? But so it is, and I have to overcome this fear! Starting tomorrow I will continue reading it each day.

20 March

I am no longer hopeful that Carlo will return. Just today, a postcard arrived saying: 'Foggy greetings from foggy Turin to the goddesses of the sun.' I seem to hear his voice in those few words. But if he sent the card, it means he's still not coming back. I don't have the strength to cry and pray anymore, dear diary, and I don't think I even have the strength to talk to you. Besides, what would I tell you? It's raining. If it weren't for Eriprando with his games and high spirits, Argentovivo says this house would be sombre as . . . never mind.

25 March, afternoon

Though Carlo hasn't returned, the Madonna has at least granted my prayer as far as Modesta is concerned: starting yesterday, she's stopped going to those socialists. I wonder why? Whatever the reason, for me it's a relief from the loneliness I had sunk into. Naturally I'm curious to know why she isn't going there anymore. If I have the courage, I'll ask her tonight. She too is very sad.

26 March, morning

I found the courage to ask her. Smiling, she spoke these words which I'm writing down in order to try to understand them, like she does with poems. What she said was: 'Well, Beatrice, that house is just like a church, filled with frescos of madonnas and saints! But as Jacopo used to say, it's best to keep away from churches after you've admired the masterpieces.' I really don't understand, talking about that house as if it were a church. To me it seemed downright filthy. And frescos? Sure, there were some paintings, but . . . sometimes Modesta is truly a mystery. Or was she perhaps joking?

Goliarda Sapienza

30 March 1921

Just a few lines, dear diary, because I am so happy my hands are shaking. Carlo is in Catania and is coming to dinner tonight. I'll leave you now. I have so many things to do and I'm also very fearful. I don't know why, but my forehead has been burning up since this morning and I've got the chills. I didn't take my temperature; I'm afraid I have a fever. Just now, of all times! And that's not all I'm afraid of. Recently I've thought and thought about what Argentovivo, in her impertinent way, told me that night. It can't be true! But she's been in love and knows more about it than I do. And if it were true? It's terrible but I'm afraid, dear diary, that Argentovivo may be right. If only I could ask Modesta! She's so intelligent, she knows so many things. But how can I? She might get jealous again and . . . I can't bear to think about it. I mustn't think about it. Because never, ever, would I leave Modesta, even if this misfortune were true. I swore to myself I wouldn't. What would she do without me looking after her and taking care of the house? She, who is always busy working with all those lawyers and notaries and who, like all intelligent people, is so distracted and impractical? Even yesterday, if I hadn't been here, she would have skipped breakfast, and she's gotten so thin lately! I will never, ever leave her; among other things, it would offend the sacred memory of my grandmother. I will stifle this love inside me, so I can at least go on seeing him with Modesta and we can be happy together, for ever.

46

'When I saw you two racing down the stairs like – if I may say so, Princess – a couple of real hoydens, I nearly fled for fear of hearing that muffled gallop over my head just like . . .'

'Nonna Valentina's marching?'

'Well, unfortunately no, Beatrice! Nonna Valentina would certainly have been preferable to the charges of the royal guard. Damn Turin, built purposely so that a few *carabinieri* on horseback or a well-aimed cannon can keep an entire district under control. Ungrateful Turin, or ungrateful continent, as you call it. How I missed this tranquil, relaxing parlour and Catania's safe streets!'

'Why do you say that Carlo? You're scaring me! Were there cannons?'

'Cannons, no, at least not for the moment. It's just that, having been gone for so long, I was able to see Turin in all its cold-blooded ruthlessness. That, however, is one of the benefits of travelling. One must periodically move away from any place where familiarity has killed objectivity. This is true of languages as well. After being forced to speak another language for many months, as I was, when you go back to your own you realize that being away from it has enabled you to rediscover its essential soul. One could coin an amusing slogan: "Study English, French, German to . . . learn Italian." And so with these pedantic, futile notions, here I am expressing my joy to be with you again, and also . . . oh, yes, the fact that by virtue of my long stay in this island's sun I have ripened into a respectable, indolent *terrone*, a true peasant. Oh! And I have also understood why those in the north are so scornful of the south: it's because they're envious, mark my words!'

'You're sad, Carlo. You're joking, but you're sad.'

'Well, let's say that the overall situation is not very reassuring.'

'Because of Mussolini? But everyone says he's just a ridiculous buffoon, isn't that right, Modesta? Didn't you hear that too, down in Catania?'

'Yes, but I also saw some broken heads that didn't seem to be at all a laughing matter.'

'How happy I am that you at least have understood, Princess, and that you haven't been swayed by the widespread tendency to belittle the adversary. As Gramsci says, "It seems to me that exhibiting this tendency is itself proof of one's inferiority. Belittling one's enemy is in fact an effort to enable oneself to believe that he can be vanquished . . ."* But enough, I'm becoming a bore. My stay in the north made me lose what little sense of humour I had. Enough, I've said too much! And you, Princess, how are you? In Catania, the comrades told me that you weren't well. But I see you are fine, I'm glad. I'm very curious, however . . .'

'Don't bother to be. With "them", I blamed my absence on illness so I wouldn't have to give unnecessary explanations.'

'Given that I have obtained your permission to be indiscreet, would you also tell me why, or am I asking too much?'

'Because of everything you've told us. There too, even if they don't exactly say "be good, be saintly, be cowards"* they say things very similar to that and . . . I got discouraged.'

'Still, I know you continue to send money to the newspaper. I don't understand.'

'That's another matter . . . but I'm afraid, Doctor, that we must try to draw Beatrice out of the silence into which she's retreated in order to please me. Come, Beatrice, open your eyes and we'll stop these serious discussions.'

'Oh God, Princess, our poor little one has fallen asleep!'

'She's burning up, Doctor! Feel her, she's feverish.'

'So it wasn't simply a justifiable, blessed sleep induced by the tedium of our conversation, but a fever! A very high fever, I would say. We must put her to bed right away.'

'I'll call Argentovivo.'

'No, no, Nonna, please! I don't want to go to boarding school, let me stay here with Modesta.'

'What's wrong, Doctor, what is it?'

'It's nothing, Princess. Don't blanch so! There's nothing alarming either in her chest or in her heart. It's just a fever.'

'Modesta, Modesta, don't leave me! I don't want to go away, I don't want to!'

'Come closer, Princess, hug her. Your being near her may soothe her.'

'Oh, you're here! Don't go away, please. I know I've been bad, but I won't do it again, ever!'

*

'One more look at our little patient and then we'll all go to bed. It's almost dawn. It's nothing serious, Princess; the salicylate has had its effect. Her fever is down. But you must exercise all your authority with Beatrice. The little one is not exactly what one would call a colossus. I would advise the utmost care. And now, if I may, I order you to go to bed as well. Come, I will accompany you to your room. You haven't slept a wink, and it shows!'

'You haven't slept either.'

'I'm used to it; it comes with my job. Come, off to bed! I really must be stern. You're awfully pale. You off to bed and me off to Catania. I have an important house call at eight, but I'll be back as soon as I'm free. Forgive me, Princess, but which grandmother was Beatrice talking about in her delirium? I shouldn't ask, but it wrung my heart to hear her imploring that way. She honestly seemed desperate.'

'You must have understood more or less, Doctor, a dreadful grandmother like your Nonna Valentina. Beatrice, however, did not have a mother like Bambolina from whom she could seek solace.'

'Such a shame! And you, Princess? Did you also have a grandmother, or were you spared? You never speak about your past, and this leads me to suppose . . .'

'No, no, it's just that my past doesn't interest me. It's only the present that counts.'

'A pity! Because if you had had a terrible grandmother too, we could have formed a league. And from a league, a party, and then on to the Chamber with a motion for the abolition of abominable grandmothers. I can't manage to make you smile. Don't be worried. As I told you, this fever is nothing critical, nor is Beatrice's delicacy serious. Don't you believe me? Don't you respect me as a doctor? Of course, when you care for someone the way you care about Beatrice, no doctor's or friend's word can reassure you,. . .

'Princess, listen to me, I love you, I love you. I know this is not the time to tell you this, but unfortunately I've tried to stifle this love for you, because your friendship and that of Beatrice mean so much to me. If you only knew how lonely we men are, constantly confined solely to the limbo of male friendships. It's so difficult to find educated, free-spirited women! It's a huge problem for me. Others, I don't know how, are content to . . . but I want to speak to you! No, no, I won't speak to you because I see that I have not been able to stifle this love for you. All night I watched you and I realized that all my effort has been in vain. With your permission, as soon as Beatrice recovers, I will not come anymore. Besides, it might be good for me to go back to Turin, to the struggle . . .'

'No, Carlo, stay.'

'Oh God! Princess, what did you say?'

'Stay, Carlo. Hold me.'

'Me? With you? Oh, yes, yes . . . but now I must go to Catania. Not because of the house call – it wasn't important but – I'm confused, Modesta.'

'Yes, of course, but stay here with me. Come.'

'I love you, Modesta, oh, how I love you! I feel, you know, that you love me too, you seem so tender, so tremulous . . . No response? You're right: silence is so sublime.'

He lifted me up and laid me on the bed, but he did not undress me. I expected it; that's how it had been once before. And like that other time, he entered me with a fervour that did not hurt me. When his head slumped heavily on my breast, I knew that he had come, like that other time, and that soon he would say: 'Sorry for the rush, *figghia*, it's just that . . .' Instead, I heard my voice saying:

'Don't your mothers teach you anything?'

'What did you say? How did my mother occur to you? What were you thinking of?'

'I was thinking of us, all of us, and at the moment us two, and how we don't know anything about making love.'

'What's that got to do with anything? . . . Can I turn on the light or will it embarrass you?'

'Embarrass me? Why?'

'Well, generally people are bashful. I'm a little bashful . . . Go ahead and straighten your clothes. I'll turn around.'

'Why won't you look at me?'

'Well, your skirt is raised and . . .'

'And I don't have my panties on? Excuse me, Carlo, but you're the one who took them off.'

'Of course, but . . .'

'But what? I swear I don't understand you. Are you embarrassed, or don't you find me appealing? It can happen, Carlo; it doesn't offend me.'

'I love you very much, Modesta. You're strange, but I love you so much! . . . How beautiful you are naked! I'll turn off the light.'

'If I'm beautiful, why did you turn off the light?'

'I don't know . . . You're strange, strange. You don't love me, Modesta.'

'Why do you say I don't love you, Carlo? Explain it to me.'

'I have to go now. You don't love me. Why won't you tell me you love me, Modesta? Tell me, I beg you!'

'I love you, Carlo.'

In the dark a shower of kisses rained down on my hair, my forehead; kisses filled with eagerness, delicate kisses from those lips that were tender and soft, like Eriprando's. With my palms, I tried to still that face, and sought his tongue with mine. But there was no tenderness from that mouth, its teeth furiously pressing against mine.

'I love you, Carlo, but go now.'

As he went away contentedly, waving a hand that now seemed small and fragile, a tremor of anxiety for Prando held me riveted on the bed: '*Your mothers don't teach you anything.*' As a matter of fact, Carmine, they don't teach anything to either us women or to you men. But just as you were patient with me, I will be patient with Carlo.

The first week of Beatrice's illness

'You don't love me, Modesta.'

'Why do you say that, Carlo? I haven't rejected you, have I?'

'No, no! But you never tell me you love me when we embrace each other.'

'When we make love, you mean?'

'There: you see how crude you are, how blunt? Plus, I sense you lying there afterwards frigid, distant.'

'Like those whores, is that what you mean?'

'What are you saying? Are you crazy? The only women I've had have been free-spirited, but respectable. Besides, what do you know about whores?'

'With these respectable women, did you ever "embrace", as you put it?'

'Of course, why not?'

'And afterwards, how did they feel? Weren't they frigid and distant like me? How did they seem?'

'Modesta, what kind of a question is that? How would I know? I wasn't in their shoes!'

'So you've made love to many women and you can't even tell me how they felt?'

'It's pointless to pretend with you. I see. You always know everything. The only women I've had before you are the ones our Turati elegantly calls the "wage earners of love".* Satisfied?'

'Ah, is that what he calls them?'

'Only once was I really in love, or at least so I thought before I met you.'

'So you've had a woman who was not a "wage earner of love"?'

'Are you out of your mind? She was a very respectable girl and—'

'You must have at least exchanged some kisses, or . . .'

'Kissed? Most certainly not! I was deeply in love and I respected her.'

'So how did it end?'

'The way these things always do: she liked my best friend better.'

'Probably this friend of yours kissed her, while you respected her.'

'You always relate everything to . . .'

'To what, Carlo? Why don't you say it? To sex? Is it such a dirty word? Do I seem so awful to you now that I see those adorable lips of yours pouting, and instead of getting angry, I only want to kiss them?'

'Oh Modesta, what full, sweet lips you have! I want to bite them.'

'Bite them then! But gently, Carlo, gently please!'

Under the sheet I ran my hand down along his chest and slim hips. His skin was almost as delicate as Beatrice's, but between his thighs the pubic hair and his penis were strong, virile. So what was the urgency that seized him and then, I could tell, wouldn't let him come effusively? Carmine's penis became small after sex, gentle. And I would play with it then.

'It's not that I don't love you, Carlo; it's that I'm left unsatisfied. Help me. You have to be less tense. Don't turn away as if you wanted to undo what you did. No, don't go! It's not a reproach; I too had to learn at one time.'

'From whom? Don't tell me you learned from the Prince?'

'No, Carlo, from . . .'

'So then it's true what they say in Catania.'

'Of course! How could I have had a child with that poor "thing"?'

'Beatrice told me you had sacrificed yourself. And I believed what she believes, the poor deluded soul!'

'Beatrice is fragile and has to be protected. But as a man, you should have realized.'

'How could I, if you never say anything?'

'There's no need for words. You watch, you observe. Or maybe you preferred to think that they had sacrificed me? No answer? Now I understand: you had created for yourself a Dantesque saint to love. Or would you prefer Petrarch, as I imagine you do? So then, you've

made me your pure, saintly Laura. You poor men! For us, Madame
Bovary, and for you, Laura. Come on, Carlo, it's 1921!'

'Who knows how many of these teachers you've had? Now I know
why you get undressed so easily and stroke me like . . .'

'Go ahead and say it! If not with the accurate word, "whore", at
least with Turati's euphemism. Go on, say it! Like a "wage earner
of love"?'

A hail of slaps – not kisses, like before – pelted my face, making my
cheeks sting, like when Eriprando had a tantrum and pounded my
shoulders, neck and face with his little fists. I had to be patient and let
him do it; it was merely the tender fury of a presumptuous child,
whose expectations have been disappointed. But after having vented
his fury, Prando sometimes understood.

The second week of Beatrice's illness

'Forgive me, Modesta. I've thought about what you said and maybe
you're right. I never let you talk; I'm always interrupting you. I haven't
slept a wink all these nights that I haven't come to you. Whenever I
fell asleep for a moment, I woke up seeking your body. Oh Modesta,
I may be a weakling – call me what you will – but I love you so much!
You won't look at me, Modesta, and you're right. I ran off like a
coward.'

'You're not a coward, Carlo. I understand you. It's neither your
fault nor mine. It's just that our pasts are so different. And it may also
be that I'm so exhausted and worried about Beatrice. Forgive me, but
I can't keep my eyes open with this headache.'

I expected a furious reply; it wasn't easy to lie to him. I sensed that
in some mysterious way that young man knew me like no one else
had ever known me.

'How beautiful you are with your eyes closed, Modesta!'

My surprise made my eyes fly open. He had lifted me up from the
chair just as he had done with Beatrice that long-ago night.

'No, Modesta, close your eyes. That's it! I'll put you to bed
myself, all right? I'll undress you like you do with children, then
you'll sleep, and I'll watch you. Will you let me stay with you and
watch you for a while?'

In his arms, in the short journey from the chair to the bed, I was hopeful. Everything ends and then begins anew; everything dies, later to be reborn. I was hopeful. His hands undressed me with meticulous care. I let go. Under the covers his naked body gently nestled against my own, his mouth resting on my breast. He couldn't see me, so I opened my eyes. I couldn't believe what I was feeling. He took hold of my nipple with his lips and sucked it. I was hopeful, and reached down – I was the one trembling now – to try and stroke his penis. Had I gone too far? No, because he entered me gently and, with the right rhythm, like long ago, took me back to a small bare room smelling of tobacco: '*Help me and help yourself, figghia; that way we'll climax together.*' I bit my lips, because a name had risen from the depths of my rapt being. But I hadn't said that name because he was moving frantically between my breasts and hips, perspiring lightly like a child, murmuring: 'Hold still . . . that's how I like you, still, with your eyes closed.' Now he reared his head, satisfied. I tried to keep my eyes closed and not say anything, but the tears I couldn't keep from trickling through my tightly shut eyelashes spoke for me.

'What is it, Modesta, are you crying?'

'It's nothing, Carlo, just emotion.'

'Emotion over what? You're thinking about that man. I'm getting dressed. I have a house call at eight. We'll talk later.'

Angrily, he gathered up his clothes and slammed the bathroom door. The door stayed closed for several minutes. He always went to wash after sex. Why? I turned off the light and whispering *Carmine*, Carmine's hands gave me the orgasm that for weeks I had been hoping for.

'Why did you turn off the light?'

'I'm tired, Carlo.'

'That's not true. I believed you earlier, but it's not true! Open your eyes. We have to talk!'

'Please, Carlo, tomorrow. You were the one who didn't want to talk before.'

'Before, it's true. But not now! Now I have to know. You were thinking of that man, admit it!'

'No, Carlo. Or rather, I was thinking about that man's freedom.'

'What does that mean?'

'It takes two to make love, Carlo. You've learned a lot of things, but . . .'

'But what? Let's hear it.'

'When you meet the right woman, let her join in, or teach her if she doesn't know how.'

'"When you meet the right woman", did you say? Does this mean that I'm not the right man for you and that you don't love me anymore? Or maybe you never loved me?'

'I love you, Carlo, even now when you're looking at me like a policeman. I love you and I think highly of you. It's just that we haven't connected physically. Or maybe, for me at least, I mistook as love the appeal you had, and still have, when we talk. It's difficult to explain it to you, but during these past weeks I've begun to understand many things about this word that we all use, but which we know so little about.'

'Excuses, nothing but excuses! You're still in love with that man!'

'Not with that man, Carlo, but with the physical connection there was between us when we had sex.'

'You're being vulgar, Modesta.'

'For you, everything natural is vulgar.'

'Oh God, I can't take any more of this! I'm leaving before I kill you! I'll kill you! But we'll talk about it later.'

47

The period of Beatrice's convalescence

'No! It's futile for you to try to avoid me.'

'I'm not avoiding you, Carlo!'

'You are avoiding me! But we should talk, given that you wanted to talk so much before, instead of loving me the way I loved you.'

'And how should I have loved you, Carlo? In silence, letting you adore me like a statue?'

'But love is mystery, silence. I venerated you in silence. Just looking at you was enough to make me happy for days and days. I didn't need to talk. Love is a miracle, and as such . . .'

'Love is not a miracle, Carlo, it's an art, a skill, a mental and physical exercise of the mind and of the senses like any other. Like playing an instrument, dancing or woodworking.'

'You're talking about sex.'

'But isn't sex love? Love and sex are two sides of the same coin. What is love without sex? The veneration of a statue, of a Madonna. What is sex without love? Nothing more than a clash of genital organs.'

'Then you deny the spiritual essence of love? You deny its spontaneity, and the fact that the more spontaneously it arises, the more genuine, pure and miraculous it is?'

'Carlo, you, too, like your comrades in Catania: "The asceticism of the Russian people, the sacredness of the working class, the

martyrology of the proletariat, nature as God, the artist as God."
How is it possible?'

'What does all that have to do with it?'

'It has everything to do with it, because all I found among your
comrades was a barely concealed aspiration for sainthood and a
vocation for martyrdom. Or else a ferocity of dogma hiding a fear
of investigation, of experimentation, of discovery, of life's fluidity.
If you want to know, I didn't find anything resembling the freedom
of materialism. And I ran away, yes, because I had no intention of
falling into a trap perhaps worse than the Church from which I had
escaped.'

'But Modesta, don't you see? You're denying the sacrifice and abnegation of those who are fighting for the proletarian cause, for a better
society without class differences, without man's exploitation by other
men, without . . .'

'I'm not denying any struggle! I'm critical of a mind-set and way of
thinking that is not very different from the old world that you seek to
oppose. By thinking the way you do, you will build a society that, in
the best of cases, will be a copy, and an inferior one at that, of the old
Christian bourgeois society.'

'But radical transformations take time. First we have to overthrow the bourgeoisie through revolution and change the relations
of production. Everything else will then follow on its own because
the superstructures created by the bourgeois ideology will collapse . . . In any case, what I wanted to talk about is us. I don't see
what this theoretical discussion has to do with it. But we'll talk
about it later.'

And talking about it, hearing myself accused in a thousand ways
of being cruel, cold, rational, being told how much I had been
loved without deserving it, hearing how love is so sacred and miraculous, I suddenly realized that I wasn't listening anymore. As I
watched his hands gripping my knees, I was thinking of all the discussions that I would have in the future, if I lived long enough,
with Alberto, Giovanni, Michel . . . Michel, his eyes green as emer-
alds. Discussions that would come up again and again, exactly the
same, for another ten, twenty, thirty years. The image of my future,

of perhaps having many more years to live, coursed through my blood like a gentle April rain, soothing the irritation that Carlo's voice now aroused in me.

But I had to show patience toward that tense, disappointed face, that of a child who will not resign himself to the fact that his plaything lies before him, irreparably broken by a gust of wind or a careless act (mine or his?). I didn't want to lose that fervent intellect that encouraged me to explore and continually gave me new insights, new concepts, new words. Having experienced disappointment myself over the end of a good thing, I began to understand. He no longer loved me either, but he couldn't resign himself to having been the cause.

'It's your fault. You're the one who ruined everything!'

'Yes, Carlo, it's my fault.'

The admission of my guilt had the power to soothe him. Now he stopped attacking. He looked at me, appeased and drained. He let go of my knees, ran his hands over his face. He didn't know where to look. He turned his head wearily from side to side.

'You have no idea, Modesta, what the men I've known since childhood are like, the men who have, so to speak, shaped me. You don't know how lonely they are, how little they know about the women they think they know all about, from the moment they first had the courage to visit a prostitute. Now I see I should have told you right away that the only women I had before you were those poor souls whom society forces to sell their body. You would have understood, and we would have quickly shattered the loneliness that for centuries has existed between men and women.'

I looked at him; he was smiling now as he finished his little speech. He was smiling his quiet, shy smile. And maybe because wispy clouds trailed uncertainly after a flight of seagulls promising unknown places, worlds and faces yet to be discovered, maybe because Beatrice, now recovered though thinner, came running toward us, one moment corporeal, bright, illuminated by the sun, the next rendered diaphanous by those timid, late winter clouds, I saw Carlo's face the way I had once seen it.

'I admire you a great deal, Modesta, but none the less, I want to tell you something, for your own good, for your future. I may be too sensitive, it's true, but you're too dramatic, far too dramatic!'

'Modesta! Oh God, Modesta, Carlo, hurry, please! Eriprando, Eriprando! Nonna was right, the curse! Run! He's on the carpet, screaming. His little foot, Modesta, his little foot, rigid like mine was. Hurry! Argentovivo went to lift him up to feed him, but he started shrieking!'

Beatrice was weeping on my shoulder, hugging me frantically. I couldn't move. An anger I had never felt before for that little slip of a thing trembling in my arms and immobilizing me made me shout, 'Shut up! Stop talking about curses and ill omens.'

I must have pushed her away violently. As I ran toward the house, I saw Carlo helping her up from the ground. But he lost no time comforting her. Once in the room, he reached out to support me just in time as I watched that little child writhing on the carpet, Argentovivo's cries resounding in my head.

'Steady, Modesta! We need a surgeon. Run to the car and wait for us, or if you don't feel you can drive, call Pietro.'

'No, no, I'll drive. What is it, Carlo, what's wrong?'

'Run, Modesta, we must hurry! There's no time! I don't want to give you any false hopes.'

Eriprando struggled with his affliction alone, wrapped in a blanket in Carlo's arms. And I mustn't scream or cry or ask questions. I must simply drive, urged on by those screams, loud at first, then fading into a long, droning, dissonant dirge.

I was left standing outside a blank, unreadable door, the nurse's impassive face regarding me as an outsider; the hospital's silence screamed more loudly in my head than Eriprando's cries, confining me behind an insurmountable wall of waiting. Or was it the slippery wall of the well, from which I was trying to crawl back up to the light on my hands and knees? . . . up there, maybe Mimmo would talk to me. I stayed in the stagnant well until Mimmo said in his unmistakable voice:

'*Don't worry, princess. It's nothing serious. It's not polio. All we had to do was cut a tendon. Carlo will explain it to you later.*'

'Modesta, may I introduce my friend and colleague Arturo Galgani of Milan? Luckily he was here!'

'Pleased to meet you, Doctor.'
'The pleasure is all mine, Princess.'

★

The headlights gingerly probed the black lava pavement polished by the rain. Carlo drove cautiously; not a jolt, no abrupt braking, so as not to disturb the sleep of the little one who lay heavily in my lap. I couldn't look at his face, which in a few hours had grown thin and pale, as if *La Certa* had paused for a moment to focus on him. I mustn't look at him. The tall blond man had smiled and said, 'Caught in time, it's just a minor episode; I suggest you take him home, however. He should wake up in familiar surroundings and if you do not appear worried or anxious, as I'm sure you won't, the child will no longer remember anything when he wakes up. It's extremely important that he forget, and accept the exercises and massages as something everyone does.'

'Do you feel ill, Modesta? Is that why you've closed your eyes?'

'No, Carlo, no. I'm just very tired.'

To reassure him, I opened my eyes and the calm, friendly face from the past smiled at me a moment before turning back to watch the road.

'What did you say the name of this muscle cramp or contraction was, Carlo?'

'Oh, they call it a *piede cavallino*, a charley horse. Are you still thinking about it? It can be serious because the contraction stunts the leg's growth, but caught in time it's nothing serious, nothing at all.'

'*Cavallino*, like Beatrice?'

'As a matter of fact!'

'Thank you, Carlo. What if you hadn't been there!'

'But I was there. I'm always there. I'm not being arrogant, believe me; it's just a statement of fact. I can't help it. Whenever someone needs me, somehow there I am, at the ready. Convenient for others, though less so for me. What can you do! It must be this damned vocation of mine as a doctor.'

He was joking. And if Carlo was joking, it must be true that Eriprando would recover.

'Vocation or not, Carlo, I'm grateful to you and . . . forgive me for everything.'

'For what?'

'So, no hard feelings, Carlo?'

'No hard feelings. Just loving ones I'd say, Princess.'

48

'May I come in? What's wrong, Modesta, why are you still in your dressing gown? Carlo is downstairs waiting and . . .'

'Beatrice, these past two months, as I promised after your illness, I've spent every evening with you two in the hope that you would make up your mind to give up your insane devotion – I find no other word for it after our talks – to outmoded customs or prejudices. But starting today, I've had enough.'

'But . . .'

'There is no "but" that will make me reconsider! I'm not coming down. You know how much time I've had to spend with Eriprando to distract him from your agitation and Argentovivo's apprehensions. Now that he's happy with Elena, I have to get back to work.'

'That Elena! You'd rather have that cold, silent stranger instead of me and Argentovivo, Modesta! Even today, she only let me see him for a few minutes and she watched over me like a *gendarme*.'

'I don't seem to recall that you spent a great deal of time with him before. Besides, Elena is cold and silent mainly because you two have certainly not treated her well.'

'But she's an outsider!'

'She's someone who's doing her job! Open your eyes and ears, Beatrice. Can't you hear how Eriprando laughs? How could we have got this result with you, when you started crying as soon as you saw him? Naturally, he reminded you of your own affliction, because that's all it was, an illness, not a curse, Beatrice! Come now, when you get over it too, you can see him as often as you want. But as long as you look so remorseful, just talking about Eriprando, no!'

'Yes, of course, Carlo said so too, but I can't help it. I'm always afraid he'll remain . . .'

'All right. Now go because I have to finish writing some letters.'

'So you really won't come down?'

'I can't Beatrice! How can I make you understand? Between your illness and Eriprando's, I've lost too much time. Look at all the letters, the documents to be signed, the accounts, the damned accounts!'

'But you'll come down to dinner at least, won't you?'

'Of course. I have to eat, don't I?'

'And afterwards?'

'Afterwards I'll see.'

'God, all these documents, Modesta! I'm really an ingrate. Here you are working for us. I hate myself, Modesta, I hate myself! And all these handwritten pages . . . such odd, tiny handwriting, it looks like a doctor's writing. It's illegible. What are these pages?'

'My work, poems, notes.'

'Oh, yes, you told me. Like Nonna used to say, I'm really a scatter-brain!'

'That's enough about your grandmother! I don't want to hear you mention her again. She's dead, Beatrice.'

'But she thought so highly of you . . . and I'm sure she still does.'

'I doubt it. Or maybe she does. Why not? You're not entirely wrong. It's typical of people like her to admire those who are able to outplay them. Remember how happy she was when the old doctor beat her at chess?'

'But you didn't outplay her, you simply disobeyed her, and I think . . .'

'Disobeyed? Did you say "disobeyed", Beatrice? You make me laugh.'

'Oh, Modesta, you're finally smiling! You're finally looking at me. It's been months since you've looked at me!'

In fact, it had been months . . . since hearing those screams of Eriprando that sometimes still woke me up at night; only the sight of his face rapt in deep sleep could drive them out of my memory. She was right too, and regaining my composure, I put my arm around her waist and kissed her wispy, hay-scented hair: the same scent as Eriprando's hair, as Carmine's. Only the texture was different. Hers still retained the softness of Eriprando's hair when he was a baby; later, after his battle with illness, his hair grew into wiry curls like those of Carmine, the father of both Eriprando and Beatrice. Up close like that, I saw a few grey strands already showing among the blond. Beatrice had inherited that premature grey hair and her bad foot from the paternal line of the family. From the peasant stock of that man of honour, Carmine, came two overly refined, exquisitely *fin de râce* signs.

'Oh, Modesta, you're smiling and stroking my hair. You don't hate me anymore?'

'I've never hated you, Beatrice, it's just that you—'

'Yes, I know, Carlo told me that it was only that you were worried, exhausted. He also used a word . . . what was it?'

'Trauma, Beatrice.'

'Yes, saying that, like me, you too had suffered a trauma. But I can't bear it, I can't stand it when you're so distant. I can't help it. I feel it's my fault, but at the same time I keep on doing things that I know are wrong. Why do I do things I know I shouldn't do?'

'I don't know. Maybe it's just that you're not used to affection. How would you know about affection? All you ever got were reprimands.'

'Oh, that must be it, Modesta, because I'm always imagining I'm unworthy of you, of Eriprando, of Carlo.'

'Fine. That's enough now! We forgot about him, and the poor thing is waiting. Come, that's a good girl, go to your Carlo, Beatrice. And don't feel unworthy because you're the best, most beautiful little girl.'

'You think so? But why did you say "your Carlo", Modesta?'

'Because we're fond of him. I said "your Carlo" just as I might have said "my Carlo". Come now, don't get upset. We're grateful to him, aren't we? He saved our Eriprando. There, you see? I said "our Eriprando". It's the same thing, isn't it?'

'Oh, yes! Our Carlo and our Eriprando. Oh God! It's already

six-thirty; I have to run. We'll expect you for dinner. Argentovivo made something you really love, but I can't tell you what it is. She asked me please not to tell you. You'll see; it'll be a surprise!'

The door closed just in time behind that lace skirt of luminous ivory, like her neck and arms. No, it wasn't a skirt. A shawl, perhaps? Where did Beatrice find those laces and silks? The door closed just in time, for already the bitter saliva she'd been holding in the back of her throat flowed over her tongue, her teeth: *'Argentovivo made something you really love.'* She ran to the porcelain washbasin dotted with tiny flowers. There, too: gleaming, shimmering ivory. The surprise must be custard, a custard pudding. With that custard wavering before her eyes, she threw up. It was a confirmation of the sweet languor that for weeks had been keeping her in bed, and that had suddenly become as gentle and welcoming as a lover's warm embrace. Or that held her for hours and hours on the chair by the open window, staring at the trees, the sky, the distant sea. Without looking at the ivory she cleaned her teeth, her tongue, and with some misgiving looked at herself in the mirror: two wide eyes stared back at her, dazed, yet serene. Her cheeks had thinned, but her breasts and hips were already pressing against her skirt, her blouse. Abandoning her image there in the mirror, she escaped to stare at the sea. She should get to work. Behind her, on the desk, piles and piles of documents awaited her. With an effort, she broke away from the window and sat down, contemplating the inkwell, the pen, the stamped paper.* Revolted by the acrid smell of the ink, she closed the bottle and rested her head on her arms. The warmth of her arms was pleasant, sweet and cool at the same time; her feverish brow found solace in that coolness . . . It was nice to let one's imagination wander between the heat of the sand and the cool shade of the woods.

'May I come in, Princess?'

How much time had passed? Hours probably, and Beatrice was behind the door calling her. No, Beatrice didn't call her 'Princess' and that was a male voice. Carlo?

'Come in.'

Pietro, standing there with cap in hand, stared down at her with his round, expressionless eyes, his marble-smooth skull bowed in respect.

What fear that man had once roused in her and Beatrice! Whereas now, if she weren't the 'Princess' she had to be, she would have run and thrown her arms around him. Another sign of the condition in which she found herself again: wanting only to be embraced, protected, cradled by the strong arms of that good man who was as gentle as a child. His eyes weren't really expressionless; they were just too docile for that massive physique, and the contrast was frightening. What did that man do without a woman, totally devoted as he was to his dear prince? He probably masturbated, and visited whores in the afternoon like Tuzzu used to say his father did: '*What was he supposed to do, as a widower, bring home a stepmother to drive us all crazy?*'

'*Vossignoria* will forgive me for disturbing her. I swear to God I wouldn't have done so, Princess, if it weren't a matter of great urgency.'

'Of course. Don't be silly, Pietro, you're not disturbing me. What is this urgent matter?'

'It's that . . . I don't know where to start. It's a matter without rhyme or reason, but it's complicated. I swear to God, Princess, very complicated.'

'Begin wherever you like, Pietro. It's up to you. You know we two understand each other.'

'So kind of you, Princess, but I'm afraid that you might take it amiss.'

'Does it concern the Prince?'

'No. It concerns Signorina Inès.'

'Signorina Inès? What about Signorina Inès, Pietro? I see you're upset. Don't you get along with each other?'

'No, it's not that. She's polite, agreeable and devoted to the Prince but . . .'

'Pietro, with me you can speak frankly, you know that. Are you perhaps in love with Signorina Inès?'

'Me, fall in love with such an educated, proper young lady? *Vossignoria* will forgive me, Princess, but you are mistaken to think that. Pietro is sensible, and knows his place, what he can have and what he cannot have.'

'Then what is it? I can see that you're worked up.'

'Perhaps the Princess hasn't looked at the expense accounts in recent months and in particular at the expenditures for my dear Prince's "amusement". And I can understand it, because you've been worried about *Principessina* Beatrice and the curse that . . .'

'Affliction, you must say, Pietro, not a curse, an affliction.'

'You're right, and the affliction that has struck the young Prince.'

'That *struck* him, Pietro. You've seen yourself that everything is back to normal now.'

'Of course, of course, a miracle, Princess, a miracle that you . . .'

'All right, Pietro, I understand. What's in the accounts? Was too much spent for the Prince's "amusement"?'

'Oh, no, Princess, on the contrary. For months and months he's no longer wanted those women. Well, I should have realized right away! But who would have thought that such a respectable, level-headed young woman like Signorina Inès . . .'

'Don't tell me! The Prince has fallen in love?'

'Seeing you smile instead of getting angry takes a weight off my shoulders, Princess. A saint is what you are! Now I feel I have the courage to continue'.

'So continue, Pietro, go on. Don't be so embarrassed.'

'The fact is that I discovered that Signorina Inès – who would have thought it! – gave . . . how can I say certain words before a woman? Well, she allowed the Prince liberties. There! I said it and now it's up to *Voscenza* to make the decision to send Signorina Inès back to Turin.'

'Why would I do that, Pietro? How is the Prince doing?'

'Oh, he's really happy about it, happy as a three-year-old child!'

'So then why should we send Signorina Inès back to Turin?'

'That's what the Princess, God rest her soul, would have done.'

'Pietro, you and I care about the Prince, don't we?'

'Oh, so help me God, very much!'

'Well then, if he's happy this way, isn't Signorina Inès better than those other women? Not to mention, how can we be certain that sooner or later he wouldn't catch some awful disease? Don't blush like that, Pietro.'

'I hadn't thought about that. *Vossignoria* is truly as firm and tolerant as a man! Like the Princess Gaia, *buonanima*, may God rest her soul!

And seeing that for *Voscenza* things are fine the way they are, I can tell you that for me it's a relief, a real relief to see my dear Prince so content.'

'Good Pietro. As long as you're content and Ippolito is content, I'm at peace. What more can you ask for? Now go.'

'Of course, of course. I've already taken too much time from *Voscenza*'s work. *Bacio le mani*, my respects, and may God bless you, Princess.'

'God bless you too, Pietro . . . Oh, listen! Tell Signorina Inès about our conversation and tell her that I must speak to her right away.'

I don't have to tell you that I sent Pietro away just in time. A fit of uncontrollable laughter shook me so that I had to throw myself on the bed and stifle it with a pillow. Gradually, the laughter turned into a deep exhaustion. *'I hadn't laughed so hard since I was six or seven years old, Princess . . . Laughing is good for you. It's tiring, but it's a good, pleasant fatigue, like after a good swim.'*

*

It must have been late, because the window panes were slowly darkening. Had she fallen asleep? Argentovivo had in fact come to wake her, knocking lightly at the door. Since she had become a princess, not by virtue of lineage but by the force of nature, as Mimmo used to say, Argentovivo no longer burst into the room, but knocked quietly, and she never spoke unless she was given permission.

Avanti, come in, *entrez* . . . She was already laughing again. *'There, that's how I like to see you, princess, laughing! Even in a bad situation, one must enjoy a good laugh.'* That's right, Mimmo, you taught me to laugh and no one will take that away from me.

Mimmo's calm, serious face gently draws away from my eyelashes and backs off toward the window. Talking with his *principessina* does him good, and he finds it hard to leave even if it is almost night. At the window, the light still lingered uncertainly, bemused by the languid season already waiting around the corner. Soon the sunsets would lengthen, exhausting the expectant sea with their caresses. The sea awaited her, as usual. Would she still be able to swim after the long winter? *'Quannu s'è*

*imparato un mestiere, principessina mia, non lu si scorda cchiù. Once you learn
to do something, you never forget it. Listen to Mimmo, who can do many things,
build tables, mend socks. . . It's the same for you. Now that you've learned to
swim, no one can take this skill away from you. Carlo says so.'*

'Oh, forgive me, Princess, were you sleeping? I'll let you rest! Forgive me, but Pietro told me that you wanted to speak with me right
away. I . . . well! I'll come back another time. When would you like me
to come back, Princess?'

Signorina Inès, frozen in front of the window, spoke of leaving, but
she didn't budge. Rigid, her silhouette stood out against the last glimmer in the sky.

'Forgive me, Inès, but I'm very tired.'

'Of course, Princess, I'll go now. I apologize again.'

That silhouette, outlined on the window panes, was swelling at the
waist, at the hips. *'You're not playing tricks on me, are you, Mody? You
must lose weight. Your peasant origins show when you're puffy like that. Eat
less, girl, if it's a matter of eating too much!'*

'No, wait, Inès. Now that you've woken me . . . There's never a
moment's peace in this house!'

'But Pietro—'

'Turn on the light, girl. I have a thing or two to tell you, and I'd better do so right away, given the situation.'

In the glow of the electric light, I was finally able to observe her,
though she kept her head lowered and I couldn't see her eyes.

'Come now, there's no use standing there stiff and contrite like a
demure goody-goody. Come over here and sit in that chair. On second
thought: go over there and get me some water. I'm dying of thirst.'

I sat up in bed, leaning against the headboard the way Gaia used to
do. A grand old woman she was! She sat paralysed in bed as if on a
throne. With her eyes, I followed the girl's movements. It was true,
the heavier waist and hips had swept away her elegant, ladylike movements and revealed her peasant origins. I was overcome by a sympathy for the girl that I didn't know I had, and I would have burst out
laughing . . . when I met her bewildered, wide eyes, full of unshed
tears. The tears made her look ugly. No, those weren't the eyes I had
once had. I had to be careful.

'So, my girl, it appears that things between you and the Prince have gone beyond "falling in love", as Pietro ingenuously told me.'

I hadn't finished speaking when she fell to her knees in front of me (she certainly wasn't me!), crying so hard – tears gushing all over the place – and uttering words so disjointed that I leapt out of bed, fearing she meant to throw herself at me. Not touching her – I felt sorry for her but I couldn't afford to lose my authority – I tried to get to my desk, saying:

'Come, come now, girl, don't be so disconsolate! Compose yourself! Have a glass of water yourself, then sit down here so we can talk calmly. That's it, good girl!'

With the desk between us – a shield that kept me from taking her in my arms and comforting her – I strove to attain an inner compromise between Modesta and Gaia so that those trembling lips and hands, not to mention the quivering curls, might stop shaking. I was still striving for that compromise when Signorina Inès, probably terrified by my silence, began crying and talking again, squirming and fidgeting like an amateur actress. I couldn't understand what she was saying. She kept wiping her eyes with a lacy white handkerchief, which she then balled up in her hands or shoved into the neckline of her dress . . . There, she pulled it out again and, rolling her eyes, pressed it to her swollen, heart-shaped lips. It was a horrifying performance! Slumped in my chair, stunned, I merely waited for the dramatic scene to be over, just as I did at the theatre. Diderot's actor!* It was true, and not only on the stage. It was true there in that room as well. That bad actress was letting her emotion overtake her and losing her detachment, making that passion of hers unpleasant to watch and to listen to. Like at the theatre, I decided to wait patiently and try to understand the script at least, ignoring the performance.

'I . . . I was going to come and confess! Today, this very day! Even if Pietro hadn't come . . . I'm not blaming him. He's only doing his duty, but I, I . . . was about to come today, tomorrow! What I've done to you, to your family, is horrible, horrible! I would have . . . I was going to come and confess everything and then disappear, go away.'

I began to understand: the script was awful as well.

'Go where, girl?'

'I don't know! Anywhere I could, to hide my shame, my sin.'

'Let's try to talk it over, Signorina Inès. Calm down, I believe you. You would have come, you're sorry, but please compose yourself, all right?'

Again the handkerchief disappeared into the neckline of her dress. Her hands, tightly gripped, were still nervous, but at least she was no longer crying, and she looked at me almost serenely.

'Thank you, Princess. You're very kind, I knew that, but I won't take advantage of your generosity and magnanimity. I don't deserve it. Tomorrow morning I will disappear!'

The idea of disappearing was an obsession, but I had to be careful, because if she disappeared, who would take my prince Ippolito?

'Inès, we've known each other a long time now. I think highly of you. Why go on tormenting yourself this way? Let he who has not sinned cast the first stone, as they say. I'm not the one who must forgive you. God will forgive you! It's not up to me to judge.'

The effect of those words was immediate in her and in me: she smiled humbly, almost radiantly, and I lost all sympathy for that bleating little curly head.

'Ooh! Ooh! Princess, what a weight you've lifted from my conscience. Ooh! Ooh!'

I had been relieving other people's minds all afternoon. I couldn't take it anymore!

'Of course, this does not lessen my guilt and I will pray to God endlessly for the forgiveness that you, in your goodness, have granted me.'

'Fine, Inès, that's good. Pray! Don't do anything else, don't get upset, don't cry, don't disappear, but pray! That's all that counts!'

'Then I can stay here?'

'That's what I've been trying to tell you for the past hour, Inès.'

'Oh, Princess, thank you, thank you!'

I gripped the desk firmly to make sure it was there to protect me from the effusion of gratitude that she heaped on me.

'All right, girl! Unfortunately now we must speak about your condition. There's no time to lose. How many months along are you?'

'Three, I think, Princess. Oh God! I'm so ashamed, so ashamed!'

'Enough Inès, don't start in again. It's nothing terrible. With a good doctor it's child's play.'

'A good doctor, Princess? Oh, no, you are too kind! A doctor is a luxury when you give birth, a midwife is good enough. At home the women . . .'

'What were you thinking, Inès?' Both Modesta and Gaia were losing patience. 'You want to keep the child of . . .'

'Yes, Princess, I know! It's a child of sin, a bastard, I know!'

'Never mind sin, Inès, come to your senses! It's the child of a mongoloid, for heaven's sake! You're a nurse; you know what that means, don't you?'

'Of course, Princess, but it's also a living creature throbbing inside me. And if God wants to punish me by making him be born like his father, it will be a sign that I have to atone, not only through prayer but also by having to look at him. This child will be my cross to bear, like our Redeemer did.'

'*We must atone, Modesta. Pray.*' I hadn't heard Mother Leonora's voice for years. As the words slipped slowly out of those swollen heart-shaped lips, like the worn beads of a rosary gliding through damp, incense-scented fingers, an acrid, sour fluid made me clamp my mouth shut so I wouldn't throw up on the desk. I lowered my head. The ink bottle was closed, the pens lined up, the letters and stamped paper waiting. I had to work; at least for an hour, I had to work. Firmly swallowing the saliva and the cloying rosary, I leapt to my feet.

'That's enough! First tears and apologies, then the most extraordinary arrogance. Stop right there! You can't expect me to let you carry a child fathered by my husband, the Prince? I didn't mean a doctor for the birth, I meant . . .'

I wasn't able to finish the sentence because she, jumping to her feet with unexpected agility, began flitting around the room like a bat blinded by the light. The dramatic plot twist wasn't bad. It managed to silence me and Gaia mainly because agitated and flying around like that, she was quite graceful and spirited. I leaned my elbows on the desk, chin in my hands, and watched her. I was actually curious to see how many times she would whirl around the room blabbering words and exclamations such as 'Ooh God! A sin! Ooh! Killing a soul! Ooh, I'd rather kill myself . . . jump in the sea! I'll throw myself into the sea rather than . . .'

That whirling pirouette preceded by the fluttering white handkerchief mesmerized me like an equestrienne's sequinned dress at the circus. As she poured it all out, I thought: shall I stop her? Give her a couple of slaps and send her back to where she came from? And Ippolito? What will I do about Ippolito? In fact, all in all she's delightful and, in her own way, she's fighting for her passionate will to exist just as I had done at one time. She wasn't the coward I had thought. In her own way, dear Gaia, she knows she is essential to the running of this household and she has managed to silence us: checkmate! Plus, it takes a good deal of courage to make love with the 'thing'! I wonder if I would have had the same courage back then!

One last cry and plop! I saw her topple over on the carpet. I knew she would faint; sooner or later it had to happen; it was customary. She hadn't fallen too gracefully, but this allowed me to observe the shape of her legs – perfect – and her lovely, plump arms, whose slender wrists boasted skin as transparent as a child's. On one of these wrists she wore a tiny, quite exquisite watch. I tried to lift her up, but she was too heavy. I didn't know what to do. I had never found myself holding a '*signorina*' who had fainted. '*If you should feel ill, signorina, look: just raise the armrest and you'll find the salts.*' Should I get the smelling salts? I didn't have any. Maybe some cold water. Her shoulders and arms, which from a distance seemed like marble, in my own had an appealing softness. The Prince, my husband, had good taste! I had doubted – like you, for that matter – that the child was the 'thing''s and I had intended to verify it. But that pale little face, slumped against my arm, gave me the feeling that while this Inès indeed had a passionate will to survive, she did not have the courage to lie. I tried rousing her gently, but there was nothing for it. That soft, talcum-scented flesh attracted me, and had it not been for the authority I had to maintain with her and with the others, I would have pressed her to my breast and kissed every inch of her. Careful, Modesta! Helpless young ladies have always been a danger . . . I was about to lay her back down on the carpet again and summon Argentovivo, when that sweet little marzipan-lamb abruptly straightened up and, clinging to my neck, stared at me with confused, shining eyes.

'No, no, Princess, don't send me away! I was going to come and confess! I was going to come, I swear it!'

'Of course, Inès, I'm sure you were. But now you must get up. You're heavy, child . . . Up!'

'But where am I? What happened? Oh God! Lying here in front of you with my legs all exposed!'

Indeed, the plump, firm legs also boasted slim, graceful ankles.

'It's nothing Inès, a momentary blackout. You were very upset.'

'Upset, Princess? It was fear, Princess, fear and shame!'

'All right, Inès. It was fear; whatever you say. But it's over now. Compose yourself, go and lie down on your bed and . . .'

'How kind you are, Princess!'

'And think carefully about what you wish to do, because afterwards I don't want any whining and tears, do you understand? If you want to keep this creature that's throbbing inside you . . .'

'Oh, yes! Princess, I do!'

'But think it over carefully, because it's the child of an idiot.'

'The Prince is not truly an idiot, Princess; he's kind and he understands a lot of things.'

Now she was offended: that pretty little chin turned up, with a stern, distant air. Simply criticizing the object of her love offended her.

'Besides, Eriprando is healthy and intelligent.'

There, she'd silenced me again. Inside me, Gaia was snarling, so that I heard myself say, 'All right, Inès. But we have to come to terms. With you women one never knows: *patti chiari e inimicizia eterna*, clear understandings breed eternal animosity!'

'Did you say animosity, Princess?'

'I meant friendship, Inès . . . So then, do you recall that Dr Civardi – now that Eriprando is beginning to take notice of the outside world – advised sending the Prince, his father, away, and concocting a white lie about his condition, since the Prince's constant presence could upset the child's peace of mind?'

'Yes, I remember.'

'Fine. Then the agreement between you and me is this: if this creature is born healthy . . .'

'With God's forgiveness!'

'Of course, of course . . . If the baby is born healthy, you will give it to me, for its own good as well. A little brother or sister can only be good for Eriprando. If it's born like the Prince, we'll put it in some institution for retarded children or . . .'

'What are you saying, Princess! I will never refuse the cross that God may give me to bear for my sin.'

'We'll see, Inès. Let's not put the cart before the horse, as they say. We'll see! Think it over tomorrow. And keep in mind that, child or no child, in a month you are going to live in the little house I showed you, which has finally become vacant.'

'But it's so far away!'

'Far from here, but closer to Catania, Inès . . . Why don't you go and see a film sometime, for heaven's sake! Or buy yourself something nice, a book, whatever . . .'

'A woman doesn't go out alone!'

'But there's Argentovivo, another one who is walled up alive.* You can go out together.'

'But two women, Princess, is the same thing, if not worse.'

'Oh, enough! Do as you please! Pietro will of course go with you and the Prince, but he will go back and forth since I may need him here more than the Prince does. The Prince is at peace, isn't he?'

'Oh, he's a little angel! He no longer gives us any trouble.'

'Fine then, if you don't let your manias and dejection get the better of you as you've done this past hour . . . It's been an hour, if not more! What was I saying? Oh, yes! I'll talk to Attorney Santangelo about what we can afford. So that even if the Prince should die . . .'

'Oh, God forbid!'

'God forbid, all right! Stop it! I'm speaking for your own good, for heaven's sake! And fix your neckline: your whole breast is showing. So then, whatever happens, happens: I, too, could die tomorrow . . . Hush! I'll leave you a small annuity and the little house. Do you understand?'

'Oh, Princess, how kind and generous you are.'

'Hush now! That's enough! Off with you! I've lost enough time with you as it is. They're waiting for me downstairs and I still have to get dressed. No, stop. There's no need to kiss my hand. Think it over, and give me your answer tomorrow.'

49

As she went contritely out the door, I could still feel the heat of those swollen lips on my hand. My husband had good taste, but I had my authority to maintain. The warm feeling that suffused me from head to toe when the door closed behind her made the nausea and vomiting disappear. The last time too, when I was pregnant with Eriprando, I felt attracted only to women. Could it be a kind of defence on the part of an organism weary of male humours and more in need of tenderness than a penetration that might disturb the formation of that little creature carried within it? In any case, that sweet warmth felt good. It would have been nice to stay there and recall that warmth, but I had to go down to dinner . . . I had to do it to keep Beatrice happy. I had had enough of womanish whining for one afternoon.

'Help, Modesta, help!'

'What is it, Beatrice? Dear God, what's wrong? Has something terrible happened?'

'Oh, no, I wish! I wish that were it!'

'Then what is it, Beatrice? You're white as a sheet. You're scaring me to death. Say something! instead of bleating like a lamb.'

'Carlo, Carlo! . . .'

'Well?'

'He kissed me, Modesta! Oh! help me, hold me tight. He kissed me on the mouth, just like you do.'

Impetuous Cavallina had not only opened the door without knock-ing, she who was always so discreet, but she had also turned on all the lights. Her usual pallor had turned all red, like when she had a fever. And though I held her arms firmly – I didn't want her to embrace me – she managed to take hold of my head and assail me with countless small kisses. In no time, she has her arms around me and kisses my forehead, my mouth, my neck, as tears fall between us. From above, not letting go of my head – how is it that she's so tall, taller than me? – she murmurs:

'At first I was so surprised that I let him kiss me. Who would have imagined it from a young man as decent as Carlo? Would you have imag-ined it? But then right away, Modesta, believe me, I immediately sent him away, and I never want to see him again! Who could have imagined it? He kissed me just the way you do. Nonna was right, men are all the same!'

Argentovivo, wide-eyed with curiosity, was staring at us from the doorway, not daring to enter or close the door. She, too, was white as a sheet. *'So sensitive those females are, they blanch and blush at will and meanwhile, with their tears and fainting, they manipulate you like a pup-pet.'* True, dear Mimmo, they're taught to do that, as our dear com-rade Bebel says.* You have to have patience.

'What is it, Argentovivo? Have you perhaps seen a ghost? What's wrong? Speak up!'

'Nothing, Princess, nothing. It's just that the doctor went off in a rush.'

'He probably had something he had to do.'

'Oh, yes, of course. Such a proper gentleman, but the soufflé . . .'

'To hell with the soufflé! Eat it yourselves in the kitchen. Now go!'

'But what about dinner?'

'Shut the door and go away! Don't you see that Beatrice doesn't feel well?'

'But . . .'

'No buts! We won't dine this evening. It won't kill anyone! We're all fully grown and well nourished, Argentovivo. Would you shut the damned door and leave us in peace?'

'Of course, Princess, of course. Forgive me.'

Look at her: another silly woman! All offended over her sagging soufflé. 'I told you to leave us, or I'll throw you out of the house!'

There! Finally, she smiles meekly and disappears behind the closed door. While my stomach of its own volition turns upside down, sniggering like an old drunk. No, it wasn't my stomach. Cavallina, hugging me even tighter, was shaking with laughter, her face buried in my neck. Unpredictable Cavallina, who now seemed small again in my arms. How did she manage to look tall, then tiny at will? She was laughing so hard she seemed to be suffocating.

'Now what's so funny, hmm?'

'I'm laughing because I was thinking about Argentovivo's face when you were yelling. She looks so funny when she's frightened. Her face gets round as an egg, and her mouth turns down. Oh God, she's so funny! She looks like one of the faces that Eriprando is always drawing everywhere. At first I, too, was afraid of you, but then I realized that you're just like Nonna Gaia, all bark and no . . . But you're right to do that. You make them respect you; I don't. And if it weren't for you, that woman would even take the keys from my belt, and that would be that! She'd be all over the house, lording it over everyone even more than she does now.'

In fact, Cavallina kept the keys to the drawers and chests on a large gold ring that she wore at her waist, along with gold, silver and ivory trinkets to ward off the evil eye. There was a coral horn, a turbaned Moor's head and a little ivory hand . . . or, no, the hand wasn't ivory, it was silver. Just as her aunt, great-aunt and grandmother had done in earlier times. Her slender chest surged with pride when she wore that ring on her belt. The keys were the medals and decorations of an obscure war, the sign of her power over us all.

'You're heavy, Cavallina!'

'Oh, how lovely, you called me Cavallina. How delightful; say it again. It's been so long since you've called me that!'

How could she like the nickname that sounded to me like a curse?

'Oh, Modesta, say it again, come on! It's so sweet when you say it!'

'All right, Cavallina, it's just that you're heavy, pressing on my chest like that, and I'm tired. Don't tell me this little Cavallina has got it into her impetuous, obstinate little head to make me stand in the middle of the room all night!'

'Will you let me sleep with you, Modesta? Oh, let me sleep with you. You haven't wanted to for months. Tonight I'm so afraid, please!'

'Afraid of what, Cavallina?'

'Oh! Afraid of thinking about how Carlo disappointed me this evening.'

'Disappointed you? How?'

'I thought he was a sober young man! I can't forget how brazen he was to kiss me. It was terrible, and I'm afraid! Let me sleep with you!'

'All right. Get undressed and let's get to bed. I really can't stay on my feet any longer!'

She undressed swiftly. She reappeared wearing one of my nightgowns and cautiously slipped under the covers.

'Can I hug you?'

Her head in the hollow between my neck and shoulder, her wispy hair brushing my chin, her hand resting on my breast . . . '*E si Beatrice nun voli durmiri coppa nno' culu sa quantu n'ha aviri . . .*' No, I mustn't sing that lullaby. Her hand lay quietly on my breast, and not a tremor came from that cool palm. She wasn't thirsty, and I was no longer her *tata*, but her sister. That was the way it should be. And as a sister, I had to talk to her.

'Listen, Cavallina, about Carlo's kiss, really . . .' She didn't answer. I looked at her in the lamp light: she was sleeping serenely, like Eriprando used to do after his six o'clock feeding. I turned off the light. This was how it should be.

*

A sharp cry of light vaulted across the ceiling. The sun was born, and in its radiance the bathroom tiles and brass fixtures gleamed with joy. But that sun lied and contrasted with the languor that spread from my belly up through my chest, arms and cheeks. I had to hurry. Soon that languor, with its mad will to live, would reach my head, and it would be useless to oppose it. I took a hot bath and got dressed to go out. I went back to the darkness that still lingered drowsily around Beatrice's slender body as she lay curled up. She hadn't moved, or just enough to hug the pillow. Was she sleeping?

'No, Modesta. Oh, you're already dressed? Come here beside me. It's early. I'm so tired!'

'It's morning, Beatrice, and we were already in bed by nine.'

'I'm hungry!'

'I can believe it. Ring the bell; a nice breakfast will do us good.'

'Oh, I can't reach it; you do it, Modesta. I'm so tired!'

This was not the time to argue or make her obey. I was in a hurry. I had to go look for that doctor whom Gaia had once recommended to me, or else a different one.

'Good morning, Princess. Oh, you've already opened the drapes! I'm sorry. If you had waited a moment I would have done it. I'm so sorry . . .'

'Of course, Argentovivo, of course! Everything is fine, don't worry. Leave the tray and go back downstairs. I said go. I'm in a hurry! Never mind the clothes. You can put them away later. I told you, I'm in a hurry, now go!'

'As you wish, Princess.'

In the sun's rays Beatrice's hair shines with a hundred colours. She won't raise her eyes.

'There's too much light, Modesta; it hurts my eyes. Oh, please, pull the drapes closed like they were before. Why did you have to open them like that? Why?'

I drew the curtains. I had to be careful. As I had foreseen, her voice had become garrulous and droning, a sign that listlessness and despondency were taking hold of her. Soon she would start wandering aimlessly through the rooms again, like the time after Carlo had gone. I wouldn't be able to stand it a second time, seeing that little face grow so thin overnight – how was it possible? – as if she had been fasting for days and days.

'Come, Beatrice; look at this wonderful breakfast! There's even orange marmalade with bits of rind in it, the way you like it . . . No, not for me. All I want is coffee.'

'Why only coffee? You're making me eat alone. At least have some bread and butter. It makes me sad to eat alone, *uffa!*'

'Oh, all right. Look at the big slice I'm buttering, okay?'

I couldn't take it. Another ten minutes and I would throw her out the window.

'Modesta, I've thought about it, you know?'

'Thought about what?'

'Well . . . about Carlo. Of course what he did last night is unacceptable . . . behavior unacceptable in a gentleman, but . . . I . . . I must be honest with you, Modesta: I love him.'

I couldn't believe what I was hearing. Was it possible that everything was resolved so quickly?

'I love him very much. And although I know that Nonna Gaia would never, ever forgive me if I left you . . . you who have sacrificed so much for us – plus I'm lame and . . .'

I had never heard her talk so much about something that concerned her personally. As she spoke, her features became animated and she seemed pretty again. Of course, if that creature growing in my belly was a girl, she would be pretty, too. A little girl, slender and elegant like Carlo . . . I looked away from those large, ever more luminous eyes, which drew me like the depths of the sea, and staring into the distant depths of my future, I read that my languor would be a boy born of Beatrice and Carlo. No, I did not want that child. I admired Carlo, but a baby by him was another matter.

'Won't you say something, Modesta? Do you think that this, too, would be impossible?'

'Forgive me, Beatrice, I was distracted. Yesterday I didn't get anything done all day, and today I have twice as much work to do. I'm sorry – what were you saying?'

'Yes, of course, I know you have a lot on your mind. I'm the one who should be sorry. I was saying that we could, or rather that you could talk to Carlo and let him know how things stand, and we could remain friends. Or do you think what he did was too serious?'

'No, of course not. It's nothing serious. Times change, Beatrice, and if he kissed you . . .'

'Oh, don't say that word!'

'All right. But if he did what he did, I'm sure it was because he loves you and not because he's a despicable, immoral man, as Nonna Gaia would say. I'm certain of it. Carlo is an honourable man, Beatrice. He's a doctor, intelligent, a hard worker, and if he wanted you to be his . . .'

'Oh, no, Modesta, no!'

'Why not, if you love him?'

'You know why not! Because I can't! Besides, he's not of the nobility. What would they say in Catania . . .'

'So let's shock them yet again, as Uncle Jacopo always tells us. In fact, it will be amusing to see them scandalized, like when we run into them at the Opera. Remember the comical, bewildered expressions on their faces? They don't know whether to look at us, whether they should greet us. Remember how we laughed, those first times with Carlo?'

'Oh, yes, it's true. Then they got used to it. So you'll talk to Carlo, won't you? Talk to him . . . but just friendship, you must insist on that – just friends. Make him come back, Modesta.'

'Of course, Beatrice. I'll speak to Carlo. Though I'm sure, as Uncle Jacopo once said – do you remember?'

'No, what did he say?'

'He said: "Even our Beatrice will find a man who is worthy of her."'

'Oh, that's right! He said it at Carmelo, but I was so little then! I had forgotten, it's been so long. You have such a good memory. What did he say exactly? Tell me, Modesta, tell me . . .'

★

'Listen, Inès. We've been talking about this for two hours and I'm very tired. Time is running short, and if, as the doctor said . . . at least you could have kept count of the months, couldn't you? Your mothers really don't teach you anything!'

'I'm an orphan, Princess.'

'All right, all right. If, as the doctor says, you're approaching the fifth month, it can be risky to terminate the pregnancy. You must make up your mind. It's ten o'clock, and at noon I have a business meeting down in Catania. I have a dinner engagement as well, and I don't know if we'll be able to see each other tomorrow, because if the dinner runs late I'll stay over and spend the night at Attorney Santangelo's.'

'Oh, Princess, I don't know what to do! I'm afraid, I'm so afraid! In the convent I heard terrible things both about giving birth and about having an abortion, and I can't make up my mind.'

'Women's prattle, Inès. Be rational. Times have changed. With a good doctor and effective anaesthesia, abortion is child's play. As far as childbirth, all women give birth. I, too, gave birth, didn't I? And here I am, alive and well, aren't I?'

'Oh, of course, Princess.'

'I repeat that you will be appropriately assisted, whether or not you decide to have this child. But remember that if you don't have it, you'll be committing a sin.'

'I've already sinned!'

Incredible, those godly little souls! They tossed the word 'sin' around and caught it like jugglers at the circus with their buoyant white balls. If the doctor weren't waiting for me, it would have been fun to watch those little balls in continuous motion. Sins that bounced from her delicate hands to her head, chest and arms and then returned obediently to the small open palms of Signorina Inès: an orphan, born in Acireale, who somehow ended up in a convent boarding school in Turin.

'And you'd like to add a mortal sin to another mortal sin? What's more, I think that, weighing one fear against the other, fear of childbirth is better. Be reasonable, hold on to this pure, spotless fear and follow God's will. Keep in mind that abortion is something monstrous for both body and soul.'

Just look at what Signorina Inès had me saying! On the other hand, I couldn't do otherwise. As Carlo had said, without knowing the number of months, the woman could die under the surgeon's knife.

'Oh, Princess, you are truly a true Christian! I, instead, I . . . even the Mother Superior used to tell me all the time: I'm not a good person. Even though I pray, I'm always praying, I'm unable to be . . .'

'Then trust me.'

'Of course, of course, like I trusted Mother Antonia, of course!'

'All right. Go then, and may God help you, child. No, no hand kissing, now go. I'm late.'

Despite the desk, which even in my sleep I now put between me and Signorina Inès, she was always trying to touch me. I stood up quickly so she wouldn't come close, and finally saw her move stiffly toward the door. Her hand was already on the doorknob, white and smooth as her skin, when she turned around uncertainly:

'And . . . about the annuity, Princess . . . it shames me, but I am an orphan and you promised . . .'

'It's all settled, Inès. It wasn't an empty promise. Tomorrow you will go to Catania with Pietro to see Attorney Santangelo. He will have you read and sign a document concerning the little house and the annuity and the paragraph of my will that concerns you, should complications arise in the future.'

'Oh, your will too. May you never . . .'

'May it never happen. Fine, Inès! Now, don't worry.'

That mournful face, which grew sombre as soon as she stopped smiling, chilled me. It had never happened to me before but once she was gone I found myself making superstitious gestures like horns and knocking on wood. All the more because a small, sterile room with pink gladioli and that shady Dr Modica were waiting for me.

50

After a lengthy silence, Beatrice formally accepted Carlo's marriage proposal, but on condition that everything take place in accordance with tradition. She was adamant about this.

'I can't see him right away. You be the ambassador. Tell him to put his mind at ease, since I have promised you, who are father, mother and older sister to me, that I will be his bride. I will see him in three days, as prescribed, in your presence and in the presence of a notary who will draw up the engagement agreement. Then, after this formal procedure, I must leave immediately.

'Following this observance, he may return every day for three months, but always in the afternoon, with the true light of day and not in darkness, which is a bad counsellor. And only for two hours in your presence or, if you're busy, that of someone you assign to represent you. During these three months, we must talk seriously about our future and get to know each other. Of course, three months is a short time. But given that there have been no recent deaths in the family, and since times have changed, as you rightly point out, and Carlo and I know each other a little, I agree to a three-month engagement.

'If it so happened that during these three months Carlo and I were to realize that we did not share enough views to face a future together – a bride and groom must become one single mind and one single heart – then the engagement must be dissolved without dishonour, either to him or to me, to our family or his.'

Opening the huge hope chest containing the trousseau, Beatrice and Argentovivo counted the sheets, pillowcases, blankets and bedspreads with the care one takes in handling glass. They placed them in large travelling bags for the day of Beatrice's departure from her home and family.

'See this blanket, Modesta? My *tata* and I crocheted it together. It was my first one; that's why I remember it. I was only seven or eight years old! See these stitches that are not quite as perfect as the others? See them? Those are mine . . .'

Beatrice spoke gravely with Carlo, never meeting his eyes as she used to do. She told him about herself, enumerating her faults and virtues. She asked him if he wanted to have children. Carlo, dazed, stared at her radiantly and agreed to everything, answering all her questions. If his gaze at times became too intense, Beatrice stood up with dignified authority and, offering him a tray without looking at him, said, 'Would you care for another pastry, Carlo?'

At the stroke of seven, no matter what they were speaking about, no matter what music they were listening to, Beatrice rose gracefully, said goodbye to Carlo, kissed me on the forehead and disappeared.

'I would like Argentovivo to stay here with you. You'll feel very lonely after I leave.'

'But Beatrice, Catania is only twenty minutes away by car.'

'Yes, I know, but I'm worried about you. I can't stand to think of you alone. Keep Argentovivo with you.'

'That will never work! She's too attached to you. All she does is cry over you. Besides, you know that with me she doesn't talk. Don't take offence, Beatrice, but I find Argentovivo a little annoying. I'll find a cook.'

'Really? If you assure me that it's all right with you, for me it will be a great comfort to have her there in that strange house.'

Carlo was not permitted to see the house that his wife was making ready for him, even though the layout of the rooms, the arrangement of the furniture and even the flower vases were described and submitted for his approval during the two-hour conversations in the parlour.

Absorbed in quiet action, Beatrice was withdrawing from me. In her solitary pursuit, she seemed young again. Her eyes grew wider and full of wonder. She cleansed herself of all past emotions so she could join her husband purified.

And never had I seen her so radiant and 'pure', as Carlo said, as on that morning in the sun's glow and in her white bridal veils. But I will stop in front of the church door, because all I remember is the great boredom I had to endure, that of all the marriages, baptisms and confirmations I've been forced to attend. And I return home just in time, because the tedium of the long ceremony had reawakened a latent hatred in my brain's chemistry that I had somehow managed to keep at bay during those months of formalities, tradition, rituals. Of course, Beatrice's beauty, serenity and happiness had compensated for it, but ten more minutes of incense and hugs and tears, and I would have hated her for the rest of our lives.

Once past the gate, the grounds seemed suddenly immense and solitary. As I entered the parlour, a tomb-like silence hung over the sofas and chairs, the piano. The gigantic Moor's head* on the piano was now merely a skull. I had to fill it with flowers, as Beatrice had always done, or throw out that lifeless vase. I looked for roses and vine shoots in the garden, but darkness had fallen, obscuring the colours, and all my fingers found were thorns. Not a sound came from the first or second floor. Maybe there was someone in the kitchen, but it was far away. I found myself crying, sucking the blood from my fingertip. A few tears, not really sad . . . a quirk of the emotions! I would have liked to run upstairs to Eriprando and have him hug me, make him laugh and play, but at that hour Eriprando was sleeping. In sleep he pulled away from me, independent.

Her fingertip was no longer bleeding. Modesta could finally take off the dress worn for the wedding ceremony and, in her robe, try to finish the little story about a fish and a seaweed that she had begun for Eriprando. But faced with her minute handwriting – why was her script so tiny? – she gave up and, lowering her head to her arms, listened to the silence that from the trees in the garden entered the parlour, ascended the stairs and now pressed its hushed palms against the door. She was afraid. A new, unfamiliar fear. In the *chiana*, the lava plain, she had feared her mother's rages, Tuzzu's indifference. In the convent, she had been afraid of being imprisoned there and later, in that other, silken convent, she had been afraid of Gaia, Argentovivo, of Beatrice herself. That's what it was: she had never been alone in an empty house, free to come and go as she pleased. That's what that fear was: she had almost mistaken it, thinking she missed Beatrice and even Argentovivo. No, she didn't miss them; she only missed a way of life that had been impressed on her emotions for so long, that couldn't be expected to change overnight. She had to accept that fear, and slowly get used to the solitude which now, she saw clearly, carried with it the word 'freedom'. To prove to herself that solitude was a treasure compared to the limitations of convention, she jumped out of bed and turned on all the lights in the room. She put on a skirt, a blouse, her shawl. And – something she could never have done for fear of upsetting Beatrice – she took the revolver with her and ran off from the house, the grounds, with Menelik happily sprinting in front of her, barking at the sea foam and at the palm trees – towers – castles – bisons awakened by the moon among sand dunes, which for miles and miles unfolded the night's sleepless dreams.

His joy exhausted, Menelik, panting, stared at the shroud the moon had cast over the sea. Or worn out by the joy of running, had he too, like me, been gripped by an eagerness to see the sun appear on the stage of the horizon, armed with shield and scimitar, to rout the pallid face that fomented grief and madness in its aimless orbit?

Behind me, muffled thuds along with Menelik's furious barking made me whirl around. I wasn't afraid. Menelik was a trusted dog, and more than once I had seen him bite someone mercilessly. Indeed, he flung himself toward the shadowy figure, but strangely enough, at the foot of that shadow he quieted down. The shadow was a horse, and when I looked up I saw the familiar white curls coming toward me, magnetized by the moon.

'Good boy, Menelik, you recognized me! Dogs, unlike people, have a good memory. See how the *Padroncina* is looking at me? What do you think? Should I greet her or not?'

'I recognized you, Carmine. What are you doing around here?'

'Ah, I've been roaming around here for three nights!'

'Why?'

'To see you.'

'Couldn't you knock at the door?'

'Carmine doesn't knock at the door. He waits for a sign from destiny.'

'And why did you want to see me?'

'I'm a condemned man, *figghia*. Here, my chest: angina. And in the time they've given me, three or four months, I got the urge to see you, assuming you still remember me.'

'I remember you, Carmine. But you're dead to me inside. I killed you.'

'I know. That's another reason why I came. My death belongs to you. I once had to wrong you, and wrong myself, but nothing ends, and Carmine has always cared for you. And now that I've seen you and spoken to you, I'll go back home satisfied, because your voice was gentle in your response. Goodbye, *Padroncina*, and may God bless you! Come, Orlando, old boy, it's time to go!'

The moon had sunk below the mountain and I could barely make out the white curls and broad back moving away behind the horse's huge shadow. It was dark, but dawn was already peeking through here and there among the low shadows of the dunes; a chill suddenly made my teeth chatter, and I shivered. Those powerful shoulders and that slow gait rose up from my past, magnified. 'A condemned man,' he had said. Not a sign of that fatal sentence, either in his calm smile there in the moonlight, or in the sure-footed trot that was already putting an unbridgeable distance between us.

'Come back! I want to see you, Carmine!'

Slowly the shadow came back toward me.

'Here I am. Look at me.'

'It's dark.'

'I can see you. Are you afraid? Is that why you're trembling like that?'

'I'm cold, Carmine.'

'It's the chill of dawn, *figghia*. Go back to the house.'

'It's a long way to the house. Like you once told me: going downhill is easy, but going back up . . .'

'You remember that?'

'I remember everything. You flushed me out of the fields like a hare.'

'Of course, you were running like a hare.'

'Take me home on Orlando, like you did that time.'

'At your command, *Padroncina*.'

'We've never been on the horse at night, Carmine.'

'No.'

'It's lovely at night. Too bad we didn't do it before.'

'There's still time to do it, for you at least.'

His arms clasped me tight and his chest seared my back; already beads of sweat were sliding down my neck and shoulders. He was silent and rode slowly. Why? I wanted to see him. I wanted to see him in the light.

'Why are you going so slowly?'

'Partly to be with you, partly because of poor Menelik. Don't you hear him hobbling along behind Orlando?'

'So leave him behind. He knows the way and I'm cold and sleepy.'

I saw him on the portico in the light of the large, moon-shaped lamp, a pale moon that was always lit, from sunset to sunrise.

'Here you are, home. I'll leave you.'

No, that light wasn't bright enough, and I wanted to see him, to look closely.

'What is there to see, *figghia*? It's not proper for you to receive a man at this hour of night.'

'In this house I'm the mistress. Come in.'

'Now that you've let me come in, can I have a little smoke?'

'Of course you can.'

'The Princess, God rest her soul, didn't allow it. She said everything stank afterwards.'

'I like the smell of tobacco.'

I watched him as he pulled out the little pouch and filled his pipe. Not a sign of that fatal sentence. I searched his features in vain, the creases of his skin. Not a blotch, not one wrinkle more ingrained, not a tremor in his hands. That iron-strong man, tamping the tobacco with his thumb as if time still had the same slow, cadenced measure it had had before he'd made an appointment with death, stood before me as though it were yesterday, and like yesterday, seeing him made me feel protected and fearful. He wouldn't speak again, or look up at me, until a small flame appeared between his meticulous, long fingers.

'One thing at a time, *figghia*. Running around left and right like that, you lose life's flavour: a good cup of coffee, tobacco, your saliva . . . Slowly, that's how I want to taste your mouth, slowly.'

Had he lied? No, Carmine was a man of honour. I had to get nearer, look at him up close, but clouds of smoke obscured his face. I had to at least touch that face of his.

'Do you want me, *figghia, ca mi tasti accussì*? Is that why you're touching me like that, as if you can't see me . . . Do you still want me? I would never have hoped! I desire you so much, but I don't want to misread your intention.'

Riveted by surprise – how could I have known if he hadn't told me? – I can't move or speak. He was dead to me. I killed him, and I want his hot, heavy body on me. I should throw him out, pound my fists on that face I put behind me, that is now back smiling. But I missed the moment, and already his arms are lifting me up, light as a feather, and the hatred dissolves, leaving only a sweet languor in my arms and in my mind.

'What are you doing, crying, *figghia*? Once, you would have got angry with me and scratched me. Did you suffer that much?'

'I didn't suffer, and I hate you!'

'And you're right to. But don't be ashamed. There's no shame in suffering when fate opposes us. I, too – and I was an old man – suffered at having to wrong you, leaving you warm and loving, the way you had grown up in my hands. But now, during the three nights that I was wandering around, I was sure there would be someone with you, and I didn't dare hope. That's another reason why I was prudent, and didn't knock on your door.'

'Cowardly. Not prudent, Carmine, cowardly! Go back to your sons! What do you mean, coming back whenever you please like this? You do your duty as a father only when it's convenient for you?'

'No, *figghia*. It's death that decides. Death has liberated me, and now that I'm free, I've come back to you.'

A tenderness I'd never felt before for that hefty body weighing so gently on mine makes my hands go to his mouth. To make him stop talking, because his voice, liberated by death, awakens a forgotten heat in my belly, and my nipples, now hard, are painful against the touch of his jacket.

'You want me, Modesta. I can feel it in your hands.'

His mouth speaks to me through my fingers. No use denying the rain or wind or sun. All you can do is accept the blaze of summer, the chill of winter. I don't answer, and with my hand, as he had done with me at one time when I didn't yet know, I guide his mouth to that swell of pleasure and pain that my breasts have become. Forgetful, my body is aroused and my thighs open beneath him, but an icy chill worms its way into the warm waves of pleasure and, against my will, makes my hand stop that blind throbbing member that gives life.

'What's wrong, *figghia*, why are you stopping me like that? Has your anger frozen you so much that you can't forgive?'

A tenderness I'd never felt before for that big body lying naked, disappointed, on my belly and tightly locked thighs almost makes me let go of his penis. But my hand will not obey me, and I'm left crushed between his sex and mine, frozen.

'What's wrong, Modesta? What is it? You can tell Carmine. If you've suffered so much that you can't forgive, Carmine can understand.'

'No, no. It's that I'm afraid, Carmine, afraid!'

'Afraid of what, *picciridda*? I don't understand.'

'There's youthful sap in the old tree, Carmine. I can feel it in my hands.'

'Ah, that's all it is! And you're right. Forgive me, *figghia*. I should have thought of it, but I wanted you so much and I was only thinking about my own pleasure.'

Gently he lifts himself off of me and drops beside me.

'You're right. I don't want to complicate your life with another pregnancy, but don't leave me like this. I'm in pain. Feel how hard I am. Here, use your hands and your mouth: give me some relief. But when you feel that I'm about to come, move your mouth away. I don't want to make you gag.'

With his hand, watchful like back then, he guides my strokes. I had never kissed him like that, and a new wave of tenderness drives away the earlier chill. A fierce heat envelops my body again and makes my senses sway with his. And now that his cock is rising and falling between my tongue and palate, I can't let go and I come with him, sucking the unfamiliar semen which bursts from the depths of his being to quench the burning thirst in my mouth. A tangy, sweet taste: tree resin, or the curdled milk of men also born to suckle.

His sex, now small again, rests passively on the wiry, curly hair. I enjoy nudging it with my finger. Like back then, he puts up no resistance, and like then I burst out laughing, an odd trick of the emotions.

'What's so funny, *tosta carusa*, my impudent little girl?'

'It's just that it looks so comical, so puny and drained! Also, I hadn't noticed it before, Carmine, but how come the hair is dark down here? Not even a single white strand?'

'If you look closely, there must be a few.'

'No, Carmine, not even one! It looks like Eriprando's hair.'

'Ah, he has our colouring? I'm glad.'

'But how can it be, Carmine, that all the hair on your head is white and the hair here is dark?'

'What can I say? It must be that I'm half old and half young; what can I tell you?'

'And your armpits? Let me see, lift your arm.'

Slowly I travel over his body. Under his arms, too, the hair is all dark, but on his chest there is some white.

'What a hairy chest you have, Carmine! Thick and curly, whereas the hair on your arms is smooth and soft.'

Slowly I make my way back down that big body. I want to see the hair down there again. I want to see if it really is as dark as I'd thought it was before I travelled upward.

'You're prowling up and down me like a kitten, *figghia*! Your hair is tickling me. What are you looking for?'

After that long journey from head to toe, I let my head rest on the dark curls. I'm tired. I close my eyes and start toying with his cock again: satisfied, it almost fits in the palm of my hand.

'First it was sooo big, now it's teeny weeny. Why, Carmine?'

'Go ask the Saracen olive tree, which enjoyed doing odd things.* Carmine knows nothing about nature.'

'Not a one; the hairs are all dark here, Carmine. How old are you anyway, old man?'

'I'll be fifty-three, if I make it to the Day of the Dead.'

'You were born on 2 November?'

'Exactly, *figghia*. My mother used to say that that year the dead brought her Carmine as a gift.* Who knows why that beautiful woman laughed and liked to think that. I didn't like the idea at first, and for many years I told everyone, outside the family, that I had been born on the 3rd. Then, little by little, I didn't mind it anymore, and like my mother, I laughed at both the dead and the living, and at God and the devil!'

I had never heard him talk so much. His cock in my hands, I was lulled by his voice. I didn't want him to stop talking.

'What was your mother like, Carmine?'

'I told you: beautiful, tall and strong like a man. She didn't know how to read or write. And when one of us misbehaved, without waiting for my father, as women do, she beat the living daylights out of us. More than once she gave me a black eye. And I had to lie to my buddies and pretend I'd had a fistfight with my brothers. What else could I say? That a woman had made me look like a boxer after a match? Especially since I wanted to be a boxer.'

'What did you know about boxing?'

'An uncle who was a boxer in America, loaded with money and women, had taught me something about the noble art the last time he came to see us. I was obsessed with the idea, and I couldn't manage to apply myself to numbers and words. And every so often I would go to my father and ask his permission to go to America, to Uncle Antonio, and eventually become a boxer. You see, Uncle Antonio didn't have any children and he often asked my father to send me.'

'And your father?'

'Oh, he wouldn't answer. Instead he told me: "Go ask your mother for permission."'

'And your mother?'

'Without saying boo, she gave me a beating, and I respected her and we didn't talk about it again for months.'

'And then?'

'My obsession with boxing gloves would come over me again. I'd lose my interest in the fields, and I'd go to my father, and he'd send me to my mother and she made me get over it with her beatings.'

'So you were little then?'

'Well, fourteen or fifteen.'

'And you let her hit you?'

'I told you: I respected her. Besides, she washed for us, she cooked for us . . . she was always laughing and singing as she cooked. And I swear to God, after she died I never again ate *maccu** as good as hers!'

He falls quiet. In the silence, his peaceful breathing draws faint sand dunes in my mind's eye. Softly, under the moon's spiteful gaze, I place my ear on the spot he had shown me with a clenched fist: the place where that bald hag had laid her eggs. But the slow beating of his heart reveals nothing, not a cry, not a moan. The veil of silence becomes heavy, and I don't feel like sleeping.

'Carmine, why are you speaking now? Before, you never talked to me.'

'Why, does it bother you, *picciridda*? If I'm bothering you, I'll keep quiet.'

'No, not at all, I like hearing your voice. But how come?'

'How do I know, *picciridda*! Or maybe I do know. You see, *figghia*, since they told me down in Catania that I might have three or four months to live, memories, good and bad, have come back to me . . . the faces of loved ones who have been gone a long time, the beautiful places I've seen. How can I explain it to you? It's a kind of nostalgia for the good things and the many springtimes that fate and good fortune have granted me. Carmine has been a lucky man, and even in bad times he has lived fully. And so, hearing the word "end", I felt a strong desire to relive my life. Take tonight, for example: what old man around here or anywhere in the world could have had the good fortune of feeling a weight as beautiful as you on top of him?'

'And you're not afraid?'

'Afraid of what, *figghia*? My father died peacefully. He, too, had been granted a full life by fate. He amassed houses and lands for us and for my mother who passed away, at a ripe old age, just six years ago. Of course, as my father used to say, if you're born weak in mind and body, and let yourself be hoodwinked by all those notions the priests hand us, then *La Certa* must naturally be terrifying. To acquire what there was to acquire, my grandfather, my father and I had to gain respect with our fists and with our shotguns. I've had a close brush with *La Certa* many times. And how those shotguns or knives flourished in the night! But I'm here with you, and I don't care.'

'Then you don't believe in God?'

'What does God have to do with it?'

His voice, set free by death, the only sign of his fatal sentence, breathes through my hair and slams me against the reef of emotion. I cling to his neck so as not to drown, and seal his mouth with my own.

'Oh, no, kitten, if you do that I'll get the urge again, and then you'll stop me with your hand – I know how you women are. And even though your lips are honey, I want to enter you all the way to your heart.'

'So what will we do?'

'Leave it to Carmine, tomorrow he'll take care of it, but for now be good. Impulsive, that's what you are. *Tosta maredda*, impulsive and impudent!* You're dead tired, and I have to go.'

'But you'll be back?'

'Of course I'll be back. When the house is quiet, like tonight, I'll be back.'

51

Every night when the house grew quiet, Carmine returned. How was that old man able to cross the grounds, pass through the entrance hall and then, in that maze of corridors and stairs, find his way to my room?

'Carmine is used to the dark, and good at remembering doors and passages and spots where danger may lurk.'

'Is there danger in this house? Why did you come back?'

'Because I forgot my pipe here.'

'I won't give it to you. No use looking for it. I won't give it to you!'

'Why not? Let's hear it. Why won't you give it to me?'

'Because you know how to light it and I can't. I tried and I burned myself. The only thing that came out was a bitter liquid, not smoke like when you did it.'

'What do you mean? You're a woman! What are you doing with a pipe and tobacco?'

'I'll tell you what I mean! I won't give it to you unless you teach me how to light it.'

'Listen to that! A sweet thing with a pipe in her mouth!'

'Just once, Carmine, show me how you do it.'

'All right, all right. But just this one time! I know you, you're stubborn as a mule, and I can't get along without my pipe! According to those in the white coats, I shouldn't smoke anymore, or drink, or . . . never mind! For what? To gain two more miserable days to live?

Forget it! . . . Come on, I'll teach you. Look: I'll humour this whim of yours, *figghia*, but you're not going to start smoking like a *carusu*, are you?'

'Why not?'

'But why? Tell me, why? Well?'

'Because I'm also a *carusu!*'

'That's really a good one! You're also a boy?'

'That's right. Half *carusu* and half *maredda*.'

'And who told you that?'

'I foresaw it. I saw it in my future, that I could shoot and smoke and run like Carmine when he was young. I saw you, you know, when you were young, and then I saw myself, old like you are now, but even older, much older. You're going to die, but I'll live three times your life. My future told me so.'

'Good for you! If your future told you so, I won't say another word! Here, look: this is how you have to fill it. Tobacco is soft and you tamp it in slowly, very slowly . . . That's it, like that. I swear to God, you make me laugh with that pipe in your mouth! Now let's see. Apply the flame and draw on it . . . Careful, the smoke should only go in your mouth! Hey, you're not going to throw up on me, are you? Don't draw so hard! Look at her! Whatever possessed you to smoke? So now that you've lit it, do you mind giving it back to me?'

'Oh, no, I'm keeping it!'

'Look, *carusa*, you're driving me crazy! I swear to God, you remind me of my son! *Lazzarolu* and *cocciu di tacca*,* like Mattia.'

'What do *lazzarolu* and *cocciu di tacca* mean, Carmine?'

'Aha, so we studied so much that we forgot our own language, hmm?'

'I asked you what *lazzarolu* means!'

'An arrogant young tough guy of no consequence.'

'And *cocciu di tacca*?'

'Same thing. Young and brazen, as if to say: a fireball.'

'Oh! And your son is like that?'

'I think so. Sometimes he seems decent, but without substance; other times he seems bold and full of fire. Who knows! A man can know everything except his own blood. Now don't make me get mad.

Give me that pipe, or I'll smack you one, like I did to Mattia, to make you behave!'

'No! I'll give it to you only if you promise me that when the house is quiet, you'll bring me one just like it.'

'Listen, Modesta, it takes years to learn to smoke a pipe properly.'

'Fine. You bring me one and in time I'll learn to smoke it properly. And why are you calling me Modesta now?'

'What? Did I call you Modesta? I wasn't aware of it.'

'Yes; first *figghia,* and now Modesta.'

'It's true. And there's a reason, but I don't know if I can tell you . . . Are you going to give me that pipe or not?'

'I'll give it to you if you promise . . .'

'All right, all right, I promise. Tomorrow I'll find you a nice one, since trying to reason with you is like talking to the wind. Stubborn and beautiful, no question about it! Give it to me!'

'Okay, but I have to put it in your mouth. You can't touch it.'

'That's fine with me.'

'No, don't move your arms. I'll put it in your mouth and I'll take it out.'

'So who's moving! Can't you feel I'm holding your waist? Such soft hips, Modesta! You weigh nothing, but your thighs and belly are nice and plump. Look at how she's making me smoke! What if the flame goes out? It goes out easily, Modesta. Like the flame of love, it has to be nourished and protected.'

'You called me Modesta again. Why? Tell me! Why won't you tell me?'

'Don't ask. And take this pipe out of my mouth! Let me stroke you . . . you're so hot, my hands are beginning to sweat.'

'Tell me!'

'It's nothing, a silly thing! A mistake I made with you. And it wasn't the first time I made the same mistake.'

'What mistake?'

'I had a woman, a wife and a treasure. And I thought this gold mine, which fate had effortlessly handed me without my having to snare her, you understand, was my rightful due. So I mined her, I mined gold from her lips and her embrace, but without appreciating her or paying attention to her. And after she had already given me two sons, I began to want a daughter. That was the only thing I wanted, without thinking about her. I should have known I was asking too much, because she was worn out and pale. But I couldn't see that, and as a result she died under the surgeon's knife. So they wrote to me. Only then did I realize what I had lost.'

'What do you mean, they wrote to you? Where were you?'

'In America, because of Uncle Antonio's will. It was challenged and contested by a woman who was half Sicilian and half American, and didn't want to give us what was coming to us. But never mind. An ugly business. Let me kiss you.'

'You've been beating around the bush, Carmine, but you haven't told me anything.'

'How can you not understand? When I got back, the coffin was already in the ground. If I had at least been able to kiss her, dead, I would have come to terms with it in my flesh. Instead, for years and years I would see her in front of me, alive, with her dark, weary eyes . . . and I avoided the faces of unknown women who wanted to take her place.'

'And so?'

'So, nothing. With you I made the same mistake. *'Na scazzittula di carusa*, a snotty little brat, you seemed like, based on my years of experience. And confused by my sons' return – Carmine is not ashamed to say – I left you without hesitation. But within a week, I reached for you at night, and by day I saw you in the fields. I didn't know which way to turn, and I ran to the *vellute*, the silken ladies who make you come if you pay.* But to come, I had to keep repeating your name in my head. So now you know. Absence teaches you: I learned your name. The more I said it, the more beautiful you grew in my imagination. I've talked too much. Don't you understand? Or is it your youth that prevents you from understanding, and lets you sleep so quietly there on my shoulder?'

'I'm not sleeping, Carmine. I just like lying here like this and listening to how much you wanted me and still want me, and not giving you what you want right away.'

'Hah, just like a woman! That's why I didn't want to tell you. My words gave you the upper hand and now you want to take revenge. But Carmine can give you the satisfaction of making him wait.'

'And with those *vellute*, did you say my name?'

'"Modesta", I said, and I wouldn't look at them.'

'Say it again.'

'Modesta!'

'Again.'

'Modesta!'

'Again.'

'Modesta, you're driving me crazy!'

'Now say: Modesta, my gold mine.'

'My gold mine, Modesta, I want to enter you all the way to your heart.'

Spoken by his voice, the word "heart" loses the ambiguity that had made me hate it. And I see my heart, the eye and nucleus, the chronometer and regulator of my carnal centre. In the dark, I listen with the palms of my hands to its violent throbbing, crying out with joy from my chest to my perspiring brow, unwilling to quiet down.

'What is it, Modesta? Why are you feeling your chest? Why are you keeping your eyes open? Love used to put you to sleep before. If you're worried about getting pregnant, put your mind at ease, because I took care of it like I promised.'

'No, no! Yesterday I was afraid maybe but now . . . now you call me Modesta, and you went all the way to my heart. I saw it, you know, my heart.'

'And what was it like?'

'Like the wooden wheel that the *carusi* set aflame at Pentecost and drag down from the Mountain. I only saw it from a window, a long time ago. At that time I wasn't allowed to go outside the walls. Around here they don't do the wheel, Carmine. Why is that?'

'No, of course not! This land is flat! What do they know about rye and wheat fields here?'

'Have you seen the big wheel up close?'

'Of course! Not only have I seen it, but for three years – at the age when the first stubble appears on your chin – just like my father and my grandfather before me – all of us Tudia have been big-boned up till this day! – I had the honour, along with one of the Mussumeci – another family of hefty stature, though dark-skinned and dark-spirited – of lighting and dragging the wheel in order to urge the sun to grant us the warmth that nurtures the wheat and rye.'

'Oh, that's what it's for? That's the reason behind it?'

'Of course! An ancient tradition!'

'But didn't you burn yourselves?'

'Well, that's where skill comes in! When the wheel is unleashed and bursts into flame as it rolls madly down the slope like an enraged beast, it takes an expert hand and quick reflexes to dodge the flames, as well as an understanding of the wind. Even when the air seems still as glass, you have to be aware of the wind. Once I had all my hair burned to ashes! That's why for three years, we wheel guys shaved our heads almost completely.'

'How did you push it?'

'I'm surprised you don't know, Modesta.'

'From a distance I couldn't tell, because all I could see was the wheel.'

'But the women and girls go to watch when the wheel is being built.'

'I was in the convent, Carmine. Don't forget.'

'Can you picture a wagon wheel? Each year, the most skilled craftsman assumes the job of making one that is as big as possible, with a wooden shaft in the centre as strong as iron. So one guy here and one guy there, holding on to this shaft, push or restrain it depending on the terrain, as you might imagine.'

'I'm afraid, Carmine!'

'It's not fear, Modesta. You're sleepy.'

'Why does sleep make you frightened?'

'Of course, a lack of sleep and food makes you cold and even causes strange sensations that can seem like fear. A weakened body can't defend itself against bad memories and gives in to the mind's imaginings. Sleep now. You'll see, tomorrow morning you won't remember. Sleep peacefully, because Carmine, as he promised you, didn't leave his mark in your womb when he made you come.'

When dawn comes, Carmine goes away . . . In my sleep I see him slip away like a shadow. How did he manage to appear and disappear, yet still be ever present?

'It's because you have me in your heart, Modesta. It's the same for me. I go away and I carry you, here, with me.'

'Do you have a pocket in your heart to carry me in?'

'Of course! the heart is a pocket, a huge basket that can hold everything.'

'Yesss . . . everything! And then it breaks, like yours.'

'When it breaks, it means that it's carried enough burdens and pleasures.'

'But why do you leave? At the first light of dawn, you leave. Even if I'm sleeping, I can feel you leaving.'

'Now I'm back, actually.'

'You're back because it's night, but then as soon as I fall asleep, you take the opportunity to leave. Don't you ever sleep?'

'Of course I sleep.'

'Yesterday you were sleeping here beside me and then when I woke up, you were gone. How can you tell in your sleep that it's getting light?'

'It's because all my life I've been waking up at dawn.'

'Then go this instant if you have to leave. Go right now!'

'But it's nighttime now, and Orlando is all sweaty from the ride. Let me get some rest too.'

'You rest and then you leave. But why?'

'Temper, temper, *figghia!*'

'And don't call me *figghia!*'

'When you throw a tantrum and start whining, you become my *figghia.*'

'Why do you always have to leave?'

'So I won't upset your household and mine.'

'Who cares!'

'You've acquired a good reputation down in Catania. They admire you for the way you've managed things.'

'But I never see them! And when I see them they look at me with daggers in their eyes.'

'The women, naturally! They envy you. Pay no attention; they don't count. But the men admire you for the way you've handled your affairs and your family.'

'That's not true.'

'Oh, no? What's the truth then? Let's hear it. How come all the Brandiforti and others came to Cavallina's wedding, hmm?'

'Don't call her Cavallina! My Beatrice is all grown up, and a happy woman.'

'I'm glad. And for this very reason, why should we upset her and everybody else with childish fits of temper? And my family too, up there in Carmelo, why scandalize them when we have our nights together? Here, let me hold you.'

'You were right, Carmine: I bled again. How did you do it? I keep meaning to ask you, and I always forget.'

'Has it been that long, Modesta? Let me hold you. So much time has passed already, and it seems like yesterday.'

'But how did you do it?'

'Never mind. Men's business.'

'Tell me.'

'I held my breath!'

'Oh, sure, your breath! You make me laugh.'

'So laugh. You're just like my Linuzza! Always curious, always asking . . .'

'Don't say that name or I'll clobber you!'

'Oh, you're just like her! She was jealous of my mother and you're jealous of a dead woman.'

'I don't want to hear it.'

'She's dead, Modesta.'

'And if she were alive, she'd be an old woman now.'

'I'm old too, but you still want me.'

'Are you saying that if she were alive, you'd want her more than me?'

'I'm not saying anything. You can't talk about something you don't know.'

'She died young so she could keep you tied to her for ever.'

'That might very well be, if you say so, since being stubborn, like her, and a woman, you certainly know her better than I do.'

'I'm your gold mine, and you should be thinking only of me now that I'm your treasure.'

'Don't you feel me holding you in my arms like my life's gold?'

He burrows between my thighs and the gold of my youth comes to light in his hands. Alone by day, remembering his face amid the fields and sunlight, at night in his arms, which smell of hay and tobacco.

'Tobacco, Modesta? Naturally, all I do is smoke! Tobacco is all that's left to me.'

'What about me?'

'You're something else.'

'What am I?'

'You're my youth, which doesn't want to leave me. It clings to your skin, youth does! Even if you're aware of the years, youth calls you, and you're driven to pursue it. And all it takes is some little thing to give you the illusion you've found it, and you let yourself be deceived. You can't help it.'

'I'm young, aren't I, Carmine?'

'Of course! What do you think?'

'At times I feel old.'

'Definitely a condition of youth! The younger you are, the older you feel, sometimes. But you have to be careful, because feeling old makes you old. Like my son Vincenzo: he came back from the war healthy and strong, and in a year he became old and miserable, living with that skinny *signorinella* who's always scowling and fainting.'

'Listen to this old man blaming his son! You're the one who married him off to that little *carusa* from Modica. All the girls from Modica are like that, skinny and dreary. Didn't you know that?'

'But this *carusa* from Modica brought us sizeable lands. And he should know the power it brought him, the joy and pride of bolstering my efforts and those of my father and grandfather with his wife's money. Today's new landowners are my sons and . . .'

'The Tudia are replacing the old estate holders, listen to that! And in time, with greater sacrifices, you Tudia will even become aristocrats, right?'

'Of course! A Tudia should take pride in riding from dawn to dusk without ever leaving the boundaries of his lands, and not let women's whining and lamenting make him miserable. Ride his horse, and seek his pleasure outside the home.'

'I hate you, Carmine!'

'That's nothing new. It's always been that way between us.'

'And it always will be that way! Why are you laughing, eh, old man? What's that laughter in your eyes?'

'I'm laughing at your hatred, *figghia*. If only I'd had a daughter like you!'

'What do you mean?'

'That you hate me because, as the Princess, God rest her soul, realized. . .'

'What did she realize?'

'That Mody is exactly like Carmine. Two peas in a pod.'

'I'm not like you, Carmine! Times are changing, and I hope that your sons, your grandchildren and all the other young people will overthrow you landowners and do away with your estates.'

'Listen to her! And who put these ideas in your head, your brother-in-law? Or did you read about them in books? And what would you gain from it, eh, Princess Brandiforti?'

'I would have a good laugh over it.'

'Those ideas are foreign, Modesta. And nothing good ever came to the island from outside. You did well to ally yourself through Beatrice's marriage to a person of some importance, who might have friends in high places one day soon.'

'Carlo would never sell himself out!'

'I swear to God, you sound just like Mattia! Always getting worked up over someone, you *picciriddi*! You with this socialist Carlo, and Mattia with his Mussolini. They're foreigners, outsiders! Just this morning, I put an end to the Black Shirt that had gotten under Mattia's skin and in his mind, with a sound thrashing! Naturally, they have to give him money, because this Mussolini is the only one who can ensure order here – he's a real Crispi, I swear to God! – but not their souls . . . He's turned to the young with subtle cunning, and inflamed their imaginations against the old. He was shrewd, because ever since the world began the young have been quick to catch fire. Sure! Give a young man an Orlando and a Rinaldo, make him dream with new words and new uniforms, let him believe that he will be boss, and he'll become your slave without knowing it.'

'There's truth in what you say, Carmine, but there's also truth in what Carlo says. And his truth agrees with me more.'

'So be it! But this truth is being told too slowly. Too many watered-down words are coming out of their mouths. Young people, since the world began, have always needed myths and heroic deeds. That's what worries me about Mattia. He must use his head, look after his interests and not let himself be taken in.'

'I don't give a fig about you and your Mattia, and all the old men like you! I know Carlo is right, and you can't understand.'

'But I do understand, and I can read, Modesta. Don't make me angry! Their plans are too grandiose, and they're moving ahead too uncertainly.'

'Not in Russia. There, heads have been broken, Carmine.'

'Well! Russia is a long way off! And it should stay a long way off from the island! I repeat my question, *figghia*: what would you gain from having the landowners overthrown?'

'I told you. I would have a good laugh over it.'

'And how would you get by without means? What would you leave your son?'

'I'm not leaving anything to my son. He'll study. He'll work like Carlo does.'

'And what about you?'

'I'll work too. I told you! I hate you!'

'And who is it that you love? This Carlo?'

'If I need to, I'll work. You can't understand.'

'On the contrary, Carmine does understand. Only one thing surprises him.'

'What's that?'

'With these ideas of yours, wouldn't you have been better off staying in the convent and becoming a nun, *figghia*?'

'I hate you, Carmine.'

'That's the way it's always been between us.'

'No! This is genuine hate, Carmine. It's no longer submission toward you, this hatred, because I've grown up and I know you're my enemy.'

'Who told you these things? Your friend from Milan?'

'A man who is not a landowner told me!'

'If I understand correctly, you love Carlo, but you want me. How can that be, Modesta?'

'I love Carlo, and my nature wants you. I've learned not to fight my nature: I satisfy it but I don't give it my soul, as you say. I satisfy it with your kisses, I satiate it and when it's sated I clear my mind and set you aside. Why do you think I let you come back? Did you think, you, with your landowner's arrogance, that I let you come back so I could be your gold mine for ever? No! It was to finish the story that you had broken off because it pleased you. To take what I had coming to me, then send you away.'

'That's what I want, too. That's why I let you beat me up and insult me. I want to have my fill of you, and when I'm satisfied, go away. I'm a condemned man, *figghia*. Don't forget that.'

'It's not true! I haven't seen one sign of it these past months, either in your body or in your mind. It was a lie so you could come back.'

'If you want to believe that, if it soothes you to think so, go ahead. But now that you're all in a lather, let me kiss you.'

'Don't act like a sheep, Carmine; you're a wolf! Take what you can get, but don't act like you have to ask. Kiss me for as long as my nature wants you, because later, maybe in a month, maybe in an hour, I'll impose the death sentence I gave you before. I'll be the one to kill you, not *La Certa*! I'm young. You said so, and I'll never let anyone own me!'

'That's what I like about you. But don't fool around with this man because, if I want to, I'll saddle you with a child. And then you'll have to think of me for at least a year.'

'You've miscalculated, Carmine. Do you think I would have been so unconcerned these past months if I didn't have a way of staying free?'

'Of course not! But the way you mean causes pain and often death.'

'I knew you'd say that! Not for someone who has money, Carmine, money and know-how. Did you find me pale and sickly the night you came back?'

'I found you stronger and more beautiful. Let me kiss you.'

'And just a few days earlier, in a small, sterile room, with a simple, painless operation, I rid myself of an inconvenience. And I'd do it again if you got the idea of trapping me. No one owns Modesta.'

'Modesta is smart and strong-willed. And Carmine declares himself beaten . . . You want to stay like that, on top of me? Stay on top and take me. Carmine is old. He's learned the wisdom of losing.'

'It's easy to afford the luxury of acting like a lamb, when nature has favoured you with being born a wolf.'

On top of him – that lamb – I set the rhythm, and come with him. But now I know that my hatred conceals envy.

'Will you teach me the wisdom of losing, Carmine? I have too much anger in me sometimes, and I'd like to learn.'

'Well, you can teach a lot of things: how to ride a horse, how to make love, but you can't give your own experience to someone else. Each of us must gain his own, over the years, making mistakes, stopping, going back and starting all over again.'

'Why is that?'

'Well, if you could teach it, we'd all be the same!'

'You know, Carmine, sometimes I think it would be wonderful to be born old and die as children.'

'The things you come up with! I like the way you think, Modesta. Of course, it would be wonderful, and it's good to dream. But nature planned things differently.'

'So, did I beat you, Carmine?'

'It's only right. A person must rebel. If Vincenzo had rebelled, truly rebelled I mean, I would never have let that *carusa* from Modica into the house. I, in my day, opposed my father's will concerning a woman. And since I wouldn't budge on that point, and had always served him most valiantly, doing his shooting and the work of four men, he had to give in. My father was a great man! You could always tell when he was coming. And when he walked out the door, he was still with us.'

'You're like that too.'

'Others may think and say that. I have no way of knowing.'

'I said so.'

'If you said so, I accept it.'

'Don't act like a sheep, Carmine, or you'll make me see red again. Now that you've given me such pleasure, I don't want to hate you.'

'So, you got rid of a child, Modesta? I won't ask whose it was.'

'I did.'

'Painlessly? How can that be?'

'Times change, Carmine. Science is discovering many things. And this one benefits us women. With knowledge and the help of doctors, women will soon be free of so many decrees that nature and over-lords have heaped on them.'

'Are those the words of that Carlo, the doctor? Is that how he talks?'

'Yes.'

'Is that why you say that word that's so difficult to say?'

'What word?'

'Love.'

'Yes.'

'Has he taught you many things?'

'Yes, many things; even how to swim.'

'Don't make me laugh, Modesta. That's impossible. You can't learn to swim unless you're a child. At one time I tried, but I was too old, and by then I was afraid of the water.'

'Because you had no one to teach you. I learned.'

'Maybe I believe you, maybe I don't, Modesta. You wouldn't be saying that just to get the upper hand and make me jealous of that man, would you?'

'Let me dispel your doubt. Come . . .'

★

I'm afraid, but I have to show him. The sea, without the sun, now seems deep and hostile like it did before. Perhaps by following the gleaming path the moon traces on that dark expanse, I can overcome my fear. On the shore, Carmine follows me with doubtful eyes, his trousers rolled up to his thighs. Waves as light as palm fronds are already lapping at my shoulders. I shudder, but I have to show him even if it kills me. I could never turn back to face his mocking wolf-eyes. I'm trembling, but I lift my feet off the sand and move toward the horizon, focused only on the moon's path. To make my victory complete, once I'm out in the open water, I roll over on my back and do the dead man's float. Maybe if I relax, the trembling will subside. With unseeing eyes, a dead man's eyes, I focus on the moon dangling there, smiling dimly . . . Someone yells from the shore. It must be him. I can't answer. What if I don't go back? He's called three times, and he must have come out after me because now he gathers me up, and the moon flings the waves against the white of his shirt.

'That's enough, Modesta! You scared me! That wasn't funny, *figghia*! Was there any need to go out that far? I swear to God you scared me! What if you suddenly fainted? You're all cold and trembling! And there I am, stuck on shore, watching helplessly!'

Now recovered, I let him carry me in his arms.

'Let's go back. There's no use my putting your dress on for you. Know what I'll do? I'll wrap you in Orlando's blanket. Look, even Orlando is pawing the ground. I swear to God, he, too, had a fright!'

'You and he were scared . . . I'm just cold.'

'Of course! That's why I'm wrapping you nice and snug in the blanket. Leave it to me. There, like that.'

'I can swim. Did you see?'

'Of course I saw! I should have been struck dead when I challenged you! You take too many chances, *carusa*! Here, let me bundle you up.'

'I'll let you bundle me up, but you have to say: "Modesta can swim."'

'Modesta can swim, but now she has to quiet down. And let Carmine take her home like a good little girl, like a sensible *picciridda*.'

Restored to life in the blanket's warmth, cradled by his arms and the deep beating of his heart, I don't want to fall asleep. I don't want to miss one step of that echoing gait magnified by the night. In the dense wood, the moon's light is blocked out and the palm grove's darkness settles on my eyelids, but I don't want to sleep. With an effort, I raise my face up to his neck and twirl my fingers around the wiry curls, motionless in the faint breeze that has suddenly begun to stir. In order to stay awake, all I have to do is take the ear hidden beneath his bushy sideburns in my teeth, and nibble on it.

'Sing to me, Carmine.'

'I can't sing, *picciridda*.'

'How far have we gone, Carmine?'

'A long way, Modesta.'

'And how far do we still have to go?'

'A long way.'

'And you aren't going to die, are you, Carmine? You lied so you'd have an excuse to come back.'

'That may be, Modesta. Who can say?'

'You can tell me, Carmine, because I recognized you when you came back . . . When was it you came back?'

'An eternity ago!'

'Tell me it isn't true. You can tell me, because you know that during this eternity I've been happy with you.'

'I can't tell you anything. But if dreaming is good for you, then go to sleep and dream. Dreams and sleep are more nourishing than bread.'

'I don't want to sleep.'

'Then don't sleep.'

'Did you see that I can swim?'

'Of course I saw! But don't try it again, not at night or by day, at least not in front of someone like me who has no love for the sea.'

'You got scared, huh?'

'And how!'

'So if you got scared, how come your heart didn't stop? No answer? I know why you won't answer.'

'Let's hear it. Why won't I answer?'

'Because it's not true that you're going to die.'

'No, I won't answer because I'm trying to restrain my imagination. I don't like falling for the uncertain plans suggested by my fantasies.'

'What does that mean?'

'It means that Carmine doesn't like the dark alleys of the mind where the dagger of suspicion can appear and stab you in the back.'

'Your words are obscure, Carmine.'

'Because obscurity has clouded my eyes since I saw you in the middle of the sea. Now go to sleep. I'll tuck you in bed. I won't be back tomorrow. Don't expect me.'

'Why won't you come back?'

'Because I have to clear away these clouds in my head that make you seem like a stranger to me. Sleep now. Don't pay any attention to me.'

'No. I won't sleep unless you tell me the reason for this sudden distance toward me.'

'Carmine isn't used to asking, to probing, *carusa*. He leaves that to the law. But if he can't see clearly, he changes his course . . . Let me go! There's no use hanging on to me. It's all too easy to first sow suspicion and then try to erase the implication with wheedling embraces.'

'No, it's not yet dawn. You can't go! You see, I'm right! It's not true that you're going to die if you can so heatedly go on your way and forget me as if you still had twenty years to live.'

'I never heard that knowing you're going to die makes you a coward.'

'Damned old man! Get out, you and your suspicions!'

'That's what I'm trying to do, *carusa*! Take your arms from around my neck; I don't want to hurt you.'

'Why can't I throw you out?'

'You know why.'

'If it's true that you can observe things, my clinging to you like this should tell you something.'

'It tells me something, that's certain, but you have to confirm it with your words. Only then will I know if my suspicion was a lover's deceitful imagination.'

'It was you, Carmine, I thought about when Carlo embraced me. And when he went away, I stroked myself and spoke your name.'

*

'I have to go, Modesta. The woods are beginning to glimmer; there's just time for me to have a smoke.'

'I want to smoke too.'

'So, get your pipe. Isn't that why I brought it to you?'

'No. I'll smoke yours and you smoke mine.'

'At your command, *Padroncina*.'

'Why didn't you want to call me *Padrona*, Carmine?'

'Because you were a *scazzittula di carusa*, a snotty little brat. I told you.'

'And now how am I?'

'A strong, dangerous woman . . . But just look at this! She makes me smoke this tiny pipe . . . Give me mine back!'

'Why did you bring me such a small one?'

'A pipe has to fit the size of the hand, Modesta. My grandmother smoked one like this, in front of the house on summer evenings, under the mulberry tree.'

'Your grandmother smoked? That surprises me.'

'Oh, yes, she and her sisters. I don't know which regions they came from before landing on the island with their father and brothers, loaded with gold and precious stones. I know little about it, because in our house we couldn't talk much about it.'

'And then?'

'Then my grandfather and his brother moved quickly and snared two of those *caruse*, loaded with gold like madonnas, keeping them here on this land.'

'And the others, the men?'

'Bah! From what little I was able to drag out of my mother over the years, they continued on their way . . . Drifters, merchants . . . thieves, who can say? I must say, that pipe suits you, I swear to God! Tell me, Modesta, why did you use that word? Love is a precise word, and one should be cautious when using it.'

'To wound you, old man. And I wounded you. For a couple of hours at least, I skewered you with doubt and made you suffer, like I suffered in your absence. How could you not see that? You're not so tough, Carmine.'

'Love sucks you dry; it makes you like glass! That's why I fled from you at Carmelo. Who came looking for me back then, all the way to my doorstep?'

'I did, Carmine. If I hadn't come, wouldn't you have come looking for me?'

'Who can say what might have happened? But knowing my nature, almost certainly no. Many times I fled from that word, which can ruin your life more than wine and gambling, turning my gaze from a balcony full of frangipani where the day before you had stared with smouldering eyes.'

'So then you love me?'

'I said I did.'

'No! You have to say: I love you, Modesta.'

'I don't like to say that word. Don't make me mad!'

'There's no use getting up. I won't let you go unless you say: I love you.'

'Of course, if you cling to me like that and breathe your life's breath into my mouth, I'll have to say it.'

'Say it, then.'

'I love you, Modesta.'

'How many times in your life have you said it, Carmine?'

'Twice before you, *figghia*, and with you that makes three. And I thank my stars for not letting me find that man with you.'

*

'I was afraid you wouldn't come back.'

'Why, Modesta?'

'Last night you threatened not to.'

'Listen to this *picciridda*! Crying, too.'

'But you threatened not to!'

'At first, sure, but afterwards don't you remember that we smoked together?'

'So you'll always come back, right, Carmine?'

'Of course! Where else would I go? I have the feeling that even dead, I'd come back to look at you. I'll come back from the eternal slumber, look at you, bring you gifts and watch that no one comes near you.'

'You don't fool me anymore, you sly old fox. You won't ever die.'

'That may be; anything is possible. We human beings don't know anything . . . Why won't you hug me? Don't be like that. I got used to being hugged. You should always treat *picciriddi* and animals in a certain way; otherwise they pine away.'

'You're neither a *picciriddu* nor an animal.'

'On the contrary, we're all *picciriddi* and animals, myself included. Will you give me a hug?'

'I don't feel like it.'

'Why?'

'Because you didn't come back.'

'What! But I'm right here! Don't you see me? Or are you saying that just to be difficult?'

'I'm saying it because I dreamed that when you passed by the house with Orlando, you turned away from my window and kept going.'

'And what do I have to do with the scenes your imagination makes up when you're asleep?'

'Didn't you tell me that a person can run from love?'

'I like the way you think, Modesta. But what you just said isn't like you. Those are the thoughts of a foolish girl, not a strong woman like you. A person can run from anything if he learns to recognize what can harm him.'

'What about destiny then?'

'A word to reassure those who are miserable! You can control destiny as you please, if you're determined.'

'That's what I think, too.'

'Then why do you say things that differ from what you think?'

'To get your confirmation.'

'*Satanasso d'una carusa!* What a little devil! You make me waste my breath, instead of embracing me.'

'And partly because I had some doubt about what I thought.'

'Let's hear it.'

'Carlo . . .'

'Don't say that name!'

'Well, I could have loved him if I hadn't been thinking of you.'

'No kidding! Too bad he wasn't able to measure up to me.'

'Damn you! Just what I wanted to hear you say. So what if after you, I don't find someone who measures up to you?'

'Your loss, if you can't find him!'

'And all the better for you, since you'd like to hold on to me for ever?'

'Naturally! Since the beginning of time, it's always been that way if you possess something precious.'

'If you could, you'd take me with you to the grave, wouldn't you?'

'No, not that! I like you alive. A lifeless body is repulsive, even for the dead. And since it's a night for words, rather than embraces, promise me one thing. If one of these days you don't see me come when night falls . . .'

'You said you would always come back. Don't lie.'

'All right. If after hundreds and hundreds of nights you don't see me, promise me you won't come looking for me.'

'Why? Are you planning to go away, like back then?'

'No, if I live, I'll come to see you for a hundred years. But if you don't see me, it means my heart has stopped, just as "they" predicted. Promise me you won't look for me. I don't want you to see me dead.'

'Why?'

'I want to remain alive for you, in your eyes! Well? Carmine has never asked you for anything; you could grant him this much at least. Answer me, Modesta. This silence of yours is like a thorn in my heart, and I can't kiss you with this thorn. Promise Carmine.'

'A promise is a promise, Carmine, and leaves a fatal stain on anyone who doesn't keep it.'

'Promise me, Modesta, if you love me.'

'I promise, Carmine, and I hope to remain unstained.'

52

As if that promise were all he'd been waiting for in order to die, I never saw him again. This was what Carmine had wanted, in order to chain my imagination to his living body. In fact, from dusk to dawn I go stumbling around the room, the stairs, the garden, repeating to myself: he's dead. But at every shadow, at the slightest sound, I see him, alive, in front of me, and hear his voice in my ear: '*If only I could have seen her dead at least! I would have resigned myself and accepted it!*'

Dawn is already lighting up the walls, confirming his death, but I talk to him as he sits in front of me, smoking calmly. '*An unkept promise is an unforgivable sin for us islanders, isn't it, Carmine?*' '*Oh, yes, Modesta. You swore, and you must keep your promise.*'

*

Lying in Gaia's big bed in Carmelo, Carmine smiles with lowered eyelids. You were hoping to hide your humiliation, but I found you, Carmine. Those who die have no say, only those who live do. And I'm alive, looking at you, you beautiful marmoreal old man, and I won't put up with rules, promises, disapproval . . .

Though my legs feel heavy, as soon as the skinny old woman who showed me into the room disappears behind the door, I move toward the imposing bed to get a better look at him dead. Repulsive: the clammy waxen brow no longer has his colour. To help my youthful

flesh forget, to resign myself and accept it, I press my lips to his forehead and on his mouth. A chill, queasy sweat trickles down my back.
But I wait for my nature to impress upon its senses that Carmine is
dead and can never come back.

'Your presence brings great honour to this house, Princess. I apologize for leaving you here, alone . . . Nunziata forgot to tell me. Nunziata is an old woman, and dazed by her master's death.'

Two tall men stare at me from the shadows. '*All of us Tudia have
been big-boned up till this day.*' That slow voice, cultured despite the
affectation of the dialect, is not Carmine's voice. But raising my eyes,
I meet a blue gaze vibrant with an irony I thought only the old man
could possess. To hide my astonishment, I turn to the other man,
who is slightly taller than the first, but he is no longer looking at me.
Leaning over, his dark head bent, he now seems frightened, staring at
the motionless body on the bed.

'I apologize for my brother, Princess, he has suffered greatly from
this tragedy.'

Again the voice and the ironic blue gaze cut through the dimness,
compelling me to look at him directly. '*No one can know his own flesh
and blood, Mody.*'

For a moment, in the severity of those eyes that make no move to
look away from mine, I can see the look that Eriprando will have in
ten or fifteen years . . . Will Eriprando be a stranger to me? Or had the
old man been lying?

'Are you Mattia?'

'I didn't hope to be recognized by *Voscenza*.'

'Carmine always held you both in his heart; you, Mattia, and you,
too, Vincenzo. I came to know you both through his heart.'

Hearing these words, Vincenzo turns his eyes on me for a moment,
but tears force him to lower his head.

'And I am pleased to see that the rumours that there was bad blood
between the Tudia and the Brandiforti were ill-founded.'

'Foolish gossip, Tudia. Carmine was a man of honour, and rendered great service to us Brandiforti. My presence here confirms what
I say. And so that everyone may know it, let us go to where vigil is
being kept.'

I sit at the oval table between Mattia and Vincenzo, with bread and salt, water for women and red wine for men, the mirrors covered by black silk shawls, and listen to the deeds and joys and sorrows of Don Carmine, while from the wide-open door men and women with flowers and fruit file in uninterruptedly until night falls.

When night comes I can say goodbye to those who remain, and leave.

'Go back alone, you say, Princess? It's too dangerous! Just yesterday a car was attacked between Malpasso and Doria, and nothing but a few charred bones was left of what had once been a family. Surely, Princess, you should know that that's how things are around here: they rob you, and to be sure they burn the rest . . .'

'But I have a revolver.'

'It's convenient, certainly, if you're faced with only one individual. But those thugs always go around amusing themselves as a gang. Allow me to insist. You cannot go alone.'

After hours of hostile silence, I can't stand to have that young man near me for a single moment more. He's nothing like Eriprando, or if he is, I don't have the courage to peer into my future. With an effort, even though my frozen legs feel as heavy as lead, I head toward my car. But there's nothing I can do to stop him. Eriprando's voice suddenly seems to leap up, blithe and shrill, before me: *'Oh, no! No way, Mama! I'm going out with lovely Elena today. It's settled.'*

Nothing can bend the stubborn will of that young Carmine. He's just like I had dreamt that night. Or had I actually seen him speed past on Orlando, head high, his curls burnished by the setting sun?

'On horseback, Princess? Oh, no! I get around on a motorcycle. This is my animal, right here. Never mind Orlando! This one has the power of a hundred horses put together.'

Either I'm confused by my exhaustion and the chill of that unnatural kiss imprinted on my flesh, or that young man, now laughing and caressing the shiny flanks of his iron horse, isn't as inconsequential as you insinuated, Carmine.

'You can barely stand up, Princess. Let me help you to your car.'

His hand clutching my arm rouses me from the mental delirium that has gripped me for hours; his fingers have Carmine's dry heat.

'You know, young man, you're exactly like your father.'

What am I saying? A deep shudder now runs through his body, and he moves away in the darkness, as though he were upset.

'What does that matter now! I have to take you home and that's that . . . and then . . .'

'Do you dislike being like Carmine? Is that why your mood changed?'

'Being like Carmine! So what was Carmine like? According to my mother, God rest her soul, he was a god! Can you measure up to a god? Look, Princess, you can barely stand up and I have to get you home. I see you rather like my motorcycle. It's nice to stroke it, isn't it? Its skin is so smooth.'

'Why shouldn't I like it?'

'Not all women like it.'

He's challenging me now, exactly like Eriprando does when he wants to race. I have to accept the challenge to learn what Eriprando will be like . . . and I hear myself say:

'Why don't you take me home on the motorcycle? I'll send someone to get the car tomorrow.'

'A woman on a motorcycle? Whoever heard of such a thing! It's dangerous. You have to know how to hold on.'

'So teach me! How hard can it be?'

'You have to have strong muscles.'

'I can ride a horse. Don't worry.'

'Yes, of course – but what if you want to now, and then you get scared? I know how women are . . . What an idea! Still, the thought appeals to me, if only to tell my grandchildren.'

'There, that's the spirit! That way you'll have something to talk about when you're an old man.'

'Witty too! Back in the house you seemed like a corpse. Why so sad over the death of a stranger, Princess?'

'Don't change the subject, Mattia. Admit that you're afraid to have a woman ride on your motorcycle.'

'Mattia isn't afraid of anything!'

'It doesn't seem like it.'

'I'll show you, Princess. Come on, climb on behind me and we'll see. Hold on tight, will you? Tighter. Feel how the engine makes everything vibrate? And that's nothing! I wouldn't want to lose you down the embankment.'

I looked at the road: it snaked along a ravine, profound darkness barely touched by the moon. My legs, tense from effort or from the jolting of that animal, were already trembling, and I almost regretted it; I was about to call out to him when a furious wrench made my heart, crazy with fear, leap into my throat. With all the strength I could muster, I gripped him like someone who's drowning, while a burst of air, inexplicably transformed into razor-sharp lava, pelted my head, making me lurch.

'Hold tight, for God's sake, Princess, hold on!'

Mattia's voice reaches me like a distant whistling. At sea, we're on the open sea, I think, in the grip of a storm . . . What is he saying now? I too am screaming but my voice breaks up in the distance – or is it my heart leaping out of me? Finally, I feel my heart revive, as if fiery fingers had torn it out and violently massaged it. And to feel it alive, no longer grieving, I fix my eyes on the yawning depths of the night in front of us . . . an abyss swallowed up by a roar of wind and brass rumbling in unison, in a sweeping metallic song never before heard.

*

'It's spectacular, Mattia! Spectacular!'

'You're fearless, Princess! If I may say so, you seem like a young girl now.'

'Oh, it's fantastic! Let's go back up and ride around all night. Afterwards you'll teach me to drive it, won't you? Tomorrow you'll come back and teach me.'

'Tomorrow? Well, who knows where we'll be tomorrow! But do you really feel up to driving it?'

'Why not?'

'So then, it's true . . .'

'What is?'

'What my father would say, not with words but with his eyes, whenever he heard you mentioned . . . *Bacio le mani*, my respects,

Princess. But just one thing; no offence. Are you like this with all men? If I may say so, you shouldn't be so quick to let yourself be accompanied by a man alone.'

'So why didn't you want Vincenzo to come with us? He offered to. What's come over you? Why are you looking at me like that?'

'I'm trying to understand . . .'

'Understand what?'

'Trying to understand, like I said.'

'There's no need to try to read me, Mattia! Stop staring at me. What do you want to know? You won't answer? I was your father's woman for a long time.'

'The old wolf! Despicable Carmine! Not satisfied with having ruined Vincenzo's life, he wanted to make me marry a silly fool as well, when all the time he had you.'

'But you didn't comply, and he had to accept it. Why are you shouting?'

'I'm shouting because I hate him, and I hate you!'

Mattia shouts as he runs to the motorcycle and kick-starts the engine, which in a flash is raring to go. I should go inside, shut the gate and leave that young man to his grief. He too must have loved him if he can cry like that . . . I see him out there, bent over his iron horse, which gleams in the moonlight. Carmine didn't understand a thing, either about himself or about others, and I should get on with my life. But the dark stretch of woods out there breathes such a strong odour of death and loneliness that the chill of that last kiss is roused in my flesh.

'Why don't you go into your house?'

'And you, why don't you leave instead of racing the engine like that?'

'I turned the engine off. Can't you hear the silence? You look like a corpse now . . .'

'Don't raise your voice, Mattia. Don't disturb my household!'

'I wish I could disturb your house like you disturbed mine! I hate you, Princess! Why did you have to reveal my father to me by telling me . . .'

'You knew everything, Mattia.'

'It's one thing to imagine, another thing to know. You killed him for me a second time.'

'No one could kill him. Carmine went when he was ready.'

'Don't say that name!'

'Watch out, Mattia. What you think is hate is envy, envy of your father.'

'What do you know about it?'

'I, too, thought I hated him, but it was only envy. Because I'm envious as well as angry at the way he died.'

'You're not a woman. You're a lava devil.'

'I must be a woman, since Carmine loved me.'

'That's not true! He only loved my mother and us sons!'

'Before. But after your mother died, he loved another woman for years.'

'That's not true!'

'Her name was Assunta, if you didn't know. There is a daughter in Acireale who is the spitting image of him. And another son of his is asleep in this house right now.'

'Shut your mouth or I'll kill you on the spot and send you with him, since you want him so much.'

'Don't come any closer. I have a gun in my hand.'

'So it's true, what he used to say, that nothing scares you. Who are you?'

'Not a step closer! I'll shatter your leg, Mattia, I'm warning you! Go home until you get over this hatred that's gripping you.'

I should back up three steps, keeping him in my sights, and close the gate, yet in spite of this I find myself moving toward him.

'How dare you, *carusu*, pass judgement on my life and that of your father? Was it lies you wanted to hear? You disappoint me. I thought I was talking to Carmine's son. Instead, I find myself arguing with an arrogant *lazzarolu* who only wants to hear fatuous words. Go away! Go console yourself with some whore!'

'No! It's you who must console me.'

'What?'

'I changed my mind about you. You told me the truth right away. You have to console me.'

'No one can console us.'

'Let me touch you the way he touched you . . . let me know . . .'

His hand suddenly on mine, without turning the gun away, ignites a forgotten heat in my chilled flesh, as he whispers:

'Shoot, go ahead, shoot!'

'Did you love him that much, Mattia?'

'He destroyed my life and that of my mother with his controlling ways. He made me leave a woman who was an angel, but I believed in him, in his word, his assurance.'

'What assurance?'

'That all his life he loved only us. But you say the old man was lying.'

'We all lie.'

'No! Not him, no! You dropped your gun, Princess.'

'So pick it up. It's a night for death, Mattia. When someone dies, he calls those he's loved to him.'

'What are you doing now? Are you going?'

'I'm going in to my son.'

'Who is also "his" son.'

'His exact likeness, you should say.'

'That's not true!'

'Come tomorrow, in the daytime, and I'll show you my young Carmine.'

'Wait. I believe you . . . before you go in, tell me the truth. If what you said is true, you must know . . .'

'What?'

'How did my mother die?'

'In childbirth. That's what your father said.'

'They told me she killed herself . . . that she killed herself in an appalling way . . . with rat poison . . . cursing Carmine and her sons.'

'I don't know anything about that, Mattia. Now go! What you say is dreadful.'

'Dreadful, is it! But you must know these things if it's true that you were his woman. Let me come in with you. I have to know no matter what.'

'Come in. I wouldn't have chased you away.'

'. . . He came here?'

'Every night.'

'Why are you lying down now?'

'I'm tired, Mattia. I haven't slept since yesterday. I waited up for him all night.'

'He was supposed to come here last night as well?'

'Yes.'

'And when you didn't see him, you came looking for him?'

'To see him dead.'

'You knew? He confided in you, a stranger! I put the gun on the table, Princess. From what I can see, given the way you live, you might need it. Well? No answer?'

'I'm sleepy, Mattia, and cold. Besides there's no use talking to you. You're afraid to know the truth and you insult me.'

'If my mother hadn't died that way . . .'

'Who told you that? Maybe it's a lie.'

'No! Her sister told me . . . and she also said . . . Or maybe you're right, you're a woman and you know about these things . . . You're beautiful when I look into your eyes. Or maybe you just have beautiful eyes . . .Who are you? A sphinx, maybe? How old are you? Let me hold you. I want to know.'

'Know?'

'How come I find you so appealing? You're round and warm . . . I liked you from the first moment . . . your hair is like silk. Did he caress it? Did he talk to you?'

'Later on, yes.'

'Later on, when?'

'When he knew he was going to die. But before that he never spoke.'

'Did he hurt you, too?'

'He's dead, Mattia.'

'Are you thinking of him? Is that why you won't look at me?'

'He's dead, Mattia. Let's accept it.'

*

'Did I fall asleep, Modesta? How could I?'

'You were exhausted.'

'He's really dead then if I fell asleep inside you.'

'Yes, but we're alive, *figlio*. Did you feel how alive we are?'

'Why did you call me that? And why are you crying now? I can't stand to see a woman cry. Are you crying for him?'

'Him too. I'll get over it.'

'Why are you touching your stomach, your breasts?'

'I'm trying to see if I'm going to have another son with you. For every person who dies, another one is born.'

'And this makes you cry?'

'No. I'd like to give a life for a death.'

'Don't be so ambiguous. Stroke my hair like you did before. I felt it while I was sleeping. No one ever caressed me that way.'

'No one was ever a mother to you? That aunt of yours?'

'Maybe she wanted to, but she was stern and cold like her brother.'

'Oh! She was Carmine's sister?'

'Yes, she was his sister, and she obeyed him like a slave. He said that no one must take the place of his wife, and on Sundays, after mass, he would bring us to her room, which had been left untouched . . . You could still smell her perfume – so he said – and he would open the wardrobes filled with her clothes. He made me and Vincenzo, who always trembled, think about her on our knees . . . what can I say? like a prayer, for at least five minutes, though it felt like centuries. It seemed like I spent my entire childhood that way. Then I rebelled, and when I saw them, him and Vincenzo, shut themselves up in that room, I felt a wild urge to run and run. And I ran through the fields for hours until I was worn out. Why, Modesta, why?'

'Your hair is wiry and curly like . . .'

'Like whose?'

'Like Eriprando's, my son.'

'Oh! Is that his name? I've never heard that name before; it must be foreign.'

'Who knows how this son of mine will grow up, with that name.'

'Does it worry you? Even Vincenzo, who is my brother, sometimes seems foreign to me.'

'Your father said the same things about you.'

'He's really dead, Modesta, if my heart can hear these things without breaking.'

'He's dead, Mattia. The woods are beginning to glimmer. It will be day soon. You have to go.'

'Why?'

'You can't stay here.'

'Do you have another man?'

'I have a son.'

'What does that matter?'

'We can't upset anyone.'

'You talk like Carmine: don't upset anyone! But meanwhile you play dirty tricks on them, right?'

'Don't shout!'

'Tell me the truth! Do you have another man?'

'No, Mattia. Use your head; we don't know each other! Tomorrow, come tomorrow. We have to give it some thought . . .'

'She goes to bed with a man and we don't know each other, she says!'

'I told you not to shout! This domineering attitude is not welcome in my house.'

'Why can't I tear myself away from you? Did you perhaps have this power over him, too? Why can't I make myself leave?'

'I feel the same way, but we have to wait.'

'That's not what you said last night.'

'It was a bone-chilling night.'

'The more I look at you, the more beautiful you seem. Will you let me come back?'

'At night you can come back whenever you want.'

'And how will I get through the gate?'

'You can find the key among your father's keys.'

'You even gave him a key!'

'Carmine and I loved each other, *carusu.*'

'Loved each other? Or maybe, it seems to me, he only came to you because you open the door to anyone at night?'

'I don't like the way you talk. We two don't understand one another. You go your way and I'll go mine.'

'Your way is contemptible. I spit on it!' Mattia shouts, rising to his feet. His naked body reflected in the dawn dazzles my pupils. I mustn't look at the beauty of those limbs. In the movement of his taut back, the trunk of a young tree, I glimpse a future that has nothing to do with me. And despite a strong desire to call him back and hold him close, I shut my eyes: I mustn't let his image worm its way into my soul. Carmine is right: you can look away and remain your own master. *'One must be cautious with that word "love"; it's a trap nature plants amid the most fragrant herbs, which even the most clever animals can fall into.'* How many hares and rabbits we found caught in the snare at dawn, Carmine, when we woke up at daybreak and ran to the woods to see, remember? But although the same light has suddenly flooded the room, Carmine will not be under the window calling Modesta and Beatrice, who must learn to hold a rifle like a couple of real men. *'As you wish, Princess! I have no doubts about the* Padroncina, *but the* Principessina *is shaking all over and . . .'* Carmine moves off between the trees and the sky . . . Or is it his son who is already passing through the gate, walking away slowly? Behind the window, I follow those steps until they disappear, swallowed up by the green.

The sun's first rays wash over my forehead, freeing me from the burden of anxiety, which for months and months had made me jump at the slightest noise or shadow. I feel like going out and running in that joyous sun which keeps repeating: you're free. The sweet pleasure of not having to expect him anymore, of no longer having to depend on someone else's bidding. No one will ever again take away this pleasure, Mattia. Tiny flowers have sprung up at the edges of the path; was it overnight? Or was I so captured by your will, old Carmine, that I didn't hear spring thumping at the ground, making its debut?

★

'Modesta, Mody! Oh, Princess, good thing you're awake!'

'What is it, Pietro?'

'Come down, come. Oh, Mody, such a commotion!'

'Has the baby come, Pietro? Is it excitement that's making you stammer?'

'It's come, yes, it's come!'

'Judging from your smile, I can tell it's a boy.'

'Yes, Mody, it's a boy! Two doctors and Signor Carlo examined him. He's healthy and strong, I swear to God! My dear Prince has fathered a giant. He was born with his eyes open, Mody!'

'All right, Pietro. Now calm down. I'll get dressed and we'll go right over.'

'Oh, yes, Mody, hurry, hurry . . .'

I was afraid that Pietro, in his joy, might be mistaken, yet seeing the ten-pound bundle that Signorina Inès had churned out, a proud laugh at having gambled against nature rose to my lips. But I couldn't let it out; holding a handkerchief to my mouth, I tried to cover up that laughter. Two doctors and a nurse were staring at me, very serious, and Signorina Inès, lying worn out in the bed, was screaming:

'No, no! I don't want to! Oh, Princess, such a state! And such pain! Tell them. You've given birth; tell them that I can't breastfeed him. An infernal night it's been, with them shouting "Push, push!"'

In bed, heavy and drenched with sweat, Inès spoke to me wide-eyed, staring at the ceiling.

'It was a difficult birth, Princess. Afterwards we made her sleep. Unfortunately the sleeping pill's effects have now worn off. But please believe me; she only just woke up.'

'So give her another sleeping pill.'

'But she has to breastfeed . . .'

Hearing those words, Inès began to writhe and scream. 'If I had known it would be like this, I would never have done it! Never again, never again!'

It had scared her so that she wouldn't try it again, so much the better.

'Leave her alone! Can't you see she doesn't want to hold him? Sister, take the baby away.'

'As you say, Princess! We waited for you to decide . . .'

'Yes, of course, of course. Make her sleep and bring the baby to me in there. I must take my time and get a good look at him! I swear to God, this room seems more like a slaughterhouse than a hospital ward.'

I escape to the little parlour just in time because, despite the hand-kerchief, I can't contain my laughter any longer.

'Listen to her! Screaming like that at the child God has blessed her with!'

'We didn't ask for your opinion, Sister Clara. Let the Princess see the baby and spare us your comments! Oh, Modesta, at last we see each other again. But why are you holding that handkerchief to your mouth? Don't you feel well?'

Sister Clara glared at us angrily.

'Put him in the cradle and leave us to ourselves.'

'Oh, Carlo! Thank goodness you sent her away. I couldn't take it anymore.'

'What are you doing laughing?'

'What else could I do? Such a fit of helpless giggles, I have to let it out.'

'Always unpredictable, Modesta. Looking at you makes me feel like laughing too. What a joy to see you!'

'Why, has it been that long since we've seen each other?'

'Well, I should say so, Princess! It's been months . . .'

'But we saw each other . . .'

'Yes, with other people . . . I wanted to talk with you the way we used to.'

Carlo, that dark mop of hair falling over his watchful eyes, looks at me reproachfully, his delicate hands holding mine tightly. In his quiet gaze I realized how much I'd missed him all those months. I had returned from a distant journey that cannot be summed up. His voice, his way of speaking, the contrast between my dark language of passion and his – lucid and elegant – which I loved so much, but which I could not reconcile with my imagination, gave me a glimpse of the struggle I would have to face in the future. Would I ever be able to sort out the ambivalence that had kept me from loving Carlo?

'Will I be able to, Carlo?'

'That's my Modesta: in a split second her expression and mood have already changed. Will you be able to what?'

'Oh, if only I could talk to you!'

'About what, Modesta?'

'About things that are so unclear to me . . . Mental and emotional obstacles that are hard to talk about.'

'Everything can always be talked about. I learned it from you.'

Hopelessly, I read in his eyes that my image would always be split by a white chalk line.

'What is it, Modesta?'

'Carlo, I need help.'

'With me you can speak frankly; you know that.'

'I know that. Thank you. That was all I wanted to hear you say.'

Hand in hand, enclosed in a circle, he drew reassurance from me and I, from him, an awareness that I was not alone.

'Who's that crying, Carlo?'

'What do you mean, who's crying, Modesta? You're strange. I've never seen you like this. It's as if you were young again, but distant.'

'He's healthy, isn't he, Carlo?'

'Very healthy! Come and see him. Then, if you want to keep him you'll have to choose a wet-nurse. Three of them are already waiting.'

'But why is he crying?'

'He's hungry, Modesta! You too had a child; have you forgotten? Come and see him.'

'I'm keeping him!'

'But you haven't seen him.'

'What does it matter! You saw him; that's good enough for me.'

'No, I must be firm about this. You have to see him for yourself and make certain he's normal. He seems sturdier than Eriprando.'

'But Eriprando isn't Ippolito's son.'

'You told me that before. Tell me, Modesta, are you still worried about the father's mongolism?'

'I, too, am the sister of a mongoloid.'

'Oh!'

'But no one knows that, not even Beatrice.'

'Is that what's bothering you?'

'Not at all. I told you because for the first time in my life I know that, with you, I can talk about anything. And I'm happy to have entrusted you with a secret that I've had to keep walled up inside me like so many others. Things we can't say fester inside us.'

'You move me, Modesta.'

'How softly he's crying . . . Eriprando wailed like a banshee.'

'But if we keep talking, without feeding him, you'll soon hear him wail all right. Come and see him. He's a beautiful specimen. It seems that nature wanted to make amends for her past sins.'

In the crib, instead of the dumpling of indistinct flesh that Eriprando had been, a well-moulded little face with pensive temples rests on the pillow.

'Pietro is right; his eyes are open! It took Eriprando several weeks.'

'Yes, but we're beginning to see many of these cases.'

'Can he see us?'

'I don't think so.'

'He has a somewhat prominent chin too . . . he looks like . . .'

'Like who, Modesta?'

'He looks like Jacopo, Beatrice's uncle.'

At the sound of that barely murmured name, the pale eyes, a faint misty grey, stared at me. Of course he couldn't see, but the conviction that he had recognized me made me lean over the crib and reach out my hands.

'What are you doing?'

'I want him, right away!'

'Crazy little thing! First you didn't want to see him and now . . .'

'Now I've seen him, I've fallen in love, and I'm taking him away with me. I'm stealing him, and I'm going to name him Jacopo. Jacopo! Don't you see how he responds with his eyes? It's his name.'

'How crazy you women are! I see. Wrap him up well, and let's go. I'll take you home, where I hope you'll have him fed.'

'Oh! Don't worry about a wet-nurse. Two days ago Stella had a baby boy as well, and I'm sure Jacopo will like her. Stella is the prettiest peasant girl around here.'

53

Carlo, eyes carefully on the road, drove slowly, like last time, to avoid the bumps and holes, the sharp turns, the sudden appearance of a dog or a bicycle. He accelerated cautiously to pass a wagon, a laden donkey or a flock of sheep that turned the air into a cloud of dust. It hadn't rained in months. But soon, at some invisible signal, the great white clouds suspended over the arid dunes would burst into cool tears marking summer's end.

Every so often, like last time, his eyes hold mine in the rearview mirror and help me carry a living being in my arms. For the first time in my life, I found myself talking about a heavy log that I had to drag, about a hovel lost in a sea of mud, about the flames of a lamp hurled against a door by my own hand . . .

'You taught me to swim, Carlo, to speak; teach me to think like you. The future lies in men like you.'

In the mirror, his soft gaze is like a gentle kiss on my forehead, but a new sadness drifted over his eyes, like a late-summer rain cloud.

'Are you sad because you see that I can never be like you, Carlo?'

'No, Modesta, I'm sad because I fear that some irreparable mistake has been committed by us men of the future, as you call us. I listen to you and I no longer dare speak to you of certainties, as I would have done only a year ago. Look over there, in front of that flock. Here, too, pennants like in Rome, with that slogan: "*Me ne* *frego"*, I don't give a damn.* In one year, this abnormal burgeoning of skulls and crossbones . . . He seized the opportunity, the Honourable Benito Mussolini. No platform for his party: *'We are about action rather than words!'* The coal crisis, England's defaulting debtors . . . to save the situation, a loan from the United States must be obtained. Only to reach the point of blackmail: *"The Fascist revolt against the intolerable Bolshevik regime".'*

'Is that why you're sad?'

'No, I'm not worried. They won't succeed . . . I'm sad because of the mistakes we made in the past, and your faith in me scares me a little. You, on the other hand, should never change. Don't try to imitate men. I have the vague sensation that there is a new strength in you and in Beatrice.'

'Before, you used to say I was immoral, and I . . .'

'Before, I didn't understand a thing . . . Now what, Modesta? Why are you laughing again?'

'I'm laughing because this Jacopo is incredibly strong. He's really hearty! We won't have problems like we did with Eriprando.'

'What problems, Modesta?'

'Well, he didn't want to suckle!'

'And this makes you laugh?'

'I wish this ride would never end, Carlo! It's nice to be driven by you like this. Beatrice told me that you two often go walking on the slopes of the Mountain.'

'Yes, often.'

'That, too, has made her become so strong and composed. Does she lean on your arm when you walk?'

'Of course.'

'I envy her, Carlo.'

'And I envy your being able to say "I envy her." Don't ever change, Modesta. Don't imitate us men!'

'Why didn't she come with you?'

'As if you didn't know her! You got her off your hands, and now you ask! Shameless!'

'I enjoy hearing you tell me what I know. She's your wife, and you have to take care of her. She gave you a hard time, did she?'

'I'll say! For months, she wouldn't even accept the idea of having a niece or nephew by that commoner, Inès.'

'I can just hear her!'

'Then, more because of concern for you, at least we were able to talk about it. But she wouldn't come. About that, there was nothing I could do to make her budge. "Me in a hospital ward like any ordinary commoner? Never!"'

'And where is she now?'

'At your house. Didn't Pietro tell you? The poor man! She chased him off rudely when he came with the news. "Only so as not to offend Modesta, I'll go to her house and see her. But never, ever will I set eyes on a bastard child!"'

'Oh, Carlo, how well you imitate her! You make me die laughing. Do it again, please!'

'"Never ever, Modesta! You can't ask me to imitate her, ever! *Uffa*, never!"'

★

In front of the gate

Pietro is pacing up and down with an alacrity unthinkable for that immense body. From time to time he wipes his perspiring cranium under the bewildered eyes of Signorina Elena who, silent and motion-less, is struggling to contain an unusual trembling in her lips and hands:

'Oh. Princess, thank God you're here! I can't take it! Forgive me, but I can't stand it. I cannot stand this tension! Look at him; he isn't even aware of your presence. He's beside himself; it's frightening!'

'What's wrong, Pietro? Tell me, what is it?'

'Oh, Mody, Beatrice chased me away again! It's a sign that she really doesn't want him! She doesn't want my dear Prince's baby.'

'Who's the mistress in this house, Pietro?'

'*Voscenza*, Princess.'

'Then calm down. Here we do what I say.'

'Yes, yes, Mody, but with bad blood, if Beatrice doesn't want him, with bad blood! There has never been bad blood in the Brandiforti family!'

'What is he saying, Princess? He's been moaning and groaning for the past hour. I should point out that all this tension is upsetting Eriprando. I sent him to play on the beach with Nunzio just in time . . .'

'That's just what Pietro is saying, in other words, Elena.'

'But he's the one who started shouting at Argentovivo.'

'Why at Argentovivo?'

'I'll tell you why, Mody: that woman from the continent doesn't understand a thing! It's because she, Argentovivo, instead of soothing the troubled waters and calming Beatrice, backs her up. It's unfair! In God's truth, she and Beatrice are unfair! Beatrice: what can you expect! But her, why fan the flames?'

'Then we'll extinguish the flames. Don't worry, Pietro, calm down! . . . Here, you take him, he's heavy. Don't you see I'm holding him? There, bring him to Stella, before he starves to death.'

'But I . . . I don't know how to hold him! What if I drop him and he breaks? Signorina Elena, you take him . . .'

'Go on, Pietro, don't make a fuss!'

'Forgive me, Princess, and you too, *signorina,* but I was upset because I had decided to leave if the right thing wasn't done. And going away and leaving my Mody and my Beatrice would have been a terrible step for Pietro.'

'As you can see, you won't have to take that step. Now go on!'

'Oh! He's crying, Mody! I didn't hurt him, did I?'

'No, Pietro, I told you he's crying because he's hungry.'

In the parlour

In the parlour's shadows, Beatrice stood waiting, with Argentovivo nearby. The drawn drapes brought back the dimness and feelings of a much earlier time.

'This house has become a barracks, Modesta! The drapes wide open, the furniture unpolished, not one vase of flowers! I don't like that Signorina Elena; she seems like a *carabiniere.* I took the liberty of telling her so, and I'm telling you as well.'

'Signorina Elena is not at fault, Beatrice. I'm the one who ordered her to open the drapes.'

'What do you mean, she's not at fault? I reminded her many times! She's a woman, isn't she? And it's clear that you, like Carlo, have so many things to think about that it's up to us women to look after your well-being and everything that concerns the home.'

'If this bothers you so much, Beatrice, we'll talk about it.'

'Of course it bothers me! I had to follow my husband, and I feel responsible seeing all this.'

Under Carlo's terrified eyes I rushed to support her. In the soft gloom of an earlier time, she clings to me and weeps. And like then, I find my hands circling her slender waist.

'Oh, Modesta, hold me close! You're not angry at me, are you? I'm so awful! I left you all alone. I was horrid to Pietro, too. I saw him looking at me hatefully. He's never looked at me that way, and he's right because I was unfair. And you, too, were bad, Argentovivo. Go away, get out of my sight!'

'Go, Argentovivo. Leave us alone.'

'Yes, that's right, chase her out! She, too, was horrid. Instead of calming me down . . . I was awful to Carmine as well. It's dreadful, Modesta. He's dead! I didn't know he was going to die.'

'No one could have known, Beatrice.'

'I should have gone to see him, at least one last time.'

'I went for you as well.'

'You're so good. You went . . . I . . . I was afraid . . . And the one . . . the one who was born? You didn't keep him, did you, Modesta? Tell me you didn't keep him.'

'On the contrary, I had to keep him. I was compelled to.'

'You, compelled? Don't make me laugh! Who can compel you to do anything?'

'Uncle Jacopo.'

'What?'

'Yes, he's come back, but not in a dream like before. In flesh and blood, a little baby, with his eyes. He's been reborn.'

'And how do you know that?'

'I saw him. And I'll bet that if you see him, you will recognize him too.'

'Oh, let's go see. It seems incredible! Where is he? Where is he? I want to see him!'

★

In the room with Stella

'You're right, Modesta, he's his exact likeness. But not the colour of his eyes. There's no way you could know this. Uncle Jacopo had blue eyes, whereas this Jacopo has grey eyes, like Nonna Gaia. Will you let me hold him, Stella, now that he's been fed? Oh, how long he is! But will you have enough milk for both of them?'

'Oh, Princess, this *picciriddu* is a blessing! Look here, my breasts are bursting.'

'Just look at his tiny hands, Modesta: such long fingers, and with oval nails! *His* hands, Modesta. Thank God you recognized him right away, thank God! And you, Argentovivo, stop crying and go and tell Pietro you're sorry. It's all your fault! But of course, everyone knows that you people from the continent don't understand a thing! How happy Nonna Gaia will be over this return. You have no idea how much she loved Uncle Jacopo. They were always bickering, but they loved each other very much.'

Argentovivo and Pietro were arguing in the corner, or rather, Pietro was repeatedly nodding his head under the flood of words Argentovivo was spewing out.

*

'Well! Did you two make up? Oh, Modesta, those two argue so much that I get the impression they might be in love. What a couple! I'm only sorry we lost Carmelo, because now we could have filled Uncle Jacopo's room, like Nonna always wanted, and not only that one . . . What if we were to buy the villa back again now that Carmine is dead, Modesta? What do you say? Think how happy Nonna would be! Eriprando in the room upstairs, Jacopo in his own room. And God willing! . . . here, haven't you noticed anything? Put your hand on my belly. Feel it?'

'How far along, Beatrice?'

'It's been two months since I've bled.'

'Does Carlo know?'

'No. In keeping with tradition, you had to be the first to know. Place your palms, like that, and bless this child for me.'

313

'I bless you, Beatrice.'

'Oh, if only God grants me a boy! Ignazio must come back. Ignazio was so handsome, the best looking of all!'

'Ignazio will return, Beatrice, but the villa at Carmelo must remain the Tudias'.'

'Why do you say that, Modesta?'

'Because we can't wrong Carmine when he's dead, and you know that.'

'I know. Carmine, dead, must be respected.'

54

'This *picciriddu* never cries, Princess. I'm amazed! He opens his eyes, sucks his milk, and sleeps peacefully. Look at him! I can't get over it: he seems like a grown man, this Jacopo . . . I shouldn't say it, but in just three months he's become more of a son to me than this 'Ntoni, who can never get enough.'

'But your 'Ntoni is beautiful, Stella!'

'Well . . . I don't know about beautiful, Princess! But he's capricious and headstrong! Just like his father. I sense that, like him, he'll give me a lot of trouble.'

'Not necessarily, Stella, if you raise him differently.'

'Do you mean that a person's destiny can be changed, Princess?'

'Everything can be changed, Stella.'

'Still no rain! This summer never seems to end! My father said that thirty years ago the heat and humidity went on until the Day of the Dead. "It's a bad sign!" he said. "The dead are thirsty." And there were great misfortunes that year. If only the rain would come to cleanse people's souls . . . Everyone seems to have gone crazy, both on the island and on the continent, chasing after these *carusi* in black shirts. We can always expect misfortunes from the continent!'

'Are you worried about your brothers, Stella?'

'Not only them! Those Fascists have captivated Melo, too, with their talk, and he went with them to Rome. I don't want to think about it. Not actually Rome, but nearby, a town called Tivoli.'

'Melo? But I thought he had gone to America.'

'Exactly! But he stopped in Rome first . . . it's raining up there, he wrote . . . and then he's going to sail from Naples. If only it would rain here too, at least!'

'It will rain, Stella. And don't worry about the men. Beatrice's husband also had to go to Rome. Melo and Carlo will be back; don't upset yourself. You don't want your milk to turn to water, do you?'

'You're right. We women shouldn't worry too much about them. Who understands them, all that running around they do? Stella is a woman, she'll calm down, she knows she must simply do her duty.'

'Good night, Stella.'

'To you as well, *Voscenza*, may you sleep well.'

Stella smiles, and the dim light that illuminates her face becomes brighter. One more glance around the big room in shadow, at the two little cribs side by side back there, where Jacopo and 'Ntoni are lying, and Modesta – like every night – can return to the quiet of her bedroom.

On the table, a small white pipe gleams among the books; she fills it. And she sits at the window, smoking in the dark and staring at the sky. '*Smoking collects the good thoughts of the day and drives out those that are as insidious as the drone of* 'u marranzanu.'* Carmine's voice coils round and round the smoke without startling Modesta. The gentleness of that voice was a sign of the fatal sentence she had sought in vain in his chest, in his eyes. And maybe, Modesta thinks, maybe this peace that has accompanied my every move for months and months is a sign that *La Certa* has decided to interrupt my journey too . . .

A distant flash of lightning, followed by muffled thunder, breaks through the heat's defences, making the trees flinch. The silent lightning unleashed on the night's broad canvas performs arabesques and Catherine wheels* as complicated as the fireworks that enthral Eriprando at Pentecost. Mesmerized, like him, by the imaginary pyrotechnics, I almost don't hear the door opening softly behind me. It's him! . . . Can someone you've met as though in a nightmare reappear before you, alive? Or have I been dreaming again? Slowly, Mattia stands before me in the dark. I can't see him but I recognize his silence . . . the ominous silence of a hostile dog or animal. Or is it youth that breathes like that? Now he takes a step toward me and I too am forced to move to the table that divides us and grab the pistol with one hand while turning on the lamp with the other.

'What are you doing here, you madman? How did you get in? Stay away from me, Mattia! One more step and I'll blow your head off!'

'I won't come any closer. I only came to bring you back the keys. Here: there were three of them. I took them from my father's key ring. Here they are, Princess, all lined up: the key to the gate, the front door and your room.'

'And you couldn't have sent them to me or come during the day?'

'That's how Mattia is! He likes to surprise people. Plus, I still had some hope.'

'What hope, you crazy fool?'

'That you were lying. We Tudias are jealous of our memories, almost more jealous of our memories of the dead than of the living. But a memory shouldn't be marred by doubt, and you made me have doubts. So I wanted to follow "his" course through the locks with my own hands, to be certain. You told the truth, and Carmine always lied to his sons.'

'Let the dead rest in peace and forget about it. Modesta has forgotten everything.'

'*Brava!* First she appears in other people's houses like a madwoman. Causes a turmoil of speculation with her insinuations, and then she forgets! Why did you come to Carmelo? Did you come to rob us? Why did you kiss him?'

'I took what your father owed me.'

'You loved him that much? Well? Do you still love him? I've watched you each day; I followed you from a distance. You don't have so many men as you made me think. You're alone, and you think about him.'

'Modesta has forgotten him.'

'Have you forgotten me, too?'

'You too. Now get out of here! What do you want from me?'

'It's you I want.'

'There are many women, Mattia.'

'I've looked, but it's your eyes I saw in theirs. Look into my eyes and put down that gun.'

On the table, three keys in a row – the gate, the front door and my room – glint in the circle of lamplight; they murmur a precise message to my mind, a course confronted in darkness without hesitation. Nunzio is always on guard duty. Lupo and Selassié keep watch.

'The dogs, you mean? Well, Mattia knows how to get around dogs and watchmen! You're the only one he doesn't know how to get around, and believe me, Mody . . . that's what he called you, didn't he?'

'How do you know that?'

'I know . . . and believe me, I tried to forget that bone-chilling night as you called it, but the more I tried the colder I felt and the more I yearned for your body's heat.'

I can't listen to that warm, pleading voice and, as though hypnotized, my frigid hand sets the gun down by the keys.

'You're more beautiful than I remembered! I understand; I asked too much of you.'

'It won't work, Mattia. You're too young, and you'll start asking questions again and disturbing the peace and quiet of this house.'

'Try me.'

His hand on mine, in the circle of light, shatters the wave of tranquillity that had lulled my senses for months. There's danger in the warmth of that hand. I stare into his eyes.

'I lose myself in your eyes. Don't make me go . . . your gaze is like a wind that sweeps me away.'

There's danger in those eyes, golden like grain. The wind in his eyes sweeps me toward him, and though my frozen body resists, my hand rebels and seeks his palm. In the circle of light, my hand loses its strength in his, and I close my eyes. He picks me up, and with that familiar touch a spell is once again cast over my senses, reawakening joy in my nerves and veins. I wasn't mistaken: *La Certa* was watching me from a distance, but only to put me to the test. I must accept the danger, if that danger is the only thing that can revive my senses – but taking my time, without the tremors of youth. And when he, blinded by his young flesh, tries to enter me, I gently stop him.

'What's wrong, Modesta?'

'If you're a man, Mattia, and not an undependable *carusu*, you know what you must do.'

'You're right, Modesta. But I've been wanting you for so long! Squeeze your thighs at least and let me come.'

I squeeze my legs tight and he comes. I wipe up his semen with my palms, smear it over my stomach and breasts, and I come too. He has the same smell as Carmine, the same sharp, salty tang of a life ripened in the sun. *La Certa* smiles, waiting. She just wants to take away the grief and the part of me, now dead, that I must leave behind. To do this I must accept my youth, that young man with the firm cheeks, unseasoned by wind and rain. Without hesitation, I grab hold of my youth in that bold, tender flesh.

'Will you let me come back?'

'Of course, Mattia. I like you when you're like this.'

'You like me! What a thing to say . . . You should love me!'

'Hush, Mattia; don't ruin everything.'

Slowly he slips the three keys in with his, watching me and letting me watch him. I could be happy looking at him for ever, at dawn, at dusk, holding him in my arms at night, that body young like mine.

'Will you let me come back?'

'You put my keys in with yours. Why are you asking?'

'So you weren't asleep?'

'No, I was watching you.'

'But your eyes were closed.'

'I saw you anyway. You're beautiful naked.'

'Don't say that; you make me want you.'

'Tomorrow, Mattia. Now you have to go.'

'You're putting me to the test?'

'You asked me to.'

'My hands are shaking; that's how much I still want you. But I'll be able to pass the test.'

'Let's hope so, Mattia.'

'You'll see!'

By now it was clear that a part of me would always belong to them, to that language with its underlying passion that at times made Stella's voice clear and warm, and at other times darkened it like a threatening sea awaiting a storm:

'It doesn't upset you, Princess, if Prando calls me Mama? I tried every way I could to make him get over this habit, but Prando is wilful and stubborn, if anything more so than 'Ntoni.'

'Why should I be upset, Stella? Let him call you that. If he's chosen you for a mother, what's wrong with that? So then, Prando, how many mothers do you have?'

'I have two mothers, and also two aunts.'

'Listen to him! And who is this second aunt?'

'Beautiful Elena!'

'And do you have brothers too?'

'No!'

'What about that one who's watching you? Isn't Jacopo your brother?'

'That one is yours!'

''Ntoni is mine . . . But Jacopo?'

'No!'

'Let him be, Stella; he's nearly asleep. Let him find his own way in his sleep. Tell me, Stella. I can see you're troubled – is your father causing you concern?'

'He hasn't accepted the idea that I'm better off here than at home. It's Melo I'm worried about. Why hasn't he come back yet and why hasn't he written? Signor Carlo has been back from Rome for some time.'

'But Melo was supposed to go to America after Rome. He must have boarded a ship.'

'Without dropping us a line? People were killed and wounded in Rome. I heard it. I can't read the newspapers, but I heard it. Signor Carlo came back gaunt and dejected.'

'But Carlo is on the other side, Stella, and he's only disheartened over the success that these ideas of Mussolini have had.'

'What does that man want, dividing our men like that? Melo is my husband. I shouldn't say so but he has a violent temper, and I can't rely on him. If, as *Voscenza* tells me, Signor Carlo is on the other side, he must be right, since Signor Carlo is a reasonable man. If only he could talk to Melo when he comes back!'

'Is that what's bothering you?'

'It is! If only Signor Carlo could make him use his head!'

'When Melo comes back, we'll have him talk with Carlo, Stella.'

'I can't stand any more of this male frenzy! What need was there for him to rush off to Rome, and then to that America, which is even farther away?'

'For his inheritance, Stella.'

'But what need is there? We're not poor. Physical separation leads to true distance!'

'He'll come back, Stella.'

'*Voscenza* comforts me, Princess, like these angelic tears that God decided to rain down on us from heaven. Such blessed coolness! Jacopo has stopped sweating, the poor *picciriddu*!'

Stella, her face faintly clouded with anxiety. Stella, with her dark slanted eyes like slits of polished stone, two bright stars even amid the din of the storm. The rain shakes the walls of the house, violently at times, then softly. The corridors and stairs glide silently under my steps. A few moments to reflect on the day, on how Prando has grown in just a few weeks. '*Jacopo's arrival made him the older one overnight*', and Mattia slowly opens the door, smiling. He's always smiling now.

'I didn't hear you, Mattia. How did you get here?'

'On Orlando. I'm sick of the motorcycle! My father was right: all that noise hurts the ears and doesn't let you hear an enemy approaching. It makes you an easy target for anyone who has it in for you. In just three days, Orlando saved me from a well-planned ambush.'

'Who was it?'

'The same ones who earlier had their sights set on Carmine. I'm the master now, and I have to be careful. *Cancia la vita quannu 'u padri mori*, your life changes when your father dies. In just a short time, Mattia has aged, and now he must plant his own roots in the land. You have to help me, Modesta, you have to teach me!'

'What do you want to know? If you can fill your father's shoes?'

'You've understood me.'

'Carmine didn't have confidence in you.'

'And you?'

'I sense Carmine's strength in you, but I can't erase his doubts about you from my mind.'

'And to think that I was the one who wanted to make him doubt me!'

'Why?'

'Who knows! Maybe it was a way to assert myself; what do I know? Make him have reservations about me at least, shake that bossy self-assurance he had toward everyone. But now that he's dead – who could have imagined it? – I feel his misgivings hanging over me. Now I can only know from you, and maybe not even from you. I have no one.'

'What about Vincenzo?'

'Vincenzo! If only Carmine were alive to see his darling blue-eyed boy! The mild, obedient boy has become a fury.'

'How can that be?'

'Clearly it was only fear that made him respect him before. Since Carmine died, Vincenzo has done nothing but curse his memory. He started drinking the day of the funeral. And now he's left the house. I'm cold, Modesta.'

'Hold me; I'll warm you up. What's wrong, Mattia?'

'Don't look at me. I can't hold back these tears. I'm not a man, Modesta. Don't look at me.'

For the first time, I feel compassion for his youth and mine, but only for a moment, because I quickly recognize the traps that lie concealed by that tenderness. *'Youth is more astute than old age and knows how to use every means.'* Only a moment, and already he presses his advantage.

'Tell me you love me, Modesta.'

'Be good, Mattia.'

'Say it!'

'The word you're asking me for, Mattia, is one that must be used cautiously.'

'But I love you.'

'You need me.'

'And that's not love?'

'In time you'll see, Mattia.'

'You're driving me crazy, Modesta! Say it: I'm not worthy of you.'

'I have two children and a husband, Mattia. Don't forget that.'

'A husband! That animal! Just say the word, and I'll rid you of that cross.'

'What do you mean?'

'I'll kill him for you and I'll marry you myself.'

'Try it and I'll shoot your hands off!'

'If you marry me, you'll own all the lands again, and with you by my side I could defy everyone. Marry me. I've given you so many assurances these past few months.'

It was true, but his youth was not my future and I didn't want land. People marry only out of need . . . Those reassurances were only the usual silken ties to bind you more tightly, afterwards. I sensed it in the force of his hands which, without meaning to, were nearly snapping my wrists. Don't lose your equilibrium, Modesta, don't listen to the warmth of those hands. Look him in the eye, where already a dark prison is outlined in his honeyed gaze. And to escape the honey that nourished my senses, I run to Carlo:

'. . . And to think, Carlo, that when I met you, I thought all young men were like you. Dreamer! I saw my future among many Carlos, with whom I could talk, grow, make love.'

'Well, there are some: Jose, for example. He and his companion are different. In Milan, they were an example for us, our pride and admiration, so to speak. Just today, he wrote me a little note that was half serious and half facetious, in which, between the lines, he calls me a traitor because of my "Puccini-like" dream of marriage: "*Un bel dì vedremo* . . ." He also says that between the two genuinely "Italiot" evils, he always prefers D'Annunzio.'

'Jose, Jose! It sounds like the same old story! And the others? Why don't you talk to me about the other comrades? Are they all like that Pasquale who is always following you around, though you don't want to tell me?'

'Pasquale is a good comrade, Modesta. Let's not lose sight of reality: we're in Sicily!'

'But did you see him at home with his wife? Did you see how he treats her? What am I saying? He doesn't pay any attention to her at all. During those few moments when she appears, poor Elisa seems invisible!'

'Yes, actually you pointed that out to me . . .'

'You're frowning, Carlo. Why?'

'Because I have to admit that before I met you I hadn't noticed these things . . . Thinking back, you're right. I must say that even in Milan he was like that, only I wasn't aware of it. There were so many more urgent things to think about.'

'Do you think my concern is too personal? Tell me the truth.'

'No. It's just that now too there are more important things to deal with.'

'You're right.'

'What you're after, Modesta, will come later. When Bebel's book replaces *Cuore*,* when, as Maria says, instead of saints on the calendar, there will be the names of Marie Curie, Louis Pasteur . . .'

'And if it doesn't happen, Carlo?'

'We will continue to cultivate our garden, as Voltaire says, and wait for the seed to bear fruit. Look at that sunset, Modesta! Let's go for a walk before the divine Beatrice, followed by her handmaiden – do you know that Argentovivo has become very charming? – comes out of the kitchen and overwhelms us with delicious morsels. She's learning how to cook. She says she wants to be the one to cook for the baby when it's born. I remember my mother, too . . .'

'The wind has picked up, Carlo. Let's run! I love the wind. Up there with the nuns there was never any wind. Everything was still, as though submerged in dense, grey water. Maybe we were nothing more than lifeless fish in an aquarium.'

'There! the poet dozing beneath the tough exterior of the pastoral *carusa* is emerging. Even your face changes. How do you do it?'

'Carmine used to say that I was like a troubadour, and Tuzzu too, I think . . . Memories fade, Carlo. It's terrible!'

'Aren't troubadours poets?'

'As soon as I get my degree, I'll do nothing but write poetry and run outside, drinking up all the wind that stirs, enlivens, wakes – how beautiful words are, Carlo! – yes, well, that impregnates this island and allows it to be reborn, ever new . . . except for the attorneys, notaries and professors.'

'How are things going at the university?'

'To be truthful, Carlo, it's horrible: they look at me as though I were a circus freak.'

'Even the professors?'

'Of course! They're so astounded to see a female creature in those hallowed halls that they hardly question me. Everything I say is fine with them. It won't be difficult to get my degree.'

'You've told me everything about yourself but . . . why do you want to get this degree at all costs?'

'When I was in the convent, it was one of my dreams, and childhood dreams should be cherished. Then, if there is an "afterwards", I'll go out and teach, like they do in Turkey. Atatürk has sent everyone to teach in the rural areas.'

'For me, teaching was always boring.'

'With children, it's a different matter! You should see how much fun it is with Eriprando! I can't wait to get back to the house and write him a delightful story I've thought up for tomorrow.'

'What's it about this time?'

'The adventurous tale of a gecko's journey along the desert of a wall.'

55

'Still reading at this hour, Modesta?'

'Oh, I didn't hear you, Mattia.'

'Are you doing the accounts?'

'No, I was writing.'

'No hugs for me?'

'*Tosto caruso*, if you hold me like that from behind, how can I hug you?'

'You seem distant.'

'No, it's just that I was thinking . . .'

'Maybe you're angry because I haven't been here for a week?'

'Why should I be? It's been that way with us these past months.'

'I want you so much.'

'It's that time.'

'So what? Blood is natural. Then if you want, if it doesn't hurt – I know that sometimes it hurts you women – I can enter you without the glove. It's more pleasurable . . . But how on earth did you get the idea of calling it that?'

I couldn't mention old Carmine. He was the one who'd called it that; it would mean a big quarrel if I said his name.

'Who knows! Have you had many women, Mattia?'

'I had one serious affair when I was a soldier, a woman who taught me a lot of things! Before that I was a squeamish *picciriddu* . . . Then the front moved on and I had to leave her. The war moves slowly but it wipes out everything. It turns everything into a desert: houses, crops, feelings.'

'What is war like, Mattia?'

'Sickening! I saw so much blood! Sickening, but also thrilling at times. It's like being in an exciting trance, challenging yourself and all of nature; when you rush out of the trenches, I mean, and go off to attack all together. Then comes the great calm of the trenches, the mud, the dust, a somnolence harbouring an eagerness for action. As you wait, you think you're resting, you think you're content with the silence, but when they start shooting, you realize in a flash that that was all you were waiting for, that you were thirsting for the screams and the exploding grenades. Well! War can even have its appeal! Sometimes this life seems like one long wait in a muddy trench.

'Not when I'm with you, Modesta. How old are you? You seem like a *picciridda* right now, or are you a sorceress? My sorceress, my little lava devil . . . Why don't you want me?'

'Why do you say I don't want you? You're inside me, Mattia. I'm holding you in my arms.'

'Your body wants me, but your mind? Where does your mind go? What is it looking for?'

'You know what I'm looking for.'

'Oh, sure! Excuses! Freedom, lack of freedom! It's that you don't love me.'

'But I do love you, you pig-headed *caruso*.'

'At night! But I want you all the time.'

'But you can come any time. I told you.'

'Oh, sure! To have tea, like a stranger.'

'Why a stranger? A friend.'

'There's no such thing as friendship between a man and a woman. That, too, drives me crazy!'

'Let's not get started on Carlo again, Mattia!'

'If only it were just Carlo! And that Pasquale, what does he come here for? And that one who is half woman, half *carusu*, who goes out by herself and goes to the university with you. What does she want from you? Don't tell me she, too, comes here. Oh, Modesta, hold me close! Sometimes I feel like I'm losing my mind!'

'Don't squeeze me so tight like that. Let me go. You're hurting me!'

'You see, you hate me! Why are you so cold now?'

'How many times must I tell you, Mattia? When you act like that, I lose my desire.'

'I'm leaving before I kill you! Never mind desire! I'll kill you, so help me God! You and all your friends. I'm leaving. Not a word, you Judas demon?* Before, you used to get angry at least . . .'

My desire evaporated, hearing that hurtful voice. As the months went by, I increasingly hoped he wouldn't appear, yet I couldn't resist that body with its smooth, firm skin, barely past adolescence.

★

'. . . Always splashing around in the water, right, Modesta? I like this dark body. I would never have believed it. Before, I used to like fair skin. Now those bodies seem pale compared to yours. Come away with me. Let's go up north, where the sun is gentle and the water is placid. I like the sea of Capri, Ischia. Have you ever been there? Let's take a honeymoon trip beforehand and then get married . . . Where were you last night? I waited two hours for you.'

'I left you a note.'

'I didn't see it.'

'Then you must not have looked carefully; it was on the desk.'

'I hate that desk, and all those books. When you're not here, everything in this room feels hostile to me. Where were you? With Prando? Was he acting up like last time?'

'I was in Catania with Beatrice, who gave birth. We were worried about her; Beatrice has narrow hips. It was a lengthy labour and I couldn't leave her.'

'Oh! But in the end it all went well, if you're smiling.'

'She's fine, but she has to stay in bed and rest quietly.'

'What was it, a boy or a girl?'

'A delicate, very beautiful little girl; she seems extraordinary, like a miniature woman.'

'Too bad! I imagine your brother-in-law . . .'

'Why too bad? I said she was delicate, but she's healthy.'

'It's not that. They say that if a girl is born first, another two or three will follow her. That it's a struggle to have a boy. What is it, Modesta? Why are you shaking now?'

I was shaking at those words that had just been spoken so scornfully. I try to understand the reason for that insane contempt which before, in my struggle for survival, I had underestimated, or rather accepted as something natural, like the Mountain, the sea, the seasons. But now I cannot contain an impulse of blind hatred for that man who stares at me, bewildered, as he keeps saying:

'What's wrong, Modesta? What did I say? What did I do?'

'Go, please, I don't feel well. If you come tomorrow, during the day when everything is clearer, perhaps I can explain it to you.'

'Is Beatrice in danger?'

'It's not that, Mattia. I'm confused. Please go. I need to be alone.'

'All right. You study too much, Modesta, you're tired . . . All right, I'll go, just don't look at me like that. By now I know my Princess. Oh, Modesta, tomorrow I'm going to Modica; I'll be there a week, I have some business to attend to, but as soon as I get back you'll see me . . . Aren't you glad I tell you what I'm doing? You should be pleased . . .'

I don't want to hate him. How could I hate him, Carmine, Tuzzu and even Mimmo, when just the day before, with my own eyes, I witnessed how the arrival of a girl is received even by a mother? Mattia kisses me gently and goes away quietly in that firm, solid body of a confident male. I no longer see him. My attention is now focused on Beatrice's desperate face as she weeps.

'But Beatrice, what does it matter? I don't understand you. She's beautiful, it's a life and . . . and then she's like us, Beatrice! Please, don't act like that!'

'Oh, sure! It's easy for you to talk. You had a boy right away.'

'But it's all the same, Beatrice! At the time I . . .'

'Liar! You're just saying that to console me. Liar!'

I don't want to hate her, but that 'liar' has haunted me for days, forcing me to revisit the past, painfully resurrecting all the words spoken by Mother Leonora, by Gaia, by my mother – words that I would have preferred to bury along with their dead bodies. But you can't bury anyone until you've fully understood what they were saying. And what were they saying? That women are women's enemy, just as men are.

*

'*Voscenza* can't sleep. Is that why you've come to see us? Look Prando, it's Mama. First you wanted her, and now that she's here you go and hide. What's wrong? Why don't you answer? It's impossible to get him to say a word when he's decided he won't talk. He was sleeping so soundly, but then he woke up. Would *Voscenza* like some coffee?'

'Call me Modesta, Stella.'

'I've tried, I'm trying to, but I just can't say it . . . Look at that! It's always that way between a mother and son. They're bound by unseen roots; twins are too, they say. What woke you up, Prando?'

'I don't know!'

'And *Voscenza*? What woke me was a foreboding, or this crazy moon that calls out the lunatics, widows and souls in torment. I don't like it when it shines too bright like this. This is a year of great changes! First drought, then torrential rains that wash away the fields. And now this wintry light that confuses night with day! What are you doing now, Prando? Why are you tugging at me like that? Do you want me to hold you?'

'No! I want Modesta to hold me!'

'And you're telling me? So go to her! What are you waiting for?'

'No more now. Now I'm going back to bed, but later I'll come back again.'

'How is Beatrice? Has she recovered?'

'She's very well, Stella.'

'And *la nicaredda*, the little one?'

'She's doing well too; at least we hope so.'

'What did they name her? You told me, but I've forgotten. I want to tell Prando about this little cousin of his . . . Ida, did you say? A lovely name! So that was the name of Signor Carlo's mother?'

'Yes, Stella, but he's already calling her Bambolina, little doll, like you call my son Prando.'

'Only because Eriprando seemed so long and sober. Maybe I shouldn't have?'

'No, no, you were right to. See how quickly he took to it?'

'My name is Prando. And also Eriprando. I have two names, two of them.'

'And now you also have a little cousin, Prando.'

''*Na femminuccia*, a girl like you?'

'Yes.'

'And like Mama?'

'Yes.'

'Why are you always holding Jacopo? Put him down!'

'Because he's little. He can't stand up by himself, like you can.'

'Oh! So I'm stronger?'

'Of course, and more capable.'

'What does capable mean?'

'Grown up like a man, big and strong.'

'And he's not capable?'

'Oh no, he's little and he's not strong yet.'

'Can I touch him?'

Encouraged by Stella, Eriprando gave in and patted Jacopo.

'How do you do it, Stella? Where did you learn the secret of how to talk to these *carusi*?'

'I had six brothers, and I'm not taken in by their empty bullying, that smokescreen of words that looks like fire but isn't.'

'Why do you say "I had", Stella? As far as I know, they're still alive.'

'Alive, but alienated by rancour and bad blood. As long as my mother was alive, she kept the peace and we spoke to one another. Later, what she said to me three days before she died came true. It wasn't foresight, it was an understanding of life. She said: "Love them, Stella, even though they will be separated by pride and a lust for money. Be strong. A woman must remain unfazed by shouting and quarrelling. In time, when the grudges heal, they come back. It's up to us to take them in and mend their wounds."

'She was a wise woman! I learned some things from her, but I don't measure up to her. Only with *picciriddi* am I able to hear her voice showing me the way, but with Pietro and Rinaldo and Melo and my father, I get irritated. I shouldn't say it, but now that Melo writes me these letters that *Voscenza* reads to me, he seems like a stranger to me, and I feel guilty about not having the patience to be able to wait for him like my mother.'

'They were different times, Stella! Everything is changing!'

'*Voscenza* always knows the right words to say to me. Everything changes by the hour, by the day. *Quann'ero nica*, when I was little, coming to Catania from the village was a long trip; now it only takes a few hours.'

'But there are benefits to these changes, Stella.'

'Benefits? For them, for their male restlessness. But for us? . . . Prando is asleep. He always wants to stay here! I hope Signorina Elena doesn't mind. Does she? I wouldn't want that. I don't want to displease her. She knows so much! And she's promised to teach my 'Ntoni like she teaches Prando, who *accussì nicu*, so young, can already speak and express himself like a grown-up. Are you sure Elena doesn't mind?'

56

The dogs are barking at the gate: it can't be Mattia. Selassié and Lupo know his scent. Maybe the full moon dancing wildly among the tree-tops woke the dogs? Behind the gate, in the darkness, two men are carrying a sack.

Nunzio: 'What's going on? Stay back, Princess. Who are you?'

Pasquale: 'Quiet the dogs, Nunzio. It's me, Pasquale!'

They're dragging a sack: empty clothes or a dummy? I don't dare ask or look. I merely follow the path their feet trace, shadowy tracks in the grass. I don't want to recognize those black shoes, and I run ahead.

Pasquale: 'Quick, Nunzio, run and get the doctor! Let's take him upstairs to Beatrice's room.'

Stella, a black shawl flung over her nightgown, and Elena, in a light-coloured flannel robe, watch us silently as we go by. At the first step Pasquale says:

'Easy, Jose, take him by the armpits and I'll carry him up . . . that's it, good! You hold his head, so it doesn't get jolted. There, that's the way, very, very slowly.'

I don't want to look, but on the stairs there are no trees to obscure the moon, and I can't help but see Carlo's swollen, bloodied face staring at me clear-eyed and seemingly smiling. He is, in fact, smiling as he now rests on Beatrice's pink pillow: silk sheets and pillowcases, pale green or blue, the same ones from her room as a girl in Carmelo. Here, too, she wanted her room left untouched. The traditional lace, delicate and pervasive, unfolds before my eyes. I shouldn't have agreed to Cavallina's terms. I close my eyes so I won't see that nauseating, sugary pink.

*

The doctor is pacing up and down the room. He's sweating, and at regular intervals he takes off his glasses and wipes them with a white linen handkerchief. What is his name? Oh, yes. Licata. Comrade Antonio Licata from Messina, that's why he addresses me informally ... What are we waiting for? Carlo speaks. We take a step toward the bed, just one step, to leave him room to breathe. I have to look. Elena is here. How did she manage to dress so quickly? Only she thought to carefully push aside the dark mop of hair from his forehead. His face, now cleansed of blood and soil, is almost unharmed. Putting his glasses back on, the doctor – what is his name? – whispers to me: 'I understand your concern, but you see I was right? There is no concussion. Do you hear him? He's talking, and his gaze is lucid.'

I can't believe his words. I have to hear what Carlo is saying.

Carlo: 'Thank you, Elena, one of these days I should make up my mind and cut my hair. I always think of it in the morning, but I must confess: I have a real aversion to barbers . . . Oh, you're all here! Did I sleep? It's light outside.'

Licata: 'You must remain still, Carlo. Don't move about.'

Carlo: 'I see. But if I recognize you all, I can presume that those gentlemen had the kindness to spare my head.'

Licata: 'Don't talk, Carlo. You mustn't tire yourself.'

Carlo: 'Hah! I always enjoyed talking more than anything else.'

Licata: 'I know, but now clear out, all of you!'

Carlo: 'Even Elena?'

Licata: 'No! She'll stay here, precisely because I know she won't let you move or open your mouth. Come on, all of you, let's go!'

Carlo: 'Wait! You can take the others away, but leave Modesta here too.'

Pasquale: 'Ever the same old ingrate! You prefer female company to us *carusi*, huh?'

Licata: 'Be quiet, Pasquale. Don't humour him. Out of the room, all of you, or I'll lose my temper, by God!'

Carlo: 'You won't say anything to me, Modesta? Were you frightened? I'm sorry.'

Modesta: 'No, no, Carlo. It's just that . . . that I'm glad to hear you speak, and . . .'

Licata: 'Come, that's enough, Modesta! Let's go. I said let's go!'

Comrade Licata was right. What was I saying? Why was I stammering? I couldn't find the right words to say to him. How could that be? For the first time in my life, I found myself sobbing incoherently behind a closed door, with three strange men, and I wasn't ashamed to be led to an armchair.

Licata: 'Don't, Modesta, don't! He might hear you, and that wouldn't help him.'

Modesta: 'But he's all beaten up, Doctor, shattered!'

Licata: 'He's young, Modesta, and we'll help him. For God's sake, Modesta, compose yourself. This isn't like you!'

Pasquale: 'Maybe we shouldn't have brought him here, but he asked us to before he lost consciousness. What else could we do, Antonio?'

Licata: 'You did the right thing. Where else could you take him? To the emergency room, crawling with Black Shirts? This goddamn country! Overnight they've all become Fascists.'

Pasquale: 'That's what Jose and I thought. We're sorry, Modesta. What could we do? Either your house or home to his wife.'

Licata: 'Oh, please, dear God! Beatrice isn't well, and unfortunately she has to be informed . . . Modesta, I insist that she should not see him! We all know what would happen. Between swooning and moaning, it would be hell!'

What was I doing? Comrade Antonio's last words brought me back to reality with a jolt, and I finally looked at them: Pasquale, his arm bracing his neck, arm and hand mangled, Jose with eyes swollen like a boxer's. I flushed with shame.

★

Licata: 'What shame! Don't be silly, Modesta! Let's not overdo it now! You've been very helpful, bandaging and treating all night long. Oh, I swear to God I felt like I was in a hospital! And now that you're smiling, either I'm going to go lie down for a couple of hours at least, or else I think I'll start crying too. Dear God! It's one thing to treat strangers, and another thing . . . never mind! I'll see you tomorrow . . . Today I have a full schedule at the hospital. I'll send Guido. He's reliable. And since you've gone this far, Modesta, you might as well go a little further and let these *carusi* stay here until things settle down in Catania. Maria is safe in prison, but they set fire to the newspaper. Now I must go. Chin up, *carusi*, I'll see you tomorrow evening. Get some rest!'

Finally I looked at them: they were young and didn't care about lack of sleep or injuries. In the course of a night Jose's lips, swollen earlier, were regaining the delicate, ironic shape they had in his photographs. It would be that way for Carlo as well: 'He's young, he'll pull through.' Comrade Licata, the doctor, had said so.

Modesta: 'Are you Jose, Maria's son?'

Jose: 'Yes, how did you recognize me?'

Modesta: 'All they talk about is you. Carlo keeps your photograph next to Bambolina's.'

Pasquale: 'Does that surprise you, Jose? You still hope to get by unnoticed with that lanky figure and . . .'

Jose: 'Big nose? Go ahead and say it, Pasquale. He's envious of this nose, Modesta. It gives me a unique appeal with the police and with the girls. It's all envy, because Mother Nature, tightfisted but wise, made me homely but intelligent, and him good-looking and . . .'

Pasquale: 'Dumb? Say it!'

Jose: 'No, not exactly dumb, but with an intelligence level that is barely normal.'

Modesta: 'He jokes around just like Carlo, doesn't he, Pasquale?'

Pasquale: 'Exactly like him! When they're together, you'd better run. They don't spare anyone.'

Modesta: 'When did you get here, Jose?'

Jose: 'Just in time for the fun and games. Luckily the train was late! I told you about it, Modesta.'

Modesta: 'Oh, really? I don't remember anything about last night.'

Pasquale: 'I was waiting for him at the station . . . the train was two hours late. And to think that I was disappointed about missing the meeting! That delay in fact caused us to arrive at just the right time. I don't want to think about what would have happened if we had all been up there, at the meeting. They would have finished him.'

Modesta: 'But didn't they hear anything up there?'

Pasquale: 'How could they, Modesta? They attacked him three blocks away. As always, all the lower floor doors and windows were bolted, at nine in the evening, damn them! And damn Catania!'

Jose: 'Don't blame Catania, Pasquale! It's the same thing up north, and to make matters worse, a great many take action against us. And if they sound the alarm, the police will even come and protect the Black Shirts.'

Modesta: 'But why Carlo, why him?'

Jose: 'From what I can see, here too the rallying cry is: down with the communists. Ex-comrade Mussolini knows his brother socialists all too well. He lets them prattle on, scares them with a spanking or purges them mildly with castor oil, like fidgety children. They enter his ranks in droves. Those who resist his invitations are often promised command posts. Many of the best have already sold out. So, with patience, he can eliminate those of us communists who have remained isolated, one by one.'

Pasquale: 'They'll never succeed, Jose, never!'

Jose: 'Do you hear him, Modesta? They'll never succeed, he says. What does that mean, they'll never succeed? Why – because progress cannot be stopped? Because history is a teacher of life? All it teaches us is to repeat mistakes, it seems. You haven't missed making one single mistake, you socialists! How can you not get it? Even if you're young, Pasquale, you should know your history . . . The same mistakes of May 1898.* The same Turati, with his words *Non mollare, don't give up!* Yet the Soviets' success said it clearly. But of course, I forgot that you only read *Avanti*: "United against Soviet crimes".'

Pasquale: 'But violence leads to more violence!'

Jose: 'That's it, Pasquale! Keep going around with that socialist bible in your pocket instead of a gun, and may your God, whom you say you don't believe in, help you. Tell me, how would we have been able to rescue Carlo from those five thugs if I hadn't shot them?'

Modesta: 'Oh, you carry a gun?'

Jose: 'Of course, Modesta, even though they inculcated this non-violence in me, too, unfortunately. I wounded two of them, but in the legs; don't worry.'

Modesta: 'I'm not worried in the least. I had given Carlo a gun and he promised me he would carry it.'

Jose: 'Clearly, he didn't have it with him.'

Modesta: 'But why, Jose, why?'

Jose: 'You know Carlo, you know what he thinks about it.'

Modesta: 'I'm sorry, Jose. I keep asking things I know the answer to. It's just that I can't come to terms with it; forgive me. Tell me, did you recognize who they were?'

Jose: 'It was dark. Plus, I've been away from Catania for some time. Maybe Pasquale . . .'

Pasquale: 'I recognized three of them, Modesta.'

Modesta: 'Tell me their names, Pasquale.'

Pasquale: 'It's not women's business. Never mind.'

Modesta: 'Either you tell me their names or I won't speak to you again. And I'll keep my eye on you constantly, as though you were a traitor!'

Pasquale: 'But I'm doing it to protect you, Modesta. If you know it, you'll be in danger . . . Oh well! Two of them I either didn't know or didn't have time to really study, but one was Ciccio Musumeci with his brother Turi, and the other one was that Tudia who rides around on a motorcycle. I saw him clearly because, when Jose shot him in the leg, he fell on top of me and I had to get him off me so I could get up from the ground and run away.'

Modesta: 'You said Jose shot him in the leg?'

Pasquale: 'And how! A serious wound, I think, because he actually collapsed on me. As you know, he's a giant. A grazing wound wouldn't even have made him sway.'

Modesta: 'Did you see his hair?'

Pasquale: 'No, he was wearing his motorcycle helmet.'

Mattia! *'I'll have you even if I have to kill everyone around you! I'm leaving, or I'll kill you and all those friends of yours!'*

*

I waited for hours at the window, peering through the moon's wintry rays, which stung my eyelids, burning with doubt and tears. The woods stretched out quietly, relishing an indifferent silence: *'I have some business in Modica. We won't see each other for a week . . .'* Would he come? Why that information? He had never spoken to me about his comings and goings before. *'We Tudias are like that. When something stands in our way, we very slowly and patiently remove it, gently or harshly, depending on the situation . . .'* Who is that son of yours, Carmine? Who is that young man who, like a cat, like a hare, is able to slink through the trees in the moonlight like that, shrinking his body into a swift, weightless shadow?

'What's wrong, Modesta? Why are you standing there all dressed? Were you waiting for me?'

'I was waiting for you, Mattia.'

'And why the gun in your hand? I sensed it. As soon as I got off my horse, I could feel that the house was different. Why the light on the first floor?'

'Better yet, tell me: when did you get back?'

'Are you jealous, Modesta? Put down that gun. I want to take you in my arms . . . You're jealous – tell the truth – and you want to scare me.'

'How is your brother Vincenzo?'

'That's what I wanted to tell you. I'm late because when I got back from Modica tonight, I found him in bed.'

'With a shattered leg.'

'How do you know that?'

'My brother-in-law saw him.'

'Your brother-in-law in a tavern in the Civita?* What was he doing there?'

'He wasn't at the Civita, Mattia! Your brother lied to you, and from what I heard, he uses your motorcycle.'

'Yes, sometimes he does.'

'He lied to you, Mattia; it happened in Via dei Tipografi.'

'What happened? Don't keep me on tenterhooks; don't make me drag it out of you. Tell me, what happened?'

'Five of them attacked Carlo, and he's fighting for his life in that lighted room you saw.'

'And my brother is supposed to be one of the five? I don't believe it. Who says so?'

'Your brother was one of the five. Carlo himself, my brother-in-law, saw him. He recognized a Tudia among those five!'

'A Tudia? So then you and your brother-in-law also had doubts about me? Well? Lower that gun.'

'No, not until you put my keys on the desk.'

'Then you still suspect me? How can that be?'

'Too many threats, Mattia! Threats eat away like woodworms.'

'Put down the gun. You're right: Mattia is a lunatic. He can't control himself. That's just what I was thinking on my way here. This damned temperament of mine! Always leading others to doubt me. The more I love them, the more . . . Goodbye, Modesta! I see only darkness before me. Nothing tells me you don't love me more than your unmoving face and the doubt that's devouring you. Farewell, I'm going to that traitor, that Judas Iscariot. I'll make him talk, and if it's true, I'll kill him and I'll kill myself, so help me God!'

★

'Modesta! Finally! Why are they treating me as if I were a child? They forbid me to do anything! I have to talk to you.'

'Why, why? Many times you treated us like children; now it's your turn, right, Antonio? What did you think, that being a doctor would excuse you from having to lie in bed and take orders? So we're getting even, aren't we, Elena? For all the times you . . .'

'You're so sweet, Modesta! You're right. But please, I need to be alone with you for just one moment. Please send them away.'

His face, unmarked until a few hours ago, was now covered with splotches and bruises, some red, some bluish. What did those throbbing veins mean? And those tortuous contusions that ran down from his forehead to his neck like crazed animals? And since Antonio was going out the door, gesturing to Elena to follow him, did it perhaps mean that now it was pointless to make him keep silent?

'Let's hear what this child has to say. What is it that's so urgent, Carlo? But speak softly; your chest will hurt.'

'More than pain, an obsession is weighing on my chest, Modesta, an obsession that won't let me breathe.'

'What obsession, Carlo?'

'I feel guilty, Modesta, toward you, toward Beatrice, and for that newborn child.'

'But why?'

'I didn't want to use your gun. You were right, Modesta, but I couldn't! Every morning I looked at it, I could hear your voice, but my aversion was stronger and I would close the drawer again.'

'It doesn't matter. Now you must only think of getting well.'

'I can't stand violence, Modesta. There must be another way. I'm sure that in fifty or a hundred years, humanity will find another way.'

'Of course, Carlo.'

'And if I were to die . . . No Modesta! Don't turn so pale! I have no intention of meeting *La Certa*, as you call her. That lady doesn't appeal to me in the least, but if she were to—'

'If she were to . . . Carlo?'

'Protect me from those black cassocks, from those crucifixes and mournful dirges, possibly even more grim than the idea of death itself.'

'Of course, Carlo. As you've seen, no priest has entered this room. They've tried, you know. But Jose chased them away.'

'Oh, really? He threw them out? How did they know?'

'"*They have a trained nose for it, and there's no way to hide from their wings*". . . as you've told me many times.'

'Oh, Modesta, your words are reassuring. Protect me from Beatrice – afterwards as well. Beatrice is strong, Modesta, I'm afraid of her.'

'But you know that I'm stronger than her, Carlo.'

'That's the reason I had them bring me here. Promise me.'

'I promise, Carlo.'

'Thank you. I'm at peace now.'

'Now you must stop talking and sleep.'

'Yes, of course. But tomorrow will you read to me a little?'

'Of course. What book would this doctor demoted to the rank of patient like?'

'Modesta, your teasing warms my heart . . . I've been so cold.'

'You taught me how to tease. Remember how serious and silent I was?'

'Of course I do! You scared me so!'

'Stop talking now.'

'But tomorrow you'll read to me?'

'Yes. What book would you like?'

'*Niels Lyhne*. Do you still have it?'

'Of course. I always keep it on the nightstand.'

'Me too, in place of Nonna Valentina's Bible.'

'Don't talk anymore. Tomorrow I'll come and read to you.'

'Oh, yes, the part where he sees his aunt on the sofa and falls in love with her. Remember?'

'Yes. Now go to sleep. Jose is watching us like a policeman . . . We've taken advantage of your kindness for too long, haven't we, Jose?'

'That's for sure! That's enough now. Off to bed, everyone! Don't worry, Carlo, Signorina Elena will be back in a few hours. Don't worry. I know you prefer her, but for a few hours you'll have to settle for me.'

*

Silence and coughing, and sudden slumbers interrupted by convulsions and blood prevented me from reading him a few lines. Elena held the basin in her hands. Instead of Jose, there was Antonio Licata.

'Is he going to die, Antonio? You can tell me.'

Antonio says nothing, busily wiping his glasses. Silence and coughing answer for him. I look away from the bloody basin. I place the book on the nightstand: Carlo might open his eyes like he did yesterday. At least he'll see it.

In my study, Pietro, standing motionless, cap in hand, is staring out the window.

'Oh, Mody, now I understand why *Voscenza* had the drapes removed: it's nice to look outside . . . Is it because of Signor Carlo that *Voscenza* called me?'

'That's right, Pietro.'

'Does *Voscenza* have any clues that might lead Pietro on the right track?'

'Not clues, certainty.'

'I knew it, Mody. Tell me their names.'

'Turi and Ciccio Musumeci, and Vincenzo Tudia.'

'And the others? There were five of them.'

'Two of them vanished unseen.'

'We'll make them reappear.'

'In time, Pietro. For now, we'll take care of these three names. Shall I repeat them for you?'

'Pietro doesn't need to have them repeated.'

'Have you heard about Beatrice, Pietro?'

'I heard. I couldn't believe that so much sorrow could enter our homes. I wanted to see her.'

'She's lost her mind, Pietro. That's why she laughs. Maybe it's best for her.'

'Maybe . . . But it's painful, her talking about Carlo, arranging flowers and preparing the evening's supper. When I left her she was getting dressed to go to the theatre.'

'And Argentovivo?'

'She's a big help. She follows Dr Licata's instructions and humours her without crying or talking too much like she used to. I left her combing Beatrice's hair.'

'All right, Pietro. Now we have to take care of those names.'

'Should we consider it a family vendetta, Mody?'

'No, Pietro, no mutilations. Just three bullets between the eyes: one for Turi, one for Ciccio, one for Vincenzo. It has to be clear that it was a political crime. How much will it cost?'

'If it's a political crime, it will take a crack marksman. It will cost a lot, my dear Mody.'

'You can't put a price on a life that's taken.'

'I'll be on my way then. And when the sun goes down, I'll find my man in the Civita. If you don't hear from me for two or three days, don't worry. We have to act cautiously. None of Carlo's friends or family members must suspect; don't let these *carusi* leave the house until I return. Just so you know, during the day I'll sleep at Donna Carmela's place. May God bless you, Princess!'

'May God go with you, Pietro, and protect you.'

'Oh, one more thing, Mody.'

'What is it?'

'I don't feel confident about Nunzio. He's basically a grounds-keeper, looking after plants and flowers. *Voscenza* shouldn't take offence: what's needed here is an armed man. If you'd let me, I would back Nunzio up with my grandson Celso, who's back from military duty. It would cost very little, and would give Pietro great peace of mind.'

★

As soon as Pietro leaves, Signorina Elena comes in.

'What is it, Elena? What's wrong? Is it Carlo?'

'No, no. On the contrary, he's gone back to sleep. His face has cleared. It's Stella who—'

'What about Stella, Elena? You've been so helpful and courageous! Please don't be frightened now.'

'It's just that I don't know whether to tell you or not. Stella made me swear I wouldn't tell, but I'm afraid for her, and I can't, I can't . . .!'

'What can't you do?'

'I'm afraid, after what happened to Beatrice. She seemed so strong, and then . . .'

'Calm down, Elena! What's worrying you about Stella?'

'I don't understand her, she's so closed, not a word about . . .'

'About what?'

'She made me promise not to tell you until Signor Carlo recovers. Oh God! I don't understand these oaths and silences.'

'Tell me. I'll take responsibility for it. What was it?'

'It's . . . yesterday her father came . . .'

'Well?'

344

'. . . with the news that they fished Melo out at the port in Naples, drowned. I didn't understand . . . tied to big rocks.'

'A Mafia killing.'

'No, Stella only said *"cinniri"*. I don't know . . .'

'Cocaine, Elena, drugs. Clearly he was working with them.'

'Oh, but it's awful! And her too, so unemotional!'

'It's men's business, Elena, and we mustn't lose our calmness. How did you hear about it?'

'She told me.'

'She told you? She must be fond of you then.'

'Oh! It means she likes me?'

'It means she trusts you; it's one and the same here.'

'Oh God, what have I done then? Now she won't trust me any-more.'

'Don't worry about it. You did the right thing. I'll go talk to her. But don't you say a word, all right? Don't worry. You didn't tell me a thing.'

★

Studying that composed profile, I knew that Elena had been wrong to worry. But I also realized that I'd been away from that room for too long.

'Your visit is a comfort, Princess. I had got used to seeing you in the evening . . . Well, one must believe in fate, because I was just thinking about making the coffee that you like so much.'

'I like the way you make it, Stella, not that tepid water that Elena serves me. If you must know, my visits have a selfish purpose.'

'I've tried to teach Elena how to do it, but she laughs and says she doesn't have the patience. Coffee has to be brewed over a low flame! Well, it's really true that destiny's predictions don't lie; it's hopeless to fight it! When I entered this house – *Voscenza* may not believe it – I knew I would remain within these walls for many years.'

'I believe you, Stella, but why are you so certain of it now?'

'Well, because of the way Jacopo smiles at me and because of Prando's caprices . . . so imaginative! Do you know that yesterday he carpeted the floor of this room with a bagful of colourful dry leaves?

And when I came in he said to me: "See the surprise I made you? I made the carpet of Santa Rosalia."'*

'Prando gives you a lot of trouble, doesn't he?'

'What trouble! The only sad thing is that they grow up, *quannu cresciuti*, their friends and code of honour take them away from you. If only I had had a little girl, a *femminuccia*, Princess!'

'Did Elena tell you that we will soon have a *femminuccia* here with us?'

'No, but I thought so. With her mother gripped by dead spirits, I imagined that we would have Bambolina with us.'

'They're bringing her tomorrow morning.'

'Poor child, removed from her mother's sight! What will we do about milk?'

'Don't worry, Stella. Carlo sent for a powdered milk from Switzerland.'

'How can that be?'

'It exists, Stella. It seems that this milk is lighter. Not only doesn't she spit it up like she did before, even with donkey's milk, but in eight days the vomiting has stopped and she's gained weight.'

'These new things scare me . . .'

'So then, Stella, are you still planning to make me that coffee?'

'Oh, Holy Virgin! Right away!'

'Tell me, what's wrong? Is your father bothering you again? Does he want you back with him?'

'No, Princess. He came to see me, yes, but to tell me that he was setting off with my brothers to avenge a death. And so it's starting all over again, like when I was a child. They leave, they come back wounded or they don't come back at all. But I don't want to talk about it. I don't want to be like my mother, crying and waiting only to learn of their death.'

'Are you afraid for Melo, Stella?'

'Not anymore! For years I cried and anticipated his death, seeing the frenzied life he led. And now if you still need me, all I want is to stay here in peace with these *carusi*.'

*

The book remained closed on the nightstand. Carlo looked at it, smiling, in the rare moments of respite.

'Tomorrow you'll read me a line or two, won't you, Modesta?'

'Of course, Carlo, tomorrow.'

Tomorrow . . . Tomorrow . . . it went on for fifteen days, that agony of silences, coughing and sudden slumbers, immediately shattered by convulsions and red blood on his white teeth. Fifteen days of struggling, never once despairing or giving in to the darkness that hour by hour crept over his eyes. Carlo was dying the difficult death of an atheist, like the hero whom he had so loved.

Already around me they were whispering: 'a hero's death'. But those who die are wrong, they're mistaken. I turn away from that error to follow Pietro's trail; his reports reach me from afar:

'Ciccio Musumeci shot in front of the entrance to Cinema Mirone.'

'Turi Musumeci found with a bullet between his eyes in the gardens of Villa Pacini.'

'Vincenzo Tudia is still bedridden because of his leg, but the first time he goes out they'll be waiting for him, my dear Mody.'

I wait patiently, staring at Carlo's serene face. Someone whispers:

'It's like he's been rejuvenated!'

He was growing younger as he died: the dark mop of hair widened the pools of dark shadow around his eyes, giving his pale face an expression of childlike bewilderment.

'He seems like a child!' Elena exclaimed in surprise.

I turn away from that child to hear Pietro finally announce:

'Vincenzo Tudia: the first time he goes out for a walk with a cane, his leg still in a cast, slumps to the ground behind his own house.'

After each name, Jose smiles and looks at me.

'Thank you, Modesta. I'm leaving tomorrow after the funeral. The only reason I had come was for Carlo, to persuade him to act or escape abroad. I'm going back up north. I'm glad I got to know you. I'm going back up there and I'll kill as many of them as I can. And if we lose, I'll cross the mountains and seek refuge in Switzerland.'

I'd like to turn away from that coffin, but I have to look, because among the red of the flags, the carnations and the shirts of Carlo's comrades, who take turns shouldering their hero's coffin, a dark silhouette replaces Jose. Is my vision dazed by the strong sunlight? Or is that big-boned man Mattia Tudia, in deep mourning over the loss of his brother Vincenzo? It's not the sun; it's the red of the carnations that's clouding my vision. When the coffin stops for a moment in the darkness of Via dei Crociferi – it was always dark as night in those narrow streets – Jose leaves my side and takes his place once more where Mattia was. They have the same build. The coffin goes on its way again without a jolt, and Mattia comes up beside me.

'You shouldn't be surprised, Princess. I came to pay my respects to a man of honour, as you had the goodness to do for my father, Carmine Tudia.'

Celso comes up alongside Mattia:

'*Vossia* will excuse me, Don Mattia, but I have orders to stay close to the Princess. Bad things are happening in our streets.'

'That's good, Celso, and I'll tell you right away that Don Mattia has not come to disturb the ceremony, but to honour this procession.'

'If he says so, it is so, Celso! We thank him and ask Don Mattia if he would like to have a glass of wine with us at the house afterwards.'

'I accept with pleasure and sorrow, Princess.'

57

'Three months I've waited, Modesta. Three times I watched the moon wax and wane with the protracted pace of a life sentence. Why do you want to condemn me to this solitude, why?'

'I'm not condemning anyone. I don't have the heart to listen to anyone anymore. My heart has become a wasteland, and the name Tudia is now stamped on me like a mark of death.'

'Damn Vincenzo for coming between us! I feel like a wolf caught in a trap. Why did he do it?'

'He was a Fascist.'

'Don't be silly; he was no Fascist! He was out of his mind! That morning before going out to meet his death – death makes you talk, you know! – he told me things . . . unspeakable things about our father, which I can't even stand to think about.'

'You see how the memory is still too vivid between us? Let's wait a little longer. Maybe in a year . . . If Beatrice would at least snap out of her psychosis and if her innocent child, Bambolina, could only swallow a sip of milk without spitting it up. Bambolina is wasting away, and I'm tormented by it. Now go!'

'For three months I've had your face imprinted on my eyes, night and day. Come away with me! There are other places outside this narrow-minded island. I've seen them . . . I'm not like those people who look at me disapprovingly because I haven't avenged Vincenzo's death. I haven't even wanted to find out who did it or who didn't. I don't want to know anymore. I don't give a damn!'

'Don't say that!'

'On the contrary, I'll say it! And I want you, even if it was a friend of yours who killed Vincenzo, even if it was that Jose . . .'

'Jose didn't leave my house even for a moment.'

'You're defending him, are you? So say it: you've changed because of him. Say it! Since he set foot on this island, you've changed.'

'I've changed because of Carlo's death, Mattia. Try to use your head.'

'No! The death of a brother-in-law can't change someone to that extent!'

'He was a friend.'

'No! I don't believe it. It was that Jose, and if you want to know, I came to the funeral to see him, just to see him.'

'So?'

'I saw him! Mattia isn't fooled. That guy has the body you like. He's a man I'd like to test my skill against, by God! Arrogant, solid as a rock, and contemptuous! If it weren't for you, I'd like to ask him a thing or two!'

'He's gone, Mattia. Stop ranting. I won't see him again. I read in his face that I won't see him again.'

'You don't fool me.'

'Like I read in your eyes that day at your father's bedside that death could come to me from you. I won't see him again.'

'Again she says it. She says it again, almost in tears! Don't you see that he's captured you, at least in your imagination?'

'That's enough, Mattia. Get out!'

'No! Not like this, you fiendish lava devil! Not with that sentence hanging over me. No! For you then, I'm supposedly a sign of death, aren't I? And what is he? He's life, right? And to think how much I loved you! I hate you! I hate you!'

I mustn't turn around . . . Before I finish the thought, I find I have the gun in my hand. From the recoil that jolts me from wrist to shoulder, I sense that I've fired, too, while a whitish flash explodes in my face and makes me keel over . . . Is it I who drop to the ground or is it the grass that rises up to meet me? Face down, I fire again, without being able to take aim because a warm liquid is now dripping into my eyes. Screams and gunshots echo behind me; bracing my hands on the ground, I try to pull my head out of the dark wave that submerges me. At night, the sea is black if there is no moon . . . But there is a moon now . . . from up above, it stares at me with its whitewashed gaze, but it isn't screaming. It's Elena who is screaming, and those swift legs, the legs of a hare, are Celso's. It seems impossible, but Celso runs like Tuzzu . . . that Celso has the legs of a hunter. He'll kill him. I find myself hoping that Mattia will manage to escape the hunter . . . I can only hope that Mimmo has seen me . . . he has long arms, Mimmo does. And although my head is now banging faster and faster against the walls of the well, I can only hope . . .

'Hope and push, Modesta. Push, that way you help yourself and you help it!'

'The position is right! . . . don't fight the wave of pain, don't oppose it, follow it with your entire body and your senses, that's the only way you'll do it!'

I push with my entire body and my senses, but that mass of flesh that stirs at regular intervals, sure as day follows night, and rams the walls of my belly, doesn't want to come out. Was it Prando, unborn, struggling inside me or was it I, unborn, who was struggling against the wire sutures of my forehead to get out? I thrashed about incessantly to be reborn . . . And one misty dawn, barely tinged with the heat's reddish glow, I gave birth to myself as though a great wave of carnal pain, washing over my body and crashing far behind me, had carried away all the sorrow, the bitterness, the joyful plans now wrecked against the rocks of Carlo's death. The disappointment over those plans that had collapsed in such a brief time was a bitter ache. It had been a bitter ache back when Carlo lay dying in bed, when Beatrice, her eyes shining with madness, kept saying:

'Just think how envious people can be, Modesta! They continue to say that Carlo is dead, when he was here just two minutes ago – you know how he is – every so often he comes down from his study to talk to me. In fact, before I forget, he told me that tonight we're going to the Opera. Would you like to come too? It's just envy, going around saying he's dead, while . . . don't you hear his footsteps up there? Listen, he's got up from his desk now . . . When he gets up, the chair scrapes on the marble floor. We should get a rug, but Carlo says it's not suitable for . . .'

A bitter ache back . . . when? A year, two years ago? When the girl Modesta, full of the untarnished hope of youth, sure of her future, pressed ahead unsuspectingly, blindfolded . . . When she walked hand in hand with Carlo, confidently, drinking in his voice, his ideas, his presence as though he were something eternal that would always be with her like the Mountain, the sky, the sea. How often with Carlo, alive, or with Jacopo, dead, had she discussed, held forth, about the contradiction that is at the core of nature. But when his death, final and unappealable, exposed that contradiction, disappointment – like an avalanche that sweeps away confidence and joy – can make you glimpse in your own end a more certain way. Could it be that young people's adventurousness, their way of rushing into deadly matches, their frequent untimely deaths, were simply the result of some earlier disappointment-contradiction? She had sought her own death confronting Mattia that night, she knew that now, and maybe only someone who has come so close to death can forget and then be reborn as Modesta is reborn day by day, staring into the mirror of dawning at that red, serpentine scar, which splits her forehead in two.

'It will take three or four years, Modesta, for the redness to fade.'

What did the years matter when you began to understand? The scar that bisects her forehead is now a sign of the healing of her being, itself divided earlier. Modesta is reborn from her body, uprooted from that earlier Modesta who wanted everything, and who couldn't tolerate doubts, in herself or others. She is reborn with an awareness of being alone. And day by day, hour by hour, she accepts the grief of Beatrice's return from her long journey through madness.

She has come back serene, but with her hair all white. In her own way, Beatrice is content, left to her memories, dressed in mourning, the locket of her beloved husband on a black velvet ribbon around her neck. Of course, Bambolina suffers somewhat in that house, what with her mother and Argentovivo who do nothing but talk about the past. But in the end, she only sleeps there, because in the morning Pietro, by unspoken agreement with his Mody, takes her to Villa Suvarita, and the sad little face quickly brightens there among Prando, Jacopo, 'Ntoni and some stray friends they picked up in the fields.

'So many children!' – she squeals happily, then always adds: 'I must tell my Mama to come and see them . . .'

She's already talking . . . Yet that moonlit night etched in my memory seems like just yesterday . . . The wound throbs at the recollection of Mattia. He too had wanted to die, but then he chose to go to America – at least that's what Pietro reported. And Jose? After having fought in the north, Jose was arrested with Pertini.

'A storm of arrests, my dear Mody! But what's most upsetting, what most casts the spirit into the deepest despondency is not seeing any news in the press. This pall of silence over everything. I swear to God! You wander around searching for news, like a dog finding a bone that's been picked clean or like a starving man seeking a crust of stale bread.'

'Yes, Antonio, arrests and indifference.'

Every solitary voice of rebellion falls into the lake of indifference, without a ripple. An indifference that slowly but steadily permeates every street, every corner, at each step of history's way: the murder of Matteotti, the Special Laws, the Lateran Treaty* . . .

Men's business, Princess, they make and unmake history as they please. Of course, Stella.

I watch her, but that gentleness and resignation I had earlier mistaken for wisdom no longer enthrals me . . . Earlier . . . when Bambolina wasn't here with us. But now that Bambolina is beginning to chase after Prando, why do they stop her and separate them? I have to leave my books and go down. She's crying inconsolably on the lawn, while Prando runs off happily toward the woods.

'What is it, Stella, Elena? Why did you separate them?'

'But she was running like a tomboy, Princess! She'll dirty her little dress.'

That's how the rift begins. According to them, Bambolina, only five years old, should already act differently, remain composed, eyes lowered, to cultivate the young lady of tomorrow. Like in the convent: laws, prisons, history erected by men. But it's women who have agreed to be the keepers of the keys, uncompromising guardians of men's words. In the convent, Modesta hated her jailers with a slave's hatred, a humiliating but necessary hate. Today, she defends Bambolina from both men and women, impartially and confidently; by defending her she is defending herself, her past, a daughter she might someday give birth to . . . Remember, Carlo? Remember when I told you that only women can help women, and you, with your masculine pride, didn't understand? Now do you see? Now that you've had a daughter, do you understand?

In the mirror – it's been a long time since I've looked at myself – Carlo's face stares back at me. Or maybe it's my habit of speaking with him that calls his features to life, moulding my smile and my eyes into his, the urge to keep those we love alive? In me, he is reborn in the mirror, alive, smiling . . . I understand why you're smiling, Carlo: the dead don't want us to die with them. They want us to keep them alive, in our thoughts, in our voices, in our gestures. With his hands, I pull a strand of hair down over my forehead . . . to be like him!

Since the morning when I woke up with my head shaved because of the wound, I've had short hair. Should I let it grow again? In a few years, I could once more have the braids which mattered so much to me as a child. A longing for those braids constantly threatened by the convent's scissors makes me want to see them again. At the time, Cavallina saved them in a drawer somewhere . . . There they are, long and thick, with a colour so vivid that touching them, my heart nearly leaps with fright. But as soon as I pick them up, distaste for that dead part of me makes me fling them in the wastebasket. You can't go back again. Besides, back then, I could hardly swim! The memory of those cumbersome braids in the water and on the pillow, the barrettes, hairpins, combs, the effort. No, I prefer that new face with its exposed neck: a boy's face, like Carlo's. I want to continue swimming without a bathing cap, like him. Even better, I want to swim to the rock of the Prophet and sweep back the mop of hair with a flick of my fingers, like him, before stretching out in the sun.

PART THREE

58

Anyone who's had the good fortune to reach thirty knows how difficult, arduous and exciting it was to scale the mountain that rises from childhood to the summit of youth, and how quickly it goes: a waterfall, a geometric flight of wings in the sunlight, a few moments and . . . Yesterday I had the unlined cheeks of a twenty-year-old. Today – overnight? – the three fingers of Time have brushed me, a warning of the brief span remaining and of the final finishing line that inexorably awaits . . . A first, false terror of turning thirty.

What had I done? Had I wasted my days? Not enjoyed the sun and the sea to the fullest? Only later on, during the golden age of fifty, an age soundly vilified by poets and registry clerks – only then do you realize how much richness there is in the peaceful oases of being by yourself, alone. But that comes later.

At the time, the anxiety of missing the past and the future gripped me powerfully: What was I doing in that study? What meaning did that search for words have, all those papers, poems, stories, notes? Was I, unknowingly, about to fall into the mystical lot of becoming a poet, an artist? Was I, unknowingly, retracing the path of Beatrice, who, in order to exist in her own eyes and those of others, moulded herself into the sacred statue of a grieving widow, beautiful and respected? Was I, with her same relentlessness and determination, unknowingly raising a temple within me? And, would I, like her, lay down my life just to comply with the subtle venom of tradition?

Imprisoned in mourning, as tradition demanded, Beatrice fell ill with 'consumption' like her husband. Little by little, and with appalling placidity, , the wax wind-up doll, which for years had wandered among the flowers and books, stopped within months: she had wound down.

What was I doing among those pens and pencils lined up on the desk? Or was it an altar? I had started it for pleasure . . . But looking within myself I saw my future: caught in that snare, legs broken by the trap of 'being someone'. Though I had escaped the convent, the piety I had sent packing was creeping out again from some hole in my room, straddling the rat of aesthetics. I saw it, that mystical rat. Its eyes, reddened by insatiable hunger, peered out from the shadowy corners, voracious. They scoured my young flesh, my breast, seeking a crack to enter me and gnaw at the backbone of my skeleton, which was held together by joy. Stopping it, I knew that I had been right to be mistrustful, and that just a few more instants of unawareness would have made me fall from reality into the grip of the 'artist' drug, a drug more potent than morphine and religion. The rat realized it, looked away and fled.

The scar throbbed from my effort to peer into my future, and in the mirror I saw it redden and writhe for a few moments. A centuries-old message from my depths, it warned me to guard against myself, and go running in the sun. I would not resume the quest for poetry until I had proven to myself that it was for fun and only for fun, like picking flowers or riding Morella . . .

Bambolina was waiting patiently beside old Morella. Her dark bangs, wispy as a shadow, fell over blue eyes that were slightly more intense than Beatrice's. I look for her across the lawn. Maybe she's just hiding behind a hedge, waiting to pop out, making her sudden laughter more dear.

'Don't you feel like riding, Zia? Staring out at the sea like that . . . It's all right if you don't feel like it. Maybe you're tired.'

The same considerate voice, Carlo's same thoughtful, caring attention . . . The scar on my forehead throbs, keeping back my tears, and I can't help hugging her and lifting her up in the air. I want her to laugh. I want to hear Cavallina's laughter again.

'Oh, what fun, Zia, you're making me fly! It's been so long since you made me fly like this! How come you're so strong? . . . Oh! Enough, stop! You're tickling me. Enough, Modesta!'

When I'm serious she calls me Zia; when I'm playing with her, I'm Modesta.

'Oh, what fun, Modesta! How strong you are!'

'You're just a *scazzittula di picciridda*, a little bit of a thing! . . . You don't weigh any more than a few ounces!'

'But Prando can't lift me.'

'In a few years, you'll see! And if you don't watch out, he'll send you flying right around the moon.'

'Oh, what fun that would be, Modesta! Then when I'm big too, will you teach me how to fly? I love airplanes a lot. You'll teach me, won't you? Like you taught me how to ride a horse and how to swim?'

Now she's rattling on excitedly like Beatrice, Carlo's careful attention forgotten. What is she saying? She's talking about some photographs she found . . .

'And who is that handsome man? Jacopo and I opened a trunk up in the attic. He took a bunch of books and a . . . what do you call that thing you look in to see everything bigger?'

'A microscope.'

'And I took some photographs. Who was that handsome man near the airplane? Prando says he was my papa, but he was joking because my papa wasn't a pilot, was he? So who was he?'

'That was Ignazio, your Mama's uncle.'

'And were all those airplanes his?'

'Oh, no! He flew them. He was a pilot.'

'What fun! When I grow up I'm going to be a pilot too!'

'Of course, Bambolina. Now let's ride before the sun gets too hot. Come on, that's it. Faster!'

★

Pietro was waiting for me in the study, cap in hand, unchanged – how old was he now? Maybe as old as the fire wheel that Carmine used to drag down the slopes of the Mountain.

'*Voscenza benedica*, my respects, Princess. Please forgive Pietro for disturbing you. But it's an urgent matter.'

'No need for apologies, Pietro. I know you come to see me for a reason.'

'I'll get to the point then, or rather, two points. One is a matter of great joy for Pietro and his wife. The other is a painful matter that eclipses the joy in my heart.'

'Tell me, Pietro! Speak freely in sorrow and in joy . . . Don't stand there mute, turning all red!'

'*Voscenza* has understood: Argentovivo, my wife that *Voscenza* was good enough to grant me . . . after two years, who could have hoped any more, Mody . . . she's . . . she's . . .'

'Is she expecting a baby, Pietro? You seem like a *carusu!*'

'Naturally, Mody; a child holds death and old age at bay. With a child to raise, as my father used to say, it's easier to close your ears to the siren songs of those old women, the lava spirits, who extol the praises of giving up the struggle and yielding to the peace of *La Certa.*'

'I'm happy for you, Pietro. And how is Argentovivo?'

'She's very well. My little sparrow sings and chatters from morning till night! And she's preparing the layette with Signorina Inès who has had the good grace to embroider with her . . . Well!'

'So why are you frowning now, Pietro? Is there some doubt, some drawback that keeps you from being happy about this lovely news you've brought me?'

'The second point, as I said earlier, Princess . . . And I hesitate to tell you because I'm afraid I acted recklessly, even though out of respect for *Voscenza* and for your tranquillity.'

'We'll see, Pietro. Explain the situation and then we'll see.'

'Does *Voscenza* recall that friend of Signor Carlo, God rest his soul, that republican Bartolomeo Inzerillo, with the heart condition, whom Signor Carlo treated with such care and concern?'

'What about him?'

'Two years after Signor Carlo passed away, he sent for me. He was at the point of death. Remorse kills, Mody, unless you are a lava demon.'

'I know what you're trying to tell me: that before dying he declared himself repentant, said that he had turned his back on the Fascists, that Mussolini had deceived them . . .'

'Not only that! He confessed to me that he was among those five men who attacked Signor Carlo and told me the name of the fifth man, a certain Serge Greco, a journalist.'

'It must be Grecò, Pietro: a Frenchman.'

'He wasn't French. He was the traitor Sergio Greco, an expatriate. His father was Giovanni Greco of Piana dei Greci, now called Piana degli Albanesi.* Now tell me, Mody, what could I do, come here and disturb *Voscenza*, grieving over our Beatrice who was wasting away? I thought it best to follow his movements from a distance, and when I had the opportunity, I nailed him here on the island, six feet under his own land: he travelled too much!'

Six feet under myself, I struggle in the dark to break out of memory's mantle of lava that Pietro has thrown over me. I stare at him and I see the rat of vengeance scurry out of the eyes of a man who is a slave to men's laws, embedded in the island's millennial Mountain. I don't want to hate him, but my revulsion for that look drives me out of the mantle of lava, out of the island.

'You won't look at me, Mody. Are you angry?'

'Weren't three lives enough for one death, Pietro?'

'A life that is taken has no price, Princess. *Voscenza* said so, and with conviction!'

'You are about to have a child, Pietro. If you are devoted to me, forget about the past and be happy over this joy that destiny has given you.'

'I am happy, but first there is an offence to vindicate.'

'What else is there, Pietro?'

'I heard from reliable friends that that Pasquale, who said he was a friend of our Signor Carlo, and who has now been made a prefect by the Fascists, knew about the attack on that cursed night. He must die, Mody. He must die!'

'That's enough, Pietro! All of Carlo's friends have gone over to the Fascists, except those who were killed or imprisoned. As for Pasquale, I'll tell you what Carlo would have said: either we all rebel together – because we're talking about politics here, and not a family quarrel

– and it may be that we'll all rebel together in five or ten years and get rid of them all – but no private retaliation!

'Back then, I agreed to those just killings because there was still hope. But to kill Pasquale today would be a personal vendetta that makes no sense. Not only that: it would compromise the many, many friends who still resist in their mind. Plus, Pasquale protects these friends out of old feelings of remorse. We as real men, and not hysterical women, pretend to believe in his partial loyalty to our ideas; we make the most of him, we use him. Who else could have saved Maria from Ucciardone,* from the blissful Villa Mori, as they call it in Palermo, where people are tortured and killed without a trial?

'This is not the time for action, Pietro, it's a time to winter, a time to hibernate. And don't worry; when the time is right, we won't fail to disillusion Pasquale, who thinks he's bought us for eternity for the few favours he's doing us. Our gratitude will be a bullet between the eyes like it was for Tudia and the others. Don't you worry.'

'You've said a lot of things, Mody, and I think I've understood. But you're angry at Pietro, since you never looked at me when you spoke.'

From the dark depths of the island his heart perceived the slightest falling shadow, the subtlest change in nerves and veins.

'If I was wrong, Mody, tell me! Pietro doesn't deserve a silent condemnation.'

'Do you trust me, Pietro? Then listen to me. Times are changing, and we have to be cautious: look around and see how we should act.'

'Oh! Is that why you've crossed the sea so many times then? I had some idea, mainly because Prince Jacopo did like *Voscenza* does. And he gained great knowledge from those trips.'

'Yes, Pietro, and it's becoming more and more plain to me that the island, our land, must abandon its isolation.'

'You mean abandon our thinking, Mody? Accept the ways and customs of the continent?'

'The train, the airplane and the radio have made the world a smaller place, and it may overtake us and overwhelm us if we're unprepared.'

'The Prince used to say that too, but the Princess, God rest her soul, didn't agree.'

'Gaia was a grand old woman, Pietro, but out of date, no offence to the dead, obsolete! Fascism might last a hundred years, but it might also end in a moment, and Carlo's world might come back. So our children must be prepared to make their way in life alone, to cope on their own, both materially and morally.'

'Is that why you send them to public schools? Now I understand.'

'And abroad in the summer, Pietro. They need to know.'

'The old timers used to say you lose your roots by wandering around the world. Prince Jacopo came back from his travels more and more stooped.'

'You lose roots that are rotten, and he became stooped because he found here a failure to understand his problems.'

'You have explained things to me, and I see that it is not Pietro who angered you, but Pietro's old-fashioned heart. And I accept that I was wrong. I'm old and I tremble at this struggle you are facing. I understand your intent, but I don't see a way forward, both because I am ignorant and because of my age. But I have confidence in you. First, because you're educated. And second, because you are my mistress and I accept your orders without question.'

'Then it's understood, Pietro? We leave Pasquale where he is. It's not the time to act, understood?'

Troubled but silent, Pietro stoops to kiss my hand. I have to look him in the eye. You can't escape the sweep of his gaze, either by crossing the sea, as he says, or by staring from the window of a train at the endless tracts of woodland and cultivated fields, laid out unnaturally and with no imagination: straight, neat towns and cities, pale faces with colourless eyes and no smile. Mouths without teeth to bite bread. I had hoped . . . by crossing the sea, I had hoped to find what Tuzzu used to say: *'There are cities full of all sorts of wonderful things, huge ports where ships come and go, laden with treasures.'* But behind the ornately painted facades of sumptuous palazzos lay the same twisted streets in the throes of hunger, the same wretched litany of poverty and constraints, only just a little more hidden and more resigned.

Following Uncle Jacopo's hunched steps, I retraced the stages of his trips and returned with yet another theatre programme, another good book, some ribbons and fabric for Stella. After years of mourning, first for her husband and then for her father, she strokes the silks and velvets, thirsty for colour. Confined in mourning, her sturdy limbs seemed to have grown thinner, giving her slow gestures an adolescent uncertainty. Stella was being reborn from the anguish of separating from her dead. Or was it habitually talking to the children, gazing into their eyes and anticipating their needs that filled her gaze and voice with that childlike wonder and enthusiasm? Modesta had never in her life witnessed such an absolute metamorphosis. Astounded, she stares at the new Stella, who laughs as she unrolls on the carpet a long stream of turquoise silk strewn with countless golden suns.

'How beautiful it is! Oh, when Bambolina comes she'll be so happy!'

'Actually, I brought it for you, Stella.'

'Oh Mody, do you think I can? Could I . . .'

'Of course you can!'

'But my older brother is ill! Maybe it's pointless to stop wearing mourning when in . . .'

'Oh, nonsense! You've worn mourning long enough! Plus, you have to think of the children.'

'It's true! Just yesterday Prando said to me: "Either you take off that black or I'm leaving". And I said: "Where will you go?" "With Mody," he said. "Abroad, where the women dress in hundreds of colours!"'

'You see, Stella?'

'Yes, yes, of course . . . but the one who surprised me was Jacopo. He doesn't seem to notice these things; he always has his nose in a book, that *picciriddu.*'

'What did Jacopo say?'

'With a very serious face he tells me: "That's right, Stella! It's about time Prando said that. I'm leaving too."'

'So, a mutiny?'

'What does that mean, Mody?'

'A rebellion.'

'Oh, right, even my 'Ntoni: "I don't want a Mama who's always wearing black. Look at this photo: that's how I want to see you!"' Imagine, Mody, it was a picture of a blond actress wearing a very low-cut neckline. Jesus, Mary and Joseph! These *carusi*! The movies, always the movies! It isn't wrong, Mody, is it? I don't know what to think. This silk is certainly beautiful. It looks like a bit of sky!'

'Good! Then with this bit of sky make yourself a dress for the mid-summer feast day; you'll see what a hit you'll be with the children!'

'All right, Mody. I'll brace myself, I'll forget about my sisters-in-law and their looks . . . oh, I can just see them, but I won't think about them.' Stella steels herself and accepts the fabric. 'Oh Mody, my hands are trembling just folding it. It isn't wrong, is it?'

'Wrong, Stella? What harm can there be in colours?'

'What harm can there be in making my children happy? As my mother used to say: "When you make your children happy, they promptly return the happiness a hundredfold." Elena was happy here with them.'

'Well, now she's found a new happiness, I would imagine.'

'Happiness, Mody? Please! Yesterday she came and she was crying, not even married one year and already she was crying, miserable, pinched, scared of everything and everybody. I felt like I was seeing myself, meeting myself as I used to be. It gave me a scare! And those two, my brothers I mean, want me to marry again! Not a month goes by when they don't show up with a match, and they keep at it. They say I've changed, that I talk like a foreigner, that . . . what do they want from me?'

'They think they're doing it for your own good. You're young . . .'

'Never! Anyone who has ever gone through serving a man once – never again! Besides, give my 'Ntoni a stepfather, I . . .'

'All right, Stella, calm down. In time, we'll see. Now why are you blushing like a little girl?'

'Because now you'll get angry, Stella knows it. You've been back one hour and now you'll get angry.'

'And why should I get angry?'

'It's that girl . . . Mela, the one whose father and mother were killed by the Fascists.'

'Yes, I know, the one Pasquale sent to us. So?'

'Oh, Pasquale did the right thing, taking her out of that convent where they first brought her. The things she's told me! And to think they're nuns, oh! No one would believe it!'

'I know all about it, Stella. Please, what are you trying to say? Why are you beating around the bush like that?'

'Do you hear the piano?'

'What does the piano have to do with it, Stella! Now I really will get angry! Of course I hear it. I'm not deaf! It must be one of Prando's friends playing so well, certainly not Bambù or 'Ntoni, who are hopeless at music.'

'It's Mela.'

'Her? She's still here? But Pasquale said . . .'

'Yes, I know, but it's hard to find a decent boarding school without money, Mody!'

'Exactly! We have no more money, Stella. Everything is in decline, another reason why I came back . . . and who knows when I'll be able to travel again! Don't make such a face. What do you think, that I'm stingy, like Prando does?'

'No, Mody, frugal . . .'

'Who would have said it, eh, Stella? That even offering a piece of bread would be a luxury! And this incessant piano playing!'

'First you said she played well.'

'She does!'

'So what do you say, shall we go and see her? She and Bambù have become such great friends. We needed a girl for Bambù! Always surrounded by rowdy boys. Do you want to meet her?'

'No, I don't want to see her! She has to go and that's that!'

'Now what? Are you going away?'

'Of course I'm going!'

'You're leaving?'

'Of course not! I'm going to my room. This idle female prattle and the thought of money have put me in a bad mood. I must find some money!'

'I've told you, Mody, I have the house, the farm. I could . . .'

'Don't be silly! Your money and Bambolina's can't be touched. I'll see you later, Stella.'

'Mody!'

'What now?'

'Wait, I . . . I didn't tell you everything. I have to tell you what happens when you're away . . .'

'What else happened? Let's hear it.'

'The fact is that there's another woman, a *signora* who . . .'

'Another woman?'

'Well, yes. She arrived four days ago. I put her in Signorina Elena's room.'

'Oh no, that's enough now! I'll phone Pasquale right away. He has to stop sending us these people. The devil take him! He's gone too far!'

'But that's the point! It's not Signor Pasquale who sent her, it's Signor Jose.'

'Jose?'

'At least, that's what the *signora* said. She said: "I have a letter from Signor Jose Giudice for the Princess."'

Jose! Although I had read in his parting smile, that long-ago evening, that we would never see each other again, I had constantly looked for him in my travels, often going miles and miles out of my way, whenever I was able, to obtain some news of him. In Basel, in that room littered with newspapers, saturated with lead and oil, filled with the din of the rotary press:

'*The editor has left, ma'am. You've come from Italy? Sorry, but we have orders not to tell strangers . . . I'm sorry, ma'am!*'

In Paris, in the barbershop of comrade Reggiani of Padua:

'*Ah, so you're the famous princess? So it's true! Just think, we didn't believe him. Forgive me, comrade, but who believes in Sicilian princesses anymore! It's really too bad, but he left a week ago. Where? You can imagine, with Jose, knowing his haunts is easier said than done!*'

'Don't you even want to read the letter, Modesta?'

'Oh, yes, Stella, of course.'

I opened the envelope. Just a few lines: 'My dear friend, I commend Joyce to your care; she is like a sister to me. She has suffered greatly over the loss of her parents. She will tell you all about it. Look after her, my dear friend. Confident of your understanding, please accept the brotherly affection and gratitude of your good friend. Jose'.

'Forgive me, Mody. I see you are lost in thought. Maybe I shouldn't ask, but is it really Signor Jose's handwriting?'

'Yes, Stella, it is.'

'Of course, I shouldn't . . .'

'You shouldn't what, Stella?'

'It's just that that lady is odd, very odd!'

'In what sense?'

'I don't know! Strange . . . looking at her flusters me. I can't express it . . . Oh God, here she comes! Look, you see! She's done that these past few days, like clockwork. Shut up in her room all day, then at this hour she goes out walking in the shade.'

'Call her.'

'Oh no, Mody, look at her. Look at her closely!'

'Well? What's so odd about her, Stella? You know I don't tolerate prejudices. How many times do I have to tell you? She's just a lot taller than our women. Maybe that's what strikes you as odd?'

59

Was it the pearl-grey pant suit with its white pinstripes, paired with an elegant white silk cravat, that cowed Stella? Or the big Robin Hood style hat which, seen from a distance like this, hid her eyes, her expression?

'If it were only the hat, Modesta, but she's wearing trousers!'

In the shadow of the heavy brown felt brim, the eyes – two large, slanted eyes – sloped up toward the dark blur of the temples. Those eyes weren't smiling, either as she came toward me, or as she displaced Stella who, ignored, quickly rushes off. In a split second, it was as if there had materialized before me one of those pretentious figures found in Parisian salons where our political exiles, between one drink and another, affected a restrained, polite disillusionment before the excited gaze of ladies delighted to have finally found a distraction from their perpetual boredom . . . I try to make out the sound those lips are surely producing, but I can only perceive their slow, elegantly composed movements. Either she is speaking very softly, or a distant storm is interfering with the imaginary cable, stretching for miles, that brings me the tremulous voice of Bambolina, somewhat breathless over the novelty of having a telephone . . . 'You're in Rome! Oh, Zia, I can't believe that you're talking to me from so far away! It's a miracle! It's almost scary. Jacopo and 'Ntoni are here tugging at me; they want to talk to you too. Come home, come back soon, we get bored without you!' Soon, in ten years, maybe twenty . . . we will surely see the face too, flying thousands of miles, on a small screen sitting on the nightstand between an ashtray and a lamp . . . The earth was shrinking into a fist while the acrid, sweetish scent of that Turkish tobacco obliterated the large unfinished wooden table and the copper splendour of Stella's pots as she now fled. I could run after Stella and forget that salon full of small naked ladies who, extending shapely arms, listlessly supported Liberty style lampshades of stained-glass, or the ladies who – crossing their long, slender, adolescent-like legs – listened, captivated and moved, to the misfortunes of our troubled country, recounted in the melancholy voice of some pale Jacopo Ortis . . .

'Who brought you there? Who sets foot in those places? Just some fake anti-fascist lackey of the bourgeoisie. You're right, they play at being heroes without taking any risks. But don't be misled, Modesta, resistance to Fascism does exist! It's here, in the factories, in our barber shops, in our bakeries! Listen to comrade Reggiani.'

I could have run to comrade Reggiani, but it was useless. I would never meet Jose. And anyway, Jose was telling me that I should respond to that woman, even though the smell of her long cigarettes was stupefying. The ashtray Stella had improvised from a flower-pot saucer held three white and gold cigarette butts. And already the long fingers were slowly fingering another one, almost gratefully. What was her name? Jose's letter, left lying on the table, told the woman's name, but it would have been rude to reopen it in front of her.

'You, Princess, are exactly as Jose described you. And I see that he did so for my own good. Always provident, Jose!'

'For your own good?'

'A concise though exceedingly useful warning: "Don't pay any attention to Modesta's sudden absences, Joyce, or you might slip into the pool of indifference which the little princess, when you least expect it, always manages to place between her and whomever she's speaking to." Forgive me for persisting, Princess, but you haven't answered, and this makes me unbearably anxious. Is it perhaps because you think it's now impossible to find passage to South America, as it was for comrade Alessandro Giudice two years ago? Do you think that by now . . .'

'If it was possible once, it will be so a second time. Don't worry! Provided of course that you have a lot of money. Back then, I was able to meet Alessandro's needs, but now that's impossible for me. Everything is in decline and I have to be prudent.'

'Oh, as far as that goes, for me it's different. Alessandro is poor and he was in Italy on a mission. In my case, the situation is less edifying: I'm wealthy, and my coming to Italy was simply a sentimental choice, and as such, a mistake.'

'If you have money, consider it done! It's only a matter of waiting for the right ship.'

'Will we have to wait long? I'm on pins and needles, and although I appreciate your discretion, Princess, my sense of guilt – which is huge, believe me – compels me to make my position clear: despite Jose's warnings, I had been under the illusion that I could travel unnoticed. The fact that I didn't have a political record in Italy . . . I'll explain: I live in Paris and I only joined the Party two years ago. I deluded myself into thinking that I could rush off to my dying sister's bedside. Certainly, had I left soon afterwards, as Jose had advised me . . . but Joland's death . . . Forgive me, Princess, I'm not used to talking about myself, but I must do so to apologize for having somehow placed you at risk with my presence here.'

'Calm down, Joyce! As Jose knows – he didn't send you to me by chance – here in Sicily, things are less severe.'

'That doesn't mean I shouldn't have left as soon as Joland died! But seeing her agonizing death, knowing that, in the last year, she had had to endure illness and loneliness, all by herself . . . Or maybe, I don't know . . . it all gripped me like a vice, and for three months I've been almost crazy with grief and remorse. I couldn't think straight anymore! Only the news that they were looking for me brought me to my senses, that – and fear of my weakness. I realized that if they were to capture me I wouldn't be able to withstand the methods they use. And unfortunately, I know many names and facts. I managed to make OVRA* lose track of me, but only because I was afraid. I'll be honest with you. It's only thanks to fear that I've emerged from a state of prostration that was about to ruin me, while implicating many valiant individuals.'

'But fear and terror, which you seem to spurn so, Joyce, carry within them the seed of courage.'

'That thought, though it doesn't convince me, calms me, Princess. I'm grateful to you.'

'I didn't say it to calm you; consoling people is not my calling. Only, I don't believe in heroes.'

'Just what Jose said.'

The shadow and hat brim were now about to blend, when suddenly those lips parted in an unexpected smile that lit up the darkness of the felt, the eyes, the shadows. Stella was right: that woman flustered you. I should have run off after Stella and got away from that deep voice whose intense pauses, underscored by long, distracted looks, made me all too aware of my awkward gestures and way of speaking. When she said again: 'Do you think, Princess . . .', the incongruence of my title with her elegance upset me to the point that, grabbing the chair, I heard myself say in a strident voice:

'For heaven's sake, Joyce, don't call me Princess! I can barely stand it at the bank and with the lawyers.'

'I understand . . . It sounded jarring to me too, when Jose talked about you. But as Jose told me: "In her, the title loses the hateful connotation custom and tradition have given the word, and revives all the fabulous legends of childhood."'

Was she making fun of me? Or, influenced by her Jose – suddenly I felt I hated him for the power you could see he had over her – did she perhaps not notice my careless dress, my neglected mop of hair, my odious voice? Indignant, I deliberately looked her in the eye. No, she wasn't making fun of me; rather, she was studying me like a curious plaything.

Full of hate for her and her Jose, I didn't answer. Rising, I dismissed her with a nod, not smiling that foolish smile, which has lingered on my lips for hours. *'I advise you to smile less, Mody. You have a beautiful smile, but when you overdo it and ladle it out on every occasion, your plebeian origins show. Be careful!'*

★

'It's true, Modesta. It was the same for me too. From the first day I had the feeling that we had known each other for ever.'

She had called me Modesta for the first time and, spoken by her, that ugly name seemed almost beautiful to me. Well, dear Carmine, I followed your advice to flee a face by looking the other way, or avoiding a back street where a partly open window proffers alluring shadows. In Palermo, at the hotel, I had managed to shun those persistent roses that offered up their red song to the sun each morning. In Paris, with that Michel and his emerald eyes it was easy to move my departure up a few days. Even now, all I would have had to do was give her Pietro's ticket, which was lying on my desk, and a ship's name and date would have silenced that voice which, day after day, filled the house with fairy tales, landscapes, stories even more exciting than the adventures of Saint Agatha and Santa Rosalia. But how could I interrupt the description of that immense, dazzling villa, its pale wood carved in tracery, whose reflection – on returning from long rowboat rides at sunset – glittered on the leaden water of the Bosporus?

'. . . to frighten us, Nazim would whisper that it was the ghost of our house that rose from the sea at that hour to greet the dying sun.'

No, I would not confirm with Pietro. Maybe later on, the next ship.

'You seem lost in thought, Modesta. Am I perhaps boring you with my childhood tales?'

Besides, she doesn't ask me about leaving either. She doesn't even ask Stella anymore. Without waiting for my reply she adds:

'It's curious, Modesta, but since I've been here – I don't know whether it's thanks to your serenity or because of Stella, or this house – all my anxiety has vanished. I'm ashamed to say it, but I'm as content here as I was with Nazim, back then, in what was our childhood home.'

You see? She doesn't want to go either. I mentally tear up Pietro's ticket with the name of the ship, the captain and so on.

'Yes, content as I was then! And maybe talking with you, I'm beginning to see why. I had never been to Sicily and I could never imagine . . .'

'Imagine what, Joyce?'

'How similar your region is to mine. The light, the harsh faces of the peasants, the ghosts!'

'Ghosts?'

'Yes. Here, every back street, every building – perhaps it's your austere, white Baroque, though that may seem like a contradiction – your fountains, your ancient melodies . . . I don't know, everything evokes ghosts and familiar voices. Often, while walking, I have the precise sensation that I'm hearing the wail of the muezzin, and I find myself gazing up, scanning for that stone cry raised to the sky, which for the pious in Turkey is the minaret. To me those cries are nothing but petrified screams, terrified of the merciless sky that crushes the frightened soul into the ground . . . How I would love to take a ship, Modesta, and show you Anatolia!'

You see? She even said the word ship, but without the slightest reference to the *San Giovanni Decollato*, which, as I've mentioned to her, definitely leaves for South America at dawn on Saturday.

'Help you get to know Istanbul! Allow me to dream, Modesta. It's been a long time since I've done so, and besides, as I told you, it's your trees that are to blame, your sky, your light. Twenty days in Istanbul, with a brief side trip to Edirne, where the most beautiful mosques in Turkey are found. And then months and months through the rugged, epic heart of the Anatolian plateau. Anatolia! A land devoid of sentimentalism. Istanbul? No, Istanbul, like all capitals, betrays the true essence of the country it represents. Capitals – only now do I understand what Nazim used to tell me – are destined to a different life, which alienates them, if you will, from the rural countryside, from the country's mountains and rivers. Perhaps that's why Atatürk, after the revolution of 1923, made Ankara the capital . . . perhaps. I never spoke about it with Nazim, and now it's too late. He's in and out of those terrible Turkish prisons, like all the comrades, for that matter. We can't take a ship to Istanbul, Modesta! At least I can't, exiled not only from Italy, but also from my second homeland.'

The voice fades out along with the light, leaving a sadness that makes me cry like Bambù when she listens to Stella's sad, sweet stories in the evening. But like Bambù, I decide to sleep a little and in my dreams change the doleful fate of my hero Giufà-Joyce* . . . Like Bambù, I'll be the one to go into the woods and get back the fox skin that the bad men stole from Giufà when he dozed off. Without the fox skin that camouflages him in the woods, Giufà can't procure food by catching the flies, mosquitoes and small worms that are his sustenance . . .

'*Bambù has two lives, Mama, a daytime one and a nighttime one. That's why I always obey her . . . if you only knew the things she does at night! She solves every problem: it's only right that she give the orders. I sleep at night! If it weren't for her, I'd be forever looking at pictures or reading. I can't think of anything else to do, not one game. Whereas she's always up to something!*'

Jacopo is right. Bambolina is like her mother. I wonder what Cavallina thinks of this Mela who plays all the pieces that I played for her at Carmelo? She's talented, this *carusa*! All I did was tell Stella she plays well, and overnight her touch has become more confident and commanding. What should I do, Beatrice? Should I send her to a boarding school? It's time to economize. Attorney Santangelo is right.

'*You, Modesta, agreeing with the sound judgement of an old bourgeois? You surprise me!*' Feigning indignation, Cavallina embraces me from behind and whispers in my ear: '*We have the attics and corridors full of Uncle Jacopo's paintings. Don't you know they're worth a fortune, Mody? That's why I kept them back then.*'

'*I know, I know, Cavallina, but we'd have to take them abroad and we need someone who is astute, sophisticated and familiar at the same time. In short, an expert.*'

'Who could that be, Attorney? Find me a man.'

'But it's contraband, Modesta! I don't see why you should risk trouble with the law when there is all the land that Carlo left to Ida.'

'No, Bambolina's money won't be touched! A woman is helpless without money!'

'Judas Priest! But why? She too has contributed to eating up your money, it seems to me, and stills does, am I right? Besides what are you worried about? Ida is a real beauty. She'll make a good match!'

'Oh, no! She won't marry for that reason, my dear old liberal.'

'She'll work then! It was you who claimed that women should work, if I'm not mistaken!'

'Before, my dear man, before, when we believed the revolution was around the corner. But the way things stand now, no! Bambolina will work only if she wants to.'

'Ah, well! That's news to me. What is it, the idea of some anarchist in your house? You want her to become a lazy, idle woman?'

'Put it however you want. Bambolina will be lazy and idle!'

'In any case, I can't help you. Find him yourself, this expert!'

An expert! It has to be an expert! Or shall I go myself? An adventure like any other. But first I must find out how one goes about smuggling . . . the techniques . . . the skills . . . Piano technique, smuggling technique, the technique of falling asleep . . . Unless I resume my technique of counting – not sheep, of course! – the beautiful sights encountered during the day: clouds at sunset, furious waves crashing on the rocks . . . Stella's and Bambolina's expressions . . . Bambolina has so many quirky gestures! And Stella, who pulls her hair up because of the heat, unknowingly imitating her ancient sisters on the Syracusan coins.* Those coins, too. . . indeed, they alone are worth a fortune.

60

I wasn't surprised when I opened my eyes and Stella told me that I had slept for nearly two days in a row; nor is she any longer surprised by it.

'It's a blessing, Mody, a blessing! Why get so upset? Even Carlo said that this sleep was good for you. What a fright, the first time! I was afraid you'd starve to death! And he just smiled . . . You know what he used to say when I got scared at something new? He'd say: "Ignorance, Stella, ignorance!" He was so right! Oh! I was forgetting Signora Joyce . . . she asked me just now if she could come up and see you.'

'Signora Joyce?'

'Yes, I found out. She's married, and widowed: she told me so. She also said that she doesn't always wear her wedding band because sometimes looking at it reminds her of the sorrow that . . . Oh, the poor thing, the way she talks! She talks like a schoolmarm, but she's not as horrible as she seemed, Mody! Recently she came to the kitchen to have coffee, like you always do, and you know what she said? "Do you mind if I steal Modesta's place for a little while, Stella?" If only she would take off that hat! Why does she always keep it on? Oh, you know what Bambù said? That maybe she's bald! . . . Oh, dear God! Bambù is waiting for me! . . . I have to go . . . So should I let her come up or not?'

I had been racking my brain for weeks trying to find an excuse to get her to come up here. Was I now going to let Stella leave without seizing that rare opportunity? Gripping the covers, I almost shouted as the door was already closing.

'No, Stella, let her come up. She'll be offended otherwise.'

Had Stella heard me or not? Did I have time to run to the bathroom and at least brush my teeth and comb my hair? Suddenly I was aware of my condition. Stella had managed to put me to bed, take off my skirt and whatever was too binding, as Carlo had taught her. But I had been under the covers with that sweater for two days . . . Touching my hair, I found it sweaty and sticky. I was already inelegant and awkward when I was washed and wearing a clean cardigan; imagine what I must be like after two days in bed. I almost prayed to any god at all that Stella hadn't heard me. But Stella had a very fine ear, and already the door was opening. Too late! I pulled the covers up so she would see as little of me as possible, and closed my eyes. In the dark 'the voice' – that's what I now privately called the only voice worthy of the name – washed warmly over my wretched body.

'Oh God, Stella! She's asleep again. Are you sure there's nothing wrong with such a prolonged sleep, Stella? Does it happen often? I'm worried about her!'

'No, she's not sleeping; my Mody likes to do this. Either she runs around like a spinning top all the blessed day, or she snuggles up in bed . . . please be kind enough to sit down and wait. Oh, I'll leave the tray.'

The 'voice' was worried about me. This revelation dissolved my hunger completely. And here I am, unworthy of her, awkward and filthy, with that awful sweater and my badly trimmed nails! As soon as Stella left the room, I opened my eyes to see her again. I stare at her as if I haven't seen her in years. But just like after a long absence, when the desire to see the beloved face becomes so strong that it blinds you, so I, blinded, stare at her but do not see her.

Is she smoking? The pale hands emerge slowly from a hazy curtain. No, they don't emerge; rather, they seem to be resting on a velvet cushion. Long, tapered hands, severed, with the perfect nails of a saint's statue. What the devil is that saint's name? Agatha? No – Saint Agatha had had her breasts lopped off, not her hands. Yet Mother Leonora had often recounted the story of those strong, transparent hands, strong enough to endure all the torture without the knuckles being marred or the nails broken. Mine, clutching the blanket, must be filthy. . .

'I shouldn't have been so persistent with Stella. I can see I'm disturbing you, Modesta. I apologize, but I was a bit sad. I'll see you later on.'

The cushion was already moving before my eyes . . . Two black infidels, blacker than hell, were raising it to carry it to the Great Khan,* blacker than his minions, who with his brutish, pitch-black paws, would rip those chaste fingers to pieces.

Forgetting my dirty nails, I quickly hastened to grab the cushion.

'Oh God, Modesta! You're not well and you don't want to say so. Are you afraid of worrying Stella? But if it comforts you to grip my skirt, I'll stay here. Don't worry! Still, forgive me for insisting, but I think I should call a doctor.'

What was she talking about? I had never heard anything so silly! Since when have doctors been able to help someone who is in love? Even Mimmo used to say that there is no cure for that pernicious plague that – to make it seem less frightening – we call love. I could hear Mela practising bass chords up and down the keyboard. The sharp clarity of those notes and a deep gentle laugh from the 'voice' dispelled the fog in front of me. And I saw her. How foolish, Stella! Not only wasn't she bald – though even bald she would have been beautiful – but she was laughing, brushing back a soft mass of black hair from her face. So that was it: the 'voice's' hair was lovelier and blacker than Stella's, and Stella was envious.

'But of course, of course I'll stay, Modesta! Now that I see you're joking, I feel reassured. How right you are! No doctor, no science, has the ability to cure that monstrous illness that fools, as you said, call love.'

Stella is not only jealous of her hair, but also of the fact that, without those trousers, a pair of smooth, slender calves led to two ankles so slight they seemed made of glass. Letting go of her skirt, I was about to grab one to see if it really was glass when that envious Stella came in, calling me back to reality. She was envious, but she cared about me. And her words – 'Would you ladies like me to bring up some coffee?' – saved me from doing one silly thing after another.

The proof was that, once I regained control of myself, simply by holding that tangible, hot cup in my hands, I noticed a tender, compassionate smile I'd never seen before hovering on Joyce's lips, now serious again. As if that new smile weren't enough, she added:

'Forgive me, Modesta, but since I've known you an indiscreet curiosity has made me want to ask you something. It's all Jose's fault, given his total inability to grasp the real core of a person, a country, an object. Everything becomes abstract when Jose tells it. To give you an example: you ask him about a given individual who's impressed him, what her hair is like, the colour of her eyes, and he says: "How should I know! I'm not interested in those useless details. I told you that she's beautiful and intelligent. Isn't that enough? Always looking for gossip!" And that's how he spoke of you. He only told me about your strength, your intelligence. And I was expecting a woman if not old, very mature, and not a young girl. Forgive me, Modesta, but how old are you?'

I felt ashamed. It was clear by now: everything I'd said and done had been gauche. I heard my voice – or was it Carlo's voice? – uncertain and confused:

'I was born on the first of January, 1900. With me it's easy to figure it out, like the nun in the convent kept saying.'

It was so easy that Joyce, wide-eyed with surprise as though seeing a dwarf or the Bearded Lady, exclaimed:

'No, Modesta! Go on, you're kidding! I'm glad, because if you're joking it means you feel all right. But you can't be thirty-three years old.'

My shame vanished. I wasn't Carlo, who never got angry and always put up with being teased about how absurd it was to be twenty-eight and look nineteen at the most. No, I wasn't like Carlo. Angrily, I insisted:

'I'm not joking. I'm thirty-three years old and I'm not kidding!'

'But it's incredible! You don't look more than twenty! Or when you turn serious, like you are now, twenty-five at most.'

Fortunately, she went straight from being astonished to telling me what Jose had said about me, staring, as usual when she spoke, at something extremely important to her that hovered over my head.

Fortunately! Because I was unable to silence the eight-year-old Modesta whom 'the voice' reawakened in me, and who now – what was that little girl doing? – who now began crying at the humiliation of not being big enough for that Tuzzu who, since he had started smoking, had got taller and more arrogant. I try to hush Modesta, but she continues crying like Bambù – all the same, these *picciriddi* – when her Prando leaves her to go bike riding with his friends:

'*I'm not crying because he's leaving, Stella, I'm crying because since his mother bought him a racing bike, even when he's here he treats me like a nobody.*'

'*But he loves you, Bambolina. Prando always says so.*'

'*Maybe, but not as much as I love him.*'

'*What does that mean? What, are we in a grocery store weighing sugar and coffee? You know what Jacopo told that silly cook who was teasing him, telling him that you, yes, you, loved Prando more than him?*'

'*No, what did he say?*'

'*He said: "Leave me alone! The important thing is how much I love Bambolina." These* picciriddi *nowadays, Modesta, it's scary how they talk! They sound like grown men!*'

'*And what was Bambolina's reaction, Stella?*'

'*She quieted down right away and went to look for Jacopo.*'

Jacopo was right, and now Modesta is no longer crying either. She's decided to take pleasure in her love for that woman even though she knows that Joyce can never love her back, captivated as she is by her friend Nazim, a Turkish poet and hero; by Silone, a writer and great anti-fascist; by Jose . . . All she does is talk about him. Could she be in love with that beanpole with the crooked nose?

Mela has resumed her practising. That girl has the power to turn the piano's mechanical keys into the live strings of a harp. Joyce laughs for the second time, removing the cigarette from her lips for a moment.

'Jose, married? In love? Please, Modesta! He dislikes these words even more than you and I do. And whereas you described love as an illness, he actually says it's a drug more powerful than religion. Oh God! I remember Angelica's irritated look when he . . .'

'Who is Angelica?'

If the idea of all those male friends of hers drove me crazy, I nearly jumped out of bed and ran when I heard that female name. Thank goodness I had only raised my head from the pillow, and to justify leaping up I turned on the lamp. She was still smiling, but she moved her head away from the cone of light that turned the sheet a dazzling white, and stared at the sunset. Was she hiding? What was she hiding when she said:

'You don't know Angelica Balabanoff? I thought you knew her. She's a good friend of Maria Giudice.'*

'No, I haven't met her. Is she beautiful like Maria?'

'Oh no, rather homely I'd say, but very interesting, with an intelligence that's terrifying in a woman, as Jose says.'

Consoled by that 'rather homely', I fell back against the pillow.

'Indeed, especially when she gets angry, and Jose is always able to make her angry.'

'How?'

'Provoking her prudishness. You know Maria, so you can understand. They are extraordinary women, but of another generation. So that day – dear God, how much time has passed! – when Angelica discreetly asked him something like: "So young man, don't you have anything new to tell your Angelica, who doesn't like thinking of you all alone? You seem more and more rumpled. Is it possible that you haven't yet found a comrade who can sew your buttons back on?", Jose bluntly replied: "Come on, Angelica, it's not my buttons that worry you. You're worried about my manly equipment, which might rust like all machines do if not used." And she – you should have seen her, Modesta – flustered and blushing like a girl: "I was talking about love, Jose!" "Never mind love, Angelica! Luckily there are our precious *hetaerae*, the only real women, the only rebels, the only women who know how to give and take from a man without sentimentalism and simpering." Poor Jose! He uses humour to fend off Angelica's free love, or legitimate bourgeois love, as best he can, but in the end he too falls for it: I've seen him, I know it for a fact!'

There, she was admitting it. Even though she wasn't in love with him, he was with her! Who could know Joyce without falling in love with her?

For the first time in my life, I slept with the worm of jealousy gnawing at me, and it kept me awake even in my sleep, making me toss and turn until morning, when for better or worse I could count the hours that kept me apart from her.

61

The light of dawn, which I had groped for in the dark, arrived to pol-ish the shapes of the furniture and Uncle Jacopo's books which, no longer imprisoned by glass and grillework, peacefully retold their stories. Since he had returned among us, I too had begun to refer to him as uncle, to distinguish between the troubled face that stared back at me from the photograph and the little boy with the pensive gaze of an adult. But the worm kept gnawing the bony vaults of my cranial chamber, making me get in and out of bed, open and close drawers and windows. It was stifling in that room, but when I opened the shutters I was met by a dense chill, without a cloud in the sky, the same unbroken, bright sky of summer in the dead of winter. How I had yearned for that gleaming brilliance during the long winters of my trips up north! No, I would not leave again. It was she who had to go away, taking the worm away with her. Though I lack the courage to admit it out loud, I know it has a name: jealousy. I said it, and for a moment this word, whose meaning had been unfamiliar to me before, stands apart from my emotions and I can see it; I can touch it like a vase, a glass, an object you can turn and look at from all sides. That's the value of saying things: materialized by my voice, the worm is more nebulous, formless and ineffectual than all the feelings I had experienced up until that day. Moreover, something that I would never have imagined before, it was a carnal sensation, a constant dull ache like a tingling, a toothache . . . That Turk Nazim, a proletarian hero despite his nobility, living in prison and in poverty despite his wealthy, influential childhood in a villa on the Bosphorus with his little friend Joyce, daughter of an Italian ambassador and a Turkish noblewoman . . . Since she wants to be unreachable, let her go! She doesn't know that even though I tore up the ticket, the ship hasn't yet sailed. It's easy enough to notify Pietro and have him accompany her to the port.

'Come in, Joyce. It's open.'

'Oh, Modesta! Just for a moment, I really need to talk to you. I must leave. Forgive me for insisting, but I must leave! Somehow or other I must join Jose in Paris. This physical and moral comfort, the exuberance of your children – such wonderful children! – and Stella's 'Ntoni as well, all so elegant and intelligent . . . in them lies the living proof of what we Marxists know: it's the environment that makes the man. Here, amid Stella's kindness and the appeal of these pines and the sea, I was about to forget my duty to Jose and the comrades. Until last night's terrible nightmares! I still can't forget Jose's harrowed face staring at me . . . I could never forgive myself for not being alongside Jose at this time of conflict within our own party. Silone, Tresso, Leonetti, all expelled! Intransigence, sectarianism toward the socialists have divided and confused the anti-fascist forces, thereby only helping capitalism which at the 5th Congress, as a result of the crisis, we had already written off.* So many hopes for the cause, so many real achievements had flourished staunchly before us in this Europe of ours! All wiped out in a few years! Atatürk's turnabout, the Spartacist movement crushed, Rosa Luxemburg assassinated! And now that petit-bourgeois Hitler, whom everyone derided until his Beer Hall Putsch, is in power by "democratically" winning the elections. A hellish night, Modesta! As though someone had taken pleasure in projecting my entire long past in a dream, all of my nearly forty years! I saw my mother's joy as she embraced me and kept saying: "You at least will be free, my child! A new era is dawning for Turkish women. From today on, you will vote and be the master of your destiny." Then the next instant I saw her face, now old and gaunt, in exile in Paris, and beside hers, the racked face of . . . Oh, Modesta, I must go! The peace and serenity of this house aren't fitting for us old, uprooted and perhaps defeated survivors. For those of us who, as Jose says, find our *raison d'être* only in the struggle.'

'I could find you a ship, Joyce, but only if I knew the real reason you are so anxious to leave. You've spoken at length about many things, but you haven't given me an idea of who you are, as a person, I mean. And that "we old survivors who find our *raison d'être* only in the struggle" prompts me not to let you leave. You say you're old, Joyce, but you're just tired and, forgive my effrontery, out of your senses. How could I take the responsibility of letting you embark in this state? It's not 1922 or 1924 anymore; it's 1933. I will only let you leave if you tell me that someone who can take care of you is waiting for you.'

For the first time, Joyce looks at me for a long time. Without her screen of words to hide behind, she lowers her head and buries her face in her arms. Her mass of black hair is spread on the desk between us: a gleaming summer night . . .

'*What is night made of, Tuzzu?*'

'*What do I know?*'

'*If you lift me on your shoulders, I'll touch it and I'll tell you.*'

'*So then, let's hear it. Now that you've touched it, what is it made of?*'

'If no one is waiting for you, Joyce, I won't let you leave.'

The hair accepts my touch – or is it just that my arm prevents her from moving? I withdraw my hand and, liberated, she rolls her shoulders. Disappointed, my hand is left lying midway on the desk.

'What beautiful hands you have, Modesta. I hadn't noticed. No, leave it there, your stroking raised my spirits, just like when I was a child and my mother used to stroke me.'

I wasn't aware of the long journey I'd made around the desk until I was seated next to her and saw my other hand, ice-cold, disappear between hers.

'And how small they are, up close like this! You're strange, Modesta. Sometimes you seem tall and strong; at other times, like now, you seem small and fragile, like a child. Before, when you said "I won't let you leave", I felt relieved – like when, as a child, I knew I could depend on the decision of someone older and stronger than me. It's been so long since I've been able to rely on anyone. Of course there are the comrades; Jose has always been close to me. But a woman friend is different, and I feel you are a friend. I've never had a female friend, Modesta.'

My hands, revived in hers, found strength and determination. Leaving the warmth of her palms and encircling her waist, I heard myself say with the forcefulness she needed at that moment (or was I going too far and would she pull away?): 'A friend, Joyce, of course. You must rely on me and put yourself in my hands. Rest.' Obeying my order, she let her head drop on my shoulder.

'What about Jose, who's waiting for me? What will he think of me? I should let him know, but how?'

'I'll write to Jose myself.'

'But it's risky! The mail,. . .'

'No, no, I'll find another way to get a letter to him.'

'How peaceful it is here, Modesta, after the suspicious looks, the innuendos, the signs of alarm every time the phone rang there in Milan, in the houses of the few friends who didn't slam the door in my face. It was terrible! Only two of the old comrades and friends took me in . . . And one of them for just a few seconds! I'll never forget. It was a Saturday; he was in black shirt, shaking, only a brief greeting before going to the weekly assembly.'*

'Don't judge them. Il Duce has won everyone over with the help of his elegant Arturo Bocchini.* Not a day goes by without witnessing the conversion of a friend, an acquaintance. Or simply entering a shop and seeing from the errand boy's determined look that he has gone over to the other side.'

'Even here in Sicily, Modesta?'

'Yes, here too, though more quietly than in the north.'

'But you're so calm, so serene!'

'It's no use squandering your energies on misguided fear. You just have to be wary . . .'

'Be wary? You suspected me, didn't you, Modesta?'

'Of course, and I still suspect you, because anyone who turns up these days – even with a letter from a trusted friend – could be an agent sent by our dear Bocchini.'

She didn't answer, but her head grew heavier on my shoulder. I didn't understand the silent language of those gestures. Until that moment, no one had ever spoken to me that way. Either that woman, perhaps sent to spy, was more cunning than I had thought, or her submission was sincere. To get past that jasmine-scented silence, I clasped her tightly to me; let her say something or move away.

'You've never spoken about Carlo, Modesta.'

'You've never asked me, Joyce.'

'Jose told me to be careful, not to reopen your grief. He told me how much you had suffered over Carlo's death. Were the killers ever found?'

'Jose was right. It's too horrible for me to talk about it.'

'Do you still suspect me, Modesta?'

'It's only been a few seconds, Joyce. Why shouldn't I suspect you?'

'Forgive me for insisting, but you've been so kind to me from the very first moment that I can't make sense of it, and only now do I realize that you've never let a single name slip out during our conversations.'

'Nor will a name ever slip out. Don't worry. That way, if you were a spy, all you would leave with was the discovery that "perhaps" I am an anti-fascist since I gave you asylum, and since you observed that this house contains neither a portrait of Il Duce nor the King, that my children do not go to the Saturday rallies and that they don't wear the uniform. But that much is well known to everyone in Catania, just as I'm known to be eccentric and perhaps a little touched. It's a preroga-tive of the Brandiforti.'

'Yet despite this suspicion, you're embracing me and stroking my hair like a sister?'

'I don't see why a spy shouldn't have a sister.'

Her deep, lingering laughter swept away the scent of jasmine like a sudden wind. No, it wasn't the wind. She had stood up, leaving the warm impression of her waist in my arms, flustering me. I got up too, but did not follow her. Laughing as she went to the window, Joyce again became tall, austere and unapproachable.

'Being with you, Modesta, brings back a gaiety I had thought I'd lost for ever. "Even spies should have a sister!" What a great title it would be for a novel! Jose told me you write.'

'Yes, but not about politics. Sorry to squash your hopes, you wouldn't find anything there either, not a name or a fact. Rather, you'd find many abstruse notions that would only confirm my eccentricity.'

'Like your way of life, right? Indeed, what could I say? No tables laid either for lunch or dinner, everyone comes and goes when and as they please. Wealthy, aristocratic children made to set the table and serve themselves, sometimes even forced to cook if by some whim they decide to eat at times that depart from the cook's schedule . . . That bird-faced Mela, all eyes, thin as a rail, alongside a young lady as elegant as your Bambù. And you let her study at your expense with the best concert artists. Oh, Modesta, besides feeling cheerful, I'm terribly hungry!'

'Hungry for information, or for food?'

'Hungry, famished, like I haven't been in years! Forget your work for today and let's have lunch together, Modesta, please. Oh, look! what an amazing sight! Look how the storm is moving in!'

'It's the Tropea screaming her fury . . . the Tropea with her windswept hair dripping blood and squalls.'

We had to shut the window tightly or the storm would hurl it open and no one would save us from the rain that was advancing, driven by the sun: fire and water were mowing down the pines, decapitating the birds and flowers. Just in time, pushing hard with my entire body, I managed to close the shutters, the windows, the jalousies and the drapes. We were in darkness now, but outside the fists and nails of that raging woman kept battering away, trying to get in.

'How strong you are, Modesta! You always amaze me.'

'Clearly I was born to amaze people. It's a refrain that has haunted me as long as I've lived. Don't be amazed, please – and turn on the light.'

'Oh, Modesta, look at the chandelier: the house is shaking!'

'The Tropea's fury doesn't last long. It blows over in the time it takes to smoke a cigarette. Why don't you smoke?'

'It's awful . . . Like you said, it sounds like the shrieks of a madwoman.'

'It's the trees and the sea responding to her shrieks, and there may have been a slight earthquake. But be assured, it will be over in a few minutes.'

'You're so calm. Does it happen often?'

'At least once a year that woman recalls ancient grievances and wages war against the Mountain. We islanders have a history of women warriors, women with swords who slaughter those who offend them.'

'Are they perhaps saints?'

'Not at all! Female paladins, valiant and fearless, equal to Orlando when it comes to swinging a Durendal.'*

'The marionettes? Jose had told me about them. But he hadn't mentioned the female puppets.'

'I'll take you to see these heroines, with profiles as delicate as Stella's and nerves of steel. You'll see how tremendous they are in their warriors' fury! For centuries, the Church has been trying to banish them, as our puppeteer Insanguine says. Just like Fascism wants to take away our dead, and with them the memory of our vital traditions.'

'Your dead, Modesta? I don't understand.'

'Yes, they declared that the only feast day for children must be the Fascist La Befana, like in the north. This greatly offended our people, who for the sake of peace and quiet formally agreed. But we continue to remember our dead and, on the night of November first, leave the door open for them to enter our homes on tiptoe, bringing gifts and messages to our *carusi*. Sweets and toys, so the children won't forget that death exists, and that our deceased live on even in death.'

'That's why there was no tree at Christmas! When I asked Jacopo if he was sorry about it, he replied: "But those are just stories. For us it's the dead themselves who bring us gifts." I admit, Modesta, that those words spoken by a child frightened me so that I didn't dare ask. I thought he was joking. Jacopo is so ironic that sometimes he makes you uncomfortable. Now that I think about it, even Bambù, when I asked her who gave her that magnificent amber necklace she often wears, told me: "Mama and Papa brought them to me this year."'

'Of course. That way Bambolina remembers her father, who was killed, but without fear.'

'In fact, she was unperturbed.'

'When they go out to play on the second of November, all the island children talk about their dead, who are neither in hell nor in heaven, but with them. Even the Church has always had to turn a blind eye to this pagan custom. And it's the first time a king or a foreign leader has dared to try and abolish this tradition. But if by November neither of us is in prison, I'll take you down to Catania and you'll see the great *Chiana dei Morti* that continues to be rekindled each year, brought back to life with lanterns and torches, mountains of toys and sweets, laughing at outsiders and at death.'

'Oh God, Modesta, what is this *Chiana dei Morti?*'

'It's Catania's large central piazza, where everyone – parents, brothers and sisters, aunts and uncles, rich and poor – spends the entire night strolling among colourful stalls, lit-up shops, teeming cafés and restaurants. And between one glass of wine and another, they look for gifts for the youngest children on behalf of the dearly departed.'

'I'd be happy to go with you to see the puppets, as well as this strange feast of the dead. Assuming they don't arrest us first! Although, I must confess, I find any idea of death very frightening. But you frighten me too, Modesta. I mean it. Since the storm you've changed toward me. I enjoyed your stories very much, but I sensed something like hostility toward me in them. Or is it the Tropea that's making you anxious?'

'No, Joyce. We're used to storms and earthquakes. It's something you said that offended me, as it would offend Stella and every other woman in the world. But perhaps I'm making a mountain out of a molehill. Don't pay any attention to me. We islanders are suspicious.'

'I don't understand. Did I say something to offend you and Stella?'

'This artificial light is gloomy, Joyce. If you want, you can open the drapes again now.'

'But the storm . . .?'

'Open them, I'm telling you.'

'Oh God, Modesta, how did you know? The sky is all blue now and calm. This silence is more frightening than the thunder and lightning. I'll never find peace, Modesta, not here or anywhere else!'

I had never seen her tremble. Or maybe she's just cold. Even the white of her blouse is trembling.

'You're cold, Joyce. Come and sit by the fire.'

She curls up trembling on the sofa, as though trying to hide. And here I've been tormenting her for hours with disturbing tales and insinuations! Her anguish communicates shivers of pleasure to me. I should at least embrace her.

'I'm not worthy of your sisterly love, Modesta!'

What does she mean? The fireplace's heat burns my mouth. No, not the fire; it's her lips pressed against mine, her tongue sliding into my saliva. I want to seize that tongue between my teeth, but:

'Oh, Modesta, I'm unworthy, unworthy!'

What is she saying? I try to follow her but all I find is the door closed behind her as she flees. My head, my forehead are aflame, as joyous laughter rises from my chest to my lips. So that's all it was, the mystery, the partial confessions, the trembling. And I thought she was a spy!

62

I don't know how long I stood there, my head against the door, laughing excitedly over my naivety, when hurried steps coming up the stairs snapped me out of my reverie. Was it her, returning? I too would have done the same. But my hand dropped from the doorknob at the sound of Stella's voice asking to come in. Jacopo and Bambù must have hurt themselves chasing each other around. No, not Bambù, Jacopo! He's the fragile one. All he does is shut himself up in his room, reading and studying.

'Mody, Mody, it's me, Stella. Please open the door!'

'What's wrong, Stella? Don't tell me Jacopo hurt himself because this time I'll give him a good spanking! Then we'll see if he makes up his mind to play some sports, and stop chasing after Bambù!'

'No, Mody, no! It's the foreign *signora*, she's distressed, and I, I . . . I'm so sorry I thought badly of her!'

'What happened?'

'I don't know! She called for me and she seemed calm. When I saw the bags in the middle of the room I thought: "She wants me to help her . . . it's time for her to leave." Wasn't she supposed to leave, Mody? Instead she told me that she wanted to sleep and didn't want to be disturbed until tomorrow morning. But as she was getting into bed I saw that she was crying. When I got back to the kitchen I couldn't stop thinking about those tears. So I went back and knocked at the door, thinking maybe she might want something warm.'

'Get to the point, Stella. What happened?'

'She didn't answer. I knocked and knocked, over and over again, a hundred times. No response. I'm worried, Mody! Maybe the *signora* isn't well.'

'Oh dear God! Princess, the water is all red. It's blood!'

Nunzio is yelling like a madman. I've never seen him in such a state. He broke down two doors: her room and the bathroom. As I hold Joyce's head, Nunzio pulls her out of the water and lays her on the bed, muttering:

'Look at this! Such a beautiful woman, and she doesn't want to live! With the Princess's permission, I'll tear up this sheet and bandage her. It has to be tight . . . like this! From the colour of the water, she hasn't lost a lot of blood . . . Oh! She did a good job with the razor blade! . . . Like a fellow from Milan at the front, who for some reason performed the same service on himself one night – without a bath tub, naturally. He slept in the bunk above me and the blood dripping on my face woke me. I wouldn't wish it on anyone!'

So I wasn't the only one who saw her as beautiful, through the filter of love that had clouded my eyes since that first day, given that Nunzio too kept saying: 'So beautiful, so beautiful . . .', as he helped Stella remove the blood-soaked nightgown.

'That's it, under the covers! Or rather, we should dry her hair first . . .'

Stella dried her hair which, wet like that, seemed longer. Her hair was slightly wavy, so naturally it would look shorter when dry.

She opened her eyes at the exact moment Dr Licata left.

From the serene gaze with which she glanced around at the walls, the drapes, the luggage still closed in the middle of the room, pausing at Stella's smiling face, I realized that between us there would be no more talk about leaving, nor unfortunately any kissing.

'Oh, Modesta, you're here too? What's happened?'

'Nothing, *signora*. You fell ill in the bathroom.'

I would never have imagined such tact in Stella and I looked at her gratefully. She, too, hoped that Joyce had forgotten. But, as the doctor had predicted, that wasn't the case, and Stella was already glancing at the hypodermic syringe ready on the nightstand: '*If she seems depressed when she wakes up, give her this sedative and call me.*'

'Oh God! Princess, Stella, my wrists . . .'

'Never mind, *signora*, leave them under the covers. It's nothing!'

But she had already slipped her arms out from under the sheet and, letting them drop, was now staring at the white bandages that covered her hands. Stella and I awaited the crisis that Licata had forecast. But when Joyce began speaking again, Stella put down the syringe she had already picked up.

'This dressing is the work of a doctor. You even had to call a doctor! How shameful!'

'Don't upset yourself, *signora*, the doctor is a close friend of Mody and the family!'

'I'm unworthy of your trust or Jose's. My God! How could I have forgotten, in my despair, that I would put you all in danger by dying?'

'Danger, did you say? Shame? Oh, Holy Virgin, why suffer like that without saying a word? We're women, friends . . .'

It was time to send Stella away. I was looking for a way to make her leave the room when she spoke up:

'Talk with my Mody, *signora*, she's able to understand anything . . . I'll go now. I have to drop in on the *picciriddi* a moment before they go to sleep. Jacopo especially becomes grumpy in the morning if I don't kiss him on the forehead in the evening. Goodnight, *signora*, and you too, Mody.'

Once Stella left, the child Modesta, who for years had dozed inside me no matter how hard I tried to ignore her, was scared to be alone with that grown woman, her mournful eyes still studying the bandages.

'I'd better go too, Joyce. The doctor said you must rest, and he'll scold me tomorrow if he knows I kept you awake.'

'Someone scold you, Modesta?'

Embarrassed, I tried to make amends for that child's gaffe.

'He's an old comrade, and I let him scold me sometimes.'

'Finally you mention someone who frequents this house. Don't you suspect me anymore, Modesta?'

'No, Joyce!'

'Because of the silly thing I did? Come here. Why are you sitting so far away?'

'The doctor gave strict orders.'

'Just for a moment or two, just enough to make me see that you're not angry with me, even though you have every right to be.'

'I'm not angry, Joyce. You can tell that I'm not.'

'Yes, I can tell. Thank you.'

In the dim light, I waited for her to go on talking, to tell me what grief – and it must be an enormous one – drove her to take her life, but she remained silent. I got up from the armchair and looked at her: she was sleeping. The deep, regular breathing was reassuring . . . Should I try to turn off the bedside lamp or not? Licata had said that she shouldn't be left alone, at least not that night: 'Often when the despair is so great that it has managed to overcome fear that one time, they realize how easy and convenient death is, and they get the urge to try again – unless the subject, upon awakening, displays a crucial fear over what he has done.' But Joyce had shown no fear over that act. Only shame and remorse toward us.

*

When I open my eyes, I'm not surprised at having slept so well in an armchair, or that someone has laid a blanket over me, or that an intense joy fills me when I meet Joyce's smiling eyes. That smile is for me, I think. And in the rush of happiness, I have the urge to leap out of my impromptu bed and cover her with kisses. For a moment, the awareness of my adult body stops me, but she continues to smile. And forgetting my legs and arms, grown too quickly, I run along the path that smile shows me and shower her with kisses – so she told me afterwards – her eyes, her forehead, her cheeks. She lets me, her eyes still smiling, but it's not enough for me. I want her to be happy, and I stop only when her lips part too, as serene as her eyes, her forehead and her neck, which throbs with silent laughter. Now my happiness knows no bounds, and I can return to my armchair.

'No, Modesta, no! Stay here! Being close to you fills me with a joy I've never felt before.'

Since she told me to – not only verbally, but making room for me – I can lie down: me on top of the cover, her underneath.

'You must have had a happy childhood if you can offer your children and me so much peace . . . You haven't answered me, Modesta. You were happy as a child, weren't you? When you're like you are now, I seem to see you as a child in a happy home like this one, with a mother as serene as Stella.'

'No, Joyce, no. My mother died early, and I was very poor before becoming part of the Brandiforti family.'

'How can that be?'

Already her eyes were losing their smile, but I didn't want to upset her with sad stories so I quickly added:

'The facts don't matter much. I've always been happy, as you rightly guessed, at least up till now. In time, if you want, I'll tell you about my adventures.'

'You're right; facts don't matter. I've always been well off. My mother died just two years ago, when I was already an adult and able to accept the loss. You see, Modesta, I must assure you that yesterday's weakness will not repeat itself, at least not in this house. But it's also my duty to warn you about me. Unfortunately, since my sister died . . .'

'Joland?'

'Yes, my sister, but not my blood-sister. You see, my father and mother . . . But never mind about me. It's you I'm interested in. Tell me, maybe even though you were poor you had brothers or sisters who . . .'

'No, I was alone.'

'Incredible! You alone, and poor! You, who are so sociable and at ease in the midst of this swarm of exceptional children, in this austere elegance! One day you'll tell me all about it, won't you? You would greatly surprise an old friend and teacher of mine, to whom I owe the mental stability that has kept me going throughout these years – at least until this shameful act. I should tell you, Modesta, that I was already tempted by death in my early years, when I lived with my father and mother. My suicide attempt drove me to press on with my studies. I wanted to find the reason for suffering that was not only physical but also emotional. I studied medicine and later psychiatry in Milan. I knew Carlo in medical school.'

'Oh! Why didn't Carlo ever mention you to me?'

'We parted ways none too amicably . . . Ideological arguments. He never spoke to you about a Jò?'

'Oh, yes, Jò! But I thought it was a man! He mentioned someone who later went to Germany, to specialize. So it was you?'

'Yes.'

'But why "Jò"?'

'Because, as I told you, I've always had only male friends. Carlo and Jose are alike, abstract or distracted, as you please. In time, in their hearts, they probably felt I was a man.'

'But why didn't you tell me right away? Now I remember this Jò . . . The nickname suits you.'

'Oh, here comes Stella with our breakfast! Modesta, please, go back and sit in your chair.'

'Why are you turning pale like that? What harm is there? We're two women.'

'But . . . really, I . . . Good morning, Stella.'

'Good morning to you, *signora*. Oh, Mody, there you are. Good thing. I couldn't stand the thought of you in that armchair. How delightful, my Mody and my *signora* chattering away like two sisters! It's a relief, *signora*, to see you so rosy. I'll bet you're hungry.'

'Very, Stella.'

'There, another good sign! I'll leave you now. Oh, how I always yearned to have a sister! But my dear departed mother, God rest her soul, produced nothing but boys!'

A flush I don't understand defiles Joyce's face. I want her for ever beautiful, with that smooth ivory brow which, tranquil or sad, has never been furrowed by doubt or stained by shame. Now I understood how a perfect face can look ugly, just as an irregular face can seem beautiful. It's the coherence that counts. When Mela's face – an amorphous triangle in which only the eyes could be called beautiful – became flushed, it made her little figure seem more attractive. The blush was somehow the logical extension of the uncertainty and insecurity the young girl bore within her.

'Why are you moving away, Modesta?'

'I'm not moving away. I just wanted to look at the sea. It's all calm and serene, as if the earlier fury had never been. Nature's imperturbability, or absence of remorse. She unleashes terror and death and then . . .'

'Your ability to withdraw to a distant place while you're just steps away from me – like yesterday during the storm – is upsetting. Did I perhaps say something that offended you again?'

'No, Joyce.'

'Or were you disappointed by my choice, like Carlo and Jose?'

'What choice? I don't understand . . .'

'They never approved of the fact that I turned my back on politics and devoted myself body and soul to the study of psychoanalysis. Jose especially was furious. He said that only the revolution can heal people's minds, and that those charming fantasies, more poetic than scientific, were nothing but the usual ingenious ideas the bourgeoisie produces to distract our thoughts from the main issue.

'Wherever he is now, he'll rejoice in knowing that only last year, even Reich published a work in which he asserts that what we psychoanalysts call the death instinct is the product of a capitalist society. Another pupil who betrayed his master . . . How we argued over it! To me, the impossibility of reconciling Marxism and psychoanalysis has always been clear. Yet I wasted years and years attempting to do so, both in my studies, and in my personal life. And today, at almost forty, I'm unable either to engage in politics or heal. I should have just studied.

'Oh, Modesta, teach me to be happy! Because you chose to be happy. When you said, "The facts don't matter much", I sensed that your serenity was a deliberate act of will. How can it have been otherwise? You've suffered losses that were perhaps graver than mine . . . Prando told me that your husband, the Prince, after a few years of marriage fell ill with a terrible malady, and that you were left alone. What was it? I didn't ask Prando – he's so young – but I imagined it was syphilis. He was a womanizer by all accounts . . . progressive paralysis, I'd guess. Why are you looking at me like that? Shouldn't I have said that?'

For the first time in my life I was seized by an intense desire to unburden myself with someone who wasn't me. Joyce watched me, waiting, and for a moment I hesitated: should I go on being with her the way I was with others – maybe she herself wanted me that way – or tell her what I was really like, and lose her? I closed my eyes.

'Why are you closing your eyes, Modesta? But what am I saying? You must be exhausted . . . a night in that armchair . . .'

In the darkness of my tightly shut eyelids I gauged every note of that voice, every slight pause or reprise, and decided that those sonorous depths, full of tortuous ravines, made no allowance for things left unsaid, for childish games or hiding places; at least not for me.

Without further hesitation, I opened my eyes again and poured into hers all the joy and bitterness of what then seemed to me my long life. And like a vase, her eyes took in emotion, tears, hardships and pleasures without cracking.

63

When my voice fell silent, an extreme weakness forced me to stop in the centre of the room and look around for something to lean on. While talking, I had probably wandered between the window and the now empty bed, which still held the imprint of Joyce's body. She too had stood up, and was staring at me from a distance so unfathomable that for a moment it made me think: I've lost her. But after that split second of dismay, the warmth of her cheek on mine pulls me back from that staggering distance.

'I can't embrace you, Modesta.'

Perhaps she can't embrace me because her wrists still hurt? But I can rest my palms on her soft shoulders, her gently arched back, and fold my arms tightly around her, to ensure that I'll never lose her.

'Unfortunately people lose each other, *bambina*! Life separates even those who are most alike. At times we are torn apart, *déchirés*, even from ourselves . . . You will send me away, Modesta.'

'Why do you say that, Joyce? Why?'

'When you know . . .'

'But I trust you now. I proved it to you.'

'Have you heard anything from the comrades?'

This reference to the comrades irritates me. I told her everything about me. Why doesn't she do the same? She does all she can to see that I always learn things from others, from the outside. Why? Why not tell her what comrade Cianca ordered me to do? This time he came to see me not just to collect his usual money:

'*You see, Modesta, in Signora Joyce's dossier there's no mention of weakness or fainting of any kind. She's described as a woman of extraordinary courage and strength. It's impressive how hard she's worked for the cause. We added it up and it seems she's spent quite a bit of time in prison, a little here and a little there. If she attempted suicide, it means she's worn out, she's given up . . . Ten years of struggle, of persecution, are a lot.*

'*We've seen so many like that! You remember Franco, don't you? Who would have expected that after his release from prison, at the first warning not to sleep at home, since it's risky, not only does he sleep at home, but at dawn, prompted by a false alarm, he jumps out the window and breaks every bone in his body . . . Oh!*

'*Mind you: assuming it's her, of course . . . From your description, it does appear to be. It says here that she must have scars on her breasts because she was tortured: that nasty little trick of putting out their cigarettes on you, while interrogating you.*'

'Yes, I have, Joyce, and I also have here with me in this note the name of the ship that sets sail Monday for Buenos Aires. They want you to leave, Joyce.'

'Oh, thank goodness, Modesta! That's very fortunate. I haven't been the same for a year now. You may not believe me, but I wasn't like this before! It's as if something has broken inside me. I can't control my nerves anymore. But all these words are useless. The fact is that I now represent a danger to everyone, and I have to leave.'

'And I, on the contrary, am telling you that your words haven't been useless. It says here that you must leave on Monday, according to them . . . And according to the absurd demands that you make of yourself, I see.'

'What absurd demands?'

'To be a hero at all costs, or die.'

'But—'

'No buts. As I've told you, I don't believe in heroes, dead or alive, and I won't let you leave. Not only because I love you, Joyce, as you think, but because I wouldn't let any comrade leave in your condition. If you help me, you're safe here. You'll regain your strength, you'll see, and in time, if your sense of duty really compels you to return to the struggle, I'll go with you. But only if you prove to me that you've recovered the strength and composure you had before.'

'I'm afraid, Modesta. I'm afraid of myself!'

'Help me, Joyce. Let's defy the verdict to which the comrades, sincere and false, have sentenced you. We'll defy them together, and I'll help you! Let's show them that they aren't infallible. Let's thwart their greedy expectation of another martyr to add to the list that's already too long. Don't listen to the flattery: a Carlo or a Joyce will only be a tiny name on a memorial plaque. Whereas if you live, I know that afterwards it will all be over; afterwards, you can resume the struggle alive and expose those who – I can already hear them – will exploit the names of Carlo, of Gramsci and of so many others. The dead are wrong if no one defends them after their death.'

'You're relentless – and maybe you're right, but I'm no longer sure of myself. Right now, I feel that I could let you help me by helping you, as you say . . . But when I'm alone, at night, or like last evening? I can't do it, Modesta! If, in a moment of weakness here . . . you, Stella, the children . . . you'd be ruined.'

'Then I'll take responsibility for that risk as well. But look me in the eye. If you betray me, not as a comrade but as a human being, by killing yourself, I will bury you in the garden, six feet under, like any common traitor, without bothering to call the gravediggers and comrades.'

'You'd do that, Modesta? By yourself?'

'I'm not by myself. Pietro looks after me, silent and watchful .'

'And my baggage? My presence here?'

'Baggage is easily burned, and as for you: a guest who left – and was never heard from again.'

'And Stella? What would you tell Stella?'

'Stella doesn't ask. At most she'll say what she said about Jose: "He seemed like such a polite young man! Who would have guessed that we'd never hear from him again, not even a postcard."'

'Since I've been in this country, I don't understand anything anymore. If someone had spoken to me in the past the way you're speaking to me now, I wouldn't have believed it and I would have been frightened, whereas your decision for some reason calms me.'

'Because I'm giving you the choice of whether to live or die. If we're denied the right to die, the pressure of living becomes an atrocious prison. You are free here, Joyce, because neither your life nor your death will be a burden to anyone in this house. Let's tear up this ship with its captain, which obliges you to live. Better yet, let's burn it! Come over to the fire. Look how easily they burn: paper, wood, constraints! I've burned many ships and their captains and crews this way!'

'Really, Modesta?'

'At least four! The last one was with Pietro. I hate ships! I love the sea – I've learned to swim – but I've remained attached to land, an inlander at heart. And no one can convince me that a heap of iron as big as a building can float . . . Will you help me, Joyce?'

'So you never wanted me to leave?'

'Never!'

'If you help me, Modesta, I think I can make it.'

'Now that you're calling me by the informal "tu", we'll definitely make it, Jò. May I call you Jò?'

'Of course.'

'You have to let me see your breasts, Jò.'

'I don't understand.'

'You must have scars.'

'I'm ashamed!'

'Who's to say whether it's shame, or simply that you're not Jò?'

'Oh God, Modesta, no, I can't! No one has ever seen me naked!'

'But the interrogators must have seen you if you're Jò.'

'Oh, yes! My shame stung me more than those cigarettes!'

'Why are you crying? What shame is there in a beautiful naked body like yours? Why the shame?'

'I don't know. I've always been this way. Even with my mother. Always.'

'Let me see your breasts. I can't force your arms open; I might hurt your wrists . . . There, take off the bathrobe, the nightgown. It's nothing terrible. Why are you covering your face like a child? I only want to gaze lovingly at the marks that will prove to me that you are my Jò. There they are: scars! Is it these scars you're ashamed of?'

'No, no! I've always been this way, always, even before!'

'Maybe you were afraid of being unappealing?'

'Oh yes, with such pale skin. And then with all these scars . . .'

'They're beautiful, Jò! They're like the veins in marble and they invite the lips . . . For each scar a kiss . . . A kiss in every wound where the pain, as it heals, deepens the pleasure.'

'Oh, Modesta, your lips are driving me wild.'

'I have a scar too. Since I was wounded, it's become the most sensitive spot on my body.'

'Yes, yes. Where? You too . . . but where?'

'No, Jò, not on my breasts . . . It's on my forehead, under my hair. But there's nothing heroic about it.'

'Oh, look at that! A long, thin scar. It looks like it was made by a knife.'

'It's only a gunshot wound from a lover, as they say.'

'Well I'll kiss it just the same, like you did with me. A hundred thousand kisses on this serpent of pain.'

Kissing her, I forget the scars. Forget for a moment, and then rediscover the beloved sharp outlines, smell more keenly the scent of her skin. We find ourselves in each other's arms after a long absence. To make certain, she touches her hand to my forehead. I take her fingers in mine . . . never to lose her! Only sinking my face between her breasts reassures me.

'How pretty you must have been as a child, Modesta!'

'I don't think so.'

'Well, I do. Don't you have a photograph?'

'No. I hate photographs!'

'Why? I would have liked to see you as a little girl.'

'So use your imagination. It's the same thing. I don't need a photograph: I close my eyes and I see you as you were.'

'How was I?'

'Hold me close and I'll show you . . . No, no. Why are you moving away? Don't you want to?'

'Yes, it's just that . . .'

'Are you cold?'

'No.'

'Are you ashamed? Back to being ashamed? All right. I don't want to see you blush. Don't worry, I won't look at you. I'll help you dress, but I won't look at you.'

'You never told me about that lover, Modesta.'

'I had forgotten about him, like so many others. I only told you the parts that matter. The rest is superfluous: incidents that are helpful, perhaps, but not crucial.'

'Incidents! You're extraordinary. A gunshot that could have killed you and you call it an incident?'

'He couldn't have killed me. I knew he couldn't have killed me. Just as I knew, on the contrary – and I've told you about it – that Carlo's death and Beatrice's subsequent madness could have destroyed me.'

'But you must admit that a man capable of giving you that wound – and what a wound! – is intriguing.'

'For that matter, I wasn't outdone myself.'

'You killed him?'

'No! I couldn't kill him either. I just left him a little memento. I've heard he has a scar all around his wrist and that he's missing a finger.'

'And you're laughing?'

'What should I do, weep?'

'But what was his name? Who was he?'

'I have no desire to dredge it all up. I told you everything, Jò, everything. Besides, what does it matter to you? After all, we won't see him again.

'I don't feel like talking. All I want is to listen to your voice. When you talk to me, I feel like I'm listening to a fairy tale. What an adventurous life you've led! You won't speak? Are you jealous of that young man?'

'Aha! He was young. I thought so.'

'Oh, how I wish you were as jealous of me as I was of you.'

'You, jealous?'

'Of course, with all those important people you've known. All those countries you've seen. Who knows how many men and how many women have loved you. And that Jose? I hate him! Did you love him? Tell the truth.'

'Most certainly not! Loving a man who thinks of me as a failed revolutionary would be the last straw. I may be a masochist, but not to that degree.'

'So then it's he who loved you, and still loves you, I know. I can't bear even the idea of someone desiring you.'

'Jose, in love with me? Jose in love with the daughter of an ambassador and a Turkish noblewoman? Jose is looking for something more heroic. If you only knew how he teased me! Affectionately, of course. But there wasn't one meeting when he didn't greet me by saying: "Oh, here's our Jò, who's somehow found the time, between a scented bath and a visit to some atelier in Faubourg Saint-Honoré, to concern herself with us." He joked, but meanwhile he was the only one who recognized the style and cut of a dress or a hat.'

'Don't you see he was in love? Those are the typical words of a man in love, someone who pokes fun in order to hide his true feelings.'

'Why are you moving away, little one? Your head was keeping me warm. Come back here on my lap. Your eyes sometimes gleam in the dark like Mehmet's eyes.'

'Who is Mehmet?'

'My Siamese cat. If it will reassure you: the only creature I've ever truly loved. Come back here, little Mehmet, let me pet you. He too has his weaknesses, however.'

'Who, Mehmet?'

'No, Jose.'

'Oh, tell me!'

'Jose denounces love, sentimentality, the idealization of women, the book *Cuore* . . . God how he hated *Cuore*! Jose has always maintained that the only women who deserve to be considered revolutionaries are the Belle Otéros: actresses or dancers, femmes fatales who exploit men and drive them to suicide.* A fascinating thesis and one with a grain of truth, although that truth is more anarchist than communist. According to him, these women are the only ones who are bringing about the revolution, by subverting the established order.'

'Well, Gramsci too in a way . . .'

'Yes, yes. For that matter, you can read something of the kind in Stendhal's heroines as well. Think about the Duchess Sanseverina, the

Abbess of Castro, Madame de Rênal herself; by falling in love with Julien, she becomes aware of the constraints.

'But the fact is that he – not satisfied with theorizing these ideas, as we intellectuals all do, but rather trying to apply them to life, poor Jose! – he too has found himself up against a different reality than he had imagined. One would be tempted to smile if he hadn't suffered so much since his youth, in his fine villa in Parma. He began rejecting the young women of his world – so girlish, as he used to say – and sought help and inspiration in brothels or on the streets. And inevitably, with a head full of romanticism, he fell in love with a certain Moira – a stage name, I think – whom he'd met in a house of pleasure in Ferrara. It seems he lost about twenty pounds studying, being active in politics, and above all by chasing after this Moira; she must have been about ten years older and had suffered many humiliations and wrongs from early childhood until the time she met Jose. "She overcame everything, always uninhibitedly, continuing her work, unashamed, bringing up her two children faultlessly, etc. . . . . etc. . . . . I've found my woman," he went around yelling in the streets. And as soon as he had a little money he went to take her with him and make her his life's companion, as he said, though as Carlo and I thought, to redeem her.

'Talking with you about it now, Modesta, I realize that his entire generation had a sentimental penchant for prostitutes. It must have to do with the widespread diffusion and enthusiasm for Russian literature after the war.'

'But even now . . .'

'Yes, of course, but with greater discretion. At that time, Slavic translations were handed out to adolescents like candy! Ah yes, Russian romanticism, and not only minor writers like Arcibasev and Kuprin, but Dostoevsky with his pure, saintly prostitutes. And what about Tolstoy? . . .

'How good it is to talk to you, Modesta. Remember *Resurrection*?* I had almost forgotten it. I have a great desire to re-read it. It can't be helped, as my mother used to say: every ten years we must re-read the books that shaped us if we want to understand anything.'

'You were telling me about Jose. What became of Jose and Moira?'

'Yes, Moira . . .'

'Did she let him redeem her?'

'I'll say! Only she insisted on an absolutely legal redemption, nothing revolutionary about it, perfectly *petit bourgeois*, with a church wedding and all the rest.'

'No! Really? And Jose?'

'According to what he went around telling people: "I let her talk and then, saying, *I was wrong about you Moira*, I turned around and walked out of the town hall."'

'And then?'

'And then nothing, I think, until he met Olga from Padua, five years ago, on a sidewalk in Paris. Olga is very beautiful, full-figured and delicate as these girls who are half Italian and half French sometimes are. A long neck, a perfectly shaped little face, fiery eyes and a smile "made in Italy". You know, those *vendeuses* who supplement their shop-girl salaries with some evening assignations, the ones you see in the metro reading poetry, maybe only French poems, but never women's romance novels.'

'Ah! So this time it was a good encounter?'

'Oh, yes! For a year, year and a half, Olga was perfect for the whore-proletarian dream Jose had been pursuing since adolescence. Given both her past and her present, that girl had the necessary credentials: her father a railway man, *ergo* working-class nobility, and not one of those troublesome, unfathomable members of the lumpenproletariat who flock to the cities to snatch up the careless leavings of those who have prospered. She followed Jose with a rapt gaze, listening patiently to our conversations, emptying the ashtrays and affirming with understanding looks and rare smiles of approval that she'd finally found the path to emancipation and the struggle. She blushed proudly when Jose introduced her as "my companion" . . . and I must say we were all stunned at the news of her engagement to François Gidot, soon to become a fashionable dentist, son of the indeed very wealthy tooth-yanker Albert Gidot.'

'How did she meet him?'

'At Jose's . . . You haven't met François? You haven't missed anything, although for years and years, Jose considered him one of his best friends in the limbo of proud Parisian democrats who, though they weren't comrades, at least absorbed the Revolution and the unassailable *clarté* that allows them to dissect any ethical, aesthetic, and, in particular, oenological issue with confidence and precision.'

'That's unbelievable! And Jose?'

'Oh, nothing. He awoke to the situation with similar Olympian revolutionary clarity: *clarté* versus *clarté*. And though he didn't go to the wedding, he sent the young Mrs Gidot a huge bouquet of flowers. Now, between one meeting and another, one article and the next, he must surely have resumed dreaming about the face of some other girl, tried by society's injustice.

'It can't be helped with us old neurotics. Just as I can't manage to quit sucking the poisonous milk of this cigarette – the hypothetical breast of an even more hypothetical maternal love that I never had – so will he continue to act out his childhood dream. Most likely, it only allows him to contend with frivolous, marginal loves, as it were, which he's now come to anticipate, and which are therefore controllable. There's nothing to be done about these personality neuroses; it's best not to stir things up. It's too great a risk to attempt to treat them. You might as well live with those small breakdowns, as long as the engine keeps running for better or for worse . . .

'What's wrong, little Mehmet, why are you bristling all over and staring at me with those big, gleaming eyes? Are you shocked, like Jose, by my theorizing? Or are you troubled by the thought that a hero like him can have certain weaknesses?'

'I've told you over and over again that I don't believe in heroes. And what you're telling me about Jose, far from shocking me, sounds like something I've always thought in some corner of my mind. It's as if you've opened a window on a landscape that I once knew and then forgot. Except that you use words and phrases that are unfamiliar to me . . . I'm so ignorant, Jò!'

'You, ignorant, Mehmet? Don't say that! I'm the one who's exploiting my specialization and becoming boring. Besides, I'm talking about new theories. Freud discovered that the mind isn't a fixed star, eternal and immutable, within us, but a whirling light that follows the pulsations of the veins and nerves, a light that dims and brightens, and that, like the heart, the eyes or the liver, is subject to curable or mortal illnesses. His discovery is a dreadful blow to man's past security . That's why intellectuals, politicians and doctors themselves oppose him with all the means at their disposal, slandering him, refuting him and – I don't even dare think about it – they might even go so far as torturing him, as they did Galileo. For now, they're content with burning his books. And this bonfire of vital words and concepts can only be a prologue to actual torture in the future. Freud said that Europe is now nothing but an immense prison, and he only hopes that Austria's cell will remain out of it. But that's not what we were talking about. God, I'm insufferable! When I get started on a subject, I can't stop.'

'But I'm happy! Oh, Joyce, tell me who this Freud is. Help me get to know him, teach me his theories, tell me about him.'

'We'll look for his books. You read French, and I see that you have Marx and Lenin in the library here. Up north, they arrest anyone who owns these books.'

'Here, not yet, at least not us wealthy people.'

'Of course! You say it with no shame, Modesta.'

'And you're blushing. Why?'

'So all you have to do is look for them in Catania, or have them sent from Paris.'

'Oh, I'll find them! You'll make me a list, won't you? And if I don't understand something as I read them, you'll explain it to me, won't you?'

'Of course, of course, *bambina* . . .'

64

When the 'voice' pronounces the word *bambina*, Modesta becomes a little girl and is compelled to run into Joyce's arms. Or when, side by side, they read those rare books made more precious by long, difficult searches and by the danger posed by simply owning them. If Modesta doesn't grasp a term, Joyce sorts out every obstacle with her melodious voice, revealing an unimagined world of renewed words, retold myths, emotions, events and passions radically uprooted from the old culture, and slid under the clear scientific glass of Freudian analysis . . . Memory, as key to a new vision, now becomes the prime means of enabling a backward journey into the subterranean woods of seemingly forgotten memories. Brought to light, rearranged and cleansed of mould and incrustations, they reveal mosaics of glittering gems for the understanding of one's own life and that of others.

Modesta, disillusioned by the old, idealistic order and by the younger but already decrepit positivism, can't help sensing the innovation and authenticity that Joyce has brought to the island, and tries to make it her own in order to survive in a world where the old God is being replaced by false, barbarian idols in the streets, piazzas and parks. Going out or travelling now means merely swallowing the venom of empty phrases, the poison of a false order and pompous heroism; whereas there, motionless in front of Joyce, beside the new gleam of intelligence that emanates from her face, the hours, months

and years glide along on the oiled tracks of a journey even more exciting than a physical one.

On this journey, Modesta was always alert in watching for the
least little hint of a smile or of sorrow on the beloved face. Her
every thought, act and wish was taken up with scrutinizing and
anticipating the desires of that face of love, driving away the latent
grief that lay in wait, and invariably came to trouble it. No, Carmine, it's not enough to take one's own pleasure and then ride off
freely through the lands and estates of the mind. That word, 'love',
had an inevitability as certain and unalterable as birth and death,
and you had to accept it, aware of not knowing why, when or how
it came to be, or toward which bleak shores or green fields it might
lead you.

Where was Joyce's faint smile leading, so promising that it filled
the days and months with an elation I'd never felt before? What was
the alluring, confident note of that *bambina* driving me to? At times,
it was so controlling that it inspired a profound terror, a sense of
being hopelessly lost with no way out. What was she thinking when
she broke free of my embrace without a word? What about those
sudden recurrences of modesty that made her cry, no longer aware
of Modesta's presence? Or when, moving close again, the great
moonlike arc of her brow compelled her to remember: to associate
images, words, events and faces in order to make sense of the fanci-
ful explosions of a dream seemingly generated by the caprice of an
excited imagination?

★

In sand that was still warm at sunset, we were digging a hole down to
where our fingers found sea water:

'Gold! Gold! . . . Bambù was the first to touch it!'

'Yes, but Mela was the one who dug the deepest, Joyce! Come and
see the mine. Put your own hands in the clear water and you'll be rich
for ever!'

Joyce no longer flushes at that word but she doesn't want to touch
the sea's gold.

'Don't you want to be rich for ever? There now, come on! Your hands have to be covered by water up to the wrists . . . That's it: Mela and I want you to have your share of this treasure too, right Zia?

'Now let's go up and prepare for this evening's big performance. The great pianist Mela Bruno . . . What an ugly name "Bruno" is, Mela! No offence. We have to find you a stage name. Can a pianist like you, by God, be called Bruno? Bruno, Bianchi, Smith! We have to find a name for Mela . . . don't any of you care? All right, I'll come up with one. Bambù has to see to everything! And please: everyone must be in formal attire this evening. I want it to be like at the conservatory. What a success it was, right Zia? Jacopo will take care of the lights. We have to reproduce everything exactly the way it was for Joyce, since she wasn't there.'

Europe is an enormous prison, and Jò can come and go in the villa, in the surrounding area, but only with great caution. To have gone to the conservatory in Palermo would have been folly. Is that why her face is growing sadder and paler? Or is it because even in summer she never goes out to the garden bareheaded? The wide-brimmed felt winter hats are replaced by shiny gossamer affairs of beige straw. Her face in shadow recedes from us: an inscrutable blur in the midst of faces and shoulders gilded by the August light. After running along the beach chased by Jacopo and 'Ntoni, a yearning for that shadow makes Modesta turn back to gaze closely into those eyes that seem about to take flight.

'Where are you fleeing to, Jò, where?'

'I haven't moved an inch, *bambina*.'

'They couldn't catch me, did you see? Look at 'Ntoni, he's panting! And Jacopo! After ten yards he quit. And to think I'm thirty-six years old, Jò! I like to challenge them. I'm quite proud of my legs and my wind.'

'And you're right. I was watching you as you ran; you look like a young girl.'

'Oh, you were watching me? So you weren't running away? Tell me again that you were watching me.'

'Admiringly besides, if you want to know.'

'Thirty-six years old! It seems like yesterday that I came back from

Catania with all those books by Freud, remember? I was so afraid I wouldn't find you here when I returned.'

'But you did.'

'Yes, yes, but I'm always afraid.'

'That's because of your childhood, not because of me.'

'Maybe, but I'm not so sure, Jò. I'm not so sure about you psycho-analysts and your theories anymore. Don't get angry, but so many things don't make sense, and not only in my case. Did you hear Bambù a few moments ago? She was talking like Nonna Gaia. Her voice is striking; it's taking on the same timbre as that grand old woman's. And she never knew her.'

'You must have spoken about her.'

'Never! Since I decided to break with tradition, that is. Since I left Carmelo, never! Though you may be right as far as Beatrice is concerned: she was the victim of her childhood or, as you psychoanalysts say, of her unavoidable destiny . . . What a great title that would be for a novel!'*

'Lovely, but you don't work, Modesta! So many splendid ideas, but you don't work.'

'I don't work? But I love you, I race with Jacopo . . . I work, and how! I work hard, but joyfully. You're laughing? Finally! Don't scold me, Jò. I'm so happy! Now it's time to get dressed. I don't want to get a scolding from Bambù as well. She's always so elegant. I wonder what name she'll come up with for Mela . . . That girl is a genius.'

★

Bambolina is waiting by the door. Her slender torso, stiffened by indignation, is drawn like a bow about to release its arrow, but Prando tilts his head of dense curls like those of a bronze statue and murmurs, 'I will never forgive myself for being late like this, Ida, never!'

'Go on, Prando, don't make matters worse.'

'My motorcycle broke down.'

'You're all greasy and muddy like . . .'

'Bambù, please . . .'

'But you're the most handsome of all, and I forgive you.'

'Thank you, little cousin. But I will never forgive myself!'

'Come on, take your place! Can't you see they're all seated? And poor Jacopo perched up there should by rights turn the spotlight on us.'

But Jacopo, aware of the importance of his role as lighting technician – rather than his walk-on appearance as a silent sentinel in the performance of *Hamlet* that was so successful just a few months ago – is serious, and doesn't take his eyes off 'Ntoni's hand, which is ready to raise the curtain. Only he knows how to seize just the right moment during the audience's silence to open the curtains. By now 'Ntoni knows everything about the theatre:

'No, I missed the right moment, Bambolina!'

'But they're laughing like crazy!'

'It was too much! Maestro Musco is right: they laughed too much. I tired them out so afterwards they didn't applaud like the other time.'

'*Uffa*, 'Ntoni! Since you've been spending time with that clown, you've become pedantic and annoying.'

'Angelo Musco is not a clown! Ask Modesta and Joyce; they're not ignorant and provincial like you. Angelo Musco is a great artist! And if you dare say it again, I'm leaving. I'd like to see what a fine show you dabblers will produce then! Amateurs!'

They must have made up sooner than usual. Generally, after an argument Bambù and 'Ntoni didn't speak to one another for two or three days. Was it the upcoming performance that reconciled them in just a few hours? 'Ntoni, dressed as Giufà, had asked Bambolina what she thought, and she had kissed him on the forehead before the first spectator entered the room. The first to arrive, shaved and wearing his formal Sunday best, was Pietro. Perhaps worried about his size, he sat down as soon as he came in in the last row next to his little daughter.

How would that child manage to see the stage, with the wall of heads belonging to all the local young people in front of her? Each year those friendships grew, and there wasn't an empty seat in the little theatre, despite the absence of so many friends . . . of Paolo, Andrea and Franco, called into the army to fight for the Empire. Only the difference of a few years had kept Prando from following them, but nothing could console him over Franco's death, not even the post-humously awarded gold medal the boy's mother had shown him:

'A hero! You had a hero as a friend, Eriprando, and you should be proud of it.'

'You're a fool as well as a woman, Donna Emanuela di Valdura, so don't be offended if a Brandiforti snubs you. And if you really must be offended, send me that other idiot, your son, to avenge the insult.'

The priest had come to Modesta to report and protest, but for the moment only knives could resolve the matter. In front of her, in the first row, Prando's marble profile seemed more flawless and dazzling for the faint cut that scored his cheek from his eye socket to his chin. The wound under Modesta's hair throbbed at the contained violence of that profile. Prando was growing up, a stranger, yet a precious part of her life. Bambù, too, was growing up, and even sweet Jacopo had grown too big to hold in her arms . . .

The lights went out. How would Pietro's little daughter manage to see now that the curtain was rising?

'Why do you keep turning around, Modesta?'

'I'm watching Pietro's daughter, Joyce; she's way back there. Look, look at her, he's got her sitting piggyback on his shoulders. That way she can see even better than in the first row . . . How good Pietro is with his daughter!'

'I find him scary.'

'I don't know what I'd give to have him as a father.'

'Because you never had a father.'

'But I did have one, and I want to have one again. Better yet, you know what? Starting today, Pietro is my father, and that tiny creature – she looks like a doll on his shoulders – is my sister!'

'Hush now, *bambina*. See how marvellous Mela looks in that tunic? Who would have thought so?'

'And wait till you hear her, just wait!'

As Modesta had read in Mela's eyes at one time, the amorphous triangle of her face, under the spotlight, was moulded into an absorbed, intense presence. A music-playing angel? An image floating up from an idea? Joyce would have said: 'An oneiric angel, evoking spaces and emotions welling up from deep within.' Modesta is not surprised when applause bursts out over the absolute silence of the hands, now motionless on the keyboard and assured as a lava flow. She wasn't surprised then, or at the Conservatory in Palermo. Because at the time they met, the nerves and veins of her body were able to read the future, whereas now Modesta is lost. Staring at Prando's wound, Jacopo's smile, Bambù's flush of pride at the success of her protégée, no image, no flash of insight reveals itself, and her senses are numbed by the sadness of no longer being able to hold them in her arms. They will go away; stopping them would mean making them hate her. For some time, 'Ntoni has hated Stella and avoids her.

'Forgive me, Modesta, I can talk freely with you . . . It's not that I can't stand her, it's just that she oppresses me with her *"Picciriddu miu . . . picciriddu miu!"* Just yesterday, I introduced her to a boy my age, not a man, mind you – a boy like me. And she, by God! asks him to look after me: "Be careful that 'Ntoni doesn't catch a chill. His throat is delicate!" Insufferable! As soon as I get the chance, I'm leaving. I don't know where, but I'm going.'

The opportunity had come: Angelo Musco's troupe. 'Ntoni was leaving in September, signed up to go on tour. Better an acting company than a regiment. Ciro, Bambù's unhappy sweetheart, had voluntarily enlisted for the war in Spain just to get away from another foolish mother. It was Prando who called almost all women *scimunite*, halfwits, including Stella: *'You're kind and dear, Stella, but* scimunita, *a fool like all women your age! Mama says it's a question of upbringing, but I have my doubts.'*

'What's wrong, *bambina*, why aren't you applauding?'

'Please, Joyce, don't call me *bambina*, at least not in public.'

'But no one can hear us. Why aren't you applauding? Don't tell me she was better in Palermo.'

'No, no, it's just . . .'

'Why on earth do you keep turning around to look at Pietro? That's all you did during the performance. It's discourteous toward Mela.'

'The play is starting now, Jò. Wait till you see how funny 'Ntoni is! Now he'll finally tell us about Giufà. I can imagine how Pietro's little girl will laugh . . . Look, look how she's staring at the closed curtain. Pietro probably told her that Giufà was about to appear.'

Pietro immediately noticed my gaze through the crowd. After

endless moments of perspiring hesitation, he decides to stand up, careful with his enormous body not to step on all the delicate dresses rustling at his feet.

'Look, Jò! Poor Pietro, he looks like an elephant trying to move among the flowerbeds in a garden.'

'And you're laughing at him! He'll be offended. How strange you people are. I really don't understand you.'

'Pietro? Offended? What are you talking about?'

'The understanding between you two is scary.'

'Is *Voscenza* perhaps in need of my services, Mody?'

'I see you managed not to knock off any heads, Pietro!'

'And God knows how I did it! Outside, this big body is useful for keeping away traitors and snakes, but here among these figurines it's a hindrance! How can I be of service?'

'You have to go back and bring me something precious.'

'Does *Voscenza* want her fan? Something to drink?'

'No! What's the most precious thing you have?'

'Crispina is the most precious thing Pietro has! Ah, you want to hold her? Oh, of course, Mody, she'll be thrilled. I'll be right back.'

Somewhat embarrassed, Pietro prepares to retrace his arduous journey. This time he stumbles . . . and nearly falls!

'Here she is, Mody, the youngest of this fine assembly.'

'And who is the prettiest one here, Crispina? Hmm? Who is she?'

'Me pretty and you pretty and Mama pretty.'

'And what about your papa?'

'Strong as an ox.'

'He's strong because he carries you piggyback?'

'No! I'm little, it's that my papa . . . my papa . . . um, I forget . . . When is Giufà coming?'

'Soon. Is Giufà strong like your papa?'

'No, he's silly!'

'Why silly?'

'He's silly. The birds aren't scared of Giufà. And he learns from the lamb, the fox and the sparrow.'

'So Mody, it's true you're really fond of Crispina and will keep your promise?'

'Did you have any doubt, Pietro?'

'It's not that I doubted you, Mody, it's that nature is unpredictable! And you might not have taken a liking to this *picciridda* through no fault of your own. I was worried! In a year she must go to school. Believe me, Mody, if she were a boy I wouldn't be bothering you: I'd take him to the fields with me. But a *femminuccia*, it's better for a girl to prepare herself by learning to read and write, as you know. Oh, they're starting! I'll take her from you, since it's so hot.'

'No, no, leave her with me Pietro. I'll give her back after the show, don't worry. Starting tomorrow, Crispina will come here every morning, Jacopo will see to this young lady. I've already spoken to him about her . . . Crispina, look . . . look how Jacopo is staring at you!'

'Is he Giufà?'

'No, Giufà is behind the curtain. Hush now, hush. I hear him crying. Do you hear him moaning and groaning?'

'Giufà is always crying!'

'No, now he's crying, but later you'll see . . . Watch, watch how he pulls his hair and bangs into the trees and walls.'

'There are no trees!'

'Of course, it's make-believe! See those coat racks? Those are the trees, and those sheets are the walls. Poor Giufà! Now hush, he'll start talking in a minute.'

65

GIUFÀ-'NTONI Oh! Such a misfortune, a misfortune! As if the first one wasn't bad enough, now this second misfortune. And then, when it rains it pours.

TREE-BAMBÙ What misfortune are you talking about, Giufà? You seem hale and hearty, very elegant in that cow-dung-coloured outfit with yellow sparrow's vomit touches on your hat.

GIUFÀ The hat was the greenest of greens: spotless. It's just that a cow shat on me. Never mind a sparrow or canary . . . a cow!

TREE How could a cow shit on your head, Giufà? Since the world began, cows stay flat on the ground.

GIUFÀ It's because I'm distressed! I'm distressed! And earlier I was even more distressed and while I was distressed, I fell asleep near the cowshed, and with this green hat on my head the cow mistook me for a meadow.

TREE And is this the misfortune that's troubling you, Giufà?

GIUFÀ If only that were all! A good many other painful events are troubling Giufà's soul. And they are so troubling that I now realize to my great horror that I've gone blind.

TREE You're not blind, Giufà. It's just that night has fallen.

GIUFÀ You're making fun of me, stranger! I'm blind, I tell you! And the proof is that you're talking to me but I can't see you. There! Giufà's logic is sharp! And logic tells me that if you can see me the sun must be up.

TREE It's night Giufà, believe me.

GIUFÀ You don't say? It's night, is it? And how could Giufà, distressed, have slept for ten hours?

TREE Young man of little faith and little intelligence. You see me and don't recognize me. I'm Tree, and I have the power to console, like all forms of greenery and stone. I belong to the race of those who stand and observe, not the human race, which fumes and frets, farts and knows no peace.

GIUFÀ Oh, Tree, forgive me! But don't add misfortune to misfortune. Call me a young man of little intelligence if you like, but don't accuse me of being a man of little faith, because Giufà has every faith and confidence in you trees, and rocks, and springs. Leave me to my despair. I just want to be upset even if I'm not blind. I believe you that it's night and not day, but I want to wallow hopelessly in this distress.

TREE There you go, falling into human error. The herb alfalfa made you fall asleep to console your sorrow.

GIUFÀ Ah, amazing miracle! I appreciate it, but nothing can console Giufà.

TREE Is it because of that bastard, your father, that the herb lacked the power to bring you peace?

GIUFÀ Worse, worse!

TREE The gendarmes then? Are the gendarmes looking for you?

GIUFÀ Worse, even worse!

TREE I see that your situation is serious. So you must immediately resort to someone who has greater power than ours.

GIUFÀ Who would that be?

TREE Here she comes now, breaching the wall of night with her scythe.

GIUFÀ Oh, Tree! You're not calling on *La Certa* to console me, are you? Let's not go too far! Giufà is distressed, but he has no love for *La Certa*.

TREE What are you saying! Immortal Tree has nothing to do with that harpy. Tree calls upon the moon or the stars or the sun. Look, here comes the moon! She's newly born, but she has the wisdom of millennia. Talk to her.

MOON-MELA Giufà, Giufà, you can't constantly pester me on my nightly journey. I have to go round and round to check on things! I'll give you one minute before I go to look for the comet and the Dolphin.

GIUFÀ Oh, Moon! What a soft voice you have!

MOON I was just born, and I have a lot to do.

GIUFÀ Forgive me, Moon, but Giufà suffered a great offence.

MOON Like that time with the figs and the Madonna?

GIUFÀ Worse!

MOON One of these nights I'll have to speak to your mother.

GIUFÀ Oh, yes, speak to her on my behalf. Because she orders me around, she tells Giufà word for word what he has to do, but when Giufà conscientiously performs the task word for word, she's not satisfied and she gets furious.

MOON She's too precise. I must muddle her thoughts a little. But tell me, what happened?

GIUFÀ At dawn this morning, she gets all dressed up and she tells me word for word: 'Tidy up the house, water the garden, then put on nice clean clothes – don't make me look bad – and come to church. Today is Santa Rosalia's feast day and all the relatives will be at Mass. But remember to pull the door behind you before you go out, Giufà; there are rogues and thieves running around! Don't forget! Pull the door behind you.'

MOON So?

GIUFÀ I struggled for three hours to unhinge the door, and then carried it, heavy as it was, on my back. And she, when she sees me in the piazza, flies into a rage, yelling at me and raving to the heavens! Of course I was three hours late and the Mass was over. But the door weighed a ton, I swear to God! Why did she have to yell at me for being late? Women! Who can understand them? Moon, I'm inconsolable!

MOON Oh, Giufà! Poor Giufà!

GIUFÀ To disown her son for being late! She threatened to crack my head open.

MOON And what did you do?

GIUFÀ Desolate, I hurled that door she wanted so much into the piazza! Besides being distressed, I was afraid of her punching and scratching. Does it seem fair to you?

MOON When I get to be a strong, full moon, I'll go visit her in her sleep and make her rant a little. Come now, I want to console you. Hop on my back and forget these things. For tonight, I'll take you around with me among the stars.

GIUFÀ Oh, how sweet it is to be riding on you, Moon! Already I feel consoled!

MOON We're taking off from the earth! Say goodbye to your friend Tree.

GIUFÀ Oh, Moon, how we're rising! We must be up a few feet or so already! Hey, Moon, I won't fall, will I?

MOON You fall when you're standing on the ground, thinking too much, not riding on me with my eyes full of clouds and comets.

GIUFÀ Oh, the comet! Farewell, friendly Tree, dear forest! What are those lights splashing so brightly down there in the sea?

MOON It's the dolphins leaping in my wake, besotted with joy under my silvery lamp . . .

*

Her attention totally focused on Crispina's tiny body as she stretches toward Giufà's flight, Modesta doesn't notice the silence beside her until Crispina falls back into her lap. She sighs.

'Giufà is gone! He disappeared behind there. Why?'

How had she missed hearing Joyce get up? The child is heavy, and the heat of her little body is making Modesta sweat.

'Yes, yes, Pietro, take her.'

'I'm not going with Giufà, Papa, I'm staying with you!'

'Of course you're staying with me. Such a wonderful show! I've never been to a theatre, but . . .'

'Let me get through, Pietro.'

'Oh, *Voscenza*, forgive me! Are you upset because of the *signora*? She left quite a while ago. Maybe because of the heat, Mody. Plus, Giufà is for *picciriddi*.'

Modesta can't join in the applause that ebbs and flows again like a warm wave. Pushing through the choppy sea that hampers her movements, she reaches Joyce's room in a few seconds. Palms on the door, she hesitates. What if she isn't there, either?

'Joyce, can I come in?'

She's there, smoking. Maybe her disappearing like that doesn't mean anything. Maybe Joyce had simply wanted to smoke, since the kids had hung large signs on the walls, so that everything would be 'just like in a real theatre': 'Smoking is strictly prohibited'.

'Come in, little one, the door is open.'

She sits in the armchair facing the window, her head tilted to the left, as always when she's smoking. On the low table are four or five cigarettes, barely started and then crushed out. Her long black hair is outlined, motionless, on the window pane which is lit by the sunset. She smokes and looks outside while Modesta still trembles about that empty seat beside her.

'What is it, little one? Sit down! Standing up like that, you're blocking my view of the sky: a magnificent sunset.'

'Why did you disappear like that? I told you I can't bear these disappearances of yours. Are you upset with me? Why don't you shout, get angry instead of disappearing like that? You do it on purpose! You know it distresses me and you do it on purpose. Yet I've explained to you that ever since that day we found you . . .'

'Oh, come on, Modesta, it's been years now. Not only has it never happened again, but—'

'But I can't bear it when you do that!'

'I can't help it; please believe me. It's in my nature. It's stronger than me.'

'Even though you know it terrifies me, it—'

'In fact, you have no way of knowing it, but I control myself with you and I try, I assure you, I try not to give in to that impulse. But believe me, what you call my "disappearances" are not covering up anything serious. At most, they're minor little foibles owing to my temperament or perhaps to my odious upbringing.'

'But can't you do it for me? I've changed so many things in my life for you.'

'It doesn't seem like it.'

'There, you see? It is something serious and not just minor idiosyncrasies, as you say. What have I done? Did I offend you? Why won't you speak? I'd rather hear you shout or have you slap me than endure

427

these silent battles, these hypocritical words! I've told you everything, everything about me. You know me as no one else does.'

'This is the first time you've called me a hypocrite, Modesta. It's a harsh word.'

'Oh! Forgive me, Jò. I wasn't thinking that. I swear to you that's not what I thought. I'm just so upset! Hold me, Jò. Can you feel how I'm shaking?'

'I know that's not what you thought, little one, but the word hurts just the same.'

'Oh, forgive me. I'll punish myself for that word and I'll kiss you until the pain goes away. Oh, Jò, hold me tight! Squeeze me, hurt me, but don't disappear!'

'You're the one who's hurting me, little one. You're biting me.'

'Yes, yes, I'll bite you . . . your neck, your lips . . . I'm hurting you, aren't I? There . . . on the neck, that way you'll have to cover yourself up so it won't show. Does it hurt? Tell me, does it hurt?'

'Oh, Modesta, yes, but a sweet pleasure too . . . Bite me, bite me!'

'I'll eat you all up, Jò: all of you inside me, even your breasts! And you'll never be able to disappear, locked inside me. Never!'

*

Wrapped up in their embrace, Jò and Modesta don't notice the dark wing lowering over the horizon.

'It's already night, Modesta.'

'And Giufà flies through the night, riding on the moon.'

'We've ended up on the carpet. How quickly day turns into night here!'

'It's only when I'm in your arms that I'm not afraid of losing you, Jò. Why?'

'I can't get used to this sudden darkness. I watch the sun sink, yet night always takes me by surprise, as if the darkness were lurking there, waiting for the right moment to leap out. In Turkey it's not like that, at least not in Istanbul.'

'We're much further south, Jò . . . Down toward the scorching heart of Africa. In Scicli, amid the mulberry vines, you can smell the tang of Africa at night: dry, sharp as a blade, a Durendal that cuts through the laurel.'

'Did you lock the door, Modesta?'

'Yes, but you know no one would dare enter. I'm the mistress here.'

'But they could spy on us.'

'No one spies on the master here on the island.'

'You people are incredible! And the kids? They might be looking for us.'

'No, no! With all the fun they're having, they're sure to have forgotten all about us.'

'How can you say that?'

'Because it's a fact.'

'They're ingrates.'

'What should they be grateful to us for?'

'You feed them. You protect them.'

'That's the rub, Pietro would say. My ability to feed them puts me in the role of master, the *pa-dro-ne*, Jò! And why should they be grateful to a master? You accuse me of being paternalistic with Pietro, then you'd have me be the same with the children. To consider oneself indispensable to young, defenceless human beings, just because you feed them, is the most atrocious paternalism.'

'Still, I hear someone coming up to look for us. It must be Bambù, or Prando, who's noticed your absence.'

'No, they'd only notice it if I left them without food and games.'

'What you're saying is appalling.'

'It's human nature. A baby is forced to love you because you feed him. Carlo wanted to organize a youngsters' union against abominable grandmothers. I would form a children's union against the formidable duo of father and mother, who demand love in exchange for a crust of bread or a plaything – too high a price for any normal individual to pay.'

'Now you're going too far, Modesta. They're knocking. It's Bambù, you'll see.'

'No, it was Pietro's stride.'

'At your service.'

'*Voscenza* will excuse me, Princess . . .'

'Go into the bathroom, Jò. I'm afraid your dress is all rumpled.'

'It was you, Modesta.'

'Go and change.'

'Just a moment, Pietro. I'll put on a robe and open up for you.'

'What is it? Is *Voscenza* not feeling well, Princess?'

'No, Pietro, just a bad headache, but I slept a little and it went away.'

'I know what you mean. What chaos with these *carusi*! It's nice to see them so cheerful, but it's exhausting . . . Stella sent me to tell you that our Bambolina has decided to have dinner on the beach. Oh, just like her mother, she's always up to something! So they've all gone to the bay of the Prophet to set things up. She's also decided to stay up till dawn to see if the Prophet's hair will bleed when the sun rises. It's the time for this mirage! Stella wanted to know if *Voscenza* agrees.'

'But of course. They're on vacation and it's their party. Stella knows they're free to do what they want.'

'Then I'll go and reassure her. She was uneasy.'

'Go.'

'We'll see you at the bay, right, Mody? You're not still feeling poorly, are you?'

'I'm just fine, Pietro. I'll be there soon.'

66

In place of the lightweight voile dress, a long white silk tunic covered Joyce's arms and shoulders. Under that white throbbed the marks of my bites. Standing on tiptoe, Modesta kisses Joyce . . . her swollen lips, their corners ending in two small weeping commas, are scorching.

'You have two little commas on either side of your lips, Jò. Or are they two parentheses?'

'They're two wrinkles, Modesta.'

'They're not! They're two parentheses that add meaning to the sentence of your face.'

'What meaning? Tell me.'

'I don't know. I'm trying to understand, but I can't seem to.'

'It's just time's warning that I'll soon be old.'

'That's not true. You won't ever be old.'

'No one can stop time.'

'Why don't you have any children, Jò? Or do you have them, and like nearly everything else about you, you're keeping it a secret?'

'What do children have to do with it?'

'Because, as Shakespeare says, if you can't stop time, you can prolong it in your children.* For better or for worse, they'll attest to you in the world.'

'I don't care about the world!'

'Or maybe like the Dark Lady of the sonnets, or the fair youth of her dreams, you're heartless and miserly? Are you miserly, Jò? I'm beginning to think so.'

'Given the way you are, I may seem miserly to you.'

'And how am I?'

'My father, a gentleman of austere Todi, would have said extravagant.'

'And yet everyone accuses me of being miserly! Poor Prando had to beg for that motorcycle . . . How handsome he is! I can't get over it. But I don't like the way he looks like a statue! Does he seem intelligent to you? He's so withdrawn that sometimes I think he's stupid.'

'He's not stupid. A young man so passionate and cogent can't be stupid.'

'You're right. It's the mother in me that won't allow me to recognize his intelligence simply because it's different from mine. But by God! mother or not, how can you understand an intelligence, or passion as you say – and you're right, passion is intelligence – for engines and speed?'

'But he studies them. He designs vehicles: improbable vehicles, yet . . .'

'But all he reads are comic books. Comics, movies and driving fast! I'm wrong, aren't I? It does me so much good having you around, Jò!'

'On the contrary, I'm afraid it's bad for you.'

'How can you say that? These past years, with your help, my head has opened up, as Mimmo would have said. Or as 'Ntoni says: "The curtains of my brain parted." Why did he say that? Oh yes, when he went to Palermo to see Zacconi in *Ghosts*. Since that day he's read nothing but Ibsen.'

'How whimsical 'Ntoni is! And such brilliance! Did you see the feeling he put into playing Giufà? Too bad Stella doesn't understand him. She's been crying ever since 'Ntoni decided to become a comic actor. She thinks of actors as depraved degenerates. You, too, underestimate Prando's intelligence, because he applies it to engines rather than books.'

'You're right, Jò. Lovely, lovely Jò! But why are we standing here talking about 'Ntoni? I have an urge to see him. Who knows whom he's impersonating at this moment. Let's go!'

★

'Oh! Look, look how funny he is!'

'He's impersonating Mussolini!'

'Yes, haven't you ever seen him do it? The speech about the Empire. It's that speech that got him the script with Angelo Musco.'

'But isn't Angelo Musco a Fascist?'

'No, but he consents to having the royal march and the Fascist anthem played before the performance: "O Sun that rises from shit", as he says.* And as he also says: "one restrains oneself" hearing it . . . in these times, it's the only way to save your hide.'

'A despicable attitude.'

'It may be despicable, but it's the same stance taken by Petrolini, by Pirandello, by Croce, by . . . Oh, Jò, you're right, but let me listen to 'Ntoni. Besides, despicable or not, given the times, I prefer to be lost in a crowded auditorium and to go on listening to Musco and Pirandello, than to know that they lie mute under a fine alabaster tomb. What are you doing? Running away again?'

'I'm not running away, Modesta, it's just that . . .'

'That what?'

'I can't stand it! All this peace, this joy, this making jokes about Mussolini, while Fascism triumphs everywhere.'

'And what would you prefer? To see the house in mourning and these young people miserable, or better yet, crying with us because we – I say we: you, me, Jose, Carlo – weren't able to bring about the revolution?'

'It's terrible. Even Russia is making eyes at Mussolini. Never mind Chamberlain, but Stalin . . .'

'So? You're just discovering it tonight?'

'No, no! But joking around, having a good time . . .'

'Not simply joking, Jò, ridiculing! It's a way of toppling a myth for those young people, an exorcism so they won't soak it up and so they can be prepared to trample it someday. A day that we two, I fear, will never see. Besides, it's an insult to them, Jò! You know very well that none of them, not even Bambù, is satisfied with just mocking him, but . . . Joyce, wait! What's wrong, what's come over you?'

'Leave me alone, Modesta! Let me go. I don't feel well.'

'Oh, no, that's not it!'

'You're hurting my wrist!'

'I'll break this wrist of yours if you don't stop running away and not speaking.'

'Let go of me. They can see us.'

'So what? You've covered yourself up like a mummy just because of a few kisses.'

'Modesta!'

'Oh, enough! Look out, I feel like untying that bow, which only a shamefaced cat would slink around in, forcing you to display the marks of my kisses.'

'Do you see I'm right?'

'See what? Right about . . . what? Say something! How can I tell what you're thinking?'

'I think your wish to display me to everyone is a desire to legitimize a relationship that can never be legitimized.'

'But that can be shared with others without this shame that's eating you up. What is it, shame or fear? Take off that foulard! Let everyone know, or at least be forced to openly acknowledge what they know.'

'But your children!'

'My children! My children are grown, and it would be a way to make them face reality and see if they can handle it, or else lose them.'

'You're insane!'

'I'm not insane, Jò, and I would never do this if you didn't feel ashamed even when we're alone. If you didn't always feel ashamed, even of yourself. At first I didn't understand the reason for those tears after our kisses and embraces. Those tears, your not looking at me, your running away, which kept me teetering anxiously for years. But now I know: you're the one who feels that our relationship is sinful, and you turn from me as soon as you're satisfied, as if my face were the sign of your guilt. You're the one who – and worse yet, not unconsciously – would like to legitimize our relationship. You let it slip out one night, you let those words *if I were a man!* slip out.'

'Enough, stop!'

'*If I were a man!* Go ahead, go! Go cry in your room. It makes me laugh to think if you were a man, or if Beatrice had been a man! I love you because you're a woman, and as a woman. So why are you still standing there? I let go of your wrist, didn't I? Go! I want to listen to 'Ntoni, or at least eat dinner, by God!'

'But for me it's the first time, Modesta, the first . . .'

'The first time what? I don't understand.'

'The first time I've . . . had an intimate relationship with a woman.'

A furious round of applause erupts from down at the bay. Il Duce has concluded his victory speech, and with his arm raised in the Fascist salute, he slowly pivots around, his back rigid as steel. Like in the frames of the Cineluce newsreel, the last sentence of 'Ntoni's speech is lost in the frenzied hail that bursts hysterically from thousands and thousands of mouths . . . They're even mocking the masses, those kids. Or are they too preparing to rush into the piazzas – yet another victory of the 'bundled rods'* – and voice their longing to be like others, to rejoice or weep with others and end the solitary struggle to be different?

'It's hard! I can't hate Cesare, even though he took the train with the other Fascist youth, the *avanguardisti*, in order to go to Rome to cheer Mussolini. Besides he's poor, and it's a free trip.'

Scores of children – all named Italo, Benito, Edda and Romana – burgeon in the countryside and in the cities. New saints replace Rosalia, Agatha, Joseph. A remaining 'Liberal' or two has asked to be called Ardito on his Party membership card . . .*

Joyce reties her foulard. What did she say? The hail of applause swallowed her last words.

'How did you describe our love, Jò? I thought I heard "intimate relationship", or am I wrong?'

'It's the first time for me, Modesta.'

'What does that mean? When you love, it's always the first time.'

'Let me go! I don't feel well.'

'I'm not holding you back. You're free to go.'

'But you're questioning me!'

'Questioning myself, Joyce; pay no attention.'

'You're pale as a corpse.'

'For me it's the first time I've felt unhappy in our relationship, as you call it.'

'What! You yourself said a moment ago that I've always kept you teetering anxiously.'

'The tightrope of love swings back and forth, forever tied between the tree of anxiety and the tree of fear. Like life, it holds a constant reminder that death must be overcome, and not this emptiness toward you that I now feel. Help me, Joyce!'

'How can I, *bambina*, how can I?'

'Don't call me *bambina*. At one time I was moved by it, but now that I understand it, your shame humiliates me.'

'How can I help feeling ashamed? I'm ashamed of just being in the world, being alive. Why was I brought into the world? Why?'

'Isn't it enough for you to think that you were brought into the world to enrich my life, to give me the joy of holding you in my arms? Well? For me this thought has sufficed during these years of confinement.'

'These years have been like a prison for you too.'

'How could it be otherwise? Not forgetting, however, that real prisons, those that swallow up hundreds of people like us in their dark bowels, are something else entirely.'

'Come back up with me, Modesta.'

'No! I'm beginning to understand you. You want me back there to cry with you, to reject those kids' joy. You've set your sights on a real cell, but I'm hungry! And from the silence that has fallen, it's clear that Bambolina's ringing voice has ordered: "And now, let's all eat!" I can just see her! Like her mother, finger raised, her tiny body whirling around . . .

'She's not lame like Beatrice, but she has the same grace when she moves. Look, see how she's lit up the beach with acetylene lamps? And surely, on the crates, the embroidered linen tablecloths she so loves set off the silver cutlery and crystal glasses. To me all that splendour is unimportant, but what does matter is the joy of that light stolen from the darkness, from the obscurantism of these years.

Besides, I'm hungry! Forgive me, Joyce, but like Beatrice, Bambolina gets annoyed if we're late for dinner, and she's right. The party languishes if there's an empty place.'

★

Bambù: 'What a pleasure it is, Zia, to see you eating with such appetite! But where's Joyce? Did her headache come back? Prando, why don't you go and see if she needs anything?'

Prando: 'Come now, my dear beautiful *cuginetta*. So beautiful that I promise you, little cousin – providing you don't change for the worse like Teresa, who was a sylph at your age and has now become squat and dumpy – I promise to marry you, if no one will have you. Or is it forbidden between cousins? Jacopo, you who know everything, is it prohibited?'

Jacopo: 'I think it requires a dispensation from the Church.'

Bambù: '*Uffa*, what unpleasant talk! Besides I'm never getting married! I asked you, please, to go and see if Joyce . . .'

Prando: 'Ah! I see that Mama's book hit the mark, *cuginetta*.'

Jacopo: 'What book?'

Prando: 'A certain little 800-page book about women and socialism.'

Bambù: 'All I asked you to do was go and see if Joyce . . .'

Prando: 'Come on, Bambù! It's hopeless! You know that when she has a headache . . . and when *doesn't* she have one? What do you say, Jacopo, maybe every other Sunday? Provided, of course, that it's not too bright or too dark or too hot or too cold.'

Bambù: 'Don't talk that way about Joyce, Prando! When you act like that, you're vulgar.'

Prando: 'Just look at how our Bambù rails in defence of the *signora*! What is it? Are you, too, perhaps in love with the beautiful foreign lady, like all the other women in this house? Hey Jacopo, do you know that everyone calls her Greta Garbo? The femme fatale who robs us of our mothers and cousins.'

Jacopo: 'Even male cousins for that matter.'

Prando: 'Ah! Have you fallen at her feet as well, my dear Jacopone? Don't tell me.'

Jacopo: 'I adore her, Prando.'

Prando: 'Even though she's always so pale and long-suffering?'

Jacopo: 'Maybe for that very reason.'

Prando: 'What a romantic!'

Jacopo: 'And I think Bambù is right. What do you think, Mama? Should I go and see if I can persuade her to join us?'

Modesta: 'No, Jacopo, don't get up. She won't come. Joyce doesn't want to be disturbed. Though, as Bambolina says, when Prando acts like that it's vulgar and irritating.'

Prando: 'Thanks, Mama.'

Modesta: 'You're welcome. And don't look at me that way!'

Prando: 'You don't like me when I do that, do you, Mama?'

Modesta: 'No!'

Prando: 'And to think I do it on purpose.'

Modesta: 'Why?'

Prando: 'Because I actually like you when you get angry. Isn't it true, Bambù, that she's beautiful when she's incensed? Remember that day we were arguing, and she came down like a fury and slapped us silly? Cesare and Ciccio too, did they catch it!'

Bambù: 'Of course I remember! I can still feel the sting of her fingers on my cheeks, even as you say it.'

Jacopo: 'I don't remember.'

'Ntoni: 'Me neither.'

Prando: 'How can you two possibly remember – your mouths were still full of breast milk!'

Jacopo: 'I never saw Mama hit anybody, did you, 'Ntoni?'

'Ntoni: 'Don't wind him up, Jacopo. Drop it!'

Prando: 'Naturally she doesn't go around hitting sheep like you two, but wolves like me and Bambù.'

Bambù: 'I'm not a wolf!'

Prando: 'You're more of a wolf than I am, beautiful *cuginetta*! Only, being female, you wear docile sheepskins to conceal the bristly hide you have underneath.'

Bambù: 'Oh Prando, that's enough! Why are you doing this? Always being a killjoy.'

Mela: 'Leave Bambù alone, Prando! Can't you see she's crying?'

Prando: 'There she is, the silent musician rushing to the defense of her little friend! Too many women in this company, my dear Jacopo! And now that 'Ntoni is leaving, and me too, what will become of you?'

Bambù: 'Will you stop it? What's come over you?'

Prando: 'Look at the fire in my *cuginetta*'s eyes! So they weren't a sheep's tears, were they?'

Bambù: 'Tears of anger, Prando, anger! When you act like this I hate you! And why are you looking at Mama when I'm speaking to you?'

Prando: 'Because I haven't seen her in ages.'

Prando's scar flares up, purplish. A roar rises from the sea, tracing a luminous crescent against the black sky.

Bambù: 'An airplane! A plane went by! Like a lightning bolt, Zia, did you see it?'

Prando: 'There's nothing to be afraid of, Bambù. Great strides are now being made in the sky. You sound like Stella, who's still afraid of trains.'

Bambù: 'But so many of them have been passing by lately.'

Prando: 'Come, don't worry! Give me your hand, and you won't be afraid anymore. Forgive my earlier vulgarity, *cuginetta*, but everything seems out of kilter to me since . . .'

Bambù: 'Since when, dearest Prando?'

Prando: 'It's obvious! Everyone in black shirts! Even this morning – I didn't want to say anything, not to spoil the party – but even Carlo . . .'

Bambù: 'Carlo, Lo Preti's son? But he was a socialist!'

Prando: 'That's right, Bambù, him too! He says that without a party membership card, he can't take part in the Mille Miglia. He says that in his heart he doesn't give a damn about it but . . .'

Bambù: 'So?'

Prando: 'So I don't believe all these people laughing it off anymore. They dismiss it as trivial, yet no foreign domination of the past has sunk as many roots into our land like this goddamn Dux! But come on! We've sat at the table long enough. There's a surprise for you, Bambù, and for you, Mela.'

Bambù: 'What kind of surprise?'

Prando: 'How can a midnight party on the island continue without . . .'

Bambù: 'Mandolins! Don't tell me!'

Prando: 'An impromptu concert by Don Ciccio the barber and the boys from his shop: mazurka vs mazurka, waltz vs waltz, duelling melodies. And the one who comes up with the most will be the only one to pluck the stars, and earn a chaste kiss from the prettiest girl!'

Jacopo: 'Who is the prettiest, Prando? Who?'

Prando: 'We'll find out! The winning mandolinist will select the whitest gardenia blooming in the heat of this night. Here they come, let's go meet the musicians.'

67

'. . . And this is Don Donato from Santa Ninfa with his *carusi*. He's the only one we were missing. He's the oldest, and an expert on the guitar. See, Alberto, we have three complete shops . . .'

Prando explains to an attentive thin face, surely a new friend from the university:

'. . . the barber and his boys sitting in a circle, like on sunny afternoons in front of the empty shop – that's the beauty of the job! Mornings are spent touching up trims and moustaches, sharpening razors – an occupation requiring a skilful hand, not hard labour. Later, waiting until evening for any customers, sitting on the sidewalk shaded by acacia trees and oaks, fingers practise on the delicate, razor-thin mandolin strings. A mason, a porter, or a dockhand can't bend his deformed wrists over the strings. In Catania, Palermo and Messina they've lost the tradition that flourishes only in the shade of centuries-old oak trees. They cut down the trees there, to pile building upon building, but here . . .'

For a moment the three shops face off silently, in tightly knit groups. At an invisible sign, the great duel of improvised melodies and rhythms splits the night, while a flock of frightened birds takes flight after the notes, revealing the silvery stars to watching eyes.

Mela: 'So many stars, Bambù, I hadn't realized it!'

Bambù: 'Legend says that the mandolin has the power to multiply them.'

Mela: 'And listen to them play! A far cry from the conservatory! I think I would have done better studying with them.'

Bambù: 'How can you say that, Mela?!'

Mela: 'Quiet, Bambù, hush. I want to soak up their nimble touch. Oh, if only I could steal it from them and impart it to my piano! The piano is impervious, by God!'

Bambù: 'What do you mean?'

Mela: 'Be quiet, Bambù! Where on earth do they get all these melodies?'

Bambù: 'They know them by heart, so Prando said; they memorize them. They hand them down from father to son.'

Mornings at the seashore, Mela and Bambù are no longer concerned about losing their alluring paleness, nor do they fear being viewed as 'indecent', as people once said: there, on that private beach, in that small realm, only local boys come – and perhaps a sister of those evolved males, students, rich and poor – daring to defy public opinion. And only because of money . . . '*Money makes the man. In fact, no poor man is ever considered valiant or esteemed.*' Carlo laughed, and afterwards Alceo brought Plato into it: 'The Republic! *Easy to conceive it on the labour and blood of the Helots! You know what I say, Modesta? That Plato is the most reactionary of . . .*'

Jacopo: 'Are you sad, Mama?'

Modesta: 'No, Jacopo, I'm listening to the music.'

Jacopo: 'Then I'll keep quiet. It's just that I wanted to ask you a question. What book was Prando talking about earlier with Bambù?'

Modesta: 'Oh, nothing . . . or rather a fundamental book for women.'

Jacopo: 'Oh, really? Is it by an Italian?'

Modesta: 'No, it's by August Bebel, a German socialist, have you heard of him? Part of Rosa Luxemburg's circle.'

Jacopo: 'Oh! And it talks about women?'

Modesta: 'The title tells you that: *Woman and Socialism.*'

Jacopo: 'And who gave it to you? Your mother?'

Modesta: 'Oh, no. My mother couldn't read or write; you always forget that. I found it among Uncle Jacopo's books. I told you about Uncle Jacopo's treasure trove, remember?'

Jacopo: 'Oh yes, of course. But I thought . . . well . . . is it because I'm a boy that you never gave it to me?'

The doleful chords of the last mandolin are echoed in Jacopo's crestfallen eyes, exposing an injustice to Modesta. Unfair Modesta! In her eagerness to protect the future woman in Bambù, she has overlooked Jacopo, Prando and 'Ntoni.

Jacopo: 'You haven't answered, Mama. Why? Is it a book only for women?'

Modesta: 'No, Jacopo, I'm at a loss. Your words showed me a mistake I made. Certainly, it's a book aimed at women, but it's written by a man, and I should have recommended it to you and Prando as well.'

Jacopo: 'That's what I wanted to know, Mama. You've always said that both men and women should read the same books, the same newspapers . . . I remember, you know, how you got angry at Stella because she didn't want Mela to read *L'Avventuroso** and . . .'

Modesta: 'Of course, Jacopo . . . I made a mistake. But we can remedy that. You'll find it among Uncle Jacopo's other books, the old ones in my study, but don't take it to school or around with you because it's banned.'

Jacopo: 'Oh – that book too?'

Modesta: 'Yes, indeed! And they're right . . . given the way they see things . . . It says a thing or two about the condition of women, and that upsets the Fascists and the Nazis.'

Jacopo: 'Is it one of the many books that have been burned? So many of them have! I'll read it, partly because I hope it will enable me to understand Bambolina and Stella a little. Well! I just don't understand women. I'm not like Prando, who says women are an insoluble mystery, but it's because sometimes they scare me . . . I don't know, when Stella accuses 'Ntoni . . . it's not that she shouts at him or anything, but it scares me.'

Modesta: 'Do I scare you too, Jacopo?'

Jacopo: 'With you it's different . . . if anything, you scare me like Pietro or like Prando. Do you know that 'Ntoni always says he feels, with mathematical certainty, that he's your son and not Stella's?'

Modesta: 'Maybe because Stella is uneducated. Don't forget,

Jacopo: culture is a privilege, and by now he's too well educated for Stella, and even for his age.'

Jacopo: 'That may be. But there's more than that, I think, more! I myself adore Stella and I'd like to be like 'Ntoni.'

Modesta: 'Why like 'Ntoni?'

Jacopo: 'You see, Mama, many times I dreamed that you weren't my mother . . . What I mean is, the mother who gave birth to me, like Stella did to 'Ntoni.'

Modesta: 'Well then? Go on, why are you trembling?'

Jacopo: 'I'm ashamed . . . But I dream that you found me when I was little, wrapped in a blanket . . . sometimes on a street corner in the Civita, sometimes on the beach.'

Modesta: 'And it upsets you to dream like that?'

Jacopo: 'Oh, no! On the contrary, I like it. I feel like having chosen me without having had me, you . . . I can't explain it, you see: it seems to me, well, a choice, not something fated. And because of this I feel like you love me more than the others. Is it awful, what I said?'

Modesta: 'Why awful, Jacopo? Dreams are wonderful. Then too, as always, there's some truth in dreams, because if I hadn't given birth to you I would have chosen you among thousands.'

Jacopo: 'Oh, Mama, I've been wanting to tell you for so long, but I was afraid. Can I rest my head on your shoulder? This mandolin is beginning to give me a headache. How about you?'

Modesta: 'Rest your head and close your eyes. The sound will fade.'

A few more notes, now furiously joyful, knowing it is the last mandolin to reach the finishing post of the stars, and Jacopo's head becomes heavy. From his breathing, Modesta knows he's fallen asleep like Crispina: wrapped in a shawl, she dozes on Pietro's chest as he sits at the edge of the sand where the rocky reef emerges. Pietro, motionless, a rock on rock, listens intently to the fireworks of those notes, mesmerized . . . It's his music. He is able to surrender to the magnetism of the Jew's harp just like Modesta, now that Jacopo is silent.

★

The last note glides off the black glass of the sky and plunges down – a shooting star – exposing the silence.

Jacopo: 'How maddening, Mama: I fell asleep! Who's the prettiest? Did the winning mandolinist choose?'

Modesta: 'No, but we'll know very soon. See how he's looking around?'

Jacopo: 'Why is he taking so long? It's so simple!'

Modesta: 'It's part of the ritual, Jacopo. Besides, maybe he really is undecided. I would find it hard to choose too. Bambù, as you say, is in the bloom of youth, but Emanuela . . . who would have said so? In a year she's become more beautiful than her mother.'

Jacopo: 'Can grown women be chosen too, Mama?'

Modesta: 'Of course. You were too young to remember: Stella was chosen three years in a row.'

Jacopo: 'Even now, she may be the most beautiful, but I'd . . .'

Modesta: 'Hush, Jacopo, we shouldn't make any noise. Pietro is glaring at us. The right decision is only made in silence, so he says. Let's go over there. The mandolinist won't choose if the circle around the musicians isn't complete.'

The winning mandolinist goes around the circle once, twice. On his third time around, he stops and stares at Bambù and Mela, who are holding hands. Then he steps back, but only to make his decision more evident, and removing the gardenia from the buttonhole of his jacket, slowly extends his arm. Everyone follows the silent trajectory of that white star, which comes to rest under Mela's chin. Bambù lets go of her hand and steps back with the others.

1st Mandolinist: 'After careful consideration, I tell you with certainty that this *carusa*, Mela, is the prettiest!'

Everyone but Mela applauds his decision. Jacopo jumps for joy, yelling, 'I knew it! I knew it! Bravo, mandolinist!'

Mela whispers, 'But why me, why? Where should I put the gardenia now? Where is it supposed to go?'

1st Mandolinist: 'On your chest. Enfold it in your musician's soul and play for us and our children and our grandchildren for ever!'

Crispina laughs. Her eyes, heavy with sleep, can't see, but she laughs at the joyous applause. That joy, though later forgotten, is destined to nourish her always.

In the parlour, the circle forms again around the piano and Mela competes alone on the keyboard against all three of the groups. No spotlight shines on her, yet she is the prettiest. Her arms, her fragile torso, filled out thanks to proper nourishment, have lost the grim scrawniness they once had. Dressed by Joyce, her hair done by Bambolina, and nurtured by Modesta, the former scarecrow in a grey smock – the Mela who first arrived – has dissolved with the past.

'Oh, Zia, remember how awful that smock was? I had never noticed orphans, but what you used to say is really true: they look like prisoners! Since Mela has come to be with us, I understand and I notice them when I run into them on the street, all grey, lined up in a row. I feel so sorry for them! How she used to eat in the early days! You know that sometimes at night she would wake up and ask permission to go to the kitchen? Once she ate a whole jar of jam with a soup spoon. Can you imagine?'

*

Pietro: 'A great honour for our Mela, isn't it, Mody? You seem sad. Or are you just tired?'

Modesta: 'No, Pietro. I'm worried about money. We're nearly penniless. I stopped the sale of the house. Selling is one thing, but being left without a roof? No. Attorney Santangelo is right about that. We have to find that man, Pietro . . .'

Pietro: 'There's only one man. But the Princess doesn't want to hear him mentioned. Or is the despondency that's come over you perhaps teaching you wisdom?'

Modesta: 'I don't know, Pietro . . .'

Pietro: 'Your hesitation tells me that Pietro was right to take the liberty of acting to hasten your decision . . .

'I'll take Jacopo and Crispina to bed. They've fallen asleep like two little lambs. Then I'll come back and we'll see.'

'*How did you save us from the fire, Tuzzu?*'

'*One under one arm and one under the other, like two sleepy little lambs.*'

Pietro ploughs through the waves of sound carrying Jacopo and Crispina to safety. Modesta follows him. But when she reaches the big window she has to stop. It wasn't a hallucination: Mimmo is now climbing the stairs at Carmelo . . . his large body sheathed in dark green velvet . . .

Bambù: 'Who is that, Zia?'

Modesta: 'Mimmo the gardener. Don't you see the big frame and the dark velvet outfit people in the country wear?'

Bambù: 'Always joking, Zia. Hardly a gardener! Stella would say he's dressed like a true gentleman.'

Mattia: '*Bacio le mani*, my respects, Princess. I hope I'm not disturbing all this joy and merriment.'

Modesta: 'Welcome! Joy, like bread, should be for everyone, Mattia. May I introduce my niece Ida?'

Mattia: 'It's an honour, *signorina*. Joy, like bread and tears, should be shared by one and all. That's what Pietro told me two minutes ago. That's the only reason I allowed myself to join your party.'

Modesta: 'I'm glad you did, Mattia. But how did you come to be in this area?'

Mattia: 'Actually, I've come by the villa several times since I returned from America, but I didn't know whether time had put things between the Brandiforti and the Tudia in a more favourable light.'

Modesta: 'Time is always favourable to us Brandiforti.'

Mattia: 'I'm pleased to hear it. And I'm also pleased to see that time and nature have bestowed health and beauty on the late *principessina* Beatrice's daughter.'

Bambù: 'I'll go now. They've stopped playing, and maybe they're hungry or will be. We still have many hours to go. I'll go help Stella. A pleasure to have met you, *signor* . . .'

Mattia: 'The pleasure is mine, *signorina* . . . I see that you have kept to our traditions in bringing up these *picciriddi*.'

Modesta: 'One must respect the good traditions and sever the bad ones.'

Mattia: 'That's right. Here comes Pietro . . . His presence is comforting, isn't it, Modesta?'

Modesta: 'Would you care to join the party and peacefully await dawn with us?'

Mattia: 'With pleasure, Princess.'

Modesta: 'Let's hope the Prophet appears so we can end with a flourish. What do you think, Pietro? Will the children's expectations be met?'

Pietro: 'The sky is like glass, and that clarity bodes well. But the world has been gripped with a mania for speed. And just one of those evil iron birds is all it takes to frighten the sky, the sparrows and people's minds . . . Here it comes again, the damn thing!'

Death caused by a mania for speed. Prando and his motorcycle. Mattia's iron horse. The scar is throbbing. Is it in his fiery gaze, in those sparks that *La Certa* lurks? If he's harbouring her in the copper-flecked blue of his eyes, Modesta must look up and face her . . .

Mattia: 'Finally you're looking at me, Modesta! And now I know how much I loved you. I've never forgotten your eyes in all these years . . . Youth bewilders us. Mistaking passion for a prison at the time, I fought you, rather than surrender to the rare sweetness of loving.'

Death no longer lurks in the stillness which suffuses his eyes, his cheeks, his smile. In time, Prando's smile will acquire the inner calmness that Carmine had as an adult. Soon Prando, too, will have white strands among the curls, a sign that the fire has subsided. Grateful for this revelation, Modesta extends her hands to Mattia. Her hands feel small between his big, warm palms . . . Crispina's hands?

Mattia: 'Thank you, Modesta. But now we should talk about those paintings. Pietro mentioned . . .'

Modesta: 'But aren't you missing a finger like they said?!'

Mattia: 'A finger? I heard that too. If you disappear for a while, legends crop up. For that matter, I actually almost lost not just my finger, but my whole hand. But all I have is a bracelet as a souvenir of your aim. Look, see under the cuff?'

Modesta: 'And I almost lost my head! Look, look under my hair.'

Mattia: 'It looks like a little snake . . .'

Modesta: 'The snake I have in my body, as you used to say, and you brought it out into the light.'

Mattia: 'And has it quieted down?'

Modesta: 'On the contrary, it's restless and makes me change direction at every step. I'll never quiet down, Mattia. I can't help it. But now let's go down to the beach. I didn't feel like waiting up until dawn before, but now I do. Let's go.'

Mattia: 'And about the paintings?'

Modesta: 'We'll talk about that tomorrow; the details can wait till day. Now I want you to meet Prando and Jacopo . . . Oh, wait, do you have children?'

Mattia: 'No.'

Modesta: 'And are you sorry?'

Mattia: 'The details, as you called them . . . Tomorrow, with the day, Modesta. Let's go.'

*

Jacopo: 'I fell asleep, Mama, how maddening! Then the light woke me. How infuriating! Did he appear?'

Modesta: 'This is Jacopo, Mattia. Jacopo, meet Mattia.'

Jacopo: 'Pleased to meet you, *signore*, a pleasure . . . Did he appear, 'Ntoni? Did he appear?'

'Ntoni: 'No.'

Jacopo: 'Too bad!'

'Ntoni: 'But you were sleeping . . .'

Jacopo: 'Well, you could have described it. You can imitate anything.'

'Ntoni: 'I've never thought of imitating a mirage. Not a bad idea.'

Prando: 'Oh, sure! Maybe with Mela accompanying you on the piano. Whoever heard of such a thing!'

'Ntoni: 'Well, why not, Prando? Always a defeatist.'

Prando: 'Look, saying "defeatist" is just as bad as saying *me ne frega,* "I don't give a damn."* It's best not to use vulgar Fascist terms, as Mama tells us. What is it you say, Mama? Oh, yes: by using the words of the Fascists you end up absorbing them. Slowly but surely they'll go to work inside you, and one fine morning you'll find yourself ready and waiting for them, with a black shirt and breeches. To me, it's always seemed like an exaggeration, but . . . How come you're not answering, Mama? Maybe I didn't express your thoughts very well?'

Mattia's smile has erased any irritation Modesta might feel toward that stony profile, so flawless even after a night without sleep. 'Ntoni's features are gaunt, like after a fever. Mela, her eyes mere slits, looks like she's wearing her orphan's smock again. Bambolina, pale, nearly asleep, is leaning against the boat, perhaps shivering. Prando's impassive profile and harsh voice are nothing but strength. Maybe the irritation she felt toward him was simply fear.

Prando: 'From all indications, my dear 'Ntoni, even though my beautiful mother didn't deign to look at us before, at least she spoke to us. Now it seems she has decided to ignore us completely.'

Modesta: 'You expressed my thoughts perfectly. Words nourish us, and like food they should be carefully chosen before they are swallowed.'

Prando: 'Such a sweet disposition my mother woke up with this morning! Or is it because she hasn't slept?'

Prando must have sensed the fear Modesta disguised as irritation; he must have been aware of it from childhood, since he's so defiant. Nature doesn't allow us to repair in an hour what we've done wrong for years, so Modesta is forced to act as before, waiting for time to apply a soothing balm.

Modesta: 'You're insufferable, Prando, and I forbid you to be a killjoy, as Bambù says!'

Bambù: 'You're right, Zia, just ignore him! Even with me he's always that way, he likes to be a naughty boy.'

'Ntoni: 'You mean a tough guy, Bambolina. The movies are to blame. He's in love with Jean Gabin.'

Bambù: 'Oh, that's true! If he didn't have such perfect features, he'd look like Jean Gabin.'

'Ntoni: 'Of course! I saw him coming out of the cinema, copying his walk.'

Prando: 'Idiot! I don't copy anybody!'

Bambù: 'But you're too beautiful, *cuginetto*, to be a tough guy like him.'

Prando: 'Oh, stop that beautiful stuff, Ida! It's offensive to a man.'

Bambù: 'Since when is it offensive?'

Prando: 'To hell with you all, and damn me for stooping to the level of such *picciriddi*! I'm going for a ride on the motorcycle.'

Bambù: 'I'll come with you, Prando.'

Prando: 'But you're so sleepy you're ready to drop!'

Bambù: 'Not any more. Take me with you.'

Prando: 'But you're shivering all over!'

Bambù: 'I'm cold! Don't go! I'm cold! Will you hold me?'

Prando: 'Hey, Mama, I have the feeling this party will end up in the hospital. I'll bet they'll all be in bed with a fever tomorrow.'

'Ntoni: 'The fishermen! Here come the fishermen!'

Jacopo: 'Come on, let's go prepare the fire. Who knows how many fish they've caught! I'm so hungry! You'll see how good the soup is when they make it.'

Prando: 'Listen to this little Jacopo of ours telling me how good the fishermen's soup is, as if I didn't know! What patience you need with these *picciriddi*, eh, Pietro? And you, my beautiful *cuginetta*, my little white dove, have you warmed up? Can you manage to walk?'

Bambù: 'I can! Mela, Stella, the fishermen are here!'

Modesta: 'Off they go, Mattia, look . . . off they go!'

Mattia: 'They're flocking toward the horizon like sparrows who've learned to fly. But you nurtured them, and that should be a consolation to you. Tell me the truth, my little lava devil, is Prando Carmine's son?'

'Yes.'

'He doesn't look like me, but he's the spitting-image of my father when he was young.'

'He resembles you, too.'

'You think so?'

'I took a gamble having you meet him. I watched everyone closely to see if they noticed anything, even Stella. But no one spotted the resemblance.'

'You like to take chances, don't you?'

'Yes, I do. No one noticed it. It's incredible!'

'If they don't know . . . No one is clairvoyant; clairvoyants don't exist . . . So, as I told you, all you have to do is remove the frames and roll up the canvases – I'm sending you an expert – then each canvas has to be placed in a tube like this. As you know, I have a history of trips to that country, and, what's more important, unsullied trips.'

'But you also said that you didn't want to go back to America.'

'I didn't want to because it was associated in my mind with the grief I carry, but deep down I was waiting for an opportunity. New York is the most beautiful city in the world if you have money.'

'Oh! Antonia died while you were over there?'

'Yes, I stayed too long that time and my wife, perhaps distraught – or maybe it's my imagination – punished me by dying along with our child. Or maybe it was fate, like with my father. Loss surprised him when he was distracted by his travels, as it did me. Or then again, maybe we Tudia males – did you hear your Prando? – harbour an egoism so absolute that it kills those who aren't strong enough to fend off the fury that constantly possesses us.'

'Carmine freed himself of what you call fury only just before he died, and he was serene.'

'Are you trying to tell me that *La Certa* is coming for me, Modesta, since I'm having doubts about the appropriateness of that fury?'

'No, your father never uttered the word "doubt"; he felt that death was a liberation from his obligations. You're not ill, nor old, as he was.'

'No, and yet I'm doubtful, as you've gathered.'

'It's as it should be, Mattia.'

'I was taught that there's no place in a man's soul for doubt.'

'They teach you that in order to imprison you *carusi* in a suit of armour made up of obligations and false certainties. Like they do with us women, Mattia: different obligations, different armour. Silken ties, but it's the same thing.'

'You must be right, because an unfamiliar melancholy came over me and has stayed with me ever since I encountered the word "doubt".'

'It's fear of this melancholy that leads man to affect certainties and impose dogmas. But man is still too young to know. He's only just learned to read and write. And those he thinks are gods are idols that only want human sacrifices.'

'This winter I was in Berlin. I hadn't been there in years, Modesta, and I saw men and women walking in the street though the sidewalk was empty. At the time I didn't think anything of it, but then I took a closer look: they all had a mark on their arm. Branded, the way live-stock is branded here. As the cars rushed by, they hurried along, hugging the sidewalk . . . I've fought in the war, and they don't fool me. Where is that branded herd being driven to? I didn't ask any questions when I came across the same sign on doors and shops, but I took the first train out and never went back to that country, which I'd remembered as clean and carefree.'

'Is that what made you doubtful?'

'That, too . . . or maybe it's because I learned to read and write, as you said, whereas Carmine couldn't, other than the accounts and his signature . . . What do you think? Did I lose my wife and treasure and my son because, as the ancients said, if you don't look after them and protect them with your presence, your watchful eye, you expose them to hail and wind, and to *La Certa*?'

'Maybe, Mattia, maybe . . .'

68

Perhaps Joyce, left to her grief alone in her room, has not been able to resist the lure of *La Certa*. Modesta had never before forgotten her friend's presence so completely. Realizing this, a remorseful anxiety makes her run up the stairs. The partly open door confirms that Joyce has waited for her. In fact, the small lamp of pink milk glass on the nightstand illuminates a pale, lifeless face, like stone. Trembling at that unnatural pallor, Modesta leans over the bed until she discerns a faint breath, so fragrant that it carries her far back in memory, to a time when Prando was just a tiny, soft dumpling of flesh. At the memory, tears inexplicably press against her eyelids . . . Jò breathes softly, gazing inward at some peaceful dream. Why, then, as soon as the sun rises, does a secret mask of sadness descend over her face?

'The sphinx, Mody, the sphinx! If you look closely, she is surely hiding gold teeth under her vivid lips, with a diamond set in her long canine.'

A foolish terror makes me run out of the house. And only when I'm far away from that room, walking up and down a deserted beach barely tinged by the sun's rays, am I able to smile at that childish fear of monsters, of sphinxes, of the ominous mirages that always gather at dawn, according to Tuzzu, to haunt the vineyards, the huge overhanging lava cliffs and the scaly backs of the sea's blue *Le Certe* . . . Even now, among myriads of sleepless, ravenous seagulls, the small island of the Prophet seems like a giant head, convulsive, half submerged by the sea . . . It's drowning, or as Stella says, it's about to be sucked back by its mother island.

Leaning against the wooden shelter, Modesta can empty her mind of thoughts, of her past and future, and follow the cries of the gulls, the deep rumble of the surf, the strident silver-gold of the sun's first rays. She almost doesn't notice the hushed whispering from inside the hut. It must be the gulls, she thinks, but then she slowly moves her head closer to the wall . . . Isn't that Bambolina's distinct voice?

'Didn't you hear footsteps, Mela?'

'No, it must be the seagulls gleefully finishing up the leftovers from our little party.'

'Still . . .'

'They have a right to their own party, don't they?'

'How beautiful you are when you smile, Mela!'

'You're always beautiful! And it's true beauty, even when you don't smile.'

'No, you're more beautiful, always.'

'All right then. Come here, on top of me, Bambù, and we'll blend together and make one single beauty.'

'Do you think we can become one single person by holding each other very tight? We've done it so many times and it hasn't happened, Mela!'

'Who says it hasn't happened? I've felt it.'

'Hold me, hold me tight. I want to feel it, too.'

'You have to keep your eyes shut and think of me, only me.'

'Oh yes, I feel you, Mela, I feel you!'

Modesta is cold, but Beatrice covers her with her silky hair.

'*Oh yes, Mody, silk warms you even more than wool. But you wouldn't know these things. I bet it was forbidden even to talk about them in the convent.*'

'*It was.*'

'*But did you hug each other? Did you kiss the way we do? Well? Was that forbidden too?*'

'*Absolutely.*'

'*Poor things! Oh Mody, don't go . . . let's do the scene from Page Fernando:* you be Page Fernando and stare into my eyes. That's it, like that, *and you'll see, we'll feel each other even without kissing. How delightful, isn't it, Mody? Now let's hold each other close and talk. I have so much to tell you.'*

'How wonderful, Mela! I actually felt you inside! No, don't get dressed, it's early. Don't get dressed – that way I can caress you and you can talk to me.'

Why can't we be happy for ever? Beatrice's diary, which has turned up again, keeps asking:

'Why can't we be happy for ever? Is it the fate of the Brandiforti, Modesta?'

'It's not fate. It's that everyone in this house only tries to be unhappy. Even when they're happy, I suspect they don't want to admit it.'

'But we're happy, aren't we, Modesta? Even though Nonna yells and we can't go to Catania, I'm happy, so happy here with you!'

Yes, Beatrice, happy for ever, like those soft voices whispering behind the wall.

*

Perhaps the effort of holding her breath makes Modesta cry, huddled up against the wood: a silent moan rises slowly to her lips, and will soon become a howl. Not wanting to disturb the seagulls' soundless flight, Modesta quietly goes away. Only when she crosses the threshold of her room, protected by the darkness of its walls, can she let go and surrender to tears.

'Where have you been? It's almost seven . . . why are you sobbing like that?'

'Oh, Jò, excuse me.'

'You look deranged! Why are you sobbing?'

'It's nostalgia, Jò. Don't worry, just nostalgia.'

'Nostalgia? I don't understand. You look like you've been through torture.'

'No. Help me, Joyce! Are you happy with me? We've been happy, haven't we? Why won't you answer me?'

'I've been awake all night waiting for you.'

'That's not so! When I came back up I saw you sleeping, peacefully too. Why the mask now?'

'What are you talking about? Come, go to bed, you're tired.'

'Help me, Jò.'

'Help you with your insanities? I've tried. You're wasting yourself, Modesta. You waste your time, your money. You know how hard I've tried to make you reason. You haven't even been able to put your poems together. By now we could have had a volume ready to publish.'

'What do the poems have to do with anything? I've told you over and over, Jò: for me written words are just a pastime.'

'Then why did you urge Mela to study so hard?'

'Because she's poor! And the poor girl can only rely on her own abilities if she doesn't want to wind up married to some lowly clerk or . . .'

'And you, on the other hand, being rich, can waste your abilities.'

'Oh, Jò! I got rid of my properties when I was twenty because I didn't want to become a slave to my estate. At thirty, I rid myself of the word "artist" because I didn't want to become a slave to my talent. I've told you that before, and I'm telling you again. And besides, this morning I discovered why Mela is so peaceful, and why Bambù has been too since Mela landed in our midst.'

'What did you discover?'

'If you hug me and smile, I'll tell you.'

'It's incredible. After all those tears your eyes aren't even red, and your face is as fresh as if you'd slept all night.'

'That's because you're holding me in your arms and smiling at me.'

'So let's hear it then. What did you discover?'

'Kiss me first. Kiss me. I want so much to feel you naked. If we hold each other tight, naked, we'll be one single person. This morning I saw the mirage, the trees told me that. . . There, come on top of me and hold me, hold me close.'

'What did the trees tell you, little one?'

69

'They were making love in the shelter? And what did you do?'

'Nothing. Why are you so pale, Jò? Don't worry, I made sure they didn't notice me, and then I came home.'

'But you spied on them if you were able to tell me everything they said.'

'Spied? What does that mean? I was dazzled by their joy! They were so beautiful, holding each other, naked.'

'You saw them, too?'

'For a moment, before I went away.'

'How disgusting!'

'What's disgusting, Jò? Me? Since, according to you, I was spying on them? Or those two holding one another?'

The mournful, enigmatic mask crumbles as a flush rises heatedly from Joyce's neck to her brow. Disconcerted, Modesta watches the composure of those marble features shatter. At one time she would have respected the silence that always managed to recompose that face.

'What's disgusting, Joyce? Disgusting, the two of us naked together a few moments ago?'

'Oh, us! We're lost, Modesta, but Bambolina, so young . . . Oh, that Mela! I never liked her, never! She should be sent away!'

Once the blanket of silence has been torn, her voice breaks as well.

'Us, lost? What are you talking about? Lost to what?'

'Normality, the laws of nature . . .'

'What are you saying, Jò? Who really knows nature? Who established these laws? The Christian god? Or Rousseau? Answer me! Rousseau, who moved God out of the heavens and put him in a tree?'

'What does Rousseau or God have to do with it? I'm worried about Bambù! Oh, Modesta, you have no idea. In Paris, in those haunts for homosexuals . . . heaps of emaciated bodies, swollen, jaundiced faces marked by shame, the dense smoke and alcohol fumes . . . a real antechamber of hell, if hell existed! You have no idea.'

'But I do, because I've been there and . . .'

'You? Me, never . . . only once – and I fled.'

'You shouldn't have, because by actually being with them and talking to them I realized what they're seeking in that "antechamber of hell", as you called it.'

'What can they be seeking? They get together and take drugs to forget.'

'No, Jò! They're seeking the real hell to atone for their sin.'

'What else can they do if society rejects them, points its finger at them?'

'Them? Nothing. But only because they're ignorant and full of prejudices, just like the society that points its finger at them. And they display their wounds only to ask for forgiveness from the society that they too – they more than anyone – consider hallowed and just, rather than fighting it. Jò, come to your senses! What have we been talking about all these years? I see that we've merely been conversing amiably about progress, about science, like people do in sophisticated salons. But at the first slight confrontation with reality you want to drag me into the panic that seizes you as it does all intellectuals at the sole idea of putting into practice the theories so often expounded.'

'I don't understand.'

'Yes, you do! In your opinion I should send Mela away, right?'

'I didn't . . .'

'That's what you said. Don't you see that by doing that I would make those girls feel that they're sinning? I would be branding them

– I, who represent, who embody society to them, as your Freud says. Afterwards, what else could they do but end up in those very places? And I wonder, Jò . . . Who was it who branded you with that shame? You weren't in a convent.'

'You know very well I wasn't in a convent.'

'Yes. One of the few things I do know about you. Was it your mother then?'

'No!'

'Then who? Your father?'

'My father! My father called himself a free thinker and didn't care about us.'

'So who was it?'

'Oh, leave me alone, Modesta. I can't take any more of this!'

'No! The time for silence and suppression is over. It's over inside me and you have to talk. You underwent analysis, which saved you, you told me.'

'Oh, forget analysis and Freud! We're talking about Bambolina's future.'

'And doesn't Bambolina's future, and Mela's too, hinge on our thinking and the few battles that have been won? Or would you rather I teach them the convenient old practice of saying one thing and doing another?'

'But Bambù will become a useless creature like me, little one!'

'And like me: say it, if that's what you're thinking.'

'Oh, with you it's different. I don't understand you, and sometimes you frighten me. You've had a child, men . . .'

'You were married too.'

'Enough! Stop this interrogation or I'll kill myself. I'll kill myself!'

'And I say stop using suicide as blackmail.'

'I would have been better off dying that night!'

'You didn't die and I love you, Joyce! Talk to me! What's this wedding band you wear on your finger?'

'A lie, Modesta, like the various false passports to get across borders.'

'I understand, but you've had . . .'

'Shut up, shut up! Don't say that word. I hate men, I hate them!'

'But you must have known some.'

'No! I hate them! They scare me. They always have, since I was a child. Don't hound me, Modesta. Since I was a little girl I've always hated them.'

'Like you hate women. That's what you said once.'

'I hated women before I knew you, but you're an exception.'

'But you've had friends like Carlo, Jose . . .'

'That's right, you're like them.'

'So for you I'm like a man. Is that what you mean when you say I'm an exception?'

'Oh, I don't know, I don't know!'

'So if I'm like a man – an exception – you are too, it seems to me. One may count as an exception, but two no longer confirm the rule. Two in this house, two more in another house, and who knows in how many others? Carlo once told me: "Don't ever imitate us, Modesta." Doesn't this tell you something?'

'No.'

'To me it does, now. You want to be like a man, so you imitate them, like he said; that's what makes you feel like a mutilated being. I feel sorry for you, Jò! Jò! I will never utter that mutilated name again. Joyce, you are whole, and a woman.'

'I'm not a woman. I'm a deviant being. For years I tried to correct this deviation through analysis, but we failed, he and I . . .'

'He who? Your analyst? Your analyst tried to correct a deviation?'

'Yes, a departure from the sound rules of nature. Even Freud says so.'

'But Joyce! Aside from the fact that it's only an indication . . . your Freud later conducted studies, proved himself wrong, insisted on being corrected over time. He keeps saying that he has only pointed out one path, as yet imperfect, for those to come after him. Joyce, you mistake him for a god, that man who even hated philosophy. Your Freud is a fine old doctor, tired and sick after years of oral cancer. Can we for once knock him off his pedestal and look at this cancer, and maybe apply his theories to him, as he did with Michelangelo?* Who knows, this cancer may be a way of punishing his mouth because he talked too much, violated taboos, codes, religions . . . You're staring at me and backing away like Mother Leonora, when she read my silent thoughts and saw that I denied her God. You people just can't live without a religion . . .

'Where are you going? To kill yourself? Don't do it. I love you, Joyce, but remember that from today on I will keep a close watch on you. I will watch your every move. Your misery mustn't touch Mela and Bambolina, because it's a contagious disease.'

'You don't love me anymore, Modesta, if you can speak to me like that.'

'A person can love someone and still watch them. I'm not looking for absolutes.'

'You don't love me anymore!'

Joyce waits with her hand on the doorknob. Outside the circle of light on the bedside table, Modesta can only make out a shadow, barely darker than the darkness of that artificial night. Beyond the drawn drapes, the sun must surely be wiping the blood off the Prophet's long hair and will then reshape his thoughtful profile. A good swim will take us to that tiny island in an hour or two, right Tuzzu? It's also a daughter of the big island, all of them nursed by the immense breast that nourishes with its fire: the sun's milk.

'*How many daughters does the big island have, Tuzzu?*'

'*Many, many of them. It's one big womb. And the belly button that goes round and round, down to the beginning of life and death, lies there where Castrogiovanni towers among the clouds and bald mountains.*'*

'*And you've seen it, Tuzzu, this belly button?*'

'*No, nobody can. Even the bravest are seized with vertigo. That's where her rules are made, and no one can scrutinize them.*'

'*Why?*'

'*Because the island is a woman, like the moon. Like your mother and my mother, who know how to steal your seed and make it sprout in their belly. My father and grandfather were right to teach us to fear them.*'

'*I'm not afraid of my mother.*'

'*What a revelation! A revelation typical of Giufà. You're not afraid because you're a woman, and even though you're a* picciridda, *you're aware of your power.*'

In fact, Joyce, her face serene when we're at the table, pretends to be kind, but she's aware of her power. Jacopo is afraid of her. 'Ntoni is terrified by Stella's tears. And maybe Prando hides his fear of me by using anger.

Why don't you want to recognize your power, Joyce?

★

'Modesta, finally you woke up! This strange way you have of sleeping frightens me.'

'But I only just fell asleep.'

'You slept all day yesterday, and it's almost noon now.'

'It seems like yesterday, doesn't it, Joyce, that I was overcome by sleep, and you came up? And to think that for weeks I'd been looking for a ruse to get you to come to my room. It was like a dream. You fall asleep hoping for something and when you wake up the gift appears . . . a dream. And now I wake up and you're back.'

'This sleep isn't healthy.'

'How can it be unhealthy if it brings me gifts and an appetite? I'm ravenous!'

'I meant it's not healthy mentally.'

'This is the first time you've told me that something in me isn't healthy. And so seriously that it would frighten me if I weren't so hungry.'

'Stella gave me a tray.'

'Oh, thank goodness! That way I don't even have to wait.'

'So then, I'll leave you to your breakfast.'

'No, no, stay here. You can have some tea. Besides, it doesn't seem kind to leave me after telling me I'm not well. You've never told me that before.'

'Even the way you cling to me . . . you're like a child. It's not healthy.'

'Why isn't it healthy, when I love you?'

'Love! Maybe it doesn't even exist between a man and a woman, much less between two people of the same gender.'

'What are you talking about, Joyce?'

'Love is an illusion!'

'All right, and I have to counter with: *La vida es sueño*, life is a dream.* But that doesn't mean that we don't live life or that I don't love you.'

'You think you love me, but it's pure transference. You identify me with your mother. Not only that, having lost her so young and through your own doing, you feel guilty, and you're always afraid of losing me.'

'And even if that were so? What's sick about searching for a joy you once knew or only imagined? I tried to find in you the serenity I had with Beatrice and I found it. Oh, Joyce, why this professional tone between us all of a sudden?'

'For your own good, Modesta. I was weak, I admit it, and I stole years and years of your youth, dragging you into a relationship that has no future for you and, as such, is unhealthy.'

'But the future doesn't exist, or at least worrying about the future doesn't exist for me. I know that only day by day, hour by hour, does it become the present. And in this present that we've had – and have – you've given me happiness, taught me new concepts, made me grow mentally and . . . And why did you call it an "unhealthy relationship"? Joyce, you're not referring to Mela and Bambolina again, are you? Well? Look, you made me lose my appetite, and that's certainly unhealthy! Let me think, you also said a relationship with no future, right?'

'Yes.'

'So, to try and understand you . . . since I assume that all relationships are without a future, given that people change and as we change relationships grow stale for us, making us require fresh emotions . . . Come to think of it, in fact, maybe people age prematurely because they limit themselves to a few hallowed relationships and scenery that never changes. But to try and understand you . . . why do you say our relationship has no future?'

'No homosexual relationship has a future.'

'Here we go again! I should have expected as much. You've picked up from where we left off yesterday.'

'The day before yesterday.'

'The day before yesterday, fine. And while I was sleeping, you changed the terms, or rather you painted them in psychoanalytic hues so you wouldn't have to relinquish your fundamental conviction, which today is clearer to me than it was before: a homosexual relationship has no future because you cannot proclaim it to the world, that is, in church, by marriage. And it doesn't bear fruit, namely, children, right?'

'Partly.'

'But Joyce, that's so conventional!'

'You have all that confidence because you've known men and you've had children.'

'One child.'

'One child, and now . . .'

'And now I love you, a woman. And I don't care about my past or my future.'

'You're an exception.'

'And what about Beatrice? For years we loved each other and later she loved Carlo. And the same can be said for countless other men and women. I know of many, and you met one of them at the party.'

'Who?'

'The winning mandolinist. He loved a male cousin and now he has a son and even . . .'

'Stop! Enough! Talking to you is impossible. That's awful!'

'But have you ever tried making love with a man?'

'Even though I can't stand the way you've taken to interrogating me in the last few days, I'll answer you: no, never! The very idea is repugnant to me.'

'You've been questioning me for years, Joyce, and this helped me to understand my past, to draw logical conclusions and to express them. So why this reserve since I started asking you some questions?'

'Because you're sick, at least as sick as me, and it's my duty to tell you so because some day this illness will explode like . . .'

'How? By my trying to kill myself? Like you did?'

'When you realize that you've wasted your time, that you didn't make use of your talent, that you didn't accomplish anything.'

'You may be right to say I'm sick, Joyce, but I don't have the same illness as yours. It's you who are identifying with me now: your illness has other origins.'

'And what would those origins be?'

'Power, Joyce, power acquired by imitating men. Your contempt for women, which at first I thought was the usual condescension acquired through upbringing, comes from imitating men, from joining the chorus of learned males; your contempt for old Gaia, for Beatrice, for Stella, is rooted in hatred.'

'So? I don't see where you're going with this.'

'It's simple. By joining this elite group that keeps telling you, "You're an exception, you are worthy of entering our Olympus". . .'

'I still don't see . . .'

'You've gone over to their side, and in you, the old bias dictated by the norms of our mothers and sisters turned into hatred for your female side, since like it or not, you have breasts and you menstruate – a hatred intense enough to sterilize your breasts and your womb.'

'I can't stand this anatomical language!'

'On the contrary, it's time we returned to this language, the only precise one for the time being. I've thought about it. What do you think? You've sterilized and mutilated yourself. But every mutilation seeks compensation. And the only compensation left to you, just as for men, was exercising power, shaping things, giving orders. Because it's not just women who have penis envy, who feel mutilated. Men also feel mutilated.'

'In what way?'

'They can't carnally create a life. And so they try to give birth to ideas. Think of Pygmalion, of Zeus, who makes up for his mutilation by impregnating his cranium and bringing forth not a naked, unformed creature, but a splendid warrior-woman armed with helmet and shield. This is because a man is a mother just like a woman, except that I have never met a mother-man who had your power. Carmine becomes a tender little mummy compared to you.'

'And you think that's funny?'

'Maternal transference!* That may be, Mama Jò, that may be!'

'Enough of this. Stop laughing! It's getting on my nerves, like your amateurish theories.'

'Now what. Are you leaving, Mama Jò?'

'Ignorant bitch!'

'Finally! This is the first time you've lost control. What is it, are you becoming vulgar on me?'

Joyce leaps at Modesta and strikes her repeatedly with her fists. No woman has ever hit me. Beatrice trembled and cried when I slapped her, but for me that slight sting on my cheeks only has the power to make me laugh even harder.

70

When Joyce, her anger spent, falls to the carpet rubbing her hands, Modesta follows her and hugs her. Maybe Joyce hurt herself like Modesta used to when she hit Carmine on the face and shoulders.

'Did you hurt yourself, Joyce?'

'Oh, I did!'

'Your hands are too delicate for hitting like that.'

'And your head is as hard as marble!'

'The bone structure of us country folk. Heads, hearts and minds as hard as stone. Tuzzu used to say, "Who knows who knocked up your mother?" Your hands are frozen. Let me rub them.'

'Oh, they hurt!'

'I'll be gentle . . . And you? Who knows who knocked up *your* mother?'

'A frigid, elegant mannequin. And to think that abroad all they talk about is the warmth and humanity of the Italians. Compared to my father, any Englishman I met always seemed like a Neapolitan to me.'

'You can never be sure whose child you are, Joyce. Only a mother knows, but in most cases she doesn't say.'

'Oh, I'm sure about me and Renan.'

'And who is Renan?'

'My sister.'

'But wasn't her name . . .? I'm sorry, you called her by another name, or were there three of you?'

'No, please, Modesta! Don't interrogate me, don't interrogate me!'

'I'm not interrogating you, Joyce! It's just that I love you. When you love someone you want to know what they were like ten, twenty years ago. That's all it is, believe me. Oh, Joyce, I've already experienced this moment.'

'What moment?'

'We two, sitting here on the carpet, talking, the light fading into darkness, and . . . you too must have felt that there are certain moments you've already experienced. Haven't you? If only we were able to remember, we could avoid all the mistakes we're compelled to make, because I'm certain these moments we've already experienced are warnings.'

'Ridiculous, Modesta!'

'Maybe . . . So, getting back to your sister . . . did you say her name was Renan? Are you sure about her?'

'Sure about what?'

'Come on, play along . . . Are you sure she was your father's daughter?'

'Yes.'

'And the other one, the one who died in Milan? What was her name? Oh, yes . . . Joland.'

'Yes . . . she was too.'

'My, my, what a respectable family! What a proper mother! Three children with the same man. Of course, times were different! Women had a lot of patience!'

'It's Timur I'm absolutely certain about. He's not my father's son.'

'Timur? You have a brother too?'

'He showed up yesterday.'

'Well, where is he?'

'I sent him away.'

'Why? Why didn't you tell me?'

'Did you tell me that your Mattia had returned? *Brava*, Modesta. You're really gifted at describing people. You could be an excellent writer if you only put your mind to it. He's exactly the way you described him to me.'

'Oh, stop it, Joyce. You have the same talent for omitting things.

How could I tell you about Mattia when all you've done since I woke up is attack me, saying awful things? Or is it Mattia's return that's bothering you?'

'Given that you spent a whole night with him, it seems to me that . . .'

'Oh, Joyce, how stupid I am! Is that what's changed you like this? Mattia's return? Of course I should have told you, but I assure you it slipped my mind. Are you jealous? That would explain your harshness. Oh, if that's the case, all those awful remarks don't mean a thing. I feel relieved. If it's jealousy, it's fitting. I too would be jealous . . . Tell me that's what it is, and I swear that if his presence upsets you, I'll send him away. Hold me, Joyce, hold me!'

'Don't be melodramatic. I can't stand these scenes. No one is asking you to make any sacrifices, and besides . . . let me up, I hurt all over from lying on the floor. It's time to turn on the light. With you, one loses all sense of reality.'

'And what would that reality be?'

'Get up off the floor! Lately all you do is go from acting childish to being sentimental.'

'Answer me, what would that reality be?'

'You know very well. Even Gramsci is dead. We're losing everything. Europe is poised between war and a peace that's more dreadful than any war, and the two of us are here basking in this gilded cage.'

'Excuses, Joyce! Don't hide your jealousy.'

'Jealousy? I'm too old for such nonsense.'

'Since when do you feel so old? Looking at you, you seem ten years younger than when we first met. Oh, no, Joyce, you could have spared yourself using age as an excuse. That's really melodramatic. As you can see, if you love someone, you can't avoid being either sentimental or ridiculous. Or maybe now you're going to tell me that I was the only one who fell into love's inescapable banalities all these years?'

'Oh, enough! I can't take it anymore, staying here helpless while our comrades are rotting in prisons or fighting to the bitter end. Gramsci's death seems to me to be a symbol of our destiny: to rot away! to waste away, impotent! . . . He was crushed in that photograph. Rather than having fallen in battle, he'd rotted away.'

'That I can understand. As I said to you back then: if you regain your strength one day, you can go. Now you're so strong that I would no longer tremble to see you go. But why repudiate all these years that have allowed you to recover your health and your strength?'

'I don't understand.'

'I'll explain it to you. Why didn't you tell me right away that it was time for you to go, instead of accusing me, disowning our years together, blaming yourself? That's ingratitude!'

'In what sense?'

'Yes, ingratitude towards life . . . I have the suspicion – I'm beginning to see you clearly, Joyce – that you're trying to tell yourself that those were lost, shameful years so you can acquire the strength you don't have. You remind me of Franco.'

'And who is he?'

'That friend of Prando who enlisted to go off to the war in Spain. Almost overnight he fabricated a Fascist loyalty so as not to admit that he wanted to get away from home and his mother. And I've seen many others go off like that. Often they enlist to escape poverty, but that's too dishonourable for a man, so they convince themselves it's for an ideal. That's just how it is, soldier Jò! But tell me, who rekindled this sense of duty in you, that brother of yours? What did you say his name was?'

'His name is Timur.'

'Is it this Timur, then, who's changed you so?'

'No, it's Jose.'

'Jose?'

'Yes. Timur brought me an old letter from Jose.'

'Well? Is he calling you back to him?'

'No! He informs me that he left for Spain with the International Brigades* and advises me not to move . . . As if I couldn't act without his protection!'

'And you're leaving with Timur?'

'Not at all! I don't need any male protection!'

'Not like fragile little Modesta, who calls Mattia back to get her some money, right?'

'Exactly! Especially since there was no need to. You knew you could count on the money I still have in Switzerland.'

'Why should I spend your money, Joyce, when someday you might need it? Why shouldn't I try to sell my paintings?'

'But to lower yourself to the point of seeking help from an apolitical individual, a mafioso . . .'

'Mattia is not a mafioso! I accept help from any hand I find to be loyal and strong, be it male or female. If I had wanted to be protected, "like a woman", to use your terms, I would have married him years ago.'

'But you're already married!'

'I told you! He would have done away with my dear Ippolito, may he live to be a hundred! Yours is a false pride that stems directly from a sense of inferiority . . . how can you not see that?'

'Spare me your cut-rate analysis.'

'I learned how to analyse from you. But I realize for the first time that we will never see eye to eye on this. I also realize that the appearance of your brother's ghost has erected a wall between us.'

'He's not a ghost. He's alive and very dangerous. I sent him away, but he'll be back, I know. We're a horrible family, Modesta. I should never have been born. I should never have come here to upset your life!'

Silent tears slide down Joyce's composed face. How had Beatrice managed to go from tears to laughter in the short distance between the chair and the sofa? She'd be huddled up, crying, and suddenly, at some invisible signal, she'd go flying across the carpet to Modesta, smiling. And how could Joyce's indifferent face dissolve into those tears, all the while remaining motionless? The loving feeling returned, always the same and always unpredictable. Except that, when it soared in the joy of the past, it was life itself, but if it brought with it that emptiness, then the time had come. Hadn't Joyce said, 'It's time to turn on the light'? All I could do was take a step back and study her, study that stranger who, consciously or not, had decided to leave, to go alone. I went to meet that little death she had chosen for us, and took her hands. I wouldn't say anything more. A good lawyer knows when it's a lost cause.

'If Timur comes back, Modesta, you mustn't see him. He's dangerous. He's in Taormina with an archaeological expedition led by Himmler.'

'Himmler?'

'He's not my father's son, I told you. He's the son of a man who appeared after my father died – a cousin, my mother said. He came to lunch every day and then stayed to talk with her in the parlour. It was he who supported us. He was very wealthy, one of the biggest bankers in Vienna. He lived in Istanbul because he had weak lungs. When he died, he left everything to Timur, who was six years old at the time. A year later my mother sent Timur to study at an Austrian boarding school. Later, much later, I found out that this "cousin" had wanted to marry her, but my mother refused in order to remain faithful to the memory of my father. Some faithfulness! She did everything she could to pass Timur off to me as my father's son. But one fine day I managed to uncover the truth on my own . . . Our family is horrible! For one thing, Timur, brought up in that boarding school in Austria, is . . . I can't tell you, he's awful!'

'Has he become a Nazi?'

'How could Timur do that?'

'Could he have done otherwise? I shudder for Prando, even though he has us as an example and has our help. Can a boy, a young man, endure always being different from everyone else? And for how long? A few days ago he asked me if he could go to Palermo for the *Littoriali*,* to see what they are. When they took place in Naples he was still too young to be interested in them.'

'And what did you say?'

'I told him to go! God forbid I should stop him from doing something, but I shudder . . . Tell me, so Timur is one of them?'

'He's been summoned by Himmler for a dig, perhaps a pointless one. Himmler insists that at the time of the Siculans . . . but what do I care about Himmler and his excavations! It's Timur I fear. If he comes back, you mustn't see him!'

71

Timur comes toward me in his impeccable suit, studying me calmly. Barely taller than Joyce, he moves in that civilian attire as if he were in uniform.

'I can't thank you enough, Princess, for having accepted my invitation.'

'But you speak Italian . . .'

'My father was Italian, Princess, and I am very fond of our country.'

It's up to him to speak, and I have no intention of losing the advantage. Not a trace of uncertainty or expectancy disturbs the composed elegance of those hands and face during the long silence I impose. The same consistent curve, from the strong chin to the high forehead, separates the unnaturally pale face from the closely cropped black hair. I hadn't been mistaken: even bald, Joyce would have been quite beautiful. The cheeks are marked by scars: rather than random wounds, they seem like precise engravings, carved by the hand of a surgeon-sculptor. Though I am familiar with the ritual known as the *Mensur*,* it's the first time I've seen those marks up close and I start counting them: one, two, three . . . As I count I meet Joyce's gaze, the same dark intensity.

'The manager of this hotel was brilliant and daring to break through the sacred walls of the convent and put in these large windows. And his daring was rewarded. This view is unparalleled! I've noticed that even the most boisterous guests fall silent upon entering this room. The hallowed past of the centuries-old walls captures them and they are absorbed in this silence; hypnotized, I would say, by the rugged, enchanting backdrop that plunges steeply to infinity – look down there – and then rises again to Etna's slopes. If you didn't have the feeling of secure walls behind you, this view would be a chasm. Is that the word? Please, come and sit down. Would you like something?'

'No, thank you, not at the moment.'

'As I was saying, I was born in Berlin, but our father was Italian and my dream is to end my days in our villa in Todi. In boarding school in Austria, my love for Italy was strengthened, as it were, and today I consider Italian to be my mother tongue. Of course, all Germans adore Italy, but for me it's different. As soon as I cross the border and my gaze falls on our land, I am reassured by the treasures of art and culture still concealed or protected – can we say protected? – beneath the olive trees and rolling hills of Umbria and Tuscany. An assurance that grips me with a different force than Goethe's over-used verses. This is what led me to study archaeology. Of course, my sister will not have had occasion to speak to you about my studies and my choices. It's not in her nature. When I was little more than a boy I had to subject her to a real interrogation to find out who her friends at the university were. I knew there were many of them, all intelligent, but that's all I knew, and this distressed me. Unfortunately as a child I was very jealous. I'm not ashamed to say that to you who have housed and protected our Joyce . . . I must confess that I once followed her.'

'You shouldn't be ashamed; all boys are jealous.'

'Do you have children?'

'Yes.'

'Allow me to thank you for what you've done for my sister. Perhaps this gratitude is why, as soon as I saw you, I had the impression that I had always known you.'

'I too had that impression.'

'Well then, as old acquaintances, may I invite you to have lunch with me, or are you in a hurry?'

'I'm not in any hurry.'

'I'm thrilled! Do you prefer the dining room or the terrace?'

'The terrace. As you aptly observed, the silence of these walls and the broad sweep of these windows is hypnotizing . . .'

As we move outdoors, the dark intensity of Timur's eyes abruptly turns into a deep, almost violet blue: the arrogant, piercing blue of the lakes of the north.

'How did we get to talking about Garda? Oh, yes! The sea, the yearning for it! The German people conceal a deep yearning under their apparent rigidity. In boarding school I learned to know them and to recognize the great longing that imbues their stupendous poetry. At times, being of Mediterranean origin, I seemed to detect the source of that longing in the absence of the sea: the sea as freedom, youth, the possibility of adventure. For us, accustomed to touching it, gazing at it, this yearning, even when forced to spend long periods in the northern forests, is never so absolute, so ferocious, so – how shall I put it? – so desperate, that's the word! Just a few more days of this bliss and I must go back to Berlin. I long to be in Berlin even though I know that a small part of this yearning awaits me. I will lap it up ever so slowly while waiting to return.'

'You'll come back here?'

'Oh, no! They only summoned me to get the excavations started. A younger colleague of mine will follow through. Without false modesty, I can say that they considered me wasted on an operation like this.'

'A younger colleague? But you yourself are so young!'

'The strength of the Third Reich lies in its youth.'

'Of course.'

'I see you knew about the excavations. I gather it was my sister who told you.'

'Yes.'

'Then I hope she also gave you the letter . . . But I see from your confusion that she didn't. Forgive me, Princess: taking advantage of a person's kindness to involve her in intimate family matters is insufferably rude. I was hoping that Joyce would have had the good grace to spare us this unpleasant situation. She didn't tell you if she intends to write?'

'She didn't tell me anything.'

The pristine blue of his eyes darkens like the surface of a lake when a storm approaches. I'm not fond of lakes: their fury, contained in such a restricted space, disturbs me. I want to return to the sea. Tuzzu never spoke about lakes, deep pits stirred by perpetually writhing black snakes . . .

'Your expression has changed, Princess, and your sadness seems like a reproach. Forgive me! But it's simply incivility on Joyce's part – believe me – and if it weren't for my mother I would never have come to add my rudeness to that of my sister . . . Since she made up her mind to act that way, I am at least obliged to explain my behaviour to you.

'After my mother discovered her daughter's place of asylum – and it wasn't easy, the poor old woman! – she urged me several times to come and look for Joyce in person, to ask her why she wasn't answering her letters. It's painful for me – the emotionalism of certain situations is painful and having to speak about them even more so – but I must respond to your questioning look. Well, when Signorina Joland committed suicide and Joyce disappeared, my mother had a stroke that left her paralysed from the waist down. If it weren't for that, she would have gone herself. She's not a woman who depends on anyone, not even a son, as evidenced by the fact that in all these years she's only asked me to come and look for Joyce twice, this being the third time. Oh, not to force her to return home, no. You don't know my mother, and it's my duty to present her in a true light. It wasn't a selfish need for her daughter; she has never once asked for an hour of our freedom. This is what angers me. Why not reply to her letters? Why? Over time, because of her forced immobility, my mother has become almost obsessed with thoughts of Joyce. Recently she began to suspect that Joyce was dead, and that we were lying to her out of pity. It's unbearable, terribly unbearable to watch the sad disintegration of that strong, beautiful woman. And so, having been called to Sicily, I couldn't refuse yet again to satisfy her curiosity, even though for me it meant a hopeless sacrifice. I knew that Joyce wouldn't see me. She told me in no uncertain terms that for her I was dead. At the time, that sentence was almost a liberation from her continual rejections of my affection. Trying to understand the reason for her rejection has haunted me for a long time. Maybe because my birth meant that I had replaced Renan, who had died? Or maybe it was an instinctive dislike, which can occur even between siblings? But I soon resigned myself to not having a sister. And for a boy in boarding school, it's sad to lose the sweet image of a sister who at least exists, even though she doesn't write or come to visit . . .

'Well, enough crying about our family! I've told you everything. One is more prone to melancholy after a delicious lunch like this, seated before – may I say so, Princess? – the most beautiful, luminous eyes I've ever seen. Your gaze contains the immense spaces of this vast sky of ours.'

Trained by Joyce's example, my emotions must have learned to remain impassive, since they don't flinch at that unexpected smile, or at the earlier disclosures, or the meticulous scars: systematic brutality marching imperturbably under the sun in the Cineluce newsreels .

'The sun has reached our table, Princess. Shall we move inside for coffee? You will have coffee, I hope? I confess that lunch and dinner for me, when I'm in Italy, are merely a prelude to our incomparable coffee. Or would you prefer that we stay here and have them open the umbrella?'

Joyce's smile, quick to be switched on and off, lingers a bit longer among those scars, following the waiter in a white jacket. With a few deft strokes he creates a circle of green shade around us.

'I confess, Princess, that I never cease to be amazed at our people's grace and style. Sometimes, forgetting an engagement, I've found myself contemplating the spare, ethereal gestures of any one of our policemen directing traffic. It may sound exaggerated, but those movements have always reminded me more of those of a great orchestra conductor than a military man. Similarly, you – it's not indiscretion, believe me, simply admiration that compels me to stare at you like this – you have an ancient, solemn grace, so rare in this era wholly intent on making women sturdy and athletic so that they can keep pace with men in the marches.

'Unfortunately, all progress requires sacrifice! And our Führer, realizing that the value of women has for too long been squandered in the shadows of the confessional, has rightly summoned woman to duty toward our people, awakening her from the erroneous, individu-alistic conviction that her guardian-angel wings should enfold only the limited, if hallowed, sphere of her own family. Hitler has shrewdly recognized the limitation of this mission, until recently imposed on women, and identified it as an attitude opposed to progress and the advancement of our peoples.

'And women have flocked to his summons. The Berlin Olympics were an exciting revelation. Having given up their binding, braided tresses, their newly released heads were worthy of our ancient Dia-nas! Don't be sad, I understand you perfectly. Freeing myself of aes-theticism and frailty was costly to me too, brought up as I was in a depleted, corrupt culture. And I'm not afraid to admit that occasion-ally, during the long process of re-education that I've set myself, in light of the absolute truth of new ideas that are vital and no longer contemplative, I am overcome by nostalgia for a world destined to perish. But I'm able to stifle these faint attacks and get back on the right track of action, which has finally been mapped out! Of what use were we intellectuals, greater or lesser? While we satisfied ourselves with abstract, poetic study, our people continued to rot away in illness and impotence! Without being modest, I, like other young people, am able to glimpse in the Führer's speeches the goal toward which he is urging us: Europe will be one great nation, led by technocrats, by intellectuals finally raised only to serve their State, and not their own sterile narcissism. Who am I? What are fifty or a hundred years to his-tory? Men like us will be swept away, and in our place men and women will grow up whole and strong, strengthened by a single will! If only Joyce had allowed a dialogue to take place between us many years ago! Men like Carl Gustav Jung have put their science at the service of Germany. Russia is willing to coexist with us . . .

'You must forgive this long speech, Princess, inspired only by the cut of your hair, so at odds with your way of moving, with your ancient beauty. Your entire person had misled me . . . It takes time to accurately date a vase, a hand, a mutilated torso. Seeing the absence of long hair that your profile brings to mind, I had thought of – how shall I put it? – a mutilation. But slowly, during this time that you've been kind enough to grant me, I caught in your chin and in your neck a glimpse of the temerity of Artemis Toxotis,* unquestionably intended by the great sculptor that is nature . . . Don't be embarrassed, it's not a compliment, simply the objective opinion of a connoisseur. And though aesthetically I can see the sculptor's intent, psychologically, the fact that you've sacrificed your hair to freedom of movement leads me to delude myself that you are not lost to our cause. We need women like you, like Joyce . . . Joyce, my ungrateful sister!

'Regrettably, even times like this must end, and the dig awaits me. Having met you, I'm more persuaded by Himmler's conviction that a Germanic presence on this island may be deduced from arrows and tools dating back to the Siculans or even earlier. I had my doubts, because when the German spirit falls hopelessly in love with a country or with a face, it doesn't accept the fact that it is not part of its own stock. In this case, Himmler is so taken by this island that he's trying to make his loving dream a reality. But who knows!

'Well, Timur, duty calls . . . The bill, waiter! Unfortunately, Joyce prevents me from accompanying you, Princess, and from . . . seeing you again, but please, on behalf of my mother, try to persuade her to write a few lines, to reassure the woman that her daughter is alive and to make her days of illness less atrocious. Promise me you'll do that?'

'Of course. I'll do everything I can, rest assured.'

'Thank you. I had no doubt that you would understand. Princess, we may not see each other again. But I will preserve your profile in my mind as the most beautiful among the many Greco-Sicilian coins I have studied.* Adieu!'

In the dense greenery of the garden, Timur's voice lingers, sealed with a smile, as black belts tight as corsets flash among the white tablecloths. Occasional pairs of officers halt, waiting patiently. From a distance, their massive boots seem to reduce the graceful orange trees to fragile miniatures.

72

When I got home, I nearly bumped into Joyce at the entrance to the grounds; she was hidden behind the gate, but I did not stop. Only when I reached the door to the parlour did my anxiety ease, comforted by the quiet of the books, the tables, the armchairs. So as not to disturb anyone, I dropped quietly onto the small settee near the French door. Mela, her back to me, engaged the soft pedal and ran her hands silently over the keyboard. Jacopo, ever taller and thinner, was bent over the table, guiding Crispina's little hand on a large sheet of paper covered with marks. Prando, stretched out on the sofa, seemed to be asleep. Through half-closed eyes, he was tracing smoke rings in the air, a cigarette between his fingers. It was the first time I'd seen him smoking. 'Ntoni, sprawled on the carpet, was leafing through a hefty volume. Bambolina, circling the oval table, was checking her masterpiece: cups, pastries, small napkins, and especially the floral centrepiece. Moving closer to straighten one of the flowers, she steps back again to get a better look . . .

Bambù: 'Oh, Zia! Do you like it?'

Modesta: 'Very much.'

Bambù: 'Will you have tea with us?'

Modesta: 'Of course.'

Jacopo: 'Dear Mama, I proclaim that Crispina has an astounding ability to learn, as professor Montaldo would say.'

Bambù: 'Oh, Zia, he made us split our sides laughing with his professor Montaldo. Go on, Jacopo, do it again!'

Jacopo: 'I'm sorry, my dear Bambù, but Paganini doesn't repeat a performance. Am I right, 'Ntoni?'

'Ntoni: 'Right! Never! Encores spoil the audience, and besides, they're so old theatre. Nowadays we tend not to ruin the mood with applause and encores. Just think: at one time Giovanni Grasso* used to perform the main scene of a play such as *La morte civile* as an encore.'

Mela: 'So! Why not? Like at the Opera.'

'Ntoni: 'But it's old theatre, Mela, excuse me for insisting.'

Bambù: 'Old theatre or not, Jacopo must do his imitation of his professor for his mother . . . what did he used to tell you, Jacopo?'

Jacopo: '. . . Astounding, young Brandiforti! Your ability to learn, undoubtedly related to your unusual height, is astounding. If I were not aware of your tender age, for obvious reasons, I would be led to believe that you are a wise old man masquerading as a child.'

Bambù: 'That was in June. If you continue growing like that, by October he, too, will have to raise his eyes to look you in the face.'

Jacopo: 'In the face? The impropriety of your language is astounding, my gentle little lass! "Face" is almost as vulgar as saying "snout"! "Countenance" is what you should have said, by gum, by golly! Besides it's not true, Bambù, you can't alarm me like that, you little Satan! You can't just toss out such an insinuation between a pastry and a smile. Or have I really grown? Oh dear God! I see the carpet as if from an airplane. Prando, get up! There, look at Prando, Bambù. He's even taller than me.'

Bambù: 'For another three weeks, maybe. But afterwards, so much for Prando's supremacy. Prando will have to pass it on to you. Look at him. Why are you stooping like that? I like tall people.'

Jacopo: 'Give me another cup of tea. You've ruined my afternoon! I'm not all that eager to grow, Bambù. It's so nice being here with all of you. Sometimes I dream that someone measures me in the headmaster's anteroom, of all places, and then orders me to leave you and this house!'

Prando: 'You dream too much, Jacopo!'

Jacopo: 'And to make matters worse, I cry in the dream.'

Prando: 'So then, Joyce is right! Or has she influenced you with her talk? I don't believe this stuff about dreams.'

Jacopo: 'I do, though. When she told me, I realized that it was true, and that my habit of stooping is a sign that I don't want to grow.'

Prando: 'Baloney! It's that you're lazy.'

Jacopo: 'And yet I try to make an effort and stand up straight. Still, you can't avoid growing up and then getting old and then . . . Just thinking about it, for me at least . . . well, I'm afraid of growing up because I'm afraid of dying.'

Prando: 'Now that I think of it, I was afraid of growing up too at your age, but I didn't dream about it. It was a waking fear, what with all the talk about pointless wars. I was afraid I'd be sent off in uniform to some faraway place, to shoot at boys like me.'

'Ntoni: 'You too, Prando? That's incredible! I, on the other hand, have always been impatient to grow up. Even now, I can't wait to turn twenty.'

Prando: 'No offence, 'Ntoni, but you are oblivious like all artists. Look at Mela. As soon as you talk about real things, her eyes start tracing musical motifs.'

Mela: 'That's not true, I was listening . . .'

Prando: 'Just look how pretty our Mela has become, hasn't she, Bambù?'

'Ntoni: 'Oh, stop it, Prando, you can't just call me oblivious like that! Ingratitude, that's all you get from the world! And to think that I chose you as a model of fearlessness.'

Prando: 'And you were mistaken, my dear 'Ntoni, because even today, subconsciously, as Joyce says, that fear has remained with me. Andrea made me aware of it.'

Bambù: 'What did that killjoy make you aware of?'

Prando: 'Here comes our Bambolina to the attack! I could tell you wouldn't like him, which is exactly why I never let him come here. Besides, the one time he came, he was disappointed.'

Bambù: 'Disappointed in what? Tell us. Disappointed in me?'

Prando: 'Don't worry, it wasn't you. Who can escape your allure? He told me man to man that when I'm here with all of you, I become dull-witted, that I talk and act like a spoiled brat. That's what.'

Bambù: 'Don't you see I'm right? See how obnoxious your Andrea is and how he causes trouble wherever he goes? He's a sour, crabby old man! Why on earth do you hang around with friends who are so much older than you?'

Prando: 'I see from your reaction that Andrea is right when he says that it was the sensible side of my nature that made me look for something outside of this house, to get away from your stultifying effect. There's no way a person can grow in this house, by God!'

Bambù: 'Andrea is not right! You insult us by submitting to him in a way that disappoints me, Prando. Your Andrea is nothing but an envious, loathsome character. That's what he is!'

Prando: 'He's not loathsome! It's just that to you – and lucky you! if you can preserve this quality – anything serious is loathsome! I'm not criticizing you. I like you that way, and you cheer us up in these dark times. But you should be careful not to make superficial judgements, because if you judge Andrea that way, you also implicate me in your judgement. It's hard to be twenty years old nowadays, Bambolina!'

Bambù: 'You're not twenty.'

Prando: 'Seventeen; it's the same thing! You're making me lose my patience, Bambù, Judas Priest! And whereas I, and you Jacopo, and you, 'Ntoni, have had the benefit of being surrounded by anti-fascists, all Andrea, Fausto and Ardito have had is the prospect of being *balillas** at age five, Fascists at ten and extreme Fascists at seventeen. Yet despite this, through their own efforts, paid for at their own expense, against their families and their schooling, they began to doubt, and from that doubt just a few months ago at the *Littoriali* in Naples they progressed to opposition. Do you know what their motto is for next year's *Littoriali* here in Palermo? "Antiracist, anti-German". And do you know what it means to think and act accordingly for students who are poor or nearly so, who have no protection? They returned from Naples excited just by having met a few other young people like themselves. That's why I decided to ask Mama to allow me to take part in the Palermo *Littoriali*, though I know she's against it.'

Bambù: 'But you'll have to wear the uniform and get a party membership card!'

Prando: 'Oh, enough of this blackmail, Bambù! You too, Mama, stop it!'

Modesta: 'Stop what, Prando?'

Prando: 'Stop pressuring me with those misgivings that cause you older people to watch our every move. You heap on us the qualms you should only apply to your failed past! You failed to oppose Fascism, and now you fear for us only because you judge us by your impotence at that time. And though I didn't intend to make a speech – I swear I didn't but here we are – I'll tell you right now that even if it means getting a card and wearing the uniform, I'm going to Palermo. I want to meet this Trombadori, this Melograni* whom Andrea can't stop talking about. And he's right. The time is past to fight outside the party, targeted like rats and thrown in jail . . . they arrest them by the hundreds, by the hundreds! It's from inside, from within the very structures of Fascism that we must fight!'

He slammed his fist on the table. Crispina jumped, unsure whether to laugh or cry. Her wide-eyed gaze flies from Prando to Jacopo.

Jacopo: 'Don't be scared, Crispina. They're just talking. Come here to your uncle's arms and let's see how the discussion will end.'

Bambù: 'Really, Prando, you frightened her banging your fists on the table like that.'

Mela: 'She doesn't look scared at all. I was more frightened, in the early days.'

Bambù: 'But you were big. Crispina is little.He shouldn't do that!'

Jacopo: 'But he should, right, Crispina? He should; your uncle Jacopo says it's right. In fact, you listen to them argue now, and later you, too, will be good at debating and answering back.'

Mela: 'That's so true, Jacopo! I've made a lot of progress since I left the orphanage, but even today . . . Now I know what I want to say but it won't come out. I can't say what I'm thinking quickly enough in the moment. Afterwards the answer may come to me in bed, but it's too late.'

Jacopo: 'Well, my dear musician! I fear that in addition to a lack of practice in the past, this also depends – and quite a bit, I would say – on your scant proclivity for grammar.'

Mela: 'There, you see, Bambù? Even now you would be able to respond to Jacopo in kind, whereas I get agitated, I feel offended and . . . and I can't find the words to toss the ball back, as he says.'

Jacopo: 'But you have music, *signorina*, music! The sublime art of sound, a universal language. You will be understood by everyone.'

Mela: 'Yes, and meanwhile you tease me and I stand here like a fool.'

Jacopo: 'You can't have everything, my dear! Come, Crispina, it's getting dark and your papa must already be worried sick about you. Oh Mama, it's incredible how Pietro frets about his daughter. The power of fatherhood! Crispina, my sweet, I'm very fond of you, but your uncle will never fall prey to those paternal anxieties that can overcome even a tried and true giant like your father. Shall I turn on the light for you, *carusi?*'

Bambù: 'Oh, no, thank you. It's lovely to follow these shadows ever so slowly until they darken, isn't it, Prando?'

Prando: 'Very lovely, my dear Bambuccia, especially knowing, as we now do, that a man's whim can wrest away our peace and quiet and our sunsets with a flick of the hand.'

Should I stop here in the peacefulness that Prando's voice suggests at sunset? Rest content with being called old, a clear sign of having given life and, with life, rebellion? He doesn't know the joy his resolve has brought me. But Prando can't be satisfied to hear the voice that whispers inside me: 'He's one of us.' His young life needs to rage in order to grow. And even today, remembering it, I have no right to leave that room and close my eyes on that difficult day. Even though I'm very sleepy, I must remain there . . .

Prando: 'And do you know who empowered the hand that with one decree can sweep away years of gains?'

Bambù: 'Capitalism, dear cousin; England, France, we know.'

Prando: 'You know, do you, Bambolina! Of course, but also the sectarianism of your communists. For a year now, my eyes have been opened; insane sectarianism that drove the socialists and all the democratic forces into the arms of Fascism.'

Bambù: 'If your eyes were opened by listening to Andrea, you could also have listened to Daniel, it seems to me.'

Prando: 'That ridiculous half French and half Italian intellectual?'

Bambù: 'Lenin, too, was an intellectual, and so is your Andrea. You're contradicting yourself, Prando.'

Prando: 'But Andrea is the son of labourers, and the only thing your Daniel's mouth is full of is his Rosselli and wails and tears over the international committee's mistakes. They were convinced that capitalism was at an end, given the economic crisis. They thought the revolution was around the corner, etc., etc. Meanwhile, the anti-fascist forces were scattered, divided. Easy to mourn the dead, Bambù!'

Bambù: 'I'm not mourning the dead – not even my father, and you know it. Now it's you who are making me angry. If mistakes were made, they can be put right. That's what Daniel used to say. And it seems to me he also showed us a different course, didn't he? You're the one who keeps rehashing and snivelling about the past now.'

Prando: 'I'm not snivelling, but I don't want to forget the mistakes and then repeat them. Plus, if you really want to know, nowadays it's not as easy as your Daniel thinks, coming here for a week, chic and elegant from Paris, to recommend an about-turn. As if it were a trick by the magician Bustelli! Talk to the communists here in Italy, and you'll see how easy it is to make them budge from the sectarianism they've been locked in for years! As soon as you mention the socialists to Lentini, to Carlentini, you'll see one spit, and the other blow his nose. You'll say: those people are peasants, okay. But let's take Joyce, your Joyce I mean – and to think I adored her! What does she do? I bring her young men ready and eager to learn, and she wrinkles her nose: a liberal! a republican! As if there were a vast meadow full of flowers from which to choose! Here we need everybody, everybody, not for the long-awaited chimera of the revolution, but to survive. You and your Joyce, dear Mama, talk a lot about Fascism, but you too are Fascists! The same fanaticism, the same stentorian speeches.'

Jacopo: 'Oh, you're at it again? Fine. But it's so dark! Shall I turn on the light, Bambù?'

Prando: 'Yes, turn it on, Jacopo. That's better.'

Jacopo: 'Sorry, but sunsets make me feel terribly melancholy. Oh, Mela's fallen asleep! And you, 'Ntoni? Why such a gloomy face?'

'Ntoni: 'It's just that . . . well! I'm afraid Prando is right. Only it upsets me to hear him call his mother a Fascist, and so help me God, Prando, I'd beat you up if it weren't a Fascist thing to do.'

Prando: 'Don't get excited, 'Ntoni. Besides, as you can see, my mother is unfazed by what she surely considers childish prattle.'

Modesta: 'Will you stop making those oblique remarks?'

Prando: 'Like what, Mama?'

Modesta: 'Number one! You know I've always let you talk without interfering.'

Prando: 'And?'

Modesta: 'Number two! A number of things have been said this afternoon that until now had been left unspoken, and it seemed appropriate for me to understand before responding.'

Prando: 'So, now why don't you tell us what you think?'

Modesta: 'Because I sense that you are determined not to believe me, Prando. But let's see: do you believe me if I tell you that I agree with you?'

Prando: 'Oh, sure! So you say! When I asked your permission to take part in the *Littoriali* you put on a face . . .'

Modesta: 'Because I didn't know the motivation driving you to it.'

Prando: 'You see? You doubted me!'

Modesta: 'I didn't doubt you. I was afraid; there's a difference.'

Prando: 'You, afraid? That's a good one!'

Modesta: 'Afraid, yes. The *Littoriali* are the breeding ground for the Fascist hounds, aren't they? How was I to know why you wanted to go if you didn't tell me?'

Prando: 'You should have had confidence in me!'

Modesta: 'You're demanding an act of faith that I don't have in anyone, not even in myself.'

Prando: 'But from the look of things you have it in your friend Joyce. Would you like a cigarette, Mama? You're very tense . . .'

Modesta: 'I don't care for cigarettes. You know that.'

Prando: 'I don't know. She smokes a lot and I thought . . .'

Modesta: 'Prando, I'm willing to answer you only if you speak clearly.'

Prando: 'Maybe this is not the time or place.'

Modesta: 'But it is! You're no longer a child, and I must remind you, and everyone else for that matter, that in this house we don't invade anyone's privacy. Did I ever enter your room without knocking?'

Prando: 'No.'

Modesta: 'Have I ever opened a letter addressed to you or Bambolina?'

Prando: 'Never.'

Modesta: 'Then I forbid you to trespass into the personal space that is due to me just as it is to 'Ntoni, Bambolina, Mela and Jacopo. Oh no! Don't turn red like that, Prando. You're a man – or would you prefer that I still call you "my baby boy"? I don't think so. So know this – all of you as well – that just as I did not put up with older people's intimidation when I was your age, now that I'm old, compared to you, I have no intention of being bullied by the young!'

Prando: 'I'm not bullying you, Mama.'

Modesta: 'Oh yes you are. Because of your youth and the fact that I am your mother, you're telling me that I should devote myself to you and only you! With your insinuation about smoking, you're asking me to choose between you and Joyce, and I reject your intimidation. I'm telling you that I am neither your property nor hers, just as you yourself are not the absolute property of Modesta. If we can love each other dispassionately, let's love each other, but if this tension – more typical of property owners – continues to worsen, I advise you to go away for a while and think about it. You were right when you said you needed more adult companions, and the *Littoriali* may be just the opportunity. You can get an apartment in Palermo starting next month, if you wish. No, let me finish. You talked all afternoon. Now it's my turn, and don't think I enjoy it. All lengthy cohabitations create tensions, and there are no blood bonds or other foolish ties that can resolve them. Fortunately we are not poor, and we can afford the cure for each of us. Tomorrow I'll telephone Attorney Santangelo so he can open an account for you in Palermo. You're always dreaming about Palermo, aren't you? Get some fresh air, Prando, and bring us good news when you return.'

*

As I leave the parlour I catch a glimpse of Joyce's face. Or is it Timur's, that gaze deep as a well, which for a moment observes the children's silence over my shoulder? My arms and legs feel heavy, but even in the dark I know the way that leads to sleep. Maybe dying is nothing more than a somewhat longer sleep, a relief that is finally never-ending . . . I barely have time to collapse on the bed before Prando's voice yells from behind the door.

'If you don't open up I'll kill myself, Mama, I'll kill myself!'

He comes toward me, tall, taller than in the parlour. Or is it the small room that makes him seem taller than Carmine?

'You want to sleep after throwing me out like that? I'll kill you, or I'll throw myself out the window to keep from tearing you to pieces!'

At the window I grab him by the arms, he's not serious . . . I just have to hold him back, without using force, and he stops and rests his head against the window pane. He's crying now, only a slight shaking of his strong shoulders, the silent weeping of an adult male. Are men unable to cry, or have they been forbidden to do so? Is it perhaps this prohibition that nurtures in them the insensitive arrogance of a master, the hostile look he gives me as soon as he is reassured by my tender gesture? Those tears, held back with some effort, are not those of a mistreated child, but the tears of a rejected man, the same look Mattia had: *'You don't love me, Modesta!'* Without taking my hands off his shoulders, I reach out and stroke the skin on his neck, as pebble-smooth as Mattia's was.

'I'm not the one who threw you out, Prando; you know that. It's you who are clearly tired of being among snot-nosed brats and old people. That's what you said.'

'You're not old! It's those appalling words that made me say I wanted to die. You're the most beautiful, Mama, the most beautiful! Even Andrea says so . . . I don't know, I don't know what came over me. Sometimes I think I hate you, at other times I can't stand not seeing you. A cursed breed, we Brandiforti, cursed! I have it in for everyone. I'll become an imbecile like my father!'

'Your father is not an imbecile. It was his illness that made him the way he is. You're not ill, are you? Or has something happened to make you afraid?'

'No, nothing, Judas Priest! I watch carefully. What do you think, that I'm crazy? But what's wrong with me then, what's wrong with me?'

'I'll tell you what's wrong.'

'What is it, Mama?'

'It's that we two love each other too much and we're too much alike.'

'You think so? Now that you're holding me in your arms I feel that's true.'

'It's true, Prando. Doesn't everyone tell you that you're the spitting image of me when you smile?'

'Oh, hold me, Mama!'

'See how alike we are, Prando? First we shout and call each other names and now I don't remember a thing, do you?'

'It's true, it's all forgotten . . . even as a child I was like that.'

'Do you remember what you always told me as a child, when you discovered that Papa was too ill to live with us? You always said: "Don't be sad, Mama, I'll marry you when I grow up."'

'It's true, now I remember. First I thought I'd dreamt it . . .'

'I would marry you, too, Prando, if you weren't my son.'

'You'd marry me? Go on! You don't think much of me at all.'

'Are we starting in again?'

'But do you really think well of me? Look me in the eye and repeat it.'

'I think the world of you, Prando, but you have to go to Palermo and spend some time on your own, look around a little. Did you know that the girls in Palermo are very beautiful?'

'That's what Andrea says, but you . . . how come you notice these things?'

'It's because I too am a little bit like a man, Prando! What do you think?'

'Certainly when you act like you did earlier, you're really a terror. You should have seen!'

'What?'

'I have to laugh.'

'Why?'

'When you walked out, 'Ntoni gestured for us to applaud.'

'You're kidding!'

'Then he said that you would have made a great actress. And I punched him, poor 'Ntoni! But I immediately apologized and I put a steak on his eye and spoke to him a bit, and . . . I feel very sleepy, Mama, why? Can I sleep here with you for a while?'

From the way his head grew heavy on my breast I realized that mentally at least he had possessed me. But I was burning all over. Who knows how much I had wanted him without knowing it!

73

Power of the imagination. As ugly as I had felt at hearing the word "old", that's how beautiful I now felt soaking in cool bath water, with Prando sleeping in the next room: beautiful and content, like a little bride in a romance novel, on her honeymoon . . . After her wedding, Beatrice became more beautiful and proud each day . . . I did not enjoy this serene bliss for long. I just had time to get out of the bathtub when Prando's voice reached me, upset.

'Hey, Mama! Where are you?'

'I'm right here.'

'What happened?'

'You fell asleep.'

'No! Tell me, how can that be?'

'It's because you're like me. First you get angry and shout, then you fall asleep. Can you imagine Jacopo falling asleep after arguing with Bambù?'

'Not a chance! He goes on and on every time! Last week, after that quarrel with Bambolina, he pestered me for three days. He gets fixated on something and that's that!'

'To us they seem like fixations, Prando, but it's just that he's different.'

'That's for sure! How long did I sleep?'

'Not long.'

'And what did you do?'

'I took a bath.'

'Was it you who put this blanket over me?'

'Of course, first I covered you and then . . .'

'You took a bath . . . What a lovely dress! It's been a long time since you've worn it. It's my favourite.'

'I know.'

'Why did you get all dressed up like that? Did you get all dressed up because of that Tudia who's coming to dinner?'

'Not again, Prando!'

'Why have you started seeing him?'

'It's business, like with Attorney Santangelo and the others; you know that.'

'Yes, but that Tudia isn't an old man and the way he looks at you incenses me. I'm all sweaty, look! Will you let me take a shower in your bathroom? This nap has left me feeling so lazy . . . I'd like to stay here even longer, but I'm hungry. What should I do, Mama? Take a shower or a bath?'

'Whichever you like.'

'If I take a bath, will you wash my back?'

How long had it been? It seemed like yesterday that Prando could have drowned in the bathtub as easily as in a lake, and Modesta had to be careful back then, very careful . . . Now his feet, big as a statue's, toy with the chain of the stopper.

'I'm famished! Who's cooking tonight?'

'Jacopo and 'Ntoni. I think it's their turn.'

'Oh God, no! Who knows what revolting stuff they'll make!'

'The last time it wasn't all that bad.'

'Why on earth don't they follow Stella's instructions? I'm hopeless at it too, but I stick to Stella's advice. Oh, Mama, did you know that last week at Andrea's I was a big success with the roast? There were ten of us, and afterwards Andrea wanted to learn how to make it. He too, a communist! Whereas before, he couldn't even make himself a couple of fried eggs.'

'That's the fault of mothers who make a mystery out of cooking and spoil their sons with their gastronomical delicacies. It took me a long time to learn too. There was no way to get Argentovivo and your aunt Beatrice out of their kitchen.'

'You're so beautiful, Mama! I'll bet you don't feel like eating 'Ntoni and Jacopo's attempts either.'

''Ntoni doesn't do too badly in the kitchen.'

'That may be, but tell the truth, you don't feel like it either, right?'

'Not in the least.'

'So listen: if you give me some cash – I'm broke, that thing isn't a motorcycle, it's a black hole that eats all your money – if you give me some cash, I'll take you to dinner in a new restaurant at La Plaia. I like it when we walk in and everyone turns around to look at us. If you give me the money, I'll make a big impression and you'll eat well.'

'Well, I might just do that. I'm starving!'

'Wonderful! Let's go . . . How light you are, Mama. How much do you weigh?'

'How should I know!'

'A feather!'

'It's you, you're so strong! Go on, put me down. You're making me dizzy.'

'I have a feather for a mother, I swear to God!'

'It must be hunger. Let's go. Put me down, Prando! You're hungry too, aren't you? Go and tell Stella, then off we go to La Plaia, as this giant commands!'

'What if we don't tell anyone and just run off?'

'That would be fun, but we can't. You know that.'

'Oh, all right, I'll go tell Stella, but you wait for me in the car without letting anyone see you. That way we can at least pretend we're running off . . .'

Power of the imagination. I actually felt like I was fleeing in the night beside that silent young man who was focused solely on his driving – just as Carmine paid attention only to Orlando's muscles – careful to shift gears smoothly so as not to alarm his beast or interfere with its running. '*An engine is a living organism, strong and delicate. Jacopo, find someone else to teach you how to drive. You lack the touch for living things. It's excruciating every time you shift gears, Judas Priest!*'

The familiar silence conveys a placid, protective power. Though raised near the sea, that young man had retained the solemn silence of the rural interior. He won't say another word until he reaches the end of his journey.

'Here we are, Mama. Just think, it took us exactly twenty minutes! What a fine lady you are in that dress. I wish you would wear it always.'

'Always gets boring, Prando.'

'I like the familiar better than the new.'

'And yet this place is new.'

'Well, since I know how much the lady likes new things, I made an effort. Do you like it?'

'It's magnificent! What a long promenade . . . it looks like a ship!'

'They tried to place the Rotunda as far out to sea as possible. We'll dine on the Rotunda, all right? You won't feel cold out on the terrace? If you're cold, tell me, and I'll give you my jacket.'

I'm not cold, but the desire to feel his arms around my shoulders makes me say, 'It is a little windy out here.'

'I knew it. Women are always like that. In order to look beautiful, they don't cover up enough and then . . . but I like it. What's wrong, Mama? You look sad.'

Right beside us, a cascade of wavy black hair caresses a young man's face. For the moment Prando doesn't look at her, but soon enough his jacket will cover those slender shoulders, barely skimmed by silk as dark and soft as this night. I'm jealous. I look up and stare into his eyes: a new jealousy, a mother's jealousy that makes me hate his youth.

'What is it, Mama? Why aren't you eating?'

'Of course I'm eating, Prando. It's just that I'm jealous.'

'You, jealous? What are you saying? Jealous of whom?'

'Of all the girls whose shoulders you'll cover with your jacket. And I want to tell you what I discovered tonight. To warn you against me, man to man or woman to man, if you prefer.'

'What did you discover?'

'That what we call a mother's jealousy exists, and it's best to recognize it.'

'What do you mean?'

'Nothing . . . I'm warning you that I will likely always be jealous of any woman you may fall in love with.'

'What are you thinking? I have no intention . . .'

'Oh, no, Prando, don't try to hedge! We decided many years ago that we would be different from all those families who pretend to love each other while instead, all they do is oppress one another.'

'Yes, of course! And as you know, I've tried to understand you. I even agreed to respect Bambolina . . . What's come over you? Don't tell me I did something wrong and you want to slap me once or twice like you did that time?'

'No! That time I slapped you because you demanded that Bambolina wait on you like a servant, and you didn't want her speaking with your friends. Why did you act like that, Prando? You're grown now. Why?'

'Oh, fine! First, because all my friends acted that way, and it seemed right. And then, because I was jealous.'

'Well, I'll give myself a couple of slaps now that I see that, even in me, the tendency to act like all the other mothers we know is so strong that . . . It must be remedied, and you've got to help me.'

'But to tell you the truth, I like the fact that you're jealous.'

'But I don't! And you have to help me.'

'Oh, great. How?'

'You're laughing, are you, Prando?'

'Well sure. I didn't expect to hear something like that from you.'

'I didn't expect it either.'

'So what do we do, Mama?'

'Nothing! Your laughter made my appetite return . . . Oh, the spaghetti got cold!'

'Mine too. Should we have them make it again?'

'Of course! Are you kidding?'

'You're so adorable!'

'Yes, but full of flaws, Prando. Me too, like all mothers. I want you to be aware of my defects, so you can guard against me in the future.'

'You devil! You know that just talking like that makes my esteem for you grow, so that other women seem silly to me, including Bambù.'

'I have no remedy for that. It's a price one must pay. I, too, having known a man like Carlo, found it hard to replace him. But that's your problem! I warned you, and forewarned is forearmed. Oh, the spaghetti. Finally!'

*

'I'm not cold anymore. It must have been hunger. Take back your jacket, Prando.'

'Are you jealous with Jacopo?'

'No! Even with you, when you were little, I didn't mind if Stella held you, or your aunt Beatrice. Do you remember Beatrice?'

'Yes, plus there are the photographs. But she was prettier than in the photos, wasn't she? I remember her fine blond hair . . .'

'You were always pulling her hair . . . But I don't think I'll ever be jealous with Jacopo, even when he's older.'

'And how do you explain that?'

'Who can understand these things! The tide has risen; do you hear it? It's slamming against the pilings.'

'Think how nice it would be, Mama, if the Rotunda were magically to break loose from the sand and the sea carried us off.'

'So many bathing establishments, Prando! When you were a child there were only five or six of them.'

'Really? Oh, what's happening!'

A hundred voices clamour in the darkness that has suddenly fallen on the white tablecloth.

'A power failure, *signora*. It's not our fault! Look, the lights are out all along the coast. I'll see to it right away. We'll bring candles.'

In a flash, a hundred tenuous flames on the tables turn the earlier joy into an agony of waiting.

'It's never happened before, captain, I apologize. The bill, of course, right away!'

'*Danke schön.*'

'A German officer, Mama. I hadn't noticed him.'

'I hadn't either.'

'Do you remember the Great War, Mama?'

'Very little, Prando. I was buried in a convent at that time.'

'What is war like? How does it start? Sometimes I find myself wishing that war would break out.'

'Because you're young, and youth craves adventure.'

'Maybe.'

'Do you remember that as a child you wanted to be a pirate, and then an explorer? Learn to question your feelings. War is not an adventure. Adventure is something an individual chooses, not something you're forced to do.'

'They say that if war breaks out everything will be destroyed. They say the Germans have new, very powerful weapons.'

'Remember Daniel? He told us that entire villages were destroyed by aircraft in Spain.'

'Yes, but he's a timorous soul! I've heard different stories about the war in Abyssinia, for example . . .'

'From the Fascists, Prando. Don't trust them. I'm certain that one day, which perhaps neither you nor I will ever see, war will be seen as an abomination.'

'But your side also talks about war.'

'About revolution; that's different! Revolution means legitimate self-defence against those who abuse you with the weapons of hunger and ignorance. How long we've talked, Prando! Please, ask for the bill and let's go home. The lights haven't come back on and I have the feeling this darkness may last for ever. Let's go home.'

'Of course, Mama. The bill, please, waiter! . . . What is it, Mama? You're shivering. Are you cold?'

'No, I'll be frank with you, Prando. Your desire for adventure upset me. Buy the car you wanted and go back to competing with males like you, or leave for America . . . Steal . . . in short, do whatever you want! As long as it comes from you and is not by order of the King, the Duce or the Führer! To want war is certainly to lead the future toward disaster, and not just your own future. Can't you see that? This is the last time I'll try to make myself understood by you and arrogant males like you. You don't belong either to the State or to me, and don't kid yourself that I'm giving orders. By God! What do I have to do to make you see that many of the things you want are instilled in you from above in order to use you? I understand that it's hard for someone poor who has to satisfy his hunger and learn to read before he can know who he is and what he wants. But you? You have food on the table and books. There's no excuse for you. You're responsible for yourself and for those whom you may drag with you tomorrow. Now, why are you just sitting there with the engine running? Can we please go home? I'm sleepy!'

74

The lights of Villa Suvarita appear through the rippling pine trees like those of a festive vessel. The gate is wide open, the dogs, silent, are circling around an ambulance. Prando brakes, pulling over to the shoulder of the drive, which is flooded with brightness; the rapid banging of doors is followed by the metallic shriek of a siren.

The door too is wide open, as if for a party. In the empty parlour, five figures wander about, spread here and there. Only Mela and Bambù hug each other tight, huddled on the red velvet sofa. On the armchairs are masks, wigs, a black silk cape, like at Carnival time.

Stella: 'Oh, Mody, finally! Pietro looked everywhere for you!'

Modesta: 'Yes, all right, but what happened?'

Jacopo: 'We were playing theatre, Mama, after dinner . . .'

Modesta: 'And . . .?'

Stella: 'I had brought tea and biscuits up to the *signora* . . . there are many times when she doesn't come down to dinner – I didn't think . . .'

Modesta: 'But what happened? Hush, Stella, let Jacopo talk! He seems to be the only one who hasn't lost his head.'

Jacopo: 'Around eleven o'clock Bambolina went up to Joyce – she needed her cape for a routine – and she found the door ajar and the bedside light on. She knocked at the bathroom door, but there was no answer. Then she noticed that there was water running out from under the door, and . . . she's still shaking over there, poor Bambù! Fortunately

Mattia was here! We had to, or rather he had to shoot the lock open and
. . . it's awful! There was so much blood, Mama! 'Ntoni fainted.'

Modesta: 'And where is Mattia now?'

Jacopo: 'He went with the ambulance. Mattia offered to give blood
for the transfusion. Oh, Mama, let's hope they can save her! The thing
that scared me the most is that Bambù came screaming down the
stairs, holding Joyce's cape tightly in her arms. Why?'

Bambù: 'I told you, Jacopo, the cape was on a chair, so I picked it
up. I had it in my hand when I noticed . . .'

Jacopo: 'But why were you holding it so tight?'

Bambù: 'How frightening, Zia, when I think that I might not have
suspected anything! Luckily I felt the carpet all squelchy under my
feet and I knocked on the door. Oh, Mela, how horrible! I don't want
Joyce to die, Mela, I don't want her to!'

Prando: 'Sit down, Mama, you're pale as a ghost. Sit down! Do you
want me to go to the hospital?'

Modesta: 'No.'

Bambù: 'Even Antonio said to stay here, because if she dies they'll
have to bring her here, on account of the Fascists. He said it softly to
Mattia, but I heard him. Oh, Prando, hold me! Where on earth were
you? Pietro has been looking for you in the restaurants for two hours.
Where were you?'

Prando: 'Well, a fine idea I had! A new restaurant.'

Jacopo: 'Such silence, Mama! I can't stand it anymore.'

Stella: 'The silence of summer's end, Jacopo. It happens every hundred years.'

Bambù: 'What happens every hundred years, Stella?'

Stella: 'This silence! During the day we move around and we don't
hear it, but it's there! And at night it takes over everything. Many years
ago, we waited until December.'

Bambù: 'Waited for what, Stella?'

Stella: 'Water from the sky, my Bambuccia! After months and
months of heat, the mouths of the rivers and streams become silent,
waiting for water. But last night around three, from the window, I saw
the first dry lightning on the horizon. It's a good sign.'

Jacopo: 'You were at the window at three in the morning, Stella?'

Stella: 'I like the night. Night reveals so many things.'

Jacopo: 'I can't take it anymore, Mama. Say something!'

Every hundred years . . . it's been a hundred years since the serpent of silence slithered around this house as Carlo fought for his life. A supple, powerful slithering around the walls, which fall silent, mesmerized by the serpents' coils, staring at its scales . . .

Jacopo: 'A car, Mama, a car!'

Bambù: 'That's impossible; the dogs didn't bark.'

Stella: 'But Nunzio is at the gate. He must have quieted them. Let's go see.'

Stella was right. As soon as we step outside, big drops, furious, like long-withheld tears, strike our foreheads, our cheeks. From the car door, Mattia hands Pietro a small bundle.

Jacopo: 'She's alive, Mama. Mattia is smiling!'

★

The bandaged hands on the white sheet have no feeling, nor do they convey emotion: repulsive relics on the silver tray kept in the blessed reliquary. What sculptor bent his talent to portray that lifeless, hopeless sorrow?

'Forgive me, Modesta. All I wanted was to die.'

'I know.'

'Why didn't you all let me die?'

'Fate, Joyce. I wasn't here. Bambolina came up by chance and Mattia broke down the door.'

'Mattia? And me, naked in the tub? How shameful! I disgust you, Modesta, I know.'

'No, I just feel a sense of helplessness and a great deal of affection.'

'When did they bring me back?'

'Tonight, around three or four, I don't recall. I remember it had started to rain, fortunately. Look how it's coming down! Stella says it's a blessing.'

'Oh, Stella! I treated her badly too.'

'Stella understands. She was just worried because you wouldn't drink the broth.'

'Really?'

'Yes, and if we can manage to send this cup back down empty, Stella will no longer remember your incivility. You'll see.'

'"Incivility"! How strange your language is.'

'So then, shall we drink this cup of broth to absolve your incivility?'

'Oh, yes, I'm so thirsty!'

Spoonful by spoonful, through cracked lips, morning after morning, until that sunny afternoon following a week of rain when Joyce, sitting beside the window, is able to bring the cup of tea to her healed lips with her own hands.

'Prando came to say goodbye to me as if he were leaving for America. He's changed a lot, he's no longer a boy, but he seemed at peace.'

'He'll have a house of his own, with his own key. He has to be free to come and go, to do as he pleases.'

'And 'Ntoni? I haven't seen him in days.'

'Well, a lot has happened! Angelo Musco's death upset his plan to escape, and now he's studying like mad because he found out that there's an acting school in Rome. Have you heard of it?'

'No, I've never been too involved with theatre.'

'Well, it doesn't matter. The important thing is that he might be able to be admitted to the courses by taking an exam, even though he's so young. And if he's good, he might even get a scholarship.'

'When will he take the exams?'

'Next month.'

'In Rome . . . And the two of us, Modesta?'

'What about us, Joyce?'

'I'm talking, asking questions, but without real interest. It's awful. It's as if I were dead and buried in your garden, as you used to say jokingly. If only I had died that morning when you almost ran into me at the gate! I thought you were returning from your usual lunch with Attorney Santangelo and . . .'

'And instead?'

'I realized that you'd seen Timur. Am I right?'

'Yes. I would have told you.'

'Oh, go, get out of here! It's as if you've killed me. I hate you all, go away!'

'And here I was hoping that, now that you're better, I could tell you about a great joy I've had.'

'What joy?'

'Prando is not a Fascist! He finally spoke to me, and if a young man like him was able to make it with our support, it gives me hope. And I owe it to you as well, if I've managed not to make him end up . . .'

'Like Timur? Say it, like Timur? He told you everything.'

'Yes, everything.'

'It isn't true! I wasn't the one who drove Renan to suicide. I loved her, more than my own life. I didn't reproach her that day. Besides, she was my twin; we were like two peas in a pod. In every country we went to as children, we were met with a chorus of admiration. Two solitaire jewels, they called us. Look, see this solitaire? Papa bought one for me and one for Renan that year there in Sofia . . . And besides, what does Timur know? He wasn't even born yet. How dare he repeat innuendoes, rumours. What does he know? When he was born my father was already dead. And with my father went all those incessant trips, never staying put! Three years here, two years there. Always new languages to tackle, short-term friends. Barely time to form a friendship, learn a language, and we had to leave, hardly enough time to finish settling into a house and we were on the train again . . . and Sofia! The most horrible city, anonymous, provincial, with all eyes fixed on the ambassador's twins. And then how was I to blame if Renan, apart from physical appearance, was so different from me? What could I do when at each embassy she'd flirt with the clerk, get bored, fail to learn the languages, wouldn't read? And "those two", so bound up in their love! I never saw my father look at any woman amorously, not a one! She and her Great Danes were the only ones he gazed at adoringly . . . us only briefly, during departures and arrivals, almost as if to check that none of his baggage was missing. And who could imagine that on the first Sunday in that new city, in that huge, freezing-cold house – who knows how long it had been vacant – with those stoves that no one could get to work . . . I was reading in bed and Renan was smoking in hers. Whenever Papa went out, she took some of his cigarettes and smoked. My father had ordered me to pro-hibit her, but I never said a word, I swear! That day I was reading *The*

Pit by Kuprin. Reading that book was forbidden, but I had taken it from Mama's suitcase. And you know how fascinating it is. I wanted to finish it before they returned for dinner. I didn't even notice . . . Afterwards, only afterwards did I remember that at a certain point Renan began pacing up and down. Why did they always make us sleep together in all those houses that were so big? . . . She started pacing, and then tried to lie down beside me. The bed was small, yes, it was small and she was annoying me, playing with my hair. Then she said: "Shall we take a walk?" How was I to know? It was the first Sunday. We didn't know our way around. I wasn't unpleasant, believe me. I simply said: "Papa has forbidden it; it's dangerous." Then it got dark, and I turned on the light to read the last lines. Renan was gone and it must have been quite late . . . I never read those last lines because I knew that Mama and Papa could return any minute, and I hoped that Renan would come back from her walk. She'd said: "I'll go by myself then." I waited at the window, expecting her to appear. That miserable square, with those dirty benches and that graceless row of sad little trees . . . I can still see that square! Until the steward knocked at the door for dinner and . . . I trembled at the idea of dinner, the three of us, without Renan. I quivered at my father's silence and decided to wash my hands, so that at least I'd have clean hands and he wouldn't get angry about that, too. In the bathroom, I found Renan hanging from one of those big heating pipes. You know, those pipes for heating bathrooms that are as big as a drawing room . . . Oh, Renan! Modesta, hold me, hold me tight, I'm so afraid! . . .'

I can't help holding her, even though the name 'Renan' whispered in the growing darkness chills my bones, my thoughts. She trembles, cowering in my lap, and clings to my neck.

'Hush, Joyce. You're right: it was an accident.'

'No! It wasn't an accident! Always reproaching her, and what's even more horrible, the censure was silent . . . What did Timur tell you, what?'

'Everything, Joyce, but I didn't believe him.'

'You're lying!'

'Joyce, I repeat, I didn't believe him. I was only frightened. You were right. Timur is dangerous.'

'You see, you see? And then too, if they really thought so little of Renan, why did they let us sleep in the same room? Why those beds, always the same, why the same clothes?'

'And Joland? She wasn't your sister?'

'He told you everything. Damn him!'

'Why did you tell me that Joland was your sister?'

'A lie, all right? A lie like everything else, like . . . go away, get out!'

'As you wish, I'll go. But Timur requested that I ask you to write to your mother. Your mother isn't dead, Joyce . . . don't look at me like that, try to understand my position too. I'm frightened. You told me your mother was dead. I, I . . . but never mind, we'll talk about it tomorrow. Will you write a note to your mother?'

'Never! What does she want from me? Isn't it enough that she tormented me? How she tormented Joland? . . . Oh, Joland, why did you do it, why?'

'What did she do? Tell me. Let it all out! If we talk about it together we can see a way out.'

'A way out of what? Talk about what? Talk, talk, talk, all nonsense!'

'But why tell me your mother was dead?'

'She *is* dead, can't you understand! Dead! I swore on Joland's body that for me she was dead. She hated Joland. She was never willing to accept her. I tried in every way I could to make her see how much I loved her, but she did nothing, disapproving and distant. Yet she knew the loneliness I struggled with, she knew everything about me . . . Besides, she brought me into the world the way I am, abnormal . . . it was she who gave me that book – I was twelve or thirteen – the book that described cases like mine . . . If she had at least accepted Joland, we wouldn't have been so alone. But she, so beautiful and flawless, with her successful life, how could she accept a relationship that was so "aberrant"? That's what she called it. If she had only accepted us, I would never have abandoned Joland . . . all alone, poor little thing, helpless. Oh, if only I had died!'

'Too easy, Joyce, too easy. Like going to prison and letting yourself be tortured for the cause.'

'What do you mean?'

'As long as people like you go to the slaughterhouse to appease their sense of guilt, the cause will be lost from the start. I no longer have any confidence in you, or in any future hero like you. Don't cry, Joyce, it was predictable. We're probably nothing but a pair of murderers like all the others. Except that I killed for my own needs, and the crime, if you can call it that, will not be discovered, whereas you, like Mother Leonora or Gaia, did so for others, arming yourselves with eternal sentiments and duty.'

'I wish I were dead!'

'You are dead, Joyce, because you finally met someone practised in killing, and more skilful than you. Not a Joland or a Beatrice, brought up to be sentimental romantics, as they used to say. . . What am I talking about? They still say it.'

'Enough! Stop!'

'Don't cry. Even if the victim has slipped out of your hand, don't despair. I love you. Not eternally, but I still love you. And now as equals, killer to killer.'

'Where are you going?'

'Well, to wash my hands. It's eight o'clock and I'm hungry. I'll send a nurse to watch over you. I wouldn't want to have to bury you in my garden – and admit that the comrades were right.'

PART FOUR

75

Cloaked in his manly silence, Prando hastens the separation by firmly removing Bambolina's desperate arms from around his neck. What does that desperation signify? And Mela's silently staring at me, biting her lip? An accusation? Is it my fault they're losing their dearest darling? I'd like to hover over them and protect them, but it's not permitted. There's a precise limit to helping others. Beyond that limit, invisible to many, there is only a desire to impose one's own way of being . . . The lie contained in words is a bottomless pit, and Modesta decides to keep silent and remain at the mercy of that empty place around the oval table of their childhood, which, seen from the top of the stairs, in the evening, is a yawning abyss. I can't go down those stairs. If I could only lean on Prando's arm . . . but Stella is crying and calling from down there. No, she's not crying; she's just upset.

'Modesta, please, come down! Ever since Prando moved out, there's no peace in this house anymore.'

'What is it, Stella?'

'How do I know! Every day it's something else! They were so quiet before. Since Prando left . . .'

'That's enough about Prando leaving, Stella! Don't make me mad. I asked you what's wrong and that's all!'

'It's just that Jacopo, ever since . . . well, for days now he hasn't been himself, and this morning he stopped eating. He hasn't budged from his room. He didn't even want to come down for Crispina's lesson, and the *picciridda* started crying. It took a hundred and one stories to quiet her down! Even now that it's time to eat he won't come down . . . Oh, you'll go? Thank goodness!'

I'm familiar enough with the room Jacopo chose, but I've never noticed that the immense bay windows almost touch the large palm tree that presses to come in. On the walls, in the dim light, are large blackboards with numbers, sketches, rows of Greek words. The lamp casts a yellow light on the table, on the book shelves, on the skeleton that belonged to Uncle Jacopo, resurrected from the attic and carefully dusted off.

'*It's dreadful! I won't come to your room anymore if you don't get rid of that appalling "thing"!*'

'*Don't be silly, Bambù! It's very helpful, more so than books! That's the only way you learn. It's fascinating to see how we're made inside.*'

'*Would you believe it, with all the wonderful things there are in the attic, he goes and chooses a skeleton!*'

'*But the gentleman interests me. I'll call him Yorick, like Hamlet. Maybe every man should have his Yorick . . . Plus, you're so irritating, Bambù! Do I say anything when you bring down those silks and laces that you like, and that I find hopeless?*'

When I touch Jacopo's shoulders, unmistakably alive under his light shirt, I feel reassured, though he doesn't move and persists in lying curled up against the wall. He always did that, even as a baby . . .

'Don't call me "baby"!'

'You're right, you're big now.'

'That's not why, and you know it!'

'What do I know, Jacopo?'

'That I'm not your baby.'

'. . . *I dreamed I wasn't your baby, and that you found me in a basket left by someone – who knows who? – under the Saracen olive tree.*'

'So let's hear it. Where did I find you this time? The last time it was in a boat at the seashore and you weren't sad when you told me about it.'

'I can't stand it anymore. I want to die.'

'So this dream has always upset you and you hid it, like you do with your teeth, so we wouldn't feel sorry for you? Is that it, Jacopo? I know you don't like to do what 'Ntoni does, making a mountain out of a molehill just so we'll make a fuss over him.'

'No, no . . . the dream has nothing to do with it. I'm sorry, but I need to be alone. I gave my word of honour. Please, go down to dinner, I need to be by myself!'

Word of honour, a man's word, a manly silence. '*A man who is a man keeps his silence when he has sworn.*'

'Didn't we decide, Jacopo, not to listen to people's prattle and to talk about everything together, as we've always done?'

'I swore on my honour. Don't insist! And besides, I already feel better. I'll come down if you really want me to. I'll come to dinner; that way we'll get it over with!'

Who could ask Jacopo for his word of honour and make him give it? '*A man who is a man doesn't go around giving his word left and right.*' Only one person had the power to do so, someone who tiptoed through our lives, someone who appeared meek, who stayed a moment and then disappeared soundlessly. The apparition of that smiling face in scenes of the past, that docile presence who for the good of her child promised to endure the cross that God had given her, took me back to a hatred long forgotten. Loathsome Inès! A woman noxious to women and to man, a vile woman incapable of giving birth . . . After Jacopo was born, she aborted four times, ever more prone; through those Calvary-like ordeals, she thought she had atoned for her sin . . . I see her now smiling there in the wings, sufficiently purified to reclaim the sacred fruit of her womb.

'Why did you allow me to be born? Why?'

'How could I not let you be born? Inès was healthy, beautiful . . . How could I force her to have an abortion?'

Jacopo's pallor becomes splotched with purple, his lanky body jerks; he gets up and seems about to bolt. I can't go after him. He's alone in his suffering and he must find a way out of it on his own . . . He circles the room like a madman, then falls back on the bed, his head in his slender hands, the knuckles reddened from despair.

'So it's true?'

'Would you rather I told you Inès lied?'

'No, no, I know she didn't lie.'

I can't add to Inès's crime by denouncing the woman's vileness and killing Jacopo's image of her. Naturally Jacopo would believe me, but I can't allow the side of Inès that lives in him to be murdered by my own hands: the sweet, smiling side that I've seen flower, year after year, grafted onto the tough, arid stock of Gaia and Uncle Jacopo.

'She's your mother, and she must have needed you to know it.'

'This is driving me mad! Why didn't she keep me with her then? Why wait fifteen years to . . . Look, I was fond of her before, I called her Zia, but you see, now that she'd like me to call her Mother when we're alone, I can't stand her anymore. I hate her. It's horrible to hate. I've never hated anyone.'

Jacopo gets up, venting a hatred that makes him pace up and down the room, rigid as never before.

'What am I, a puppet that you can pass from one to the other? Don't I have eyes to see and ears to hear, as Pietro says? Don't you think I know? In fact, now I'm connecting a lot of things that Pietro couldn't rightfully say. She got an annuity, and not an insignificant one, to give me up to you. And you know what she had the gall to tell me? That she will leave it to me . . . to me, do you understand? As if I needed her money or yours. I'll work and I don't want anything from anyone. And then . . . this too fills me with hatred toward life! I won't even need very much money now because . . .'

'Because what, Jacopo?'

'Because now I know that I shouldn't have children, ever! That illness is hereditary. I know that's why you didn't tell me about Inès. I was born when he was already sick with syphilis, not like Prando, who was born earlier. Oh, Mama, why, why? . . . And why are you crying? Don't cry! I won't ever have children, but I'll never call that woman Mother, never! You're my mother, aren't you? You used to say – and I didn't understand – that Bambolina was more your child than Prando, that 'Ntoni was your nephew even though Stella isn't your sister . . . You're my mother, aren't you? Hug me, Mama . . . and you always will be, won't you? Say it!'

He cries in my arms at last, and to calm the tremor of dismay that's come over him, I can say the meaningless word that – when used in appropriate doses, like certain poisons – has the power to relieve pain.

'Always your mother, Jacopo, always near you.'

I found myself sobbing on his chest, and his arms supported me. How could Jacopo seem so fragile a moment ago and now be so strong? Once before I had cried like this, but I could no longer remember . . . It had been on a beach, at night, and the glow of the fishing lights had illuminated two moist eyes, like those of a grateful dog. Or had it been when they had brought home Carlo's empty shell? That mannequin whom they had jokingly dressed in Carlo's jacket, pants and shoes. I'd never cried like that again.

'That vile woman! And I'm supposed to call a woman who makes you cry like this Mother?'

'I'm afraid, Jacopo! Why does everyone always have to try to make us unhappy?'

'Don't be afraid, Mama, I'm here with you.'

'All this time you've suffered alone, and I'm afraid. Please, if you feel despondent again, don't hide it anymore. Talk to me, like we did about your teeth, remember? You were hurting but at least we were together.'

'You held my hand.'

'There, you see? It's solitude that makes suffering so awful. Others take advantage of solitude to hurt you even more. Promise me, promise me. We have to fight together.'

'I promise, and to fulfil my promise without delay I have another ache to confess to you.'

'What is it now?'

'My stomach hurts; it must be hunger. It's embarrassing, but I'm hungry.'

'Me too.'

'How can that be, Mama? Can you feel hungry even when you're suffering?'

*

Eating Stella's roast, the pain seems to disappear.

'How delicious it is, Mama! I'll never be able to make it this good.'

'Me neither.'

But once his hunger is satisfied, the despair returns to haunt him and his eyes seek escape, like moths banging against the kitchen walls. In the silence, his anguish has the subdued vibration of brass instruments, or is it the muffled beating of his heart, pressing to burst through his chest? He must give birth to himself or die from the foreign body that has crept into him. He clears the table as he struggles, seeking help from familiar objects, from customary gestures.

'For me, just being able to cook something gives me joy. The day before yesterday, you weren't here, Stella was busy, Bambù and Mela were studying, and I was glad I knew how to make scrambled eggs in milk for Crispina, who was hungry.'

He stares, hypnotized, at the big empty table. Jacopo can only pound his fists on the wood before sitting down again, head in hands, and looking at me resentfully. For a second Inès's mask is superimposed on my face, and he can't find a way to reach me. Maybe that mask will have the power to settle over the face of every woman in the future, locking him in a cell of mistrust for his entire life. He mentioned Crispina . . . Perhaps that little face can slink through the bars Inès has planted all around him.

'Crispina cried today.'

'I know, I know. That's what upsets me, but I couldn't stand seeing her!'

'Others make us suffer unjustly, and instead of putting a stop to the injustice, do we continue it against those who are younger and more defenceless?'

'You're right, I know! For her sake too I had tried to be strong, but that, that . . . oh, Mama, that woman is evil! And now that I know she's my mother it's as if . . . as if I've discovered that everyone is evil, everyone!'

'Why is she evil, Jacopo?'

'Because she is! Not only did she reveal what by this time she no longer had the right to tell me, but all she did was criticize you, Bambù, us. She said you're a madwoman. That in order to live as you please, you've squandered all the money and . . .'

'She's not the only one who criticizes us, Jacopo.'

'I know . . . Why does it hurt so much, Mama?'

'Because knowing that you're her son, you're afraid that you, too, are evil. She's not evil, she's ignorant. Kindliness, not being cruel, is a luxury. The poor have no time to be kind. I was poor so I know it.'

'But Stella is kind.'

'She's an exception, Jacopo! And not much of one at that. Stella is the daughter of prosperous farmers. She's remained here by choice and will stay as long as she wants, but she's not forced to. It's different! Inès, on the other hand, grew up in an orphanage, not knowing who her parents are.'

'I didn't know that.'

'That's what I'm trying to tell you, Jacopo. Each of us is the result of a unique past and of our upbringing, and Inès has had the worst upbringing.'

'So you're saying she's not evil?'

'She's just ignorant . . . and maybe she has a weaker character than Stella or me. Who knows? If I were to tell you, for example, that Bambolina might have many selfish or stubborn qualities if she'd been brought up differently, would you be surprised?'

'Oh, not at all! I never thought about it, but it's true. Mela is stronger, although she doesn't appear to be.'

'You see? And Prando? Let's look at the truth a little, Jacopo. What would you say about a Prando who was left free to take charge and give orders?'

'Oh, dear God!'

'I myself am neither all good nor all bad. I'm good when I can be and bad when I have to defend myself or defend you, or defend Crispina from you . . . You yourself were "evil" to Crispina, to use that dreadful, irrevocable word.'

'It's true.'

'Well then? It happens, but we can make amends.'

'I'll apologize to her.'

'Apologizing or saying you're sorry is fine with grown-ups, but with a child you have to act, do something that will make her forget the wrong.'

'You know what I'll do tomorrow with the money you gave me for my lessons? I'll buy her a present. What would a little girl like, Mama?'

'Don't think about the fact that she's a little girl; think about what you would like.'

'Tomorrow I'll ask 'Ntoni, he's very good at these things. Tomorrow? Today! Look, Mama, it's dawn! How can that be? And I'm not sleepy . . . how come I'm not sleepy?'

'Because you're upset, Jacopo. It was the same for me whenever I was distressed: sleep vanished.'

'Did I suffer at other times, Mama? I don't remember.'

'Oh, yes. Remember when Bambù had diphtheria? You were little, but you were aware of everything and you were always crying.'

'Oh, yes, that's right. But where was Prando then?'

'Here.'

'So he suffered too?'

'No, Prando is different. We're all different; that's what complicates things. Prando believed Antonio's lie . . . a doctor's lie so as not to scare all of you. But you saw through it and there was no way to soothe you.'

'Look how light it's getting! Shall we go outside and see the sun come up?'

'Of course, but let's hurry because it doesn't take long for the sun to rise out of the water.'

'Let's see if it rises first or if we get to the shore before it.'

76

As we run along the sand bleached by dawn's frosty dew, a clear glass rises before us like a pale unbroken wall.

'Hurry, Mama! If we run we can make it!'

'Run, Jacopo, run. It's good for you.'

'How do you escape fate, Mimmo?'

'By letting your thoughts outrun its designs without ever looking back! You have to be quick, until you leave it behind you, that jackrabbit of a destiny!'

'We made it, Mama! It's all white. You can't see a thing; even the head of the Prophet has disappeared. Or is it me who doesn't see it? Don't tell me I need to wear glasses, like Antonio says?'

'No, Jacopo, I can't see a thing either. How cold it is! Or am I just getting old? I hate old age almost as much as you hate glasses.'

'Don't be silly. Old age! It's just that we didn't get any sleep. But Jacopo is provident. Look.'

'Oh, no! You just want to distract me so you'll be the first to see the sun's eye.'

'Jacopo is provident . . . Stare at the horizon all you want, but raise your arms so I can slip this pullover on you.'

'Oh, yes, I'm freezing to death!'

'There . . . look at her: she won't even turn around to thank me.'

'Oh, no! I'm not falling for it. If I turn around you'll see it first . . .'

'There it is!'

'You little devil! You did everything you could to distract me.'

'Now what? Why are you hitting me, Mama?'

'It's obvious! You've been unsportsmanlike, and I'm giving you a spanking.'

'And I'm stopping you, dear Mama. We're past the time when you could spank me whenever you pleased. There we are: shoulders pinned to the ground. Now let's see you move if you can . . . Do you surrender or not? Watch out! If you don't surrender, I'll stake you to this beach with some pegs and you'll have to cry for help.'

There was no way I could move. Where had all that strength come from? Until only yesterday he would run panting behind me whenever we raced. And where did he develop that triumphant laugh that streaks his grey eyes with silver? Uncle Jacopo, in the photograph, barely smiled behind his spectacles. That shrill, unrestrained laugh, those dark curls, that silver gleam that spread from his eyes to his voice had come from Inès's veins.

'You have to say it three times!'

As we struggle, his distress subsides, but it soon returns and changes that laughter into an icy whisper:

'Mama, I hate that woman and I know she's evil . . . I'm so cold.'

'Me too.'

'Let's go home. I'll make you some nice hot milk.'

*

The hot milk, as it quickly eased the chill in my bones, made me aware of my complete exhaustion, both in my legs and in my head, after a night without sleep.

'I can't stay awake another minute, Jacopo. I'm dead on my feet! Help me go up; I swear those stairs seem like Mont Blanc to me!'

'Just lean on me and we'll scale it. Oh, Mama, either you've lost weight, or I'm still growing . . . how long do people keep growing, Mama?'

'Until they die. Oh, please, Jacopo, close the shutters! I can't stand any more light!'

'Right away, Mama. Better now?'

'What a wonderful invention the bed is, Jacopo!'

'Can I lie down too?'

'Yes, if you take off my shoes, I'll let you.'

'Such tiny buttons! It's hard to unfasten them.'

'It's not enough that we have priests and philosophers; even shoe-makers enjoy complicating things so as not to be outdone.'

'You said we continue growing until we die?'

'And maybe even afterwards.'

'What do you mean, afterwards? The one thing Joyce and Andrea agree on is that afterwards there's nothing.'

'Oh, as far as that goes, so does our Antonio, a fine doctor and professor.'

'An atheist . . .'

'You said the magic word!'

'What do you mean?'

'An exclusive label, like those shoes with the tiny buttons. In fact, Joyce gave them to me . . .'

'But you, Mama, aren't you an atheist?'

'Oh, Jacopo, why do you, too, want to put a label on me?'

'Well, in order to understand each other, to use words correctly . . .'

'Words are deceiving: as soon as you utter a word, it falls on you like the lid of a coffin. If you really want me to give you a word, it would be "agnostic". Now that you're older you know what it means, don't you? Those continentals, no offence to anyone, possess all that certainty because they aren't surrounded by the sea; they don't realize that they, too, are an island encircled by space. Believe it or not, I have the feeling that they still haven't understood Galileo Galilei, even though they see planes flying over their heads.'

'And what does this have to do with atheism?'

'They're related of course! Excuse me, Jacopo, but isn't an absolute denial exactly the same as an absolute affirmation? I don't understand mathematics but, by God, you're wearing me out!'

'You're right! That's why I was so afraid of death. Why didn't you tell me before?'

'Well, Jacopo, I too still have to grow a lot more to merit my death.'

'Mama, I'm sleepy. Will you let me sleep here a little while? I don't feel up to going back down Mont Blanc. May I?'

In sleep, his suffering subsides. The pulsing of his veins slows down, recomposing the faint outline from his forehead to his cheek, where sparse tufts of hair are sprouting. He has Inès's hair and Uncle Jacopo's blond beard.

When his hunger for sleep is satisfied, the serpent of reality returns unaltered, strangling his chest. He jerks and his eyes open wide, fixed on a distant point in space. Until yesterday, the pensive eyelids would linger as if to savour the light's soft lips. *'It's a joy to wake Jacopo up, Modesta! He lies there with his eyes closed, and then he smiles.'*

'That woman is evil, Mama.'

'What are you trying to tell me, Jacopo?'

'She's horrible!'

'Is there something else?'

'She called you a whore.'

'Well! So much for Inès. I'm afraid that as *simpatica* as I find her, you're right in saying that she's a little evil.'

'And you're not offended?'

'About what? Did I ever pretend to be a little saint with you children?'

'No!'

'Well then? Clearly for her, a normal woman is a whore. What can I say? Or does it pain you because you heard it from others as well?'

'Of course not! Others criticize you, sure; some say you're eccentric. Prando's friends say you're a femme fatale.'

'Right, Greta Garbo . . .'

'But how come it doesn't offend you, Mama?'

'Taking offence is narrow-minded! Everyone going around being offended! I'm trying to understand why she said that to you.'

'Because that's what she thinks.'

'I don't give a damn whether she or others think that. Everybody thinks, and they have a right to think whatever they please. But how stupid of me! We're a couple of idiots, Jacopo!'

'Why?'

'Well of course! She said it because she wants you all to herself, and she thinks she can achieve that by telling you that I'm a whore. That way, you won't be able to help losing respect for me. It seems obvious, doesn't it? And maybe I really am . . .'

'God, Mama, you're so funny!'

'Naturally I've had relationships, and even a fling or two . . .'

'Couldn't you have asked for an annulment and remarried, Mama? You didn't do it for us, did you? Not remarrying?'

'Whose sublime idea is that? Stella's? 'Ntoni's? Wait, don't tell me! No, on second thought, poor 'Ntoni, how can it be otherwise, with Stella always saying that she didn't remarry so as not to give her son a stepfather . . . Ah, my darling Jacopo, it will never end!'

'What will never end?'

'This Fascism inside us. Even in Russia, "free love" has done an about-face and they've gone back to marriage. But that's not what we were talking about . . . Oh, yes. I didn't do it for you, I did it for me, you see. Imagine bringing a master into the house!'

'But you must have met men who were different.'

'No one. Up till now, not a one. Maybe you, the new generation . . . Marriage is an absurd contract, Jacopo, that debases both the man and the woman. As far as I'm concerned, if you meet a man you like, you love him until, well as long as it lasts . . . And then you leave each other as good friends, if possible. Oh, Jacopo, talking with you is a font of insights for this whore-mother of yours! You know, an idea just occurred to me about love!'

'What idea, Mama? Tell me.'

'If you were forced to be alone always, with only your own company, how would you feel?'

'Well, I can just imagine! I'd go crazy. I'd be bored stiff.'

'Exactly! I think that aside from sensual attraction, which is even more obscure than many of the things that have been said about it . . . Schopenhauer, for instance . . .'

'Oh, really? What does he say?'

'You'll see for yourself; I don't feel like going into it now . . . Aside from . . . no! not aside from, *because* the senses follow the intellect and vice versa, it seems to me that we fall in love because over time we get bored with ourselves and we want to enter into someone else. Not because of the charming but fatalistic idea of Plato's apple* – you know it, don't you?'

'Yes, of course.'

'We want to enter into an unknown "other" to come to know him, make him our own, like a book, a landscape. In fact, later, once you've absorbed him, after you've fed on him until he's become part of you, you start to feel bored again. Would you always read the same book?'

'Oh, please!'

'There, you see? You get bored! And before you realize it, you start getting hungry for something else, other worlds, other fantasies. Of course, a sailor who comes ashore with his head filled with landscapes can last a year or two wandering the streets, but then the longing for a ship takes hold of him again, and you find him at port staring wistfully out to sea. What do you think? Is it a ludicrous idea?'

'I've never been in love, but you, Mama, how many times?'

'Whenever it was necessary.'

'Besides, I . . . I know you'll get mad, but I really like the idea of eternal love between a man and a woman.'

'Why should I get mad?'

'Bambù got mad when I told her that. It's a shame it isn't like that, though!'

'Oh sure, for you old timers brought up on absolutes.'

'We old timers, Mama? You make me laugh . . . me? I'm only fifteen!'

'But you're old, Jacopo. You're older than me. And you know why?'

'No.'

'Because you're more intelligent, so much so that I feel like asking you to adopt me as your daughter.'

'That's a good one, Mama. Me, adopt you?'

'Would you adopt a little girl like me? Make believe you found her wrapped in a shawl outside your door, like in your dreams?'

'Oh, yes, in a heartbeat!'

Pride crushes the serpent of sorrow. With it off his back, Jacopo comes to me in the sun from the window, and with the stern, gentle hands of a father, turns my face up toward his.

'Why are you bowing your head, Mama? Are you sad? You're right: it's all narrow-minded bigotry. I've made up my mind!'

'About what, Jacopo?'

'I was undecided between philosophy and medicine, as you know. I'll become a doctor. You're right: there are still too many tangible ills to lose myself in abstractions. While you were speaking I remembered, you know . . . or did I dream it? I remembered Bambù in bed, writhing and clutching her throat . . . when was it?'

'In '32 I think. You know I have no memory for dates. There was a diphtheria epidemic. I remember that when Bambù went back to school, all she did was cry because in her class of thirty-seven, only five or six were left. Remember all the houses with the black silk mourning ribbons down in the Civita?'

'Yes.'

'All children.'

'Oh, Mama, how tiny you are without your heels.'

'It's you who are sprouting up like a beanpole! Besides, Uncle Jacopo was nearly six feet tall   absurd for this island of midgets! Maybe that's one of the reasons why he was always so sad.'

'You seem like a child . . . He was an atheist too, wasn't he?'

'A heretic. At that time the word "heretic" was used as an affront.'

'And Carlo, Bambù's father, was also a heretic, right?'

'Yes, you know that. Why do you ask?'

'I'm keeping count . . . So with me, there are actually three generations. We could start a new nobility if the word weren't so distasteful. Chekhov says: "To forbid a man to follow the materialistic line of thought is equivalent to forbidding him to seek truth. Outside matter there is neither knowledge nor experience, and consequently there is no truth . . ."'*

'Yes, but what does that have to do with it?'

'He was a doctor too, a new nobility! I'm teasing, Mama. How little you are!'

'That's why I asked you to adopt me.'

'And I'll kiss you on the forehead like a true papa. Oh, Mama, I see you're no longer cutting your hair. Prando is right; you look nice with long hair, like when we were children. I hadn't remembered that.'

'And to think that all you did was yank it when you were little.'

'Naturally! Even now I have the urge to pull it. It's so soft! Oh, Mama, don't cut your hair anymore. Come, look in the mirror, see how nice you look.'

In his eyes I saw myself reborn along with him.

77

Jacopo's gestation lasted several months, and now he was reborn from his intellect as new flesh. Meanwhile, I stopped thinking about myself. I overlooked Prando's coming and going with gifts for Stella, for Bambù and Mela, then quickly leaving again, locked in his silence. I hadn't been wrong: each time, there was no regret, no hurt, in his hasty departure as he turned away irritated by Stella's tears, only a desire to be free. And Joyce?

Ever more beautiful in her apparent death, she roams around the house, jealously peering at faces and throwing fits. But we on the island know how to live with the dead, how to quiet them if need be, and never to believe it when they say, '*We were so happy, Modesta, what happened?*'

What happened was that you were never satisfied with anything, chasing your dream of perfection, and now you lie buried six feet under in my garden and you'd like to go back to yesterday. But for the living, yesterday served only as fertilizer for this new today, tangible and filled with sunshine. I have all that sunlight inside me, and Jacopo's arms around my neck, his caresses in my hair.

'*Why are you always with Jacopo now?*'

A jealous rage seizes her. The jealousy of a possessive master reddens her cheeks, and as before, I look away from the purple splotching that turns her ugly. But one must be patient. After all, she's right: until yesterday, I was a faithful little wife, and she, confident of her power, boasted to herself that unlike other mortals, she was not jealous. Well, Joyce, what good was all that intelligence of yours, all that knowledge, if you weren't able to scratch the surface of even a tiny fraction of your guilt? How arrogantly you stated: '*My mother? A masochist who sought her persecutor in that country squire from Todi.*' I see you with Renan, and then with Joland, parading through the streets of the living as you take turns scourging one another. And I myself almost slipped into that secular *via crucis* of purification. Now I see that your anger isn't jealousy, it's simply anger and envy toward someone who looks at you joyfully and refuses to suffer with you. I turn and walk out of the room. It's dark in that room and outside the sun is shining . . .

'Where are you going now? What are you doing with Jacopo? Did you sleep with him? The boy has assumed a masterful air. You're capable of anything! You never loved me, I was only a diversion for you at a time when you were bored. It's men you're drawn to . . .'

How can I make her see that I loved her as long as she seemed like a woman to me, as long as my hands found that skin delicate, those breasts full, that abdomen soft. But now that I see her locked in the impervious armour of an impotent male, my illusions are over and I run to Mattia, who after so many months has finally returned from America with the money.

★

'How did it go, Mattia?'

'What happened? . . . Did you suddenly fall asleep while we were talking? What do I know! Who knows what goes on in that little head of yours! I only phoned you about the paintings and you ran over here; you didn't ask how or why, with everything I went through to do you this favour, and then you fell asleep.'

'Who put me in this bed?'

'I did. You slept a night and a day! I called Stella, I got scared, but she told me it was nothing to worry about . . . You certainly gave me a scare! You were tossing and turning in your sleep. Once you said they wanted to separate us. Who can understand you women! You're not a sleepwalker, are you? Do you remember the telephone call at least?'

'I felt like seeing you. You were away a long time, Mattia.'

'Well, these aren't matters that you can take care of in two days, Mody.'

'How come you called me Mody?'

'Whenever my father said "Mody" I'd become jealous and I felt a hatred for you that now seems strange to me. How things change when *La Certa* passes through and clarifies the past!'

'Why did you put me in this room? Why is it so quiet here at Carmelo?'

'They're all dead, so I closed everything up. What did I need all those bedrooms and parlours for? I only keep this wing open: three rooms and an electric kitchenette, like they have in America.'

'And who looks after you?'

'A woman comes in and cleans, careful not to let me notice her. I've had enough of dinners and lavishly set tables. Why, don't you like this room?'

'I grew up in this room, Mattia, but it was different then. I recognized it by the big window.'

'Well, I had them remove all that junk: mirrors, vases, velvets! Why are you crying?'

He smiles, pulling his pipe out of the pocket of his blue velvet jacket, and I know he won't say another word until the small flame is well lit. Slowly, the scent of tobacco rises up, reducing the room to that bare, distant one with its roughhewn planks, redolent of resin, and Carmine's white curls. Another year or two, and Mattia's salt-and-pepper hair will also be a bright snow white.

'What is it, Mody? Why are you staring at me like that?'

'Will you let me take a puff?'

'Oh, right, this little she-devil even smokes a pipe! I'd forgotten! Take this one – I'll fill another one – but treat it carefully because it's my favourite pipe you're holding. Just look at her smoke! How did you learn how?'

'Now that *La Certa* has passed by and clarified things, as you said, I can tell you: your father taught me.'

'I knew the answer when I asked you, Mody. But you were wrong to say "your father"; you should have said "Carmine the *padrone*, the lord and master".'

'You still haven't made your peace with him?'

'No! When it comes to *padroni*, not even *La Certa* has the power to reconcile us. And these days I hate him more than before. I've thought about it, you know – alone, in this house of the dead, I've thought about it – and I hate him even more, because by following his example of greed I lost my wife and children. And I buried him a long time ago, no longer part of me, in a field far removed from my heart. I've suppressed his voice and I don't want any part of what he left behind. That's another reason I came back to you. You, sphinx-like, had seen my error and you warned me. You rejected me back then because you didn't want masters, and I came back to you to learn. Oh, I don't want answers in words; these aren't things you learn from words. I've watched you, I've watched your children and I'm looking at you now . . .'

'And what do you see?'

'Enormous freedom of thought and action! How did you manage to achieve such freedom? Down at Villa Suvarita they weren't even surprised by your departure.'

'I got them used to it.'

'How?'

'By allowing them the same freedom. When they were little – partly so I wouldn't have to listen to them, partly to accustom them to it – I would go to a hotel in Catania. You have to put some distance between you and those you love. Distance clarifies things almost better than *La Certa*.'

'Ah, I see. Is that why you sent Prando away?'

'The weed of dominance was beginning to grow in him, and if this weed grows persistently in Tudia soil . . . Go find your slaves elsewhere, the world is full of them.'

'The problem is that we Tudia aren't fond of those whom you call slaves. It's the mania to subjugate those who are free that drives us.'

'I know. There's that tendency in me as well, but I don't nurture it. It doesn't get you anywhere, Mattia! When you subjugate, you become a slave yourself, watching over those you've rendered power-less to look after themselves, clinging to you like leeches.'

'Is that how you talk to your children? Aren't you fearful for them, for their future?'

'When you've fertilized the soil, the plant will grow, Mattia. You've brought me money for fertilizer.'

'I thought you wanted to amass it.'

'Now you're talking like your father. Money is useful so you can be free in the present, not in some uncertain future.'

'One night in Las Vegas, I was about to lose everything that Car-mine had stored up. I was overcome by a mad urge to fritter it away and I lost and lost, but then something stopped me . . . a kind of oppression, rage at all those concrete and gleaming glass walls rising to the heavens. For many years they'd seemed like magnificent cathe-drals of power, and then . . . I don't know, Mody . . . That night I was dead drunk, and at the window where I went to get some air – it was sweltering inside – I had a sudden longing for our valleys of almond trees and orange groves sloping down toward the sea, and for a moment I seemed to be whirling in the scent of orange blossoms. They told me I fainted and fell to the ground. Naturally when I came to, I realized that I had to fertilize what little land was left, and I came back. Even if this house of the dead was the only thing waiting for me, the plants were still alive, and I knew I had to nurture that scent.'

'You lost that much?'

'Nearly everything. But, as you say, I feel liberated and I can sleep again. Why is that? That's what I wanted to ask you.'

'You're asking what you already know. All that wealth was super-fluous.'

'Those years when I was well-off, always wheeling and dealing, went by without my remembering a single day. Now, like someone risen from the dead, I'm rediscovering everything, and that midsum-mer evening with you seems like a baptism. Though I was a mere bystander, there to watch, I drank in the sound of the mandolins, your wine, your joy, finally experiencing the sounds and tastes. Why is that, Sphinx?'

'You're asking me to put in words what you already know, Mattia.'

'As confirmation. One must touch the Mountain's true stone and the water of the Simeto* of words to know what water is, what stone is, what words are. I'm sleepy again. Even the whisper of pain, which like a snake was slithering slowly from my arm to sting me here in my heart, has been dulled by sleep. What is it, Mody, why aren't you answering?'

'Did it go away when you slept?'

'Yes.'

'Then sleep, *caruso*. That way the painful serpent will glide away in your slumber.'

'Did you say *caruso*?'

'Yes, and *picciriddu*.'

'Last night you embraced me. Was it gratitude because of the money?'

'No. It was to touch the truth of stone and water, as you said before.'

'What's wrong, Mody? Why are you so pale? Why are you trembling? Come here. Sit down again.'

'Oh, Mattia, I thought I saw a white figure coming through the trees down there.'

'Where?'

'Back there, among the branches of Nonna Gaia's weeping willow. She loved that sad tree, and in the midday heat she would read for hours and hours in its shade . . . She didn't sleep in the afternoon.'

'I don't see anything, Modesta. Maybe you thought of her and she appeared to you. The dead find their way in during the struggle between sun and shadow: it's noon, the hour when the sun turns black.'

'As a young girl I was always afraid in this room. It seemed immense to me, and instead it's small. Even the grounds seemed endless . . . Maybe it was a ray of sunshine on one of those white statues. I had forgotten those statues. Let's go outside. I want to see them again.'

'Come on. I'll take off my jacket if I may. I'd put it on because coming from outside, it's chilly within these walls.'

'Like back then, Mattia. I too used to look for a shawl when I entered the hall.'

Outside the walls the sun is dazzling. The sun always blinds me when I go out, and the white statues shimmer in a silent, frenzied dance: '*One, two, three . . . one, two, three . . . Quick, let's gallop down to the sun.*'

'Where are you running to? You'll perspire and catch cold, Mody! What are you looking for? There's nobody here. Hey, *tosta carusa*, where are you, you impulsive girl?'

In the distance, Mattia's voice rises higher and higher. Or is it Beatrice calling me, frightened by the hour when spirits appear? It's not Nonna Gaia stirring the branches of her willow tree. Joyce, motionless, stares at me, her gaze dilated: she does not speak.

'What are you doing here, Joyce?'

'That's a question I should be asking you.'

'I fell asleep.'

'How convenient for you to fall asleep.'

'How did you get here?'

'The same way you did. By car.'

'When I was a girl, shut away in that convent, I thought it took days and days to get to Catania. Then the first time I saw Catania in little more than an hour, with the sea just beyond it, I couldn't believe my eyes.'

'I'm not interested in your stories, Modesta. I'm leaving!'

'Wait. Come up to the house. I'll show you where I grew up.'

'Don't touch me! Go to him. Don't you hear him calling you?'

'You have no reason to be suspicious, Joyce. Wait! Mattia and I just talked and . . .'

Joyce whirls around, ashen. Arms rigid at her sides, she swerves behind a marble pedestal and disappears among the weeping branches of the willow.

'She's gone.'

'Who, Mody? Now you're scaring me. I saw something too.'

'It's Joyce.'

'Why is she running away?'

'She's jealous, or rather she acts jealous now. Before, I could stay out for three days and she wouldn't even notice.'

'What's between you and her, Modesta?'

'You already know the answer: love, Mattia. On my side, a deep love that made me believe she loved me too. It happens. But then I understood, and now she's dead to me . . . You were right; I shouldn't have run. I'm perspiring and I feel dizzy.'

'Running at high noon can make your blood go haywire! Don't move. Lie down in the shade – that's it – and don't talk.'

In the silence, the green canopy of the branches battles the black sun.

'This is where she was standing before. See? The grass is crushed.'

'Don't talk, lie quietly. I don't like your colour.'

'She was here.'

'Who, Mody?'

'The apparition . . . She stood here motionless and spied on us.'

'The apparition has vanished, and if you lie still and rest it won't return.'

In the silence, the green shade of the tall willow stoops over my forehead.

'Your hands are cool, Mattia. How can that be?'

'I didn't run and I didn't see any apparitions. Hush, Modesta. If she's dead to you, forget her or she'll come to haunt you for ever.'

'She's evil, that woman, like Inès. They don't know the art of forgetting and they take their revenge on everyone: on themselves, on men, on children. Do you know why she came here? Like Santa Rosalia, she wants to wear the gold, diamond-studded mantle but also be a man with a sword.'

'Your pulse has stopped racing.'

'And your hand has grown warm.'

'Now just be quiet, and Mattia will pick you up and carry you to the house. We'll face the heat together and then at home we'll put a nice cool cloth on that troubled brow.'

*

'You're feeling better with the damp towel, aren't you? You're smiling again.'

'Yes, and I don't want to go out in the midday heat anymore, Mattia.'

'Of course, no one should go out at this time of day. Only stray dogs are out and about . . . They slink along the meagre shadow of the walls or stand stock-still like goats. Have you seen goats at this hour in the stony fields? If you don't look closely, you almost don't notice them; they seem like statues. Not even their eyes move as they wait for the midday heat to pass, so they can breathe again.'

As I wait for the hour when the heat abates and apparitions vanish, I cling to his chest. At dusk, lava radiates the heat it has absorbed throughout the day, and if you lie on it, it warms you as the wind becomes glacial.

'You're trembling now, Mody. What is it? Are you cold again?'

'A little.'

'I'll find another blanket for you.'

'You're trembling too.'

'Yes, but not from the cold. I wanted you, Modesta. Your touch aroused me.'

'So why did you hide it?'

'One doesn't take advantage of an embrace that comes from gratitude, or sleepiness or sorrow. So while you slept, I went to a *velluta* to quench my burning thirst.'

'You still call them *vellute*?'

'What should I call them? Those offensive names foreigners call them?'

'*Velluta*, a silken lady . . . I hadn't heard that word in so long! We're losing our language, Mattia, and the island will be left with great regret. Tuzzu used to say: "Colours come from the heart, thoughts from memory, words from passion."'

'Who was Tuzzu?'

'A *carusu* who knew all the words and taught them to me. Do you like words, Mattia?'

'No, I like silence.'

'And you absorb it . . .'

'It's going to rain tonight; the heat was so extreme . . . You don't feel cold anymore?'

'No, and you? You don't feel desirous anymore?'

'It subsided as we talked, Modesta.'

'Why are you way over there?'

'I know I could have you now; you told me so. But I don't want to mix things. I'm still sated from the *velluta*'s attentions. Go to sleep, and tomorrow we'll see if you've caught a cold or if it was just the stress of coming back.'

'And where are you going?'

'To my own bed.'

'I'm afraid. This house is becoming more and more silent. While you were making me race through the heat, I saw that all the balconies and windows of the house were deserted.'

'There's no one here. Rows of rooms closed on the emptiness of a man alone. If you're afraid, I'll sleep on the sofa. Don't be frightened. I won't leave you by yourself. Now go to sleep.'

As if sleep had been awaiting his command to bend over me with its forgetfulness, I fall asleep, lulled by the reassurance of his breathing. And I'm not afraid when he leans over me in the grey dawn and whispers softly: 'I told you so, Mody: it rained all night. For four or five hours it will be cool. Do you want me? Or shall I take you home while it's still cool?'

'No, I want to stay here.'

I place first my palms, then my cheek on the warm rock of his chest and he takes me in his arms. How could I have known if he hadn't told me that even amid the grass of quiet friendship a pleasure stronger than passion can grow? A sure, carnal pleasure, no wounding, no uncertainty. He doesn't believe it either. He looks at me, surprised. I feel his hands exploring my body to understand, blind hands that see for the first time. I was right to run away from that swamp of false sentiment. I was right to run to him. After looking at me, he drops back down on me, heavy yet light, confident of my body's equilibrium.

78

'I thought you had gone, Joyce.'

'No, first I wanted to see if you had the guts to tell me. Well? Do you insist on saying that all this time all you did was talk?'

'At first, yes, but after you appeared we started making love.'

'You're disgusting! I knew you were just waiting for the chance to return to normality.'

'I'm a woman, Joyce, and for me being normal means loving men and women. If I want to give birth, I have to love the one who can plant a seed in my womb. It may be different for a man; he can perhaps look the other way after sowing his seed.'

'What are you trying to say?'

'That I'm expecting a son or a daughter. Who knows!'

'Bastard! As soon as they can, they grab the chance to make you a slave.'

'You're wrong. He's able to make love without enslaving anyone: he knows how to use the little glove, as Carmine called it.'

'How repulsive!'

'Weren't our kisses and our caresses just as repulsive, Joyce? I'm the one who asked him. While I'm still fertile, I want all the children my body and my fancy demand.'

Don't pay any attention to this dialogue. I was lying to unmask her entirely and give her the strength to leave. But now that's she gone, indignant and fierce – some cultured, refined individuals find the strength to act only in moral indignation – now that's she gone, I can tell you the truth: I'm not the one who's pregnant, it's Stella. Swollen and dreamy, she's been roaming distractedly around the house and is expecting a baby without even knowing it. For five months Stella has been thinking she's ill, but she's serene. How did I fail to understand the dewy languor of her dark-ringed eyes, those remote gestures, the way she slips into quiet concentration more and more often, her face bowed as she listens to her own body?

For a month we wandered through white corridors, glass doors closed softly on the word tumour . . . Long trips on dark velvet seats amid the clamour of the rails, that word repeated by the whoosh of the train until we met the amused smile of a young doctor up there in the distant north, in that vast city that intimidated Stella . . .

'Nothing serious. She's just expecting a baby. It's not the first such case. Here too – in the countryside, of course – they think they're in menopause and . . . but I won't bore you with useless details. She's in excellent health, but by now the pregnancy is quite advanced and I'm afraid she'll have to carry it to term.'

'Afraid, doctor? If you tell me there's no risk for Stella, I think it's wonderful.'

'No risk. I could see that she has the tissues of a girl despite her forty-four years. If anything, what I'm afraid of is that the lady will be shocked. But it seems that Signora Stella is in good hands with you.'

*

'How shameful! How can it be? Doctor Antonio and even the midwife told me that I was in menopause. Such a disgrace!'

'Enough of that refrain! I'm happy that you're not ill. What would I do without you, with that house to look after?'

'Aren't you going to ask me who he was?'

'You have no obligation to tell me if you don't want to, Stella.'

'But I . . . I have to tell you even though I'm so ashamed. If I've done wrong, I feel I must take responsibility for my lapse. But you mustn't tell the *carusi*. I'll tell you, and afterwards if you don't want to look at me anymore I'll go back home. Because Stella made a huge mistake, becoming pregnant by Prando. He mustn't know, but you must, and if you want to get angry at me, and justly so, you have a right to be angry and to even raise your hand to me! Stella won't say a word, whether you insult me or hit me. It was a mistake.'

As she spoke she stood up slowly and now, sadly but without shame, she looks me in the eye. Her direct gaze makes me set aside my earlier shock and emotion and stand up straight in front of her . . . Foolish surprise caught you, Modesta. I read on her face that it could not have been otherwise: in the familiarity of living together, I had forgotten her beauty. Dazzled by that perfect face, I'm spellbound as I fantasize about her and Prando . . . I should be jealous, I tell myself. I had been jealous of Prando on the Rotonda at La Plaia, but even if I wanted to, I can't seem to call up that jealousy. To clearly understand my feelings and hers, I move closer, and with my palms feel the perfection of those cheeks, that neck . . .

'You're caressing me, Mody? Then you're not angry.'

I put my hand over her mouth to stop her words. Words seem out of place on those warm, perfect lips. She expects me to judge her, but I can't speak because instead of jealousy, I envy the young man who was able to conquer such beauty.

'You, Stella, nursed my Jacopo and raised Bambolina and Prando, and this devotion of yours is priceless, you know that. And you know that any mistake, as you call it, was one of affection, and neither I nor anyone else can condemn you for it.'

'Could I have possibly denied that *caruso* consolation? Maybe I should have, but I'm not strong, and I would have done anything not to see him cry after that night.'

'What night, Stella?'

'The night you two went at it, and he felt he was thrown out of this house.'

The exact logic of life appeared to me so clearly that I heard myself say: 'The ways of desire are infinite.'

'The ways of the Lord, did you say, Mody? Do you mean to say that this creature is blessed?'

I mustn't correct her feeling. She has a benign Lord made of flesh and blood, that starry-eyed woman.

'Yes, Stella, for me this creature is blessed.'

'*È arrivato l'ambasciatore a cavallo d'un cammello . . . È arrivato. . . ,*' Crispina sings, the Ambassador has arrived, riding on a camel* . . .

'Oh God! Here comes Crispina! The *carusi* . . . I'm so ashamed! What will we do about the *picciriddi*, Mody? What a disgrace!'

'Calm down, Stella. I'll see to the *carusi*. You pack our bags. Ample ones; count on us being away for six months.'

'Six months, Mody? Why?'

'Because I don't trust the doctors around here. Remember how *simpatico* that young doctor in Milan was?'

'Oh, yes, yes! I didn't feel ashamed with him.'

'There, you see? We'll do what he suggested: your baby will be born in Switzerland.'

'But I'll be lost up there alone!'

'I'll be with you the whole time. Jacopo and Bambolina will take over the reins of the household. They're grown now, and it's time they had to face notaries and tax documents. I can use a rest myself.'

'If that's the case, it's all right with me. Only the continent is so expensive!'

'Mattia took care of matters for me in America. He came back with a fortune. Bambolina will have to deal with this too . . . Come in, come in, Crispina. Jacopo, come in! Have you finished studying?'

'All done, Mama. Teaching Crispina is a joy. It nearly makes me want to go into teaching . . . How beautiful you look this morning, Stella! Seeing how well they restored you up there on the continent, I'm glad I've decided to become a doctor.'

Stella's eyes stare at me terrified as Crispina clambers up on her lap, still singing, 'The Ambassador has arrived, with a feather in his cap! The Ambassador has arrived, riding on a camel . . .'

Stella is afraid of the *carusi*, and she's right. To my surprise, I realize that I too fear their judgement. But I have Gaia inside me, whispering to me: 'Don't discuss it with them! Do what your conscience tells you to do.' I would never have imagined that growing old brought with it a fear of young people. Was the anxiety I felt inside a sign of old age perhaps? When did it begin? Too many problems fill my head as Jacopo shouts and laughs, chasing Crispina around the room: he's gone from being a teacher to being a child again . . . they're playing cowboys and Indians.

*

I thought about it as I walked with Stella along the clinic's opulent, sterile lane, which lacked any fragrance, or wandered with her through the spotless streets of that odourless, sparkling village with its small shops like those of a crèche . . . and I would have been able to make sense of it, I would definitely have come to terms with it if Stella hadn't died while giving birth to a tender dumpling of flesh – so he seems, now that I hold him in my arms – though too big for her weak heart: *'Yet we operated right away! . . . Too big, Princess, nearly nine pounds . . . A weak heart!'* the doctor repeated.

The heart of a girl, a traditional heart pierced by shame, I add mentally. Naturally, her *carusi*, whom I informed by letter – four gentle but direct letters – responded immediately with kind words. 'Ntoni, pleased to have passed the entrance examination to the Royal Academy of Dramatic Arts with a scholarship – 'Just think, Modesta, 800 liras per month! I'm independent!' – even joked about the matter, saying the only problem was that it reinforced his envy of Prando who – damn that guy! – always won the affection of all the beautiful women . . . But she, Stella, in her heart of hearts . . . what would she have felt that morning listening to her children's replies? She, who could neither read nor write?

The terrible doubt that it had been shame alone that killed her was so overwhelming that for months and months I could no longer think of myself, nor of the newborn child whom Bambolina named Carlo after her father, and whom she allowed no one to touch . . . What are they saying, sitting around the old oval table of their childhood, radiant with lights, crystals and flowers? Oh, yes! After six months of mourning for Stella's death, Bambolina decided to celebrate little Carlo's arrival here among us . . . Even 'Ntoni has come to pay homage to his little brother, and as usual he holds forth like a true leading man: 'A far cry from an autocratic feast, my dear Bambuccia! Here we eat! In Rome, people are starving to death. I must be truthful: more so than for Carluzzo I came to *sbafare*, to scrounge a free meal as they say in Rome . . . The Academy is a real centre of Fascist resistance . . . There are some amazing people, from the director Silvio D'Amico to Vito Pandolfi, the Da Venezia . . . I finally met your Jose, Modesta, and here I thought he was made up! He's a true hero. He came to see me and he sends you his warm regards. He travelled down from Paris in disguise to get in touch with the workers in Turin.'

Why are they shrieking like that? I'd never see Jose again. Or is it 'Ntoni I'd never see again? I miss Stella so much and I'm so tired . . . Dear Stella, in our day we spoke quietly at the table, the candles weren't strident. They were a gentle light, respectful of the meal . . . Light bulbs screech in your brain, the radio blares, forgotten, on the other side of the room, the telephone rings: other guests, maybe . . . A low-flying plane thunders by. For some nights now, that punctual phantom plane has flown around the house, and they don't even hear it. Or am I getting old? How does old age begin? With sharp scratching sounds in your head? The elderly, in fact, squint sometimes, perhaps to ward off sounds or lights that have become too shrill for their weary senses. How does the term 'old age' herald itself? It has a gentle sound, that dreaded term, a reassuring sound. Does one let oneself go and hide in the folds of that sound, unemotionally?

She flees up the stairs, slowly, into old age: a slow escape into the silence of that word, shutting herself in her room and not listening. The door turns on well-oiled hinges, revealing a dark, bottomless well. I must jump! To come out into the light, I must once again climb up onto the old corroded rim and let myself fall, but fear grips me like it did then. There are no trees in that orderly room, where Mimmo can hide and keep watch. Jump or let go and forget? That's the hidden meaning of the words 'old age': deserting a life that's comforting, leaving the field clear, mowed down by the rapid fire of young voices, young emotions. The young remind you that you must grow old, maybe they want you to get old and perhaps even to die, and you tell yourself: they're tiresome, a foolish word that conceals envy and fear. And fear leads you to make yourself old, to inspire their awe via the flame of wisdom. And through that awe to drive them back: fight fire with fire, like in war. A long-standing contention that no socialism will ever be able to heal. I've barely had time to slip into bed when Ida knocks on the door:

'Zia, Zia, are you sleeping? May I come in?'

Let her come in? Or, like Gaia, give in to fear and chase her away with harsh words? No, you took the coward's way, Gaia! I won't follow you any further.

'I'm not sleeping, Ida. Come in.'

'Did you say "fear", Zia? You, afraid? Of what?'

'Of everything, Ida, and you know it.'

'I'm always afraid too, but as you taught me, even fear can be useful.'

'Indeed, I was just thinking about that before you came in.'

'I'll leave you then.'

'No, why? I can continue later. I have all the time in the world.'

'How beautiful you are lying there! The bedside lamp makes your skin look so delicate and your hair shiny, vivid . . . It was Mama who chose the colours of the furnishings, wasn't it?'

'Yes, Beatrice had an extraordinary aptitude for colours, as do you, for that matter. I'm afraid all of it will soon have to be replaced though. When I came back from Switzerland, everything seemed worn out, aged.'

'To some degree, it's true! And if you think we can afford the expense . . . what I mean is, don't worry about it. I'll take care of it. You'll see, with new, more modern fabrics, I'll be able to recapture Mama's beautiful colours and that way everything will be new and at the same time like it was before.'

'That's your dream, isn't it?'

'Oh, yes!'

'But I think maybe you didn't come to talk about the furnishings.'

'I'm afraid now that I'm here with you.'

'Why?'

'Well, if you hug me maybe I'll have the courage to tell you.'

It must be something very serious to make Bambù take on such a grave, proper look. But no! I'm forgetting that when Ida speaks with Modesta she becomes more adult, more composed and self-assured.

'I'm forgetting . . .'

'What are you forgetting, Zia? You're strange!'

'Oh, nothing! But what is it? Tell me. You're trembling too.'

'Oh, hug me, hold me tight, and don't get angry at Prando.'

'What does Prando have to do with it?'

'I'll tell you if you promise me you won't be angry with him. He doesn't mean any harm. It's the way he is; he can't help it!'

'What did he do this time?'

'Well, yesterday morning after we took a walk he slapped me.'

'Slapped you? Why?'

'Well, he doesn't like Mattia. Who knows why! Sometimes I have the feeling that they resemble each other. I'm not sure why . . . something in their eyes, the way they walk. Maybe that's why . . . I've thought about it, you know? Maybe that's why I've fallen in love with Mattia.'

Bambolina had thought about it. You could tell by the shadow that widened her eyes to dark circles, giving her a striking resemblance to her father.

As she repeats softly, 'Seriously, I've thought about it, Zia,' the resemblance to the sorrowful Carlo now imbues her voice, her gestures, until she suddenly rears up, freeing herself from the embrace in order to face Modesta fearlessly, eye to eye. It was Modesta who hadn't thought about it. I'm getting old. I'm becoming deaf to others if something so predictable hadn't even crossed my mind.

'It's not infatuation, as Prando says, Zia. I'm in love and even for me it was like a bolt out of the blue. It took me months to realize why I was so happy when I was with him. How could I have imagined it? He seemed like an old man when I saw him the first time at the party. An old man with all that white hair . . . What's wrong, Zia? Why are you staring out the window and not saying anything?'

'It's nothing, Ida. I have an awful headache.'

'A headache? So bad that you won't say anything? I know you; you're stalling because you're against it! You too are opposed to Mattia, like Prando, like Mela.'

'Mela too?'

'Yes! Oh, why can't we be happy for ever, Zia, why?'

As Bambolina utters her mother's words, Beatrice, evoked by them, sweeps away Carlo's voice like a wind, invading Bambolina and making her fall on the bed, beating her fists and weeping desperately.

'Everyone is against Mattia, all of you! I can understand Prando, but she really has no right.'

'She who?'

'Mela! I didn't say a word when she became attached to that cold statue, Ippolita. All she sees is her, always studying with her. What does she expect from me? Now that she's got her diploma, she'll leave, she'll go out into the world! Why does she continue to disapprove of my love for Mattia? Why is she so harsh? Why destroy all the memories of our friendship? Why? I don't want to hate anyone, no one. Oh Zia, help me. I don't want to hate Prando, or you. Help me!'

'*Help me, Modesta, help me!*' Once again Beatrice has returned and weeps in my arms: her despair fervent and fragile, like when she runs along the sand or whirls round and round the silk-covered walls of the parlour, by herself, to show me the exact steps of the waltz. Yet those small, trembling hands irritate me, that wispy hair makes it hard to breathe.

'What are you doing, Zia? Are you pushing me away? Why?'

'I'm not pushing you away! I'm tired, I told you. Go to bed!'

'Like this, without your consent?'

'You're a big girl, Ida. You don't need anyone's consent.'

'You're vile. You know I need it! You're abandoning me by doing this, you're letting me know that I'll lose you. It's either you or Mattia, isn't it?'

Ida was right, and being right made her bearing solemn, her face intent, unafraid of her decision. Or is it the moon that makes her seem so tall and beautiful? I must stall for time against that sudden beauty that pains me.

'You're right. It's just that I'm upset because I have to leave soon.'

What am I saying? Where must I go?

'Leave? Where are you going? You're frightening me, Zia.'

'Well, I'm frightened too, Ida. Be patient, at least until tomorrow.'

'Zia, are you ill, maybe, and haven't told us?'

'No, no, I'm in very good health.'

'Oh, thank goodness! What with everything that's happened!'

'There now, go to bed. Let's wait till tomorrow. Please, Ida. Tomorrow we'll talk it all over.'

The moon must have hidden itself, because darkness has fallen over the spot where Ida's slender body stood, perfectly sculpted by her white tunic. The absolute darkness announces the diaphanous spectre of the coming dawn. I can't get to sleep, partly because now that the house is sleeping, the noise I thought I had dreamt the night before starts lapping against my closed window again. The muffled sound of giant paws raking the distant sand: one, two, three long scrapes, then a silence quickly followed by a deep rumbling (the waves or an engine?). From the window that rumble now moves to the door, crashing into it forcefully, or is it still the paw that resumes its scraping in the distance, hidden in some cove along the beach? No, I'm not dreaming, the door is thrown open and two silent giants enter, followed by a tall, slim young woman, perfectly sculpted by an opulent dressing gown of white silk. Her mother, too, always wore white.

79

They're not so tall now that they're standing beside me. It's the uniform that makes their legs seem longer and the epaulettes that create those enormous shoulders. Leaning on someone's arm as I climb into the big black car, I feel the muscles of a man, yes, but someone like Mattia, like 'Ntoni, not giants. It's the specially fitted uniform that makes those chest muscles, those back muscles, look huge. I turn away to the window opposite me so I won't have to hear Mela crying in Jacopo's arms, or see the terrified, blank stare in Ida's eyes. It's been many years since I've gone outside at dawn and maybe this is a chance to find out who's been digging in the sand the past two or three nights ... There, once we turn the corner, massive German trucks are parked along the road, loaded with sand, their engines running, while among the dunes huge bulldozers descend to dig up the 'sun's flour'; that's what Tuzzu used to call the sand. Are the Germans stealing our sand ... to make fortifications?

'Could I have a cigarette?'

'Of course, Princess.'

I need to smoke, but only so I won't smell the scent of lavender on those impeccably shaved cheeks. I wonder why I waited so long to savour the fragrant smoke that envelops the foreign faces in a serene fog and focuses the mind. The leisurely act of bringing that little white cylinder to your mouth soothes your nerves, and you can distract yourself by following the tiny blaze as it unhurriedly approaches your lips. Joyce was right when she would carefully, almost reverently, pull her treasure out of its case. But hers weren't white and blond like these; they were dark tobacco, wrapped in yellow paper.

'Another cigarette, Princess? But of course, of course, I'll leave you the whole pack.'

The big black car has stopped in front of the entrance to the Prefecture. The journey is over. It must be Sunday if so many black pleated skirts, two by two, crowd the sidewalks. *'The Duce has liberated us from corsets and cumbersome clothing. He wants us limber, in low heels, our stride brisk to serve the country.'*

We have to wait for them all to troop by before we can go inside.

*

'It's a disgrace, Princess, an outrage!'

If Pasquale the traitor hasn't called me by name, there's a reason for it and I have to listen to him. By using that title, he is advising me to be regal. I had forgotten that I was a princess and this armchair in the Prefecture is very comfortable. My head is heavy, but I dispel my drowsiness, and straighten my shoulders. I must not have smiled until now, because when my lips part in a condescending smile, the two non-uniformed officers stare at me, puzzled.

'That what I think too, Prefect. And I won't stoop to ask the reason for the disturbance you are causing me. I have been inconvenienced and affronted!'

Hearing these words, the two officers lean toward one another, whispering. Then the taller of the two murmurs sadly: 'Orders from above, Princess, but we can assure you that we very much regret it.'

'Of course, of course. A misunderstanding! I have done everything possible not to cause you any disturbance. A princess in contact with those good-for-nothing communists, just imagine!'

'Exactly, Pasquale! I may address you informally as I do in private, may I not? It reassures me . . .'

'But of course, Princess. I am honoured by your friendship. And I feel it's important for me to state that I've had nothing to do with any of this. Orders came from Berlin to Rome: a misunderstanding, surely!'

'From Berlin?'

Timur seemed so gentle, but Joyce is right to keep warning me: *'He's dangerous, Modesta, dangerous like all the young men of the left who went over to Fascism . . . They're the most dangerous, as though they want to cleanse themselves of a shameful past.'*

*

'We're in serious trouble, Modesta, done for!'

'But they went away, Pasquale.'

'To telephone, just to phone . . . We're finished, damn it! May I ask what you were thinking when you revealed our friendship? If they check into it, they'll discover who I was.'

'Exactly! That's what I wanted.'

'Some gratitude! But what do you mean? Do you realize that what you did was stupid, plain stupid? If they suspect me, how will I be able to help you?'

'That's not true! You're part of the norm. You were all with us, before. And that, as you well know, won't harm you in the least. Declaring my friendship with you, on the other hand, means you have no choice but to help me, like it or not.'

'Shrewd! I would have saved you regardless.'

'I never believed you, Pasquale, or rather, I believed you kept a foot in both camps as long as it seemed that Fascism might end in five or ten years. But now you're better off just throwing us all overboard.'

'Clever, damn you!'

'I only wanted to take precautions.'

'Then listen carefully: your situation is a matter that lies outside my jurisdiction. The order to investigate your case came from Berlin. And one of those two came down from Rome purposely for you!'

'Was it Timur?'

'Who is Timur? What are you talking about?'

'Joyce's brother.'

'No, Joyce has nothing to do with this, nor does this . . . what did you say his name was? But who gives a damn! This is all much more serious! They've arrested someone in Paris, an informer, a certain

Marabbito who claims that over the years you've done nothing but finance comrades abroad, act as a spy, and who knows what else!'

'That's it? Is that what you're getting all worked up about? I was afraid . . .'

'But it's enough to throw you in jail for years and years!'

'Well, I thought it was something worse.'

'What else did you do, you goddamn, idiotic woman! What did you do?'

Pasquale shouts and runs around the room like a crazed chicken. In just a few years he's gone bald. Without the thick mass of blond ringlets – like a little angel! – his small round pate looks like a perfect ostrich egg. He doesn't even have those few black strands that Mama carefully combed over Tina's head . . . And for a moment Modesta is tempted to lop off that scrawny neck with a knife, the big one that Mama used to kill the hens. It wouldn't be bad to watch that egg roll among the dark, opulent furniture in the Prefect's office, enjoy the amusing spectacle a little while, smoking a cigarette . . . thereby putting a worthy end to his sweaty, drawing-room performances in uniform, when he entertains everyone with anti-fascist jokes, winking at some big shot: '*All winds blow over the island and we are excellent sailors!*'

'Good God, are you crazy? Have you forgotten the special tribunals? They suspect you of espionage. Do you or don't you understand?'

'Are you reminding me that the death penalty has been reinstated?'

'And you're looking at yourself in the mirror?'

'Luckily in my haste, I grabbed Bambù's purse. She's pretty, isn't she, Pasquale? Look at these beautiful pearls . . . Fortunately there's powder and lipstick! Bambolina is right about these things, like her mother. I've been neglecting myself for some time, and that's not wise.'

'What are you doing? Putting on makeup? Look, I won't be able to go with you to Palermo. You'll be in the hands of men who will interrogate you. They won't give you a moment's peace, never mind powder!'

'On the contrary, you're wrong! Powder and lipstick! I'm not so bad yet, am I, Pasquale? The tall one was giving me a certain look!'

80

'Princess, Princess, *Voscenza* will do us the favour of sleeping here for tonight. You may close this curtain. That way you won't see that woman over there . . . Anyway, all she does is sleep! Unfortunately we haven't had any instructions . . . If she bothers you, have them call me at once. But tomorrow, you'll see, we'll arrange for a room just for *Voscenza*.'

That voice – do you hear it? – isn't gentle like Mother Leonora's, but I have to listen to it and do just what it suggests. For now it's telling me to be sickened by the sight of that ageless, unkempt woman who lies shaking, hands in her hair, facing the wall. And I, like the voice tells me, make a face of disgust, but not too much so: disgust tempered by great compassion. I am in the hands of people who say they believe in compassion.

'*Voscenza* is too good to be moved by that woman. There's no call to pity a subversive communist!'

'But who is she?'

'Someone from the continent, a wretched fool! She's not even a teacher like the one in the next cell, who's rumoured to be an organizer of the reds. A woman leader of the reds – what will we see next! Oh, Princess, I see you are upset . . . *Voscenza* is tired, I'll let you rest.'

She turns away with a slight bow and a hint of a smile, repeating: 'Good night, Princess.' You can tell she likes to call me that. Jacopo, Bambolina, tell all the children not to kid themselves: even in prison, princesses and leaders are treated differently. As soon as Sister Giuliana disappears behind the door, the woman leaps to her feet and starts talking to me like someone forced to remain silent for years, rushing at me like a starving person reaching for bread.

'Who are you? Why did that slut Sister Giuliana make such a fuss over you? Plus, I'm not from the continent: I'm Roman!'

The voice is husky, maybe due to the long silence, but beneath the bruises and scratches (knife wounds?), the face, lit by flashing yellow-green eyes, doesn't seem unattractive.

'Who are you? Do you mind answering me?'

Pinned by that implacable yellow gaze, Modesta is tempted to respond just to close her eyes and have a little darkness.

'*No, Modesta, the danger lies precisely in the cells: for every two real pris-oners there is one, maybe even more convincing-looking than the others, who is an informer instead.*'

Joyce has had some experience with prisons, and what she says should be noted; it might be useful.

'*You never can tell, Bambù.*'

'*But she's boring when she starts in on that subject, Zia!*'

'*We should listen, and then remember.*'

'*Besides, you? in prison? Just imagine!*'

'*You never can tell, Bambù, never!*'

Modesta remembers and opens her eyes again to observe that relentless creature, who talks and talks and asks questions . . . And when she turns to the wall and pounds her fists on the damp, flaking plaster, it's even more excruciating to the eye and ear than the flood-light pointed at Modesta, and the individual sitting behind the desk:

'Why, Princess, do you force me to sit at this table? It pains me more than it does you, you must believe me! Under this uniform is a man who is saddened to see you so exhausted, but unfortunately it is my duty. I beg you once again: try to remember something specific. Did someone perhaps want to seek revenge by involving you in matters that pertain to men? A rejected lover? With your charm, it would come as no surprise! Sometimes men who are rejected can become ruthless . . . Try to remember. All we need are two or three names. We'll hand them over to the law, and you'll be back home in less than no time!'

Behind the dark grille of the confessional, the thin voice of the priest in Palermo coiled like a snake and made me tremble with fear and horror, more so than Mother Leonora's shouts or those of this officer, who for three hours has been pacing around the room shrieking like a lunatic.

'No, no sitting today! Today we'll talk better on our feet! Outside, the sun is shining . . . talk . . . You are so beautiful, Princess, so young! Why let your silence prolong a conversation that is so distasteful to us both?'

Now what is he doing? Why has he stopped? I had just got used to the steady gallop of those short bowlegs. Now though, at regular intervals, he stops and clicks his heels together, as if on parade.

And in the days that followed, each time I entered and sat down: 'No, no sitting, we'll talk better on our feet.' . . . The cigar! Why does he now stare at the small ember of his cigar, then look at me lingeringly as he twirls it between his fingers and feigns a smile? Years later, Joyce's breasts were still scarred by a faint tracery . . . 'I'm sorry, I see your eyes are closing, but we have to talk.' Now, he too sits down, but he's no longer smoking . . . They haven't even changed my clothes yet. I've been here for several days.

'Well, my dear Modesta, my discovery was horrifying and my decision even more horrific. It's chilling to sit in a cell and see those poor women come back beaten and raped, and realize with disgust that you, being privileged, remain healthy, with your clothes intact. Of course, they use words like weapons with the leaders, but that's not saying much: words don't cut the flesh like the razor blades they often use.'

'And you?'

'After a month I realized that I would lose all my credibility with those comrades who were farm women and workers. To get them to do these "embroideries" on me, as you poetically call them, I had to insult them personally and in any way I could. Only after days and days of this was I able to return to the cell with my head held high. It's incredible to have to fight to be tortured, but the suspicious looks finally stopped, and we were united again.'

The *Romana* is silent now. She bends over me, the yellow beacons of her pupils peering closely at my forehead, my neck, and on her resolute face I see subtle cuts. Joyce was right; they use razor blades.

'Nothing, sure! Mummy's little darling, not a mark! You come and go from there without a scratch, not a hair out of place, not even your lipstick is smudged, is it, Princess! Who are you, an informer? Tell Nina! Either you tell me or I'll beat you up but good. Who are you?'

I'm sleepy. I could have followed Joyce's example, but I have no intention of being a hero, and when she rushes at me with her sharp fingernails I grab her wrists with one hand – Nina is tall, but she has slim wrists – and slap her with the other, once, twice, three times. The slaps reopen the cuts, and she's finally forced to get off of me and stop talking.

'That's so you never try it again. Remember that! Keep in mind, I'm convinced that you're the one who's an informer. Yes you, with your bruises, an informer! Bruises make informers more convincing, right! Who are you? Tell me or I'll start slapping you again. Who are you?'

'*Cazzi mia!* My fucking business!'

I had never heard that word on a woman's lips, and maybe because I instinctively smile, or because of the dialect that breaks the words into gentle, hesitant pauses, I'm left flabbergasted.

'*Cazzi mia*, bitch! You made me bleed. But I'm glad. You're no informer if you're so incensed. Get some sleep now. Tomorrow we'll talk, the two of us . . .'

'*Please, Princess, tomorrow let's try to make our conversation more productive. Think about it: if we can see a way to resolve one or two things, tomorrow could be more pleasant, with this beautiful sunshine outside, being able to talk with you in a café, in a park . . .*'

★

'Do you have breath to spare, Princess, that you want to talk? Save it for those *signori*. From the looks of things, we'll have plenty of time to chat!'

Never had Joyce been so sympathetic and smiling, despite the numerous grim cuts that blur her features in the dark room; bringing a long, shapely finger to her lips she gestures me to be silent to save my strength after my return from those discussions with the lawyers

. . . No matter what time it is, she waits for me, still on her feet or lying down, but always attentive, her huge eyes wide open. And she doesn't get upset if I make noise trying to find my cot.

'*Thank you, Jò, for your understanding. Thank you, my love.*'

'They worked you over but good, didn't they, Princess? Wake up! Who is this Jò? your husband?'

'I killed her . . .'

'Oh, no, Princess! You have to wake up! Up to now I went along with you. I left you in peace because you weren't raving, but talking nonsense like that is dangerous! Shit, if only there were a real lamp instead of this dim blue light from purgatory . . . they think of everything! Come on, sit up and open your eyes. That's it: take a good look at me – good, so to speak – look at me: I'm Nina, not your husband.'

'Oh, yes! . . . What did they do to your face? You look like you ran into a cheese grater.'

'Just don't touch me. Ignore it; otherwise you'll make the goddamned stinging worse.'

'But what did they do to you, Nina?'

'Nothing. They went to town with the razor blade. You know, the usual fun and games . . . if only that were all, Princess!'

'For God's sake, what else, Nina?'

'Ah! I see the subject has brought you back down to earth. Good!'

'For the love of God, what else did they do to you?'

'Think about it: when it comes to games men in uniform play, what else can they do to reduce you to a colander, front and back, huh?'

'And you can smile about it?'

'What should I do, cry about it? Crying doesn't fill the holes.'

'How many men were there?'

'That's what I'd like to know! I have the impression there were three of them – you know how it is in all the confusion – but I'd swear that a regiment marched over me, a regiment with sabres and brass bands!'

'You're so funny when you talk, Nina!'

'Oh, if you only knew, *fijetta*, how much I like to talk, kid! Like my father, who was an anarchist and taught us to be plain-spoken and not to worship false prophets. I remember at the time Italy entered the war – I was only seven, but I remember because at home we didn't cook and I was so hungry – I remember my father at the window, spitting as he kept saying: "Don't believe it, Nina, those people who want to go to war aren't socialists, they're traitors."'

'Oh, but you're young then!'

'I was born in 1908. Are you shocked? I can believe it! And don't look at me that way! You think I don't know I look like an old lady? But as soon as these cuts heal and I can dye my hair again . . . it's these dark roots that make me seem old . . . I could use some henna! Tomorrow I'll ask Sister Giuliana, just for laughs!'

'What's henna?'

'Well, a balm! It gives you a nice reddish colour without damaging the hair like other dyes do. In fact, it nourishes the hair since it's made from a plant, and since when has a plant ever done any harm, right? While we're on the subject of health, I have to tell you something but . . . I know you're going to get embarrassed.'

'Me? About what?'

'Naturally, you landed gentry aren't taught. Like my father used to say, they spoil you. It was okay before, because who could take your privilege away from you? But now . . . Who would have thought that even you might sometimes end up in jail!'

'What are you talking about? I don't understand.'

'It's that I've noticed your modesty – I've watched you, what do you think! – and I don't know how to tell you but . . . To make a long story short, can you feel how hard and bloated your belly is? It looks like a drum. You need to take a crap, *fijetta bella*. You have to shit, kid, or your head will split and your bowels will be on fire.'

It's that plain talk or the warmth of Nina's hand as she palpates the taut surface of my belly that makes me cry so hard and repeat in a distant, long-forgotten voice: 'I can't, Nina, I can't.' When had I last heard that childish voice echoing in a dark room? Was it Prando who kept saying: 'I can't, Mama, I can't', or was it Bambolina? Jacopo never cried; he just frowned like a sobre, mindful little old man.

'When you're done crying – crying is good for you – we have to do it, *nennella*!* Come on now, what are you ashamed of? It's only the two of us. What if they had tossed you in with ten others – all having to shit in the same bucket in the middle of the room – what would you have done then, huh?'

'One bucket for ten women, Nina? What a horror!'

'And not women who are as delicate as you . . . all staring at you to see how you make out.'

'Ghastly!'

'No, it's just that by the time you get there, they've already spent years and years inside, and inside you get bored. So a newcomer is a novelty, a sensation. How can I explain it? She takes your mind off things, like at the movies. If only they were satisfied to just look. On the other hand, what can you expect? Common prisoners, thieves, whores. Oh, not that I have anything against thieves and whores; hating them doesn't fit with anarchist thinking. We hate the masters who reduce them to stealing and make them become whores. As the song rightly goes: "*Son nostre figlie le prostitute, son . . .*, the prostitutes are our daughters".* But what the hell! I try to hold to an ideal, but they become hyenas! If this sainted lady hadn't come, this teacher in the cell next to ours, they'd have eaten me alive! She was the one who made them send me here to the infirmary . . .

'Come on, don't worry! I'm going to bed now – if you can call it that! – and I'll turn and face the wall. You pull this filthy sheet that Sister Giuliana calls a curtain closed and take a crap. Okay? No? Get over it now – what's your name, anyway? Goddamn it! – this princess stuff isn't for me . . . Modesta? Hell, what a name! Who named you that? It's worse than Princess. Imagine calling such a beautiful lady Modesta, especially one who's crying because she doesn't want to poop . . . I can call you Mody, you say? Oh yes, that's better . . . Look, Mody, will you make up your mind? What are you worried about if I swear I won't look at you? The sound you might make? Or the stink? Listen, for the stink do this: take this piece of newspaper and while you go, burn the newspaper with this match – don't waste it now! we only have a few of them – burn it in the bucket, I mean, and the smell will disappear, you'll see. All right? Come on, get up and don't think about me. Make believe I'm not here, pretend I'm blind and deaf: look how well I can act blind and deaf. I could even play a cripple when I performed. I wanted to be an actress when I was little

. . . But what's wrong, why are you gripping me? What is it? Are you in pain?'

'No, no, it's just that maybe from laughing or because of the massage you gave me . . . Oh, Nina, I'm so ashamed, I can't hold it! I can't move, I can't hold it in!'

'And you're upset? It's a stroke of luck! Lean on my arm. Good thing you're not heavy! Here, take off your panties . . . no, I won't leave you, there's no need to cling like that . . . Let go of my hips! I won't leave you, but let it all out. For God's sake, don't hold back. You can die from intestinal blockage. Don't hold it in!'

Whether because of that 'don't hold it in' or the warmth her hips conveyed to my arms, I let myself go, sinking my face between her thighs . . . I let it all out and she stood there stroking my hair and whispering: 'There's a good girl, *brava*, let it all out, all of it, it will do you good! . . .' And, something I would never have imagined: as I let myself go, a pleasure sweeter than *rosolio* or Tuzzu's tongue now makes me sigh and weep, not from shame, but from joy, as I say over and over again: 'Nina, Nina, don't leave me . . .'

81

'"Don't leave me," she says. In jail! I swear, if I get out I'll have to tell about it. Oh, how funny, a real joke!'

Throwing her head back, Nina laughs out loud, recalling endless fields of rye and poppies.

'I'm hungry.'

'I can believe it, given what you evacuated! I mean, good for your health, but for your stomach it's a different story! We have no choice, either die of toxicity, or . . . You were less hungry before, huh?'

'Not hungry, just nauseous.'

'Of course, then after the nausea you would have become feverish.'

'I'm starving!'

'I heard you – don't wear me out! Talking about it makes it worse. I have a blade where my stomach should be! But it's time for soup . . . "è ll'ora che . . . "'

'". . . che volge il disio al . . .", it's the hour that turns longings to . . .'*

'Never mind Dante! Belli, our own poet! "Che or'è? ccheor'è? È una cosa che tt'accora. Nu le sentite, sposa, le campane? Lo sapete che or'è, ssora siggnora? È ll'ora che le donne sò pputtane . . ." What time is it? . . . It's the hour when every woman is a whore . . .'

'I'm not familiar with him.'

'Where have you been living? I'll tell you about the great blasphemous poet. They, the Jesuits, that is, say he repented before he died, but it's not true; they say that about everybody. I was there when my grandmother died and she wasn't at all repentant. She was just angry at having to die too soon, that's what she said. And she was eighty years old! Well, after not even a month, all the relatives said – they should be beaten for it, that's what! – they all said that she had repented . . . It's just that with these schools . . . the crucifix . . . if only they'd kill him!'

'Who? Christ?'

'No, I meant that traitor Mussolini, and to think he even wrote a book against the papacy . . . It was he who made peace with the Jesuits and delivered our Rome back to the priests. Damn him! But what was I saying? Oh, yes . . . What can you expect from Ottavia and Grazia, my younger sisters, educated in these schools, with the crucifix in front of them, religion lessons, and then at home too . . . before, when I was little, if you grew up in a house of atheists, all you had to do was stay away from church and you wouldn't have to listen to the priest's voice: walls protected you then! Now they come into your house and talk to you even if you don't want them to.'

'What do you mean, they come in?'

'Come on, Mody, through the radio! A diabolical invention, the radio. Suppose my *fijetta* and I are there cooking, straightening up the house, and we don't mind listening to, let's say, *"Illusione dolce chimera sei tu. Che fa sognare, sperare e amare tutta la vita. . .".** A nice song, huh? Well, you're humming along unsuspectingly with the radio, you relax, when suddenly you hear a mournful chanting so associated with the song that offhand you pay no attention. And by the time you realize it's the Holy Mass, even if you run and turn off that infernal contraption, you've already swallowed some of it. Well, at a certain point didn't Ottavia and Grazia, who grew up with this poison, start saying – yes, them too! – that my grandmother had repented? Repented! Did I already tell you this? Sorry, I'm repeating myself. It's hunger. I talk and talk, partly because I haven't spoken to anyone in three years and partly to fill this emptiness in my stomach. Sorry.'

'No, Nina, keep talking. I like it. My mother never spoke!'

'Why not?'

'Maybe because she had to sit there sewing those filthy rags. She sealed up her lips.'

'What, are you joking? Your mother sewing rags? Maybe you meant that she was obsessed with embroidery? . . . Ah, here comes our Sister Giuliana! Soup, huh, Sister? How wrong you are . . . Slop! It may be because I've had a nice chat with a friend, but you don't look as bad to me as you did yesterday, Sister. And the smell of this soup isn't so repulsive. What happened, did you get a new cook in this house? Oh, Mody, did you hear what she calls this prison? House, she calls it.'

'Shut up, you ill-bred creature, and take your hands off her! Oh, Princess, it's a disgrace! – I've reported it to the Mother Superior – a disgrace to keep you here with this woman, but we're all full. All the rooms are filled!'

'While you're at it, why don't you say "the hotel has no vacancy", eh, Sister? You know I dreamed about you, Sister? I dreamed we met in Hell, in a naked embrace!'

'If only you had come just three days earlier, Princess! But the world seems to have gone crazy! It must be because of this war, which one day is coming, and the next day isn't! We were told that yesterday a rumour had spread that war had broken out and everyone fled Palermo; they all went to the countryside, but then they came back . . . It seems they're also distributing gas masks . . . But if this creature bothers you, all you have to do is say the word and, regardless of that lady's protection, I'll see to it that she's removed! You're too good. Tell me the truth: does she bother you?'

'Don't be silly, Sister Giuliana! For us women raised in obedience and humility it makes little difference whether or not we're alone. And then too, we must understand and forgive ignorance. We are all God's sheep! And I sense that even Nina, deep down, isn't as bad as she seems. I will help her, and my stay here may perhaps be a sign of the Lord. Maybe I was called to lead this lost sheep back to the right path! In fact, I would beseech the Mother Superior to please grant me the consolation of caring for this soul. It will serve as atonement for my sins.'

'Sins, Princess? You? Defamation, I'm certain of it. I was just speaking about it with the Mother Superior.'

'We are all sinners! Tell the Mother Superior that I feel I must remain with this lost soul until she finds her way.'

'A saint! I tell you, you're a saint! I'll go and tell her right away . . .'

'A saint, my eye! You nearly had me convinced, Mody! I was about to lose my temper. Here she comes again. What is she, a train?'

'Oh, Princess, the Mother Superior says that you are too good, much too good! She also says not to concern yourself because the teacher offered to share her cell – oh, forgive me – her room with Nina. What's more, she says . . . but no, no, don't be upset!'

'What? You want to deny me the consolation of atoning for my sins by seeing to . . .'

'What sins!'

'Sins, Sister Giuliana! Or do you feel you are without sin? Let he who is without sin cast the first stone! And if God sent me here, it's a sign that I failed at something. It cannot be otherwise, because the Lord sees everything.'

'Oh, Holy Virgin! How well the Mother Superior understands you, even if she's never seen you! It's always that way among higher souls; she talks just like you do. With those very same words she said to me: "Go and try to persuade her. But she'll refuse, you'll see." Excuse me now. I'll go and ask for her confirmation; that way we'll put an end to it, because I have a lot of work to do! We have to finish putting up the blue paper for the blackouts and . . . then there's such a crowd, it's like the end of the world. This is the end of the world, not just a war!'

The slamming of the door makes me open my eyes: when Argentovivo leaves my room she slams the door. No, she wasn't the one who slammed the doors; she's the maid. Gaia shouts and slams doors, and now that she's decided to send Beatrice away to boarding school, it won't be easy to make her change her mind . . .

'It's all settled. Oh, what a day! God forgive me, I can't take it anymore, all the blessed day up and down the stairs! Nina can remain here . . . What are you doing, Princess? No, no, please, get up!'

On the ground, on my knees, hands over my eyes so I won't see the struggle in Nina's face, flushed from the effort to keep her mouth shut and not laugh. It's she who makes me want to laugh. And it must also be my empty stomach tickling me with airy fingertips . . . It can't be joy; I never heard that you could find so much joy in prison.

'Princess, please, get up. I'm not worthy!'

'God sees us, Sister Giuliana. None of us are worthy, yet all of us are worthy. Give my thanks to the Mother Superior and leave me to pray to the Lord who has granted me this grace.'

'Pray, pray. I'm going. Such humility! And you, you ill-mannered creature, let her pray, do you understand? Let her pray!'

I have to dig my nails into my forehead to keep from laughing. It must truly be joy, because when the door slams shut and I can finally give in to laughter, the putrid walls, the wretched cots, the bucket no longer exist, just Nina's flushed face. Now that her scars are beginning to fade, her strong features have a gentle turn. Maybe Nina is beautiful under that frightful mask. And when she, too, starts laughing – maybe she sensed my joy – and whispers 'You were great, Mody', I can't help throwing my arms around her neck – she's tall and I have to stand on tiptoe – and kissing her on the mouth, a mouth brimming with minute white pearls that dazzle my eyes and my mind. When I bite them her lips have the tart, sweet taste of blackberries faintly chilled by the dew. Nina must be strong since, as we laugh, she can lift me off the ground and whirl me into a spinning waltz: one-two-three, one-two-three! *And now, the grand finale, the galop. Headlong among the unsteady walls, the armchairs, the chandeliers swaying over my head like so many suns . . .*'

'Are you dizzy? I can believe it: on an empty stomach! We're crazy to squander our energy this way! Come on, let's eat the soup before it gets cold. We shouldn't squander our energy in here. No, it's not your fault, you're a novice, but me . . . Christ! It's just that, if you must know, you touched me, that's what. Who would imagine! Nina, moved. *Annamo bene!*. . . That's a good one!* Okay now, that's enough, let's eat . . . Oh, Mody, for a second I forgot where I was. Don't look so disheartened! What's wrong? Are you offended by what I said? I'm not angry with you, *nennella*. How can I explain it? I'm angry with Nina. It's Nina who's experienced with jails, not you. Now do as I say! It's awful, I know, but it's nourishing . . .'

Maybe because I'm no longer nauseous, or maybe because after stirring the soup she takes a spoonful and brings it to my mouth, I hear myself say with conviction: 'You're right, Nina. It's not so bad, and it warms you.'

'There, you said it. In here, Nina is always right, at least as far as –
how can I put it? – physical matters are concerned. We should also
walk back and forth. We'll start tomorrow. Wash as best we can, not
let either dejection or euphoria take hold of us. Euphoria is especially
harmful: at first you think it's good for you, like wine, but then it can
be more tiring than giving yourself a hand job, for God's sake!'

'We shouldn't?'

'Of course we can, but not every day. It wears you out. You have to
establish an exact time. Hey, I know a thing or two about it!'

'So we can't dance anymore like we did before?'

'You're too much, Mody.'

'Then we can't?'

'Prudently . . . Oh, no, all of it! you have to finish all the soup. What
was I saying? Oh, yes: you're too much when you come out with
things like . . . what do you call those bullies when they come to get
you? "Those *signori*! . . . those *gentlemen* have invited me to have a
friendly chat." I like you, Mody, and now that I've found you I wouldn't
want to lose you for anything in the world. Let's make a pact. As you
saw, I realized that you were right and I changed my tune with Sister
Giuliana, so you should also change how you act when Nina is right
. . . Here they come, to invite you to have a chat. You'd think we had
called them! Come on, gulp it down quickly, finish it all up.'

'If I finish it, will you kiss me when I come back?'

'Of course, but prudently. We can't wear ourselves out.'

With that sure promise singing in my mind, the shouts of those
signori no longer hurt my ears and 'chatting' becomes easier day by
day. So easy that they sometimes fall silent, amazed, in their soiled,
badly sewn uniforms . . . Now, after the blinding lights, the shouting
and the silences, I return safely to the cell's darkness, reach out my
hands and I know that, in a matter of seconds, I will find two warm,
open arms, and a breast on which I can sink my head, drowning all
thought.

'Did you put the pillows under the covers?'

'Yes, Nina, like you taught me.'

Nina thinks of everything: my cot lies in the path of the peephole.

'Can we touch each other?'

'No, go to sleep like a good girl. We have to wait for a day when they give us an egg.'

'Is it tomorrow that they'll give us one?'

'I don't think so. Let me think: it must be the day after tomorrow. Be good now, sleep! Tomorrow I'll find out . . .'

'But can't we make an exception? I want so much to kiss your breasts.'

'I told you, no! Now sleep, don't make me mad!'

Nina is terrifying when she gets mad, and whether it's fear or the warmth of her arms holding me tight, I slip into a sweet, peaceful sleep.

82

Nina saves up her sugar and mine: 'You can drink the so-called coffee without sugar – or even pour it into the bucket; it's nothing but dish-water, whereas this precious white powder, mixed with an egg, increases its nutritional value a hundred per cent.' Day by day the paper packet grows and ends up between Nina's bra and her breasts. Only she has the discipline not to open it, not even during the longest hours of hunger, from noon till seven.

'So much sugar, Nina! You're really strong willed. I wouldn't be able to resist.'

Nina smiles, and my admiration makes her more beautiful. Hour by hour, the ugly mask of scars, now healed, fades away, partly because of my caresses and my breath.

'Oh, yes, Mody, keep doing that. It relieves me. If you only knew how these scabs itch! Just like when I had the chickenpox, and my mother tied my hands to the bed. It was torture! Don't stop! Now that I've met you, I don't want my face to be scarred. Before, when I thought you were an informer, all I did was scratch myself. If only there was a mirror! You say most of the scabs have disappeared with-out leaving a mark? Oh, Mody, is it true, or are you just saying that to make me feel better?'

'I'm your mirror; you can trust me. I'm the only mirror that doesn't lie. Your skin is becoming flawless again, and if it weren't for the dark circles under your eyes . . . Your colouring has an amber tone like

when you come back from a walk on the first sunny day after winter
– it seems impossible here inside these walls.'

'I'm not just saying this, but Nina has always been admired for her
complexion. As for the dark circles, yours are no joke either, *nennella*!
We wore ourselves out last night.'

'You said we could.'

'And it's not a criticism. It's nice to think back, knowing that in a
few seconds Nina can make things better . . . Hold on a minute.
Hey, I don't want to brag, but no one can whip up a *zabaglione* or a
mayonnaise like me. You like mayonnaise, huh? I dream about it!
Not to brag, but none of the women in my family or in the neighbourhood could make two eggs yield so much. Look, they seem
like ten! Now, there's a good girl, suck it slowly, it's more nourishing that way.'

We look into each other's eyes as the thick liquid stolen from the
sun goes down, warming the tongue, the palate.

'The last spoonful for Mody because she's more *piccina*. Little
minx! Come on, mmm . . . all done!'

'That was so good! I feel all warm inside. Will you let me kiss the
hiding place where you keep the sugar?'

'No!'

'At least let me touch it.'

'Okay, touch, but then it's time to walk. Come on, get a move on,
Mody. Apart from everything else, at this hour that bitch Sister
Giuliana could arrive. Come on, we have to go from one wall to the
other at least ten times . . .'

'It's boring!'

'I know! Close your eyes part way, and imagine that Nina is taking
you for a stroll through the woods.'

'No, not the woods!'

'Listen to her! And where would you like to walk? You just have to
ask: there's something for everyone.'

'The beach, Nina. I haven't seen the sea in so long! Take me to the
seashore this time. Let's walk along the never-ending strip of sand . . .'

'About-face! Oh, no, you can't lean on me like that! Come on, turn
around and let's start over . . . You like the sea, eh?'

'Oh, yes . . . that isn't the wall . . . that's where the reef begins. Can you make it?'

'Let's try.'

'If you can do it, Nina, maybe we'll make it there . . .'

'Make it where, *micia?*'

'To see the sunset.'

'Of course, pussycat, whatever you like. Come on, just a little farther and we're done for today.'

'A little farther, yes. Look out there, do you see the little island, the Prophet?'

'It looks like clouds to me.'

'Because you can't see it.'

'Actually, I can't see far away.'

'Then trust me, and we'll get there quickly. If we're lucky, we'll see the sun bend down to kiss the Prophet's brow.'

'No!'

'Then in an instant, the sun drags the head down with it into darkness . . . Why are you stopping, Nina? There's time before the soup. The sunset is far off. Let's keep walking a little more.'

'Too hot for me, too much light!'

'Let's at least go as far as the top of the rise. There are trees and shade up there.'

'All I see are white rocks and yellow rocks, then more white and yellow. God, what misery!'

'The yellow isn't rocks, it's yellow blossoms, broom. You're really myopic, Nina!'

'That's right, keep it up! I've told you a hundred times I'm nearsighted.'

'Then trust me and keep walking. There are trees and shade up there.'

Nina lies down in the shade and closes her eyes. Now I know I can lie down beside her and lay my head on her breast. Her ample bosom doesn't feel my weight and I can travel, as I did then, from her belly to her neck without disturbing that deep, regular breathing. How can Carmine go on sleeping while I move up and down his body?

'*You're light as a feather,* figghia! *Besides, how can a big animal like me feel the weight of a little* micia, *a pussycat?*'

'You're not an animal, you're a beautiful column! Once I saw them on the other side of the island. They're scattered in the fields, sleeping in the sun.'

It's not Carmine who is caressing his pussycat with a parched marble hand. He used to call me *gattina*, kitten, or *micia*, pussycat, like the voice that keeps saying: 'What is my minx of a pussycat doing, sleeping? Or is she getting ready to play a naughty trick on me?'

'And you, what are you doing with your eyes closed?'

'I'm trying to get over this fatigue that's come over me. Clearly, though I yearned to see the sky, I don't appreciate it now that I see it. I don't feel it. What can I say? I can't enjoy it. Well, four years in a cell are four years! I'm not used to the fresh air, and my eyes hurt. If I hadn't met you, I might have rotted away in that jail awaiting trial. Shit, I had given up hope of any kind of sentence. It seems like a joke! Hoping for a trial as if it were a prize! Then you come and everything is resolved: relocation, books for you, ink, paper . . .'

'And for you, yarn and a crochet hook.'

'. . . A trial in a jiffy. It was all so quick, like in the movies, that I still feel confused. Oh, Mody, keep an eye on the time! At sunset we have to go back in. I have no intention of losing this paradise for a walk.'

'It's allowed, Nina. Don't get excited. You were so strong in prison!'

'True, I have to get used to it . . .'

'And find something to do.'

'That's also true. You write, teach, but what do you write?'

'Twaddle, Nina, to pass the time.'

'And you earn money too! Didn't you give a lesson today?'

'No, I want to be free at least one day a week.'

'Impudent minx! On an island the breadth of a hand, she wants to be free! Hey, I like it, because when I'm alone I don't know what to do with myself.'

'You have to keep busy.'

'That's what I wanted to talk to you about. Yesterday at the market I saw that they were selling badly crocheted red and blue berets. I can get by with a crochet hook . . .'

'Exactly. That's what I was saying.'

'I want to try!'

'And you could also make baby blankets. All they do is have babies on this island.'

'That and die. Not one day goes by that you don't see a funeral. It must be all these rocks and the lack of water. I'd really like to try! Yesterday, with two berets, an old woman took home a litre of water. I really should give it a try. Are you sure they'll send us yarn from your house? What's happening at your house, anyway? All you do is get letters, read them and say nothing. Nina is curious, very curious. It's a defect of hers.'

'You can read them.'

'Oh no, not that! My father said it's a violation of privacy. It's not part of the anarchist "Ideal".'

'If you want, I'll tell you.'

'It's about time!'

A succession of iron birds streak across the sky, ignoring the wretched piece of land in the middle of the sea. Where are they headed, to spew out their deadly breath? To more attractive places, of course, full of people and life.

'That's why they ignore us, Nina. Their metallic hunger craves young, wholesome flesh, not a few acres populated by shrunken bodies and spent eyes. Oh, Nina, have you seen the man who sells lemons? If you can call him that. He has no nose, no lips, and two slits for eyes. He looks like he was eaten by insects.'

'Only him, Mody? I counted about a dozen of them and then I got tired. It must be leprosy, even if they don't say it. But never mind, tell me about things at your house . . . Bambolina is going to marry your Mattia? Are you upset about it?'

'When she told me about it that night – it seems a century ago – I was sad at first, but then as I waited for dawn, I realized that I wasn't sad because I was losing Mattia but because I felt vanquished, old: forty years!

'You, forty years old . . .'

'Forty-two today, Nina . . .'

'. . . I don't believe it. Not even if I were to see it in writing!'

'Yet I felt every one of those years that night. Because youth and old age are only hypothetical.'

'What does that mean?'

'It means that even age is something that you choose, that you convince yourself of.'

'You think so? But nature also comes into it.'

'Of course, and hard work, and poverty, the privations that age people prematurely. But for those who have had the privilege to be spared that, like me, old age is only a concept instilled in you, like so many others.'

'I like you, Mody. I like the way you acknowledge your privilege.'

'It's the primary duty, it seems to me, for those who think like we do.'

'But tell me about that night.'

'I told you: I was falling into the trap of cliché. Oh, no matter how much you rebel, it's hard to overcome the rules of society that tell you: this is how you are at ten; then at twenty, like this; at forty, with children, you're old . . . I'm ashamed to say it, but that night I was losing my rebellion. I was about to enlist in the army of sheep ambling through the world.

'But not for long! Before dawn I'd realized it, and if they hadn't arrested me, I would have gone in search of something else. The world is big, as Carmine used to say.'

'You still think about your old man?'

'When he helps me.'

'When are they getting married?'

'Oh, they're not getting married. I said that to make you understand. They're already together, and things seem fine, even in bed. Read this: "And don't worry, Zia, even though everything is fine between me and Mattia, I won't ever become one of those legitimate . . . whom our friend talks about."'

'What do the three dots stand for, Mody?'

'Whores. She didn't write it because she was afraid of censorship.'

'And who is this friend?'

'August Bebel . . . Here, there's more: "I got to know him well, not like Mela, who only pretended to read him. And now I know that Papa was right when he said that our friend's words will be the new bible for the women of tomorrow. But enough of these serious matters. I want to tell you how wonderful the villa has become with all the rooms full of life. Even Pietro and Crispina are with us because of the bombings. Catania is an inferno." And so Carmelo has returned to the Brandiforti, as Beatrice hoped it would.'

'And Mela? Crispina?'

'Crispina is studying with a real teacher, and Mela has had a series of successes. In America, life goes on.'

'Still with her Ippolita?'

'Still. Who can understand nature! I think that she will always love only women, although for the press she passes as a virgin devoted solely to Music. Maybe in time, she'll take a husband as a cover . . . unless the world changes.'

'Oh sure, the world is going to change tomorrow! Please!'

'Still, it might change.'

'We're comrades and we can say it, Mody: where do you see that it's changed? In Russia, they've discarded everything that mattered to our individual freedom. After only a few years, they forgot about free love and went right back to marriage. And that's not all!'

'I like it when you talk like that, Nina.'

'Well I don't! I'm sick and tired of talking virtuously and reading books full of dreams. It's easy for you to talk, but in Spain the man of my life was killed by our communist comrades!'

'Are you sure?'

'Sure as can be: eyewitnesses. You yourself know that when the time came, they did away with all the anarchists, and not just them.'

'The dream was too far ahead of its time, Nina. Anarchy is a destination, not . . .'

'Oh sure, too far ahead! And when is it that we'll really decide to take a small step forward, eh, my worthless Princess? And your Gramsci? You condemned him! Arminio, my brother, saw him, you know! Always alone in a cell, or outdoors, isolated from the comrades and scorned. The jailers had a free hand.'

'So?'

'So Gramsci suffered from insomnia, and the guards banged on the bars every hour to wake him up. You're as good as dead in prison if the comrades abandon you. "They" killed him!'

'But even though Arminio knew these things, he continued the struggle like you, it seems to me.'

'Thank you kindly! One must always stay on the side of what's right! But with your eyes open, don't make me angry, Mody!'

Nina is terrifying when she gets infuriated. Her eyes flash yellow sparks and her deep voice echoes cavernously.

'I don't want to lose my temper, Mody, over these stories from the past! Tell me about 'Ntoni. I like that young man from your descriptions of him. Have you heard anything about him?'

'No. I only know that he fled after my arrest.'

'Many were arrested in Rome. I heard it yesterday at the port where the ship that unloads water is docked. They were talking about Rome.'

'What were they saying?'

'That in Rome all you see are women, children and the elderly, and that people are starving in the streets . . .'

83

'Ntoni drags his pale, swollen legs through the streets of Rome, shoved about by indifferent old people and women. He is just one of many who are doomed: the flesh swells with water and the skin becomes taut and white, whiter and whiter before you starve to death.

'What is it, *micia*, why are you screaming? Open your eyes. Nina is right here. Wake up!'

'I had a bad dream, Nina . . . and my stomach hurts.'

'It's nothing, *micia*: it's hunger.'

'You're right. You can't find anything anymore on this shitty island!'

'They're bombing everywhere, Mody.'

'They've forgotten us. Did you see them yesterday, Nina, those pale, swollen children?'

'I've told you over and over again that you shouldn't look at them.'

'You're right. It's just that, like Carmine – how could I understand it at the time? – I'm worried about my children. I dreamed that 'Ntoni was starving to death in Rome.'

'I shouldn't have told you about Rome. Stupid Nina! But 'Ntoni is strong, you said.'

'Yes.'

'Then is it Jacopo you're worried about?'

'No, just yesterday a letter arrived. Luckily they found he has tuberculosis.'

'*Porco cane*, bloody hell. Happy about a son who has tuberculosis!'

'It's not serious, and it's always better than going to war, like Prando.'

'The hell it is!'

'Prando is strong. Have you seen the fiery letters he writes from the front? In our coded language, that patriotic passion means they're doing everything they can to bring about a defeat.'

'Wishing for the defeat of their own country?!'

'That's the only way Fascism can fall, Prando says. But he's different. Jacopo would be dead, Nina, dead for sure.'

'Hey now, don't cry, *micia*.'

'It's partly hunger.'

'So do this for me. Even if I have to pry open your mouth with a knife, you're going to eat this cat. Nina pickled it: it's a delicacy. There are people who are eating rats . . .'

'Oh no, Nina, no!'

'Do you think I like the idea? It must have been the last one on the island! They're eating everything and anything, like in Russia after the revolution. Everything, even the rats. Angelica used to tell me about it when I was a little girl. But the hell with Angelica and her revolution! Now it's you who have to steel yourself. After months of roots and some lentils, Mody, your complexion looks like something out of *La Traviata*, and I don't like it one bit!

'Do you like *La Traviata*? I was crazy about Verdi. When my father opened the shop in Rome, he told me "in Rome there is the Opera" and so my sorrow over having to leave Civitavecchia – I was little at the time – vanished in a flash. And then he kept his promise. Every Sunday afternoon, up there in the gallery – with all those eccentric old people leafing through the scores and singing under their breath – he would always say: "You see, little one, to prepare for the revolution one must soak up lots and lots of fantasy." A great anarchist, Ottavio! To keep Nicola quiet when he started shouting – Nicola was his cousin, a raging, all-out Leninist – he would whisper very, very softly: "It's not your fault, Nicola, it's that you don't have any imagination! We agree that everything depends on the economy, but then the real revolution has to be invented!"'

'And now it's our turn, Mody, or rather the cat's! Don't run away!

Would you rather I had lied to you, maybe? And then what would I do? You have eyes to see, don't you? They've eaten everything, and I can't blame them. The birds are gone . . . Because of the bombings, you say? Oh well . . . Come on, another little piece. Think of it as medicine! Remember the whipped egg? Damn, it was good! Who would have said we'd be longing for an egg we had in prison, eh, Mody? If it weren't for your horrified face, I'd laugh. How comical you are! Now swallow, or you'll choke on it! Did you chew it, at least? Oh God, this one is going to choke herself! I apologize for laughing, little one, but I just had a crazy thought! Given the way things are going, don't you think that before long – and despite all your grimacing – we'll end up looking back with longing at this little creature too?'

*

'Nothing at all, Nina? Didn't you sell the berets?'

'One question deserves another. Didn't those *cialtroni* bring you anything, the bastards? Yet they gobble up your lessons.'

'The poor things, they can barely stand on two feet! But it heartens me to see how, despite their hunger, their interest is stronger. They lap it all up as if it were *rosolio*! In the convent, I dreamed of being a teacher, mostly because of Mother Leonora's lectern, her pointer . . . When Jacopo was five, he dreamed of being pope.'

'Damn! He's no slouch, your Jacopo.'

'It's because of their age. They have so much energy, they don't know what to do with it. All you have to do is not oppose their dreams and then in time, having had their fill, they come to understand; dreams satisfy you like another life. In fact, afterwards Jacopo began to dream of becoming a pirate.'

'I dreamed of being an opera singer.'

'Indeed, you have a stupendous voice.'

'Yes, but seeing how big and fat they were, I got disgusted. I wanted to be slim!'

'You can be happy: we're in the right place here.'

'Funny! But do I see a little packet?'

'Really, Nina, it's only the usual handful of lentils. And besides, there's no water!'

'That's why they let you have them, those little buggers.'

'That's not true!'

'Of course it's not true. I said it just to say something.'

'How well they catch on if you speak clearly to them! At first I thought my own children were so bright because of the way I raised them. But I see that isn't so. Except for that Mazzella, who is really deficient, they all get it, and that helps.'

'They even understand too much! Watch out, the parish priest has complained, I wouldn't want them to send us to a worse island. Things can always get worse!'

'I'm not afraid, Nina. Prando was right: all hell is breaking loose, and they have other things to worry about . . . As I was saying, I wanted to be a teacher.'

'You already told me, *piccoletta*. Hunger isn't doing you any good, little one.'

'If you tell me I'm repeating myself, it means you don't love me anymore, Nina.'

'What are you saying, *micia*, come here . . . There, that's it, on my lap, my little pussycat. Oh, you're burning up! Don't tell me you've got a fever?'

'No, no, you don't love me anymore. Even yesterday, you didn't want to kiss me.'

'Well now Nina will kiss you. Come! Yesterday I went up and down four times for the mail, *micia*, don't forget that!'

'But before you always kissed me, even when you were tired.'

'So? What does that mean? Naturally the flesh always calms down little by little in these things, but in return there's so much tenderness, right, *micia*? So much tenderness it almost makes me cry . . . Come now, a small kiss on these beautiful eyes, this face, this mouth that goes on and on, just to make it stop chattering . . .'

'And also on my firm, arrogant chin, as you used to say . . . Do you still like it, Nina?'

'Of course I still do, like this beautiful serene brow, just barely marred by a scar that changes shape, colour . . . what shape does it have today, do you know? It looks like a small pale brook full of little stars.'

'Oh, Nina, don't mention water. I'm so thirsty!'

'I can't blame you. So then let's say that today it has the shape of a comet. You've told me everything, but not how you got this scar.'

'I don't feel like talking about it. I just feel thirsty.'

'Then you know what your Nina says? It's time to get a move on!'

'You're so funny when you say that!'

'Get a move on, then. Come on, shake your ass! Lazy bones! Not to brag, but we Romans are really elegant spirits, almost worthy of Sir Eden, or stylish Bond Street, as Arminio used to say.'

'What pronunciation, Nina! Say it again: Strreeteh'.'

'What does pronunciation matter? As long as you get it! Besides, I live by reflected light and I'm satisfied with that.'

'Whose reflected light?'

'My Arminio's. He knows foreign languages and all that. I revolve around him. I look at him and swell with satisfaction!'

'You still think about your brother, eh, Nina?'

'Like you and your old man: when I need him.'

'Listen, Nina, you haven't told me everything either, like why you stopped studying.'

'Who knows! Arminio says it's because of the usual old female self-deprecation. It's true. I let myself get discouraged! Oh, not at home. At home, to my father, we were all equal . . . and in fact, damn if he wasn't right! All dead or in jail, women and men alike! What was I saying? Oh yes, not at home but outside, in school. He also said that maybe it depended on your date of birth. I was born too soon, and he must be right because Licia, the youngest, studies and she's quicker than a locomotive . . . Come on, move. I really hope I hear from Olimpia: with Licia she's in good hands, but you know how it is! A mother's anxiety doesn't let up. Come on, let's go.'

'No, tell me about Arminio. What is he like?'

'Again? You must know it by heart.'

'Yes, but I like to hear about him.'

'Not to brag, but he's my brother!'

'Is it true that his eyes change colour, or did you make it up?'

'Look at mine. What do you think?'

'Will I get to meet him?'

'How should I know! It seems to me that we won't meet anyone here anymore except in the next world! Come on, let's go.'

'I feel weak, Nina. What is it?'

'Then stay here. I'll go. Today is a good day, you'll see. You'll see, I'll come back with a lot of letters and something to eat.'

I'm sure that's true. When Nina says she'll be right back, she means it. She's never been late, not ten minutes or an hour. But whether due to thirst or hunger, or because of all that salt water – even from a distance you can tell it's salty and bitter – today I'm afraid I won't see her face again. To calm the trembling of my knees, even if I had to crawl over the scorching rocks on all fours, I race after her and grab her hand . . . I can't see anything, yet it's broad daylight. All I feel is the warmth of her hand urging me down toward what was once a quiet cove of pale blue water, with rows of white houses like the ones Jacopo used to draw when he was five or six years old . . . Why has Nina stopped? And why, instead of the usual silent, empty streets, are there so many people pushing and shouting? Why is that man who has climbed onto the ledge now plucking at the wall and hurling stones at us?

84

'They weren't trying to harm us, *micia*. They were tearing down Mussolini's bust, and they were elated! When you slumped to the ground like in the movies, I realized, damn if Nina didn't realize, that it was serious! But now you're out of danger, and that's what counts.'

'What danger? And why is it so dark?'

'Because your eyes hurt. Nothing serious. It's the fever and weakness.'

'It's from hunger, isn't it, Nina?'

'Well, I wish! You had typhus, *micia*, and what a fever! Is it possible you don't remember anything? What a fright! Hour by hour, I was afraid you would die in my arms.'

'Nina? I've never seen you cry.'

'Hell! It's you who are making me cry, with those fleshless ribs and these tiny little hands. They look like my Olimpia's hands when she had diphtheria.'

'Olimpia! Have you heard from your daughter?'

'She's here with us . . . you really don't remember anything?'

'I only remember that I followed you and that it was hot . . .'

In the dim light, I stare at Nina's face and try to remember. Maybe if she'd turn on the lamp . . .

'Why the lamp, *micia*? It's still daylight. I'll open the window.'

To open the window Nina has to move aside waves of white tulle, like the veil the novices wear when they become brides of Christ. The gauzy white makes me nauseous. Who knows why Beatrice insisted on that fatal symbol, and why Carlo didn't rebel? '*No one can defy Beatrice. You know that, Modesta.*'

Nina moves away from the curtains, satisfied, and goes over to the large mirror framed by gilded vine leaves and flowers. Who can defy Cavallina? She insisted on that mirror until she got her way, and now, like every morning, Nina looks at herself in the glass and brushes her hair as she gazes at her image.

'It's beautiful here, *micia*, lovelier than you'd described. Eh, you rich folks! Either you don't realize what you have or you mock the rest of us: the country house, a cottage . . . Hell, this place is a palace!'

Nina combs hair that shines like burnished gold – or is it the sun?

'Naturally, your Bambù got me some henna! Hey, it's not true that everything natural is always good. Sometimes nature needs some touching up.'

She's right: that silky golden mass softens her somewhat plebeian features, as Nonna Gaia would say, and gives Nina's face 'a certain something sweet that's touching'. Right, Carlo?

'*Un po' di luna, un po' di mare, un po' di musica nel cuor. . . Solo così potrò scordare il mio dolor . . .*, a little moon, a little sea, a little music in my heart . . . only then can I forget my sorrow . . .'*

Nina is singing a new song.

'Oh, did you know I met your famous Jose?'

'Where?'

'Here. He landed with the Americans. He found us some penicillin and left again. Who could have imagined it, an Italian in an American uniform fighting against his country! He sends you his warm regards. What a magnificent man! Your Nina, for two days at least, was in love, and not because she's a *cottarola*, as her father used to say, someone who loses her head easily. The truth is, that guy is a real man!'

'Everyone falls in love with Jose.'

'Look at that! You too?'

'No, not me.'

'Why not?'

'Because I was certain I'd never see him again. I won't see him again. It's Timur I'm going to meet up with.'

'Timur! Come on! You said every German helmet we saw was him.'

'Yes, it's the only thing I remember: faceless helmets and shiny metal badges on their chests. A hundred, two hundred, maybe a thousand helmets and badges with that cruel slogan.'

'Actually, we only saw a few of them, *micia*! "Only the essential quota of Germans!" that's what your Jacopo said.'

A warm rush of pride when Nina talks about Jacopo that way always clears away the fog of lethargy. To hear her speak about him, and for that reason only, I have her tell me the story of our liberation, which I know by heart . . .

'Yes, yes, it was him. While everyone was celebrating the fall of Fascism, deluding themselves that it was all over, that very morning, with Pietro, he began pulling strings, and didn't let up . . . Yes, he was the one who persuaded your friend Pasquale to help them. Hardly timid or hesitant! He planned the trip, dealt with everybody. And after bringing us here, he quickly departed again for Rome to bring back my Olimpia. Just in time, too!'

To hear it again and make certain of Nina's admiration for my Jacopo, all I have to do is ask, 'But is it possible that he carried me in his arms for so long?'

'Of course he did! He and Pietro, but nearly always him.'

Nearly always him! . . . Even though he's far away (Jose took him along to fight in the north), in Jacopo's arms I'm transported tenderly from bed to chair. And if it's not too hot: 'You mustn't sweat,' she told me, her gentle hands supporting my waist as we move toward the window, so distant; it's a struggle to reach it, but it's clean, no bed-bugs or rats that scratch.

'It's nice here, isn't it, *micia*? All these trees are restful on the eye. Greenery outside, and so clean inside! Remember how those dark bastards used to scratch? You were really brave to never mention them, Mody, I have to tell you.'

'All we could do was ignore them.'

'Sure, but now that I see all this cleanliness – almost excessively spotless – I realize even more how courageous you were.'

'And how about you? You never told me about your seasickness or island sickness, whatever you want to call it.'

'I still dream about that little scrap of land the size of a handkerchief! Oh! You couldn't raise your eyes without seeing that fearful water constantly in motion.'

'That's why you often kept your head down. So it wasn't a headache!'

'Oh sure, you must be joking! You're talking about the kind of headache a *signorina* gets! It was as if my head was stretched and pulled by the waves. Oh, they know that being confined on the island has this effect on almost everyone, except you, my fine little one!'

'Nina, hold me. You're right, but I'm still afraid. I'm ashamed, but I'm afraid!'

'Come, stay quietly in my arms and the fear will go away. Not to brag, but Nina is a master at calming her *micia*.'

Nina is a master at soothing every quiver, her stroking sure and confident on my burning forehead. And that's why today, too, I look into her eyes to endure the long waiting, the anxiety, the fear, the lack of news, bombarded by echoes of massacres, torturing, mass killings that only those who have lived through can know, and afterwards have the right to tell.

But that comes later . . . Now, if it weren't for Nina, I would remain supine, waiting, suspended in a void of anxiety and fever, trying only to decipher the closed faces, sealed by terror, of those who return amid the indecipherable chatter the radio constantly blares . . . And nothing can console me, not Bambolina's beauty, a new beauty, her face tanned, proud of her work in the fields, nor Carluzzu, Stella's son, who when he falls already knows how to get up by himself without crying, not the birth of little Beatrice – all white and golden – the daughter of Bambù and Mattia, nor the sight of Olimpia, Nina's daughter, as she plays with Crispina.

'They're always together, aren't they, Nina?'

'She's a force of nature, that Crispina! In a few months she's transformed my Olimpia. When she got here, her eyes were those of a terrified sheep. She wouldn't speak. Now she runs and leaps around like a little goat . . .'

At night I continue to reach for Nina's hand, the dark-haired, serious Nina of the island who still lives in my memory. By day: the golden, smiling Nina who runs through the delicate green of the vineyard at sunset. Finally I can run beside her and drink in her stories, her jokes.

'God the hare, Nina? That's a new one!'

'No, little one, old as madonna eight!'

'What do you mean, eight?'

'Eight! Like the number eight. Or madonna the ballerina, or if you prefer, God the tightrope-walker, whatever you like.'

'You make me laugh, Nina. Where do you get these things? Do you make them up?'

'Make them up? Not a word! They're all passed down as part of the family legacy. It takes centuries to arrive at such refinements. In his serene old age my grandfather, a pure-blooded product of Viareggio, enjoyed digging up and collecting various oaths. "Now that Italy has finally been united" – he used to say – "and now that the parasitic papacy has been chased out, it's our duty to gather together the expressions of revolt that rose spontaneously from the oppressed people . . ." That's right, like popular songs and poems: part of the cultural heritage, he said. Poor *Nonno*! He was completely unshakeable. I only saw him cry twice: over the Concordat* and over Sacco and Vanzetti.'*

'For God's sake, Nina, don't start in with Sacco and Vanzetti!'

'Yet if the Allies win, we'll have to take a look at that ugly crime, my dear Mody.'

'No, Nina, no! Instead, tell me: any news of Arminio?'

'Nothing, not about Arminio or your 'Ntoni. But we can be happy to have heard something about Jacopo and Prando. And if I'm happy, not being part of the family . . .'

'You *are* part of the family!'

'How I love your Mattia! If it weren't for Bambolina I would gladly spend a couple of hours one-on-one with him. But though Nina may be a *cottarola* who loses her head easily, she gives in to her fancies, yes, but not with men who are taken.'

Nina, Nina . . . The dark-haired, feral Nina of the island, the golden-haired, smiling Nina of Carmelo. Finally I can run beside her, enjoy the sight of her harmonious freedom, her step that sketches melodious whorls of vital energy. Now she stops, preoccupied. She must have something to confess to me.

'I have a confession to make, *micia*. Last night I had a relapse, so to speak. It's just that that dark-skinned guy appealed to me, plus this morning, he was leaving. Well, now you know, it wasn't so bad . . .'

Each time she confesses, my surprise at not being jealous makes me run into her arms, grateful. How can that be? Thinking of Joyce, I realize that jealousy is always provoked by those in the habit of using it out of pointless, venomous cruelty. Besides, after her confession, her arms tighten around me with new warmth.

'You're not mad at me, are you, *micia*? What can you do? That's how Nina is! She's a bit of a *maschiaccio*, a hoyden, as Arminio used to call me when I was a little girl. And was he ever right! Don't pay any attention. They're just passing fancies, nothing serious, things that only render the affection I have for you purer. Even with my husband, it was the same. Of course, he got worked up a little . . .'

'And if he did it?'

'Oh well, it doesn't work both ways!'

'And if I do it?'

'It works both ways, *micia*, don't worry. Nina keeps her word.'

'But you're all I want.'

'Bullshit! It's just that you don't know; you have no experience. You, Bambolina, you're the first to have had a little freedom. Not to brag, but we, in these things, had it really easy with my mother, and my mother with my grandmother . . . But then come to think of it, maybe each of us is the way we are. Any rational thinking stops when it comes to love, and it's best not to talk about it. What a time your Nina went through, torn between you, who were dying, and that little one so far away! Only Jacopo understood me. That young man understands everything. How could I leave you to go and bring Olimpia back from Rome? "Well, then we'll send Pietro," he said, without batting an eye. "If you feel you can rely on him, write a letter to your sister and Pietro will go and get her." What a decision, my *micia* with that giant who never looks at you directly. I trust him, but would Licia trust that beast? And so Jacopo, as if he had read it in my eyes, said: "All right, I'll go. For some reason, everyone trusts me." For some reason, he says! He looks like an angel!'

'But Jacopo will come back, right, Nina?'

'Of course, like they'll all come back. Even Arminio, I'm sure of it.'

The magical balm of her certainty spurs us to keep Carmelo's rooms ready and waiting, and nothing else exists around us, neither the unbridled joy of those to whom everyone has returned, nor the ashen, death-like grief of those who have lost everyone and wander like blind men through the ruins, the markets, the shops. It's horrifying to meet their gaze, eyes dilated in a question that has no answer.

'Don't look at them, Mody. Do as you did on the island with those who were starving. It doesn't help them or us.'

And without looking, we waited through winter, then summer. And then another winter and another summer.

85

That opulent golden summer, unforgettable for its harvest and its light . . . as if the earth, anticipating the end of that deluge, was ready to rejoice in a silence brimming with grain, which had suddenly fallen over the fields.

Mattia: 'Never in living memory has such a rich harvest been seen on the island! Down in Catania everyone is wild with joy. They cheer for peace just like they called for war before.'

Modesta: 'Always the same reckless lunatics, Mattia. Reckless and vulgar, Nonna Gaia would have said. They don't see that, once again, it's a foreign military rousing senseless hope in them.'

Pietro: 'Everything has stopped, Mody . . .'

Bambù: 'Not a single plane flies over anymore, Zia. I thought war would break out with all those airplanes passing over us, especially at night.'

Mattia: 'In 1918, at the end of the Great War, we young people were joyous because we thought everything would turn out well. And it annoyed us to hear the old people who kept saying: "Peace has broken out, and it will be worse than war".'

Pietro, on the other hand, is calm. He has managed to prevent at least one former prefect from jumping onto the platform and speaking again.

Pietro: 'How that traitor Pasquale pleaded! "I was young when they decided to beat up Carlo. What did I know? They only intended to teach him a lesson." And on and on, pleading and reminding us of all his good deeds. Good deeds! Five years in prison for my Mody! And he, fat and slick, keeps saying that there was nothing more he could do: "How could I have saved her from a proven charge of financing a clandestine party?" If everyone had done as I did and as *signorino* Jose ordered, something could certainly have changed. At least we would have got rid of the old faces, although now new ones are coming from America. Yesterday I nearly got myself in trouble; I saw the notorious D'Alcamo brothers in a jeep.'

Mattia: 'And who are they, Pietro?'

Pietro: 'Two mafiosi, vicious as sin, so vicious that first they were called angels. Then they disappeared. But as we know, angels fly around, and just as they vanished earlier, now they're back in the arms of the foreigner. And this tells us that nothing is going to change.'

Bambù: 'Oh, stop, Pietro! that's enough! *Uffa*, you make me want to cry! You older people are right, but I want to be serene like Zia. I want to have hope! Hope, at least, that Prando, Jacopo and 'Ntoni will return. Oh, Zia, they must return!'

In the silence of an indifferent peace that envelops the endless fields, I find myself wandering alone in the midst of an irreverent abundance of lush fruit, vegetables and fleshy flowers that mocks the dead buried under the rubble. Like at the time of the Spanish flu, big rats (nourished by the corpses? I shudder to think of it) prowl through the half-ruined stables, menacing our livestock. Yesterday we heard about another child found at dawn with his little feet gnawed by those creatures, now as big as cats. Shotgun in hand – it's now the rule at Carmelo – anyone who has time goes hunting for that primal enemy. And so I too skulk around to flush them out, my head deafened by the blast of the pellets, my wrists sore.

I've been crouching for ten minutes, smoking a cigarette, when a furtive rustling from behind the fence makes me instinctively raise the barrel of the gun.

'Damn, it must be my fate! Wherever I go, all I find are guns pointed at me. Hey, Mody! Is this any way to welcome me back?'

''Ntoni!' I hear my voice scream. 'What on earth were you doing behind the fence?'

'Well, I was trying to recover a little before making my appearance. I felt so fearless as I was walking here! But once I saw the house I was ashamed to show up like this . . . I don't know! I was hoping I'd seem more decent if I rested up a little.'

'What are you saying, 'Ntoni? Come here! Where are you going?'

'But I have lice, too! They torment me, Mody, they're a torment!'

'Ntoni runs off. He must have noticed the horror that came over me, fool that I am! What did I expect – to see them return as they were before? I mustn't be scared by his appearance. It's 'Ntoni, it's his voice! I run after him and grab him by the arms. He didn't go far; he hasn't got the strength. All I had to do was touch him and, there, he falls into my arms crying.

'Oh, Modesta, finally you're holding me! So long without a woman's face, without a woman's arms! A man can't live without such tenderness. He can't live!'

'Ntoni trembles in my arms the way he trembled in Stella's arms when he was a baby. And nothing can warm him up, not a hot bath nor a cup of honeyed chamomile tea. '*Quannu pigghia friddu 'stu carusu diventa siccu siccu comu fussi manciatu du so stessu trimuri! . . . comu a so patri*' – Stella's words – 'When this boy catches a chill, he becomes skin and bones, like his father, as if his own tremors were eating him up.'

Day by day, 'Ntoni grows more gaunt under the covers. And when night falls, the chill reminds him of atrocious scenes from a past known only to him, which makes him shout out orders, entreaties, words in German . . . Those words erect an icy barrier between him and those of us who are impotent spectators before his struggle.

Bambù: 'Oh, Zia, it's awful! He has a scar. What can it have been? And you, Antonio, what kind of a doctor are you? Why don't you say something?'

Antonio: 'It's not clear, or rather it's plain as day: torture, experiments . . . I know of some, but only he can tell us.'

Bambù: 'Look, even his hip! It seems like he can't move his legs properly.'

Antonio: 'No, no Bambolina, he's not paralysed anywhere; the scars have been closed up for some time. He's just very malnourished, and that doesn't help any. The physical wounds will heal soon enough, but the wounds of memory won't! Don't cry, Bambù, the important thing is that . . . well, the important thing is that there's nothing . . . well, he's still a man.'

Bambù: 'Yesterday he asked about Stella. He must have forgotten.'

Antonio: 'It's possible. Probably his body couldn't handle that other sorrow and erased it. So much the better!'

Bambù: 'I'm afraid, Antonio, so afraid! What about Prando and Jacopo? Why haven't they returned? So many have come back . . .'

Antonio: 'Don't get upset, Bambù. Try to stay calm like Nina. She's waiting too. Many have yet to return. I got the numbers down at the town hall: there's still hope.'

Bambù: 'Oh, Antonio, it seemed like it was all over!'

Antonio: 'War is quick to come and slow to leave. Italy looks like a heap of ruins; the fields are still mined. In Milan, they've allotted a kilo and a half of coal per individual, twice a month. They're warm this winter in Milan, Bambù, in the midst of armed gangs who ransack everything. In Naples, gangs of kids, one of them ninety-strong, attacked a train: the oldest member was seventeen.'

Bambù: 'I'm scared, more scared than before, during the war. The house seems empty since Prando has been gone, and Modesta doesn't talk, doesn't smile. She comes and goes from Catania looking sadder and sadder.'

Bambolina speaks about me as if I weren't there, and she's right. In the evening I sit with them around the table and bring food to my mouth but I'm unable to speak. My mind is focused solely on a deep disappointment. On those men in Palermo, in Catania, who receive me with open arms as they slip around the old desks of power, the same gestures barely softened by white-striped grey suits, the same heads, though not wearing the Fascist beret: *'You, Princess, are a heroine, and today more than ever we need women like you. The future will belong to women! Like in America. With your past, you will attract crowds of women to us. You'll be one of the first women deputies . . .'* Except for Pasquale, and I almost feel sorry for him, they're all still there: their cheeks smoothly shaven, fragrant with bergamot. And though at home I'm silent, there at least I enjoy blanching those cheeks: *'You mean the first woman paid to collaborate? Why, isn't the word "collaborate" used anymore? But of course, collaborate with the landowners, the barons, the priests?'*

'But Princess, democracy! It will be a democracy! All we have to do, as America has suggested, is demonstrate first through local elections that we Italians are capable of establishing this democracy! And with a democracy we . . . you'll soon see . . . You're not turning communist on us, are you, Princess?'

'Oh, Zia, please, say something!'

'Sorry, Bambù. I was thinking about what I should say to those *signori* tomorrow.'

'Did you say that with the fall of the Parri government and with the Americans in Italy there will never be a revolution?'

'Yes, that's right, Bambù. Parri falls and that Jesuit De Gasperi takes over the government.* The Jesuits will reassume their influence, as Jose would have said.'

'But there's also Togliatti!'

'For as long as it's convenient, and certainly to circumvent the risk of revolution. Ah, that's what I'll say tomorrow! I want to have some fun.'

'It doesn't seem like you're really having fun, Zia!'

'I'll say that I'm a communist and that I believe only in the revolution. We have to side with the opposition. I've thought about it. Nina is right. Especially women: we're always part of the opposition.'

'Why are you crying now, Zia? For the love of God, why are you crying?'

'Because I've made up my mind! But above all, because . . . because I knew I would never see Jose again. I knew it, but he shouldn't have died, he shouldn't have!'

'Oh, Modesta, is he dead? How did it happen?'

'Yes, fighting at Cassino. He had enlisted in the Fifth Army. With him, this war took away one of the best. *'And if you two foolish little ladies thought for even a moment about celebrating this unfortunate peace, you were mistaken! I will never tolerate the sight of those shirkers who, while profiting from the absence of the best men, prepare to enjoy a peace based on theft and lies. War carries off the best men, always!'*

Nonna Gaia's grey eyes pierce my pupils like daggers, and I have to lower my head to escape the pain they inflict . . . Months of abject conversations, full of inflated rhetoric, good intentions, plans. Meanwhile, in the countryside people are starving to death. And already, invisible shotguns are aimed at the heads of the godless reds. No, that's what they said before; now they're called 'Bolshevik emissaries'. Already heads are falling in this time of peace, and now we can put a name to a few heads among the countless who have vanished into thin air: on 7 June 1945, union leader Nunzio Passalacqua is killed in Naro, with instigators and perpetrators acting in broad daylight, out in the open, so that everyone might see and reflect on it.

*

'Indeed, the noblewoman we know gave everything she had to Don Calò. Yes, the same Calogero Vizzini from when we were young, Modesta. The Mafia in Palermo and Monreale encouraged her, let's say, to support EVIS:* a kind of militia formed by the right wing of the separatist party, the party of those who want to separate from Italy so they can steal better. And in the absence of a Mussolini, they finance and arm a certain bandit, Giuliano. Don Calò dealt with him personally. I've had confirmed reports.'

'They don't lose any time, do they, Mattia?'

'The *signori* are always prompt to act, as Carmine used to tell me when I was a boy: "This is something you must learn from them, only this. Because we peasants are slow, but with the strength of our arms and their alacrity you'll be riding high like your father Carmine for your whole life and that of your children." Only now do I understand why it gave me so much joy to lose at the gaming table. It was like a beneficial blood-letting, Mody; it drained away all the bad black blood of us ill-fated Tudia!'

'You Tudia may be ill-fated, but not us Brandiforti! Thanks to our mother's teachings, we found ourselves on the right side, and we will make the price we paid – first, through anti-fascism and later, fighting in the war and in the mountains – count for something. I warn you, Mattia Tudia, that nothing is solved by such defeatism.'

'Defeatism was a Fascist word, Prando.'

'We'll find another one, don't worry! We'll find other words, right, Mama? The important thing is to act!'

'How beautiful you are, Mama. I'm ashamed to say so, but I was afraid I'd find you old. It's strange, but in the midst of that inferno, my only concern was that I wouldn't find you as I'd left you. Mama, you know what I'll call you from now on? And maybe it will help to make you stay young for ever . . .'

'What, Prando?'

'My *mamma bambina*, my child-Mama . . . What a strange creature man is!'

'Why, Prando?'

'Oh yes, strange! Before, I had you all to myself and I didn't understand you. Then, when I was far away I realized who you were and I was afraid of losing you: a kind of remorse for not having understood you earlier, as if fate wanted to punish me for my inattention. That was the only thing I was afraid of, not killing or being killed. Let me rest my head on your lap. Touching you is the only way I feel sure I've found you again.'

As soon as he lays his head on my lap he falls asleep. His face, unchanged, shows no signs of distance. As if he had gone and returned from a ride on his motorcycle. Only his eyes have become more thoughtful. Another wound, still red, can be seen parallel to the long scar on his cheek that has now faded. His skin has lost the gloss of stone polished by the sea, but even in sleep it is still firm and smooth under my fingers. Why can't I rejoice in his return? Is it Nonna Gaia's refrain perhaps? '*In every war the best are lost . . .*' Or maybe it's the presence of 'Ntoni who, cloaked in his sorrow, wanders distractedly in the garden without speaking? From a distance, his restored body makes him look just as he was before, but when you get closer, his eyes bleed from a wound that is still open.

An airplane passes overhead, obscuring the sun, and Prando's eyes open, somewhat troubled. 'You're here, Mama? Thank goodness! I always fall sleep. I wonder why? It's as if I never get enough sleep and . . . But are you sad, Mama? Oh, I'm sorry, what a moron! Your Prando will always be a self-centred idiot! Is it because of Jacopo? Are you

worried about Jacopo? But he must come back, Mama, he must . . .
He was the best of all of us.'

Those words make me cry out loud in his arms. If Jacopo is dead, I
won't add another line to these memoirs of mine and I'll remain
silent for ever.

86

And just as silence fell over the brief reminders of my life in that distant 1945, I fall silent again now as I write, trembling as I search for Jacopo's name among the papers. I'm afraid I've lost the date of his return.

Waiting makes us impervious, distracted . . . Here it is: 6 August 1945, Hiroshima. Jacopo returned at just that time. Clearly that was why I didn't note the date. The A-bomb was able to distract even me. Merely a bomb more powerful than the others, they said. And later on, in fact, they gave the name 'bikini' to a bathing suit and the uplifting nickname 'atomic' to a movie star.

I close my eyes and hear only the memory of that waiting, which draws out the seconds and minutes in a single bleak sound. And I don't notice 'Ntoni coming toward me on the beach at Villa Suvarita . . . From a distance – his body strong again, his hair trimmed – he looks like he did many years earlier. But as soon as he comes closer I have to look away to avoid seeing his bitter, unsmiling face.

'You really missed the sea, didn't you, Modesta? You don't even seem concerned about the mines.'

'Don't worry, 'Ntoni. I settle for going back and forth along the permitted space. See, there are signs posted. Besides, sooner or later we have to decide to fix up this villa.'

'It's seen a lot, poor Suvarita! I haven't had the heart to go inside yet. Bambù sounds like a madwoman when she talks about it, yet no one can say that Bambù isn't strong, right, Modesta?'

'No, that's for sure.'

'Is it true that all the walls are smeared and soiled in the room we used as a theatre? Are there bloodstains on the walls?'

'We cleaned everything, 'Ntoni.'

'Are the stains gone?'

'They're gone.'

'Good.'

'Nina helped me.'

'Nina is the dearest, most beautiful woman I have ever known. Poor Nina! You can tell she's suffering over her Arminio . . . how she waited for him! War is atrocious! After the news, she became thin and old. But now she seems like a young girl again. How can it be? How old is she?'

'I don't know, 'Ntoni. You know I can never remember anyone's age.'

'Where does she get that strength? From her daughter, maybe? She's certainly a wonderful girl. It would be nice to have a daughter like her! But I think – I spoke with Prando about this and he agrees – I think it will be better, I'd say appropriate, not to have any more children. Not to bring any more unfortunate creatures into the world. What kind of a future can children have in these times? All we needed besides everything else was this bomb, Mody! What a death: disintegrated, pulverized in an instant! Plus, who knows what else they're not telling us . . . We owe this to our American friends.'

'Please, 'Ntoni . . . it's really all so sad.

'Oh, forgive me, Modesta, you're right, it's just . . . I can't help it! What were we saying? Oh, yes, Nina is fantastic! And can she sing! It's a shame she wasn't with us when we used to put on performances; she'd have driven everyone wild. Too bad she didn't know us then, right, Mody!

'Let's go, I can't stand to see our house destroyed like this. Yet even now, if I stare at it, I can see you all the way you used to be: My mother in those funny outfits, part peasant, part *signora*. Prando always muddy and tattered, trying to be like Jean Gabin,* the big snob! Bambù always the prettiest in her white dresses . . . oh, I can still see her coming down the stairs! Then behind her, the starring couple:

the Princess arm in arm with her favourite . . . even though you never said so, did you, Mody? . . . arm in arm with her Jacopo, tall, lanky, with his childlike face and old man's walk . . . There, now the Princess and her darling deign to come down the stairs. Oh, Modesta, I'm losing my mind, losing it! Look, I see you there, dressed in white, with Jacopo, and yet you're here. Modesta, help. You look too!'

A deep terror makes me turn toward him at once: his face is ashen, like that of someone who has seen a ghost.

'Look, I haven't lost my mind. It's Bambolina, with Jacopo! It's him, Modesta, it's him! There can't be anyone else that tall but him!'

Can joy transfix you like lightning, and rip through your body? Riveted by that joy, I barely have a chance to see him before I faint in his arms.

When I open my eyes again, years seem to have passed, even though the sea is there, lit by the same dazzling sun.

'Oh, Mama, thank goodness you're opening your eyes again! For a moment I thought you had blacked out.'

It's his voice, but that robust chest, those strong arms that almost lift me off the ground must be Prando's arms. It's best not to look; it must be an illusion. I shouldn't have listened to 'Ntoni and his madness.

'No, Mama, no, I'm not Prando. Here, look at me closely. I'm Jacopo, can't you see? It's this American uniform that's to blame, but I wanted to come right away rather than waste time changing. Besides, what would I change into, Bambù? Nothing fits me anymore.'

'Oh yes, Zia, even Prando's shirts are too tight for him!'

Why don't I recognize him? Yet Nina had alerted me: '*Of course, Mody, your Jacopo carried you in his arms all the way when you had the fever.*' But it's one thing to imagine and another thing to see, to touch. With my hands on that broad chest, I search for my Jacopo. With my palms, I inch slowly up toward the straight, broad shoulders. And only when I meet the grey eyes behind the misted glasses do I find him. It's ridiculous, I know, and I can see why Bambolina bursts out laughing. But I can't help taking off his glasses to be sure. Stripped of them, the pupils widen, gentle and shy, and the sad, demure gaze – as Beatrice used to say of Uncle Jacopo's – stares out at me intently as if from the photograph. '*Oh yes, if it weren't for his thinness and that stooped, solemn gait, Uncle Jacopo would have been a very handsome man*' . . . Uncle Jacopo moves off, bent under his burden, while my Jacopo sighs and settles his eyeglasses on his slightly aquiline nose with its thin nostrils.

'Oh, thank you, Mama, now I can finally see you again! That's right, Bambolina: I'm really blind as a bat! Just think, from a distance, even with my glasses on, I mistook you for Modesta.'

'It's just that she's all you think about. You see her everywhere.'

'And what about you, then? A fine welcome! Mama, do you know that until I was right under her nose, she kept staring at me suspiciously?'

'I mistook him for one of those giant Americans.'

'You should be ashamed! And how about 'Ntoni, staring at me as if I were a ghost? And you, Mama, so pale you can't say a word? It's all because of this damn uniform. Come on, let's go, I want to take it off. I can't stand it anymore!'

Gradually, as he speaks, the lightning bolt of joy that struck me dissolves into a happiness I'd never felt before. But as soon as he loosens his hold and starts to let me go, fear of the soft, unsteady sand underfoot makes me say foolishly, 'No, Jacopo, don't let me go. Carry me in your arms like you did when you came with Pietro to free me from the island.' And Bambù laughs.

'Of course, of course, but do you remember that? How can you? You were delirious.'

'No, I don't remember. Nina told me about it.'

'Of course, Nina! Where is she? I'm really eager to see her again. What a courageous woman, Bambù. You can't imagine.'

'Oh, tell us about it, Jacopo, tell us and hold me tight.'

In Jacopo's arms I listen again to the adventurous stages of our journey, and only now do my senses feel certain that the time in prison, the war, is over. Only now do I hear in his voice that it's possible to think about a future. Indeed, as Jacopo says, settling me in an armchair and covering me with a shawl . . . What is he saying?

'Yes, Mama, the worst horrors are over, at least for us here in Italy. But later on I'll tell you about the things I've seen among these Allies!

I couldn't wait to come back here and discuss them with all of you. There is no Marxist thinking among their intellectuals, and I'm talking about intellectuals, students like me: peculiar students, who specialize in only one field. Of course, Roosevelt is a great man, but similar to our old Antonio, a rose-water libertarian socialist. But the things I've seen among the young people! Inhibitions, discrimination, racial hatred. Just think: there was a certain Bob, whom I came to like – he was in the hospital with me – I didn't find out until later that at night, despite his poor condition, he would go out with a group of guys to beat up any fellow soldier who was black. The first one they came across, he told me afterwards with an innocent, disarming air: 'The first black mug we run into' . . . But that part of my past is over now, and though we shouldn't be pessimistic, neither should we think – as most people unfortunately do – that with the end of Fascism, all will be well. In the year I spent in that hospital, Mama, I felt like I had gone from a real cell to a somewhat more spacious one, with enough food and a newspaper or two: a slightly more permissive cell, as Joyce once described Italy in comparison with Hitler's Germany.'

*

'. . . Twenty years, only to start all over again. The revolution did not happen. And it will be all we can do to get rid of the Savoia. There's a price to pay for twenty years of ignorance and the regime. On my trip back, all through Italy I heard talk that would make you shudder. I've become convinced that we'll pay for these years, all of them, day by day, hour by hour.'

'If it weren't for how happy I am to see you alive, Jacopo, I swear to God I'd start arguing with you again! But I don't want to spoil my joy and Mama's. Look at her, Mattia. She looks like a different person; she seems ten years younger! Come here, Jacopo, hug your brother Prando. Welcome back.'

As they clutch one another, motionless, there in the sun, a joy-filled silence emanates from their embrace. That silence must have a certain pull, because one by one, all the residents of Carmelo pause at the door, almost on tiptoe: Pietro, old Antonio, who takes off his glasses and concentrates on wiping them with a freshly laundered handker-chief, Argentovivo with little Beatrice in her arms, Crispina holding hands with Olimpia, pointing out her hero to her little friend, and other faces new to me, the faces of *carusi* who work in the fields with Mattia; among them is an elderly man with big blue eyes set among deep creases, holding little Carlo by the hand. The beauty of that old man's face captures my gaze. Or maybe I'm looking for an unknown face so I won't be overwhelmed by emotion? Even Bambolina clings to me tightly, like when she was a little girl and we would walk side by side on the sand, facing the sun and then wading through the morn-ing's silent waves. With water up to her chin she'd whisper: '*Oh, Zia, I'm still too small. I can't wait to grow up so I can get close to the sun like you.*'

She isn't talking about the sun now, and even though her arm encir-cles my waist as it did then, I don't have to stoop to hear her.

'Oh, Zia, in our joy we forgot about 'Ntoni. He's disappeared! Let's go look for him right away!'

Without a word we go looking for him, searching through the immense rooms, the vast corridors, up and down those endless stairs that, given the anxiety that comes over me, suddenly assume the fear-ful quality they had when I wandered through that intimidating house as a girl.

'I knew it! He's locked the door. Quick, Zia! Good thing I real-ized . . .'

'Realized what, Bambù?'

'That's why I had him sleep in Uncle Jacopo's room . . . Come on! I know a way to get into the room. Here, behind this painting there's a passageway that leads to the big tapestry in there. Come on, help me take it down.'

Going from the darkness of the passage to the room's dazzling light, all I can make out is a silhouette framed against the open win-dow: one arm raised as if to greet someone down in the garden. I barely have time to turn to Bambolina and see her rush toward that arm. A shot makes me instinctively bring my hands to my ears and close my eyes.

'Put down the gun, 'Ntoni! Give it to me; it's over now! You could have shot me, did you know that? Shot your Bambù!'

Your Bambù must be a magical expression between the two of them since it has the effect of turning the laboured panting of that cornered animal into convulsive weeping, as 'Ntoni falls to his knees crying, 'Oh no, no, Bambù! You? Never, I would never want to hurt you, never! I'm insane, a lunatic! A lunatic and a coward! I even left the door unlocked!'

'You locked it, 'Ntoni, unfortunately you locked it. But your Bambù is cunning, sly as a fox. Remember how you used to call me your sly fox?'

'Oh, yes, yes . . . How did you get in?'

'There's a secret door.'

'I'm so ashamed, Bambù! Don't tell anyone: I'm a coward! I want to die! You're so beautiful, a good person like Mama. I don't want to hurt you like I hurt her. She died because inside me I had rejected her . . . I had judged her, put her out of my life. I'm like my father. Mama was right: like my father, I destroy what I love most.'

''Ntoni, 'Ntoni . . .'

For a second I'm tempted to take a step toward him and tell him the truth: that he's not to blame. But my knowledge is theoretical, and those young people must discover their lives on their own, through their own senses, their own language. Indeed, like blind men trying to see, they hug each other now, touching one another in silence.

Quietly, so they won't hear me, I leave the room.

87

On the long journey back through the endless corridors, stairs and more stairs, the anxiety that I might lose Jacopo too in that other struggle he has withstood for years – against a gentle face framed by graceful curls – makes me tremble; he hasn't mentioned Inès, hasn't asked about her. Only when I return to the parlour, now rustling like a crowded theatre – the same murmuring, the same occasional voices interspersed with a few silvery notes of an instrument as someone tunes a guitar, a mandolin – only when I see Jacopo where I left him, no longer hugging Prando but Nina, does my anxiety subside. And my surprise at how little time has passed between the peace his return brought us and the war that erupted in 'Ntoni – and which perhaps lies invisibly coiled in Jacopo's serene smile as well – gives way to the first mandolin player's melody. It charms Prando, who throws his head back as he listens. At every event, big or small, Prando always demands music and his gaze becomes tender, distant. My scar throbs under my hair at the sight of the beauty of that absorbed head, the large head of an adult man. I can't sit still; I'm better off going back to 'Ntoni. But as soon as I turn to leave, Prando grabs me by the waist.

'Where is my *mamma bambina* running off to? Always running away, always full of mysteries! Or is it just that, however you may do your duty as a mother, you really can't stand me, can you?'

He forces me to turn around. When I meet his gaze, now bold and scathing again, I realize that he can't help it. He will always be that way: he loves me just as I love him. Could it be otherwise? The love between a mother and a son is the ultimate romantic melodrama, simply because it cannot be consummated.

'It's no use running away, little girl, because this business of trying to escape me makes me love you more. At the front I was the laughing-stock of everyone! Oh, not that I spoke about you a lot, but they all noticed it and laughed at me. Oh, with respect, mind you . . . and you know how I responded? "Go on, laugh, laugh, you guys with mothers who are real dogs!" Then they'd start talking nonsense because they were all in love with their mothers as well. See what my *mamma bambina* does? I hardly say a word to her *ca già gira l'occhi scappannu pi banni e banni*. Already she's looking all around, not knowing which way to turn. *Ma unni vai? Ccà vicinu a mia hai a stari: madre mi sei e miniera mia!* Where are you running to? Stay here with me, you're my mother and my treasure. Come on, Pippo, play a courtly serenade! Maybe it will melt that precious stone she has in place of a heart.'

How did Prando come up with that forgotten language? Did he ever hear Carmine's voice?

'Oh, Pippo! She's trembling against my chest like a frightened dove.'

'You're hurting me, Prando! Let me go! I can't breathe!'

'Do you know that if I really squeezed you, I could break you in two? But then if I needed it, where would I find a suitable glue to reattach this porcelain neck? If only I could find such a glue! I would enjoy breaking you into pieces to then have the pleasure of reassembling you piece by piece afterwards. Where to find it? I'll have to look for it at the Civita, in that no man's land. They say you can find everything there. You can buy anything: from the finest silks to candles for the dead, from one-hundred-carat gold to the sharpest knives, from a faceless *picciotto* – a thug who for a few liras will kill whoever decided to snub you by crossing the street – to silken ladies, *vellute* with perfumed hair . . . even fresh new corpses, if you really want to study anatomy on your own . . . You're laughing! Laugh, *bella*, because when you laugh – no offence to decent, married women – you become the most beautiful of all!'

It must have been the guitar and mandolin that caused that spring – silent, earlier – to flow. Even his voice changed. The guitar, at first delicate, became deep, as though scoured by underground winds.

Pippo and Cosimo stand up as they play, and behind Prando's back stare at my face or at some apparition behind me that enchants and transports them. Prando is silent. He knows that, after delivering his offer of love to everyone, it's time to listen to other voices, other requests for love. And indeed, a jasmine-sweet voice breasts the wave to declare its anguish over an unrequited love:

'*Bedda p'amari a tia 'stu cori chianci. Sinceramenti senza ca si fingi* . . . *Cugghiennu alivi pi 'sti munti santi* . . . *bedda p'amari a tia 'stu cori chianci* . . . My sweet, for love of you my heart cries, sincerely, it's no lie . . .'*

To whom is Crispina singing? Where did that mature voice come from? Or had the pall of war, marked only by anthems, silenced that living sap? After the sorrow over her unrequited love, Crispina, now pushed by unseen hands into the centre of the room, starts singing spitefully:

'*Quantu è laria la mi zita, malanova di la sua vita* . . . *Ah, laria è, cchiù laria d'idda nun ci nn'è* . . . *Havi i spaddi vasci vasci ca mi parunu du casci* . . . *Ah, laria è, cchiù laria d'idda nun ci nn'è* . . . How ugly my fiancée is! No one is uglier: her shoulders are so stooped she looks like a hunchback . . .'

At that expression of liberation from the shackles of a tormented love, Carluzzu widens his eyes, easily frees himself from the old man's arms and toddles toward us. Held by that old man, he seemed small. Now, as he slowly approaches, the big-boned structure of his hips and shoulders makes him seem like a little man.

'Oh, Mama, look at my son! He's tugging at me! He must not be used to seeing me hugging a woman. What's the matter, Carluzzu, are you jealous?'

'Papa, I sing too!'

Stella's voice seizes me by the throat; her trusting dark eyes stare at me. I have to bend down and touch him to feel her in my arms . . . The small sturdy body doesn't struggle as he keeps saying, 'I sing . . . I sing too with Crispina. Why are you crying, Nonna?'

'Because I'm moved, Carluzzu. Crispina sings so beautifully.'

'Me too, Nonna, I sing good.'

'I'm sure you do.'

'Nonna, Nonna . . .'

Already I was a grandmother . . . As I reflected on the idea – inevitably more upsetting than any war – I looked away from Carluzzu and saw Inès enter through the parlour's French door.

I hadn't seen her in years, and if it weren't for the perception of danger that her name, whispered beside me, carried with it, I wouldn't have recognized her. The smiling charm that had made her seem beautiful had vanished, along with the dark curls, now wound tightly around her head in a harsh braided crown. The small swollen lips, pinched in a disdainful expression, had thinned to a rigid blade of command, and her body, bolstered by the 'position' she had won, had lost its agility and grace.

'Eh, Mody, a new broom sweeps clean! You should see her now, a harpy with her maid! And something Pietro cannot tolerate: despotic and harsh with the *signor* prince. That woman has decided to kill him so she can marry: I can see it in the way she rolls her eyes right and left! All she does is hoard money. Plus, she no longer satisfies the *signor* prince and he's itching for her, the poor creature! I've talked to her, but she doesn't want *vellute*. Why not? I thought. If you accepted that arrangement, back then, why won't she, instead of making the poor soul suffer? By this time, he trembles and runs away when he sees her. Action is needed here, Mody. Listen to me!'

'And what is that, Pietro?'

'It's simple: get rid of her by natural means, using her own venomous ways.'

Inès comes forward with regal bearing and stops in front of Jacopo, who is still arm in arm with Nina. Jacopo hasn't seen her, so taken is he by Nina's smile. I can believe it! What else can matter to him when Nina is talking and laughing? But Inès raises her hand – at one time delicate and tremulous, now loaded with rings – and places it firmly on her son's shoulder, separating the two. Jacopo turns pale as a corpse and abruptly pushes Nina away. Staring at him in surprise, she exclaims, 'What's come over you, my dark-haired boy? Is this your girlfriend perhaps? Is that why you're flustered? Look how red he is! Oh, Mody, come and see!'

Nina laughs louder, staring at Inès defiantly. Inès, chin raised, hisses: 'You see filth everywhere, *signora*. Or is it *signorina*?

'*Signorina, signorina!*'

'Oh, now I see, *signorina*. But things here aren't like they are on the continent! I've known Jacopo since he was a baby, and I've come to embrace him as a mother.'

'Sorry, I was just joking. Besides you're so young and beautiful I thought I was paying you a compliment!'

'Such compliments aren't appreciated here, isn't that so, Jacopo? Have you nothing to say to me?'

'But Inès, I came to see you as soon as I returned . . .'

'Yes, but only for a minute.'

'Well, to reassure you and then . . . then I had to reassure the others as well.'

'Of course. But afterwards I waited all day for you.'

'Well, I would have come back later on, after . . . You see? They're playing music. Crispina was singing. Come on, Crispina, go on with your singing! Besides you're here, aren't you, Inès? You're here with us now. Cheer up, Inès. Don't be like that!'

Jacopo's voice becomes uncertain, stammering. It's time to act. As if Pietro has understood my intention – maybe from my stride, certainly not from the smiling expression on my face – I find him standing silently by my side, and I hear myself say, 'Oh, Inès, a pleasure to see you! Come, let's not ruin this party in Jacopo's honour. Our Jacopo is happy. You should be happy as well. Come, let's hug. It's also been a long time since we've seen one another.'

Rigid and hostile in my arms, she whispers, 'Jacopo is mine, mine alone, and I don't like this slut. Why was she holding him so tight?'

'All right, Inès, you're here now, aren't you? Stay with your Jacopo . . . and you, Nina, come and see how amazing Carluzzu has become. He says he can sing like Crispina. Let's see if it's true. You too, Pietro, you were certainly right: your Crispina must study music. You were right about that other matter as well: we've wasted too much time, we must resolve things.'

'Of course, Mody! I'm relieved to hear it, and with your permission everything will be arranged in the best possible way.'

'I don't doubt it, Pietro.'

'What's wrong with that Inès, Mody? Why did she get so incensed? Is she in love with Jacopo, maybe?'

'Come on, Nina! Have you forgotten she's his mother?'

'Oh, right. But how does that change things?'

'Territorialism. You invaded her colony!'

'Hell, Mody, you've restored my good mood! Olimpia, come here, my precious colony! My adored Somalia, my Abyssinia! You crack me up, Mody! I'd like to write a song about it and sing it in the streets . . . Oh Bambuccia, there you are, finally! Where were you hiding? Come and hear your aunt's latest . . . Come, you too, with your lands, your plantations! How is your colony?'

Nina and Bambolina laugh, and Bambù goes along with that amiable moment. And when Nina, looking around the crowded room, exclaims: 'Where is your chosen twin? Your 'Ntoni? Uh-oh! Something has happened here. It's the first time I've seen you two apart,' Bambolina answers calmly: ''Ntoni had a slight indisposition, but he's asleep now. I think it's best to let him sleep. But afterwards, Zia, later on, when this delightful impromptu party is over, 'Ntoni has asked to speak with Jacopo.

'Now let's go get more wine, Nina. What kind of hostess are you, for heaven's sake! Don't you see they've drained every drop and are looking for wine and other drinks as if they were dying of thirst?'

*

'So, Mama, will you make up your mind or not? Are you going to run for deputy, yes or no? You'd be at the top of the list. Down in Catania, they're insisting on it. It would be a matter of pride for us: a communist deputy, a Sicilian woman, in Rome. Plus, I would love to have my *mamma bambina* side by side with me.'

'No, Prando. Joyce wrote to me as well: no! Despite the fact that we have only a little money, and a salary wouldn't hurt. But if they pay you – and from what I've seen, the pay isn't paltry – they become your masters and tie your hands. No, Prando, I want to be free to speak.'

'You're unpredictable, Mama, as unpredictable as you are irritating! The communist cause . . .'

'I enrolled, didn't I? I support it. In fact, since I've discovered this gift of public speaking that I didn't know about . . .'

'Oh, you're simply fantastic!'

'Fine, I'll work for you, but on a grassroots level: in the piazzas, with the crowds, not in a building where there are already a great many of you to defend us.'

'That's true too. Young people don't know how to speak in public. It's strange.'

'Twenty years of silence have an effect.'

'In fact, the few who are able to speak are those who did so like me at the *Littoriali* – that is, in a Fascist setting.'

'Exactly. So you'll fill a void with me. Is it a deal, Prando?'

'Still, I'm a little sorry. I dreamed of seeing you there in Rome alongside Joyce.'

'Such a fine party, wasn't it, Prando?'

'Oh, wonderful! Whenever a party is unplanned, it turns out well.'

'Too bad it's over, right, Nina?'

'Too bad. But why haven't Jacopo and Bambù come back? They've been up there with 'Ntoni for an hour. I'm a little worried.'

'Here they come. I'm off.'

'Why, Prando? Stay! Don't you want to hear about 'Ntoni?'

'Hey, Nina, excuse me but I have other things to do than worry about these spoiled *picciriddi* and their crises!'

Prando gets up slowly and heads for the French door; on the way, he rights an overturned chair upholstered in red silk. For an instant, the silk focuses the sunset's hundred tongues of fire and those of his hair; for a moment, his tall, lithe body pauses as he stares in silence at the tables full of glasses, pitchers, dishes . . . Maybe he noticed the dismay in our eyes over what he said. Perhaps he, too, was somewhat struck by his own words, since he is moved to add, 'It was lovely, Mama! A party after years and years! I should give you all a hand cleaning up, but, well . . . I have to run. Forgive me. See you later.'

'What can I say, Mody? No offence to anyone, but the more I see of these men, the happier I am to have had a little girl. Tell me, didn't you have him read Voltaire?'

'Of course I did!'

'Are you sure? Including the terms "fanaticism", "tolerance"? If I were in government, I'd see to it that the various Prandos were settled down nice and comfortably, amid fresh meadows and spouting water fountains, and I would make them read over and over again what Voltaire said about fanaticism . . . What a fanatic, wow! As if he were the only one who had gone to war!'

'Oh Nina, you make me feel cheerful again. Do you know what I would do if I were in government?'

'What would you do?'

'I would give a lifelong income to people like you who have the talent to cheer others up.'

'Don't even mention income, please! What can I do to earn a living? Shit, the only thing I'm experienced in is prisons! Say, Mody, isn't there some school where I can teach that subject?'

'Stop, Nina, or I'll die laughing!'

'But there should be, or it should be created. Because, well, Fascism is over but the prisons are still there. Yesterday I took a little stroll through Catania . . . those prisons must be protected by God! Everything destroyed, Mody, bombed, but the prison is untouched, as if nothing had happened . . . But what are those kids doing? Those *carusi*, as you people say. I really like *carusi, meschini, picciotti* . . . There, I could study Sicilian and go teach it abroad.'

'Abroad, Nina?'

'Sure, in Italy . . . It's given you some bitter disappointments, hasn't it, this Italy! Tell me, Mody, couldn't we have gone directly from the earlier little states to socialism?'

'Apparently not, Nina.'

'A pity! But what on earth are they doing? They've been standing there chatting on the stairs for an hour . . . Now look at that, instead of coming down, they're going back up. Hell, who can understand them! Daytime parties are really nice, but like everything else, they have their downside: the sun sinks, and after the warmth of all that company the shadows deepen and you think . . . you think about the fact that there's an entire night ahead of you, and melancholy slips in *en pointe* like a sad ballerina. You too, Mody, shit! If I don't fire up the engines to make you smile . . . I see you, don't you realize it? Even in the dark I see you. It may be because I feel like I've spent a hundred years with you! I see you all huddled and pale, as if harbouring bitter thoughts. My beautiful, sad Mody, what's come over you?'

'You're sad too, Nina, come on!'

'It's because the party's over, I think.'

'It's not because of the party and you know it.'

'Of course, you have to admit that it seemed more like a farewell party than a welcome home party.'

'When Prando stalked off that way, I had the same feeling I had when he left for the war.'

'Certainly, imprisoned down on the island, we weren't hoping for such a quick end to Fascism. We were thinking of a different kind of peace.'

'That's exactly right, Nina.'

'And yet my father and his old buddies had warned us.'

'Yes, you told me many times, and Maria down in Catania said so as well.'

'I'm afraid comrade Angelo was right.'

'Angelo who?'

'Angelo Tasca, when he said back then that with the Lateran Treaty, the Church wasn't so much forming an alliance with Fascism as preparing to assume its legacy . . . Oh, damn! You startled me, Bambolina! Are you all crazy, appearing like ghosts and turning on the light so abruptly?'

'Are you angry, Nina?'

'No, no! But I have to say something. Sorry. It must be because of being in prison; six years take their toll, after all! Every time the light is suddenly switched on or someone yells, it makes me jump. May I ask what you were all doing, going up and down the stairs? Hey, don't tell me something serious has happened?'

'It's just that we had to make some decisions, Nina, Zia . . . Or rather, Jacopo had to make them because I can't do it. I . . . I'd dreamt of this moment so often. I was so happy! All of us here together like before, and instead . . . oh, Nina, I can't believe it! Just reunited and we have to . . .'

'Come, sweetheart, come. Don't cry. What am I saying? Cry, cry, let it all out here in Nina's arms.'

Bambolina sobs in her arms, and her shoulders, toughened by the outdoor air and sunshine, become fragile and tremulous again, shaken by those sobs. Nina holds her gently, tenderly. She knows, as I knew, that that slim waist, barely marked by a black patent-leather belt, can break under the pressure of a harsh gesture, an unkind word. Like my Beatrice, Bambolina strives for absolute joy as a natural right, and she knows how to achieve it and how to offer it to others. Even Mattia, who slowly enters through the French door and looks at me gravely – why hadn't I noticed him before? – even he, despite the problem with his heart, seems like a young man again, his skin and his gaze soothed by Bambù's caresses.

'*Happiness is a right.*' Yes, Carlo, like bread, water, sunshine. And together we will fight for Bambolina and for little Beatrice who, we can already see, '*lacks the shrewdness and ruthlessness needed to fight, which fortunately you have, Modesta*' .

Jacopo studies an overturned pitcher, trying not to listen to Bambolina's sobs. '*Oh, Mama, when I hear a woman cry I want to die. I can't take it!*' Jacopo, his tall body once erect, now humbled, takes off his glasses and wipes them. Jacopo, like Bambolina, lacks shrewdness and ruthlessness. It's for them that we must fight, Carlo, only for them . . . for that Carluzzu, who fell asleep on the sofa and is now rubbing his eyes, staring at the chandelier. '*. . . Well, Mama, with this child about to be born to Stella and Prando, we're at the fourth generation of atheists. I know you don't like the word, but four generations are already almost a nobility.*' '*What do you mean, Jacopo?*' '*Uncle Jacopo, then you, Mama, then me, Prando and Bambù. And Carluzzu makes four . . .*'

Look at him there: a big-boned little man, sliding off the sofa and running, dazed, toward his aunt. In that wide-eyed gaze you can read everything, those eyes still full of the earlier fun and games, the cheerful singing. Clearly undecided whether to leave the joy behind and cry too, he clings to Bambolina's skirt, asking for help in his own way.

The tiny hands have the power to rouse Bambù, who lets go of Nina and exclaims: '*Ma che semu pazzi*, are we all crazy in this house! Carluzzu, what did they do, abandon you? Just look at that, forgetting about such a sweet *piccioletto*! My little one, my little kitten! What are we today, eh, Carluzzo? Come, tell your aunt what you are today: a kitten or a little ant?'

'I'm a *sciccareddu* today, Zia, a little donkey.'

'You mean an *asinello*, right, Carluzzu? Sooner or later, we have to learn an Italian word or two, don't we?'

'*Asinello, 'u sacciu*. I know the song too: *Sciccareddu di lu me cori* . . .'*

'Oh, Zia, when you were away I thought I might be mistaken, but now seeing you two side by side . . . Did you know that Carluzzu looks just like you?'

'Well, what a surprise, Bambù! Prando is Mody's son.'

'Of course, of course, Nina. But Prando doesn't resemble Modesta. And you Carluzzu, do you love your *nonna*?'

Carluzzu doesn't answer and stares at me, serious. Indeed, I was a grandmother . . . how did it feel? Nina had asked me many times, but I had no answer. Even now, with that overly serious face, the big wide eyes staring at me, I don't feel anything, but I'm beginning to understand. Up till now, my inattention toward the last born concealed envy toward someone whose youth reminds you of a time that is past for you, and of a future that you will not live to see owing to biological constraints. And everyone's insistence on the fact that that small creature looked so much like me? Sensing an old person's envy which, if badly directed, might explode, they were probably trying to arouse my tenderness in order to protect him. His little face, so intent on studying me, was further confirmation of my conclusion: Modesta must seem tall to him, powerful . . . like Nonna Gaia, Nonna Valentina. Of course, it would be easy to intimidate and dominate him with authority, just as it would be easy to suffocate him with excessive love, thereby protecting oneself against the ever-present threat of a 'league against abominable grandmothers'.

'Just look at them, Jacopo: two peas in a pod!'

How can I resist the temptation of power that makes my brow throb now that he, perhaps sensing my doubt and confusion, smiles with my smile and touches his hand to my face to feel through my flesh where the danger, or tenderness, of my being lies? His palm reads me, and as soon as I decide not to use that power, the little hand gains strength and pretends to slap me.

'You must like your *nonna*, don't you, if you do that! He always does that when he likes someone, even with Olimpia.'

'Olimpia! Where is Olimpia?'

'It's really an obsession. Always fixated on Olimpia! Just look at him. That's always the way: first a slap, then he kisses you.'

I feel like I've been able to strip the word *nonna* off my skin – or transform it into something small and tender like him.

'Oh Zia, he's just like you: always restless, always up to something, and he asks so many questions! You must have been like that as a little girl. I can just see you! And then too, he has a mania for dragging . . .'

'Dragging, Bambù?'

'Yes, he drags tree limbs, gathers leaves, and he never stops asking questions. He's alert, intelligent, but what worries me is his fear that everyone may disappear at any moment. What do you think, Jacopo? Could it be because of the war? Because he saw you all leave one after the other?'

'That could be. But at the moment it's 'Ntoni we need to worry about. Right now he's sleeping, but he's in bad shape, worse than you think. And as I told you earlier upstairs, your loving care, your words, won't help him. He needs medical care and that's that. The soul can fall ill just like the body. He was wounded inside and the wound will only heal with the help of a physician who specializes in these things. It's not solely because of the war, the concentration camp, as you thought. There's also Stella . . .'

'So you've really made up your mind, Jacopo? I was hoping you would have second thoughts.'

'Bambù, you're really stubborn, you know? If he himself realizes it and he's not well . . . Did you see how he asked to go when he saw a glimmer of hope? If he realizes it, all of you should realize it as well. When I returned, I too dreamt of nothing but studying here and enjoying the sunshine, our home! What did you think? I dreamt of it for years, but clearly it's not possible.'

'But he could go to Milan himself, to that doctor.'

'No! He asked me to go with him, and all in all it will be best for me too that way: I'll study and quickly become apprenticed . . . I'd say this is a warning. As always after a war, times speed up. Yes, the pace has quickened and this is probably a sign that we shouldn't waste a moment. We're behind Europe by at least twenty years! Mama, please, you talk to Ida. I know you understand.'

'I understand perfectly. But we have to consider the accounts: we have very little money now.'

'Damn! With the newspaper having risen to thirty liras in a year! Shit, Mody, I'll accept the offer of that bitch who's loaded with money. I'll go into business!'

'Into business, Nina?'

'That's right, Jacopo. Back there, on the island, I started knitting, and crocheting hats, scarves, sweaters and shawls isn't bad. Plus, with that shitty Esmeralda we'll have helpers. I like to choose and match colours. I've always had a passion for colour, maybe because I'm *begalina*, half blind, as my mother used to say, and colours stand out.'

'Oh, dear Nina, thank heavens you're staying here!'

'We'll work, Mama! And it will be a good thing for both 'Ntoni and me to start looking after ourselves, financially speaking as well.'

'Anyway, I'm going to bed. What a day this has been! I have to bolster my strength so that tomorrow I can face Esmeralda's favours and her intentions to save me through redemptive work, concepts that motivate that aristocratic lady. She's beautiful though; damn, she's gorgeous! They talk a lot about proletarian beauty . . . to console us and keep us in line in our poverty. Before, I didn't look at the rich, or I looked at them and didn't see them, since my eyes were blinded by that populist platitude. Until I realized, damn if I didn't realize, that they are not only rich but beautiful, fragrantly scented and often intelligent! Like you, Jacopo. Damn this rotten world!'

'You're making me blush, Nina. Come, I'll take you up.'

'Oh sure, go ahead, take me up, give me your arm. Not everyone has the chance to be accompanied by a young man like you. Good as gold! At least I'll be able to tell my grandkids: "So, you won't believe it, my dear grandchildren, but your grandmother, long ago, had the good fortune, thanks to incarceration and prison cells, of landing among the most elegant and refined people . . ." And they'll say: "No, really, Nonna? How did that happen? Tell us!"'

88

Nina's voice trails off toward the darkness of the parlour. I'd like to follow that voice and go on dreaming while she talks. But the buzz of voices, the clanging of trains, the muffled sound of pressing throngs branch out from my future and invade the room, keeping me pinned in my chair . . . I'd like to drive off those crowds and go back with her to a small cell, where being more than a few feet apart from one another is unthinkable. Why is that? Is it nostalgia for that lost cell that's making me cry like this? How could I have known it if life hadn't shown me? How could I have known that my greatest joy lay concealed in the seemingly darkest years of my life? One must surrender to life, always without fear . . . Even now, between train whistles and the slamming of compartment doors, life calls me, and I must go.

The ability to speak and to transport my listeners, which had suddenly revealed itself in me, exciting my senses and my mind as though I were under the influence of a drug, kept telling me that this natural gift – most likely firmly ripened in the fertile soil of years of silence, study and reflection – could serve to bring us women like Nina, like Bambolina . . . To awaken them from a twenty-year lethargy, let them know that they aren't the first, acquaint them with examples from the past.

'Look, Modesta, you can't fall back on that Alexandra Kollontai in every speech . . . Balabanoff, did you say? Maria Giudice? Come on, Modesta. They're problematic figures, nonaligned. Sensational more than anything else, at least for the time being. When we learned that Maria was ill, I'll be frank with you, it was a relief for everyone. It's awful to say so, but all she did was create confusion. You can't just suddenly start talking about free love, about abortion and divorce. You have to take it gradually, as comrade Giorgio says.'

Right, Giorgio . . . On the desk, his photograph stands out among the books.

'Your husband, you mean?'

'As you wish, Modesta. I see you haven't changed.'

'Nor have you.'

On the other side of the desk, polished and without a trace of dust, Joyce (or her ghost?) smiles at me with mild detachment.

'Here, there are other, more urgent things to worry about.'

'But why did I have to call you by your husband's name in order to see you?'

'What of it? True, you've never had a political mind, Modesta. We have to reassure the public, we have to show the country that we are respectable people in all ways, not those lawless reds, those rabble-rousing reds, and so on, like you still see written on walls in the rural areas.'

Where had she learned that winning, democratic smile, just like the one you saw on celebrities and politicians overseas? Before, she'd never smiled, and the grave sadness of her eyes had made her beautiful. Now, with that strange smile seemingly pinned to the corners of her mouth, her white hair expertly cut by skilful hands – a cut just barely longer than a man's – her beauty had become rigid, reduced to an abstract image of mortuary solitude. Modesta had sensed it years before, but the living embodiment of her intuition makes her tremble with anger, and with fear.

To overcome the repugnance that Joyce's words spill into her being, Modesta searches her memory for the faces of other female comrades she's met on platforms, at assemblies, at rallies during those years . . . Luciana? Carla? Renata, maybe? Renata, only twenty-two years old, with that eternal refrain repeated yet again just last night? '*But women, barring some exceptions, are silly fools. A waste of time, Modesta! I really don't understand how a person like you can waste your time going to dinner with one of them.*' Watch out, Bambolina, Crispina, Olimpia: beware! In twenty or thirty years, don't blame men when you find yourselves crying in a cramped room with your hands rubbed raw by bleach. It's not men who have betrayed you, but these women who were once slaves themselves, who have willingly forgotten their state of bondage. By disavowing you, they can align themselves with men in various positions of power.

'So what have you decided, Modesta?'

'Decided?'

'You never change! It's hopeless to try to get you to think. The minute you don't like what someone is saying, you lose yourself in idle reveries and amen! You had a lot of promise, Modesta, but I see that your exquisitely female obstinacy got the upper hand.'

Watch out, Bambolina, Crispina, Olimpia . . . Be careful, you who have had the privilege of culture and freedom, not to follow the example of these perfectly allied slaves. Instead of hands worn away by bleach, years of dismal mannish training await you – training in how to chain the poorest women to the assembly line – along with atrocious sleepless nights: efficiency at all costs. And after twenty years of this training, you will find yourselves trapped by distorted acts and thinking, restrained by emptiness and regret for your lost identity – like this shadow of herself who smiles out of official duty, an embodiment neither male nor female.

'I told comrade Giorgio that it was hopeless to try to persuade you, but he insisted. He has a strange respect for you, and in the name of our old friendship, I decided to talk to you. But I see it's no use, that you will not accept the cuts that have justly – I repeat, justly – been made to your article. It's too violent, Modesta. We cannot today, in 1950, entitle an article: "We are all murderers".'

'Why not, Joyce? According to you and to what we Marxists have thought for decades at least, weren't we all – I who speak to the crowds, you who sit behind that desk, the doorman who, content with his paltry power, ushers me in with reactionary bows – weren't we all to blame for leading that woman from Salerno, for driving her to drown herself with her three children because of the wretched living conditions that—'

'Mentally unbalanced, Modesta! I'm a doctor; don't forget that.'

'No, that wasn't it! I spoke with everyone. I saw the photographs. She looks like Stella. Think about that, Joyce: Stella.'

'And who is she?'

'Stella. Jacopo's wet nurse.'

'Ah yes, that pretty little peasant girl, somewhat faded . . . how is she?'

'It doesn't matter. Just as this article doesn't matter.'

'So then we won't publish it?'

'Under those conditions, no!'

'Modesta, you don't intend to create a furore, do you?'

'If it were possible for me to create one, I would, but I know that it isn't possible because you are a gang of traitors, Joyce. And as such, powerful as usual.'

'You mean we're not insane. We can't alarm citizens that way. We have to win the Catholic voters! We're in a Catholic country, Modesta. You're forgetting your history!'

'An article in a magazine doesn't have the circulation of a newspaper, and as I see it, the specialized press is exactly the place where we should begin discussing the most weighty issues in order to keep the tradition – *our* tradition – alive, and prepare to disseminate it tomorrow. The way you're acting, you're not merely showing respect for the Catholic electorate, you're meeting it fully and distorting the very roots of our struggle.'

'Fine! We've finally seen each other, but now I have work to do and I'd like an answer.'

'Yes, Joyce, we've seen each other . . . and now I know why I tried to avoid seeing you these past years.'

'Why is that?'

'I knew that if I saw you I would understand things clearly, and I didn't want to. I wanted to delude myself, and that's because . . . damn! how hard it is to see clearly when you're doing something that in itself satisfies you, gives you joy, drugs you.'

'I'm trying to be patient with you, Modesta. What is it that you like so much?'

'Well, speaking, feeling the vibration of the crowd, the applause!'

'You never change. For me it's not a pleasure.'

'Oh, really?'

'No, for me it's a duty.'

'Are you sure of that?'

'That's enough, Modesta, enough!'

'You taught me the little bit of psychology that we should all know, Joyce.'

'Oh, enough about the past. I have a lot to do.'

'And I, on the other hand, no longer have anything, and I feel like a deflated balloon.'

89

So it was that Modesta had to decide to leave the most exciting pursuit that she had ever experienced. There was no sweeter liqueur, no freshly baked bread, no lover's saliva that could compare with that breath of life, that intensity, which for years had sent her flying through the country, sweeping away every memory, every sorrow. Determined not to collaborate with the enemy, which, though disguised in a hundred modern ways – what was the face of that new power, which unfolded in the many silent tentacles of an octopus camouflaged in the various colours of science, the arts, the professions? – was still the same power in every respect, wearing the elegant uniform of an arrogant warrior.

Determined, Modesta managed to get up from her chair and stand up straight, but she still had to cross the hall and go down the grand marble staircase. And though in Joyce's presence irony had helped conceal the emptiness that slowly rose from her chest to her head, once she was outside in that broad, marmoreal avenue, in a Rome that stood intact among the wasteland of rubble throughout the peninsula, a Rome protected by the vast, roseate wings of the papacy, she could not help giving in to despondency. So as not to fall, she groped around for a seat in a bar crammed with people from many different regions who continually flowed through those streets seeking refuge, hope, among the untouched walls . . . The unsettling crowd milled around her as in a dream: starving Italians side by side with the plump, rosy faces of Americans looking for business. Men from East-Central Europe shoulder to shoulder with former inmates of concentration camps: emaciated Jews followed by the barely more secure steps of ex-prisoners . . . Starting a year or two ago, women have been walking in the streets without hats or stockings. Back there, a small blond woman, timid perhaps, still wears a kerchief on her head and hugs the wall, trying to pass unnoticed: a new treasure is clutched to her chest, the glossy American magazine *Grand Hotel*, which is all the rage. On the tables are gelati, espressos, and a jungle of slim bottles of Coca-Cola.

'What would you like, *signora*?'

'An espresso, please.'

The round, smiling eyes, still rimmed by hunger's dark circles, cast rapid glances in search of opportunities, the darting eyes of a former shoeshine boy skilled in picking out the big, blond prey: an American. For those of us who were deprived of it for so many years, coffee is still a miracle, of course, and fills the emptiness of confusion. I have to hurry to the hotel before the stench of our soldiers' wretched bodies, mixed with the scent of hundreds of American bath soaps and musty French fragrances, suffocate me. But I don't have the strength to walk. Drained, Modesta stares at her image in a shop window. For years she hasn't had time to look at herself in the mirror. Does she look older, maybe? Is her weariness merely the first sign of old age, perhaps? All in all, it was time: she's fifty years old. Look at her there, Modesta: her breasts are heavier, her cheeks full . . . but she was always a little too thin. And the rounded hips, slim legs and trim torso don't give the impression of a mature matron, but rather a *carusa*, a young girl who aged overnight, but gracefully, as her Nina the shopkeeper says. What does she say in her letter? 'I saw you in the newspaper. You were really funny, Mody! Lots of kisses from your shopkeeper, who's loaded with money. I can't wait to tell you how good I've become at robbing those *citrulli*, those American fools. All you have to do is tell them that something is traditional, antique, and they're ready to shell out . . .'

A young girl grown old! But there in the shop window she can't see her wrinkles, her hair. Therefore, Modesta, if you want to know more about that weariness, you must have the courage to look at yourself in a mirror at least once. '*Oh, shit, you're far-sighted, Mody! You see everything cloudy and indistinct . . . Will you, or won't you wear these glasses?*' So Modesta had better wear the glasses that Bambolina gave her. '*You'll get a crick in your neck, Zia, every time you have to read!*'

Reassured by the lenses, all she sees are the usual white strands and a few more wrinkles. Her teeth? Strong. And if she smiles, the wrinkles are erased by magic. That smile at the end of her speeches had sparked cries of enthusiasm and applause. It was satisfying and comforting to be understood, to be loved. That was the reason – she realized it now – why each day she acquiesced to watering down her ideas, impoverishing their content, reducing her language. Even so, success was certain; in fact, even more certain than before. That was the catch! In recent months, the less she said the more applause she received from the crowd. And she, content, tried not to see it. Now she realized that during those years, all she had had was personal success. Like an actress who, just to please the audience, passes off even the most hackneyed or reactionary script as good. She understood Mela; she finally understood the radiant eyes, the confident demeanour of that girl . . . Surrounded by applause, accepted and loved by the crowd, Mela had no need for anyone, except for some casual affair with a woman. Lucky her! But Mela made sounds spring from her keyboard: exquisite, classic sounds, not words that spewed fire more terrible than cannons . . .

With her arms on the mirror, Modesta's happy smile vanishes, and she weeps in despair. She's never felt so despondent, not when she decided to stop getting richer and richer by accumulating money, nor when she felt called to poetry. With her face buried in her arms, she tries to find the strength not to be corrupted by herself, that self who says: 'Besides, if you don't do it, someone else – surely worse than you – will promptly do it.'

90

'What do you plan to do, Mama?'

'Enjoy the sunshine, can't you see? I feel like I've been away from this sun for a hundred years!'

'Do you think it's fair to keep me in the dark? Make me look bad?'

'Bad how, Prando?'

'Like a fool, down in Catania and in Rome. Is it possible that I always have to hear about things from other people, from strangers?'

'Did Lucio phone you?'

'He was desperate! You left without even calling him, and he wanted to know from your know-nothing, idiot of a son if it's true that you intend to drop everything.'

'Nonsense, Prando; an excuse to call you. I cancelled all my engagements properly. I spent an additional week in Rome, in that bogus peace, to call off all my commitments. A nightmarish week! Gilded clouds, celebrations! And to make matters worse, Via Veneto, with those "happy few" who feign a grim cheerfulness when they meet one another.'

'Never mind Rome! Why won't you answer me? What's the story about the article?'

'Why are you bothering to ask, Prando, when you know everything?'

'All because of ten lines in an article!'

'For that matter, twelve lines and a title. And even if it were only one line, I don't accept censorship of any kind. You people are young, but for me twenty years was enough. I feel all censored out, as Nina would say.'

'Nina this, Nina that! Forget about her! It's she and that spineless existentialist Libero who gave you a swollen head.'

'I can tell you that Libero is one of the few genuine Marxists I met in Rome.'

'A beaten individualist, that's what he is!'

'Naturally, compared to your absolute triumphalism. Drop it, Prando; I'm tired of controversy. Who would have said that after only four years – imagine! – I'd have to agree with that warped Jesuit, Sartre!'*

'What does Sartre have to do with it?'

'It's related, listen. In Milan, in 1946, I think, it was summer and everyone was suffocating . . . such heat in that sunless northern city, you wouldn't believe it!'

'Spare me the poetic descriptions, Mama!'

'I'll spare you. Sartre said that a little angst wouldn't hurt against your triumphalism, and he attracted all the young people to him.'

'All the spineless young people you know! I know other young people, like me . . .'

'You, Prando, young? You're as old as the power of this island, and you're handsome too, like its ancient beauty. I like looking at you. You remind me of an old man, as wise as the sea and as calm as the Mountain, who enchanted me as a little girl.'

'If one could talk rationally with you women. Judas Priest!'

'I talk rationally, Prando, if you speak to me clearly and don't beat around the bush like you've been doing for an hour. What is it you want? Spit it out.'

'Lucio wants to . . .'

'Marry me, you mean?'

'Because he's a man of honour.'

'A man of order, you mean?'

'What is it you don't like about Lucio?'

'A small detail that today is no longer in fashion: I'm not in love with him, my darling Prando.'

'In love! Haven't the years, experience taught you anything? Yet they say you're supposed to grow calmer with age.'

'That's what they told me too.'

'Aren't we enough for you? Me, your shitty Jacopo, Carluzzu, Bambù? All the women envy you. Carluzzu wants no one but you. He's always pestering me! Amalia is dying of jealousy because she can't win over Carluzzu, no matter what.'

'She'll get over it, Prando. As soon as your little bride has her baby – I'm certain it's another boy – she'll calm down, you'll see. Amalia is sweet. She just needs to have a child of her own.'

'I don't give a damn about Amalia. I want to know what you've decided.'

'Decided? About what?'

'Lucio is going to call tomorrow. What the hell should I say to him, do you mind telling me?'

'That he should phone me. I'll see to Lucio.'

'Look, if you don't marry him, you're coming to live with me in Catania.'

'And why should I do that?'

'Why, she says! Villa Suvarita has been sold, right? In three months you have to leave. Where do you intend to go? You don't have a red cent, Mama, can you get it through your head?'

'You really want to put me out to pasture, right, Prando? That's how it is: an old man wants to force you to be eternally young and a young man wants to see you old before your time, out of his way.'

'What are you talking about? Everyone adores you!'

'Exactly. You pamper a child, you adore the old man in a corner. You tempt me, Prando! To grow old among books, my grandchildren, taking pride in your beauty and strength. You're successful in court, right! Not like Lucio or Libero!'

'Don't say that name!'

'Why not surrender to the sublime love a son can give you? I could lord it over your meek Amalia and when your baby is born, effortlessly steal him away from her like I did with Carluzzu.'

'You're crazy, Mama, crazy!'

'Of course, and like all crazy people I'll repeat what I told you many years ago: just as I did not tolerate being pressured by my elders, so I will never stand for being pressured by you young people. Now go away. I'm going back inside. I need a nice hot bath! It's incredible, but I will never cease to be amazed at how by effortlessly turning a small tap with two fingers, you can have streams of hot water ready and waiting for you. Do you know that at one time you had to heat water and fill tiny little tubs? That's if there was any water! Awful times, Prando! The smell of sweat, bedbugs, itching.'

'Oh no, Mama!'

'No, what?'

'No, I know you! When you start digressing, it means you have a specific idea in mind, and I'm not moving until you give me an answer. Judas Priest! I can't stand this constant worrying! What do you plan to do?'

'Take a hot bath, Prando. I told you.'

'What now? Are you smoking, too?'

'Well yes, to make up for . . .'

'Make up for what? That's all we needed, a cigarette in her mouth . . .'

'I started smoking the morning they arrested me and I loved it! Then I realized that it was better not to continue. And it was just as well, because in prison and on the island it would have been an added torment. Now here on the big island with these Americans we have plenty of cigarettes . . . a cigarette lets you dream and keeps you company.'

'But it's not good for you!'

'When I feel it's harming me, I'll quit. Nina is right: acquiring and breaking habits, that's how we should live. All right, I see you won't desist. *"The wife would not desist."* Such amusing language you lawyers use! And to think you got your degree on a whim.'

'Well, I had to do something!'

'Yet you're content and proud of your profession. It shows. That's the beauty of life. The best things can come to you out of the darkest corner where you never thought to look. So then, dear son, will you let me take my bath or not?'

'I'm not letting go of you, Mama.'

'Fine, let's go in then . . . Oh, look, Mattia's here! Come on now, let go of my arm. Will you let me welcome him or not? Mattia, you're back at last! Give me a hug! I haven't seen you in a year, you old man! It's hard to hear *'sta camurria di parola,** that horror of a word, isn't it? Who would have said we'd grow old together!'

'I knew we would, Mody . . . Hello, Prando . . . Is it true you're staying here with us, Mody? Nina told me, and I can't tell you how happy this makes me. Is it true?'

'Of course! And you, are you done travelling?'

'Yes, everything is settled. I sold all those frozen houses . . . Bambù is right: not much money, but liquid, to use for seed, fertilizer and machinery. We're better off bolstering what little land we have. I was a little reluctant because of the girls. But Bambù is right: they'll make their own life. Fortunately, this at least has changed: having two daughters is no longer as worrisome as it was before.'

'That much at least, Mattia! . . . How nice the shade is! Beatrice had that wisteria planted. The building foreman didn't want to. He said that over time the roots, voracious as beasts, would eat away the walls of the terrace and the house, but Beatrice kept telling him: "This house will live even longer than we will, and I want a plant that will get out of the way like a theatre curtain in winter, and in summer will give me shade: a violet and green canopy." You won't believe me, but Beatrice's eyes were violet in the summer . . . Thank you, Nina; by now you make tea just like Beatrice did.'

'Well, by associating with the rich you grow refined and decadent. But how sweet this decadence is!'

'How come you're still here? I thought you'd gone to the shop.'

'It's Sunday, Mody! Shit, I can tell you've never worked!'

'True. You'll teach me all about it, won't you, Nina?'

'Teach you what, Mama? You're exasperating! Do you mind telling me what you two have concocted?'

'What do you say, Mody, shall we tell him? Your mother is opening a shop next door to mine, and since she knows more about books than yarns, it's a bookshop!'

'I want to create a bookshop that is also a gathering place, like the one in Rome on Via Veneto. A few select books and someone you can ask for recommendations. At least my reading will be put to some use.'

'You, behind a counter? Not on your life!'

'What's wrong with it, Prando? I told you, Nina: we would have been better off not saying anything to him.'

'You, a Brandiforti, working as a shopkeeper?'

'You know, Mattia, sometimes I really feel like creating a domestic revolution and saying what should be said to this *caruso*.'

'Drop it, Prando. Leave your mother alone! She knows what she wants to do.'

'You always side together, you two! But what need is there to work? I earn well, Bambolina is wealthy. With the proceeds . . .'

'No, Prando! The proceeds from the sale of this villa have already been invested in books and in the small shop adjacent to Nina's.'

'And where will you live?'

'I've paid the Brunos a deposit. I'll live above the shop.'

'In that rats' nest? In that shady neighbourhood? Are you crazy?'

'Nina lives there, doesn't she? And if she's there . . .'

'Nina, always Nina! I won't allow it. Never! I'll never consent to seeing you behind a counter!'

'I have to earn a living, and in the least unpleasant way. At a guess, we'll have roughly twenty years of white Fascism.'*

'What are you talking about? The gradual revolution . . .'

'The reformist shambles, you mean? Like the joke about agrarian reform, right, Mattia?'

'I don't know much about politics, Prando, but it's true that agrarian reform was all smoke and mirrors, a sop: a few feet of stony ground improperly allocated and no money for seed or machinery. So to cultivate those few feet of soil, farmers went into debt. They fell into the hands of loan sharks everywhere, and already the young people are leaving the land.'

'You're all crazy, Mattia! What can you expect overnight? I've had enough. You with the land, this one with the women's issue!'

'All right, Prando, I've told you before and I'll say it again: I want to be independent from men like Lucio. And watch out, because at this rate when women realize how you leftist men smile smugly and paternalistically at what they say, when your Amalia realizes she isn't being heard and that she's wearing herself out doing two jobs, at the stove and in the laboratory – how come you never speak to me about Amalia's work, huh? why do I only hear how sweet, or pretty or jealous she is? – when they realize all this, their vengeance will be awesome, Prando, like in America. They will turn their backs on you and . . .'

'That's enough!'

'Exactly! I don't want to hate you. I love men like Jacopo, Mattia . . .'

'Sappy fools, Mama!'

'Careful, Prando! Because I might break your neck if you say that again.'

'Calm down, Mattia. Don't take offence. It's not his fault; he grew up in the Duce's breeding ground.'

'You'll never see me again, Mama. One more word and you'll never see me again!'

'It was to be expected, Prando. The last time, too, our brothers, our children deserted us. It's a time for big decisions. Think about it. I've made mine . . . What did your Malatesta* do when Fascism arose, Nina? And he was seventy-one years old. I'm a young girl by comparison.'

'He went back to his work as an electrician in a small shop in San Lorenzo.'

'There you are. I'll take advantage of it to read Bakunin and so many others. What did your Arminio rightly say, Nina?'

'He said that a Leninist doesn't read out of self-censorship. It's incredible, but that's how it is!'

91

In front of the small artificial pond that has miraculously risen before her, Modesta stops and ripples the green water with her hand. But no joy comes from that miracle. Prando turns his back and stalks away. 'You'll never see me again, Mama, never!' To rebel against a son . . . This was something she hadn't known: that rebelling against a son produces unbounded sadness, doesn't it, Modesta? Why? Think hard, Modesta; don't fall into a trap. If you think hard and don't lose your head – just like during the bombings – you'll find the answer. Here: sit down on the small gilded stool where your Beatrice used to sit while you splashed about in the water: *'I'll set it here, Modesta. It's charming, such an antique in this modern setting . . . It's original, plus this way we can go on talking.'* There, sit on the stool and light a cigarette. The bathwater can wait. Amid smoke and tears Modesta thinks: rebelling against a father occurs when you think you're young and have all eternity ahead of you, but rebelling against a son – when you are perhaps nearing the end of the journey – reveals thoughts of carnal loneliness that smack of death. So then, what to do? I'm still dressed. I can run outside and call him back, and by so doing decree my own living death, submitting to words and actions contrary to my own thinking, watching the systematic destruction of that poor Amalia, who's confident like all intelligent women yet new to the art of being an adult. Watching the reverse destruction to which Carluzzu is subjected day by day: *'You're a man.*

You have to prove how manly you are, Carluzzu! Not womanish like today's young men!'

They're not even thirty and already, as always, they're railing against fourteen- and twenty-year-olds. No, Modesta! To accept this is vile, more vile than siding with the jailers there on the island. If you held out on that windswept scrap of rock . . . if you held out then, you cannot nullify that action now by totally surrendering to Prando (or the fear of death?) or to the fear of old age that has been instilled in you to preserve order in society, just to safeguard that first line of defence which – Fascism or not – is still the family, the training ground for future soldiers, soldier-mothers, grandmother-queens. Besides, why that eternal glorification of youth? The young work, produce, bear children, go to war, all before gaining self-awareness. But at forty, at fifty years of age, a human being – if he hasn't perished in the incessant social war – becomes dangerous: he poses questions, he demands freedom, rest, joy. Even the term 'old age' is a lie, Modesta. It's been crammed with scary ghosts, like the word 'death', to make you be quiet, deferential to the established rules. Who knows what old age is? When it starts? In Stendhal's day, a woman was old at thirty. At thirty I had just begun to understand things and to live. How many have dared cross the threshold of that word without listening to the preconceptions and clichés? Maybe more than you imagine, since among those cast aside you can find serene faces and calm, wise gazes. But no one has ever dared speak out because of fear – always that eternal fear – of toppling the bogus equilibrium that has been established. Standing before the closed door of that frightening word, the temptation to go in and look around takes hold of you, doesn't it, Modesta? Of course, after entering that door, you could meet your death just around the corner. But why wait for it out there, shoulders hunched, hands limp in your lap? Why not go and meet it? Challenge it day by day, hour by hour, stealing all the life you can from it?

The cigarette between your fingers has gone out and the water inspires you to fight. Glowing pink, green and blue on the shelf in the shadows are scented soaps straight out of *The Arabian Nights* – who would have imagined it back then, eh, Beatrice? Bambù put them there to bring me joy. Perhaps she understood my fearfulness? *'You seem distant, Zia. Why? Distant and distracted. Please, go back to being your old self!'* Soaping myself is pleasurable; my firm body only needs some exercise. It's time to move, to fight with every muscle and every bit of brain power in the chess game with *La Certa* that awaits me. Every year that's stolen, won, every hour wrested from the chessboard of time, becomes eternal in that final match. Think, Modesta: maybe growing old is nothing more than an ultimate act of revolution . . .

Revolution? Modesta smiles, trying to float in that small pool of artificial water.

'You float in the tub as if you were out at sea, Mody!'

'It's raining outside, Beatrice. It's winter, but all I have to do is close my eyes and remember . . . It's just that I'm afraid I'll forget how to swim. What do you think? When summer comes, will I still know how to swim?'

'Once you've learned to swim, Mody, you never forget how.'

'Once you've learned the joy of revolution, you mean.'

Beatrice must really be afraid of that word, since her face becomes small and pinched and turns pale, so pale that it vanishes in the steam rising to the ceiling from the hot water. Has she gone? Don't be afraid, Beatrice. Even the word 'revolution' lies or grows old. We need to find another one. If Carlo were alive, he'd find one. He was so good at it, a fount of new words . . .

92

A few strokes, and already my hand is touching the Prophet's beard: long ringlets combed by the waves, where swarms of fish drift in the green silence of the algae. You can stretch out between the beard and the forehead, and the giant's large hollow eye won't blink, riveted as he is by millions of years looking out at sea. Before Modesta was able to swim, the distance of that gaze made her tremble with hope and misgivings. Now, only a profound peace invades her mature body at each sensation of her skin, veins, joints. A body that is its own master, made wise by an understanding of the flesh. A profound awareness . . . of touch, sight, taste. Lying on her back on the rocky ledge, Modesta observes how her developed senses can take in the entire blue expanse, the wind, the distance, without the fragile fears of childhood. Astonished, she discovers the meaning of the skill her body has acquired during the long, brief course of her fifty years. It's like a second childhood, but with a precise awareness of being young, an appreciation of how to, touch, see, enjoy. Fifty years: the golden age of discovery. Fifty years: a happy age unjustly maligned by poets and birth records.

How to describe that summer afternoon lying on the rock, touched by the last caress of the setting sun? How to describe the joy of that discovery? How to tell others about it? How to communicate the happiness of each simple act, each step, each new encounter . . . with faces, books, sunsets and dawns, Sunday afternoons on sun-drenched beaches? '*Good for you, Nonna, I envy you! I've discovered that envy is the right attitude for wanting things. By envying you, I'm trying to imitate you, and maybe someday I'll be like you.*' How to describe the joy of listening to that boy? The emotion his voice communicates when he tells me: '*With you, Modesta – will you let me call you that? – with you, I feel like I have a buddy. So, buddy, the boss – my father – paid me. Shall we go to the movies and pass some time? I just have to see* The Asphalt Jungle; *everyone is talking about it! The movies have now become a must. Come with me. It only lasts a couple of hours; then we'll walk around and talk. I have so much to say about that Julien you introduced me to . . .*' It may be that after the movie we won't talk about either the film or about Julien Sorel,* but we'll go to Nina's instead and laugh and eat, and Carluzzu and Olimpia will play the guitar endlessly, passing it back and forth along with a glass of wine . . .

*

Stop here, in this joy bursting with the senses and the mind, and thus freeze for ever in me, in you, the best ten years of my life, those between fifty and sixty? The temptation is strong, but life doesn't stop, and Carluzzu has entered the bookshop. His face has changed. His eyes blaze with hatred and he wipes his perspiring brow. He stares at me, and for a moment his gaze grows calmer. He needs me.

'What is it, Carluzzu? What's happened?'

'What happened is that I had to beat up your son, that is, according to the civil registry – my father I mean, if you believe that stinking birth certificate! I didn't mean to, I know I didn't want to! But all of a sudden he slaps me. I tell myself: be good, Carlo, it's just the usual little slap. But then he starts yelling, and I can't stand being yelled at, Nonna, you know that. So I made him shut up by force. And I could have killed him too!'

'And then?'

'I went to the port to vent my anger, walking up and down amid the fishmongers' cries. Then I stopped at the mussel stand and I must have eaten a hundred raw mussels, I think! I downed them with a glass of wine and the steam went out of me. Oh, Mody – it may have been the mussels or the wine at midday – I felt like I was flying in the sunshine, light as a gull among the white walls and the shouts, the hot sun pressing at my back and the cool wind on my forehead. And I told myself: "Why lose all this for that animal? And then it's no use thinking about taking a train, a steamship – you've already done that so many times – you'll always come back here, like Zio 'Ntoni and Zio Jacopo." Then I think about that animal again, your son . . . I see him slammed against the wall by my fists, his head lowered like a tired lion, and I feel a little sorry and I tell myself: "Let's go see if he's lost a few teeth . . . He cares a lot about his teeth: that dazzling smile he can flash at the jurors." I know, it's no use you smiling, we all went to night school, as Nicola says: I know it's age-old remorse, ancestral. Who would dare raise a hand against his own father's mane, white or not, be he a believer or an atheist? Fine, so I go back home, I open the door without making a sound, I go into the hall and what do I hear? You won't believe it: his voice, pompous and persuasive like in court, saying on the phone: "Yes, it's true, Mattia . . . he beat me up, that's all there is to it! When you have a son of your own blood who is not a weakling, but a real man, this, too, can happen. Lucky you, you only have two girls!"'

'And what did you do?'

'*Fischia!* Damn! Hey, Mody, do you know that in Rome it's popular for young people to say *"fischia!"*? Nicola told me. It's awful, but it sticks in your mind like the lyrics to a bad song.'

'And so?'

'*Fischia!* Oh, sorry! So I uttered a string of dithyrambs à la Miller, the great blasphemous Henry,* and completely satisfied with my cultural skills, I came straight to you, the one who gave them to me . . . Now let's go! I'll take you to a restaurant. Your grandson is rich today.'

'Why is that?'

'I finished the thesis for Nicola. Remember, I came to you for information? I steal your ideas on Anglo-Saxon literature, add a little something of my own and sell the product to Nicola, who is rich and doesn't know a damn thing! Then he looks good at home and with his professor. Complete thievery, Nonna, on your shoulders . . .'

'What could be better in this case than to be robbed? If they rob you, it means you're rich, right?'

'So, *ragazzaccia*, what will you have, naughty girl?'

'Spaghetti!'

'Me too! Hey my friend, two spaghetti *alle vongole* and torrents of white wine!'

'What sunshine, Carlo! One more week and then we can swim until October.'

'Do you know that you're a fabulous little *nonna*?'

'You gave me a stunning account of your morning, Carlo, but you didn't tell me why you beat up my Prando.'

'Are you fond of your Prando?'

'No, but I love him.'

'You have a clarity, Mody, that's scary, as Nina says.'

'So then, what did your old father want this morning?'

'The same old story: "You're young . . . you don't know what it means to . . ." And always at the same time, at the table, when you're famished and not in the mood: "Not everyone, son, has the good fortune of having a father who paves the way for him. Why pursue impossible things like archaeology when you have a law practice that yields like an oil well right here at your fingertips?" That was five years ago, remember? And to keep the peace, I said to myself: "Let's make him happy; after all, he's the boss, and with a boss, either you kill him right away, or you dupe him." So I skip classes and repay him for what it cost him to raise me. Because that's the point: all they want is for the money they spent on you to pay off. Forget paternal love! But is it true he was an anti-fascist, Mody?'

'Of course, and a communist as well.'

'If he was a communist, then why did he leave the Party when the 20th Congress* took place? What did he think, that a revolution is all sweetness and light? Uncle Jacopo didn't drop out; on the contrary, he told me back then in Milan that it was time to fight harder, to stay in the Party and finally make Gramsci's ideas heard . . . I know, I'm sorry, we've talked about it so many times and I'm being a pest. It's just that it's hard for us young people to understand. Take Nicola . . . Outwardly, in public, his father declares himself communist, then on Sunday he goes to Mass. And in the evening they say prayers. What a screw-up, as Nina says! I can't talk to Nicola anymore, Mody. It's awful, but I'm going to lose him! It's like he's deflated, worn out. One day his mind seems clear, the next day he starts saying it's all hopeless. Did you know he only reads Indian texts now? I read the *Autobiography of a Yogi* too, to try and understand him, but all I found in it was the usual warmed-over mysticism. How can people not see that it's just another opiate packaged in America? What can you do? At least it's not found in our house, thanks in part to the wife your son really doesn't deserve. She's on the ball, all right! I don't know how she slaves away all day looking after Papa and still keeps up on things. Such a sharp mind! I don't understand how a woman like her can put up with your son, Nonna, I just don't get it! You didn't stand for it.'

'It's because Amalia lacks confidence in herself, Carluzzu. She doesn't know it, but she lacks confidence because she's a woman.'

'You know, sometimes I enjoy teasing her. I cosy up to her and ask her to run away with me. She pretends to be indignant, and in a beautiful full voice says: "But Carlo, I'm your mother!" And I say: "No, Amalia, I'm Stella's son." "But I'm old." And I: "Stella was old too when she had me with your husband." At this point, she flushes and says: "How awful to tell *carusi* the truth, they take advantage of it!" And she laughs . . . those are the few times I see her laugh. I feel so sorry for her that sometimes I almost feel I love her. Is it true, Mody, that love is so very, very close to compassion? It's partly for her that I got my law degree. I tell myself: "Now that you're a lawyer, Carlo, your father will be mollified. He'll give you money and you can go to Greece for three months before you get into uniform." Instead, this morning he comes out with: "So then, beginning tomorrow you'll come to court with me and start learning the ropes." And I: "But Papa, in six months I have to leave for military service!" And he says: "No, no, we'll get you an exemption." Resorting to nature as evidence, I reply: "But Papa, at over six feet tall and with a chest this broad it will be impossible!" And him: "Everything is possible for a Brandiforti!" I lose my appetite, and on my plate I see battlefields, compulsory calls to arms, crusades, and I realize why wars break out . . . it's one way to escape from home. But Judas Priest, Mody! How can he talk like that at his age? How can he say: "You'll see the moral satisfaction you'll get from having an innocent man absolved!" For every one you save, there are a hundred in the prisons . . . Doesn't he understand that here, everything should be called into question, starting with his morals, which are at least a thousand years old?'

'Carlo talked like you forty years ago.'

'Carlo who?'

'Bambolina's father.'

'Right, and he was killed. But they won't kill me, Mody! They won't kill us, thanks to you, and to Jacopo. I met his students up in Trento, young people with their eyes open, guys like me determined not to be seduced by any false idealism. It's just that . . .'

'What, Carluzzu?'

'There are so few of us, Nonna, so few!'

'It's always been that way.'

'And the few I've met, in Milan, in London, in Paris, are sad.'

'It's always been that way, Carlo.'

'I don't want to be sad like them.'

'But there is still joy in knowing that you are different, Carluzzu, if you know how to find it.'

'It's true. That's what they don't want to understand! As if they were ashamed of being happy, as if happiness necessarily meant being like all the others: superficial and vain. Look at Uncle 'Ntoni, up there in Rome: a success with the public and with the critics, streams of intellectuals, of cultured people waiting to congratulate him in his dressing room. As soon as we're alone, a tragic mask falls over his face!'

'But 'Ntoni is a comic actor, Carlo. Don't forget that.'

'What does that mean?'

'There's also temperament. Don't become fanatical about joy, for heaven's sake! The temperament of a comic is terribly sad. There's something mysterious, unfathomable in people, in the professions they choose. Nature itself is unfathomable, Carluzzu, for crying out loud! Let's let others be the way they are, or how they want to be!'

'You're right, Nonna. I'm a fanatic like your Prando and before you get mad – I can see you're getting angry – give me your hand. Peace! I'll take you to see what a great bar they've opened near the *Pescheria*: all mirrors and glitter.'

Hand in hand we walked down to the port to take our minds off things, following the white wings of seagulls chasing lingering clouds.

'Is it true, Mody, that if you occasionally let the mind wander, it opens its wings and glides over colours, sucking up their nectar as if it were a butterfly?'

The same thought at the same moment there along the quay in the shadow of the port. Can a sixty-year-old woman have the same thoughts as a young man of twenty? I look at him: in the last of the sun's light, his dark eyes are veined with green and violet.

'In the daytime your eyes are light, Carluzzu.'

'Mama, I mean Stella, had dark eyes, didn't she?'

'Yes. Black as a starless night.'

'Too bad I can't remember her.'

'I remember her for you, Carlo.'

Yes, a sixty-year-old woman can have the same thoughts as a boy of twenty. Still amazed, happy as a child, Modesta throws her arms around that boy's neck and he takes her by the waist and lifts her, swinging her around among the fishermen, the stalls, the cries of the vendors. Carlo later told Nina and his friends that a few people turned around, surprised, but not indignant or scornful:

'Imagine a serious, elegant lady who suddenly flies off the ground as if she had wings, hugging and kissing me! In a flash, the considerable conformist in me tells me: "Stop, or they'll lynch you here, Carlo!" But the other Carlo quickly replies: "Coward, face up to them like she does. Better yet, reinforce her gesture by swinging her around, and let it be a lesson to you and to this stern, arrogant race from which you come." My heart explodes as I make her go flying, and for interminable seconds I await a raspberry, some snide comment. Instead, not a word . . . And when I set her down and dare glance around, I see a few people almost fearfully avert their eyes, and one individual staring at me, transfixed by a sharp doubt that maybe, yes, maybe that odd couple is happy and has the courage to show it. It's that old man from the port, the one as big as an armoire, with two shaggy little brushes for eyebrows. Well, after a moment that mountain of wrinkles smiles at me. It's a victory!'

Nina laughs and is beautiful, perhaps more beautiful than before.

She must be in love again. With whom? Maybe the tall, thin man who stares at her with the eyes of a music connoisseur who can listen effortlessly to the most complicated rhythms? Or is her new love Cesare, with his languid body and a face flashing with imagination? No, it must be the musician whom Nina is attracted to . . .

And I'd like to stay there for ever, but Bambù is calling me. I'd like to stay and go on listening to Carlo, who has the gift of telling stories, of captivating you and transporting you far away. But life moves swiftly in this conscious youth, it calls and I must go. Life cannot be stopped. Pietro is dying and he needs me.

93

But none of us would have known it if the doctor hadn't whispered to us as he hurriedly went out: 'Indeed, he has little time left now!' Seated in a roomy armchair, his head barely supported, Pietro is staring at something beyond the open window.

'Pietro has never stayed in bed when the sun is high, and this little worm tickling my chest certainly won't put me there.'

'Are you in pain, Pietro?'

'No, Mody, *staiu aspittannu me figghia*, I'm waiting for my daughter. Afterwards, when I've seen her, I can go . . . How long have I been waiting for her, Bambolina?'

'Two days, Pietro. But she should be here soon. She's stuck at the airport.'

'America is a long way off, Bambù!'

'But Crispina is in Palermo now, and if it weren't for the strikes . . .'

'Strikes, Mody?'

'Yes, Pietro.'

'It took some doing, didn't it, Mody, to be able to say that word out loud and in broad daylight! You're young, Bambuccia, but at one time you could only talk in the dark, and you couldn't even feel secure within the walls of your own house. You remember Pasquale, don't you, Mody? He was slender and *bionnu*, fair as an archangel, then thanks to betrayals and kowtowing to the Fascists, he became bloated and sweaty like a pig, and like a pig this hand of mine got rid of him

. . . Bambù, will you hold my hand like you did yesterday? Bambolina's hand sees, heals and restores. That's why she can then recount whatever she touches in poems, like the balladeers. My father used to say that a person born with the talent to tell stories is also someone who heals . . . What is my little sparrow doing, Bambù? My Argentovivo isn't off crying somewhere, is she?'

'No, she's making a *cassata* . . . Crispina will be famished.'

'That's my little sparrow, she listened to me. You'll take care of her for me afterwards, won't you, Bambù? You'll guide her along? That's how she is. Many people are like that. It's not that they're less capable than others, it's that they're meek by nature and they need to be steered along.'

'Of course, Pietro.'

'I knew you would. I'm just talking to pass the time while we wait.'

'Speaking of talking, Zia, if you knew what fantastic stories Pietro has told me these past few days! I'll write them all down, Pietro. You'll let me, won't you?'

'If they stir your imagination, they're yours.'

'Never mind imagination! You should hear all the things he knows about Nonna Gaia, and about Uncle Jacopo and the time he came to liberate you from the island. Tell Zia too about the island, Pietro.'

'I've told it all by now, Bambuccia.'

'But about that German who was kind . . .'

'Well, I don't know if he didn't see us on purpose, or if he really didn't see us, but certainly if he had stopped us we would have been done for.'

Timur! . . . so I had encountered Timur? A chilling terror fills me at the thought of that name that I myself had summoned up. They only mentioned a German.

'What is it, Zia? You've turned pale.'

'What did that German look like, Pietro? Tell me.'

'How should I know, my dear Mody! With those helmets, all their faces looked alike.'

'Let's not talk about Germans. I don't like Zia's expression when we speak of them. Tell us about your masterstroke, about how you routed Inès . . . Pietro considers it his greatest work, Zia.'

'Of course! I can fight forcefully with my hands and legs, but with a woman, well! With a woman! . . . Pietro had to make himself small as a snake and spy on her . . . But Mody knows everything, Bambù. I had nothing against Inès, but she was tormenting my Ippolito so I blackmailed her. She had a *cascamorto*, a lovesick suitor, but she couldn't make up her mind to run off with him. She kept accumulating money, so I made her decide in a jiffy. But afterwards she too was happy. Women! Who can understand them! She said she couldn't leave her son Jacopo, that her duty was to stay close to him. But while we're on the subject, Mody, I shouldn't, but . . . for my peace of mind can I be sure that you'll find a companion for my dear Prince, to go fishing, walking with him?'

'Of course, Pietro.'

'Go open the door, Bambù. Crispina is here! She's come just in time. I'm tired, and this languor that's come over me even while talking about happy moments is a sign that I am truly exhausted and must sleep.'

*

Pietro sleeps deeply, and faced with that profound sleep, no one dares weep or shriek. His composed body, the smile that Crispina's arrival fixed on his face for ever, inspire only respect.

Everyone was notified by Bambolina's elegant script with its irrevocable words . . . Like back then, at Carmelo, when we could do anything we wanted, right, Cavallina? but only during the hours that Gaia's calligraphy had firmly penned on that piece of paper, shiny as silk. Jacopo squeezes my arm for a moment. His clothes have a new smell of aseptic wards mixed with the whiff of a train – they've travelled all night – and he holds his Olimpia by the waist, as if to support her. That's right, I had almost forgotten; even good things are forgotten. For every life that's taken, another life is born: Olimpia is expecting a baby with my Jacopo.

'How lovely Crispina is, Nonna! Every time she comes back, she's even more beautiful! Is it true that I was in love with her as a child? Pietro always told me so.'

'Yes, Carluzzu.'

'I don't remember being in love, only her singing. I have two Crispinas in my head: the one 'Ntoni used to push into the middle of the room to sing, and the impressive, confident woman on that immense stage. Remember how Pietro was sweating? Where was that, Nonna?'

'In Milan, I think; it was so long ago. Pietro was happy! Life flies by when you're happy.'

'It's true. But what are you looking at, Nonna? Why are you so pale?'

Prando is back there, standing near 'Ntoni and smiling at me. After so many years, he wants to talk to me. I'd rather stay there with them, listen to the stories about Pietro, drink some wine. But Prando needs me. I have to go to him.

'What is it, Mama? Why are you looking at me like that? Your silence is humiliating me. Prando has come, and by coming he is apologizing for his past behaviour. Let's put it behind us.'

Why is he speaking in the same voice he used as a child, when his foot in a plaster cast made him fidget and fret?

'I had to see the doctor. Something is wrong with my heart. They tell me I have to make up my mind: either change my life and live another thirty years, or . . .'

With my hands I grasp the wiry curls and look closely at him: not a single white strand, not a shadow on those marmoreal features. But Prando isn't lying. Only this warning could have bent his pride and made him return to the one who gave birth to him.

'But you know what I told that blatant idiot? That without my work, which is more intoxicating to me than wine, and without my motorcycle, I can't live. What should I do, end up like that wimp Mattia, who looks after himself like a delicate, sickly woman?'

'But he's happy.'

'That may be, but I'd rather . . .'

'Whom do you want to spite by dying, eh, old man?'

'Old man, you call me – and you're right. Why did you bring me into this world if you knew I would have to grow old?'

'So, you want to take your revenge on me?'

'That too. If a son dies, your son, you'll regret giving birth to me.

And you'll be an old woman with regrets, for ever bound to my memory.'

'You've loved me that much, Prando?'

'That much. But you haven't!'

'Why do you say that?'

'Because you lived for everyone else, always travelling around, damn you, giving speeches and cosying up to everybody.'

'Was I supposed to choose you, and reject a life?'

'Yes.'

'Prando, you have always wanted it all, even as a child. "Prando has two Mamas: Mama Stella and Mama Mody, and two aunts besides." Remember?'

'Yes.'

'So then tell me: what could I do, I who am so much like you, who, like you, want it all?'

'That's true too! Finally a smile, Mama. When you smile, you become young again, like when I was a child. Prando is a bastard, but he's also proud when you smile and look like a young girl . . . I want to hold you in my arms, and don't protest, right, because I'm not well! Here, close to me, my *mamma bambina*, or did you lie? Maybe it wasn't even you who gave birth to me? Maybe you're my sister? With you, anything is possible. That's what drives me wild! Even when I'm dead, it will drive me crazy!'

'Yet you know that if I had been docile, all yours like Amalia, you would have tired of me, as you have of her.'

'It's true. Prando tires easily of the things he possesses. Money only bores me now that I have it, and even the motorcycle. I pretend it's important to me, but I've lost my taste for it now that everyone can have one.'

'I know you, Prando. Shall we put our cards on the table?'

'Let's put our cards on the table. What are you trying to say?'

'Knowing your greed is insatiable, it seemed pointless to me to sacrifice myself.'

'You mean you realized that the more slack you gave me, the more you bound me to you?'

'Maybe, if you feel that way about it. Maybe . . . Who can fully understand their actions when it comes to love or affection? I only know that nobody likes the idea of being cast aside, and you, you're a man who takes and discards . . . Who could you have got this from? The old man wasn't like that. He knew how to love the things he won.'

'Don't talk to me about the past. The past is boring!'

'You see? You rob life with both hands. With both hands you seized it – admit it! – and now you want to throw it away.'

'Yes.'

'Don't your children mean anything to you?'

'Very little! I like Carluzzu: he's tough, he knows what he wants. Did you know he beat me up once?'

'Yes.'

'What a keen mind he has!'

'Why didn't you prevent him from seeing me all this time?'

'Damn if I didn't try! But you know what his reaction was? Didn't he tell you? He replied abruptly with a few harsh words: "You will not stand in my way. You're just an old Fascist has-been." That's exactly what he said. Just between us, Mama, I had to laugh. You like Carluzzu, don't you?'

'I've never liked anyone more.'

'Then you have to give me some credit, because he's my son after all, isn't he? What resolve that boy has! And what integrity! Take military service . . . With a little money, I could have had him declared unfit and instead . . . Well, he's leaving! In a few months he's leaving and there's nothing I can do about it. But why?'

'He's right. He says that having been raised in a privileged setting, the military will help him understand his country.'

'Yes, yes, he says things like that but . . . when he comes back he has to join the practice with me! Otherwise who will I leave it to?'

'Get it out of your head, Prando. Try to understand once and for all . . .'

'You always side together, dont you! I knew it, and to tell you the truth, this is the only thing that has consoled me during these years and allowed me to keep tabs on you. Through him I kept up with you. Your affection for each other gratified me – who knows why? We

647

really are a mystery to ourselves when it comes to matters of love and affection . . . Who said that, you or him?'

'I did, a few minutes ago.'

'Oh, right. I'm not a good listener, I know. Even Bambuccia is always telling me that. But he knows how to listen, right?'

'Of course, and you should hear him tell stories!'

'Enough, or I'll get jealous! Instead tell me, you old sorceress, what do you think of Ignazio?'

'He's your spitting image and you know it. Why even ask?'

'Yes . . . my spitting image.'

'Why are you frowning like that? Why do you avoid him? Bambù told me.'

'What can I say to someone who is just like me? I've been fed up with myself for years! Oh, Mody, listen . . .'

'Why are you calling me Mody now?'

'I want to explain why I really came back to you. I didn't come back to my mother, but to my best friend. Because you've been a friend to me, Mody, I have to tell you. I need an ally now who knows about my heart condition – a complete secret is heavy to bear and you, I know, will not annoy me by whining and offering advice as Amalia, Bambù or even Mattia would.'

'You know you can count on me.'

'I know. But you must swear to me on Carluzzu that no one will ever know anything.'

'I swear.'

'Come here; look me in the eye. You're tough, old lady! How is it possible that I don't see any dismay, not a tear in your eyes?'

'You'd like me to cry now? To be worried about you?'

'No. My esteem for you would lessen. But will you be able to keep it up tomorrow or a month from now as well?'

'Try me.'

'Look at that! Now she's challenging me! And to this challenge, my dear Mody, I add another. Listen, I've had an idea: Once the mourning for Pietro is over, would you be willing to arrange a party for me and my heart? A party for us two and our secret? I want a very grand party. The whole island must feel the joy. You must prepare it with your own hands, and I'll see if these beautiful little hands I'm kissing tremble. Can you do it? If you're up to such a contest – and whoever heard of such a thing, celebrating your own son's engagement to this slut of an illness clinging to his heart? – if you can do it, Prando will reward you by wanting to live, you can be sure of it. The excitement he feels for this wager is already causing life to flow back into his veins. But watch out, old woman, it won't be easy. I'll follow you step by step, watch your every gesture, your every expression. And if you so much as quaver or grow sad, you'll lose.'

94

The grove of orange and lemon trees lit by thousands of little light bulbs – back then we couldn't have done it with candles, could we, Beatrice? – slowly fades in the glow of dawn. Yet couples holding one another tightly continue circling in the marble dance area where the two staircases meet. Prando slowly climbs Carmelo's broad steps, looking for his mother. All night he's watched me; soon we'll know who won the contest. I did not tremble as I feared I would, and now I know the reason for this serenity of mine in the face of Pietro's death and Prando's illness. It's not indifference, a blunting of the senses due to age, as I had suspected. It's the complete mastery of emotion and a supreme awareness of each precious moment that life rewards you with if you have courage and a steady hand . . . Carmine slowly climbs the stairs of Carmelo. Now I know, old man, the deep sense of freedom and joy you felt before dying, and I no longer envy you. I've acquired your skill, and from now on there will only be joy for me. I see it in my future and in your eyes, Prando.

'What do you see in my eyes, old woman?'

'I see that you won't die before my eyes are closed.'

'And how long do you think you'll live?'

'Who knows? A long time, I hope.'

'So my life depends on yours?'

'If you want it to. If you don't, kill yourself! But do it sooner, with

a revolver. Waiting for death whining and snivelling is for the mediocre, and you've been a lot of things, but never a coward.'

'You won the wager and Prando will repay you by wanting to live.
What else can he do? What fun is it to die if you know that the one
who gave birth to you won't even shed a tear?'

*

'Ntoni: 'What a fantastic idea to light up the garden bright as day, and
inside, where most of the party took place, keep the parlours dim. All
night I went around as though I were in a dream. A dream is what it
is! Congratulations, Mody. This party is a dream!'

Bambù: 'Carluzzu, hug me. I feel so deserted!'

'Ntoni: 'You always feel deserted whenever a party is over, or a performance ends. Something is gone, leaving many small deaths inside
. . . cold, rosy little pearls like the ones you're wearing around your
neck, Bambù.'

Carlo: 'Always up to date, our 'Ntoni! You can sense it, can you, you
old wolf, that they're reassessing D'Annunzio?'*

Bambù: 'No, Carluzzu, let 'Ntoni speak. I like it. Maybe he's the
only one who hasn't changed.'

'Ntoni: 'And how was I before, Bambuccia?'

Bambù: 'The most amusing and original.'

'Ntoni: 'And do you know why I haven't changed?'

Bambù: 'No.'

'Ntoni: 'Because I haven't married . . . What is it? Why are you crying, Bambù? My comment was meant to be funny.'

Bambù: 'I want to see Jacopo! He never sends us news except once
in a blue moon.'

Jose sends word of himself more and more rarely . . . He's fighting
far away and Jacopo follows him . . . For a moment, Modesta fears she
will never see him again and clasps Prando's head tightly to her breast.

Prando: 'What is it, old woman?'

Modesta: 'I'm afraid, Prando.'

Prando: 'For me?'

Modesta: 'No, for Jacopo. Always alone, fighting!'

Prando: 'I actually envy him! It's fate's good fortune to have a head that allows you to fight with your mind. I could only fight with my arms, but the time for that is past. Maybe that's why my body has come to weigh on me.'

Bambù: 'Your body has come to weigh on you because you eat and drink too much.'

Prando: 'That's also true.'

Bambù: 'Even now, instead of lying there on Modesta's lap, why don't you see to Ignazio? He's fallen asleep on the rug. Go and put him to bed. He's your son, isn't he?'

Carlo: 'Oh Zia, how contentedly he's sleeping! I, I don't know . . .'

Bambù: 'What?'

Carlo: 'Seeing Ignazio in this dim light . . . for a second it was like seeing myself. Yes, as though I too . . .'

Bambù: 'Naturally . . . if you only knew how many times you fell asleep like your brother!'

Carlo: 'And I was afraid too, wasn't I, Bambù?'

Bambù: 'You were afraid everyone would leave and never return. But then we gave you so much warmth and affection and . . . you got over it. We always had to hold you in our arms.'

Carlo: 'Imagine! Now that you tell me that, I can feel powerful arms lifting me up in my sleep.'

Bambù: 'Oh, of course, it was Pietro who, very quietly, without a word – he knew your father would never do it – would lift you up and carry you upstairs.'

Carlo: 'Pietro! I can feel him still with us. I've seen him many times in my dreams, walking around among us with his impassive face . . . I'll go and get Ignazio – or Ignazio-Carluzzu – and take him upstairs. I want to see what being a father feels like. Because Pietro was a father, right, Bambù?'

Bambù: 'Yes, a father and a mother, Carluzzu . . . I'll go and take a stroll around to see who's still here. Parties are always like that! Until the sun rises and extinguishes the lights, no one has the heart to put an end to the enjoyment . . . Oh Carlo, look how beautiful! Everything is all white and shining, and the light bulbs against the greenery seem just like gleaming oranges . . . you too, 'Ntoni! Come on, get up, look!'

'Ntoni: 'I was falling asleep. Good thing you woke me. I'll come with you. You can't miss a sunrise like this.'

Prando: 'Shall we go too, Mama?'

Modesta: 'Of course, Prando. A sunrise like this should never be missed.'

'Until the sun rises, no one has the heart to put an end to the enjoyment.' It's understandable. Who would dare commit such a crime? . . . Did I say that or did Prando, who's whispering meaningless phrases in my ear? Or was it Bambù, running nimbly ahead of us, her slender hand raised – the wing of a dove – to point the way? Her slim torso sways back and forth in the silence.

Bambù: 'Why is it so quiet, Prando?'

Prando: 'The musicians are sleeping. Look at them: fallen like vanquished paladins.'

Bambù: 'But people are still dancing . . .'

Prando: 'Sure, everyone sings something, a waltz, a tango, whatever he likes.'

Bambù: 'We should tell Argentovivo to bring us something hot. Look at those two huddling inside the niche; they're numb with cold.'

Prando: 'I already did. Here she comes, tottering with her tray. How fat and comical Argentovivo has become!'

'Ntoni: 'She must be happy fat, because she talks less. There's no avoiding it: either sex, or food, or incessant chatter.'

Argentovivo: 'What's that, *signorino*?'

'Ntoni: 'I was saying that plump and speechless you're delightful, Argentovivo, delightful!'

Argentovivo: 'You're too kind, *signorino*.'

'Ntoni: 'For you, I'm always a *signorino*, right, Argentovivo? What a comfort to remain young, for someone at least! Come, come dance with me.'

Modesta: 'All of Carmelo's rooms filled . . . If your grandmother were here, Prando, you'd hear it! Shouts of rage! Maybe it's because I'm sleepy, but in this silence I'm afraid I'm going to hear her voice explode at any moment. Who's yelling like that?'

Prando: 'It's Nina, Mama, and she's not yelling. She's singing, in the arms of her gallant beau. How repugnant I find him! Look out, they've seen us. Come on, let's run behind the hedge. Maybe we can avoid the simpering of that pathetic gentleman.'

Nina: 'Oh, no you don't, Prandone! You have to stop keeping Modesta sequestered like that. We have a right to her company too. Oh, from a distance, don't worry. But where are you taking her?'

Prando: 'To bed, Nina.'

Nina: 'To bed? But we're just getting started! Stay, Mody, stay with your Nina.'

Prando is holding me tight. The hundreds of stairs, drapes and corridors of that house have transported me back to a deathly past. Nina must have sensed it because she loosens Prando's arms firmly and laughs.

Nina: 'Oh no, mummy's darling boy! We let you have her all night, but now Mody is staying with us.'

Prando: 'But she's worn out, Nina!'

Nina: 'You'd like that, my dear boy! You know what I think? That she's tired of being sucked dry by your problems. Oh, these babies, Marco! The more you suckle them, the greedier they grow up to be.'

Prando: 'You're a bitch, Nina, a bitch, I swear to God!'

Nina: 'Why don't you go to Amalia? Look at her over there, how she's looking at you . . .'

Prando: 'Believe me, I'm going. Are you coming, Mama?'

I'd like to go. I'm tired, but by now Nina has taken me in her arms, and besides, I can't be impolite to her friend. Prando is always rude to outsiders. To make amends, I hold out my hand to that gentleman, though I don't catch his name.

Modesta: 'What did you say his name was, Nina?'

Marco: 'Marco Clayton, *signora*. Clearly, Nina, your Modesta doesn't want to know me.'

Nina: 'Go on, Mody, I've introduced him to you a hundred times! What, are you getting forgetful on me now? Don't you remember that evening when you came to my house with Carlo, and then to the theatre? You have to forgive her, Marco. When Mody is with Carluzzu, she doesn't notice anyone else.'

Of course, that evening . . . Pietro was still alive and Olimpia was still here with us. Nina is right; he was also at the wake and at the funeral service. Now I remember that face, always there beside Nina . . .

I'm sleepy and Prando is calling to me with his eyes. I should follow him. But what about that gentleman? '*Remember, Mody, that a princess, even if she isn't one, must never offend anyone, not even the humblest of men.*'

Marco: 'Well, Nina, how about a nice cup of tea? I have the feeling your Modesta is very tired. We should go.'

He's offended. He smiles, but you can tell he's hurt. I have to say something.

Modesta: 'Forgive me, but I really am tired . . .' Now why do I hear my voice saying, 'You're a musician, aren't you? Can you swim?'

Nina: 'What's got into you, Modesta? You crack me up! Didn't I tell you, Marco? She seems oh-so-serious and then . . .'

Modesta: 'Let's go for a swim, then!'

Nina: 'But the sea is far away, Mody.'

Modesta: 'It seemed far by carriage. But now, by car, it's less than an hour,. . .'

Nina: 'What do you say, Marco? Should we make her happy? Jump in the car and take her to the sea? Look at that impudent face! She's always like that, my Mody. Even in jail she managed to come up with some wacky idea, and you could kiss peace goodbye!'

Marco: 'Really?'

The two of them laugh, and it's clear that they're only staying with Modesta to be polite. You can tell by the way they look at one another that they're just waiting to be alone so they can laugh and joke around. I've become too serious! By trying to imitate Nonna Gaia and make people respect me, I've become possessed by her, and now I'm old and harsh. Or is it because I don't fall in love anymore? After me, Nina had a grand affair – *à la Grand Hotel*,* as she described it – and then another sublime or springtime love . . . '*What are you living for, if you don't fall in love in springtime?*' But it must not have been so sublime if after three months, at the height of August, she's letting that musician look at her that way.

Nina: 'So what should we do now, Marco? This one has fallen asleep.'

Modesta: 'I'm not sleeping. I just closed my eyes because I don't feel like talking.'

Marco: 'It's not a problem, Nina, we'll take her upstairs. I'll do it . . . Look, she's taken off her shoes and curled up as if she were already in bed. How lifeless she is! Are you sure it's nothing serious?'

Nina: 'No, no, this always happens! She can go for days and days without sleeping, even back then in prison, then all of a sudden she can sleep for two days and two nights.'

Marco: 'How strange!'

Nina: 'Carluzzu told me it's a talent great leaders have. I don't know if he was joking – Carluzzu is always kidding around. Actually, he told me that when Caesar – Julius Caesar, I mean – didn't know what to do, he would fall asleep.'

Marco: 'Don't make me laugh, Nina. I'm afraid I'll drop her or wake her up.'

Nina: 'Not a chance! When she's like this not even an earthquake could wake her.'

I can't be sleeping if I can hear their words. And I could make him have an apoplectic attack, as Nina says, if I were to start screaming or laughing. But I don't feel like talking, especially now that Carluzzu has joined the procession and is having a good time teasing Nina about how strong her musician friend is.

Carlo: 'Hey, Nina, for once you have a strapping guy. How come? Have you changed your views on virility? I've always seen you with fairies and nymphets.'

When Carluzzu jokes like that he sounds a little like 'Ntoni. Why does that surprise you, Modesta? One way or another, they're both Stella's sons, except that Carluzzu – don't tell 'Ntoni, he'd be offended, poor thing! – is much, much more intelligent than 'Ntoni.

95

'Good morning, Zia.'

'Oh Bambù, have they gone?'

'Of course, it's been two days!'

'Go on, stop kidding. I heard it all perfectly. Carluzzu was teasing Nina . . .'

'Sure, two days ago!'

'I see: I was asleep and dreamt I wasn't sleeping. In fact, I'm ravenous! This sleep hasn't happened to me in a long time. I must have wanted to escape from something . . . but what?'

'Maybe, as Nina says, you wanted to get away from our carrying on. She gave us quite a talking-to, good-naturedly I'd say, your Nina! And she's right, because I myself have been very irritating lately. Even for the party, you had to do everything yourself.'

'It was a lovely party, wasn't it?'

'Just the way Prando wanted it! The whole island is talking about it, and will do so for quite some time.'

'Oh, Bambù, it's *déjà vu*! I've already experienced this moment: me eating, you looking at me, the big window, the mirror with the vine leaves and gilded fruit. I woke up in this room that other time too, when I had typhus after being in prison. I wanted to ask you, and then I forgot . . .'

'What?'

'Maybe you don't remember . . .'

'Of course I remember! How could I forget the fall of Fascism and you about to die?'

'That mirror, Bambolina – who put it there?'

'I did.'

'This was my room when I knew your mother. Did you know that?'

'Really?'

'What made you choose that particular mirror to hang there?'

'I don't know. It was in the attic.'

'Now I know why I fell asleep. I wanted to stay here, now that the dead are gone and the house is lived in. It's nice here. The girls must be awake, Bambù. Hear them laughing downstairs? How many are there?'

'Beatrice, Gaia, and two or three of their friends who slept over . . . They can't stop talking about the party. In their own way, they're continuing it.'

'Yes, I wanted to stay here!'

'Oh, I wish! Stay here, Zia, stay!'

'I'd like to stay here with you, Bambù, but life goes on. Someone is knocking at the door. Let's see who it is . . .'

Carlo: 'Oh, Nonna, you had us worried. The whole island is worried! Everything is at a standstill in the bookshop! Your secretary – how pretty she is, wow! I almost don't want to leave, so I can flirt with her – your secretary says she's terrified without you . . . But you, how lovely you are, oh! You must stay like that for ever.'

Modesta: 'A little exaggerated, don't you think, Bambù?'

Carlo: 'Well, at least until I've captured your image by having a daughter identical to you, or until I've written a great novel that depicts you to a tee.'

Bambù: 'I'll see to the latter!'

Carlo: 'Oh, no, Bambù!'

Bambù: 'Oh, yes I will!'

Carlo: 'Oh, all right. What if we wrote it together?'

Modesta: 'Together or not, don't write it right away, please, because I plan to live until I'm a hundred. You don't write about the living.'

Bambù: 'What beautiful roses, Carluzzu! Why did you toss them on the table? I'll put them in a vase. They're suffering.'

Carlo: 'Hey, Bambù, give me a hug before you take care of the flowers. This is the first time we'll be far apart for so long.'

Bambù: 'Listen to him! And the time you went to America?'

Carlo: 'Just look at her, Modesta. She has tears in her eyes!'

Bambù: 'Have some pity, Carluzzu! You all leave. I know it's only right, but it saddens me.'

Carlo: 'But I'll be back. Military service isn't for ever.'

Bambù: 'You will come back, won't you?'

Carlo: 'Of course! And I'll tell you all about what's happened to me. What good is experiencing things if you don't come back and share them in the piazza, talk about them at the bar and tell all your friends?'

Bambù: 'You must be a bit of a sadist, Carluzzu, let me tell you. I bet you're going away just so you can enjoy seeing us suffer. But I'm not falling for it anymore! I'd rather go over there and take my mind off of it with the flowers.'

Carlo: 'Aren't you going to come with me to the station?'

Bambù: 'Sure, so I can watch you enjoy my tears. He's a monster, this *carusu!*'

Carlo: 'You do know that you're a sweet little aunt, Zietta Bambù?'

Bambù: 'Why? What is it, an excuse to make me stay here and suffer a little longer?'

Carlo: 'You're right when you say I like knowing that you worry. And I think it's because when I was a child, everyone always left, and sometimes they didn't come back. It must be a form of revenge: subjecting others to the abandonment I went through.'

Bambù: 'That may be, Carluzzu, but it seems a little too pat to me, even from a psychoanalytical point of view . . .'

Carlo: 'Hey, Mody, why are your eyes shut? Are you feeling moved?'

Modesta: 'Well of course! There's no escaping someone who delights in moving you to pity.'

Carlo: 'Oh, Mody, I brought you a book by a certain Pierre Daco, a shitty priest, as Nina would say. Look: *What is Psychoanalysis?* I spent all day yesterday reading it. This bastard turns it into Christianity. I couldn't believe my eyes.'

Modesta: 'And this surprises you? Before long, we'll even have

Christian materialism. Those priests weren't born yesterday, as Nina says.'

Carlo: 'We have to do something!'

Modesta: 'You will, Carluzzu.'

Carlo: 'But I'm also very fearful. They're powerful, Mody! Oh, I almost forgot. Here: look at this cover.'

Modesta: 'Why did you buy the *Economist*?'

Carlo: 'Look, the person here, next to Brandt . . . Isn't he a male copy of Joyce?'

On the cover is a perfect head, bald, with two dark eyes that stare at me intently, dolefully slanted toward the delicate temples. Timur smiles ironically and confidently, as if only a few hours had passed since our lunch on the terrace of the San Domenico in Taormina.

*

'You haven't changed a bit, Princess . . .'

Who else but he could call me that now? I knew I would meet him again, but I never would have imagined hearing his voice in this remote café in Istanbul, surrounded by tombs like decayed tree trunks.

'I never for a moment doubted it.'

'You haven't changed either, Timur.'

'People who possess great moral intensity grow old, yes, but stay intact, like the immortal marble of the temples. No, don't go! Grant me a few more moments of your precious time. Your smile is a balm for my nostalgia.'

'Nostalgia, Timur?'

'Yes, I confess: nostalgia for your expanses of sun and shadow, for your human and metaphysical spaces . . . De Chirico* could only have been Italian.'

'Your Italian, if possible, has improved.'

'Distance is a good teacher. You only fully understand that which you have lost.'

'You never returned to Sicily?'

'No, the destruction I saw in Rome and Naples was enough for me.

I fear I will no longer find the land that our Goethe extolled, *our* land. A land, as well as art, belong to those who understand them. Is De Chirico Sicilian, Princess?'

'I don't know.'

'He must be, because the key to everything is to be found in Sicily . . . We would have made your island into a garden, not the rubbish heap – is that how you say it? – that I saw in Naples. But why talk about the past? This radiant sun scatters the clouds and impels us toward the future, and the future will be ours. Too bad, though: thirty years lost. We would have made quick work of it, clean and scientific, not this slow blood-letting they call democracy. Hitler was betrayed, but his dream will come to pass: a united Europe led by Germanic genius . . . But must you go, Princess?'

'Yes, I really must.'

'You're trembling. It's my fault for keeping you here at this table. Here on the Bosphorus, I sometimes delude myself that I'm in balmy Palermo. Temperate, majestic Palermo, cradled in the rosy corolla of her mountains . . . but as soon as the sun goes down, the barbarous cold wind of the Asiatic plains brings me back to reality.'

I'm cold and I don't want to listen to his words or look into his eyes anymore. I have to return to Catania. I feel cold, and I don't understand why I'm listening to that slimy creature with the eyes of a snake . . .

★

Bambù: 'Carluzzu, Carluzzu, what's happened?'

Carlo: 'I don't know; she suddenly fell asleep again.'

Bambù: 'And you're just standing there, not doing anything?'

Carlo: 'Nonna, Nonna, for God's sake!'

Bambù: 'She's opening her eyes, Carlo, she's opening them! But run and get a doctor!'

The *Economist* has slid off the bed. Its cover, which had showed me a glimpse of my future, lies face down on the floor: a flashy advertisement for a tropical drink makes a fine showing amid sand and palm trees . . . That encounter took place later, much later, when I had also learned the art of travelling, and finding joy in observing a vase, a statue, a flower . . . In my eagerness to live, my mind raced ahead too fast.

Bambù: 'Modesta, Zia, what happened?'

Modesta: 'Nothing, Bambù. A momentary blackout. I slept too much. Help me get up. You'll see, with a nice bath and some coffee . . .'

Bambù: 'And a doctor, my dear! This time, either you let a doctor see you or I'll get angry. I mean it, Zia! Carlo, how come you're back? I told you to go find a doctor!'

Carlo: 'Calm down, Bambù. Our lucky day! I was about to go and look for a doctor, and who knows where I'd find one. Since Antonio died we can't seem to get one! It was so reassuring to have a permanent doctor around, dropping by every night . . . How nice it was! Why did he have to die?'

Bambù: 'He was eighty years old, Carlo! You're driving me crazy! Is that all you're worried about?'

Nina: 'Look at her, how well she looks. She's even laughing . . . Come, Marco. Here she is, our impulsive little girl.'

Bambù: 'Oh, Nina! Forgive me if I don't kiss you, but I have to go find a doctor.'

Carlo: 'But here he is! Marco is a doctor, I told you . . .'

Bambù: 'You didn't tell me that, Carluzzu! When will you stop thinking that you said something you didn't say!'

Carlo: 'Didn't I tell you I met Nina and Marco at the gate and that she said, "Where are you running off to?" and I said, "To look for a doctor and blah-blah-blah"? Come on now, so I glossed over it, Bambù. How old-fashioned you are!'

Bambù: 'Listen, Marco, you have to examine her.'

Carlo: 'But there's nothing wrong with her, Bambù! It's not as if it were the first time she fell under a spell and flew off to other shores!'

Bambù: 'Nevertheless, I insist that she be checked.'

Modesta: 'It's all right, Carlo. Let's put Bambù's mind at ease. How lovely you look, Nina. What's different?'

Nina: 'It's just this white dress, my dear Mody; white makes you look younger. Whenever I put on this dress, she thinks I look nice.

Face it, Bambù, our Mody will never understand anything about clothes. No one is perfect, you know . . . Oh, Carlo, I saw *Some Like It Hot* again. The more times I see it, the more I like it.'

Nina is right, my dress tossed on the chair is a sickly colour. It might be fine in artificial light, but in the sun like that it has the putrid colour of a poisonous mushroom. I'm embarrassed, and I don't dare take my eyes off that purplish mushroom. And then who knows what colour undergarments I'm wearing! I'm embarrassed in front of that tall, tall stranger who stands silent, motionless at the foot of the bed. I pull the covers up and with my hands try to guess the colour of my slip. My only hope is that Bambolina put something of hers on me, like the time when they arrested me. It must be so, because I touch a fabric as light as silk. It must be one of those glamorous cotton nightshirts they wear now.

'So, shall we proceed with this examination?'

From the looks of him I thought the musician would have a faltering way of speaking, as many Englishmen do. How annoying when they start in with "that . . . um . . . er . . . and . . . um . . ." But he must be an exception, because after palpating me all over like a rabbit, he pronounces seriously in a deep, well-modulated voice:

'In my opinion you are quite healthy, but I advise you to have some tests done. Today the clinical eye no longer exists . . . Tell me: did either of your parents suffer from diabetes?'

'But aren't you a musician?'

'A musician? What makes you say that? Truthfully music is a mystery to me; it sounds like noise and nothing but noise. But you haven't answered my question.'

From a distance, his musician's face seemed too smooth and perfect, but up close it has myriads of anxious, elegant lines that enchant the eye.

'You have such elegant wrinkles, Marco. I've never seen wrinkles like that.'

'It's taken a lot of work, Modesta: fifty-eight years of dogged effort! But you haven't answered me.'

'My parents?'

'Yes.'

'Who knew them! I may have exchanged four or five words with my mother. She was a woman who didn't know if she was alive or already dead. My sister was a mongoloid. Does that have anything to do with diabetes? Why are you laughing? Is it related or not?'

'No, it isn't. And your father?'

'I met a man who claimed to be my father, but I didn't have a chance to ask him if he had diabetes or not.'

*

'Are you done in there? If you're laughing like that, it means the examination is over and I can come in. Nonna, please. I have to leave, and as is customary, a grandson can't leave without his grandmother's blessing.'

Why are they making such a fuss? She had been tempted to stay at Carmelo, but now she saw that it was a foolish idea; she craved the silence of her little room, her simple objects and her papers. That nightshirt was nice, but it cut into her armpits. And Carluzzu too, why was he so effusive? All that joviality made you think of birds of passage, who slam into the lighthouse on stormy nights . . . *No, that was a poem, a poem learned many years ago. The discovery of poetry! That was what she should do: go back to her room and take up reading again. New voices called to her from the book covers: Kerouac, Burroughs and that other one . . . She was always glad she had learned some foreign languages; even now that the world had shrunk to a small piazza, translations were always slow in coming . . .

I'm slow too, I want to get up but Carluzzu hugs me, the vein on his forehead throbbing against my neck. Whenever Carluzzu is sad, he covers up his sadness with those jokes that make others laugh so much. I like him better when he's serious.

'You're right, Mody, I'm very nervous about the journey. All in all, I'm just a neurotic – like the rest of my generation.'

'We were neurotic too, Carlo – only we didn't know it.'

'I'm taking away this magazine that caused you to pass out suddenly . . . Just one question, Mody: what was it that upset you like that?'

'Look at the cover, Carlo; it's obvious.'

'Well then, Nonna?'

'Well, I think we were presumptuous. I think it's time we realized that we're still nothing but a small, meagre group of anti-fascists, exactly as we were all those years ago.'

Why is everyone so silent, eyes cast down, like at Pietro's final sleep? Am I perhaps ill and, as always in these cases, they're hiding it from me? That stranger – musician or doctor, whatever he is – is pleasant enough now that he's moved away and is looking at Bambolina. But he's too tall and perfect, too polished, as we say.

'You really won't come to the station with me, Nonna?'

'No, Carlo.'

Finally they've gone, and I can take a leisurely bath, get dressed, and – why not? – even smoke a cigarette gazing at those beautiful red roses, vibrant in the sun.

The cigarette burns down between my fingers, and I remain suspended there between a death, a party and a departure. I had been tempted to stay at Carmelo, but now the silence of those walls chills my blood. Even at the window, the sun fails to warm me, nor does Pietro's slow wave reassure me as he rounds the corner of the villa with his steady step, unsmiling.

'Oh, *micia*, what are you doing there all alone? Come, we'll take you home . . . Marco, come back, my *micia* will come down with us now. Right, *micia*?'

For a moment I stare at that man, stopped midstride. His indecision is becoming comical.

'And this villa seems deadly to me when isn't full of people. Come on, Mody, come down and we'll get out of here!'

Nina is right. For the young people there's air, space and light here, but for me that light is darkened by ghosts. Besides, even though she's joking, I hear Nina's apprehension for me loud and clear; she knows about desertions, all of them, she knows the thickness of each wall. She's the one I must follow.

'Finally! How about a nice swim, Mody, so we can shake off these departures and funerals? How strange life is! For years we're all together, then in a flash Olimpia leaves, marries, has a child . . . and now Carluzzu. And your head becomes a whirl of speeding trains and station masters' whistles!'

In the close space inside the car, the man who's driving seems like someone I've known for ever. But maybe it's just because I always saw him in a crowd of people before. Is it the 'Marco', whispered by Nina, that makes him seem familiar? Or is it simply because he's laughing now as he chases Nina on the beach?

They laugh, and in the meantime I've learned to dive. Bambolina taught me. I rise up on my toes, get a running start and plunge into the water. *'When you're under, give a forceful lunge, and there's nothing to fear. The water itself brings you up.'* The cold water must have washed away the mists of sleep, because when I open my eyes I find myself fully alert, and I can finally see the blue sky racing over the expanse of sea.

Without his clothes, the man appears to be smaller and more agile. Nina too, with her long, girlish legs, runs toward the waves, pretending to be afraid of that man as she once did with Carluzzu, and yesterday with little Ignazio. The deserted beach encourages the game; plus there are arms, teeth and claws of lava extending beyond the sand where one can hide. *'Come on, Nina, let's play hide-and-seek! Count to a hundred, and Nonna, make sure she doesn't peek . . . There! I found you, Nina. There's no use hiding . . .'*

'Oh no, *micia*, sleeping in the sun, no! How do you feel?'

'Fine, Nina, but why such a sad face? You're not becoming anxious about me like Bambù is, are you?'

'But why are you sleeping so much, Mody? I . . .'

'For heaven's sake, Nina, I'm fine. Your friend even confirmed it.'

'Well, as a friend I trust Marco a great deal, but as a doctor less so.'

'Don't disparage me in front of Modesta, Nina. I was a doctor even in the army.'

'Sure, in Africa. Some guarantee of reliability that is! And then, it's not as if it were yesterday! You've probably forgotten everything.'

'Doctors are born, just as denigrators are – is that the right word?'

'Yes, and you know it.'

'Denigrators like you.'

'You can't say that. As far as your body goes, I admire you a lot, as

Carluzzu would say. It's quite a scene going out with Marco, Mody: everyone turns their head.'

'Class, Nina! You can't beat class!'

They joke around as if they've known each other for years. To my surprise, I find myself listening to his voice, which sounds to me like a refrain I once knew but later forgot.

'He seems like one of us, doesn't he, Modesta?'

'Yes, but how did you meet him?'

'Prowling around, *micia* . . . Damn, it's late! Speaking of prowling reminded me of an appointment. I'm going up to get dressed . . . No, Marco, why are you getting up? Stay, I'll have the gardener call a taxi.'

I'd like to go back up with Nina, partly because heavy clouds are darkening the Prophet's brow, and that profile is frightening when it's angry. But Marco says nothing; his silence has a familiar rhythm. Plus, he must know everything about us since he calmly murmurs, 'I agree with Nina. I find this villa more agreeable than Carmelo. Bambù was wise to buy it back. I can't forget the joy in her eyes when she told me: "Go, Marco. Go and see how beautiful our childhood villa is! You'll see, every room still echoes with our songs and games." Then, too, it's a way of preserving something in this race to destruction that's seized everyone. I want to photograph it. Bambù gave me permission.'

I don't feel like talking. Maybe they're right to be concerned about me. I hear myself say with effort, 'Don't tell me you revel in looking back on the past as well, Marco? It's become stylish, this nostalgia, a real bore.'

'No, I don't mourn anything from the past, but for some time now I've also understood the lie that masquerades behind the word "progress", and I console myself by going around photographing things that will soon disappear . . . Rome's last trattorias, the last of the taverns . . . I have hundreds of photos of the Civita . . . They've demolished street after street, house after house.'

'How come you speak Italian so well?'

'It's simple: my mother was Sicilian and my father British. And in the battle that parents always wage to have you all to themselves, my mother won; that's it. And so I rejected a specialist's life – that of a

667

doctor, in my case – as my father wanted, and returned to my maternal Eden.'

'Poor Marco! That path must have cost you dearly.'

'As it does all outsiders: hunger, a variety of jobs, adventures.'

'Now I remember. Nina insisted that I meet you this winter, and to entice me she said: "My Marco is one big adventure!"'

'Nina exaggerates. Basically I'm just a photographer . . . But you're cold, Modesta.'

Yes, I'm cold. And grateful for his silence, I let him take my hands and help me up from the sand, which has become damp beneath me. When I stand up, my head spins – I must be really unwell – and it's no wonder he holds me close against his chest to support me. Maybe *La Certa* has decided to keep her appointment right here on our beach, still filled with the cries of children, the fluttering of Beatrice's white skirts, the sound of Carlo's voice, and Pietro's slow, solicitous step . . . Could be.

I open my eyes to decipher that message, but I encounter a calm gaze, as though he were intent on listening to some melody. That gaze prompts me to rest my head on his shoulder and listen with him.

'You have an intense feeling for life, Modesta, which I now understand because I followed you this entire past year.'

'You followed me, Marco?'

'Yes. Not that I was really aware of it. I was very intrigued by your way of speaking, your way of falling silent. You were silent a moment ago as well, but I could see by your face that you were thinking. About what, Modesta?'

'I was gripped by an intense curiosity about my death. Yes, as if another biological adventure could be read in that word, yet another metamorphosis that awaits us, Marco: me, you, Nina.'

'I'm frightened by it . . .'

'Naturally. But there's also an intense curiosity to *know*. You're a man, Marco, and you don't know – or you knew and then, in your haste to act, forgot – the material transformations in your body, so the word makes you tremble a little. But if you hold me close, I, a woman, will help you remember, and not be afraid of that which must change in order to continue living.'

As he holds me tightly, his tremor disappears, and between my body and his, the eternal, shivery heat rises in waves until his eyes widen in mine with pleasure. Now I understand: I've learned many things in life, but never how to inhibit love . . . Can you inhibit love, Mimmo? *'You can inhibit the intelligence of others, the facts of history, even destiny – I grant you, even destiny – but never love!'* And if Carmine hadn't told me, how could I have known that the indifference I thought I felt for that man, the apathy and boredom, were merely my attempts to evade the mysterious imperative that always inspires fear, and which the scalpel of human speculation has not yet managed to dissect?

'How could I have told you, Modesta, when I myself didn't know it yet? But now that we've discovered it, if you like, we can be together for some time. I've been alone for many years, and wandering the world alone is tiring. Will you come with me?'

And so it was that with a simple gesture, abetted by Nina, life handed me the most beautiful gift a child's mind could ever imagine. And from a man I had mistakenly thought to be a former golden boy, grown old in comfort and ennui, I discovered day by day, year after year, the wealth of knowledge and experience that only a mature body can possess.

From him I learned that I did not know my island – its powerful, secret physical body, its hot nocturnal drafts that fuse stone upon stone to solidify the spirit of the drywalls into a single block, the mystical breath that keeps the columns of the temples alive and makes them throb in the sunsets: 'Here, Mody, this is where the stone widens so that the column breathes and produces the optical illusion of levitation'; the white silence of abandoned fishing nets, cast away by the sea and by man, yet for ever pervaded by the ghosts of the tuna that stop there, seeking the reason for their life and death; the eternal currents of the seas that converge around the island, at times enclosing it, at times releasing it, ever changing in intensity and colour. 'That emerald coloured strip over there is the sea of Africa.'

From him I learned the art, which I still did not know, of coming and going from my land, forgetting it at times, travelling to different continents and oceans, then rediscovering it: new, and even richer with layered memories and sensations. And what can I say about our evenings and nights together? If only I could freeze them! Being alone together, holding hands, looking into each other's eyes, recounting impressions, intuitions, talking . . .

'They say so much about first love, don't they, Marco? Lies, like all the rest.'

'That's true, Modesta. I never would have imagined it either, and unfortunately you have to reach our age to find out. Did you see how those kids were looking at us on the bridge today? I was almost tempted to tell them, but they wouldn't have believed me.'

No, it's impossible to describe to anyone this joy, full of vital excitement, at defying time as a couple, being partners in stretching it out, living it as intensely as possible before the hour of the last adventure strikes. And when this old youngster of mine lies on top of me with his beautiful body, heavy yet light, and takes me as he's doing now, or kisses me between my legs just like Tuzzu did back then, I find myself thinking oddly that death might simply be an orgasm as satisfying as this one.

'Are you sleeping, Modesta?'

'No.'

'Are you thinking?'

'Yes.'

'Tell me, Modesta, tell me.'

Rome, 1967–76

In Modesta's World . . .

A Translator's Note

The daughter of Giuseppe Sapienza and Maria Giudice, Goliarda Sapienza was raised in an atmosphere of absolute freedom from social constraints, in accordance with her parents wishes. Her father did not even allow her to attend school, lest she be exposed to Fascist forces and influences. Goliarda's protagonist, Modesta, creates a similar world around her, resisting society's rules, rejecting conventional norms and opposing Fascist restrictions. Sapienza's book was written over a nine-year span, from 1967 to 1976, and published by Stampa Alternativa in 1998, and Einaudi in 2008.

Notes to pp. 9–29
A *chiana* is a plain or flat expanse: in Italian it is a *pianura*, from the Calabro-siculan *chianura* or *chianu*. (9)

A *coppola* is a traditional flat cap worn by men in Sicily. (10)

Ceusa is the fruit of the *ceuso*, or mulberry tree. (16)

Voscenza is a dialect term that is used to express one's respect toward the person being addressed. A shortened form of *Vostra Eccellenza*, Your Excellency, it is sometimes accompanied by hand-kissing and can mean anything from Your Grace, Your Lordship, Your Highness . . . or simply a deferential Sir or Madam. Serafina, a character in Tennessee Williams's *The Rose Tattoo*, says: 'They said to his uncle "Voscenza!" and they kissed their hands to him!' (Tennessee Williams, *The Rose Tattoo: Play in 3 Acts*, Dramatists Play Service, Inc.: 1951, Act I, p. 16). (20)

Sister Teresa's words paraphrase the Bible: 'A good man out of the good treasure of his heart bringeth forth that which is good; and an evil man out of the evil treasure of his heart bringeth forth that which is evil.' (Luke 6:45, King James Bible, Cambridge Ed.) (29)

Notes to pp. 32–87

When Sister Teresa refers to a novice from the continent, she means the mainland. As can be seen elsewhere in the book, it was customary for Sicilians to refer to the Italian peninsula as the continent, as distinct from the island of Sicily. (32)

The *fagoniu* that makes the reeds toss and stir is the west wind, the zephyr; from the Latin *favoniu(m)*, *faògna* in Siculan, also known as *foschia sul mare*, mist over the sea. (38)

The first of many references to *La Certa*, Death, which are found throughout the novel, may be an allusion to the Latin proverb *Nihil morte certius*, nothing is more certain than death, or *mors certa hora incerta*: death is certain, the time uncertain. (42)

The verse *'E caddi come corpo morto cade'* is from Dante's *Inferno* V:142, and its translation, 'And fell, even as a dead body falls', is by Longfellow. (The Project Gutenberg Etext of *The Divine Comedy of Dante Alighieri*, Henry Wadsworth Longfellow, tr., at http://www.gutenberg.org/cache/epub/1004/pg1004.txt) (47, 67)

The orphanage in Pietraperzia, where they want to send Modesta, is in the province of Enna, in the centre of Sicily. (52)

The expression 'Happier than God Himself in His paradise' echoes Théophile Gautier's words in his short story *'La Morte amoureuse'* (1836): 'If thou wilt be mine, I shall make thee happier than God Himself in His paradise' (*The Mummy's Foot and Other Stories*, Aegypan, 2008, Lafcadio Hearn, tr.); Gautier was a sceptic of Christianity. (55)

The real tears Modesta weeps are a reference to Dante's words in the *Vita Nuova*, XXIII:6: *'Allora cominciai a piangere molto pietosamente; e non solamente piangea ne la imaginazione, ma piangea con li occhi, bagnandoli di vere lagrime.'* 'At that I began to weep most piteously, and I wept not only in my dream, I wept with my eyes, wet with real tears.' (*Dante's Vita Nuova*, Mark L. Musa, ed. and tr., Bloomington and London: Indiana University Press, 1973) Cf. also the prologue to Leoncavallo's opera, *I pagliacci 'ed ei con vere lacrime scrisse'*, 'and with real tears he wrote' (from the English translation of the original Italian text, EMI, 1954). (56)

The Sicilian proverb *'Chi lassa la strata vecchia pi la nova, sapi chiddu ca lassa, ma non sapi chiddu ca trova'* is roughly equivalent to the English 'Better the devil you know than the devil you don't know', and literally means that a person who abandons a familiar path knows what he's left behind, but not what he will find. (86)

The mention of Doré's Beatrice (here and again on p. 103) refers to one of Gustave Doré's series of illustrations for Dante's *Divine Comedy* which shows Beatrice pointing, arm raised. See http://www.worldofdante.org/gallery_dore.html. (87)

Notes to pp. 93–122

Modesta croons a lullaby to Beatrice in Sicilian dialect: *'fa la 'O"* (or *'fa la vò'*) is baby talk for 'go to sleep'; the *coppa* is a ladle, used here to spank the child who won't go beddy-bye. (93)

The saying *'catanisi soldu fausu'* means that people from Catania are false or insincere: a *soldu fausu* is literally a false coin, or counterfeit money. (95)

The *gabellotto* was a figure somewhere between an administrator and an overseer, a man of considerable authority and power, quite different from a gardener or an armed guard (*il campiere*) of an estate. The *gabellotto* always carried his shotgun (*lo schioppo*) with him, a symbol not only of authority, but also of distinction. The *campieri* constituted a kind of private police force for the feudal estate and reported directly to the *gabellotto* and indirectly to the *latifondista*, or feudal landowner. These armed field guards and the *sovrastanti* or *soprastanti*, the *gabellotto*'s trusted men, are mentioned throughout the book. According to information provided in 'Storie di Sicilia di Fara Misuraca: I Fasci Siciliani', the figure of the *gabellotto* dates back to the nineteenth century, when the Sicilian aristocracy began moving away from the interior to the city of Palermo, leaving their lands in the care of tenants, who paid a tax, a *gabella*, and were therefore called *gabellotti*. The *gabella* trade in west-central Sicily was largely controlled and run by mafia organizations, and many *gabellotti* were affiliated with these organizations, as were the aforementioned *soprastanti* and *campieri*. The *gabellotti*, in turn, would sublet the lands to the *contadini*, peasants, for a fee much higher than the *gabella* which they were required to pay to the landowners. During periods of work, *braccianti*, farm hands or labourers, offered themselves each morning in the piazzas of their villages, hoping to be hired by the feuds' *campieri* or *soprastanti*. (http://www.ilportaledelsud.org/fasci_siciliani.htm) (110)

The words *'fui amata amando'* recall Violetta's aria *'Ah, fors'è lui'* in Act One of Verdi's *La traviata*: *'O gioia / Ch'io non conobbi, essere amata amando!'* , 'Oh, joy . . . I never knew . . . To love and be loved!' (From the libretto by Francesco Maria Piave after Alexandre Dumas, Jr.; online at www.dennisalbert.com/Opera/latraviata.htm) (113)

The line 'the Love that moves the sun and the other stars' is the last verse of Dante's *Divine Comedy*: *'Amor che muove il sole e l'altre stelle'*, *Paradiso* XXXIII:145, http://dante.ilt.columbia.edu/comedy/. (114)

The term *'pedi 'ncritati'*, literally 'feet of clay', derives from *incretato* or *creta*, meaning clay, and is used to refer to a coarse, ignorant peasant or boorish lout. (118)

Princess Gaia's words, *'Patti chiari e inimicizia eterna'*, or 'Clear understandings make for eternal animosity', are a sardonic take on the popular saying *'Patti chiari, amicizia lunga'*, 'Clear understandings breed long friendships'. (122)

Notes to pp. 129–209

Gaia's reference to Carmine as *quell'uomo d'onore* recalls the 'Men of Honour' in the Sicilan mafia: 'made men', or 'soldiers' in the family structure. (127)

The quotes from Diderot's *Interpretation of Nature* are from Denis Diderot, 'To Young Persons Preparing to Study Natural Philosophy', in *Thoughts on the Interpretation of Nature and Other Philosophical Works*, David Adams, ed., Lorna Sandler, tr., Clinamen Press, 1999, pp. 34 and 59. (129)

The words 'Never lose old friends, as Shakespeare says' are perhaps a reference to a line in Sonnet 30: 'When to the sessions of sweet silent thought . . . For precious friends hid in death's dateless night'. (139)

Figghia, the Sicilian word for *figlia*, daughter, can also be used more broadly to indicate any young woman or girl (like *carusa*) or even a child or a kid. Carmine initially calls Modesta *figghia* to tease her and emphasize her inexperience and youth, though later in their relationship it becomes his affectionate pet name for her. (143)

The *spagnola* is the Italian for Spanish flu, or the influenza epidemic of 1918–19. (162)

The Lancia Trikappa passenger car was produced between 1922 and 1925. (174)

Picciotta, like *picciridda* or *carusa*, is one of several Sicilian words for a girl or young woman. The masculine form, *picciottu*, plural *picciotti*, has passed into the Mafia's lexicon with quite a different meaning, referring to minor killers, inconsequential 'soldiers' in the Mafia ranks. (175)

The walls of the palazzos in Catania were adorned with sculpted floral elements carved from the sharp lava of the island of Sicily. In addition to flowers and vines, many of the palazzos and churches, built from soft tufa stone, were embellished with sirens, winged horses, monstrous masks, and grotesque figures which sprang from the facades. (179)

Cabiria here refers to the 1914 film directed by Giovanni Pastrone, not the later 1957 version by Fellini. (180)

The Holy Father is said to be a prisoner since the popes opposed the 'liberal' Italian state and were 'prisoners of the Vatican' between 1870 and 1929 (the year here is 1921). Most Italian politicians were openly anticlerical and Mussolini himself was extremely anticlerical, both as a Socialist and later as a Fascist. His Fascist formula was simple: 'Nothing above the state, nothing outside the state, everything and everyone to serve the state.' The later Lateran Treaty of 1929 was an attempt to end the conflict between the Italian state and the Roman Catholic Church that had existed since 1870. (180)

Notes to pp. 209–20

The lines are from Ecclesiastes 10:19–25: 'A feast is made for laughter, / wine makes life merry, / and money is the answer for everything. / Do not revile the king even in your thoughts, / or curse the rich in your bedroom, / because a bird in the sky may carry your words, / and a bird on the wing may report what you say.' (New International Version, copyright © 2011) (209)

The *Carbonari* were an influential, revolutionary group of Italian patriots originally formed as a secret society to fight for the unification of Italy (achieved in 1860). (209)

The 'Blond Tiber', *il Biondo Tevere*, as Romans call the river, dates back to Horace in the *Odes*, Book I:viii. Horace's word is *flavos* (an earlier spelling for *flavus*), meaning yellow, golden, tawny or blond. The Tiber was often described as yellowish because of the mud it contained. (209)

The gentleman king, the *Re Galantuomo*, with whom Garibaldi met in Teano, was King Victor Emmanuel. In the famous Handshake on 25 October 1860, Garibaldi handed the Two Sicilies over to the Kingdom of Italy. (209)

'May of 1898': the phrase refers to a spontaneous uprising to protest inhumane working conditions, the Bava Beccaris massacre, named after the Italian General Fiorenzo Bava Beccaris. The repression of widespread riots by workers in Milan in May 1898 resulted in 400 dead and more than 2,000 injured. Filippo Turati, one of the founders of the Italian Socialist Party in 1892, was arrested in 1898, accused of inspiring the riots. (211)

The Dante verses, '*Nessun maggior dolore / che ricordarsi del tempo felice / ne la miseria*', are from the *Inferno* V: 121–3, Mandelbaum, tr.: http://dante.ilt.columbia.edu/comedy/. (215)

The description of the comrade who had worked with unions since she was a young girl and was imprisoned and tortured many times alludes to the fact that Mussolini's Black Shirts regularly attacked Socialist Party headquarters and newspapers as well as union halls. (216)

Beatrice wonders why Marx chose the dreadful word 'spectre' because she's reading the Communist Party Manifesto, which begins with the words: 'A spectre is haunting Europe – the spectre of communism. All the powers of old Europe have entered into a holy alliance to exorcise this spectre . . .' (217)

The quote attributed to Antonio Gramsci is from his *Prison Notebooks* (volume 3, Joseph A. Buttigieg, ed. and tr., Columbia University Press, 2010, p. 324). (220)

The words 'Be good, be saintly, be cowards' are Modesta's way of referring to Filippo Turati, who early on preached passive resistance and patience ('*Non raccogliete le provocazioni, non rispondete alle ingiurie, siate buoni, siate santi . . .* '), which Modesta finds cowardly. (220)

Notes to pp. 224–72
The term *le salariate dell'amore*, literally 'wage earners of love', is attributed to Filippo Turati in Antonio Gramsci, *Prison Notebooks* (volume 2, Joseph A. Buttigieg, ed. and tr., Columbia University Press, 1996, Notes to the Text 53, p. 452). (224)

Stamped paper, or *carta bollata*, was used as an efficient way to collect taxes on documents requiring stamping, such as leases, agreements, receipts, court documents, etc. (238)

Diderot's actor refers to Diderot's essay, 'Paradox of Acting' ('Paradoxe sur le comédien', written 1773, published 1830), known for its famous paradox, namely, that in order to move the audience, the actor must himself remain unmoved and detached. (243)

Modesta calls Argentovivo a *murata viva*, literally someone who is walled-up alive. The expression recalls the Middle Ages, when it was supposedly common practice for nuns to have their cell doors bricked up, leaving just a small opening for food to be passed through. (248)

Comrade Bebel, or Ferdinand August Bebel (1840–1913), was a German Marxist politician, writer, orator and author of *Women and Socialism*, published in 1879. (251)

The gigantic Moor's head on the piano is one of the colourful ceramic vases from the Caltagirone region of Sicily. (261)

The Saracen olive tree is the name often given to ancient olive trees in Sicily, which can be hundreds of years old, and whose huge gnarled trunks are twisted into bizarre shapes. The name reflects the period of Arab rule in Sicily. (267)

On 2 November, the Day of the Dead or All Souls' Day, it is traditional for children to be given small gifts purporting to be from the family dead. (268)

Maccu is a traditional, very thick soup (almost a puree) made of dried fava beans in most parts of Sicily. It is usually cooked in the winter months and has been a staple dish for the *contadini*, peasants, since ancient times. Also known as *Maccu di San 'Gnuseppi*, according to Pino Correnti in his *Il Libro d'Oro della Cucina e dei Vini di Sicilia*, it is a ritual soup for Saint Joseph's day, 19 March, as well as a custom handed down from the celebrations of the spring equinox in classical times, when the housewife would clear her pantry of leftover dried legumes in the expectation of the new harvest to come. (269)

The word *maredda* in the expression '*tosta maredda*' (here and elsewhere in text) is Sicilian slang for girl; in dialect, *morella* and *moredda* are diminutives for the Sicilian *moru*, meaning dark-haired. (270)

Lazzarolu and *cocciu di tacca* are dialect: a *lazzarolu* is a rascal, scoundrel or thug, an arrogant young tough guy or someone young and attractive but of no consequence. A *cocciu* is a scamp or little rogue; a brat. And *di tacca* means insignificant or small-time. The two expressions basically mean the same thing: someone young and brazen, a fireball. (272)

Vellute (here and throughout the book) are whores, prostitutes; literally 'silken ladies'. (274)

Notes to pp. 309–37
The slogan '*Me ne frego*', 'I don't give a damn', was written on Fascist banners: black pennants with a skull and crossbones. In the same passage, Mussolini is sarcastically referred to as '*l'onorevole Benito Mussolini*', 'honourable' being the title used for a Member of Parliament; Mussolini became the 40th Prime Minister of Italy in 1922 and began using the title *Il Duce* by 1925. The 'blackmail' ('*The Fascist revolt against the intolerable Bolshevik regime*') may refer to the fact that when Britain reacted to Italy's invasion of Ethiopia by stopping the exports of coal to Italy, Italy had to rely more and more on German coal and this had political consequences, pushing Italy into the war as Germany's ally. (309)

'*U marranzanu*, Sicily's traditional Jew's harp, is also known as a *scacciapensieri* or *marranzano*; it is a rudimentary musical instrument that produces monotone vibrations. The word *marranzanu* can also mean a chirping cricket. (316)

Catherine wheels, *girandole*, are a type of firework consisting of a powder-filled spiral tube; when ignited, it rotates quickly, producing a display of sparks and coloured flame, like a pinwheel. It is named after the instrument of torture, the breaking wheel, on which, legend has it, St Catherine was martyred. (316)

Cuore was a book for elementary school children written by Edmondo de Amicis and published in 1886. Set during the period of Italian unification, it includes patriotic themes and topics of moral edification and is considered a classic of children's literature. (324)

Mattia refers to Modesta as a '*satanasso d'un Giuda*', a Judas demon. The expression echoes the gospels, which say that Judas Iscariot was possessed by Satan. Luke 22:3, for example, states: 'Then Satan entered Judas, called Iscariot, one of the Twelve'. John 13:27 also talks about the possession of Judas by Satan: 'As soon as Judas took the bread, Satan entered into him.' (New International Version) (328)

For the events of 1898, see note to p. 211. Filippo Turati was accused of inspiring the riots which led to the Bava Beccaris massacre. *Avanti!*, meaning 'Forward!' or 'Onward!', is an Italian daily newspaper, born as the official voice of the Italian Socialist Party. Published since 25 December 1896, it took its name from its German counterpart, *Vorwärts*. Turati's party was the Partito Socialista Unitario; after the 1924 murder of Matteotti, one of the brave men who dared to speak out against Mussolini, there was a push for a more active opposition to Fascism and the clandestine publication *Non mollare* was founded; Fascist violence towards the left became increasingly severe. (337)

Notes to pp. 339–84
The Civita is an ancient quarter in the historical centre of Catania. (339)

The carpet of Santa Rosalia recalls the *infiorata*, a traditional springtime event in many Italian towns, in which flower petals are used to create works of art in the streets or in front of churches. (346)

Matteotti's murder, the Special Laws and the Lateran Treaty date from 1924, 1925 and 1929 respectively. (353)

Piana dei Greci, later called *Piana degli Albanesi*, originally took its name from the fact that the Greek language was used in the Byzantine rite professed by the inhabitants. In 1941, during the Fascist regime, the name was changed to *Piana degli Albanesi*. (363)

Ucciardone is a prison in Palermo; it was called Villa Mori after the prefect Cesare Mori. Prefects in Fascist Italy were in control of party districts and were loosely in charge of party doctrine within their districts. (364)

OVRA, the Organization for Vigilance and Repression of Anti-Fascism, was a secret police force formed in 1927 under Mussolini. Led by Arturo Bocchini, it was the equivalent of the German Gestapo. (373)

Giufà is an Italian folklore character (mainly southern Italian and Sicilian) whose antics have been retold through centuries of oral tradition. Scholars suggest that the character developed from stories about Nasrudin, an Arabic folk character, which were absorbed into the Sicilian oral tradition during Islamic rule of Sicily. Although Giufà is most often recognized as the 'village fool', his actions and words usually serve to provide a moral message. It is his peers' reactions, rather than Giufà's outrageous behaviour, that are judged at the end of each story. (376)

Stella is said to resemble her ancient sisters on the Syracusan coins. The portrait side of those coins bears a striking image of Syracuse's patron water nymph, Arethusa. The naiad, seen in profile, generally wears an elaborate earring and beaded necklace, and her hair is gracefully bound up in loose tresses with leaves of corn. The coins of Arethusa are said to be the most beautiful minted by the ancient Greeks. (378)

'The Great Khan and his black infidels' is a reference to the Emperor Kublai Khan and his great mastiffs in *The Travels of Marco Polo*: 'The emperor hath two Barons who are . . . "The Keepers of the Mastiff Dogs". . . . And when the king goes hunting . . . 5,000 dogs go towards the right, whilst the other go toward the left . . .you will see these big hounds coming tearing up, one pack after a bear, another pack after a stag, or some other beast, as it may hap, and running the game down.' (381)

Maria Giudice, Sapienza's mother, was the first woman to be elected head of the Turin Chamber of Labour in 1916. During the Fascist period, despite the official subjugation of women in society – their role limited to the kitchen, children and the church – she and other women advocated the emancipation of working women, the right to vote, an eight-hour working day and equal pay for equal work, as well as complete control over their own bodies. (384)

Notes to pp. 387–481
At the 5th Comintern Congress, held in July 1924, the Comintern proclaimed that the capitalist system was entering a period of final collapse. The Spartacists, led by Rosa Luxemburg and Karl Liebknecht, were a group of radical socialists. Adolf Hitler launched his Beer Hall Putsch (coup) on 8 November 1923. (387)

The weekly Saturday assembly refers to Fascist Saturdays for Fascist youths, during which paramilitary training was conducted. (389)

Arturo Bocchini (1880–1940) was head of the Italian secret police formed in 1927 under Mussolini's Fascist regime; see note above. (389)

Orlando (Roland) was Charlemagne's paladin and Durendal was the name of his sword; the reference is to Ludovico Ariosto's *Orlando Furioso*. The puppets are the large marionettes of the Opera dei Pupi, the Sicilian Puppet Theatre, a traditional form of entertainment on the island; the marionettes are a representative symbol of Sicilian folk-art and as integral to Sicily's cultural identity as painted horse carts and *cannoli*. (392)

The Belle Otéros refer to Caroline Otéro, who gained fame in the theatres of Europe and became known as La Belle Otéro. Her career as an actress, singer, dancer and courtesan took her around the world, and she was said by the press to be the lover of no fewer than six crowned heads of state; at least two men supposedly fought a duel over her, and another committed suicide when she rejected his advances. (409)

Resurrection, first published in 1899, was Leo Tolstoy's last novel, intended to be an exposition of the injustice of man-made laws and the hypocrisy of the institutionalized church. (410)

The term 'unavoidable destiny', which Modesta says would be a great title for a novel, became the title of a posthumous volume of stories by Sapienza: *Destino coatto* (Empiria, 2002; Einaudi, 2011). (417)

The Shakespeare reference to stopping time and children may recall Sonnet 3: 'Thou art thy mother's glass and she in thee / Calls back the lovely April of her prime . . .' The heartless or 'black' Dark Lady figures in twenty-four of Shakespeare's sonnets, addressed to a woman whom the poet describes as 'a woman colour'd ill', with black eyes and coarse black hair. From the poet's perspective, he is treated badly by her; in sonnet 114, for example, he describes this temptress as 'my female evil' and 'my bad angel', who ultimately causes him anguish. The Dark Lady Sonnets are also referred to as The Bard's Black Beauties: – e.g. : 'In the old age black was not counted fair, / Or if it were, it bore not beauty's name. / But now is black beauty's successive heir, / And beauty slandered with a bastard shame' (Sonnet 127). (431)

Notes to pp. 433–61
The line 'O Sun, that rises from shit' is a twist on the words of the Fascist 'Hymn to Rome': '*Sole, che sorgi libero e giocondo. . .*', 'O Sun, that rises free and joyful'. (433)

The 'bundled rods', or *verghe del fascio*, refer to the Fascist symbol: a bundle of rods bound together around an axe with the blade projecting. It was based on the ancient Roman fasces which the magistrates carried as an emblem of authority and which consisted of a bundle of birch rods. (435)

The remaining 'Liberals' who asked to be called *Ardito*, brave or daring, on their Party card were holdovers from the Italian Liberal Party. When the Liberal Party's government could not control the debt, unemployment, strikes and other forms of social discontent in Italy at the time, including anarchist, socialist and communist insurrections, the Fascist Revolutionary Party led by Mussolini took matters in hand and combatted those issues with the Black Shirts, paramilitary squads of veterans from the First World War and ex-socialists. (435)

L'Avventuroso was a periodical in comic strip format, based on American adventure comics. (443)

Using the term 'defeatist' is criticized because *disfattista*, like '*me ne frega*', 'I don't give a damn', was one of many Fascist slogans. It refers to the defeatist attitude of the revolutionaries who did not succeed in bringing about the revolution. (449)

Page Fernando appears in a short story by Giovanni Verga, 'Paggio Fernando'. (455)

The suggestion of applying Freud's theories to Freud himself, as Freud did with Michelangelo, alludes to Freud's 1914 essay on Michelangelo's statue of Moses. The essay is the only one of Freud's works whose authorship he sought to conceal, until he agreed to have it included in his *Gesammelte Schriften* in 1924. Although the essay bears no relation to psychoanalytic theory as such, Freud characterized the method of inquiry that he employed therein as one that has 'in point of fact a certain resemblance to the methodology of psychoanalysis', and a number of authors have since proclaimed the essay to be paradigmatic of Freudian interpretive methods. Freud's stated purpose was to discover Michelangelo's intention in creating the statue: what was the mental constellation or emotional attitude that the artist had aimed to awaken in the viewer? Answering that question required finding the meaning and content of Michelangelo's representation, that is, interpreting it. See Malcolm Macmillan and Peter J. Swales, 'Observations from the Refuse-Heap: Freud, Michelangelo's Moses, and Psychoanalysis', *American Imago*, vol. 60, no. 1, 41–104, copyright © 2003 by The Johns Hopkins University Press. (461)

Notes to pp. 462–80
The Castrogiovanni that towers among the clouds is Castrugiuvanni, or Enna (Latin: Henna or Haenna), a city and commune located roughly at the centre of Sicily. Soaring above the surrounding countryside, it has been given the nicknames *belvedere* (panoramic viewpoint) and *ombelico* (navel) of Sicily. After the Islamic conquest of Sicily, the name for the city became Qas'r Ianni (Fort of John), a combination of *qas'r* (a corruption of the Latin *castrum*, fort), and Ianni (a corruption of Henna). In Sicilian dialect the name remained Castro Janni (Castrogiovanni) until it was renamed by order of Benito Mussolini in 1927. (462)

La vida es sueño, Life is a Dream, is a Spanish play by Pedro Calderón de la Barca, dating from 1635. (463)

In Maternal Transference, a person who has had a difficult relationship with his or her mother during childhood may come to regard someone else as a mother figure. In the eyes of that person, the mother figure assumes wisdom and authority, providing reassurance that all will be well. The mother figure feels good as a result of this, since the childlike respect and admiration she gains boost her self-esteem, and give her power. In her position of authority, she provides protection and control in return for loyalty and obedience. (466)

The International Brigades were military units made up of socialist, communist and anarchist volunteers from different countries, who travelled to Spain to defend the Second Spanish Republic in the Spanish Civil War between 1936 and 1939. (471)

The *Littoriali* were a type of Fascist youth competition held in different cities. (473)

The ritual known as the *Mensur* was a fencing match considered a rite of passage for German students who were members of university fraternal organizations (*Verbindungen*, also *Burschenschaften* or Corps). Before the Second World War, the vast majority of German students belonged to such organizations, which after the war were banned by the Allies until 1956. The facial scars inflicted during the *Mensur* were often considered to be a badge of honour, and the *Mensur* has been classified as a subcategory of Ritualistic Combat. (474)

Artemis Toxotis is one of the oldest known and most widely worshipped of the Greek goddesses; of the many epithets associated with her, *toxotis*, the archer, was one of them. (480)

The *monete siceliote*, the many Greco-Sicilian coins Timur has studied as an archaeologist, are coins dating back to the time of the Greek colonies on the island of Sicily. The noun and adjective *sicelióta* (from the Greek Σμχελιώτης) was a denomination used by Greeks in the homeland to designate their fellow countrymen who settled in the numerous colonies founded in Sicily in the 8th century BC. (480)

Notes to pp. 482–559
Giovanni Grasso is considered Sicily's greatest tragic actor and one of Italy's best. (482)

Balillas, boys aged eight to fourteen, were members of the Italian Fascist Youth Movement. (484)

Antonello Trombadori and Carlo Melograni were both anti-fascists. Trombadori, an art critic and journalist, participated in a secret propaganda effort to convince Italian youth to abandon Fascism. Melograni, an architect, wrote a book about Italian architecture under Fascism: *Architettura italiana sotto il Fascismo. L'orgoglio della modestia contro la retorica monumentale 1926–1945*. (485)

Plato's apple is said to be fatalistic, because to throw an apple at someone in ancient Greece was to symbolically declare one's love, while to catch it was to show one's acceptance of that love. The reference is to Plato, Epigram VII: 'I throw the apple at you, and if you are willing to love me, take it and share your girlhood with me; but if your thoughts are what I pray they are not, even then take it, and consider how short-lived is beauty.' ('Epigrams', *Plato: Complete Works*, John M. Cooper, ed., J. M. Edmonds, tr., Indianapolis: Hackett, 1997, p. 1744) (524)

The quote from Chekhov is from the *Letters of Anton Chekhov*, Constance Garnett, tr., Echo Library, 2006, letter of 7 May 1889 to A. S. Suvorin. (525)

The Simeto, the largest of the Sicilian rivers, skirts the base of Mt Etna and falls into the sea a few miles south of Catania. (532)

The words Crispina sings are from the song '*È arrivato l'Ambasciatore*' (1938) by Nuccia Natali: '*È arrivato l'Ambasciatore / con la piuma sul cappello, / è arrivato l'Ambasciatore / a cavallo d'un cammello. / Ha portato una letterina / dove scritto sta così: / 'Se mi piaci, Nini, / ti darò tutto il cuor'. / È arrivato l'Ambasciator! . . .*' (540)

When Nina calls Modesta *nennella*, it brings to mind the girl in the story 'Nennillo and Nennella' in *Lo cunto de li cunti* (literally *The Story of Stories*), also known as the *Pentamerone* (1634), a Neapolitan fairy tale collection written down and embellished by Giambattista Basile. (556)

The lines of the song 'The Prostitutes are Our Daughters' are from *La marsigliese del lavoro (L'inno dei pezzenti)*, a Socialist anthem. The song goes: '*Son nostre figlie le prostitute / che muoion tisiche negli ospedal, / le disgraziate si son vendute / per una cena, per un grembial'*, 'The prostitutes are our daughters, who die of consumption in the hospitals, the poor wretches sold themselves for bread, for clothing'. (557)

Dante's verse '*É ll'ora che volge il disio al* . . . is from the *Purgatorio* VIII:1–2: '*Era già l'ora che volge il disio / ai navicanti e 'ntenerisce il core.*' 'It was the hour that turns seafarers' longings / homeward – the hour that makes their hearts grow tender' (tr. Allen Mandelbaum). Dante, of course, is a Florentine, and Nina, being from Rome, responds with verses by Giuseppe Belli, a poet whose 2,200 sonnets in the Roman vernacular expressed the voice of the common people of nineteenth-century Rome: '*Che or'è? ccheor'è? È una cosa che tt'accora. Nu le sentite, sposa, le campane? Lo sapete che or'è, ssora siggnora? È ll'ora che le donne sò pputtane . . . .*', 'What time is it? What time is it? It's a sorrowful time. Don't you hear the bells, wife? Do you know what time it is, my dear lady? It's the hour when every woman is a whore . . .' (my translation). (559)

Notes to pp. 560–92
The lines '*Illusione dolce chimera sei tu. Che fa sognare, sperare e amare tutta la vita . . .*', 'Sweet illusion you are that makes me dream, hope and love all my life', are from the song '*Signora Illusione*' by Aurelio Fierro. (560)

The expression '*Annamo bene!*' recalls the line '*A-aaah annamo bene*' used by Sora Lella, played by the late Elena Fabrizi, the calm grandmother in the film *Bianco, Rosso e Verdone*, a 1981 comedy directed and starred in by Carlo Verdone. (563)

The song Nina sings may be the Neapolitan song '*Canzona Doce*' by Roberto Murolo: '*Nu poco 'e luna, / nu poco 'e mare . . .*'. (581)

Italian Concordat, one of the Lateran Pacts of 1929 (also known as the Lateran Accords or Lateran Treaty), granted the Church immense privileges; Catholicism was declared the only religion of Fascist Italy. The Church wholeheartedly supported the Fascist regime: prayers were said in churches for Mussolini and for Fascism, priests became members and even officers of the Fascist Party, and so on. The Lateran Treaty is also mentioned further on in the book. (584)

The Sacco and Vanzetti case was highly controversial and believed to have been politically influenced. Nicola Sacco and Bartolomeo Vanzetti, both Italian-Americans, were convicted of robbery and murder in 1921 and eventually executed. Although the arguments brought against them are said to have been largely disproven in court, the fact that the two men were known radicals – and that their trial took place during the height of the Red Scare – may have prejudiced the judge and jury against them. (584)

Ferruccio Parri, an anti-fascist and activist in the resistance movement against Mussolini and Nazi Germany, was Prime Minister of Italy briefly, from June to December 1945. He warned: 'Beware of . . . reopening the door to Fascism . . . There are rumours that Washington and London have no trust in me.' Alcide De Gasperi, a conservative Catholic and founder of the Christian Democratic Party, succeeded Parri as Prime Minister from 1945 to 1953. Communist Party leader Palmiro Togliatti acted as vice-premier when De Gasperi became Prime Minister. (591)

EVIS stands for *Esercito Volontario per l'Indipendenza della Sicilia*, the Volunteer Army for the Independence of Sicily. (592)

Notes to pp. 596–651
Jean Gabin was a very popular French actor of the prewar era. The essence of world-weary stoicism, he was a classic anti-hero whose characters ran the gamut of society's victims and losers, outsiders damaged by life with no hope of survival. (596)

The lyrics '*Bedda p'amari a tia . . .*' are from a Sicilian song called '*Liu-là*'. The gist of it is: 'My sweet, for love of you my heart cries, and it will be free of these chains only when you decide to love me . . . and we'll gather olives on these hallowed hills . . . sincerely, it's no lie . . .'. (604)

The lyric '*Sciccareddu di lu me cori . . .*' is from the well-known Sicilian song '*Avia 'nu sciaccareddu / davveru sapuritu . . .*'. (612)

The reference to Sartre as a warped Jesuit or literally, having the Jesuit strain injected the wrong way, calls to mind James Joyce's *Ulysses*, Chapter I: 'Stately, plump Buck Mulligan came from the stairhead, bearing a bowl of lather on which a mirror and a razor lay crossed. [. . .] Because you have the cursed jesuit strain in you, only it's injected the wrong way.' (James Joyce, *Ulysses*, Oxford University Press, 2011, Chapter I) (625)

The Sicilian term *camurria* is a distortion of *gonorrhea*, and can refer to venereal disease, which once required a long and difficult treatment, as well as to any annoyance, trouble, bother, nuisance and so on. Here, '*'sta camurria di parola*', 'that horror of a word', refers to the word 'old'. (628)

The term White Fascism, *Fascismo bianco*, was applied to the successors to the Black Shirts. Though not the Fascism of the regime, *Fascismo bianco* clearly violated Article 21 of Italy's postwar constitution guaranteeing freedom of expression. (629)

Enrico Malatesta (1853–1932), born in Santa Maria Capua Vetere in the province of Caserta, was a major anarchist leader in Italy and a friend of Bakunin. (630)

Julien Sorel is, of course, the young protagonist in Stendhal's *The Red and the Black*. A starry-eyed dreamer from the provinces, Sorel is fuelled by Napoleonic ideals. (635)

The great blasphemous Henry is Henry Miller, whose supporters supposedly referred to his *Tropic of Cancer* as a 'dithyrambic novel', meaning written in an exalted or enthusiastic vein. Dithyrambs were hymns sung to the Greek god of decadence, Dionysus. (636)

The 20th Congress of the Communist Party of the Soviet Union was held in February 1956. It is remembered for Khrushchev's so-called 'Secret Speech', which denounced the dictatorship and personality cult of Joseph Stalin. (637)

Gabriele D'Annunzio was a Fascist poet, novelist and playwright. His reassessment was viewed as a kind of return to Fascism, which many anti-fascists felt had not been entirely defeated and seemed about to return to Italy. 'Ntoni's words are reminiscent of D'Annunzio's characteristic bombastic, extravagant style. (651)

Notes to pp. 655–64
Grand Hotel was a 1932 film based on a 1930 play of the same title which was adapted from Vicki Baum's 1929 novel *Menschen im Hotel*. The film won an Academy Award for Best Picture and made famous Greta Garbo's line 'I want to be alone'. The 'grand hotel theme' came to describe any dramatic film that portrayed the activities of various characters in a large bustling setting such as an airport, ocean liner, hotel, etc., where some of the characters' lives overlapped in strange ways while they sometimes remained unaware of one another's existence. (655)

Giorgio de Chirico (1888–1978) was a Surrealist painter born in Volos, Greece, to a Genovese mother and a Sicilian father. He founded the *scuola metafisica*, the metaphysical art movement. (660)

The migrating birds of passage recall the lines from Montale's poem 'Dora Markus': '*La tua irrequietudine / mi fa pensare / agli uccelli di passo / che urtano ai fari / nelle sere tempestose*'; 'Your restlessness reminds me / of those migrant birds that hurl themselves / at lighthouse beams on stormy nights' (Eugenio Montale, *Collected Poems 1920–1954*, Revised Bilingual Edition, Translated and Annotated by Jonathan Galassi, Farrar Straus & Giroux, 1998, 2000). (664)